River Deep™

Where powerful passions rise...and a new dynasty dawns

Welcome to a rich and verdant land—where rugged, sexy men and bold, strong women flourish. One powerful family has been living and loving here for generations. Watch as twelve passionate tales of old fortunes and new futures thrill this close community...

Available now

After the Lights Go Out by **Barbara Kaye**—Scott Harris is Valerie Drayton's boss, and yet against the rules, he's attracted to her. Now he has to prove to her that they belong with each other...

Hearts Against the Wind by **Kathy Clark**—Jeff Harris has always been a drifter, but then he meets gorgeous Beverly Townsend. And all of a sudden he wants to settle down!

About the author:

Kathy Clark gets ideas from photographs, newspaper articles and even from gossip columns. She likes to take a little piece of a real-life event, or even a scene in a film, and turn it around, add some background and people, then create a whole situation. Kathy lives in Colorado, USA, with her husband and three sons.

Hearts Against
the Wind

KATHY CLARK

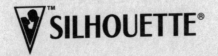

*Silhouette and Colophon are registered trademarks of
Harlequin Books S.A., used under licence.*

*First published in Great Britain 2000
Silhouette Books, Eton House, 18-24 Paradise Road,
Richmond, Surrey TW9 1SR*

© Harlequin Enterprises II B.V. 1993

Special thanks and acknowledgement to Kathy Clark for her
contribution to the River Deep series.

Special thanks and acknowledgement to Sutton Press Inc. for its
contribution to the concept for the River Deep series.
This series was originally called Crystal Creek

ISBN 0 373 82519 6

113-0010

*Printed and bound in Spain
by Litografia Rosés S.A., Barcelona*

River Deep™

A Note from the Author

I was born and raised in Texas, so the River Deep series has a special meaning for me. Handsome cowboys, beauty queens, oilmen, cattle barons and plain old country folk are more than fiction…they're Texas traditions.

I now live in Colorado with my family, but my roots will always be in Texas. I hope, through the wonderful stories of the residents of this town, you'll fall in love with the beauty and majesty of that great state, too.

Kathy Clark

CHAPTER ONE

"THERE JUST AREN'T any good men left." Beverly Townsend leaned against the solid oak bar inside the lounge at the Hole in the Wall Dude Ranch. Her gaze followed the bride and groom as they swirled among the other dancers on the dance floor.

"Yeah, I agree," Jeff Harris said, then as Beverly cast him an amused look, he hurriedly revised, "I mean there aren't any good women left either." His attention returned to the newlyweds who, wrapped in each other's embrace, were oblivious to the crowd around them.

For several minutes Jeff and Beverly stood silent, weighed down by their thoughts— thoughts that were running on a parallel course. The groom, who happened to be Jeff's brother, and his smiling bride continued to move around the floor, dancing slowly in the intimate circle of each other's arms.

Beverly sighed as they passed directly in front of her. Scott, the groom, was handsome, intelligent, wealthy—he owned the Hole in the Wall. He could have been her Mr. Right. Why, then, had fate chosen that same time to drop Valerie Drayton—now Valerie Harris—into his life and into his arms?

If Val hadn't entered the picture, Beverly was certain she and Scott could have made a terrific couple. If only they'd had a little more time together, Beverly was sure he would have fallen in love with her. If only...

But, as disappointed as she was, Beverly couldn't dislike Val. It was easy to see what Scott saw in her and why he had, just an hour earlier, made her his wife. Val was pretty, in an outdoorsy sort of way, and she could hold her own with anyone around the ranch. In fact, it was mostly due to her energy and expertise that the Hole in the Wall had become such a successful guest ranch so quickly.

When Scott had first hired her to coordinate the building and day-to-day operations of the twenty-five-hundred-acre resort, the people around Crystal Creek had watched skeptically.

Actually, the locals were more concerned because Scott, an outsider, had come along, bought the land and built, of all things, a dude ranch, complete with gift shops, restaurant, tennis courts and swimming pool. And something that had caused Beverly's mother particular anxiety—an exotic game preserve. But Carolyn Townsend and the other locals had accepted Valerie, who had been working on ranches since she was a teenager and who fit into the rural routine with ease. And through her, the townsfolk had gradually warmed to Scott, whose sophisticated reserve had taken more time to adjust to the casual life-style of the Texas Hill Country.

Everyone had encouraged the romance between the ranch manager and her handsome boss.

"Do you want to dance?"

Beverly jumped and turned to Jeff. She'd completely forgotten he was standing beside her.

"No thanks. I'm not in the mood." She didn't try to hide her melancholy. Of all the people in the room, Jeff would best understand how she felt at the moment. After all, he'd been interested in Val until Scott staked his claim.

"But it's a tradition that the best man dances with the maid of honor." Jeff gave her a wolfish grin and adjusted the silver clasp of his bolo tie with exaggerated care. "It's not often you're going to see me dressed up like this. I'm more of a jeans and T-shirt kind of guy." His bold gaze drifted down Beverly's ruffled rose cowgirl blouse and calf-length denim skirt that had followed the theme of a country wedding. "Although I suspect you're used to getting all dolled up for parties and things," he added, an unexpected hint of disapproval shading his voice.

Beverly studied the man next to her. She still found it difficult to believe that Jeff was Scott's brother. They were as different as night and day, not just in looks, but in temperament and attitude. Scott, with his ash-blond hair and gray eyes, was tall and gorgeous, besides being as steady and reliable as the huge, ancient oak trees that grew on the ranch.

Jeff, on the other hand, could only be counted on to be unpredictable. A little taller than his brother, Jeff was certainly no less handsome than Scott. Beverly could easily picture him in the role of a rogue with his dark brown hair, a little too long in the back and always falling across his forehead, and his mischievous blue-gray eyes. In fact, Beverly had noticed a good percentage of the female population of Crystal Creek drooling over the younger Harris brother. And Jeff, in turn, was living up to his reputation by charming every woman between the age of puberty and death.

If she could believe the gossip, which was the lifeblood in a small town like Crystal Creek, he'd almost killed a man in a bar fight and he'd left behind a string of broken hearts without the least sign of remorse. He'd blown into town about a month ago and no one knew when he would disappear again, riding off into the sunset in search of adventure. Jeff, it seemed, was as determined to remain footloose and fancy-free as Scott was to put down strong, deep roots.

If only Scott had fallen in love with Beverly. But, with the crumbled remains of a partially eaten wedding cake serving as a depressing reminder, it was too late.

"I think I've had enough *fun* for one evening," she stated, placing her half-empty glass on the bar. "I'm going to give my regards to the happy couple, then go home and cry myself to sleep."

A slow, sexy smile stretched across Jeff's face. "Beverly Townsend crying over a man? Ah, come on, darlin'. I can't believe that."

"I'll bet there's a tear or two inside you right now for ol' Val, even if you won't let it out."

"Don't be silly. Val's just a friend," he said with a casual shrug.

But Beverly caught a glimpse of regret as Jeff's gaze involuntarily moved to his brother's new wife. Somehow it made her feel better to know someone was sharing her pain, however selfish that might be.

"How long will you be staying in Crystal Creek?" she asked.

"I haven't made any plans."

"I heard long-range planning wasn't one of your strong points."

"Long-range, short-range—I'm just not a planning kind of guy. I like to listen to the wind as it whispers the names of places I've never been, things I've never done and people I've never met." He leveled a measuring look at her. "You had your chance. You could have made a clean break from this town. Why did you come back?"

Beverly blinked, caught off guard by his sudden seriousness. "Because all my friends and family are here," she answered with only a slight hesitation.

"That's a crock..." he exclaimed. "You came back because you didn't have the guts to break away from the security of your little cocoon. Crystal Creek isn't the real world, you know. There's excitement, endless possibilities and new horizons out there. You won't drop off the edge of the earth if you go past the city limits sign."

"You don't know what you're talking about." Beverly bristled, straightening and meeting his eyes with a disdainful glare. "I *chose* to come back here because there were people who loved me and were waiting to welcome me home. But you wouldn't understand about that, would you?''

A frown twitched across his dark eyebrows, then quickly disappeared. ''I like to keep things simple. No roots, no regrets...''

''And no responsibilities,'' Beverly added.

''Yeah, sort of like you, huh?''

''Don't try to turn this around. I'm not afraid to take on responsibility.''

''Such as?''

She opened her mouth to give him a hot retort, but couldn't think of an honest reply. Even though she was twenty-five years old with a master's degree from the University of Texas, she still lived at home with her mother. Volunteering at the hospital at least two afternoons a week and taking on an occasional modeling job didn't exactly qualify her as the responsibility poster girl.

Still, Jeff was the last person who had the right to accuse her. ''You wouldn't know responsibility if it bit you on the...''

''No, but at least I'm honest with myself.'' One corner of his lips curved up in a grin that seemed to imply he knew a lot more about her than she thought. "And I'm not afraid to push the boundaries to see how far I can go. I let my intuition guide me, stopping me in one place for a while, then telling me when it's time to leave."

"Yeah, you already told me—you listen to the wind." Beverly gave a scornful laugh. "Well, you should listen to it saying that it's time you grew up!"

He flashed her that killer grin. "Why should I? I enjoy my freedom." He paused a few seconds, then added, "Envious?"

"Of course not!" she retorted, but deep inside, she knew he'd touched a raw nerve. She *wasn't* living the life she wanted to live. Not that she wanted to travel from town to town, never putting down stakes. She just wanted to find her own place in the world.

"You should give it a try. Do something just because you *want* to and not because it might somehow affect your career or your future. Listen to that Texas wind. It's more eloquent than the wind in any other part of the world. It's filled with tall tales and sad stories. It carries the voices of men and women who were brave enough to break away from their secure, predictable lives and strike out for something better. It's out there, Beverly. All you have to do is listen.''

Beverly could scarcely contain her anger. How dared this man, who made a joke out of everything, presume to tell her what to do? ''If I want your advice about my life, I'll ask for it. You just arrived here a few weeks ago. You don't know anything about anyone. Least of all me.''

''Can't we leave the two of you alone for five minutes without you coming to blows?''

Beverly whirled around. She'd been so caught up in her argument with Jeff that she hadn't noticed Scott and Val's approach. ''We...uh, I was on my way over to congratulate you two and wish you a lifetime of happiness,'' she managed to say, her usual poise shaken. ''And to tell you that I've got to leave.''

''You're leaving so soon? But the party's just getting under way,'' Val said. She looked genuinely disappointed.

''I've got a splitting headache. Must be some sort of allergy,'' Beverly responded. At least the headache part was true, but it had nothing to do with the pollen count.

Beside her, Jeff snorted and Beverly tossed him a warning glare.

Beverly gave Valerie a hug, then hesitated a split second before giving Scott a clumsy embrace. God, she wanted to get home, away from all this happiness and love. "Thanks for asking me to be your maid of honor, Valerie."

"Thanks for accepting. It meant a lot to both of us," Valerie said, unconsciously snuggling closer to Scott as he slipped his arm around her waist. "I realize we planned this wedding pretty quickly, but once Scott and I decided to get married, we didn't see any sense in waiting."

"Besides, tourist season will soon be at a peak, so this was the last chance we'd have until fall," Scott added, giving his bride an affectionate look. "I didn't want Val to stay in that guest cabin a minute longer than necessary."

Valerie smiled at her husband, then turned back to Jeff. "Oh, by the way, you can move into the cabin as soon as I get the rest of my things moved to Scott's next week.''

''Thanks.'' Jeff accepted the offer, but hurried to add, ''But I shouldn't be needing it long. I plan on being on my way in a couple of weeks.''

Beverly couldn't take any more of the cheerful chitchat. ''I've really got to go... good night.'' She brushed past them and hurried toward the door, anxious to get away before she embarrassed herself in front of everyone. But luck was not with her as her cousin, Lynn McKinney, stepped into Beverly's path.

''Doesn't Val look beautiful? And that cake! I haven't seen anything that big since Dad's wedding to Cynthia. And isn't Val's mother sweet? To think, they hadn't seen each other in all those years, but now they're close again....'' Lynn's chatter stopped abruptly as she peered more closely at Beverly. ''What's wrong, Bev? Are you sick?''

''Just a headache,'' Beverly answered, trying to force a smile.

''Well, go home and take a couple aspirins or something. Sam and I will pick you up in the morning at nine," Lynn continued, still watching her friend carefully. "Is that too early?"

"What?"

"We're going to the lake house tomorrow, remember? Now don't tell me you forgot about it! This is the first weekend we've been able to plan something together in weeks."

Beverly noticed Lynn's brothers, Tyler and Cal, approaching with their respective fiancés, and she became more desperate than ever to escape. "Yeah, sure. Nine o'clock's fine. See you then."

It wasn't until she was in the parking lot, sitting safely in the solitude of her new white sports car that Beverly realized she'd committed herself to going. While Scott and Val were spending their honeymoon in the Bahamas, Beverly would be suffering through a whole day of watching Lynn and her fiancé, Sam Russell, share sweet, private glances.

It seemed like the love bug was biting everyone in Crystal Creek...everyone but Beverly. She gave a mirthless heart-wrenching chuckle. They all thought she had her pick of men. Wouldn't they be surprised to find out she'd *never* been in love!

It might have been a different story with Scott. Oh, she'd known what she felt for him wasn't real love. But the attraction had been there. Maybe it could have developed into genuine affection over time.

She'd known she and Scott were not really suited to each other. Scott liked quiet evenings at home. His idea of a good time was to throw a steak on the barbecue, open a bottle of wine, perhaps put on some classical music and enjoy the company of whomever he was with. Beverly, on the other hand, was the original party gal. She loved noise, excitement, crowds and dancing. How many times had she been irritated with Scott for refusing to go out?

So why had she felt so sad at his wedding? She was Beverly Townsend—used to men falling at her feet. She knew she was beautiful. It would have been stupid to deny it or pretend not to know it. Her beauty was completely natural. When she was a child, people would stop her mother in stores and comment on Beverly's perfect features. Her father had taken her everywhere with him, bragging about how pretty she was and getting her to show off her equestrian skills.

Beverly had always enjoyed the attention. But most of all she'd enjoyed knowing how proud her father was of her. She'd always been Daddy's little girl. His death a couple of years ago had been a crushing blow. But the pattern had been set. She knew what to do to make people notice her.

But, with the years, had come the realization that no one seemed able to see beyond her huge, deep blue eyes or flawless complexion. No one tried to see if there was anything of value beneath that perfection.

Whether it was because she didn't think she would be able to change their minds or whether she didn't want to make the effort, Beverly had accepted their attitudes. She knew her beauty was God given. She certainly hadn't done anything other than use it to her best advantage. Getting by on her looks became a habit. It made her popular. It helped her get better grades. It was her security blanket.

She brushed away the tears that were

threatening to spill, and turned the key in the ignition. She had to get home.

The ranch house at the Circle T was quiet when she arrived. Her mother was still at the wedding and the staff were probably already asleep. After parking her car under the carport, Beverly walked around to the back of the house where she had a private entrance to her bedroom through a French door. Centered in a flagstone patio and surrounded by a rock garden, the oval swimming pool sparkled in the moonlight like a polished opal.

Deciding a few laps might clear her head, Beverly quickly changed into her swimsuit and poised on the end of the diving board. A full June moon dominated the velvet sky and danced on the surface of the pool as if teasing her with its shimmering double image.

I'm nearly thirty, Beverly thought. *And what have I accomplished?* Beverly knew that, figuratively, she was poised on the edge of the rest of her life. Oh sure, she had her beauty contest trophies. From the first one she'd won as the rodeo queen when she was a freshman at Crystal Creek High, to the assorted beauty awards she'd collected while in college, then through her progression from Miss Austin to Miss Texas to the Miss America contest, Beverly had used her looks to get her whatever she wanted. That included two full scholarships to college, a constantly expanding wardrobe, money in the bank and her car. But when she'd finished as first runner-up in the Miss America contest, Beverly had suddenly realized there were no more rungs to climb on the beauty-queen ladder.

And now, two years later, Beverly was no closer to finding a satisfactory career than she had been in high school. And she was certainly no closer to a meaningful relationship with a man. But then, how could she hope to find a man who would love her for the woman inside when even she didn't know who that woman was?

With a lithe jump, she pushed herself upward, arched and shattered the moon's reflection into a million ripples. The water, still holding the heat of the day, curled around her, sensuous in its intimacy. Beverly's arms reached out in rhythmic strokes, pulling her to the opposite end of the pool. She touched the concrete wall and immediately turned and began another lap. If the soothing liquid didn't ease the strain from her, at least the exercise would help her get to sleep.

THE MUSIC from the country and western band spilled out the door as Jeff opened it and walked outside. As the door swung shut behind him, the party noise was muffled, replaced by the nighttime sounds of the ranch.

Horses shifted, stomping the ground and nickering as they settled for the evening. Soft bellows of cows and the answering cries of their calves traveled through the still night air from the pasture.

Jeff's boots clattered against the wooden boards as he walked along the porch that ran all the way around the lodge. An owl hooted from the branch of a nearby live oak tree.

A lonely cloud drifted across the full moon, shrouding the yard in darkness. When a match scraped across the rough cedar rail and flared into a tiny blaze, the owl spread its wings and disappeared into the darkness. Jeff jumped, startled to discover he wasn't alone.

"All the excitement's inside," a voice commented.

Jeff peered into the gloom, but it wasn't until the cloud freed the moonlight that he was able to make out the figure of an old man sitting on the porch swing.

"Thanks, but I've had enough excitement for one night," Jeff replied. "Do you mind if I join you?"

The old man shrugged. "Suit yourself."

Jeff sat on the wide top rail, one leg resting on the rail and the other braced against the porch. He leaned back against a rugged wooden post. For several minutes he sat quietly, watching out of the corner of his eyes as the old man smoked a hand-rolled cigarette.

"You're Hank, Lynn and Tyler's grandfather, aren't you?" Jeff asked.

"*Great*-grandfather."

Jeff had heard a lot about Hank Travis. He was a living legend in Crystal Creek. His ninety-nine years had spanned decades of change in the world. And his mind was sharp enough to remember it all from the time he was old enough to take note of current events.

But what interested Jeff was Hank's history in oil exploration. He'd been a very successful oilman in his prime.

"And you're Scott Harris's brother," Hank stated, more as a fact than a question. "How long you plan on stayin' in Crystal Creek?"

"I'm not sure. Maybe tomorrow...maybe after my birthday in a few weeks. I've got no real reason to stay. But I don't have a reason to leave yet, either."

"I heard you're an oilman," Hank said, apparently reading Jeff's thoughts.

"I like to think so," Jeff answered, and one corner of his mouth lifted into a self-deprecating grin. "But next to you, I'm a rank amateur."

"Hell, don't knock experience. Every minute a feller spends on a site, he learns somethin'. Why, I remember ridin' up to take my daddy his lunch and seein' the top blow off the Spindletop well. Yep, only seven years old I was then, but I remember it clear as day. That black gold just come gushin' outta there like a fountain. Wasn't but a few minutes till we were all covered from head to toe in oil." Hank chuckled. "Shoot, I'll never forget the lickin' my mama gave me when I got home. But I was hooked. From that day on, I knew I didn't have blood runnin' through my veins—I had oil.''

"Yeah, I know what you mean," Jeff agreed. "Ever since the bottom dropped out of the oil industry, I've been trying to think of some other line of work to get into. But there's just nothing like the anticipation of the search or the excitement of the drilling. It's like a treasure hunt. The clues are all there. All a person has to do is read them correctly, then choose the right spot to sink the casings.''

Hank leveled his steady gaze at Jeff. Even though they were shielded by the thick lenses of wire-rimmed glasses, Hank's eyes were not those of an elderly man. They were keen and observant, and Jeff felt as if he'd been weighed, measured and thoroughly evaluated by the time Hank managed a companionable smile that barely disturbed his tanned, creased cheeks.

"I'm tired of all this noise," Hank said, pushing himself to his feet. "You got a car?"

"Uh…yes," Jeff answered. "Actually, it's a truck."

"Even better." Hank nodded. "Gimme a good ol' pickup any day. Let's go. You can take me home now."

Jeff stifled a smile at the old man's imperious attitude. He noticed that even though Hank used a cane to walk, his movements were surprisingly spry for a person of his age.

"I don't get off the ranch much anymore," Hank continued.

"Why not?"

"Well, for one thing I banged up my hip in an oil well blowout—must be close to forty years ago now—and then I broke the same hip twenty-five years later."

"You look like you get around pretty well to me."

"Some days are better than others. It weren't so bad when I still could get around in my pickup. But they said I was too old to drive. Can you imagine that? Take away a man's keys and you take away his freedom. Hell, I don't feel any older than I did when I was in my sixties." He held on to the railing, waving off Jeff's offer of a helping hand. "It's hell gettin' old. How old are you, boy?"

"I'll be thirty in a couple weeks."

"Thirty. Ahh...to be thirty again. I was in my prime."

"Yeah, well, I feel like I'm all washed up," Jeff commented. He and Hank walked slowly across the manicured lawn that bordered the pathways from the main lodge to the guest cabins and the parking lot.

"Havin' some tough luck?"

"You could say that." Jeff sighed. Actually, that was an understatement. Out of his past six jobs, he'd come up with four dry holes. That was less than a fifty percent average. And that was why he was killing time at his brother's ranch, waiting for a job offer or even a hint of a job that would take him back on the road. "My methods are a little unorthodox in today's scientific society."

"So you're not one of those geologist fellas that makes your decisions on facts and figures?"

Jeff gave Hank a curious look. It was a casual question, but something in Hank's attitude told Jeff it was a more complex inquiry than it appeared. He hesitated a moment, because his approach was unconventional, and some people didn't understand. But Jeff could feel a kinship with the old man.

"I guess you could say I'm more of a traditional wildcatter," Jeff said. "I look at the maps and study the statistics. But what I really go by is my gut feeling. It's like there's a vibration leading me to the oil. No one else can feel it, so they think I'm nuts. But I *know* whether or not there's oil under the ground as soon as I step on it."

Hank stopped walking with a suddenness that made Jeff look at him with concern. But instead of pain on the old man's features, Jeff saw unmasked delight.

"Hot dang. You *are* an oilman." Hank nodded and his thin lips spread into a wide grin. "I've got this piece of land down near the Gulf Coast...."

CHAPTER TWO

"IT LOOKS LIKE perfect weather today," Lynn commented as Sam drove her and Beverly out of Crystal Creek toward Lake Travis.

Thoughts of the weather were the farthest thing from Beverly's mind. She still couldn't believe she'd let Lynn talk her into tagging along. How much fun could it be to spend all day on a relatively small powerboat with a couple who were wildly in love? In her current mood, being the odd one out would only accentuate her loneliness.

The car stopped in the driveway next to the lake house that was jointly owned by the McKinney and Townsend families. Actually, the land had been inherited by Carolyn and her sister Pauline, Lynn's mother, from their father. They'd decided to turn it into a family retreat and had had the large, airy house built when their children were very young so they would always have a place to go for family gatherings away from the constant demands of their ranches.

Beverly climbed out of the car and stretched. She was still tired. Even after what must have been thirty laps of the pool, she'd taken ages to fall asleep last night. She suspected that as soon as she sprawled out on the cushions of the open bow with the sun beating down on her, she would doze off.

Already, the air was hot and heavy with humidity. The hum of cicadas vibrated from the oak trees, and dozens of birds flitted from their nests to the ground as they searched for food to feed their fledglings.

Beverly felt the reluctance to enjoy the day ease out of her. This had always been one of her favorite places. There was a peace and calm here that she never felt at the ranch.

"Remember when we were kids and would come here for the weekends?" Lynn asked, apparently sharing Beverly's thoughts. "We would take Grandma's quilts out on the porch and make a giant pallet."

"Then we would lie on our backs and look up at the stars, waiting for one to streak

across the sky so we could make a wish,''
Beverly continued the story.

"Tyler would always try to count them,''
Lynn added.

"And Cal would watch for UFOs." Beverly laughed at the memory. She and her cousins had had so much fun together. She'd always been close to Tyler in spite of the nine-year age difference between them. And of course Lynn was her dearest friend. There had sometimes been friction between Cal and Beverly. Probably because they'd been quite similar as kids—both attractive, popular and sure of themselves.

"Remember when Cal swore he saw a UFO hovering over the lake, but everyone else missed it?"

"So we never believed him," Beverly agreed. "He always did like to stretch the truth."

"But he could do tricks on water skis that would make everyone else green with envy. I don't think he's ever felt a moment of fear."

"Why else would he have been crazy

enough to stick it out on the rodeo circuit for so long?''

Sam came back from carrying a load of supplies down a steep pathway to the boat, which was tied to the floating dock. "Okay, you two. You're just avoiding helping by standing around reminiscing."

Lynn lifted a grocery bag filled with potato chips and other snacks and handed it to Sam. "We're busy supervising."

Sam leaned over and gave Lynn a kiss. "Slave master. And I suppose you're going to make me drive the boat, too."

"Of course. Why else do you think I brought you along?" Lynn answered with an intimate smile.

"I'll drive." A new voice joined the conversation.

Perfect Beverly thought. *This really makes my day.*

"What are you doing here?" she asked bluntly.

"Well, good morning to you, too." Jeff grinned.

Wearing only a pair of cutoff jeans and old tennis shoes, he had a kind of loose-limbed grace Beverly had to admire. He had a six-pack of cola in one hand and a canvas duffel bag slung over one broad, bare shoulder.

Her breath caught in her throat as she looked into his twinkling eyes. The reaction was so quick and unexpected that she took a step backward. Ducking inside the back of the car, she grabbed her bag and the small thermal chest that held some fresh fruit and the chicken salad for their sandwiches. Of course she'd always noticed that Jeff was an extremely handsome man. But somehow, until that moment, she had felt no attraction to him.

Stop it, Beverly, she chided herself. *You're just so anxious to fall in love that even Jeff, the lady-killer, looks good.* She turned her head, glancing over her shoulder as Jeff lifted a large ice chest out of the trunk. His arms tensed, the tendons tightening into iron cords. Obviously, his work in the oil fields had toned his body. There was a hardness and a symmetry to his muscles that dedicated bodybuilders would kill for.

The shorts rode low on his slim hips, revealing a tantalizing line of curly dark hair

that began just above his navel and disappeared into his waistband. His legs were long
and almost as tanned as his chest. Even
though she'd often seen him in white tennis
shorts as he instructed the guests at the Hole
in the Wall, Beverly had never noticed just
how well developed his body was.

At that moment, he looked up and caught
her studying him. Impudently, he gave her a
slow, roguish wink.

*God, he was insufferable! Did he think
every woman in the world was attracted to
him?* Beverly gave an audible snort. But as
he turned away, he hoisted the ice chest
higher and sent the layers of bulging muscles
across his back into motion. Beverly found
she couldn't tear her gaze away. Looking
didn't hurt, she reasoned. At least she would
never succumb to his flirtations. She wasn't
that desperate.

IRONICALLY, not even Jeff knew why he was
there. He had no reason to join this little out-
ing and every reason to avoid it. Although
he'd struck up an easy friendship with Cal
McKinney, he'd never really gotten to know

Lynn or her dentist boyfriend. And what he knew of Beverly, his survival instincts told him to avoid.

He'd been filling in for the tennis pro at the Hole in the Wall for about a month now. Scott had originally given him a job as a ranch hand, but Jeff had shown no aptitude for the work. In fact, Jeff had already told Scott he would be leaving as soon as the regular tennis coach returned. Now that he and Scott had mended a few of the bigger conflicts between them, Jeff would feel comfortable stopping for a night or two whenever he happened to pass through town on his way to his next job. But he couldn't imagine staying indefinitely with Scott and his new wife.

Just that morning, Jeff had gotten a call from Buck Dalton, one of his old friends, telling him about a new oil field that was under consideration in South Texas. He hoped Jeff could come in as a consulting partner, giving his expertise instead of a monetary investment.

Finding oil was what Jeff did best. Of course, it was a hit-and-miss situation, but until lately, his average had been higher than most. It was as if he had a sixth sense for it.

Unfortunately, the rumor had gotten around that he'd lost his touch. Since he had no idea what gave him that "touch," he was having a difficult time disproving the rumor. But this new job would give him the chance to try once more.

Why, then, was he still in Crystal Creek? It certainly wasn't because of any woman. Initially, Jeff had been attracted to Valerie, his new sister-in-law. But after the first rush of disappointment that she'd chosen his brother over him, Jeff had had to admit that he hadn't really been in love with her. He liked her and was glad they would remain friends.

He carried the ice chest to the boat and rested it on the top of the seat while he stepped over the side into the boat. He and Sam took the last of the bags from the women, then helped them get on board.

"Could you untie us?" Sam asked as he turned the key and started the powerful engine.

Jeff leaned over and slipped the ropes off

all four brass cleats, then tossed the ropes inside the boat. "All clear, captain. Anchors aweigh."

Sam eased the boat out of its cushioned stall, and soon they were motoring down the narrow inlet to the lake. Already the water was dotted with brightly colored sailboats trying to take advantage of what little wind there was, and fishermen trolling their lines, trying to find an unsuspecting largemouth bass.

"Okay, who's going first?" Lynn asked as they worked together to unpack the ski gear.

Sam volunteered and stripped to his swimsuit. Jeff took over the controls of the boat and idled the motor while waiting for Sam to get ready. The other man positioned himself behind the boat, floating in the water, his skis pointed upward at an angle and his hands firmly gripping the towrope's handle. As soon as Sam gave the sign, Jeff eased the throttle forward. The boat increased speed until Sam was on top of the water, gliding smoothly along.

Jeff's attention was divided among the RPM gauge, the skier behind the speedboat and the lake in front of them. It wasn't until he reached a steady speed that he glanced at the other occupants of the boat.

The midmorning sun was hot, and Lynn and Beverly had taken off their shorts and T-shirts and were lounging against the cushions across the back of the boat, laughing and taunting Sam.

Jeff's mouth suddenly went dry.

His gaze riveted on Beverly. God, he'd never seen anyone so beautiful. That hair, those eyes, that figure...her perfection literally took his breath away.

This wasn't the first time he'd noticed her. She was like a glowing star, brightening every room she entered and causing every red-blooded male to ache with desire.

Her hair was a rich golden color, threaded with strands of palest ash-blond. Its thick, wavy length tumbled down her back, reaching almost to her waist. As he watched the wind persistently carry it across her face, she reached inside her beach bag and pulled out an elastic, cloth-covered band. Her hands gathered the silken mass and secured it into a ponytail.

Whoa boy. Jeff forced his eyes away from the intoxicating sight. *Remember this is Beverly. Spoilt, self-centered, shallow Beverly— to whom looks are everything.* Despite his warning to himself, Jeff glanced back at her. Now that her hair was tied back, he had a much clearer view of a figure her bikini did little to hide. Jeff felt his body automatically respond to the swell of soft flesh that threatened to spill out of her skimpy top.

"He's down," Lynn yelled.

Jeff jerked his attention back to the job at hand. He steered in a wide circle and went back to where Sam was floating in the water with a ski under each arm.

"Hey, you picked up a little too much speed there, Jeff," Sam commented as they helped him climb into the boat.

"Sorry. Something distracted me," Jeff answered, carefully keeping his eyes focused away from Beverly.

"That's okay. I was getting a little tired anyway," Sam said congenially. "Who's next?"

They took turns skiing until one o'clock when Sam guided the boat back into its covered slip in front of the lake house. While the men secured the mooring, Lynn and Beverly walked up the steep path to the house.

"DID YOU SEE the way he was looking at you?" Lynn asked in a conspiratorial tone.

"Who? Jeff?" Beverly pretended surprise, although she'd been quite aware of his scrutiny.

"Oh course I mean Jeff. If it had been Sam, I'd have slugged him." Lynn unlocked the door and they walked inside the cool interior of the house.

Beverly shrugged. "Oh...Jeff looks at all women that way. You know, he reminds me of a wolf with those predatory eyes and that hungry curl to his lips. I always have the impression that he's waiting to pounce. But not on me," she hurried to add. "Jeff and I are exact opposites. We could never be attracted to each other."

Lynn smiled. While she would never deliberately hurt her cousin, she couldn't help thinking how alike Beverly and Jeff really were. Both were very attractive and somewhat self-centered. Neither seemed to have a care in the world. Lynn knew, as far as Beverly was concerned, there was another side that most people never saw. Of course, she hardly knew Jeff, so she couldn't speak for him.

"He's one gorgeous hunk. You two would make a beautiful couple, like in one of those sexy magazine ads for perfume or romantic vacations in the Caribbean."

Beverly glanced out the front window at the two men who were walking across the large deck. No, she couldn't argue with the fact that Jeff was one of the best-looking guys she'd ever seen. And he had the charm to use those looks to get anything he wanted.

"Do you want me to make the salad or the sandwiches?" Beverly asked, intentionally changing the subject.

"I'm not sure you should go into the kitchen at all," Lynn teased with a frown. "I'll never forget what you did to the home economics lab...."

"That was years ago."

"Yes, but has your cooking improved since then?"

"Well, no, but even *I* can slap chicken

salad on bread and make a sandwich.'' Beverly took her cousin's joking lightly. It was common knowledge that Beverly's talents didn't include anything remotely related to a kitchen. And the damage to the home economics lab hadn't been all *that* bad...just some smoke stains, a gutted oven and a melted pan. Of course, it had all looked a lot worse than it really was after the fire department got through flooding the room with water and foam. At least Beverly accepted that she couldn't be great at everything.

The men entered the house and Sam immediately went to Lynn and gave her a hug and a long kiss. Beverly's gaze shifted self-consciously away from them and she found herself looking directly into Jeff's eyes.

He was studying her with the same intensity he had been all day. Beverly was used to being stared at, but the way Jeff was looking at her made her uncomfortable. And it wasn't because there was anything lecherous in his manner. It was as if he was searching for something, and not quite finding it.

Beverly lifted her hands to smooth back her hair, but her fingers tangled in the wet, wavy mass. She knew she must look horrible with her soggy hair, no makeup and a shapeless T-shirt hanging down past her hips.

Jeff thought he'd never seen anything so beautiful in all his life. Beverly looked like a mermaid just pulled from the sea. For the first time he noticed something vulnerable about her.

Jeff realized that just as she now stood several steps away from Lynn and Sam, no matter where she was or whom she was with, Beverly was always standing at the edge of the group. Even when she was the center of attention, there was a distance, either physical or emotional, between her and the others.

How odd that a woman so exquisite should always be the outsider. As he continued to look at her, he saw a flicker of uncertainty in her eyes.

"Sam, be good," Lynn chided, but the affection was clear in her voice. She pushed him away with a halfhearted effort.

Beverly glanced at them, then back at Jeff. Her expression softened and she nodded toward Lynn and Sam with an indulgent smile.

Jeff felt his own lips curve in response to Beverly's compelling grin.

"Here, Jeff and I will fix the sandwiches while you two fill the glasses with ice," Beverly said, gently pushing Sam and Lynn toward the refrigerator. "I think you can handle that."

"I don't know," Jeff teased. "Love can be a powerful distraction."

"Well, since *we* don't have that as an excuse, we should be able to put together the best sandwiches ever made," Beverly responded as she flipped her long ponytail back over her shoulders.

"And I would have guessed you'd be the one doing the kissing instead of the cooking." Jeff washed his hands and joined her at the kitchen counter.

"Then you'd be wrong." She gave a mirthless chuckle.

"Hmm...do I hear disappointment? Regret?"

Beverly shrugged. "Sure, I suppose I keep wondering when it'll be my turn."

Jeff leveled a serious look at her. He watched as spots of color washed across her high cheekbones, but her eyes didn't waver from his. Jeff fought the impulse to reach out and touch her lovely face. There was a lot of pain in her expression, but it was the insecurity he saw there that surprised him. "Your turn will come, Bev."

"Well…maybe." She looked down at the container of chicken salad in her hands and focused on opening the snap-on lid. Her fingers fumbled on the tight closure and Jeff reached toward it.

"Here, let me help you with that," he said, meaning to take the bowl from her. But the second his fingers touched hers, they froze. Her skin was soft and still warm from the sun. But it was more than simply the feel of her beneath his hand. It was like a small jolt of electricity.

His gaze jerked upward, and as he met her startled eyes, he knew she had felt it, too.

They both dropped the bowl at the same instant. Being securely sealed, it bounced harmlessly on the floor, rolling to a stop between them. Jeff and Beverly bent to retrieve it, moving in awkward unison so that their hands touched again as they reached for the bowl simultaneously.

The reaction was exactly the same, except as they squatted on the floor, their faces were in much closer proximity. He could hear a faint gasp as she inhaled through slightly parted lips. He focused on those lips and felt his own breath catch in his throat. God, what gorgeous lips. Full, soft and a delicious shade of rose, those lips were made to be savored.

The rattle of ice cubes brought him back to his senses. He even managed a shaky grin as he picked up the bowl and stood. "I guess it should be stirred enough."

Beverly rose, too, and began laying out the slices of bread. "Lettie Mae makes the best chicken salad this side of the Mississippi."

She took a knife out of a drawer and began to spread chicken salad on the first slice of bread. Jeff decided he dared not chance another encounter until he'd had time to recover from the last two, so he concentrated on opening the bags of chips.

Lynn and Sam, with much more whispering and intimate giggling than was absolutely necessary, finally got the glasses filled with ice, quickly put together a green salad and carried glasses and salad to the table. Jeff took the chips and Beverly followed with a platter of sandwiches. Everyone was famished after the morning's exercise, and they quickly filled their plates.

"So, I thought we'd take a run to the other side of the lake this afternoon," Sam began as he lifted his sandwich to his mouth. "The crowds seem to be thinner over there. We should be able to get in another five or six hours of skiing before—"

The piercing tone of his beeper interrupted. Sam picked up the small black box and glanced at the code flashing on it. "Damn," he muttered, putting down his sandwich and standing. "It's my office. Where's the phone?"

Lynn pointed across the room to a table beside the stone fireplace, and Sam hurried to it.

"A dental emergency?" Beverly asked and Lynn shrugged.

Sam put down the receiver and turned to Lynn. "I'm sorry, honey, but I've got to go in. One of my patients got his front teeth knocked out in a Little League game.''

Lynn immediately stood up. "I'll go with you, if that's all right.''

"I'll take you home,'' Jeff offered.

"No, thanks,'' Lynn responded with a smile. "Sam and I haven't been able to spend much time together lately.'' She turned back to Sam. "It won't take me but a minute to change clothes.''

"I guess I'd better change, too,'' Beverly said. "I wouldn't want to get Sam's car seat wet.''

"Oh, Jeff, would you mind taking Beverly home?'' Sam asked, gathering his clothes. "I hate to ruin the day for all of us. You two stay and enjoy the sunshine. Besides,'' he added, "I really don't have time to backtrack through Crystal Creek. I need to get to Austin as quickly as possible.''

Jeff's gaze darted back to Beverly. There was a panicky expression in her eyes that very closely reflected his own feelings. But they really had no choice.

"I'd be glad to,'' Jeff agreed, leaving it up

to Beverly to protest if she had any major objections.

With a helpless look as if her friends were tossing her into the Gulf of Mexico in the middle of a school of tiger sharks, Beverly nodded. "Sure, that'd be okay with me."

"Thanks, Bev," Lynn said, as she and Sam made for the bathroom.

Five minutes later, the door shut behind Sam and Lynn, and it was quiet. Too quiet. Beverly and Jeff still sat at the table, sandwiches still on their plates.

At last Beverly took a small bite and began chewing with deliberate determination.

Jeff followed her lead and began eating.

Beverly returned the sandwich to the plate. "Pass the chips, please."

Because she hadn't been specific, Jeff handed her the bags of all three varieties.

"Thanks," she murmured and selected one of the bags. She shook a few chips onto her plate, then selected one with the studied precision of a jeweler choosing a perfect diamond for Elizabeth Taylor's newest necklace.

Jeff watched with breathless interest as her

straight, white teeth nibbled tiny bites of the chip. Then the pink tip of her tongue circled her lips, licking off the salt. It was all so innocent, and yet one of the most erotic gestures he'd ever seen.

He stood, so abruptly that the chair tumbled backward onto the carpeted floor. Beverly jumped as if she'd been shot.

"Sorry," he mumbled and carried his plate to the kitchen. "I guess I'm not as hungry as I thought. You go ahead and finish your meal and I'll clean up in here."

Jeff dumped the uneaten food into a garbage bag and piled the dishes in the sink. He squirted a generous amount of dish soap on top, then turned on the water full blast. "Want to take a few more runs in the boat?"

"Just you and me?" There was a startled note in Beverly's voice.

"Sure, why not? I haven't been waterskiing for years."

"Yes, but..."

Jeff's hands were submerged in the sudsy water, but he turned his head until he could see Beverly's face. "An hour ago, you were having a great time. Now you act as if I'm asking you to walk naked over hot coals. If you don't watch out, you'll give me a complex.''

Her mouth twitched into a smile. ''Yeah, like anything I could say would give *you* a complex. You're the most self-confident man I've ever met.''

His expression sobered. ''It's all an act, darlin'. How about you?''

For several seconds, Beverly's sapphire blue eyes stared into his gray-blue ones. ''I suppose I've done my share of acting, too. Sometimes, it's easier to pretend to be self-confident than it is to actually get rid of all those insecurities, isn't it?''

He grinned. ''I guess everyone has insecurities. Some people deal with them and some people cover them up. I guess you and I belong to that second group. Actually, Beverly, you and I are a lot alike. We've both gotten a lot of mileage out of our looks, which has its advantages and disadvantages. The advantages are obvious, but the disadvantage is that no one really takes us seriously.''

Still a little cautious, she studied him as

she answered, "No, they don't. So what should we do about it?"

"Well, I don't exactly have the answer to that, but I think if we put our heads together, we could think of something."

"Together...you and me?" she repeated skeptically.

"Sure, why not?" As her mouth opened to protest, he quickly added, "Nothing serious, just friends. We seem to be the only two singles left in a world full of couples. Maybe if we team up, sort of partners against this passion that's raging through Crystal Creek, we won't feel so left out."

"Strictly platonic?"

"Absolutely."

"I suppose we could give it a try. It's not like I have an overabundance of friends right now."

"Good," he said, his smile returning full force. "Then let's begin by spending the rest of the day out on the lake."

There was an intrigued sparkle in her eyes as she answered, "Sure, why not. As long as you keep your mind on the boat and don't run over anything."

"Then maybe you'd better keep your T-shirt on. That bikini you're wearing is pretty distracting."

"Ahh...but a friend wouldn't notice that."

He chuckled. "Of course a friend would notice. And it's my duty to tell you that that bikini is a hazard to the health of every man on this lake. Now wouldn't you feel bad if you caused some old guy to have a heart attack or if you distracted a skier and made him slam into something?"

"Gee, I didn't realize this friendship thing would extend to offering advice on my wardrobe."

"Oh sure, and tomorrow we can talk about your hair," he joked. "Have you ever thought about becoming a redhead?"

Beverly jerked the dish towel away from him and threatened to pop him with its fringed corner. "Don't press your luck, *pal.*"

"Okay, okay." He laughed, as he fended off her attack. "I'll stick to more generic subjects. Like, why don't you pack us a lunch while I finish these dishes."

She looked at the sandwiches he'd just

dumped into the garbage and reached for the
bread to start over. "I never argue with a
man who's volunteering to do the dishes. Do
you want one sandwich or two?"

CHAPTER THREE

"IT'S LOOKING GOOD…damn good." The man speared another big piece of chicken-fried steak with his fork and pushed it around his plate until it was coated with thick, white gravy. "We should be drilling by the end of the summer."

"Hey, that sounds great." Jeff leaned forward and rested his arms on the table as he watched Buck Dalton shove the huge bite into his mouth. "When do you want me on site?"

Buck chewed the steak thoroughly, much longer than he had the piece before. He seemed reluctant to swallow. "Uh…that's why I wanted to meet with you today. I was just passing through Crystal Creek on my way to Danbury, and thought you'd rather hear it from me."

Jeff didn't have to hear any more to know

he was not going to like Buck's news. He pushed away from the table and reclined against the back of the booth with a nonchalance he wasn't feeling. His association with Buck went back several years to when they were both roughnecks on their first job for a company out of Houston.

They'd spent twenty-four hours a day working on that well. Because of their youth and inexperience, they'd been given all the worst jobs. They'd laid board roads over muddy cow pastures while trying to avoid rattlesnakes and water moccasins, so the heavy equipment could drive across the soggy ground. They'd carried countless lengths of pipe up to the platform. They'd retrieved tools that had been forgotten at the warehouse and had driven into town for carry-out lunches.

And, more important, they'd learned every aspect of the drilling process. Caught up in the excitement as the drill bits dug through layer after layer of soil and rock, they'd pushed exhaustion aside, catching catnaps in the back of their pickups so they wouldn't miss the big moment. When the well finally came in, they'd tasted their first drops of oil and were immediately hooked.

But, eventually, they'd branched off in different directions. Jeff preferred the challenge of exploration and the variety of free-lancing, while Buck had moved up through the executive ranks until he was the vice-president of operations of PetroCo.

It was in that capacity that he sat across the table from Jeff in the Longhorn Coffee Shop on this steamy June afternoon.

And it was in that capacity that he was about to deny Jeff the job that could have resurrected his stagnant career. It would have been his ticket out of Crystal Creek, and out from under his brother's critical eye. With the petroleum industry still moving in slow motion, there weren't a lot of offers from which he could choose. In fact, this was the first project in several months that was open to outside bids. The truth of the matter was, Jeff *needed* the job.

He swirled the rapidly melting ice cubes around in his glass of cola and asked, "Tell me what?"

"I'm sorry, Jeff, but they decided to go

with GeoTex.'' There was genuine regret in
Buck's voice.

"GeoTex! That group of anal-retentive,
pretentious jerks!'' Jeff exclaimed. ''All
those geologists…all those tests. They'll delay drilling by at least a couple of months.''

''All those tests will save us a lot of time
and money in the long run. We have to take
as much of the guesswork as possible out of
the equation before we can give it a green
light.''

''Green light? What are you, an oilman or
a traffic cop? You *know* I can find that oil,
and for a hell of a lot less than GeoTex.''

''Hey, I have faith in you, buddy. That's
why I called you earlier. But the company's
been putting pressure on all of us lately. We
don't have the capital to take the risks we
used to. And your success rate lately hasn't
been great.''

''So, I made a couple of bad calls. But I
still say there was oil in those holes if they'd
kept drilling.''

''We went down fifteen thousand feet on
that last one.'' Buck shook his head. ''Do

you have any idea how much that dry hole cost us?''

"It was down there," Jeff repeated stubbornly.

"Maybe so. But we couldn't afford to go any deeper."

"Yeah, but remember all the times I was right."

Buck leveled an apologetic look at his friend. "I know, but your methods are a little—" he paused, obviously searching for a word that wouldn't offend Jeff "—a little unorthodox. I've seen you in action and know that when you're hot, you're hot...."

"And when I'm not, I'm not," Jeff muttered.

"It's just that it's difficult to explain to a roomful of executives and bankers who've never been closer to an oil well than when they have to pump their own gas at a station, how you *feel* the oil. Companies like GeoTex offer solid facts and figures. On paper, their proposals look very impressive...."

His voice trailed away as the glass door of the café opened and Beverly walked in. With a toss of her head that sent her golden hair back from her perfect face, she seemed to light up the room. There were a few seconds of silence as all conversations were suspended. Beverly seemed totally oblivious to the effect her arrival had had, as she held open the door for Lynn, who followed her inside.

"Thank God for air-conditioning," Beverly said to Lynn in a voice so low it wouldn't have carried around the small room had its occupants not been so silent. As if on cue, the conversations resumed.

"Speaking of *very* impressive..." Buck murmured with obvious appreciation as Beverly approached them, heading toward an empty booth by the window.

She called out greetings to everyone as she passed, and everyone answered with the indulgent affection of a relative or very close friend. Actually, that was one of the things about Crystal Creek that both fascinated and repelled Jeff. On the one hand, it would be nice to belong to such a large, extended family. On the other hand, it could get very annoying not to be able to sneeze without everyone calling out a "God bless you."

Beverly's gaze drifted in Jeff's direction and—was it just his imagination?—her smile widened.

"Hi," she said. "It looks like you got a little too much sun yesterday, too."

Jeff automatically touched his sunburned nose and shrugged. "A little. You'd think with all the time I spend outdoors, my nose would get used to the sun."

"I guess it was the reflection off the water." A mischievous twinkle danced in her blue eyes as she added, "Or it could be from that blaze in the barbecue pit. We were lucky to rescue our steaks before they were consumed by the flames. I'm surprised the neighbors didn't call the fire department."

His lips stretched into a grin at her irresistible charm. He suspected he'd never seen that charm turned up to its full wattage, and he hoped he never would. If the way his body reacted to her when she was just being friendly was any indication, he hated to think how he'd feel if she ever directed that powerful charisma at him.

"You did say you liked your steaks well-done," he teased.

"There's quite a difference between well-done and burned to charcoal."

"Ahem." Buck cleared his throat in an apparent effort to draw her attention and he was rewarded with a dazzling smile.

"Hi, my name's Beverly," she said. "And this is my cousin, Lynn."

He took Beverly's extended hand and gave her a warm smile. "Actually, we met last time I was in town. I'm Buck Dalton from PetroCo. Jeff and I have worked together on quite a few jobs."

"*Worked*...as in past tense," Jeff muttered, but Buck didn't seem to notice as he continued his campaign.

"Why don't you two ladies sit down here with us," he said, sliding around in the corner booth and patting the empty spot next to him while his gaze focused charmingly on Beverly.

Her incredibly long eyelashes fluttered, then lowered as she tilted her head. "Why, thank you for the offer, but Lynn and I have a few things we need to discuss that wouldn't interest you gentlemen at all," she drawled.

Jeff shook his head and slumped against

the back of the booth. Where had the Scarlett O'Hara act come from? How many sides of Beverly had he not seen? This one, he had to admit, he wasn't particularly fond of.

Just then, Beverly looked back at Jeff and gave him a private, conspiratorial wink, then rolled her eyes. With that single, intimate exchange, she assured him that it was just as he'd thought—an act. With one last dazzling smile at the two men, she swept past them to the booth where Lynn, who was obviously used to being ignored while in Beverly's presence, was already seated.

Buck was the first to recover. "Hell, what's a babe like that doing in a hick town like this?" he exclaimed, when Beverly finally sat down and was out of their line of vision. "No wonder you've stuck around here as long as you have."

"She had nothing to do with me staying here," Jeff replied.

"Yeah, sure," Buck drawled. "And the sun's going to set in the east tonight."

Jeff knew it would be impossible to make his friend believe he hadn't spent more than fifteen minutes alone with Beverly before yesterday, so he shrugged it off.

But Buck wouldn't drop the subject. "She's gorgeous. How long did it take you to get her to bed?"

Jeff's fists clenched, but he managed to stay cool. "I told you, she and I don't have anything going on. I barely know her."

Buck gave Jeff a skeptical look. "Well, that's not like you at all. You've been here a month and haven't found out what that body looks like under those clothes?"

The image of Beverly's body, barely covered by that tiny bikini, pushed its way into Jeff's mind. Actually, the picture had been slipping in and out of his thoughts for the past twenty-four hours, but he'd have bitten his tongue off before he would admit that to Buck. For some reason—and Jeff had no idea what that reason might be—he felt compelled to defend Beverly's honor. The feeling was so unusual and so powerful that Jeff was momentarily silent.

"If you don't have any claim on her," Buck continued, completely oblivious to the turmoil raging in Jeff, "then maybe you can set *me* up for tonight. Does this bump-in-the-road place have a nice restaurant?''

"What do you mean, *nice restaurant?* I don't see any food left on your plate.'' The waitress had chosen that moment to walk up to the table and slap the bill on the red-and-white-checked tablecloth.

Startled, Buck glanced up at the middle-aged woman, but she was already walking away.

"Hell, you'd think she owned the place,'' Buck retorted.

"She does,'' Jeff informed him. "That's Dottie Jones. She owns this café and the motel.''

"Speaking of motels, how about doing an old friend a favor, and help me get better acquainted with that sex goddess.'' He nodded toward Beverly. "I wouldn't mind spending an extra night in this place if it could be with her.''

Before he even realized what he was doing, Jeff's hand darted across the table and grabbed a fistful of Buck's shirt. "Leave her alone.''

Buck tried to pull away, but Jeff had a firm

hold on him. "Hey, buddy, if she doesn't belong to you, why should you care?"

As the logic of that statement sank in,
Jeff's fingers slowly relaxed until he released
his hold and moved back to his side of the
table. Why *should* he care? He glanced over
at Beverly's table and could get only a
glimpse of silky golden hair, falling away
from her face as she tossed back her head and
laughed along with Lynn.

There was no denying that Beverly was
very beautiful and incredibly sexy. Jeff
wasn't immune to her obvious feminine
charms. However, yesterday he'd seen something else. He knew that beneath the glossy
glamorous shell was a lonely, vulnerable
woman. Jeff felt no compulsion to protect
that polished jewel on the outside, but he'd
go down fighting to keep the fragile china
doll on the inside from getting broken.

"Just leave her alone," Jeff repeated in a
tone that left no doubt that he wasn't joking
around.

Buck straightened his shirt, trying to
smooth out the wrinkles over his chest.
"Doesn't sound to me like a guy who isn't

interested," he grumbled as he scooted out of the bench and stood. "I think I'll hit the road now. I can make it home by dark."

Jeff stood and held out his hand in a conciliatory gesture. "Thanks for stopping by. Just keep me in mind for future jobs."

"Sure. You know I will." Buck took Jeff's hand. "You're the same old hot-blooded roughneck," he said with a companionable smile. "It was good seeing you again."

"Yeah, you too." Jeff watched as Buck left the Longhorn and got into the black Corvette parked by the curb. It wasn't until the car turned the corner and disappeared behind the courthouse that Jeff realized his good friend had left him with the check.

He glanced at his watch and saw he still had an hour to kill before he was due back at the ranch for his afternoon session on the tennis courts. He picked up his half-full glass of cola and took it to the counter where he sat on a stool while he fished enough cash out of his billfold to pay the check.

"Couldn't help overhearing your conversation with that city boy," Earl Waddell, the grizzled foreman at Hole in the Wall said as he pulled out a cigar from his pocket. He glanced up in time to see Dottie nod pointedly to a No Smoking sign. "Damn rules," he muttered, as he put the unlit stogie in the corner of his mouth. "You'd think a grown man could do what the hell he wants."

"You can," Dottie retorted. "As soon as you pay your check and walk out the front door."

"Sassy broad," Earl said to Jeff, not really caring that Dottie could overhear his comment. "If I was a few years younger, I'd be after her like a duck on a June bug."

"If you were a few years younger, I wouldn't look at you twice," Dottie stated, with just a hint of a smile. "I like my men older and experienced."

Earl slapped his hand on the Formica counter with such force that everyone in the café looked around. "Then hell, woman, there ain't no one older or more experienced than I am, except old Hank. What're you doin' after you get off from work this evening?"

"I'm going to kick off my shoes, watch 'Roseanne' and go to bed early."

"I like that last part," Earl agreed.

"To sleep, you old goat. I need my beauty rest."

"Nah, from what I see, you're purty enough."

Dottie picked up Earl's check and tore it in half. "Okay, it worked again, you scoundrel. Compliments will get you a free meal here any day."

Earl slid off the stool and took his weathered Stetson from the hat rack by the door. With a wink at Jeff, he said, "Let's head back to the ranch, son. I need your help to load some feed into my truck." He gave a pointed glance toward the corner booth as he tugged his hat low on his forehead. "And while we're at it, I'll teach you a few ways to handle women, too."

Jeff looked over Earl's head to where Beverly still sat, sipping a big glass of iced tea. Tempting as Earl's offer was—not that Jeff thought the older man could teach him anything where women were concerned—Jeff had other, more important decisions to make.

Somehow he had to get back in the oil business. There was no denying that Buck's

news had been a major blow. Suddenly, looking at Earl, Jeff thought of another wise old
man he'd met here in Crystal Creek. What
was it Hank Travis had told him? Something
about oil and a piece of land he owned.

Maybe it was time to pay old Hank a visit.

CHAPTER FOUR

BEVERLY WALKED into the Crystal Creek Community Hospital the following morning staggering under the load of magazines and paraphernalia she'd brought for her favorite patients. Her arms were filled with large-print romance novels for Mrs. Goodwin, the elderly heart patient whose condition was worsening daily, puzzles for Jackie, a nine-year-old boy with leukemia and color books for dainty little Carrie, a four-year-old girl on dialysis because of bad kidneys. She immediately noticed the air of chaos in the corridors. Beverly made her way to the elevator with her burdens and managed to push the Up button with her elbow, then stood back to wait.

The elevator arrived with uncharacteristic speed and Beverly stepped aboard, juggling her armload so she could press the button for the fourth floor. When the doors opened to let her out, she was met with the sounds of patients' buzzers beeping at the nurses' station and a cry of joy from the station's lone occupant, Glenda Wong.

"Beverly, thank God you're here! You're a sight for sore eyes—not to mention sore feet and frazzled nerves. Are you up to bigger and better things today?"

Beverly carefully eased all the books and things in her arms onto an empty cart and grinned at Glenda. "Sure, anything short of brain surgery. I just don't think I'm up to that today."

"But anything else, right?" Glenda answered with a weak smile and stuck her tongue out at the blinking, buzzing board behind her.

"I have the feeling I'm going to be sorry I said that, but what did you have in mind? Am I moving up to the nursery? I've never spent much time around babies, you know." She surveyed the relatively deserted hallways. "Where is everyone?"

Glenda put her fingers to her forehead and rubbed her temples. "I have four nurses and three aides out with the flu—or spring fever. That can be deadly this time of year, too.''

Connie, another nurse, hurried up to Glenda and Beverly. ''I can only do so much, Glenda. It's either bedpans, clean sheets, baths or medicine. Take your pick.''

''The cavalry has arrived, Connie. Or at least a willing recruit. If you can do the scheduled vitals and the medication, I'll get Beverly started on her new career.'' Connie gave Beverly a sympathetic look and hurried off to get the tray of medicine and the blood pressure machine.

Glenda turned to Beverly. ''You don't have to worry about working in the nursery because that's about the only station that's fully covered.''

In spite of her protests, Beverly was a little disappointed. It was true that her experience with babies was extremely limited, but she'd found herself drawn to the glass-enclosed room every time she came to the hospital. She looked at Glenda. ''No babies? No magazines and letter writing either, huh?''

Glenda shook her head. ''Sorry, kid, nothing so glamorous. Think more along the lines of bed baths, bed changes and bedpans.''

"I don't know, Glenda. I've only been volunteering here for a few months, and—''

"What? You don't make your own bed? Shame on you. What kind of wife and mother will you make?'' As she spoke, Glenda guided Beverly down the hall toward the room on the end.

"Of course I make my own bed,'' Beverly declared with indignant pride.

"And you smell like you bathe,'' Glenda continued, "so that just leaves the bedpans. Common sense should cover all you need to know along those lines.'' She stopped at the linen closet, pulled out a cart that was loaded with clean sheets, towels and cleaning products and pushed it down the hall. When they reached the end room, she parked it outside the door. "Everything you need should be on this cart. Just put the dirty linens into the laundry bag on the end.''

"Dirty linens?'' Beverly echoed, as it began to dawn on her that her own slightly rumpled sheets and the sheets on the bed of a critically ill patient would be two entirely different experiences.

"Start here and work your way up and down each hall on this floor." Glenda gathered an armload of linens and thrust them into Beverly's reluctant arms.

"But…"

"You've been taking the volunteer classes, haven't you? By now you should have had at least some instruction on all of these things."

"Yes, but I haven't *actually*—"

"Then today's a good day to get some practice. And remember, neatness counts," Glenda added, already hurrying back toward the central desk where the noise of the buzzers continued.

"Neatness counts?" Beverly muttered. She hadn't counted on doing *real* work when she took up volunteering at the hospital. She'd thought all she would need to do was smile, hand out meals and magazines, amuse child patients and let someone else take care of the dirty work. Assuming she wouldn't really be dealing with the three B's—bedpans, bed baths and bed changes—Beverly hadn't paid much attention to demonstrations in the classes. But now she had no choice. They needed her, and she would just have to do the best job she could. She could only hope the patients would be patient.

Beverly knocked and hesitated a moment to compose herself before entering the room. There were two names on the door, neither of which Beverly recognized from past visits. With a confidence she didn't feel, she pushed open the door and swept inside. She had a sneaky feeling she was going to be earning her candy stripes today.

Instead of being welcomed warmly, she was greeted by a chorus of complaints.

"It's about time, nurse." Mrs. Leonard, the old lady in the first bed looked anxious. "I just had my foot operated on, dearie. I can't walk to the bathroom."

"Uh...I'll help you." Beverly waited until the woman had eased her legs over the side of the bed. "Here...lean on me," she told her and wrapped her arms around Mrs. Leonard's plump waist. Slowly, they crossed the few feet of bare floor to the bathroom. After waiting for the woman to settle, Beverly stood awkwardly, not knowing what she should do next. Fortunately, Mrs. Leonard spoke up.

"Now go away," she retorted. "I can't do anything with you standing there gawking at me. I'll call you when I'm through. And close the door."

Beverly quickly exited the small bathroom and found the other elderly lady looking at her expectantly.

"Good morning, Miss Wilson. How are we today?" Beverly felt like an idiot for the "we," but justified it because that was the way the nurses talked to the patients on "General Hospital".

"I don't know about *you,* but *I'm* used to having *my* bath right after lunch, young lady. I finished lunch more than a half hour ago. What's the holdup?" Miss Wilson fixed Beverly with a steely gaze.

"Well...I..." She heaved a deep sigh and gave the woman an apologetic look. "I'm going to give it to you straight. I've never done this before, but I'll give it my best shot. So, what comes first, a bath or a bed change?"

The dragon leveled a deprecating stare on her. "The bath, of course. You wouldn't want to get clean sheets wet, would you?"

Beverly smiled at the woman. "You remind me of a teacher I had once," she said, adding the silent thought that that teacher had also been a dragon.

The woman replied with a pleased expression, "As a matter of fact, I *am* a teacher. I've taught third grade for forty years at Crystal Creek Elementary." She squinted near-sightedly through her round bifocals at Beverly. "You know, I think I recognize you, too."

Beverly was momentarily speechless as she studied the woman. "You are *that* Miss Wilson, aren't you?"

When the old lady nodded with obvious delight at being remembered, Beverly asked, "But how on earth could you remember me? You must have had hundreds of students over the years."

"I'll admit that some of the students' faces and names have blurred. But I remember you as clear as day, Beverly Townsend."

Beverly started to protest modestly, ex-

pecting her old teacher to mention what a
lovely child she'd been.

"You were a holy terror," Miss Wilson
continued, clearly enjoying the memories.
"You always wanted to be first in line. And
when someone else's drawing won first place
in the art contest, you sat in the corner and
cried. When you lost that beauty contest a
few years ago, I wondered how you reacted
because I remembered how you used to pout
whenever you didn't get your way."

"Thanks for reminding me," Beverly muttered. But she couldn't deny the truth of what
Miss Wilson was saying. She'd never liked
to lose, even when she was nine years old.
Determined to change the subject and hesi-
tant to try her first bed bath on an old school-
teacher, she announced loudly, "I think we'd
better forgo the bath today. But I have to
change the sheets."

Miss Wilson volunteered without hesitation. "Once a teacher, always a teacher. I'll
teach you how to make a bed any marine sergeant would approve of."

Beverly proved to be a quick learner and
finished Mrs. Leonard's bed before the elder-

ly lady was ready to leave the bathroom. After helping her into the fresh, clean bed, Beverly changed Miss Wilson's linens while she took her turn in the bathroom. If the sheets were a little loose, neither patient complained.

"Not bad for a beginner," Miss Wilson stated in her finest schoolmarm voice.

"She did a fine job," Mrs. Leonard added. "Beverly, dear, you should consider becoming a nurse. You're so good with people."

Beverly gave them a weak smile as she began gathering up the huge pile of dirty linens from the floor. Aloud, she told them goodbye, but under her breath, she was muttering, *Me become a nurse? Not in this lifetime. I'd rather muck stalls.* Already her back was aching and she'd broken two fingernails.

She stuffed the linens in the bag on the cart, moved on to the next room and repeated the routine until she reached the end of the hallway. Parking the cart to one side she staggered to the nurses station.

"A Coke. I'd kill for a Diet Coke."

Glenda looked up from her stack of charts. "Ready for a break, Bev?"

"You mean we have time to take one?" Beverly was decidedly relieved. "What about all the other patients?" Her sigh was tired, but she managed a smile.

Glenda smiled back. "We were able to call in a few temporaries, and some other nurses and aides volunteered to come in early. But don't look too relieved. We still need you. But first, we deserve a break. Let's go down to the dining room."

"You're on." After Glenda turned the desk over to Connie, the two women started toward the elevators.

"This will have to be quick, Bev. We have to be back before the dinner trays arrive so we can pass them out and help the people who can't feed themselves. After dinner, all the water jugs need to be filled and the trays picked up. Then, not coincidentally, there always seems to be a bedpan or a help-patients-to-the-bathroom rush."

"It's a vicious cycle. How can you stand to do this *every* day?" The list of upcoming duties made Beverly even more tired than she'd been before. They stopped at the rest room and freshened up before going into the cafeteria. "It's certainly different from the soap operas where nurses slink around the hospital in short, tight uniforms seducing doctors, and holding an occasional sick patient's hand until they make a miraculous recovery. Another romantic myth in the Dumpster."

"Disappointed?" Glenda put a piece of pie and a cup of coffee on her tray.

Beverly eyed the pie hungrily, but picked up a salad instead. Then she stopped at the soft drink dispenser and got a diet cola. "Of course I'm disappointed. I grew up watching all those romantic soap operas about hospitals. And, of course, I believed dozens of handsome, eligible doctors would be competing for the honor of making me a doctor's wife."

Glenda gave her a quizzical look. "Is that what you want? Is that why you volunteered?"

Beverly laughed and shook her head. "No. I volunteered because my cousin Lynn twisted my arm. She told me I needed to get more involved in my community. But I think

the real reason is that she's as determined as
my mother to find me a suitable boyfriend.''

"You mean you're not interested in having
a doctor for a husband?'' Glenda raised a
skeptical eyebrow. "With your looks, your
mother's and your cousin's dreams could
come true, you know.''

"Oh, it's not that I have anything against
doctors. It's just that I've already found the
perfect man. He's tall, handsome and successful, perfect husband and father material.'' Beverly sighed and took a bite of lettuce.

"So when's the wedding?''

"It was last week. He married another
woman. I was her maid of honor.'' Beverly
shook her head and suspected her expression
was as wistful as she felt.

"Did you love him very much, Beverly?''

Beverly knew the answer. She'd been considering the question for some time now.
"It's not that I *loved* him so much, because
our relationship hadn't really gone that far.
It was just that he *was* so perfect for me. He
was everything I needed.''

Glenda took a big bite of pie, chewed it

thoughtfully and swallowed it. "But you didn't love him?"

"I would have learned to love him."

"Don't kid yourself. You might have talked yourself into believing you did, but thirty years down the road, you'd be stuck with a perfect, boring husband and no good excuse to get rid of him. Is that how you'd want to live your life?" Glenda took a sip of her coffee as she watched Beverly over the rim of the cup.

"Would that be any worse than spending the next thirty years trying to find myself? At least I'd have someone to be miserable with. Isn't that better than being miserable alone?" Beverly reasoned.

"No. Trust me, it isn't." Glenda shook her head emphatically. "I went through that with my own marriage, and let me assure you, it's twice as miserable if you're living with someone who doesn't love you or you don't love than if you're living alone." She took another sip of coffee. "What you need is for some guy to come along and sweep you off your feet. Believe me, you won't be expecting it, because he won't be a *perfect* man."

"There aren't very many *perfect* men out there," Beverly agreed.

"I doubt there's *any*," Glenda retorted. "In fact, your Prince Charming probably won't have any of the qualities you're looking for, but he'll take you to the heights of paradise and the depths of hell." Glenda paused as she finished her coffee. "At least you won't be bored." She got to her feet and picked up her tray. "Time to get back to our floor. I hear the rattle of dinner trays. And I want to thank you for staying a little longer than usual today. You've been a real lifesaver."

Beverly and the rest of the volunteers, plus the nursing staff, spent the next two hours working at a frantic pace. Beverly followed the dinner cart and delivered the meals while listening to complaints about everything from the food to the color of the floor tiles. Then she helped settle the patients for the evening.

After all her chores were done, Beverly decided she had time for one more visit. She picked up some of the items she had brought with her.

Beverly knocked on the door, but didn't wait for an invitation before tiptoeing inside the room. She peered into the semidarkness at the motionless figure on the bed, trying to see if the patient was awake.

"Beverly, I figured you'd already gone home." A frail voice barely carried to Beverly's ears.

"It was a zoo around here today," Beverly explained as she pulled a chair closer to the bed and sat down. "They needed all the help they could get." She reached out and took the old lady's bony hand. "I'm sorry I wasn't able to get by to see you earlier."

"You shouldn't be spending all your spare time with an old woman." Her pale lips moved into a shaky smile. "A pretty girl like you should be out having fun with her beau."

"You know I don't have a beau, Mrs. Goodwin. And I visit you because I *like* to, not because I *have* to."

Mrs. Goodwin's long, thin fingers squeezed Beverly's hand, but her grip was so feeble, Beverly barely felt it.

On her very first day as a volunteer, Beverly had met Mrs. Goodwin. The elderly lady had just been transferred to a room on the fourth floor after spending several weeks in intensive care, recovering from her third heart attack. Beverly had been instantly drawn to the sweet-tempered patient who never complained. Then, when she noticed Mrs. Goodwin never had any visitors, Beverly had started spending as much time as possible with the old woman, bringing her anything that would brighten her day until she could get well.

But Mrs. Goodwin didn't get better. Instead she became weaker and more fragile. Glenda explained to Beverly that Mrs. Goodwin's heart was almost totally dysfunctional. If she were younger, she could have been a candidate for a transplant. But because Mrs. Goodwin was in her seventies, with no one to fight for her and no real reason to fight for herself, all she could do was wait to die.

"Look at the beautiful flowers I got today." Mrs. Goodwin glanced toward the cheerful arrangement of Shasta daisies, roses and ferns.

"Hmm...so that secret admirer is still around?" Beverly teased.

Mrs. Goodwin's faded blue eyes twinkled, momentarily breaking through the film of pain that always clouded them.

It had become a running joke between them. Twice a week Beverly had fresh flowers delivered to Mrs. Goodwin's room, but had never admitted being the one to send them. And Mrs. Goodwin, whose mind, when not dulled with medication, was as bright and quick as ever, had guessed right away who was responsible for the flowers.

"So, how are you feeling today?" Beverly asked.

"Fine," Mrs. Goodwin answered, but the grimace that furrowed her forehead belied her claim.

"Is there anything I can get for you? Some water? Or juice?"

"No, I'm okay," Mrs. Goodwin said, but there was an unspoken question in her eyes.

"If you're not too sleepy, I brought you something special today." She didn't have to hear Mrs. Goodwin's excited reply to know the older woman had been waiting for this. Beverly reached into the bedside drawer and pulled out a cassette player. She picked up what looked like a book from the stack she had brought with her to the room, opened it and took out an audio tape. "I found something new in the bookstore yesterday. It's a romance on tape. I listened to part of it on the way over here, and it's really good. There are actors speaking the parts and music and sound effects, just like hearing a movie."

After putting the tape into the machine and turning it on, she leaned back in the chair and watched her elderly friend's expression as the story unfolded.

Ever since Beverly had found out Mrs. Goodwin loved romances, she had brought her a half dozen every time she came to the hospital. But Mrs. Goodwin's eyesight was weak, so whenever Beverly had time, she would read the stories aloud. The tapes seemed a perfect solution to keeping Mrs. Goodwin entertained when Beverly couldn't be around.

When the tape ended, Beverly tried to turn off the machine as quietly as possible because she thought Mrs. Goodwin had dozed off. To her surprise, the old woman reached out and touched Beverly's hand.

"Would you leave it here, please? I'd like to listen to it again tomorrow."

"Sure," Beverly answered, pleased that Mrs. Goodwin so obviously liked her surprise. "Listen to it as often as you want. It's yours. They had a few others, and I'll pick them up the next time I'm at the bookstore."

Mrs. Goodwin nodded and her hand relaxed as her paper-thin eyelids drifted closed. She whispered, "You're a real blessing, Beverly."

"Good night," Beverly said softly, turning away so the old woman wouldn't see the tears in her eyes. She busied herself tidying the blanket before turning off the overhead light and slipping from the room.

She called her goodbyes to the relief nurses on duty at the desk and rubbed the small of her back as she waited for the elevator. It had been a long, rough day. Beverly couldn't remember when she'd been so tired.

The elevator doors opened and she stepped inside without even noticing there was someone already there. With a sigh, she leaned against the back wall and shut her eyes as the small compartment jerked into motion.

"So you're the beautiful angel of mercy the patients have been telling me about," a deep, amused voice said, making her eyes snap open.

She turned her head, startled to find a drop-dead gorgeous man in a white coat with a stethoscope around his neck standing across from her, watching her with open curiosity. Her hand automatically rose to her hair, smoothing the loose tendrils back from her face. She could only imagine how awful she must look. Here she was, riding down in an elevator with an incredibly handsome doctor who, if his lack of a wedding ring meant anything, was not only interested, but eligible, and she looked like she'd spent the day running a marathon…and losing.

"It couldn't be me," she answered, even managing an exhausted grin. "I almost lost one patient in the sheets when I was changing her bed, and I dropped a tray of food on poor Mr. Robbins."

"Hey, those are minor infractions considering the pressure we were all under today." He tilted his head and flashed her a wide, perfect smile. "I don't think we've met." He extended his hand. "I'm Gregory Sinclair. Today's my first day here."

Beverly took his hand, briefly wishing she'd taken the time to rub on some lotion after she washed up. "Welcome to Crystal Creek. This is a wonderful hospital."

"So I've heard. I did my residency at Dallas General, but I wanted to work somewhere smaller, more personal so I could spend more time with my patients."

Beverly blinked, wondering if she had dozed off and was caught up in a dream. Surely, this man couldn't be for real.

But he went on, "I'm just getting off, too. Why don't we go someplace for a drink?"

Beverly glanced down at her wrinkled, soiled uniform and shifted to ease the ache of her exhausted feet. As much as she wanted to accept his offer, she knew she would make poor company. "I'd love to, but I can't tonight. I'm beat."

"Another time then?" He didn't appear to be the least bit discouraged by her refusal.

Beverly nodded. The elevator settled to a stop on the ground floor and Dr. Sinclair stood to one side and allowed her to exit first, then insisted on walking her to the parking lot.

As she drove off, she glanced in her rear-view mirror at the tall, attractive, *eligible* man getting into a sparkling silver Corvette convertible. Maybe her timing wasn't so bad after all. Maybe there was one perfect man left.

CHAPTER FIVE

"YOU HAVE TO RUN up on the ball, Mrs. Kramer. You're not supposed to let it bounce three times in your court before you hit it." Jeff tried not to show his irritation as the woman on the other side of the net stood several feet behind the foul line and waited for the ball to reach her.

"But if I move up, then you can hit the ball over my head."

"Then you'll just have to move around, following the ball wherever it goes," he explained. What on earth was he doing here anyway? He wasn't a tennis pro; he was an oilman. He should be standing on the wooden floor of a derrick instead of the asphalt surface of a tennis court. "That's how the game is played," he informed the woman calmly, but he could feel his nostrils flaring in rebellion. "If you just want to stand there and hit balls, I'll hook up the ball machine.'' *And go to a bar and get drunk while you're out here screwing around,* he added to himself.

Of course, it didn't help his concentration that a camera crew was shooting an ad on the adjacent tennis court. It wasn't the cameras that were distracting him. No. The source of his distraction was the star of the shoot— Beverly Townsend.

Dressed in an extremely short white tennis outfit with her glorious hair swirling loose around her shoulders, she was pretty enough to sell disco records to Garth Brooks.

Jeff wasn't sure what product was being promoted. It wouldn't have mattered anyway. All he could see was Beverly.

Beverly, too, was trying gamely to keep her mind on the matter at hand. But trying to ignore the tennis lesson taking place on the next court was taxing *her.*

Beverly submitted once again to the hairdresser who was making a gallant but futile effort to keep the Texas wind from blowing Beverly's hair. The makeup artist joined her, brushing yet more powder on Beverly's already well-covered skin.

"One more time, kids," came the gravelly voice of Mike, the photographer. "John, try not to look like you have morning sickness. You're supposed to be enjoying this. Remember, you have the woman of your dreams in your arms, you've just completed a rousing game of tennis, and there isn't a sign of sweat anywhere on her gorgeous body. The message here is she can go straight from the court to the bedroom without a stop in the locker room for a shower."

The male model pasted a shaky smile on his pale face and took his place behind Beverly, putting his arms around her, and attempting to nuzzle her neck. His lips were clammy against her skin and she had to force herself not to wince. This shoot was taking more acting talent than a full-length major motion picture.

John suddenly grabbed his stomach and moaned. "Where's the bathroom?"

Beverly pointed toward the clubhouse and sighed as John sprinted away. With a glance at her watch and a groan when she discovered how slowly the hours were passing, she sat down at one of the umbrella-shaded tables scattered around the tennis court area. Mike glanced at the sky and shook his head as he made his way over and collapsed loosely on the chair next to her.

"What's wrong with John?" Beverly asked. "I've never seen a man look so pained at having to put his arms around me. Doesn't he like women?"

Mike managed a dry chuckle. "That's definitely not his problem. John's a regular Lothario with the ladies. But right now he's got something else on his mind. He just got back from a shoot in Mexico. I think Montezuma's taking his revenge."

A tennis ball bounced over the fence and rolled to a stop at Mike's feet. He picked it up and turned around to throw it back.

"Dammit, if John doesn't get his act together, we're going to lose our light!" he exclaimed as he stood. "Dodie, go get the nurse and see if she can do something for John...some Alka-Seltzer or a couple bottles of Pepto-Bismol. We can't afford to lose a whole day."

The makeup girl hurried to obey his commands, and Mike tossed the tennis ball back over the fence.

Jeff caught it on the first bounce and waved his thanks.

Beverly was trying not to be obvious about watching the tennis lesson in progress, but her gaze was drawn to Jeff's lean, muscular body like a magnet. As she waited for John to return, the plump, matronly Mrs. Kramer's lesson ended and a sassy redhead, whose bosom was too large for the halter top she was wearing, joined Jeff on the court.

"I just can't seem to get any power in my backstroke, Jeff. Can you show me one more time?" The woman's whiny, flirty tone grated on Beverly's already frazzled nerves.

"It's back*hand*, Buffy. Back*stroke* is a swimming term. Okay, let's try it one more time. Try to concentrate, now." Jeff's deep, sexy voice, combined with the fact that he was standing close behind the lovely Buffy and guiding her arm in the proper position for a good, strong backhand, caused Beverly's teeth to clench.

Buffy's shrill giggle was the last straw. Beverly got abruptly to her feet and walked over to the refreshment wagon. As she sipped a cool glass of sparkling water, she called to Jeff.

"I don't think that's the back*hand* she's worried about, Jeff."

Jeff glared at Beverly and handed the tennis racket back to Buffy. "You need to practice, Buffy. I'll turn on the ball machine so you can hit a few."

Buffy smiled coyly up at him. "Could you show me again, Jeff? The racket doesn't feel right in my hand."

"You just have to get used to your racket." Jeff turned his back on her and positioned the ball machine. "Get ready," he warned before adjusting the speed and turning it on.

He walked over to where Beverly was leaning against a tree and stopped, braced his arms on each side of her, effectively pinning her in place without touching her. "What's the matter, Beverly? Jealous?"

Beverly almost choked on her drink. "Jealous? Me? Of you and Bambi?" she sputtered.

"It's Buffy," he corrected, his lips curving into a knowing grin.

"Bambi, Buffy, bimbo…" she countered, in a voice low enough for his ears only. "What difference does it make? They're all the same. I've never seen women make such fools of themselves around a man. What is it, a secret hormone in your after-shave or that come-on-I'm-a-real-stud look in your eyes?"

Jeff refused to rise to the bait. Instead, he asked suggestively, "And is it working on you?"

"I have more willpower than that." Her words were bold, but Jeff's nearness was doing frightening things to her nervous system. She had no logical explanation for why the thought of Jeff giving *private* lessons to overdeveloped bimbos like Buffy made her heart constrict in her chest. Jeff meant nothing to her, so how could she be having these feelings that did, indeed, very much resemble jealousy?

"Right." Jeff continued, the warm flirtation in his eyes replaced by silvery disapproval. "You're holding out for a country-club jock with a fat wallet and a big diamond engagement ring in his pocket. Anything cheap isn't in your scheme of things, is it?''

"At least I have ideals and goals. All you care about is your ability to sniff out oil and available, willing females. And not necessarily in that order.''

Jeff's lips relaxed back a sexy smile. "I've turned over a new leaf. Since the last time we talked about this, I've decided that my long-term goal is to be an oil baron. And my short-term goal is—'' his gaze shifted from her eyes to her mouth "—to kiss you.'' His last words came out in a warm caress as his lips moved closer until they pressed against hers.

She wanted to push him away and tell him never to kiss her again. She really did...but somehow her resolve didn't transmit itself to her body. Her eyelids fluttered closed and her hands rose until they clutched his biceps in what was more of a gesture of encouragement than of rejection.

What was it about this man? No wonder the women flocked to him. He had a sexuality that was almost palpable. As much as Beverly tried to resist, she, too, was affected by it. The touch of his lips or his hands or even the intensity of his eyes was enough to set off a wildfire of emotions raging inside her. Emotions Beverly had never experienced with any other man and couldn't quite define. Emotions that delighted her, yet scared her to death.

"Now that's the kind of action I need!" Mike's voice jarred both Beverly and Jeff apart. "I'm afraid John's out of the picture, so to speak. Unless you want to continue the shoot in the bathroom." Mike looked Jeff over appraisingly. "How would you like to make a few quick bucks?" ·

"You're going to pay me to kiss a beautiful woman?" Jeff asked, obviously amused by the offer. "Hey, I might have to rethink that long-range goal."

"You'd make a great gigolo," Beverly agreed. Her comment was meant to be sarcastic, but her voice sounded soft and breathless even to her own ears.

Mike gave her a curious glance, then turned back to Jeff. "How about it? You're already dressed like a tennis player, and you look appropriately sweaty. It won't take too long, and you'll have an extra five hundred bucks in your pocket.''

''I don't think it's a good idea, Mike,'' protested Beverly. ''Not even your skill with a camera can make the public believe that Jeff and I are attracted to each other.''

Now it was Mike's turn to look amused. ''You could've fooled me. You two were shooting off enough sparks for a Fourth of July picnic.'' To Jeff, he explained, ''Our male model is sick, and we'd like to salvage today's shoot if possible. This location is expensive, and we're operating under a tight budget. Have you had any modeling experience?''

''No, but I'll try anything once,'' Jeff answered with a shrug and a pointed glance in Beverly's direction. ''Sure, I'll do it. I can always use the money.''

''Great!'' Mike motioned to the hairdresser and makeup artist. ''Do your stuff, gang. Let's get this show on the road and get this shooting over with. I have a hangover that needs a little tender loving care. All this standing around in the sun is making *me* sick.'' He wiped his forehead on the back of his hand. ''Damn, is it always this hot in Texas?''

''Only between the months of March and December,'' Jeff replied as Dodie rushed up, set a chair behind him and pushed him onto it. ''Hey, none of that stuff,'' he protested as she tried to put a layer of pancake makeup on his face.

''Yeah, he's a natural beauty,'' Beverly said, only half in jest.

''Well, even natural beauties need help in front of the camera,'' Dodie declared in a tone that clearly said she would tolerate no resistance. ''Now sit still and take this like a man.''

''That's the problem,'' Jeff grumbled as Dodie spread a thin layer of foundation over his face and patted the shine off his nose with a fluffy powder puff. ''Real men don't wear this stuff.''

''No one will know but you and me,'' Beverly teased, ''and, of course, *I* would *never* tell anyone.''

Jeff turned his head to give her a horrified look. ''You wouldn't...''

Dodie turned his head to face the front so she could comb his hair, and then used a toothbrush to tame his eyebrows. "It's just not fair for a man to have such thick dark eyelashes," Dodie commented with a shake of her curly head.

Jeff didn't know how to respond to that since it hadn't really been stated as a compliment. He felt this was above and beyond the call of duty and that, in spite of the fact that he was feeling more foolish by the second, he was being incredibly cooperative. But when the makeup artist reached for a container of blush, he slipped out of the chair and stepped a safe distance away from her. "That's it," he stated firmly. "Either they take me like this or they find another guy."

Mike hurried over and stood between the stubbornly advancing Dodie and the equally determined Jeff. "Okay, Dodie, that's fine. We want that rugged, sweaty look." Mike nodded toward Beverly. "Why don't you touch her up while I give Jeff a few tips?"

Once again, Beverly submitted to being fluffed and powdered, while Mike explained what he wanted Jeff to do.

"You're hot for her...but you're trying to keep to the business at hand. You're giving her a tennis lesson...."

"And see what a fine teacher he is," Beverly couldn't resist commenting as Buffy missed another easy backhand shot.

Both Mike and Jeff gave Beverly a look of censure. "We want you up close and personal," Mike continued. "And try to look like you have plans for a different kind of lesson after the game. You know what I mean?"

Jeff flashed that deadly grin that never failed to send Beverly's traitorous heart fluttering. "I've got the idea. Come on, Bev, let's work on your serve." He stood and pulled Beverly to her feet. Before she could protest, he whipped his arm around her slender waist and pulled her against him until her back was plastered against his front.

Mike thrust a tennis racket into her hand and propelled the two of them to the spot on the court where the cameras were set up.

Jeff's free hand wrapped around hers on the racket and he whispered in her ear, "Now try to concentrate." His breath filtered through her thick hair and brushed against her skin like a gentle night breeze.

Damn the man…and damn her reaction to him! "You're too close," Beverly warned through smiling lips.

"Not as close as I'd like to be," Jeff returned as he crossed their arms over her chest and guided her into a smooth overhand serve, his body moving perfectly with hers.

The camera clicked and clicked and clicked. Mike moved around constantly, changing the angles, adjusting the focus, switching lenses. "This is great stuff. Keep it up."

Beverly could see that Jeff was enjoying his role. He knew his presence was annoying her, and he was deliberately pushing his luck.

It was time he was taught a lesson—one that was totally unrelated to tennis. She moved, rubbing her buttocks slowly against his groin and was rewarded to feel he was, indeed, affected by her.

"You're not playing fair," he murmured, his voice noticeably shaky.

"You're the teacher. I learned all the rules from you."

"I don't think I could teach you a thing, darlin'."

Dodie rushed up and squirted Jeff in the face with a bottle of water.

"Hey, cut that out!" he exclaimed, reaching to wipe it away, but Dodie caught his hand.

"You don't look sweaty enough," she explained.

"That's funny—it felt like I was covered with it."

"Maybe she thought you needed a cold shower." Beverly tossed him a taunting look over her shoulder.

"Relax, Beverly, and smile. We'll be done here in no time. This is really great stuff. *Great* stuff."

Mike's instructions forced Beverly back into alignment with Jeff's body.

"See?" Jeff chuckled as he nuzzled her hair. "Even Mike recognizes greatness when he sees it."

"Conceited ass!" Beverly commented.

"Beautiful broad!"

"What?" Beverly was totally unprepared

for Jeff's retort. "Didn't you hear me? I called you a conceited ass."

"I *am* a conceited ass, and you *are* a beautiful broad. And I think we'd be great together." Jeff tightened his grip around her body and turned her into his embrace for another deep kiss, forgetting that Mike was photographing his actions.

"Perfect!" Mike's triumphant shout along with more frantic clicking of his camera brought Beverly to her senses.

"It's a wrap! You guys are beautiful together. Wow! I've never seen such chemistry. I hope it comes across on film." Mike began gathering up his equipment while Dodie and the hairdresser packed their supplies. "We need you to fill out a few forms, Jeff. Your check will be in the mail in a couple of weeks. Thanks a lot! We appreciate you filling in for us."

Jeff and Beverly were still standing dazedly, the tennis racket hanging loosely from Beverly's hand and their arms around each other. When they realized their rather compromising position, they dropped their arms to their sides and took several steps apart. Beverly turned and started to hurry away.

"Bev, wait."

Beverly took a couple more steps before her feet stilled. "What do you want?"

"Hey, I'm feeling rich tonight. How about going out to dinner with me?"

She wanted to refuse. Just as much as she had wanted to push him away when he kissed her. She wanted to refuse...but somehow when she opened her mouth, she said, "Sure, but I need to go home and take a shower."

"So do I." He glanced at his watch. "How about seven o'clock? Can you get dressed in an hour?"

"What's that supposed to mean? Do you think I need major help to look decent?"

"You two are dynamite," Mike said with a laugh. "Do y'all always joke around like that?"

Jeff grinned and shook his head. "Yeah, neither of us likes getting serious."

Beverly swallowed past the lump that had suddenly and inexplicably risen in her throat and headed toward the parking lot.

"You did good today, babe," Mike called

after her. ''I'll be in touch if something else comes up.''

''Thanks,'' she answered and gave him a casual wave as she got in her car.

As soon as she was out of sight of the tennis courts, she pushed down on the accelerator. Only an hour. It took twice that long for her hair to dry. Well, she just wouldn't take the time to wash it. She was determined to be dressed to the nines and sitting on the porch when Jeff arrived.

Why had she accepted his invitation? There was no logic to spending time with him. Even if he had *any* of the qualities she was looking for in a husband, he'd made it clear he had no intention of settling down. At best, they would have a short, hot, sexy affair, dripping with a passion she'd never felt before...but still just an affair.

Beverly wanted more. So, thank goodness she wasn't attracted to Jeff. That man was dangerous. He was the worst kind of villain, the kind that would take all she had to give, then ride off into the sunset. Beverly knew better than to get involved with him. She was

smarter than that. Her plans for her future
didn't include Jeff or anyone like him.

But then, she doubted there was anyone
else like Jeff. He was definitely one of a kind.

HE WAS LATE. Beverly sat on the porch
swing, swatting mosquitoes and trying to ignore the hands of her watch as they ticked to
ten minutes past seven, then fifteen, then
twenty. Was there a more annoying man on
earth?

A truck turned off the county road onto the
driveway and wound its way around the
curves until it stopped in front of the house.

"Sorry I'm late. Mike and I got to talking
about our favorite islands, and the time
slipped away," Jeff said after hopping out
and approaching the porch.

Beverly bit her tongue to keep from blast-
ing him with what she thought of him and
Mike chatting about the Caribbean while she
was being sucked dry by mosquitoes the size
of hummingbirds.

He opened the passenger door for her, then
jogged around to the driver's side. "We have
reservations for eight o'clock. We're going
to have to hustle to make it on time."

They arrived at the trendy Austin restaurant at five after eight. It was a deceptively ordinary-looking place on the outside, but Beverly had eaten there often and knew the food was excellent.

"I'm hungry for a big steak," Jeff said as he took the menu from the waiter.

"We have a delicious beef Wellington," the waiter offered, "or you could try our lamb tartare."

"No raw sheep for me," Jeff said with a decisive shake of his head. "Don't you have just a plain ol' steak? You know, maybe a thick rib-eye, medium rare?"

"I'm sorry, sir. But these are our only meat entrées. Would you like to see a wine list?"

"Sure, why not? Although I'm not sure what wine goes with raspberries and asparagus."

"Jeff!" Beverly scolded. To the waiter, she smiled and said, "Yes, André, bring us a wine list, please."

As soon as the waiter left, she leaned across the table and glared at Jeff. "Would you please act nice, or I'll ask for a booster chair for you.''

"When I asked Scott to recommend a restaurant, I assumed it would be a place that serves *real* food. What is this stuff, anyway? And look at the prices!"

"Jeff…" she warned.

He lifted his hands. "Fine, I'll find something my poor starving stomach can tolerate. But next time we go out, *I'll* pick the place."

"Next time? Who says there'll be a next time?"

Slowly, his lips curved into his sexiest grin. "I do."

"Oh, you do, do you? And do you always get what you want?"

He leaned forward, resting his elbows on the table until their faces were only inches apart.

"I have hopes that I will."

A sensual shiver of anticipation streaked through her, and Beverly abruptly sat back in her chair. "Why don't you let me order the wine?"

He leaned back with a nonchalant shrug. "Sure, knock yourself out."

André returned and Beverly ordered the wine and her meal. It took Jeff a couple minutes longer, but he finally decided on the beef Wellington. André brought the wine and, after Beverly approved it, he poured them both a glass, then left.

"So, Bev, is your life filled with one exciting photo shoot after another?" Jeff asked, leveling his disconcerting gaze on her.

"I wish," she admitted. "But this isn't exactly a hot spot for modeling assignments. Actually, I'd like to get into the movies eventually."

"As an actress?"

"No, as a baby wrangler!" she retorted sarcastically. "*Yes*, as an actress."

"Was that your talent in the Miss America contest?"

Beverly shifted uncomfortably. The talent competition was something she'd rather forget.

"No, my acting coach didn't think I was ready."

"What did you do then? Sing? Dance? I don't think I've ever heard anyone mention it."

"Dammit, if I could sing or dance, I'd have won that contest!" she snapped. "That was always my weakest score."

Jeff seemed genuinely surprised. "You can't sing, dance or act?"

"I didn't say I couldn't act. I just said, I wasn't ready at the time of the contest."

"Okay, I stand corrected. But with all your pageant experience, I would have thought you'd be able to sing like an angel."

"I think the term my singing teacher used was that I couldn't carry a tune in a bushel basket."

She could see he didn't realize how serious her lack of talent was.

"So, what *did* you do?" he persisted.

"I did a sort of comedy act." She met his gaze defensively.

"You cracked jokes?"

"Well, not *me* exactly. I was the straight man. Dinky was the comedian."

"Dinky?"

She lowered her voice until it was barely audible. "Dinky is my dummy."

Jeff was trying very hard not to smile.

"Well, I can see where that would be most impressive."

"Are you making fun of me?"

He must have noted, at last, her sensitivity to the subject because his eyes gentled. "No, of course not. I might tease you, Beverly, but I'd never make fun of you. You're too special for that."

Beverly was momentarily speechless at the unexpected compliment. Jeff didn't pass them out lightly, so when one came out of his mouth, she was astonished. And she didn't know how to deal with it. Not from Jeff.

"Actually, if they'd let me ride my horse on stage, I would have knocked their socks off," she rushed to add, trying to hide her confusion. "Dandi was my good-luck charm all through my competitions up to the big one. All of a sudden when I hit the big leagues with the Miss Texas title, I had to scramble to come up with something acceptable, and I was a lot better at comedy than drama."

"I'll bet you were a cheerleader, weren't you?"

She nodded.

"And the school's 'most beautiful,' and 'most popular'?"

Again she nodded. "But none of those had anything to do with *me,*" she said softly.

He reached across the table and took her hand in a genuine burst of concern. "Poor Beverly. Caught in your own image. When you look in the mirror, what do you see?"

"I...I don't know what you mean," she hedged, not wanting to face the answer she would have to give.

"You know what I see?" His expression softened as he answered his own question. "I see the sad, beautiful face of a lonely woman who wants to be loved for herself rather than for her body."

Beverly's mouth opened, but she couldn't find honest words to deny any part of his assessment.

"Not that it's a bad body," he said, his grin returning as if he sensed the conversation was getting too heavy. "Combined with the brain that you don't want anyone to know about, the tart, sassy tongue and a heart as big as Texas, it's a pretty powerful package.

I don't understand how some guy hasn't wrapped you up yet.''

''I told you, there aren't any good ones left,'' she responded lightly.

''What am I—canned ham?''

She managed a shaky smile. ''No, you're just passing through.'

André arrived with their dinners and placed them in front of Beverly and Jeff with a dramatic display of his serving skills.

The conversation remained more neutral as they ate, and Beverly watched with amusement as Jeff cleaned his plate.

''Okay, I'll have to admit, that was pretty good,'' he said when every last bite was gone. ''There just wasn't enough of it.''

''You're still a growing boy.''

Jeff glanced pointedly at the food still left on her plate. ''And I suppose you're going to say that you have to diet constantly to watch your figure.''

''If I don't watch my figure, no one else will want to.''

''No wonder no one can see past your body. You won't let them.''

''What is that supposed to mean?'' she

asked, bristling at his tone. "And I suppose if I got fat, people would be able to see the *real* Beverly and like me for what's underneath all the blubber? That is, if they would take the time to look."

"You're selling yourself short, Beverly. If you start to take yourself seriously, other people will, too."

"I take myself seriously. I'm realistic when I believe that my body is my future. Any career I pursue will relate to the way I look."

"Then maybe you're pursuing the wrong careers," he said in an annoyingly calm voice.

Once again, he left her speechless. Beverly had never seriously considered any career that didn't relate to her beauty. Oh sure, she'd once toyed with the idea of becoming a veterinarian. But that had just been the dream of a child.

It struck Beverly that she'd never really decided what she wanted to be when she grew up.

CHAPTER SIX

"DOES THIS THING still run?" Jeff asked as he looked at the ancient, battered pickup truck that was parked under a tin-roofed shed on the Double C Ranch. God only knew how many hundreds of thousands of miles the antique truck had on its odometer. One thing was obvious—time had not been kind to the vehicle. Held together as it was by rust and layers of mud, its original color was impossible to determine.

"Well, it did the last time I drove it."

Jeff glanced dubiously at the tires, which were definitely showing signs of dry rot. "How long ago was that?"

Hank paused, mentally calculating before he answered, "About 1980. That's when I broke my hip and J.T. decided I was too old to drive anymore. Shoot, I was only eighty-six or -seven then."

The hood groaned in protest as they lifted it. Jeff peered at the dust-covered parts with an experienced eye. He'd done his share of fiddling with all sorts of vehicles and knew his way around the mechanical complexities of a combustion engine. "It doesn't look too bad," Jeff commented. "A little dirty, and you're going to need to replace all these hoses and belts, but we can probably have it running in a few weeks."

"A few weeks, hell!" Hank exclaimed. "I'm goin' to the library today to check some charts and maps—to compare them to my map."

"We can go in my truck."

"Nah, I need to get this baby runnin' again anyway." Hank sucked in a deep breath and straightened. Ever since he and Jeff had spent an evening talking oil and speculating on how they could put together a crew and the equipment, should there actually *be* oil on his property, Hank had gotten a new lease on life. Jeff reminded him of himself when he was much younger. And their conversation brought back the memories of his glory days. He was reveling in it.

They spent the whole morning working on the truck, cleaning the engine, changing the oil, spark plugs and filters and charging the battery. With any luck, the belts would hold until they could get into town to buy more.

When the moment came to try starting it, Hank climbed into the cab and turned the key. The engine growled several times, then sputtered to life. With a tired cough, it died, and Hank turned the key again. Jeff made some adjustments and the engine caught and smoothed out.

"Get in," Hank called.

"Why don't I drive?" Jeff offered after shutting the hood and looking in the open passenger-side window.

"Nah, I've been drivin' since before you were born. Hell, probably since before your *grand*dad was a gleam in his papa's eyes." Hank stomped on the clutch and shifted the gears with a metal-to-metal growl that raised the hair on the back of Jeff's neck.

"Needs a little transmission work, too," Hank added. "Been meanin' to get it fixed, but the mechanic in town can't find the parts. Says the truck's too old. Can you imagine that?'' He shook his head. ''Too old! Damn, I hate to hear someone say that.''

Jeff wisely decided against adding his voice to those who thought Hank was too old to still be driving *any* vehicle, much less a truck that probably hadn't been roadworthy since the sixties. That would explain why there was no Texas inspection sticker on the windshield.

Against his better judgment, Jeff got in the passenger side and slammed the door shut. It immediately popped back open.

''Oh, you gotta hold down on the handle and ease her shut,'' Hank explained. ''She's like a woman—you gotta treat her gently.''

Jeff complied and the door latched, but a generous amount of space still showed between it and the frame. Automatically, Jeff felt for a seat belt.

''You won't find any of those dang belts in here, son,'' Hank said, guessing what Jeff was doing. ''Harnesses were meant for animals, not people.''

Jeff settled for a death grip, out of Hank's line of vision, on the edge of the threadbare seat. ''Where did you say we were going?''

"To the library," Hank answered. He reached under the seat and pulled out a rolled map. Its tattered edges and yellow color testified to its age. "I've got somethin' to show you, and I thought we could look at some current geological maps of the area. This baby might be a little out of date."

Not old, just out of date. Jeff smothered a smile at Hank's understatement.

Hank returned the map to its place on the floor and gave Jeff a wrinkled grin. "I been savin' that map all these years, waitin' for one of my grandsons to take an interest in the oil business. But Cal was too busy—first gettin' his butt busted in the rodeos and then gettin' involved in the boot business. And Ty's out playin' around with grapes. Wine!" the elderly man said with a snort. "It's a sissy drink. All that sniffin' and garglin'. Hell, they should take a shot of Jack Daniel's and get it over with."

Hank pulled out onto the county road and headed toward town, punching down on the accelerator until they were traveling at ten miles over the posted speed limit.

Jeff never would have believed the old

truck capable of moving so quickly. He only hoped it didn't self-destruct right there in the middle of the road.

"Anyway, none of my blood kin care about oil like I do," Hank continued, completely oblivious to Jeff's worried glances. "They wouldn't appreciate my little secret. And even if I gave them the land, they wouldn't know what to do with it."

"You want me to help you get a well drilled?" Jeff asked, finally guessing the direction of the conversation. Hank had a tendency to wander a bit, so it was often difficult to keep up with his train of thought.

"It's there, son. I *know* it's there." Hank's bright eyes danced with excitement. "I was puttin' together the money to wildcat it when my wife died. I guess I just lost the heart for it. Then I banged up my hip and J.T. moved me, house and all, to the Double C. But the past few years, I been wantin' to get back to it. You know how it is with the oil business...I miss it."

"Yeah, I know," Jeff agreed. "I've been missing it myself. But I'm not having any luck finding a job."

"Then you've got time to go check this out with me," Hank stated.

"Well, sure, I suppose so. Where is this land?"

"In Brazoria County, just outside a little town named Alvin. Ever heard of it?"

"Other than it's Nolan Ryan's hometown, I've heard there's a few good oil fields in the area. A friend of mine who's with PetroCo is about to start a job in Danbury, which is only a few miles from Alvin."

"This one's gonna be more than just a *good* oilfield. It's gonna be a gusher that'll put Spindletop to shame."

"Have there been any tests done on it?"

"Nope, don't need 'em. The oil's there," Hank answered positively. "I can *feel* it. And once you're there, you'll feel it, too."

In spite of the overwhelming likelihood that Hank was just blowing hot air, the old, familiar rush of adrenaline at the thought of finding oil swept over Jeff.

He turned to Hank, eager to continue the discussion. But the old man's face was twisted in a strange expression. All of a sudden, Hank's gnarled fingers tightened on the wheel and he slumped forward, jerking the wheel sharply to the right.

Jeff leaped forward and tried to grab the wheel and dislodge Hank's foot from the gas pedal at the same time. But it was too late. The truck was traveling too fast as it plowed through the carpet of pink buttercups and yellow dandelions that lined the road. The ditch barely slowed them down, but the soft mud jerked the truck to the left. The vehicle slid several more yards before slamming into a three-foot-tall concrete drainage culvert.

BEVERLY SAT at Mrs. Goodwin's bedside, reading aloud from one of the romance novels the old lady enjoyed so much. Her condition had worsened to the point that Beverly could scarcely tell if she was even conscious. Only a faint smile on the woman's face when Beverly came to an especially racy scene gave her any hope at all. Finally, when the old woman's breathing became so deep that Beverly knew she was truly asleep, Beverly stood and stretched her aching back.

Her shift as a volunteer had been over an hour ago, but she couldn't bear to leave Mrs.

Goodwin. She pressed a kiss on the woman's forehead, whispered goodbye and crept out of the room.

In the hallway, Glenda ran past, obviously in a hurry. Beverly automatically fell into step, more out of curiosity than because she thought she might be of help.

"What's going on?" she asked once they were in the elevator, going down.

"There's been a bad car accident and the emergency room is understaffed, just like the rest of this hospital."

A chill chased down Beverly's spine. Since Crystal Creek was such a small community, the chances were good that she would know the accident victims. "Do you have any idea who was involved?"

"I'm not sure, but I think they said it was that old man, Hank, and a young guy...Jeff Something."

Beverly's heart leapt into her throat. Hank and Jeff? *Oh God, please don't let them be dead,* she prayed as she watched Glenda rush through the swinging doors at the end of the emergency-room waiting area.

As soon as the emergency-room nurse re-

turned to her desk, Beverly rushed over to it.
"How are they...Hank and Jeff? Do you
have anything on their condition? They're
not...?" She couldn't bring herself to speak
the words as tears filled her eyes. It was
amazing how much feeling she had for that
cocky Jeff. Suddenly, all she could think
about was his gorgeous smile and deep,
warm laugh and the way those blue eyes
studied her and how good his lips felt on
hers.

The sympathetic nurse smiled and said,
"They're both alive. But the old man's in
bad shape. They think maybe he suffered a
stroke before he lost control of his truck."

"What about Jeff?" Beverly asked anx-
iously.

"You know him?" the nurse answered.

Beverly nodded eagerly. "Is he okay?"

"He'll be all right. He's pretty bruised up,
and he might have a couple of broken ribs.
He's in X-ray right now."

Beverly breathed a sigh of relief and
smiled her thanks to the nurse before hurrying to the X-ray department to await news
about Jeff. She paced nervously in the

sparsely furnished waiting room. Then, unable to bear the tension, she ventured up the hall to listen at the door of the X-ray room where Jeff was. Her ear was pressed against the door and she was unaware of anyone's presence until a deep voice spoke to her.

"Well, Miss Angel of Mercy. Are you working on this floor today?"

Beverly whirled around and found that she was almost nose to nose with the handsome doctor she had met in the elevator two days ago. She glanced at the door again. "I have a friend in there. I just want to know what his condition is."

"*His* condition?" A look of disappointment crossed Dr. Sinclair's face.

"Yes, Jeff's sort of an old friend of the family. I couldn't go home without knowing how he is."

"Jeff Harris?" he questioned. "I've just been assigned to his case. Let me check his X rays and I'll get right back to you. If he doesn't require emergency surgery maybe we could go get a bite to eat afterward?"

Beverly nodded. "I suppose that would be

okay. If you don't mind being seen with a lowly volunteer.''

Dr. Sinclair winked at her and disappeared into the X-ray room. In moments he was back. "Just some badly bruised ribs and a mild concussion. We'd like to keep him under observation overnight, but he refused. Your friend's pretty hardheaded—in more ways than one.'' He gave her another big smile. "He'll be out in a couple of minutes if you want to wait to see him. Then we can be on our way.''

Almost immediately, the doors opened and Jeff was pushed through in a wheelchair. His face, hair and jeans were splotched with mud. His shirt had been removed and already a big bruise was appearing on his right side. His swollen, blackened eyes brightened somewhat at the sight of her.

"Hi, Bev. Have you come to hold my hand and nurse me back to health?'' Jeff managed a pained grin that nevertheless was quite dazzling.

Beverly wiped a blob of dried mud off his face. ''Are you all right, Jeff?''

"I'm gonna be fine. The doc here says I

can go home. Want to give me a lift, darlin'?''

Dr. Sinclair stepped forward. ''Maybe I've
been too hasty. Maybe I should *insist* that
you stay here a couple of days for observation. I don't like the way your pupils are di-
lating.'' He turned to the nurse pushing Jeff's
chair. ''See to it that he's admitted for the
night, nurse. And don't take no for an answer.'' He then took Beverly's arm and led
her away.

Jeff shifted painfully and watched the couple walk away. Just as they were turning the
corner, Beverly heard him mutter, ''Well,
shoot!''

GREGORY WAVED AWAY the menu that Nora
Jones brought to the table and took a sip of
water. To Beverly he said, ''I've spent so
much time in here since I moved to town a
week ago that I know the Longhorn's menu
by heart.'' Then, turning to the waitress, he
smiled and asked, ''How are you doing today, Nora?''

''Just fine. And how are things at the hospital? I heard ol' Hank got himself in an accident. Damn fool, driving at his age.''

Gregory ordered grilled chicken and Beverly a salad. As soon as Nora left, Gregory focused his full attention on Beverly.

"So tell me, Angel. Are you engaged, or otherwise romantically involved?"

Gregory studied her over his glass of mineral water, giving Beverly the feeling she was a specimen under a microscope. "You're certainly direct, Dr. Sinclair," she hedged.

"Please call me Gregory," he said with a charming smile. "Doctors are notoriously short of time. We have to cut to the chase, or lose out altogether. How about that young man in X-ray?"

"Jeff? Jeff and I are just friends."

"If he's not in the running, is there someone else who's special in your life right now?"

"Not a soul in sight, Dr.—er, Gregory," Beverly said lightly. "I have no serious suitors. There aren't all that many eligible bachelors left in Crystal Creek."

"I just happen to know one."

"Oh, really?" Beverly bantered back. She was on firm footing now. If ever there was something Beverly was good at, it was harmless flirting. She could certainly hold her own with the self-confident doctor. She glanced around the room, then let her eyes slowly slide back to meet his. "Where?"

"Beverly, there's a dance at the country club on Saturday night. I'm off that day, so would you like to go there for a real meal? I know it's soon, but...well, I'd like to get to know you better."

Beverly remembered the conversation she and Glenda had had the other day. Was Dr. Gregory Sinclair the one who would sweep her off her feet? She looked into his handsome face and noted each of his perfect features, the perfectly layered blond hair, the perfectly shaped sky blue eyes, the perfectly straight nose, the perfectly white teeth. And to top it all off, he was a doctor! She couldn't ask for a more stable, successful career than that.

"I'd love to go to the country-club dance with you," she said, giving Gregory a look she knew would make his mouth water. She knew, because *she* had practiced it in the mirror. Perhaps that was why she recognized the characteristic in him. It appeared she and Dr. Gorgeous were two of a kind.

Oh God, why didn't that make her happy?

"So, Beverly, other than volunteering at the hospital, what do you do with your time? Do you work anywhere else?"

"Actually, I don't have a *real* job right now, just a little modeling," she explained, reminded once more how empty her life was. "My mother owns the Circle T ranch and I help out around there, too."

"Oh, isn't that the huge ranch just north of town?"

"No, that's the Double C. The McKinney family owns that. Our place is a little smaller, about eighty-five hundred acres. We raise cattle and quarter horses."

"I don't know much about ranching. I'm just a city boy from Dallas. I went to University of Texas in Austin and fell in love with this country."

"I went to University of Texas, too. Class of '89."

"I was five years ahead of you. What was your major?"

"Business and a minor in science," she

answered. "I was thinking about becoming a veterinarian."

"And what changed your mind?"

"Oh, I was busy with the pageants and having a good time in college." She shrugged. "I guess I was like a lot of kids then, more interested in partying than in studying."

"And I'll bet you were really popular on campus," Gregory commented, studying her with an approving look. "Now *I* spent all my time studying."

"Yeah, right… I went on a few dates with some doctors-to-be, and they found time for fun."

"I would have too, if you'd been there with me."

Nora arrived with their dinners, and their conversation switched to tales of his residency.

They were about halfway through their meal when Gregory's beeper went off. He grimaced, excused himself and dashed to the telephone to check his message. When he returned, he gave her a disappointed look.

"I'm sorry, Beverly. One of my patients is having some problems. I have to go."

"Don't worry about it, Gregory. Duty calls."

"That's the glamorous life of a doctor." He smiled and shrugged. "I'll pick you up at seven-thirty sharp on Saturday. At the Circle T?"

She nodded. "I'll be ready."

He stopped at the cash register and hurried out after giving Beverly a parting wave.

Nora stopped by the table and commented, "Such a nice-looking man."

Beverly nodded. "I suppose so."

"You *suppose* so? He looked perfect to me."

"I think that's his biggest flaw."

Nora gave Beverly a look that clearly said she thought Beverly had lost her mind. "He seemed pretty taken with you."

"A lot of men are taken with me...then they marry someone else. No sense in getting too excited until they put a ring on your finger."

"Well, maybe this one will be different."

GREGORY STRODE into Jeff's room, flipping the chart as he walked. He slid to a stop when he found Jeff sitting up in bed watching television. "So, what's the emergency, Harris? Why did you have the nurse call me?"

Jeff gave the doctor a knowing grin. "Oh, I was just wondering how long you plan on keeping me in here and away from Beverly."

"Beverly told me she's not involved with you," stated Gregory.

"Oh, she's involved, all right. She just doesn't know it yet." Jeff clicked the television to another station.

"Just what are your intentions toward her?" Gregory demanded.

"Purely dishonorable. How about yours?" Jeff changed the channel again.

"We've just met. But I plan on getting to know her a lot better."

"Just keep in mind that she's one of those high-maintenance babes. She's pretty enough, but...never mind. She'd never forgive me if I told you everything."

The doctor took a step forward. "But what..."

Jeff held up both hands defensively.

"Nope! Not another word will pass these lips. Where is Bev, anyway?"

It was Gregory's turn to smile secretively at Jeff. "Now that's for me to know and for you to find out," he taunted as he turned and walked out the door, leaving Jeff with the clicker in his hand and a curse on his lips, for the second time that night.

CHAPTER SEVEN

"WHAT ARE YOU DOING here today?" Glenda asked late the next afternoon, looking up from the desk as Beverly got off the elevator. "No, don't tell me, let me guess. You love it so much here, you just can't stay away."

"Wrong." Beverly shifted the two packages she was carrying to her other arm. "I just wanted to check on some of the patients. How's Mrs. Goodwin doing?"

"Not too good. Her heart stopped twice last night. She's in intensive care today."

"Oh no." Although Beverly knew Mrs. Goodwin's condition wasn't improving, she hated to think of losing her friend.

"And Jackie?" she asked Glenda.

"He went home for the weekend. His blood tests are so encouraging, we think his leukemia might be in remission."

"And how are Hank Travis and Jeff Harris?'' Beverly asked with studied nonchalance.

''Hank's still in intensive care—''

''Is he *that* serious?''

''Actually, he's doing pretty well, all things considered. Do you know that guy is ninety-nine years old?'' Glenda chuckled. ''I've never seen a man more determined to make it to a hundred.''

''So, he's going to be okay?''

''He should be. His cuts and bruises will heal relatively quickly, but he's going to have to take it easy for a while. He's lucky that stroke didn't paralyze his left side. As it is, it's just going to be weak.''

''And Jeff?''

''Ah...Jeff. I think the nurses have voted him the man they'd most like to give a bed bath to and keep as a patient for the rest of their lives. Is that the Jeff you're talking about?''

Beverly rolled her eyes. ''Yes, that's the Jeff I know. What is it about that guy? Women can't resist him.''

''Is that why *you're* here today?'' Glenda gave Beverly a curious glance. ''Is he your Mr. Right?''

"Jeff Harris?" A dry, harsh sound that was a cross between a snort and a chuckle burst out of Beverly's mouth. "The only thing he's got going for him is a nice smile—"

"And a fantastic body," Glenda added. "Not to mention enough sex appeal to stop a herd of wild horses."

"Not as far as I'm concerned. Sometimes he's the sweetest, funniest guy I've ever met, and other times he's the world's biggest jerk."

"Well, around here, he's been a real joy. I just wish more of our patients were like him."

"So, which room is Mr. Wonderful in?" Beverly forced herself to ask. "I brought him a present."

"Oh, he checked out several hours ago. Dr. Sinclair seemed anxious to get him out of here for some reason. Last night he wouldn't let Jeff go, then this morning he practically kicked him out."

Beverly sighed and glanced down at the books in her hand. "So, I guess I'm out of luck. I'll just have to deliver these later."

"Well, if it isn't Crystal Creek's very own

Angel of Mercy. This isn't one of your regular days, is it? Or did you stop by to see me?"

Beverly turned to find Gregory standing behind her. "Oh, hi, Gregory."

Out of the corner of her eye, she caught Glenda's curious look.

"I'm on rounds right now or I'd buy you a cup of coffee," Dr. Sinclair said. He flashed her one of his perfect smiles, pulled his pen out of his pocket and picked up one of the charts from the top of the desk. "I'll see you tomorrow night," he added before heading toward the hallway.

"So, how long has this been going on?" Glenda asked, watching the interchange with interest. "Is this why you're not interested in Jeff?"

"*Nothing's* going on. At least, not yet. All we've shared is some conversation and half a meal."

"Well, that's more boring than my love life." Glenda glanced down at the pile of charts. "If you stick around any longer, I'm going to assign you to bedpan duty again."

"That's it, I'm gone." Beverly was in the

elevator before Glenda could make good her threat.

AS BEVERLY APPROACHED the Hole in the Wall ranch she decided, on impulse, to drop Jeff's present off at his house.

Jeff was living in the cottage that had been Val's before the wedding. Beverly parked her car in front of the small log house and got out slowly, almost changing her mind a half dozen times between her car and the front porch. Oh well, she and Jeff *did* have moments of friendship, and this was certainly a *friendly* thing to do. Either that or she was taking this nursing business a little too seriously.

She knocked and heard a muffled thud, followed by a very distinct curse word. Almost a minute passed before the door opened and Jeff appeared, wearing only a pair of jeans with just the bottom three buttons hastily fastened.

"What are you doing here?" he asked, not attempting to mask his rudeness. In fact, he seemed to be trying to magnify it. "Was the doctor busy this evening?"

Beverly thrust the package at him and

turned around. ''I don't need this hassle,'' she stated as she stalked across the wide, open porch and down the first step.

''Bev, don't go,'' Jeff said, his voice soft and full of pain. ''I'm sorry. I didn't mean to snap at you.''

Beverly hesitated, her foot on the second step.

''*Please* don't go,'' he repeated with a groan.

She turned back to see if he was playing another game, but from the grim expression on his face and the way he was gingerly holding his side, she knew he was genuinely in pain.

''Go lie down,'' she ordered, returning to where he was leaning against the doorjamb. ''I'll get you a heating pad.'' She helped him loop his arm around her shoulder, and he leaned heavily on her as she assisted him across the living room and into the bedroom. It was more difficult to ease him onto the bed, but finally, he was lying on his back.

Beverly paused for a second, looking down at him. His eyes were closed and his face was pale except for two spots of color high on his cheeks. His dark hair was tousled and falling across his forehead. She reached down and ran her fingers into its thick strands, pushing them back.

His eyelids fluttered open and he looked up at her. "Your touch is so gentle. I can see why you're such a good nurse's aide."

That little heart dance she'd been expecting when Dr. Gorgeous made his move was happening now, filling her chest with a longing and an emotion she didn't want to feel. Not for this man. Not for Jeff Harris.

She jerked her hand away. "I'll be right back."

It took several minutes of rummaging through his house to find the heating pad on the top shelf of the linen closet, the bottle of pain medication the doctor had prescribed and a clean glass.

"When did you last take these pills?" she asked as she carried the supplies back into the bedroom.

"I haven't taken any," he mumbled. "I don't like to take medicine."

"Well, too bad. You're either going to take these voluntarily, or I'll have to force them down. And I know how to, too. Do you want me to show you?"

"There are *many* things I want you to show me," he said, a hint of the rogue twinkling in his eyes for just an instant. "But forcing pills down my throat isn't one of them. Here, give me those damn things."

"Now, now, cursing won't help." She handed him two pills and helped hold the glass steady while he took a drink.

He lay back down on his pillow with a groan. "This hurts like hell. I can't remember ever being in this much pain, and it's just my ribs."

"Bruised ribs can be very painful. Just be glad you didn't break anything. With a little rest, you'll feel as good as new in no time."

Jeff managed a crooked smile. "You sound just like one of the hospital staff. Bev, I think you've missed your calling."

"Yeah, and you should be a banker."

His eyes closed again, and she searched the walls for a plug for the heating pad. She adjusted the temperature and placed it carefully on the purple bruise. She tried not to stare at his broad chest and the ridges of muscles running down his torso. Bruised, battered and weak, he was still the sexiest man she'd ever seen.

She sat by his bed until the pills took effect and he was sleeping peacefully. Then, in a move that would have shocked her mother and everyone else who knew her, Beverly did something totally out of character. With a dish towel tied around her waist, she washed Jeff's dishes and tidied up the kitchen. Next she straightened the living room, his bathroom and even—careful not to disturb him—his bedroom. She did stop short of vacuuming, reasoning that it might wake him up. Besides, she was exhausted. This housecleaning was hard work.

By then she was surprised to see how late it was. Jeff was due another dose of medication in a half hour, so she decided to wait, give him the pills, then leave. That was the least a good nurse would do...or a good friend, she reasoned as she stretched out on the sofa and flipped on the television.

BEVERLY AWOKE to the smell of coffee brewing and bacon frying.

"Good morning, Sleeping Beauty," a masculine voice drawled, pulling her attention to a pair of denim-clad legs. Her gaze followed his body up to the amused grin on

his bruised face. "How about some breakfast?"

Beverly pushed her tousled hair back from
her face and sat up. "Thanks, but I rarely eat
breakfast."

"Oh, come on. It's the only meal I can
cook with any proficiency," he coaxed. "At
least, have a cup of coffee with me."

She wiped the sleep from her eyes and
hoped she didn't look as disheveled as she
felt. She knew she should be getting home,
but the coffee smelled too good to refuse.
"Okay, that sounds good. Let me freshen up
first."

He returned to the kitchen while she went
to the bathroom, washed her face and
combed her hair. Feeling somewhat more
presentable, she joined him at the kitchen table. In spite of her refusal of breakfast, he
had set a plate and silverware at her place
beside a cup of fresh, hot coffee. Beverly
looked at the platter of fluffy scrambled eggs
and crisp strips of bacon, and her stomach
growled.

"Sure you won't have anything to eat?"
he asked as he spooned a generous portion
of eggs onto his own plate.

"I guess I will," she said, giving in to her appetite. "I didn't have a chance to eat dinner last night."

"You were too busy with your patients."

Beverly helped herself to the eggs and bacon and savored her first bite. "These are really good."

"Thanks. Eggs and chocolate chip cookies are the only things my mother taught me how to cook."

"Hmm...I love chocolate chip cookies."

"I'll remember that. They say that chocolate is an aphrodisiac, you know." His eyes twinkled as he openly flirted with her.

"I've heard that. But I don't believe it."

"Then I guess I'll have to make you some of my special-recipe cookies. They'll melt in your mouth and make me irresistible."

Beverly laughed. "And with bruised ribs, you wouldn't even be able to do anything about it," she teased.

One corner of his mouth lifted into a crooked grin. "You wanna bet?"

"As your unofficial nurse, I say you require bed *rest*. In a couple of days, you'll be as good as new."

"And then you'll be willing to try my secret recipe?"

The gleam in his eyes made Beverly's breath catch in her throat. "Uh...so what were you and Grandpa Hank doing in the truck?" she asked, choosing to change the subject rather than answer his question. "The two of you have been very mysterious."

"We're talking about going into a partnership to drill a well on some property he has down near the Gulf Coast."

"Oh, that old land," Beverly scoffed. "He's been talking about that for as long as I can remember. Mother told me J.T. even financed some sort of survey down there many years ago, and it came up with nothing."

"Well, Hank's convinced there's oil there, and he wants me to check it out."

"You're wasting your time. That's been Grandpa Hank's dream, but that's all it is. I think it reminds him of his days in the oil business. I've heard he was very successful and made a lot of money. But, like most wildcatters, he lost it all in the ongoing search for one more gusher. Oilmen are like gamblers—they may strike it rich, but they have to keep dropping those dollars in the slots, looking for more, never satisfied with what they've got.''

''I guess there's a grain of truth in that,'' Jeff admitted. ''It's a constant challenge, and it does get addictive. Hank and I understand each other and can talk about the oil business for hours. He's a nice old guy, and even if it doesn't pan out, I've promised him I'd check out his place for him.''

''Just don't be too disappointed if it's all hot air.''

''Oh, well, I'm not busy right now, so I don't mind taking a trip down to see it. Besides, I have a few contacts down there I can drop in to see, and maybe get a job lined up.''

Beverly looked at him curiously. ''Still nothing, huh?''

''No, not yet.''

''So, are you going to keep working here until something comes up?''

''I've decided to stay until my birthday in two weeks. I'll be getting a small inheritance then that will tide me over until I get a job.''

For a long moment their gazes met. She could see questions and indecision in his eyes, and knew her own must contain the same confusion. They both were very aware of the sexual attraction between them, which made them view his leaving Crystal Creek with mixed feelings. In one way it would be good to have the decision made for them, but on the other hand, they would never know what they had missed....

GREGORY GUIDED Beverly through the large double leaded-glass doors of the Crystal Creek Country Club. They passed across the marble-floored entry area and waited for the hostess to show them to their table.

Pausing in the doorway, Beverly looked across the room. Dozens of tables, dressed in their crisp white tablecloths, fresh floral centerpieces, sparkling silver and pointed mauve napkins added to the elegant atmosphere. Ever since she was a young girl, she'd loved going to the country club. Her mother and father had always made it a treat taking her out for her birthday, Easter or to celebrate something special. They'd all dressed up in their fanciest clothes and ordered whatever they'd wanted from the menu. She remembered her father's deep, rich laugh and the way he'd looked at her mother. They had been so in love. When Beverly's father died, Carolyn had grieved as if her broken heart would never mend.

Beverly wanted a love like that. She wanted a man who would adore her as her father had adored her mother. She wanted a man for whom she would feel such deep emotions that she would know she would die without him.

"Are you ready, Bev?"

Gregory's hand on her elbow and his voice in her ear startled her. She'd been so deep in her own thoughts that she'd forgotten he was there. They walked into the dining room and Gregory held out her chair as she sat. He seated himself and smiled across the glowing candles at her.

"I'm glad you agreed to go out with me tonight," he said. "Seeing you at the hospital all week and barely having a chance to talk to you has made me really look forward to this evening."

Beverly looked at him, forcing herself to concentrate on the very handsome doctor. "It's been a busy week there. What with half the staff being down with the flu and Grandpa Hank's accident.''

''I didn't realize that old man was your grandfather.''

''Well, no, he isn't really. Actually, he's my cousin Lynn's great-grandfather. He's been living at the Double C Ranch ever since I can remember and I spent a lot of time over there when I was younger. So it was just natural that I started calling him Grandpa Hank.''

''He's a crusty old codger, but sharp as a tack. Now that young guy who was with him—''

''Gee…I sure am hungry,'' Beverly interrupted and picked up the menu. ''What's the chef's special tonight, Danny?'' she asked the waiter.

''The beef Stroganoff is good and we have boneless barbecued ribs,'' Danny answered. ''By the way, it's good to see you here again, Miss Townsend. It's been a while.''

''Thanks, Danny. It's good to get back here. It's my favorite place to eat in Crystal Creek, you know.''

''It must be nice growing up in a small town and knowing everyone,'' Gregory commented after they had given Danny their order and he'd headed toward the kitchen.

"It has its advantages and disadvantages."

They kept up a lively conversation as they waited and throughout dinner. Beverly relaxed and realized she was having a good time.

"How about dinner and a movie on Wednesday?" Greg asked while they dawdled over dessert and coffee. "There's a new Kevin Costner romance out, and I'll be off work early that night."

"Great...that sounds great," Beverly answered with a little too much enthusiasm.

Beverly pointed out all the landmarks of her hometown as they drove back to the Circle T. Gregory walked her to the front door.

"Would you like to come in for a drink?" she asked, not really wanting to extend the date, but not particularly eager to end it, either.

"Thanks, but I'd better not. I'm on call in a couple hours, and I'd like to get a little sleep," he answered. "Will I see you at the hospital tomorrow?"

"Yes, I'll be in after noon. I promised the kids I'd bring a rabbit in for them to play with, and I've got a few new tapes for Mrs. Goodwin.''

''I'll try to catch you then, and we'll have a cup of coffee, okay?''

Beverly nodded, then before she could react, he took her into his arms and pressed his lips against hers.

She tried to respond. She even tried to enjoy it. If there were no bells, no sirens, no shooting stars, at least there were no alarms cautioning her that it wasn't wise to fall in love with this man. This was real life, not one of the romance books that Mrs. Goodwin loved so much. There was no such thing as a perfect hero.

As if to taunt her, the image of Jeff's sexy smile popped into her mind. There was certainly no chance of a happily-ever-after ending if she didn't get over her attraction to the wildcatter.

CHAPTER EIGHT

BEVERLY WAS PLEASED to find Mrs. Goodwin's condition had improved and she had returned from intensive care to her own room.

"You're looking wonderful today," she told the woman as soon as she neared the bed.

"And you need to get glasses, Beverly," Mrs. Goodwin responded pertly, but her weak voice showed just how much her latest attack had affected her.

"Do you want me to open your blinds? It's a beautiful day, but *really* hot. They're predicting it'll get up to the mid-nineties this afternoon."

"I used to love to sit in my backyard under a big old live oak tree in the afternoons," Mrs. Goodwin reminisced. "No matter how hot it got, it was as cool as springtime under that tree. I could sit and watch my babies playing on the grass or in the garden. They were only two years apart, you know. Mary Ellen was such a pretty little thing, all blond and pink and soft. And little Charlie was always wandering off, searching for new adventures from the first moment he could toddle around.''

Beverly was used to these ramblings about the children, so she quietly sat on the chair next to the bed and listened. During the past few weeks, Mrs. Goodwin had often talked of her children and her beloved husband. Tragically she had lost them all. Her daughter had died when she was just a little girl and her son had been killed in Vietnam. Mr. Goodwin had passed away several years ago. Beverly listened sympathetically at first and then found she enjoyed the stories. The time always passed too quickly.

''Oh, do you have to go so soon, dear?'' the old woman asked.

Beverly didn't mention that she'd been sitting almost motionless for more than an hour. Instead she said, ''I'm sorry, but I've got to check on Carrie before I leave. She's the little girl I was telling you about who's on dialysis and waiting for a kidney transplant. I want you to meet her as soon as you're feeling up to it. She looks a lot like that picture of Mary Ellen you have in your locket.''

Mrs. Goodwin raised her thin, heavily veined hand to her bare throat. ''Please, Beverly, would you help me with my locket before you leave? It's in the drawer of my nightstand. They always take it off when I go to intensive care.''

''Of course I will,'' Beverly said, retrieving the antique gold locket from the drawer and looping the long chain over Mrs. Goodwin's neck.

The old lady's hand shook as her fingers closed around the large oval. ''My children...'' she whispered and relaxed back against the pillow.

Beverly pressed a light kiss on Mrs. Goodwin's forehead before hurrying off to finish her visits.

It was a pleasant surprise to discover that Jackie was back and was sitting with Carrie in the sun room. Both children greeted Beverly with big smiles.

''A friend of mine wanted to meet you two.'' Beverly sat down and placed on her lap the small suitcase she had been carrying.

She snapped open the clasps and lifted the lid, being careful to block the children's view. "I've been telling him what good patients you are." As she continued to chatter, she slipped one hand inside an opening in the back of a dummy and gripped the mechanism that would move the doll's mouth and eyes. With a flourish, she moved the suitcase to the floor and seated Dinky on her lap.

He was dressed in his usual cowboy outfit, complete with tiny fringed chaps, a red checkered shirt, a leather vest and a straw cowboy hat. His painted smile and large, rolling eyes made the children laugh even before he spoke.

"Hi, my name is Dinky," Beverly said, her lips almost still as the dummy's mouth snapped open and shut. "I'll bet you're Jackie and Carrie. Beverly's told me you are the bravest kids in the whole world."

The children scooted closer, their delighted gazes focused on the lively face of the dummy while Beverly conducted a three-way conversation between the kids and Dinky. When her father had first suggested she take up ventriloquism, Beverly hadn't been too enthusiastic. After all, how much call could there be for people who could crack jokes without moving their lips?

But she had been surprised at how much children loved her act. Once her pageant days were over, Beverly had continued giving impromptu shows whenever she was invited to speak to a group of children. Then when she began volunteering at the hospital, Dinky had become a valuable communication tool, especially with children who didn't feel comfortable talking to strange adults. It was amazing how quickly and easily the kids would open up to the dummy's cheerful prompting.

"You're looking way too healthy to be in the hospital," Beverly said, speaking to Jackie through Dinky.

The little boy's sunken eyes sparkled with excitement. "My doctor says I'm in remission. I might even get to go home soon."

"Well, that's great news!" Beverly exclaimed, momentarily forgetting to throw her voice. Quickly correcting her mistake, she lowered her tone to Dinky's husky, boyish voice and added, "I'll bet you'll be glad to get back to your own room. I'll bet you even have a Nintendo, don't you?"

Jackie nodded eagerly. "Yes, and Mom said she would buy me the new Mario Brothers game cartridge." His expression became somber as he shrugged. "I love playing baseball, too, but I'm not very strong anymore."

Beverly's heart twisted. At his young age, the child had felt more pain and disappointment than she had in her entire life. But she managed to keep her voice cheery and upbeat as she spent another half hour entertaining Jackie and Carrie, as well as a couple other children who rolled into the sunroom in wheelchairs or hobbled in on crutches.

THE LAST PERSON on Beverly's list was Grandpa Hank. She hoped he'd be awake. Both times she had tried to visit before, the old man had been fast asleep.

What she didn't expect to find was a very chipper Hank, sitting up in bed, having a lively conversation with Jeff. The discussion ended abruptly at her arrival—almost too quickly, making her wonder just what the topic might have been.

"Hello. How are you two Indianapolis 500 drivers doing today?" she asked, forcing a smile on her face. This was the first time she'd seen Jeff since...well, since she had woken up in his house last Saturday.

"I hope you brought me some clothes, so I can get out of this place," Hank declared. "I'm gettin' downright claustrophobic cooped up in this room. All this white! I hate white. Why don't they paint the walls a nice shade of blue or green, you know, somethin' that would make a fella think of the outdoors?"

"I'll put that in the suggestion box."

"And you know what else I miss," Hank continued, unable or unwilling to stop until all his complaints were heard. "I miss the smell of an animal. Everything here smells like alcohol and death." He leaned closer to Beverly. "'Cept you, gal. You smell pretty damn good. But you're the only thing in this place that doesn't stop up my nose. Give me the good, clean smell of a horse any day."

"I'll see what I can do about that, too, Grandpa Hank. I brought you a book." She handed him the package and he tore the paper off with the eagerness of a child.

"You brought me a present? Why, hell, that's mighty sweet of you, gal. *Tales from the Derrick Floor*," he read aloud. "Why, it's about the olden days of drillin'. See here, son. You'll have to read this.''

''I will, Hank,'' Jeff agreed, flashing Beverly an approving smile. ''Just as soon as you finish it.''

Hank's wrinkled face was inscrutable, but the mistiness in his eyes told Beverly just how touched he was by the unexpected gift.

''I've got to get home,'' Beverly said. ''I'm already two hours over my scheduled time and Mother has invited Vernon to dinner tonight.'' She paused, then impulsively reached out and rested her hand on top of Hank's. ''Is there anything else I can get you before I leave?''

''Nah, I'm just fine.'' Hank was back in total control of his emotions and gave her a fierce stare. ''You plannin' on comin' back and visitin' me again?''

Beverly returned his steady look without wavering. ''Yes, I thought I would. Do you have a problem with that?''

One bony shoulder lifted in a careless shrug. ''Nah, I don't suppose I could stop you anyway, could I?''

''No, sir, you couldn't.''

''Then I guess I ain't goin' nowhere.''

"No, sir, you're not. I'll see you tomorrow then."

"Fine."

The door opened and the small room instantly became filled to overflowing with McKinneys as J.T., Cynthia and J.T.'s children arrived. They all exchanged greetings with Beverly and Jeff, then crowded awkwardly around the bed.

"Well, hell," Hank muttered. "You'd think I was fresh road kill and you folks was a flock of buzzards the way you're all crowded around me like this." He lifted his thin hands and shooed them away. "Step back and gimme some air. All this concern ain't healthy."

"He likes to complain, but just look at that smile," Lynn whispered to Beverly. She glanced at her watch. "Wasn't your shift over an hour ago? What on earth are you doing still here? No hot date?"

Beverly picked up her suitcase and was barely able to stifle a yawn. "I've got nothing more exciting than tucking Dinky into bed tonight."

"Why don't you stop by the ranch later?

You've been so busy that I haven't had a chance to talk to you.''

"Not tonight," Beverly said with a tired shake of her head. "I'm beat. But I'll try to catch up with you later in the week." She gave Hank one last smile. "I'll see you tomorrow," she promised him, then added, "goodbye, everyone" and turned toward the door.

"Wait, I'll walk out with you," Jeff called.

"Don't forget, son. Go get that map." Hank's voice followed them.

"Yes, sir, I'll do that right away," Jeff replied. "I'll try to get back here later this evening."

Hank didn't answer, but they could hear the pages of his new book turning as they walked into the hallway.

"Bev, I tried to call you yesterday."

"I went to Austin with Mother and Vernon to a quarter horse auction." As she answered, she continued walking, barely looking at him—actually, barely *able* to look at him. Around Jeff, she always lost every ounce of self-confidence she had.

Jeff must have noticed her attitude and

misjudged it to be coolness. He caught her arm, pulling her to a sudden stop.

Beverly took a step backward but encountered the solid obstacle of a white corridor wall. Jeff took advantage of her position and braced an arm on either side of her head, effectively blocking her escape. Little did he know that, when he was this close to her, escape was the *last* thing on her mind.

"Beverly, what are you still doing here...?" Glenda's voice trailed off. "Whoops, did I interrupt something?"

"Uh...no," Jeff said, moving away a little and letting his hands drop to his sides—but not before he trailed his fingers down Beverly's arms. "I was just about to ask Beverly to have dinner with me on Wednesday night."

"Uh...I can't that night," she answered. "I already have a date."

Jeff exclaimed. "Don't tell me you're going out with Dr. Kildare again."

"It's Dr. Sinclair, and I—well..." Beverly hedged. But her lack of an answer was apparently all the answer Jeff needed. A chill chased the tenderness from his eyes.

"Never mind, I forgot I already had plans

for Wednesday,'' Jeff said in a flat mono-
tone. ''See you around, Bev.''

Why don't you ask me out for Thursday or
Friday or any other damn day of the week?
she wanted to call after him. Of all the
luck...the first two real dates she'd been
asked for in a month, and they had to be on
the same night!

JEFF'S PATIENCE was particularly thin that afternoon as he tried to teach the proper way
to serve to a teenage girl who was more concerned with attracting the attention of a
young wrangler.

''Karen, you have to toss the ball higher
and follow through. Watch me...again.''

The girl fluffed her hair and licked her lips
as she struck a pose. ''Yeah, sure, Mr. Harris. I'm watching.''

Mr. Harris! Lord, that sounded old. He
wondered how old she thought he was, then
remembered when he'd been sixteen, he'd
thought turning thirty was a fate worse than
death. And today, he felt every one of his
almost thirty years.

Frankly, even if he lived to be as old as
Hank, he would never understand women.

When he'd awakened last Saturday morning and found Beverly asleep on his couch, the thought had flashed through his mind that he really wouldn't mind waking up with that woman for the rest of his life. It had gone as quickly as it appeared, but it had sneaked back in several times in the past few days.

He tossed the ball into the air and slammed the racket down so hard the ball sizzled across the net, barely missing Karen.

Karen screamed and dropped her racket in her haste to get away.

Jeff muttered an oath and walked around the net to pick up the racket. He was sure Scott would hear about this one. And then Scott would feel compelled to discuss it with Jeff, who was bored beyond words with his stint as tennis pro.

Obviously, it was time he moved on. He'd hung around Crystal Creek longer than he'd planned. Surely, once he hit the road, a job would open up for him. There was certainly nothing...or no one...holding him here. His birthday was in two weeks. After that he'd be gone, following the Texas wind once more.

He was in the shower when he remembered his promise to Hank.

A promise was a promise. Jeff knew Hank wouldn't rest easy until that map was recovered.

He drove his pickup through the wide elaborate archway marking the entrance to the Double C Ranch. As he parked outside the sprawling ranch house, he saw Cal standing in the middle of the corral, holding a lounge line and putting a nervous colt through his paces. Jeff walked over and stood watching, marveling at the silent communication Cal was telegraphing through the nylon rope to the young horse.

Cal noticed Jeff right away and waved. "Hi, you want to take a turn with this guy?"

"You've got to be kidding. I may dress like a cowboy and walk like a cowboy, but I could count the number of times I've been on a horse on the fingers of one hand."

Cal gave the rope a little jerk and the colt slid to a fidgety stop. He walked up and patted the horse's neck with his gloved hand, then unsnapped the rope from the animal's halter. "So, how's it going at the Hole in the Wall? Killed any dudes yet?"

Jeff chuckled. "Funny you should ask. I almost wiped out my first one today. And there have been others who have seriously tried my patience."

Cal's loud burst of laughter startled the colt, who circled the corral, kicking and bucking. "Sounds like you weren't cut out for public relations."

"Actually, I'm kind of soured on relations of all kinds at the moment."

"Sorry to hear that," Cal said. "This love business is a lot more fun than I ever imagined."

"Yeah, that's easy for you to say. You found a woman who has both feet on the ground. I seem to be attracted to women who have their heads in the clouds." Jeff shook his head and knew he'd better change the subject before his mood dipped below sea level. "Anyway, Cal, the reason I dropped by was to ask what y'all did with Hank's truck."

"That old piece of scrap metal? Daddy had it hauled to the junkyard."

"Which one?"

"Stan the Salvage Man's Wrecking Rodeo over on Tower Road."

"Thanks. Tell that pretty lady of yours 'hi' for me."

"Sure thing."

Jeff waved goodbye and got back into his pickup truck. He was glad he wasn't the one who would have to tell Hank about his most prized possession. Now, if only Jeff could get to the junkyard before Stan compacted the vehicle into a rusty cube.

The junkyard was surrounded by a six-foot wall, hiding its jumble of auto parts and partially dismantled vehicles from the road. Only a faded sign and an impressive number of hubcaps mounted all over the front of the building testified to Stan's business.

The man at the counter was busy taking apart a carburetor. "Can I help ya?"

"Is Stan here?"

"Nope. I'm Lou. Stan sold me the business about ten years ago. But Lou the Salvage Man doesn't have the same ring to it, don't you agree?"

Jeff would have assumed the man was making a joke, except that his dour face never changed expression. Jeff shrugged. "I'm looking for a truck."

"Just *any* truck?"

"No," Jeff answered. "A specific truck."

"Make?"

"Chevy."

"Color?"

"Rust."

"Year?"

"Uh…late thirties, maybe?" Jeff sighed. "Look, it was involved in a wreck last Thursday. I'm not sure when you would have picked it up, but you couldn't have picked up that many ancient pickup trucks since then."

"Just picked up the one."

Jeff swallowed hard, resisting the urge to reach across the counter and shake Lou. He pulled out his wallet and fished out a twenty-dollar bill. "Would you be so kind as to let me look at it?"

Lou picked up a rag that was almost as filthy as his hands and wiped off the top layer of grease before taking the bill and stuffing it into his shirt pocket. "Follow me."

They wound their way around stacks of threadbare tires and piles of corroded batteries until Jeff saw Hank's truck parked in front of the crusher. Considering its recent intimacy with a culvert, the truck was in surprisingly good shape. Well, at least it wasn't

in much worse shape than it had been before
the accident.

"That it?" Lou asked.

"That's it." Jeff started toward it, but Lou
reached out and grabbed his arm.

"You can't go over there."

"Why the hell not?"

"Insurance. They got rules, you know."

"Look, all I want to do is get something
out of the front seat. It won't take me but a
few seconds, then you can get back to
your...whatever it was you were doing."

"My business is selling parts. You want to
buy something, I'll sell it to you."

Jeff's already stretched patience snapped.
He yanked out his wallet, pulled out two
more twenties and held them out. "I want to
buy the whole damn truck."

"Are you kidding? It's an antique."

Jeff took out the rest of the bills and added
them to the others, then with his best poker
face firmly in place, stated, "Here's a hundred and forty bucks. It's all I have. Take it
or leave it."

Lou squinted at Jeff, trying to guess if Jeff
was good for a larger amount. Apparently de-

ciding he wasn't, Lou nodded and took the money.

"She's all yours. For another fifty bucks, I'll tow it to your place."

"No thanks. I'll tow it myself." He wasn't sure how he would accomplish that. All he knew was that he wasn't giving that worm another dime. He didn't want to ask Cal or any of the other McKinneys for help because, until he decided what he was going to do with the truck, he didn't want Hank's relatives to know he had it. And Scott was in Austin.

Beverly. He hated to ask her, but she was the only person he could think of who would sympathize with Hank's loss. She might be coldhearted and calculating when it came to men, but she had a soft spot for the hospital patients.

Hopefully, she wouldn't be out with Dr. Marcus Welby Sinclair. Frankly, the mood Jeff was in right now, he wouldn't have minded knocking out a few of the perfect doctor's perfect teeth. In fact, it would have made Jeff's day.

CHAPTER NINE

"OF COURSE I CAN DRIVE a pickup truck. Why?" Beverly gave him a look that clearly said she thought he was losing his mind.

"Good. Then my next question is, would you let me park a vehicle on your ranch for a few days?"

"I suppose so, but..."

"Would you go with me to rescue Hank's truck?" Jeff asked, then went on to explain the whole situation to her.

"And you don't even know if the map is still in the truck?"

"Well, no. But it's more than just the map. You don't know how attached Hank is to that truck. I think it would kill him if it were crushed."

Beverly, who had just returned from a long ride, swung out of the saddle. With one hand on the reins and one hand resting on the palomino's golden neck, she nodded. "Okay.

Just let me unsaddle Dandi.'' As she walked toward the barn leading the horse, she called over her shoulder, ''You owe me one for this, though.''

It had been difficult enough for Jeff to come to her this afternoon after the scene in the hospital hallway yesterday. But she seemed determined to complicate it even more. He jogged along until he caught up with her at the barn door.

''What did you have in mind?'' He gave her a wary, but intrigued glance.

''I've decided to take Dandi and maybe one of the llamas from your brother's ranch to the hospital day after tomorrow to visit with the patients,'' Beverly explained. ''I think the kids and some of the older folks will get a big kick out of it.''

''Darlin', you never cease to amaze me.'' He flashed her a sincere grin and she answered it with a look that was almost embarrassed that she'd been caught doing something so un-Beverlylike.

''So, will you help me?''

''Sure. It sounds like fun.'' Jeff leaned against one of the heavy oak support posts and watched Beverly unfasten the buckles and swing the saddle off the horse's back. He took it from her and carried it to the tack room, where he hung it from a looped rope that was suspended from the ceiling. Returning to the post, he couldn't keep his eyes off her. As she stroked the horse's sleek hide first with a currycomb, then with a stiff-bristled brush, Beverly's body moved with a sensuous grace. Her beautiful hair tumbled over her shoulders and down her back, swaying rhythmically with each long, smooth motion.

The horse and the woman were a stunning pair, both golden, gorgeous and spirited. Jeff could well imagine that, had Beverly been allowed to ride Dandi onstage during the Miss America pageant, the judges wouldn't have been able even to consider anyone else. He'd watched her ride for several minutes before she'd noticed him, and the sight of her in the saddle, her sexy, slender body moving gracefully in perfect harmony with the animal beneath her had brought an immediate physical response from him.

Jeff refused to consider the fact that he just might be a little in love with her. That didn't fit into his plans at all. So why was he so angry at the thought of Dr. Perfect kissing, touching, loving Beverly? He, Jeff, had no idea what he would do if Beverly said she loved him. He only knew that, at the moment, he was consumed with a passion for her heart and her body that pushed aside all other considerations. And one of those considerations was that he wasn't being fair to her. She deserved much more than he could offer.

"All finished," she said after dumping a measure of grain into Dandi's feed pan. "What exactly am I supposed to do?"

IT HAD TAKEN all Jeff's powers of persuasion to get Beverly behind the wheel of Hank's truck.

"This looks dangerous. What if his brakes don't work and I ram into the back of your truck?" she asked.

That thought had also crossed Jeff's mind. "I'm really hoping that doesn't happen. We'll be traveling slow, and if you want me to pull off the road, just honk."

Still she looked skeptical, but gave a good-natured thumbs-up sign. Jeff double-checked the chain to his trailer hitch after it was fastened to the frame of Hank's truck. Then, pushing aside the map he'd retrieved from under Hank's seat, Jeff climbed into his cab and started the engine. Easing forward slowly, he watched in his rearview mirror as the chain tightened, then jerked Hank's truck forward.

Beverly grimaced, but kept her hands on the wheel as they continued moving. The front end of the truck had suffered the worst damage, and she was obviously struggling to keep it heading in a straight line behind Jeff's vehicle.

It seemed to take forever to drive the five miles to the Circle T. Making the turns was the trickiest part of the trip, as Beverly had to fight the truck's urge to wander in the wrong direction. When they finally pulled in behind the barn and stopped, she slumped forward, her head resting on the steering wheel.

"I hope you know what you're doing," she muttered as Jeff helped her out of the cab. "I don't think there's a mechanic in the world who can fix this thing. Maybe you can talk Hank into filling the back with dirt and using it for a planter."

"I've always been handy with engines and mechanical things, and I just thought it was right to give Hank the option. A man doesn't like to have his most prized possession taken away without warning."

Beverly leveled a curious look at him. "And just what is *your* most prized possession?"

For a few seconds, he was lost in the crystal pools of her intuitive eyes.

He forced his voice to sound light as he answered. "I suppose my truck is, simply because it's been my home for so many nights. I'm not really a possession kind of guy."

"No, they might hold you down."

"That's right.

For several long minutes they studied each other, silently asking questions to which neither had answers. Jeff wanted her to know that his feelings for her were different. But how could he expect her to understand when he didn't have a clue what they were? No, it was better not to say anything than to say something that the dusty Texas wind might blow back in his face.

"Would you like to stay for supper?" she asked, breaking the silence first.

Jeff was tempted. But things were getting too complicated. If Beverly only wanted to be his friend, why was she flirting with him? It was obvious that she was as attracted to him as he was to her. Then there was Gregory, the great doctor. Did she have her sights set on him? Where did Jeff fit into the picture? Or did he?

And why the hell did it matter so much? Once he was out of town, Beverly would find her Mr. Right, whether it was Dr. Kildare or some other pillar of society. So maybe it would be best if Jeff started fading out of the picture now. It was time to leave Crystal Creek...and Beverly, behind.

"No, thanks," he answered. "I've got other plans tonight."

"Oh? A date?" Was that a note of jealousy in her voice? Or was it merely curiosity? "Yes," he lied. His gaze lowered to her full, rosy lips and he wanted, more than anything at that moment, to pull her into his arms and kiss her until she begged him to stay and never leave her.

Drawing in a deep, ragged breath, he spun on his heel and headed for his truck. After shutting the door, he rolled down the window and called out, "And thanks for helping me today. What time do you want me here tomorrow?"

"About two p.m. I want to make sure I arrive between lunch and supper. The patients complain about the food, but they'd be furious if they were late for a meal."

Jeff nodded and soon was heading down the driveway toward the main road. He glanced in his rearview mirror and saw Beverly still standing by the barn, her hand lifted to shade the sun from her eyes as she watched his truck drive away.

Would she miss him? Even a little? Jeff reached up and pressed his fist against the strange ache in the center of his chest. As much as he hated to admit it, he knew her memory would be with him for the rest of his life.

BY THE TIME Jeff arrived the next afternoon, Beverly had groomed Dandi until she glowed like a new gold coin. She'd decided at the last minute to save the llama for another visit, after she saw what kind of reception Dandi got.

Jeff was in a quiet mood and had the

pained look of a man with a hangover. She didn't ask and he didn't volunteer any information about the previous evening.

When they arrived at the hospital, Beverly was glad Jeff was there. She left Dandi in the trailer until all the patients who were able to had gathered in the courtyard. Then while Jeff looked after crowd control, Beverly rode Dandi in front of them and put the horse through the set of tricks she had taught her. Instead of the worn brown leather saddle she used at the ranch, Beverly had brought the elaborate silver-studded black saddle and bridle her father had given her for her thirteenth birthday.

The children were wildly impressed, clapping and cheering and wanting to pat the "horsie." Dandi, with an intuitive patience, allowed them to tug her mane or stick their fingers into her large velvety nostrils. And while Beverly held the horse, Jeff gave each child who was able a chance to sit on that beautiful sparkling saddle while Glenda took their pictures with a Polaroid camera. Even Carrie was able to make a brief visit.

The older patients reacted with more reserve at first. But once they loosened up, they were louder and wilder than the young kids. Jeff even had to run to the store for more film as each elderly person insisted on posing for a photo with the horse *and* his or her favorite nurse's aide, Beverly.

Beverly worked tirelessly making sure everybody had a good time. *Interesting,* Jeff thought as he watched quietly. *Beverly doesn't realize that, for once, her physical appearance has nothing to do with the people's love for her.*

All afternoon, Beverly had noticed Jeff's gaze focused on her. When she caught him off guard, she was certain she saw a genuine spark of approval and...something more. A kind of wistful longing.

Or was she reading more into his look than was really there?

CAROLYN FACED her daughter across the breakfast table. "So, how did the big date go last night?"

Beverly shrugged. "Oh, it went okay. We had dinner at that French restaurant in Austin and saw a movie."

"Just okay? Didn't you go out with Dr. Gorgeous?" her mother asked, picking up on the nickname Beverly had christened him with.

"He's a nice guy." Beverly nibbled on a piece of whole wheat toast.

"Just *nice?* I would have thought there'd be a little more enthusiasm in your voice than that."

"Mama, I *am* enthusiastic. It's just that..."

"What?" Carolyn prompted after Beverly's pause lengthened.

"He's just nice," Beverly repeated.

"But I thought you were looking for a *nice,* successful man. And it probably doesn't hurt that he's very good-looking."

Beverly shook her head and shrugged in complete confusion. "He's perfect. He's exactly what I've been looking for. You're right—I should be dancing in the streets."

"You're not even *skipping,*" her mother pointed out.

"I don't know what's wrong with me. Who was it who said, 'be careful what you wish for because you might get it'? Well, that's how I feel right now."

"So, are you going to participate in the box-lunch auction at the Frontier Days celebration Saturday?'' Carolyn asked, trying to steer the subject in a more cheerful direction. ''All the money is going to build a recreation center for the kids, you know.''

''There's not that many bachelors left in Crystal Creek, Mama. Do you want to risk wiping out what's left of them with my cooking?''

''I thought maybe I could help you with the cooking, dear. No one ever has to know.'' Carolyn smiled at her daughter.

''You know that would be against the rules. Besides, anyone who knows me would guess the truth. My lack of domestic skills is common knowledge. You can't keep little things like flunking home economics a secret.''

''But Dr. Gorgeous wouldn't know,'' Carolyn persisted.

''He'd find out soon enough.''

''Well, you should participate. It's for a good cause and it should be fun. Nobody takes it seriously. I doubt whether Dr. Gorgeous would judge a woman by her ability to make a good box lunch.''

Beverly drained her coffee cup and stood. ''I guess we could look at the bright side,

Mama. If I don't marry, you'll have a devoted daughter to take care of you in your old age." She headed toward the back door. "I'm going to take a ride. I'll be back in a couple of hours."

She went to the barn and saddled Dandi, then rode toward her favorite part of the ranch. In the far northwest corner where the land was the hilliest, underbrush and trees had been left untouched to form a forest that provided a protected habitat for all the wildlife native to that part of the state. Beverly never went there that she didn't see whitetail deer, a wild turkey or two, Spanish goats, several armadillos and possums, as well as javelinas or feral hogs. Before Scott had found a way to keep his exotic game on the Hole in the Wall property, other species of deer and sheep had been crossing the fences for the thick grass and abundant cover.

But today, as she let Dandi wander through the forest, Beverly barely noticed her surroundings. She was lost in thought. What was wrong with her? Why wasn't she jumping for joy over Gregory's obvious interest in her? Had she met Gregory sooner—about a month earlier, to be exact—she probably would have been thrilled. He was one of the nicest, most eligible men she'd *ever* met.

But Jeff had messed things up. Why was she so attracted to him? Why did her heart always start to race when she heard his voice? Why did she wake up in the middle of the night thinking about the sound of his laughter or the way his eyes twinkled like a mischievous little boy's, then burned with a passion that heated her very soul? Damn him. Now she could no longer settle for "nice" and "eligible." She wanted that undefinable "something special."

Two hours later, she returned, no closer to an answer than she had been when she left. After unsaddling Dandi and letting her out in the pasture, Beverly went in search of her mother.

"I've decided to enter the auction, Mama. And I'm going to make the lunch myself." She even managed a little smile. "God help the poor man who bids on my box lunch."

"Consider peanut butter sandwiches, honey. I don't think anyone ever died from eating peanut butter."

"There's always a first time."

BEVERLY WALKED OUT of Mrs. Goodwin's
room, and Gregory Sinclair instantly appeared beside her.

"Are you going to the Frontier Days celebration?" he asked.

"*Everyone* in Crystal Creek goes to that.
Any excuse for a get-together, you know."

He gave her one of his charming smiles.
"So tell me how to know which box lunch
will be yours."

"That would be cheating." Beverly gave
him a wry grin. "Besides, you're probably
better off not knowing."

Gregory chuckled and Beverly waved as
she turned away, heading toward Hank's
room. She enjoyed her visits with the old
man. Their sparring matches seemed to perk
them both up.

She poked her head around the door of
Hank's room. "Hi there. I hear you've been
causing the nurses grief again."

A chuckle came from the bed. "Well, if it
isn't little miss Goody Two-shoes come to
spread sunshine and good cheer. I think I'm
gonna be sick. Get me the bedpan, Jeff."

Beverly's head snapped around and she
saw Jeff sitting by Hank's bed.

"Hi, darlin'. Where's Dr. St. Elsewhere? I can't believe you're here without him breathing down your neck. Beverly without her adoring lapdog doctor. And people say there's no such thing as miracles anymore."

"His name is Dr. Sinclair, Jeff," she corrected stiffly.

"You certainly can't fault his taste in women," Hank piped up.

Beverly pointedly turned her attention to the old man. "Thank you, Grandpa Hank. And how are you feeling today? Do you want me to have the ladies' auxiliary come and visit you?" She smiled at the old man.

"Don't you let those Bible-totin' old biddies anywhere near me, Beverly. They get within thirty feet of this room and they'll hear language that'll burn their ears off." Hank crossed his arms over his chest and glared at her.

"Did I ever tell you about the time the nurses turned me loose on their patients? Bed baths, bed changes, bedpans? They've been trying to get enough money together to bribe me into taking care of you all the time. Wouldn't that be fun?" Beverly leaned against the end of the bed, plumped his pillows enthusiastically, ignoring his grumbling at being disturbed. "See you later," she sang out as she left the room.

Dr. Sinclair was waiting in the hall for her. Jeff, who had followed her out, nodded as if to say, "I told you so."

"Did you hear that Beverly was entering the box-lunch auction, doc? It's a B.Y.O.S.P affair," Jeff commented casually.

Gregory looked confused. "B.Y.O.S.P.? I guess I'm not up on local lingo." He smiled at Beverly, then looked back at Jeff. "What does it mean?"

Jeff flashed his crooked grin. "Bring your own stomach pump." Before either Gregory or Beverly could respond, Jeff retreated into Hank's room.

THE FRONTIER DAYS celebration was in full swing. A marathon volleyball game that had been going on for hours had just ended, and a large group of hot and sweaty softball players had just decided the heat was too tough an opponent and were returning from the field, as the auctioneer announced that the box-lunch auction was about to begin.

As if most participants didn't already

know whose box belonged to whom, the auctioneer made all the women stand on one side of the park in front of the gazebo and the men on the other so there would be no unfair prompting. He picked up a box from the table behind him and sniffed it dramatically. "Umm...umm, does this smell good. What am I bid for this culinary delight?" He held up the box. "Do I hear five dollars?"

Beverly stood beside her mother. "I can't believe I let you talk me into this. I'm going to be so humiliated. I'm going to the refreshment stand to get a beer."

"But you don't like beer, Beverly," Carolyn reminded her.

"I've decided to develop a taste for it...in the absence of anything stronger. Maybe it'll cushion the blow when nobody buys my lunch." Beverly left Carolyn's side and made her way toward the refreshment stand.

Gregory had seen Beverly carry a pink-wrapped box to the platform and put it on the table. He'd watched as she tucked a fresh daisy into the bow. And now, as he watched her head for the refreshment stand, he noticed the auctioneer pick up the box with the daisy and put it up for bids.

The auctioneer tugged at the edge of the box, but the ribbon held it securely, so he gave it a cursory sniff. "Well, it smells interesting, anyway," he said. "What am I bid for this very attractive box lunch?"

Gregory raised his hand. "Five dollars."

"I've got five dollars," the auctioneer droned. "Who'll give me six?"

"I'll give you ten." Jeff's voice snapped Gregory's head around.

Gregory raised his hand again. "Twenty."

"Thirty," bid Jeff.

"Fifty!" countered Gregory.

The auctioneer looked at Jeff. Jeff shrugged and shook his head. The auctioneer turned and pointed at Gregory. "Sold for fifty dollars to Dr. Sinclair. One terrific lunch prepared by Crystal Creek's own Bobby Sue Warner. Enjoy yourselves, kids."

Gregory's mouth fell open as perpetually perky Bobby Sue picked up the box and headed in his direction. She grabbed his arm and dragged him toward a big shady tree. As they passed, Gregory glanced at Jeff, who gave him an innocent grin.

"You switched the daisy, didn't you?" Gregory accused in a low voice.

"Would I do something like that?" Jeff asked with a chuckle.

The auctioneer picked up the next offering, which was also wrapped in pink. "Another pretty box. Now what am I bid for this one?" He sniffed it. "Uh...I think it's peanut butter."

Some people in the crowd looked in Beverly's direction and smiled knowingly. Beverly downed her beer with a grimace and ordered another one.

"Come on, men, let's be good sports about this. It's for a good cause, you know. Someone give me a bid."

"Fifty dollars." Jeff's voice rang out, sounding extraordinarily loud in the silence.

The auctioneer quickly snapped up the offer. "Sold for fifty dollars to Jeff Harris. Good luck, Jeff. The little lady is over by the refreshment stand."

Jeff took the box cautiously and headed toward Beverly. With a grin he handed it to her.

Beverly wrinkled her nose and shook her head. "No thanks, I'm not hungry." She took another swig of beer. "You shouldn't have done that, Jeff."

"You're telling me. I don't have the fifty bucks. Hey, I don't suppose you could loan me fifty until I get my modeling check."

"I'll *give* you the fifty, Jeff, and thanks," she said, giving him a relieved smile. She looped her arm through his and led him down the row of booths. "I'll even buy you a hot dog."

"What about this?" Jeff shook the box cautiously as if afraid it might contain a bomb.

"I know exactly what we'll do with the box lunch from hell. We'll deliver it right after we have our hot dogs...and maybe some cotton candy."

"You're on, darlin'." Jeff tucked the box under his arm and they headed for the hot dog stand.

BEVERLY AND JEFF stuck their heads around the door of Hank's hospital room. The old man was watching "Wheel of Fortune" and had a sour look on his face. "Idiots! Can't get a damned easy puzzle like that. Where do they find these jerks? All they know how to do is buy vowels. It's Tumbling Tumbleweeds. Can't you see that, you fool? Humph!''

"Hi, Grandpa Hank," Beverly said brightly. "We thought you might be feeling left out because of not being able to go to the Frontier Days celebration, so we brought you a little something."

Jeff stepped forward and handed the box to Hank. "Here you go, buddy. I hope you enjoy this."

Hank looked up at them and squinted suspiciously. "Did you make this?" he asked Beverly.

"Well, sort of," she admitted, giving Jeff a significant grin.

Cautiously, as if he were examining a bomb, Hank slid the ribbon off and lifted the lid an inch at a time. When he got a good view of the contents, he tossed aside the lid and his expression brightened.

"You brought me a chili dog. Damn, that was thoughtful of you. I ain't had any decent food since they hauled me in here." He lifted out the chili dog and took a big bite. "And french fries." He rummaged around to the bottom of the box and took out an ice-cold bottle of beer.

"Now don't let the nurses catch you with that," Beverly cautioned, glancing toward the door. "They'd have my candy stripes if they found out I helped sneak that in to you."

"It'll be our secret," Hank assured her. "Here, open the beer for me, then you two git outta here and have a good time. And thanks." He gave them one of his rare smiles.

"Well, don't blame your heartburn on me," Beverly added after Jeff twisted the top off the bottle and they headed toward the door.

"I'll enjoy every minute of it."

Jeff and Beverly escaped to the elevator, hoping to be out of the building before the smell of french fries brought the nurses running. By the time they tracked down the source, the evidence would be long gone. And so would Beverly and Jeff.

They couldn't keep from laughing as the elevator doors slid shut.

"Did you see his expression when he saw that beer?" Jeff asked.

"It was a nice touch. I'm glad you thought of it."

"But you thought of the hot dog. That was really sweet, you know."

"Yes, well, I doubt he'd have appreciated my sandwich."

"You know, it seems like a long time since we ate," Jeff said, his voice suddenly lower and huskier.

As she looked up at him, her heart leaped into her throat. The laughter in his eyes had been replaced by a hunger of a different kind.

"What did you have in mind?" she asked breathlessly.

"I made a batch of chocolate chips cookies this morning. How would you like to come over to my place...and taste them?"

"I thought you'd never ask," she whispered. "It's been a long time since I've had a chocolate chip cookie."

"Then I think we should do something about that right now."

When the elevator doors opened on the ground floor, Beverly and Jeff were so engrossed in their kiss they didn't notice the crowd of people standing outside, watching with interest.

CHAPTER TEN

"MMM, THESE ARE delicious." Beverly took another bite of the cookie and held it in her mouth, savoring the taste.

They sat on the couch in Jeff's living room with a plate of cookies on the coffee table in front of them.

"You sound like you weren't sure they would be," Jeff joked. He was enjoying watching her as her eyelids drooped from the pure pleasure. "I told you chocolate chip cookies were a natural aphrodisiac."

Her eyelids fluttered open, but there was no censure in her expression. "I think you could be right."

"As a purely scientific experiment, let me kiss you, and you can tell me if it's any better," he suggested.

"I guess, in the interest of science, I'd agree to that."

The kiss was meant to be light and teasing,

but as soon as their lips made contact, the intent changed. Her mouth was soft and sweet beneath his, and the delicious flavor of chocolate served to fuel his hunger. The tip of his tongue slid around her lips, licking off the crumbs before slipping inside her mouth, touching her tongue and causing her to moan with pleasure.

His hands moved to cup her face and draw her closer and she responded by eliminating the open space between them on the couch. Her fingers slid up his arms and across the planes of his shoulders, then threaded themselves into the blunt ends of his hair at the nape of his neck. She cradled his head, subtly encouraging him not to move away.

Beverly knew she was approaching the point of no return. If she was going to stop this before they actually ended up in his bedroom, she knew she had to do it right away. But she had been wanting this for too long. Ever since the first moment she met Jeff, there had been a spark. At first, she'd thought it was hostility, but now she realized it was an animal magnetism as age-old and powerful as life itself. When his fingers slid down her neck and across her breast, lightly brushing one nipple, all thoughts of resistance scattered.

Her reaction was intense and immediate, and as his hand moved under her blouse and returned to cup her breast in his palm, her moan was muffled by his mouth. Even through the layer of lace on her bra, his fingers burned into her skin...and she wanted more. When she felt his other hand working the buttons of her blouse free, she didn't protest. All she could think about was feeling Jeff's wonderful mouth on her body.

There was a rush of cool air as he pushed open the front of her blouse. A flick of his fingers released the fastener of her bra and he lifted it, freeing her breasts to his eager lips. He kissed one nipple, gently pulling it into his mouth, then moved to the other one. Circling its hardened pink tip with his tongue, he nibbled and suckled it until Beverly thought she would explode.

Her body was beginning to ache from the desire he was creating. His hand slid under the waistband of her slacks and into her panties, until his fingers found the source of that throbbing need. He caressed her, moving his fingers back and forth over that oh so sensitive area until her body arched against his hand. In response, his finger slipped inside her, sending her to a whole new level of anticipation.

"Jeff...oh, Jeff..." she gasped.

"Beverly, I want you so much," he whispered, his voice husky as he returned to capture her lips again.

"Yes..."

He gently eased her backward until she was lying on the couch and he was stretched out on top of her. Her full breasts pressed against the soft fabric of his T-shirt, and Beverly could feel the hard, swollen evidence of his desire pushing hotly against her.

"We can't..." she somehow managed to breathe as a fragment of sanity penetrated her foggy brain.

"We were made for each other, Beverly. Feel how perfectly we fit together."

"Yes, but your ribs—"

"They're fine now. It's been more than a week." His words were breathless whispers against her lips as he continued to kiss her. "You're a candy striper. Make me feel better."

"You should be in bed..."

"Ah…good idea." He stood, and with no apparent strain or pain, lifted her into his arms. He bent his head for one more long, hot kiss, then carried her into his bedroom. Laying her on the bed, he looked down at her. "You *are* beautiful, and incredibly sexy. God, Beverly, I want you more than I've ever wanted anything in my life."

Beverly sat up and let her fingers trail over his chest and down his flat, muscular stomach to his jeans. The buttons opened easily and she eased the denim pants over his hips.

With a groan, he stepped out of the jeans and kicked them aside. He made quick work of removing the rest of his clothes, then slowly, teasingly undressed Beverly, one piece of clothing at a time, kissing and caressing her thoroughly as he went.

Finally, just as neither could stand any more, he moved on top of her and found that spot between her legs that was wet and ready for him. He stopped long enough for another deep, passionate kiss before he pushed into her aching femininity. When, at last, he was buried deep inside her, he paused, allowing them both time to savor the moment.

Ecstasy swept closer and closer until Beverly felt that tension burst within her. The room swirled around her, and when she closed her eyes she felt herself floating into the dark weightlessness of the star-studded universe. Her body tensed, automatically trying to hold on to the intensity of the feeling that was an odd mixture of pleasure and pain. She arched against him, and he thrust deeper still, pulled along by the ripples of her orgasm until she heard his ragged cry and felt the heat of his passion pumping into her.

They clung to each other, bound together for an eternity and yet strangely alone, wrapped in the padded isolation of their own personal reaction to their lovemaking. Slowly, they relaxed, returning to the solid cushion of the bed. Jeff rolled onto his side, but pulled Beverly with him, keeping her wrapped in the comfortable security of his arms and not breaking their most intimate connection until absolutely necessary.

Beverly snuggled closer, burying her face in the curve of his neck, breathing in and adoring his masculine scent. Jeff might not be the perfect man she had thought she was looking for, but she couldn't deny that he was perfectly a man. There could never be anyone else who could make her feel what she had just felt.

And now, could she ever settle for less?

"GOOD LORD! Has my watch stopped or is the world about to come to an end?" Lynn exclaimed as she led a rangy chestnut gelding out of his stall and tied him to the hitching post.

"Okay, so I don't get up early very often," Beverly admitted.

"What's so important to get you out of bed at the crack of dawn?" As Lynn spoke, she began brushing the horse's sleek reddish gold back.

"I couldn't sleep," Beverly answered and picked up a currycomb from the bucket. "Need any help?"

"That dapple gray needs some exercise." Lynn nodded toward a stall several doors down.

Beverly took a lead rope off a hook and brought the horse to the hitching post, where she began cleaning the dust and straw off his speckled hide.

"Since when do you have insomnia?" Lynn asked. "I remember when we were kids, you had the uncanny ability to fall right to sleep as soon as we went to bed. Boy, you were a real dud at slumber parties.''

"Yeah, well, I'm a real dud at falling in love, too." Beverly slipped a bit into the dapple gray's mouth and pulled the bridle over his ears.

"Ah…man trouble. So, who's the lucky guy this week?"

"That's sort of the problem." Beverly smoothed the wrinkles out of the saddle blanket, then centered the lightweight racing saddle on the horse's straight back. "I need some advice from a woman who knows what love is."

"Right, like I'm the expert," Lynn snorted. "I've been in love exactly once in my life."

"Yes, but you knew it right away, didn't you?"

"Not *right* away. But I did know there was a special spark between Sam and me."

Yes, Beverly thought. She knew all about those special sparks. That was part of her problem.

"So, tell me, who's got you thinking of the L word?"

"Have you met that new doctor at the hospital?"

"The one who looks like a young Robert Redford? The one who was in a bidding war to get your box lunch? The one who zips around town in a silver Corvette convertible?" Lynn bent down and pulled the girth under her horse's belly. "Yes, I think I've heard a thing or two about him. Is he the one?"

"He's exactly the kind of man I *thought* I wanted."

"But?" Lynn prompted.

"But there's this other guy who challenges me. He doesn't let me sit back and get by on my looks. He doesn't pull any punches about telling me I should be doing something else with my life." Beverly thought of all the discussions she and Jeff had had, but also of the way he could make even a commonplace thing fun. She added, "He makes me laugh and he makes me cry."

Lynn checked the girth one last time, led the horse to a mounting block, then swung into the saddle. "Yes, but the real question is...does he love you?"

Her cousin glanced back over her shoulder

at Beverly and gave her a look that dared her to tell the truth.

Beverly sighed, amazed that it mattered so much. "He's never actually said it in so many words, but I'm sure he cares a lot about me. However, he's made it perfectly clear that he isn't in this for the long haul. No promises. No plans. Just a good time while it lasts." Beverly mounted the gray gelding and the two women rode side by side to the large oval racing track.

"And you're settling for that?"

Beverly gave a wistful sigh. "I don't have any other choices. Have you ever heard that Garth Brooks song called 'The Dance'? It's about a guy who can't regret the pain of losing his lover because at least it was fun while it lasted. He's grateful for the time they had and the memories they shared."

"This doesn't sound at all like you." Lynn stopped her horse and turned her full attention on Beverly. "You've always had such definite goals and you've never let anyone sway you from your course. What is it about this guy that tempts you to accept anything less than a wedding ring and a white picket fence?"

"I wish I could answer that." Beverly shook her head in total bewilderment. "If I knew, I could stop thinking about him all the time."

"So who is this mystery man?"

Beverly hesitated. It wasn't that she was ashamed to admit being attracted to Jeff. Rather, it was that she didn't want to put him up for comparison with Gregory. Even though he'd never know his attributes had been discussed and clinically measured, it somehow didn't seem fair to him.

"It's Jeff Harris, isn't it?" Lynn said, then chuckled when she saw she'd guessed correctly. "I thought so."

Beverly was amazed. "How did you know? Why, not even *I* would have guessed I'd be attracted to Jeff."

"Are you kidding? You should see your face when you look at him. I've never seen such a goofy look—on you, at least."

"No!" Now Beverly was amazed *and* horrified. If her feelings were that obvious, she must be the talk of the town.

"Calm down. I can see it because I know you so well," Lynn hurried to reassure her. "I haven't heard anyone else mention it, so your secret's safe as long as you want to keep it that way.''

''I don't know what I want. The only thing I'm absolutely certain of is that I don't want to miss 'the dance' with Jeff. I'll just have to deal with the pain later.''

''Then that's your answer. Have fun while you can. You'll have plenty of time to settle down later. And you'll always have the memories.''

''That's all I'll ever have. Just memories. Memories of my father. Memories of the pageants I won and the big one I didn't. Memories of falling in love with the wrong guy.''

''Yes, but like Garth said, it's better to take the chance than to miss out.''

''I just hope ol' Garth knows what he's talking about.''

''He must know something. Look how happy his marriage is.'' Lynn clucked to her horse and started him moving again. ''What's going on between Grandpa and Jeff? Each time I visit Grandpa in the hospital, Jeff's there.''

''You won't believe it, but somehow

Grandpa Hank has gotten Jeff wrapped up in that land he has down by Galveston.''

"You're kidding! I thought he'd given up on that."

"Well, I guess the two of them just hit it off. I think oilmen live in their own little world, anyway."

"I have to admit that it's doing Grandpa Hank a lot of good. I haven't seen him so excited about anything in years. It's given him a whole new lease on life. I just hope he isn't too disappointed when this oil deal doesn't materialize, or too devastated when Jeff leaves town."

"Yes, that makes two of us."

Lynn gave her cousin a sympathetic smile. "We'll breeze the horses one lap around the track, then when we reach the quarter pole, we'll race flat out to the first turn, then cool them down the rest of that lap. Okay?"

"Be prepared to eat my dust," Beverly challenged.

"Ha!" Lynn responded as both women urged their horses into an easy canter.

JEFF RAN HIS FINGER along a line that Hank had drawn on the map. "Are you sure that's where the boundaries are? I don't want to be caught trespassing on someone else's property.''

''There's a little pond in one corner, the ruins of an old cabin in the other and a road runs across the front. Even if the fences are down, you oughta be able to figure out pretty close where the property lines run.''

''Hank, now don't take this wrong, but suppose you and I *both* believe there's oil there. How could we afford to drill? No big company's going to bankroll such a small project and under mere speculation. And I'll be honest with you. I barely have two nickels to rub together right now.''

''Don't worry about money, son. You find the oil, then we'll find the money.''

''Are you going to bring J.T. into this?''

''Hell, no. Sure, he'd loan or even give me the money. But he'd be doin' it to humor me, not 'cause he cares about the oil. And if there's one thing I hate, it's bein' patted on the head and told to go off and play, like I was a child.''

There was a knock at the door and Beverly stepped into the room without waiting for a response.

"Well, if it isn't the Hardy Boys, studying their treasure map," she commented. "So what are we looking for today? Gold? Indian artifacts?"

"Dammit, woman. Ain't you got anything better to do than to make my life miserable?" Hank growled. But the smile dancing around in his eyes told her he was as glad to see her as she was to see him.

Beverly reached into the pocket of her pink uniform and took out a small plastic bag of cookies. "Here, I brought you something to help harden your arteries," she said as she handed them to him.

Hank looked at the bag with suspicion. "Did you make them yourself?"

"Hardly. I haven't been allowed to bake cookies since I set the home economics kitchen on fire in the eighth grade."

"What happened—too much kerosene in the cookie dough?" Hank teased. He took out a cookie, examined it from all angles, then bit gingerly into it.

"You heard about that, huh? I thought it would give them a little more kick." Beverly grinned. "It did, too. I mean really, kerosene…Karo syrup…it was an easy mistake. Could have happened to anybody.''

''No, I think it could only happen to you,'' Hank said with a dry, hoarse chuckle.

''And I brought you some good news,'' Beverly added, drawing out the suspense. ''But after all those cracks about my cooking, I don't think I'll tell you.''

She gave him a saucy smile and turned toward the door. ''I guess you don't mind waiting until tomorrow afternoon to find out.'' She waved. ''See you around.''

Jeff looked from one stubborn person to the other, then quickly crossed the room to stand in front of the door and block Beverly's escape. ''If you don't tell us right now, I'm going to kidnap you and take you to Alvin with me.''

''Oh, God, no. Not Alvin!'' Beverly exclaimed in mock horror.

''Oh, yes.'' He leaned closer so that only Beverly could hear him. ''And I'll lock you in your hotel room and make wild, passionate love to you until you cry for mercy.''

''Was that a threat or a promise?'' She wasn't sure if it was his nearness or his

words that caused the hot flash of desire to
streak through her body.

"I don't make promises. That was a prophecy." Jeff's whisper was husky and provocative, stirring memories of all the kisses
they'd shared in the past four days.

Each afternoon he'd dropped by the ranch
and spent a few hours working on Hank's
truck. He'd hammered out most of the dents
and sanded off at least three layers of rust.
He'd confided in Cal and enlisted his help in
tinkering with the old engine to bring it back
to life.

Beverly had always been able to think up
an excuse to wander out there to watch and
even to help Jeff when there was something
she could do. They talked about everything,
from their childhood to politics. But the one
thing they both avoided, by silent but mutual
consent, was any discussion of the future.

And somehow, no matter what the topic,
they managed to end up in each other's arms,
drawn together by some force that neither
was strong enough to resist. And it rarely
stopped with just kisses.

She wished she could regret their lovemaking. But just thinking about it brought a

smile to her lips. It had been wonderful. It had been special. It had been absolutely natural, as if they'd been lovers for years.

And it was evident Jeff felt the same way. She often caught his gaze on her, and there was more than lust shining in his silver-blue eyes. He never looked at her that his expression didn't reflect his genuine affection and a certain amount of wistful longing, as if he knew there were promises she wanted to hear. But these were promises he couldn't keep, so he kept silent.

He'd never said it out loud. But Beverly had seen it in his eyes, felt it in the tender way he made love to her and the crushingly possessive hugs he gave her when he didn't want to let her go. She suspected Jeff, like herself, had never been in love before. It frightened, yet fascinated him.

She wanted to talk about it. She wanted to pour out her heart to him and confess her feelings to him. But she didn't. And he didn't. Whether it was pride or fear or reluctance to press the issue too far, she kept her words of love inside and hoped he could tell she loved him by her actions.

"Oh well, if I *have* to go with you, then I

guess I'll make the best of it,'' she responded in a slow, sexy drawl while her fingers slid down the row of buttons on his shirt and ended by hooking on the top of his waist-band.

A hot spark leapt into his eyes. ''You'll go with me?''

''If we can arrange it around my schedule here at the hospital and a modeling job I have at the end of next week, sure, I'll ride along with you.''

Oblivious to Hank, Jeff pulled Beverly into his arms and gave her a long, steamy kiss. By the time their lips parted, her knees were so weak, she was glad he kept his arm around her waist as he turned her toward Hank.

''Hey, did you hear that? Beverly's going with me.''

''If y'all are through smoochin' over there, maybe Beverly will tell me the news.''

''The news?'' Beverly echoed, all other thoughts driven from her mind by Jeff's embrace.

''Yes, dang it, girl. *The news* about me that you were so all-fired excited about.'' He straightened the top of the sheet and pretended nonchalance. "Not that I really care or anythin'. But you might as well tell me and get it out of your system."

"Oh, *that* news," she said, remembering what Glenda had told her earlier that afternoon. "Grandpa Hank, I hope you haven't gotten too used to being waited on and pampered...."

"Pampered, hell! They treat me worse than I treat a sick horse."

Beverly continued, ignoring his outburst. "You'd better pack your things because you're going home as soon as the doctor signs the release."

"Hot dang!" He tossed back the sheet and swung his legs over the side of the bed. But as he sat up, he began to sway.

"Whoa, slow down," Beverly said, rushing over to steady him until the dizzy spell passed. "You haven't completely recovered from that stroke, and you're still going to have to take it easy. Just because you've been walking around and you're getting to go home doesn't mean everything's back to normal yet. You're going to be weak and unsteady on your feet for quite a while, so don't push yourself."

"You sound like a doctor, missy," Hank said, accepting her help in getting out of the bed. "In fact, you've got a better bedside manner than those docs that have been pokin' and proddin' me like I was some sort of medical freak."

Jeff stepped closer and dropped a kiss on top of Beverly's golden head. "I've been trying to tell her she should think about becoming a real nurse...but you might have hit on an even better career."

"Yeah, right, like I could be a doctor," Beverly scoffed. "I'd have to go back to school, and really study. Then there's residency and internship and—"

"If you wanted it bad enough, you could do it," Jeff encouraged. "You're young, intelligent, motivated, compassionate—anything you want, you can have."

Beverly's expression sobered as she looked up at Jeff's beloved face. *"Anything?"* she whispered.

"Almost," he answered in a soft, slightly apologetic voice.

"I ASSUME you've thought about this." Carolyn sat on the edge of Beverly's bed and watched her daughter pack.

"Actually, Mama, I'm trying *not* to think about it. For the first time in my life I'm listening to my heart and not my head."

"You know I've always been supportive of you in everything you've chosen to do," Carolyn said thoughtfully.

"Uh-oh. I hate it when you start a discussion like that." Beverly took a bikini out of a drawer and put it in the suitcase next to a couple pair of shorts and some panties.

"No lectures, Beverly. You know that's not my style." She reached over and picked up a blouse Beverly had laid on the bed. As she talked, she folded it neatly and placed it in the suitcase. "I'm very proud of you. You haven't always made the choices I would have made. But then you and I are very different people."

"Are you saying you wouldn't go if you were me?"

"I have no idea what I'd do. Love has a peculiar way of throwing things all out of proportion. You do love him, don't you?"

"Against my better judgment...yes, Mama, I do."

"And how does he feel?"

"I think he cares for me, too...as much as he can."

Her mother was silent for a minute, then sighed. "I just don't want you to make a mistake, honey. I don't want you to get hurt."

"I think it's already too late for that." Beverly turned away so her mother wouldn't see the tears that always welled in her eyes when she thought of life without Jeff.

"How can you be so calm about all this? I've seen you more upset when a guy forgot to bring you a corsage."

"I'm not really calm. I've just accepted that this is the way it has to be."

"But Jeff doesn't *have* to leave town."

"There's nothing for him here."

"You're here. His brother's here. He could find work somewhere and settle down."

"But, don't you see, Mama? It would have to be his decision. I can't ask him to stay. I can't ask him to give up his dream."

Carolyn shook her head. "But what about *your* dreams?"

"What dreams? I don't have any. I thought I wanted to marry a rich, successful man. But now I realize that's not what it'll take for me to be happy. I thought I wanted to be Miss America. But what would that have gotten me but a rhinestone tiara and a year of traveling around the world, giving speeches and opening malls?''

She turned back to her mother and cried, ''Until I find out who *I* am and what *I* want out of life, I can't ask someone else to change their plans.'' Beverly straightened and took a deep, steadying breath.

''The one thing I do know is that it's time I grew up.''

CHAPTER ELEVEN

"HANK SURE DID WANT to come along with us." Jeff glanced over at Beverly as they drove east on Interstate 10. The air conditioner inside the truck's cab was on full blast, in an effort to combat the ninety plus temperature outside. But Beverly, as usual, looked cool and beautiful in khaki shorts and a peach-colored sleeveless blouse.

"His doctor would never have allowed it," Beverly stated positively.

"If his doctor was Dr. Sinclair, I'll bet he would have *insisted* Hank go."

Beverly unfastened her seat belt and moved to the center of the bench seat. She snuggled against Jeff's side and ran her hand along the top of his thigh. "Still worried about Dr. Sinclair, are we?" she teased.

As her hand brushed his thigh, he groaned. This constant state of arousal was something he was learning to live with around Beverly.

Her scent, her touch, the sweet sound of her voice, the music of her laughter, all kept his libido in high gear. No other woman had ever affected him as she did. No matter how often he saw her or kissed her or made love with her, he simply couldn't get enough. She was in his blood. And she was in his heart.

They stopped for lunch on the way and arrived in Alvin in midafternoon. They found a nice motel right off the interstate and Jeff parked his truck outside the registration office. Turning to Beverly, he captured her mouth in a long overdue kiss.

"One room or two?" he asked, his lips moving against hers.

"I suspect we need only one," she whispered back. "How can you fulfill your prophecy from across the hall?"

"Hmm...yes, the prophecy. Wild, passionate love, wasn't it?"

He felt her lips curve into a smile. "I'm counting on it."

"I'll be right back," he said, reluctantly pulling away and opening the door. He paused outside the truck for a minute, trying to catch his breath, and to will his body to relax and calm down so he wouldn't embarrass himself. His tight jeans did nothing to hide his condition. Finally, he gave up and pulled his shirt out of his waistband and hoped it would help cover him long enough to get them checked in. And once in their room, he and Beverly could "fix" the problem.

An hour later, Beverly was lying in the curve of his arm, idly running her fingertips in lazy circles on his chest.

"So when do you think you'll be finished with Hank's truck?" she asked, her voice low and sleepy with the exhaustion of complete satisfaction.

"I'm not sure. But probably within the next couple of weeks," he answered.

Both knew they weren't talking about the vehicle, but about Jeff. Both knew it was inevitable. And both were very sorry this moment wouldn't last forever.

JEFF STOPPED his truck on the county road, and he and Beverly stared at the cluster of tract houses.

"Is this it?" Beverly asked, glancing from the map to the neighborhood and back again.

"God, I hope not. Hank didn't say any-

thing about these houses. But then, they
don't look very old. They couldn't have been
here when the map was made. As I interpret
his map, this overgrown stretch of land next
to the housing development is Hank's.''

"How many acres are there supposed to
be?''

"About twenty-five.''

"Isn't that kind of pushing it for an oil
well?''

"I've seen them drilled on as little as five,
but usually they like to have at least fourteen
or fifteen acres because of all the equipment.''

"I'll bet it's pretty noisy. How do you suppose the people in this neighborhood are going to react to having an oil well in their
backyards?''

Jeff grimaced. ''I think they're going to be
madder than hell. But, we've got to find out
if there's oil here and make sure Hank owns
the mineral rights before we stir that hornet's
nest.''

"And how are you going to do that—find
the oil, that is?''

Jeff gave Beverly a measuring look. ''This

might sound a little weird to you, but I can feel it."

Beverly's expression was skeptical, but she didn't voice any doubts she might have had. "So, I suppose we're going to have to get out and walk around."

"I'm not too crazy about the idea of walking through that myself," Jeff admitted. "It reminds me too much of my younger days when I had to fight off the snakes to build the roads to where they wanted to erect the derrick. However, *I've* got to do it, but not today. I'll come out early in the morning when it's cooler. You can sleep late, then I'll take you out for breakfast."

"You want to do this alone?"

"Yes, if you don't mind." He gave her a crooked grin. "Somehow I always have trouble concentrating when you're around, darlin'."

She leaned over and gave him a long, deep kiss. "You got yourself out of that one, fella. So what's on the agenda for this afternoon?"

"I thought we'd go to the Brazoria County courthouse and check their records."

JEFF AND BEVERLY stood in the lobby of the courthouse and studied the directory of offices and services located there.

"Okay, so where do we start?" he asked.

"How about the tax records? Surely they would show if Hank's name is still on the property."

"Who said blondes were dumb?" Jeff teased.

"A brunette, no doubt," Beverly responded with a sassy grin.

They rode the elevator up to the correct floor, then joined a line of people waiting to speak to the clerks. When it was finally their turn, the clerk, whose name tag said he was Jerry, could barely take his eyes off Beverly long enough to acknowledge Jeff.

Jeff swallowed back a surge of possessiveness, and tried to keep his cool. "We have the legal description. Perhaps you could tell us the name of the owner."

Jerry tore his attention away from Beverly and wrote down the legal description, then seemed to take an eternity to call it up on his computer. Finally, he leaned back and announced, "It says here, a Henry Travis of Crystal Creek, Texas, is the owner of that property, and all taxes are paid up to date."

"Then where would we go to see a deed?" Beverly asked. "We need to check on the mineral rights."

"That would be down the hall in records." The clerk melted under the powerful wattage of Beverly's smile. "I'll call a friend of mine in that department and he'll have the book pulled for you by the time you get there."

"Thanks, Jerry." Beverly stood and held out her hand. "You've been very helpful."

"It was my pleasure," the young man gushed, holding her hand as if he were honored to touch her.

"His pleasure," Jeff grumbled when they were back in the hallway. "Am I going to have to get used to every guy fawning over you?"

"Jealous?" Beverly's blue eyes sparkled.

"Of that kid? Ha!" Jeff exclaimed, then caught her gaze on him. "Okay, yes, I am. Isn't that stupid?"

"Absolutely crazy," Beverly agreed. "But I love it."

They arrived at the records department, and true to Jerry's word, the book was open to the correct spot. The records clerk was just as eager to help. He made them copies of the deed and an up-to-date map of the entire area around Hank's land.

"Did you notice the way those guys were looking at you?" Jeff muttered as they left the courthouse.

Beverly stopped at the top of the steps and slid her arms around his waist. "Jeff Harris, unless you're blind *and* stupid, you should have noticed by now that the only guy *I'm* looking at is you. Besides, I've noticed quite a few females trying to catch your attention, and you don't see me foaming at the mouth with jealousy." She stood on her tiptoes and kissed him. "I just keep it hidden better than you do."

Jeff chuckled. He hadn't even noticed any women looking at him. That was a first. Usually, his radar was tuned in to the feminine frequency. But somehow, Beverly had shorted out his system.

They drove back to Alvin and had a leisurely dinner at a local steak house before returning to their motel room.

The next morning, it was all Jeff could do to force himself out of Beverly's arms and into the Gulf Coast humidity. A few minutes later, he was parked in front of Hank's land, surveying the waist-high weeds. It didn't take him but a minute to decide to make a trail with his truck before attempting to walk through the thick growth.

He shifted into four-wheel drive. There was no driveway, so he angled the truck diagonally to cross the shallow ditch. The tires spun in the slick mud before catching and thrusting the vehicle forward.

Mosquitoes rose in gray clouds from the tall grass. Cottontails, disturbed from their hiding places, bounded away as Jeff tried to locate the pond or the cabin that Hank had mentioned.

He finally found a pile of burned logs and guessed it might have been the cabin, long ago destroyed by kids or transients. A little further investigation found an almost dry pond about four hundred yards across the back of the acreage.

Parking his truck in the middle of the property, he opened the door. For several minutes he sat, hesitating to take that first step.

What if he didn't feel anything? How would he break the news to Hank? Jeff suspected that the hope and planning for this project's success was one of the main things keeping the old man alive.

Even worse, what if he *thought* he felt something, and he was wrong? He couldn't forget that his past few jobs had come up dry. Of course, he still believed oil was down there, deeper than the crews had gone. But there was always the possibility that he could have been wrong.

Coming to check out Hank's land was more than just a favor to the old man. Jeff was testing himself, trying to regain his confidence in his own abilities. It had definitely been shaken during the past couple of years. He *needed* to be right about this one. If he wasn't, not only would his career be, for all practical purposes, over, but he would waste every penny the old man could raise, as well as breaking his heart.

Hesitantly, he stretched out his leg. First one booted foot touched the ground, then the other, and he straightened, standing tall in the middle of the prairie grass.

He felt it immediately. It was as if the compressed energy beneath the earth's surface sent up vibrations.

Just to make sure it wasn't the truck affecting his sensitivity, Jeff started walking. But even when he was dozens of yards away from the vehicle, he could still feel the oil. It was down there. He was sure of it. And, just as he felt the oil lying patiently in the bedrock, he could feel the stirrings of excitement within himself—a different kind of excitement than Beverly generated.

It was the thrill of the hunt, the mystery of discovery, the ecstasy of success. The feeling was almost as good as sex.

Jeff chuckled. He certainly couldn't say that to Beverly. Women—no, not just women, almost no one—would understand. Only another oilman would know how it felt.

He looked around the property, visualizing how it would look with its wooden platform and steel derrick stretching into the clear blue Texas sky. Lights would be strung all the way to the top and around the entire area, so the crews could work around the clock.

Jeff had no idea how deep they'd have to go. That wasn't one of the things he could "feel." Soundings would be made and core samples taken to determine the best location to drill. And with both his and Hank's intuition being so strong, Jeff knew they would stick to it until the oil was reached.

And there were plenty of obstacles to overcome. Getting the oil out of the ground was going to be a much more difficult process than it would have been several years ago. There were sure to be protests from the subdivision's residents, and this property was now within the city limits and would require all sorts of permits. There was also the cost factor. It wouldn't be cheap to put together an independent drilling operation.

A fresh attack of mosquitoes finally forced Jeff back to the truck. But for several minutes longer he sat and considered the possibilities. Could he be wrong? No, he was positive there was oil, so sure he was willing to invest his inheritance. If the well was successful, he'd be set for life. If it failed, he wouldn't be much worse off than he was now.

Sure, it was a gamble.

But it was his big chance. Not only would he be instrumental in fulfilling an old man's dream, but Jeff would earn the respect of his peers. And last, but certainly not least, with his share of the money the well would bring in, as well as the renewed proof of his oil-finding skill, he could sit back and wait for the job offers to come his way. Maybe once Beverly saw that he could be successful in the oil business, she wouldn't object to becoming the wife of a wildcatter. Sure, they would both have to do a little compromising, with Beverly being willing to accept a new life-style and Jeff being willing to curb his wanderlust as much as possible. For the first time since he'd met her, Jeff could see a chance that he and Beverly just might be able to make their relationship work on a more permanent basis.

Buoyed by the thought, he hurried back to the motel room and slipped into the room, finding Beverly, just where he'd hoped, still in bed.

"So, is it there?" she asked, covering a lazy yawn. "What time is it?"

"Are you always so full of questions when you wake up?"

Her smile was slow like a Southern drawl. "The only question I should ask is why it's taking you so long to kiss me."

He leaned over and let his tongue trace around the full curves of her lips before covering her mouth with his. "And I regret every second I wasted," he whispered as he pulled away. "But yes, there's oil down there. I can't wait to tell Hank."

He kissed her again. "And to answer your other question, it's after nine. How about some breakfast, and don't tell me you don't eat it because I've seen you."

"Now that you mention it, I think I *am* hungry." She sat up, looked in the wall mirror and frowned at her tousled appearance.

"Don't change a thing," he told her, his voice soft and adoring.

"But I look like I just woke up."

One corner of his mouth lifted in a grin. "I know," he murmured as he kicked off his boots and crawled back into bed with her.

Quite a while later, they checked out of the motel, ate breakfast, then headed toward Galveston. It took them almost an hour to reach the island city.

"My parents used to bring me here almost every summer," Beverly recalled as they crossed the causeway from the mainland. "We stayed at a beautiful old hotel called the Galvez. Have you ever been there?"

"I've spent a lot of time in Galveston, but

never at the Galvez,'' Jeff answered. ''That was always a little above my means.''

''Where are we staying tonight?''

''Hey, I'm temporarily wealthy since I got my modeling check, so why not the Galvez?

JEFF DROPPED their suitcases on the dresser and joined her at the window that faced the Gulf. Wrapping his arms around her waist, he pulled her back against him and rested his chin on top of her head. ''I'm glad you came with me.''

''So am I.''

He groaned and turned her around so he could kiss her. ''I think we'd better leave now if we want to do any sight-seeing. I'm afraid I can't be responsible for my actions if we stay like this much longer.''

''Just wait until you see me in my bikini,'' she teased and stepped away.

They spent the day driving around the island, stopping to tour a tall ship that was in the harbor and several old historic mansions. After a wonderful fresh seafood dinner, they returned to their room to enjoy their view of the Gulf.

Outside the full moon was reflected on the

rolling surf, sending a shimmering streak of silver toward the beach. In the distance, lights twinkled from offshore oil rigs and ships that were navigating the Intracoastal Waterway.

"This is like a whole different world from Crystal Creek," Beverly said as she reached around and lifted her heavy hair off her neck. "That breeze feels wonderful...so cool and fresh."

"And humid."

Even though it was almost midnight, the traffic along the tall concrete and granite seawall was still heavy as teenagers drove as fast as they dared and shouted and honked at the cars they passed. There were quite a few pedestrians still out, some walking hand in hand along the top of the seawall and others sitting on its edge, swinging their legs as they looked out at the water.

"I'm glad I came with you," Beverly said, turning in Jeff's arms and looping hers around his neck.

"I'm glad you did, too." And for just a moment he thought how good it would be if no matter which hotel or which city or even which state he was in, Beverly was always with him. He wouldn't mind waking up to her face every morning or lying down next to her body every night.

CHAPTER TWELVE

"LET'S GET OUT of here," Jeff said, as they waited while a large family paraded into the water, following the father like a procession of ducks. "I know of a more private beach."

Even though they were several miles down the shore from the city of Galveston, the beach was packed with people. Some lay on towels, soaking in the sun's rays, while others had set up elaborate sun shades of tarps or blankets under which they sat on lawn chairs. The odors of grilled hamburgers and hot dogs mixed with that of countless buckets of fried chicken and the fresh fragrance of watermelon. Frisbees whizzed past Beverly and Jeff and small children screamed and laughed as they floated on blow-up toys or built sand castles just above the water line.

Beverly nodded her agreement. They returned to the truck and drove south. They crossed another bridge, leaving Galveston Island, but continued along a road that followed the beach. The farther they drove, the fewer houses there were. Finding a deserted section, Jeff turned onto a road that had been formed between the sand dunes.

Since they could drive directly onto the beach, Jeff parked the truck as close as he dared to the water's edge, backing it up so the tailgate faced the Gulf. He retrieved the towels they had brought from the hotel and spread them out on the sand.

Beverly took the suntan lotion from the glove compartment and handed it to him. After stepping out of her shorts and pulling off her T-shirt, she asked, "Would you mind putting this on my back? I don't want to burn."

Jeff's lips curved into that killer grin. "It'd be my pleasure."

Beverly sat on one of the towels and pulled her hair forward over her shoulder, holding it loosely in a ponytail. Jeff shook the bottle of lotion, then squirted some on his hand.

The thick liquid felt cool against her skin, and his fingers felt wonderful as they massaged her shoulders. She sighed as he spread the lotion, but her sigh turned to a moan when she felt his lips nibbling along the tender skin at the base of her neck. The tip of his tongue touched her earlobe, sending lightning bolts streaking through her. She turned her head, eagerly seeking those lips she loved to taste against her own.

His breath was hot as he opened his mouth, devouring hers with an insatiable hunger. No matter how many times they made love, the sparks still flew as soon as their gazes met or their hands brushed or their lips touched.

"Oh, Beverly, I can't believe what you do to me."

"Do to you!" she exclaimed in gentle dispute. "Just look how you affect me."

He rolled her onto her back and his hand slipped inside the cup of her bra and pulled one of her breasts free. "Let me see, darlin'." His tongue left a wet circle around her desire-hardened nipple. "And, oh, how I love it when you get aroused," he murmured, his lips moving against her soft skin. He drew her into his mouth and suckled her as his hand squeezed and stroked her other breast.

Beverly's fingers raked through his hair, holding his head to her. She could feel him pressing hard against her leg and she breathed a ragged sigh. "How deserted is this section of the beach?"

Two trucks full of teenagers with their radios on full blast barreled past, spinning out in the soft sand.

Jeff lifted his head and moved away. "Not *that* deserted, apparently," he said and reluctantly rearranged her top.

They stretched out in the sun, Beverly still lying on her back and Jeff rolling onto his stomach.

"Tomorrow we have to go back to Crystal Creek," she whispered, obviously as unenthusiastic about returning to the real world as he was.

"Yes, I guess we do. I've got to tell Hank the good news, then see about collecting my inheritance so we can get moving on the project."

"Then what?" Beverly turned her head and peered at him through the dark lenses of her sunglasses. "You're going to invest your inheritance in Grandpa Hank's folly?"

"Yes, I am."

"How much money are we talking about?

I don't know much about oil wells, but I *do* know they're expensive.''

''I'm going to invest all two hundred thousand dollars.''

Her mouth opened, then closed as she turned her head away.

''Beverly, I know you think I'm throwing my money away, but you've got to understand that this is a terrific opportunity. If we hit oil—and I'm sure we will—then I'll be able to write my own ticket. All those oil companies that wouldn't give me the time of day will be beating down my door. I'll be doing the kind of work I love. Plus, I'll be financially set, so I can offer you a future.''

She sat up and looked down at him. ''Thanks a lot, Jeff. You make it sound like all I want out of life is a rich husband. Has it ever occurred to you that I might just want to be with the man I love?''

Jeff turned over and sat up so he could face her. ''You've never made any bones about wanting a man who could give you a comfortable life.''

''Yes, but that was before I realized that love was more important.''

''But no one can live on love alone. I

wouldn't even think of discussing the possibility of a future with you until I was financially secure.''

"But I have some money, and my modeling contracts should provide a pretty good income for several more years," she offered.

"Your money is your money. It may be old-fashioned, but *I'm* going to be the provider in my family. You might think love is enough now. But someday I might look into your eyes and see regret and resentment for me not carrying my own weight. And I couldn't stand that."

"Jeff, if you really felt that way, you wouldn't throw away your inheritance. It would make good seed money. We could live off the interest or the dividends. Or maybe you could even start a company of some kind."

"I *am* making an investment," he repeated.

For a few seconds longer, Beverly's eyes searched his, looking for some promise, some sign that he was joking. In one breath he was telling her he wanted to provide security for her, and in the next he was throwing away all his money on an old man's dream. Apparently, all the things Scott had told her about Jeff's irresponsibility and inability to handle money were true. He was willing to risk a guaranteed future with her for the remote chance of striking it rich. And Jeff, of all people, should know the odds were against him.

Beverly couldn't help but believe that, if he cared enough for her, he would go for the sure thing. But then, he'd never made any pretense that Beverly was his first love *or* his last love. In fact, he'd never mentioned love at all.

It wouldn't take him long to finalize his plans with Hank, and then, probably in less than a week, he'd be gone.

A cold chill raced through Beverly, totally chasing away any remnant of passion. She crossed her arms over her chest and turned away, suddenly feeling more naked and vulnerable than she'd ever felt in her life.

"I think we'd better leave," she said, wishing the tears weren't so evident in her voice.

"Beverly, I..." His words trailed off.

"Jeff, when it's time to go...it's time to go."

She could feel his hand stroking her hair, tenderly, gently touching it as if he was trying to remember the texture and curl of every golden strand.

"Maybe someday..." he began again, but she shook her head.

"You don't make promises, remember?" she said. "And I'm not asking for any. I respect your honesty." Her bare shoulder lifted in a shrug. "I may not have always liked it, but I can't say you've ever lied to me or told me something just because you thought I wanted to hear it. Please don't start now."

The ride back to the hotel was silent. But it wasn't a tense silence, it was one heavy with melancholy.

"Do you want us to drive back to Crystal Creek tonight?" Jeff was the first to speak. He glanced at his watch. "If we get started right away, we can make it before midnight."

"If you don't mind, I'd like to do that," Beverly confirmed, not quite meeting his eyes.

And since he'd seen the glitter of unshed tears in her eyes when they left the beach, Jeff didn't want to look too closely anyway.

He'd always been a sucker for tears. And Beverly's were doubly painful for him to witness. He knew he'd hurt her. And yet he knew there was nothing he could do to change things. He had to do what he felt was right.

Oh sure, he could get down on his knees and apologize. He could tell her he loved her more than he'd ever thought it possible to love another person. He could beg her to wait for him...for God knew how long until he could give her the kind of life she deserved. Or he could buy a small business and settle down to the life of shopkeeper in Crystal Creek and be bored out of his mind.

But Jeff knew none of those options was viable. If he didn't find oil he would have nothing to offer Beverly *except* his love. If he didn't try for the oil on Hank's land, the old man would never forgive him, and Jeff himself would always wonder whether his instinct had been right.

No. There was only one way to accomplish all his goals, and that was to strike oil on Hank's land!

But for now, he had to keep silent. And hope. More than anything, he hoped she would be there when—he refused to even think if—the well came in.

They broke the journey only for a quick supper in a truck stop and to fill the gas tank. Beverly leaned against the passenger door and slept, or pretended to sleep, most of the way. Jeff tried to concentrate on the road. But the fragrance of her perfume filled the cab of the truck. And every once in a while he heard what sounded suspiciously like a muffled sniffle. Jeff reached forward and turned on the radio, scanning until he found a good country and western station. He knew he was being cowardly, but he couldn't stand to hear her cry.

As he'd predicted, it was eleven-thirty when he drove through the Circle T's elaborate gates and parked in front of the sprawling ranch house. Beverly opened the truck's door immediately. Jeff took her suitcase and overnight bag out of the back and carried them onto the porch, standing behind her as she fumbled with her keys, finally unlocking the front door.

All the lights were off except for a low-wattage lamp in the living room. Everyone had obviously already gone to bed. Normally, Jeff would have welcomed the opportunity to spend more time alone with Beverly. But tonight, she didn't even invite him in.

Instead, she took the suitcases from him, flashed him a shaky smile and said, "Thanks, Jeff. I..." Her voice faltered and she took a deep breath before continuing. "I suppose I'll be pretty busy the next few days.... I might even have to drive to San Antonio for a modeling job. So, I guess I'll just say goodbye now...and good luck. I hope you and Hank find that oil."

She leaned forward, obviously planning on pressing a platonic kiss on his cheek, but Jeff turned his head and met her mouth with his. Startled, she began to pull away, then sighed and returned his kiss with a sweet wistfulness that touched him more deeply than any passionate response ever could.

"Goodbye," she whispered, her words hot against his lips, then she was inside the house and the door had clicked shut in front of him.

"Goodbye, Beverly," he said softly, and with the safety of the heavy, soundproof door between them, he added, "I love you, darlin'."

THE NEXT MORNING Beverly barely took the time to say hello to her mother and tell her where she was going before packing her bags to leave town. At first she'd considered actually going to San Antonio, even though there weren't any modeling jobs planned as she'd told Jeff. All she wanted to do was get as far away from Jeff as she could, so that she couldn't go to him and either throw herself into his arms and beg him to reconsider or admit that she loved him and would wait an eternity for him. Either way, she would be setting herself up for humiliation. Whether he accepted her offer or granted her plea, it would be because she'd pushed him into a corner and he had no graceful way out.

As much as Beverly loved Jeff, she wanted him because he chose to include her in his life, not because she had forced her way in. And part of her knew he *had* to seize this chance to prove he could still find oil. Perhaps at some point he actually *would* come back for her. There was even a remote possibility that the well could hit. She didn't want to think what would become of Jeff if it didn't. But she had to get on with her life...a life *without* Jeff.

Carolyn must have sensed her daughter's dilemma because she wisely made no mention of Jeff, but did offer a little motherly advice. "Gregory Sinclair has called here a dozen times, asking about you," she told Beverly. "He's a very nice man, you know."

"I know, Mama. He's exactly the kind of man I thought I was looking for. But I've made a startling discovery during the past couple of weeks. You can't pick who you love. And I don't want a marriage without love."

Her mother frowned, concern written clearly on her face. "So, what are you going to do?"

"Right now or long term?"

"Right now for a start."

"I don't know. I just have to get out of town for a few days."

"Why don't you go the lake house?" Carolyn suggested. "I don't think anyone's using it. I'll give J.T. a call to make sure."

Beverly considered the idea for a couple of minutes before nodding. "That might be just what I need. But," she said, leveling a serious look at her mother, "don't tell *any-*

one where I am, okay? I need the time alone.''

Carolyn nodded. ''Sure, whatever you want.'' She reached out and covered Beverly's hand with her own. ''Baby, it's not the end of the world. I know it hurts now, and you'll never forget him. But in time someone else will come along. I'm sure there's the perfect man out there for you somewhere.''

''I know,'' Beverly agreed. ''But it doesn't make it any easier to get over him. I just know I need to get away so I can think more clearly.''

''I'll call J.T. while you finish packing.''

''Thanks, Mama. Just remember—''

''I won't tell *anyone*.''

WHEN BEVERLY ARRIVED at the lake house, she unloaded the car, changed into a bikini, then went out on the deck. She tried to get interested in a book, then tried to catch a nap in the sun. But her attention kept straying to the driveway. Would Jeff come? Would he somehow pry the information about her whereabouts from Carolyn? Or maybe he'd simply sense that she was here.

She finally dozed, not waking until the

shadows of evening covered the deck. Trying not to feel too disappointed, she went inside, showered and put together a salad for supper.

There was nothing interesting on television, so Beverly put a videotape movie into the VCR and tried to get interested in it, all the while waiting…waiting for her Prince Charming to come to his senses. At midnight she gave up and went to bed, telling herself that surely tomorrow he would arrive on her doorstep. She would try to be angry at him for waiting so long, but he would flash that sexy smile at her and her heart would melt.

But Jeff didn't come to the lake house the next day. Or the next night. Or the day after that. In fact, when Beverly finally broke down and called home to see if anyone had called her, she got the unhappy news that Jeff had already left Crystal Creek.

He was gone. And he wasn't coming for her.

Beverly slumped on the couch and felt her heart tighten painfully in her chest. The tears she'd been holding back for four days began spilling over, flooding down her cheeks.

That was the trouble with dreams. They never came true.

CHAPTER THIRTEEN

"HEY, STRANGER, it's good to have you back," Glenda called as Beverly stepped off the elevator.

A romance novel slid off the top of the pile in her arms and Beverly nudged it with her foot, sending it sliding through the open doorway toward the nurses' station. She dropped the pile of magazines and books onto the desk, then bent and picked up the one on the floor.

"And it's good to be back. When I signed up as a volunteer, I never would have believed I'd actually miss coming here."

"So, how was your vacation? You look tanned and rested."

"Well, I don't know how rested," Beverly admitted. "I got caught up on my reading, but I didn't get much sleep."

"That Jeff guy kept you awake nights?"

"You could say that—except he wasn't with me for the past week."

"I thought I'd heard he'd left town, but I assumed it was to be with you," Glenda commented.

"No, he wasn't with me." Beverly busied herself straightening the magazines, aware that her hair fell forward, effectively hiding the pain she knew would be reflected in her eyes. "He's moved on to a new job."

"But I thought—"

"So, what's going on today?" Beverly interrupted, anxious to change the subject. "Are there any special requests?"

"We've had quite a turnover in patients since you were here last." Glenda handed her a clipboard across the desk. "Here's a list of who's in which room and their condition. As usual, some are well enough to be entertained, but some are better off resting."

Beverly glanced down the list and recognized very few names. "How about Mrs. Goodwin? I don't see her listed here. Did she get to go home?"

Glenda looked up from the chart she'd been updating, a startled, then regretful expression on her face. "Oh, I thought you

knew. Mrs. Goodwin died five days ago.''
She reached into the desk drawer, brought
out an envelope and handed it to Beverly.
''She asked me to give you this. I'm so sorry,
Beverly. I know how close the two of you
were.''

Without even glancing at it, Beverly took
it and stuffed it into the pocket of her uniform.

She must have looked as stricken as she
felt because Glenda rushed to add, ''You
knew she was terminal. It was just a matter
of time.''

''I know…I guess I was hoping for a miracle…or at least a little extra time.'' Beverly
felt her throat tighten. Mrs. Goodwin had had
her bad days, but usually she'd been sweet,
funny and undemanding. It had been a joy
spending time with her, reading her the romances she loved so much and listening
while she talked about her family. It was
more than losing a friend, it was like losing
a member of the family.

''Bev, you can't let the patients get to you
like this.'' Glenda's tone was sympathetic,
but the warning was clear. ''Some of them
are going to die. We've talked about this in

the volunteers' classes. If you're going to keep working here, it's something you to have to learn to accept."

Beverly dropped the clipboard onto the desktop with a clatter. "Then I'm not sure I can work here anymore."

"Don't make any hasty decisions, Bev. This has been a shock. But the patients love you. They ask about you every day. You have a way with them, and I'd hate to see you give it up."

"I can't stay today, Glenda. I'll think about it and give you a call." Beverly whirled around and headed toward the elevator. Just as she reached it, the doors whooshed open and before she could react, a small boy ran out and threw his arms around her legs. His body, while frail for a child his age, carried enough momentum to almost knock her to the ground.

"Miss Beverly, I'm so glad you're here," the boy said. "I've really been missing you. Every time I come for a checkup, I come here to see you. But you've been gone."

"Why hello, Jackie." Beverly smiled down at the little boy whose leukemia had so recently gone into remission. "Have you been eating lots of cheeseburgers and chocolate shakes?''

His thin face beamed. ''I sure have.'' He lowered his voice. ''And thanks for sneaking those candy bars in to me when I was here.''

''I was glad to do it,'' she told him in a conspiratorial whisper and gave him a thumbs-up sign. ''I heard you're doing great.''

He released her legs and took a step backward, swinging his arms wide. ''See, I've gained ten pounds. And look...'' He took off his Texas Rangers baseball cap and bent his head toward her. ''Hair. I've got real hair. Isn't it cool?''

Beverly reached out and stroked the sprigs of hair that were struggling to grow. Seeing the children with bald heads from chemotherapy and eyes that looked several sizes too large for their gaunt faces had been one of the most startling things she'd had to adjust to when she first became a volunteer. And now as she looked at Jackie, who still looked as if a stiff wind would blow him away and whose wispy hair was barely noticeable against his shining scalp, she thought he was the most beautiful thing she'd ever seen.

Kneeling in front of the boy, she looked directly into his eyes. "You're going to have so many girls chasing you in school next year, you'll have to run really fast—that is, unless you *want* them to catch you and give you a big kiss."

Jackie shifted uncomfortably, but there was an intrigued expression on his face. "Really? Do you think so?"

"I certainly do. I know if I was a little girl, *I'd* be chasing you."

That comment brought a blush to his pale cheeks. "Heck, I wouldn't mind if *you* kissed me," he said.

Beverly leaned forward and pulled Jackie into her arms. She gave him a big hug, then kissed his forehead.

The elevator doors opened again and Jackie's mother walked out. "I figured you'd be here," she said, shaking her head with affectionate exasperation. To Beverly she added, "He was supposed to wait for me outside the doctor's office, but by the time Dr. Holland and I finished talking, Jackie was gone. It didn't take Sherlock Holmes to figure out where he might have gone."

Beverly stood, but Jackie slipped his hand

in hers and she squeezed it gently. "Jackie and I were having a little reunion."

"Well, I'm glad he finally caught you. He insists on looking for you every time we come here." She held out her hand toward Jackie. "We've got to get going, son. I've got a dozen errands to run, and we're stopping by Baskin-Robbins first thing."

Jackie reluctantly let go of Beverly's hand. "Will you be here next time I come in?"

She looked down into his pleading brown eyes, eyes that were much too serious for a child his age. "I'm not sure what my schedule will be, Jackie. But I'm sure we'll bump into each other every once in a while. Crystal Creek is a pretty small place, you know."

He seemed partially satisfied by her answer, but continued solemnly, "Okay, but you won't forget me, will you?"

"Of course, I'll *never* forget you, Jackie. You're my favorite little boy, remember?"

He flashed her a toothy grin and said, "And you're my favorite grown-up friend, Miss Beverly." He pulled his baseball cap back on and gave her a jaunty wave before following his mother into the elevator.

Beverly turned around to see that Glenda

had witnessed the whole incident. "Don't say it," Beverly cautioned.

"They love you," Glenda said, ignoring her friend's warning. "And you love them."

Beverly shook her head and punched the Down button with a little more force than absolutely necessary.

She stopped by a florist, then drove to the cemetery. It wasn't difficult to locate Mrs. Goodwin's grave because it was the only new one on the well manicured grounds.

Beverly walked across the thick, emerald green lawn and stopped in front of a pile of fresh dirt. The pungent odor of the moist soil filled her nostrils, competing with the fragrance of the flowers clutched in her fist. With barely restrained grief, she read the words chiseled on the granite headstone: *Charles Edward Goodwin, Beloved Husband and Father 1911–1984,* and next to that on the same large stone, *Mary Gladys Goodwin, Beloved Wife and Mother 1914–.* There obviously hadn't been time for the year of Mrs. Goodwin's death to be added.

Beverly gently placed the flowers at the foot of the new grave. There were far too few sprays of flowers scattered over the mound.

She noticed that on either side of the main headstone were two smaller ones. One that read *Mary Ellen Goodwin, The Angels Sent You, Then Took You Back Too Soon 1935– 1942;* the other *Charles Edward Goodwin, Jr., Dear Son, We Miss You and Love You So Much 1937–1967.*

All the stories Mrs. Goodwin had told Beverly came flooding back. She thought of how little Mary Ellen had died of tuberculosis when she was only seven. And she remembered the old lady's pride in her precious son Charlie who had been a pilot in the Air Force, as well as her tears, even after all those years, when she told how Charlie's Phantom jet had been shot down in Vietnam and he'd come home in a flag-draped coffin.

Except for a few cousins and scattered distant relatives, the old lady had been all alone in the world.

"I'm sorry, Mrs. Goodwin...so sorry," Beverly sobbed. She knelt at the edge of the soft dirt, and the tears began to flow. She cried for Mrs. Goodwin's last lonely years and her pain. She cried for not being there to hold the sweet lady's hand as she died.

Beverly reached into her pocket for a tissue, but her fingers pulled out the envelope instead. She'd forgotten all about it until that moment. For several long moments, she stared at it, not sure she wanted to open it, but knowing Mrs. Goodwin obviously wanted her to or she wouldn't have gone to the trouble of leaving it for her.

Finally, she slid her finger under the flap and tore it open. A light breeze tugged at the stationery as she removed it and unfolded the single page.

Dear Beverly,

I don't think I'll be on this earth much longer, so I wanted to tell you how much I've appreciated all you've done for me these past few months. Your sweet smile and cheerful voice always brought sunshine into my darkest days. And when I bored you with my memories, you always were kind enough to pretend you were interested.

I think my daughter might have grown up to be just like you. Anyway, I'd like to think so. You've brought so much happiness into my empty old life. I hope you will continue to brighten other sick folks' lives and make their recoveries or their deaths easier by just being there.

I'm sorry I won't be able to hold on long enough to tell you this in person. But I feel so tired. Thank you, Beverly dear. You'll never know how much you helped me along this last, lonely path.

Please accept my locket as a token of my affection. It wouldn't mean anything to anyone else, but at least I know you'll know what it meant to me.

Goodbye and good night, dear friend,
Gladys Goodwin

Beverly turned the envelope upside down and caught the shiny gold oval-shaped locket and chain that slid out. She snapped open the tiny doors and smiled as she recognized the faded photos of Mary Ellen and Charlie that Gladys had shown her countless times before.

"Yes, Mrs. Goodwin, I'll cherish this always," Beverly said as she clutched it in her fist and held it to her chest. "I wish I could have done more."

A big black thundercloud rolled across the sun and sent out a blinding flash of lightning, followed a few seconds later by an ominous rumble. It hadn't rained for several days, but from the looks of the rapidly gathering clouds, quite a storm was in the works.

Beverly snapped the sides of the locket together and looped the chain around her neck. "Goodbye, Mrs. Goodwin. I'll take good care of your memories for you," she said before standing, dusting off her knees and heaving a heavy sigh as she walked back to her car.

BEVERLY STARED out the window of the plane at the cloud cover that still shrouded Texas, and wondered what it would take to lift her sagging spirits.

Actually, the phone call should have done it. A month ago she would have killed to get such a call. But the past few weeks had made her reexamine her goals. She was no longer sure a career in modeling was what she really wanted.

But when her agent had offered the deal with Belle Cosmetics, Beverly recognized it as her big break. How could she turn down such a plum opportunity when she still had no other, more worthwhile plans? At best, being the latest Belle Beauty would help her get bigger and better jobs should she decide to stay in modeling. At least, it would occupy some time and put money in her savings account while she was trying to decide what her next step should be.

She reached New Orleans in late afternoon and took a taxi to the Sheraton at the edge of the French Quarter, where the photographer, crew and ad agency representative were also staying.

The bellboy showed her to her room and opened the drapes, revealing a lovely view of the Mississippi River. Beverly handed him a tip, then walked to the window and looked out. In the growing dusk, a large paddleboat looked very festive with twinkling white lights along its rails and cabin roofs as it floated up the river.

It wasn't the Gulf. It didn't look anything like the view she and Jeff had had in Galveston. And yet it triggered memories. Happy smiles. Passionate embraces. And a tearful goodbye.

Jeff. Where was he now? Was he back in that motel in Alvin, surrounded by maps and lists? Was he in a conference with oil executives, trying to negotiate a deal to trade crew and equipment for a percentage of the well? Was he rounding up the crew and equipment on his own? Was he relaxing with a cold beer in a bar? Was he alone?

Her mind always veered off in that dangerous direction. Jeff wasn't the kind of man to be without a woman for long. He'd admitted he loved being around females. Even when there wasn't a romance involved, he felt comfortable talking and flirting with women.

The thought of Jeff with another woman brought a fresh grip of pain tightening her heart. But it was inevitable. And Beverly knew she had better get used to the idea or else push it completely from her mind.

Awash not so much in self-pity as in despair and loneliness, Beverly yanked the drapery cord and the curtains slapped together, shutting out the view of the river and any memories it might resurrect.

She flipped through the messages that had been waiting for her at the front desk. She was to meet the others in the lobby at five o'clock the next morning so her makeup and hair could be done before they all headed for

the site of the shoot at eight. She was delighted to find a hello from Mike, the photographer on the project. And there was a
fruit basket and a bottle of wine from the
Belle representative.

Beverly yawned. It had been a long day
and she had to look fresh very early the next
day. She changed into her gown and pulled
back the sheets. It seemed that she could
never get enough sleep anymore. No matter
how long she stayed in bed, she could barely
rouse enough energy to get up. Sometimes it
hardly seemed worth the effort.

She flipped off the light. Well, as Scarlett
O'Hara said, tomorrow would be another
day. Hopefully, it would be better than the
past few.

"BEVERLY, move a little to the left. We're
getting shadows from that big bush," Mike
called, studying her through the viewfinder
on his camera. "Yes, that's it. Perfect."

The camera began clicking as Beverly
smiled, posed, moved slightly, changed her
expression and generally ran through all the
motions she'd done countless times before.

The first day's shoot was at a beautiful an-

tebellum mansion that looked as if it had
been frozen in time.

And, as usual, that night Beverly fell into
bed, exhausted. Modeling looked deceptively
easy, but it was hard work sitting for hours
while getting made up to look ''natural,''
then standing in awkward poses, trying to
look cool and cheerful in temperatures that
would melt candles. But now she welcomed
the extreme fatigue because it kept her from
lying awake, thinking about things she'd
rather not think about.

The next day, the location was Jackson
Square in the French Quarter. Special permission had been obtained for Beverly to
pose on the statue of General Andrew Jackson in the center of the park, sitting behind
him on his horse. With St. Louis Cathedral
in the background and a group of street mu-
sicians in the foreground, there was an interesting blend of new and old New Orleans.

It was another hundred-degree day, and
Beverly sat limply on a park bench, barely
touching her food during the lunch break.

''Hey, kid, why so down?'' Mike asked,
sitting beside her and balancing his plate on

his lap. "I would've thought you'd be all smiles at getting this assignment."

"I'm smiling on the inside," she said with a weak attempt at an outward grin.

"Terrific. That'll really show up on film."

Beverly groaned. "Am I looking that bad? Are the photos—"

"They're fine." Mike hurried to calm her fears. "Actually, they're better than fine—they're great! You're beautiful, as usual."

A muffled scream pierced the air. Beverly turned around in time to see a young man pulling a bloody knife out of an elderly lady's stomach. Before anyone could move, he'd jerked her diamond rings off her fingers, grabbed her purse and fled, disappearing quickly into the crowd on the sidewalks that surrounded the Square.

"Oh, God! She's bleeding like crazy," one of the lighting technicians cried. "Someone call a doctor!"

Beverly didn't stop to think, but ran across the manicured grass to where the older woman lay. As she knelt next to her, Beverly pulled off the expensive designer scarf that had been loosely knotted around her neck.

"Don't try to move," she told the woman. "They're calling for an ambulance."

"He stabbed me," the woman gasped as she struggled to sit up, obviously teetering on the verge of shock. "Did you see that? He stole my rings…and my purse."

Beverly pressed the wadded-up scarf against the woman's wound with one hand and pushed against her shoulder, forcibly making her lie back down. "Don't worry about those things. You need to lie still now. Help will be here in just a few minutes."

"But—"

Beverly smiled gently, but didn't relax the pressure on either the wound or the woman's shoulder. "No buts. I've had first-aid training, and I know it's difficult, but you need to try to relax. My name's Beverly. What's yours?"

"Wanda. Wanda Anderson."

"Do you live around here?"

The old woman peered into Beverly's eyes and must have seen something that reassured her, because she actually did relax a little. "I'm from Miami. My husband and I are here on vacation. He's taking a nap and I thought I'd do a little shopping. He's going to be so upset I lost all my credit cards...."

"He's going to be so glad you're okay, he won't care about those silly old credit cards," Beverly said positively.

"Oh, you don't know my husband. He'll have a fit. He told me not to leave without him."

"Which hotel is he at?" Beverly looked up at Mike, who was standing beside her, and he interpreted her silent request. He pulled a piece of paper out of his pocket and a pen, then wrote down the name of the hotel Wanda mentioned and sprinted off. "My friend Mike will tell your husband, and I'm sure he'll meet you at the hospital."

Beverly kept the conversation going until she heard the wail of the siren as the ambulance approached. "See, they're almost here. It won't be long now."

The paramedics rushed through the gates, following the directions given by curious bystanders. As soon as one of them knelt down and reached for the scarf, Beverly started to move away.

"Don't leave me...please," Wanda begged.

Beverly looked up at one of the paramedics and he nodded before joining his partner in a quick examination of the wound. Then he jogged back to the ambulance to get a stretcher while the other paramedic started an IV in Wanda's arm.

She kept an ever-weakening grip on Beverly's hand as they lifted her onto the stretcher, pushed her through the crowd and loaded her into the back of the vehicle. "Thank you," the elderly woman whispered to Beverly just before she released her hand and they closed the doors.

"Will she be okay?" Beverly asked the man as he latched the door.

"I think so. You did a fine job," he said as he gave her a quick smile. "You probably saved her life." Then he jumped into the cab, turned on the siren and pulled back into the traffic on Decatur Street.

The crew crowded around Beverly, some staring at her in amazement and others pounding her on the back. She looked down at her blood-covered hand and noticed, for the first time, the stains that were splattered across her outfit.

Belle Cosmetics wouldn't be too happy

about that, Beverly knew. But suddenly she smiled. It was the first genuine smile to break through the unhappiness that had been hanging over her for the past week. She felt good, really good.

Her smile widened. For once, she had actually done something that made a difference.

CHAPTER FOURTEEN

JEFF LEANED FORWARD, resting his elbows on the bar as he nursed his fourth bottle of beer and stared moodily into the mirror that stretched across the back wall.

"Hey, cowboy. You new here?"

He'd seen the woman approach, so he wasn't really surprised when she spoke. But he took his time swiveling on his stool to face her.

"I've been in town a few days," he answered as he let his gaze boldly slide over her.

The black leather *bustier* pushed up her breasts until they were almost overflowing the lacy cups. The bodice was snug and short, leaving a couple inches of bare skin between its hem and the tight black miniskirt that barely covered her butt. Her long, shapely legs were bare and a pair of red leather boots covered her feet. A month ago, Jeff would have appreciated her beautiful figure, young, firm, voluptuous...but now...

Now, he longed for Beverly's body. How wonderful it had felt pressed again his. Her breasts were so soft and full and her skin as smooth as velvet. His hands ached to touch her again. But, he reminded himself sternly, he might never have the chance.

"Beverly." The word escaped in a husky sigh between his lips before he could stop it.

"Beverly? No, my name is Marla," the woman said, a flirtatious smile curving her lips. "What's yours?"

He blinked and his vision focused on the woman in front of him. "Jeff," he answered and patted the stool next to him. "Let me buy you a drink."

"Sure, I'll have a beer." She slid up on the bar stool and crossed her legs, causing the miniskirt to ride even higher on her thighs. She took the bottle the bartender put in front of her and tilted it to her lips. After taking a big swallow, her tongue circled her lips in an intentionally provocative gesture. "So, tell me, cowboy, how long will you be here?"

"Until I get rich," he muttered, "or die trying."

She frowned as if she was trying to decide if he was joking or not. "What do you do?"

"I gamble with other people's money." At her confused expression, he added, "Oil. I'm putting in a well south of town."

Her eyes brightened. "I just love men who know how to use their tools," she said with a suggestive glance at the front of his tight Levi's.

"How about a dance, Marla?" He slid off his stool and downed the last of his beer.

"I didn't think you'd ever ask." The leather skirt stuck to the vinyl bar stool cover, revealing a flash of black bikini panties as she took her time pulling down the hem to a semirespectable level.

Jeff noticed and was mildly surprised that the sight had absolutely no effect on him. Attributing this to one drink too many, he draped his arm around Marla's shoulders and led her to the dance floor. She melted against him, immediately looping her arms around his neck with the intimacy of a lover. A Garth Brooks song flowed from the jukebox. Jeff tried to ignore the words as he held

Marla much too close and tried to forget the woman he'd rather have in his arms. When Garth sang about being able to walk away from everyone except the one woman he loved, Jeff tightened his grip. As the song continued with Garth saying he'd never been in love like that before, Marla found Jeff's mouth and kissed him. Hard. Hungrily.

"What's the matter, cowboy? Don't I turn you on?" she asked as he turned his head away.

He stepped back. For a long moment he stared at her, noting every beautiful curve of her body and wondering why she was having absolutely no effect on him. She was sexy, had a great figure, long blond hair, an attractive face. Normally, he would have responded to her immediately. Marla had everything he usually looked for in a woman.

But she wasn't Beverly. The components were the same, but the finished product was different. Marla didn't have Beverly's sassy sense of humor or Beverly's vulnerability or Beverly's surprising innocence. The truth of the matter was, no other woman would ever measure up to Beverly.

And as his thoughts again drifted to her, it

wasn't her physical perfection that made him ache for her. Instead, he smiled at memories of her charming the children with that silly dummy of hers and of the many hours she had spent with Hank and the other patients even after her shifts were over. He was impressed by her gentleness and patience regardless of the task she was given at the hospital. He doubted he could have lasted there more than a day.

The more he got to know Beverly, the more obvious it had become. Beneath that beautiful body was a heart as big as Texas, and Jeff's own chest tightened.

Garth had been right...Jeff was in love as he'd never been before, and Beverly was definitely the one woman from whom he couldn't walk away.

"Cowboy? Are you okay?"

Jeff's head snapped up. He'd forgotten about Marla.

"No, as a matter of fact, I'm not. I'm feeling a little sick," he told her. "Why don't I just take you home?"

"No thanks. I rode with a friend, and I'll head on back over there to meet her."

"I'm sorry," he muttered.

Marla snorted and tossed her mane of blond hair over her shoulder. Without another word, she marched across the room.

LYING ON HIS BACK with his hands behind his head on the pillow, Jeff stared at the ceiling and tried to think how he was going to get through the next fifty or sixty years without Beverly. Would this pain that was wringing all the life from his heart ever ease? Would he ever be able to say her name without his breath catching in his throat? When he heard the inevitable news that she'd met that perfect man and married him, would he ever be able to smile again?

God, what had she done to him? What spell had she cast? He couldn't even concentrate on negotiations for the well, which was extremely unusual for him. Oil had always dominated his life, his thoughts, his dreams. Now a sweet, exciting woman had become a permanent part of all those things.

Had they really been such a bad match? He remembered the happy lilt of her laughter and the sparkle in her eyes. He remembered the shaky moans that had shaken her body as she reached an orgasm beneath him. He remembered the fun they had had at the picnic, visiting Hank, meeting behind the barn to work on the old truck, and all the times they had gone for long walks to the horse pastures or the evenings they'd spent in each other's arms. Those certainly weren't the actions of a woman who didn't care for him.

She'd never told him she loved him. But she wasn't the type of woman to get so deeply involved with a man if her heart wasn't involved...at least a little. Surely all those emotions he'd sensed stirring within her hadn't been his imagination.

Of course, he'd never told her he loved her, either, and look how deep his feelings were. Several times, the words had been pushing against his lips, dying to burst out. However, he'd held back, knowing that once he actually said them, he'd be leaving himself wide open for her to break his heart. Somehow, as long as he kept his feelings to himself, he could protect himself from the pain and the humiliation. Once the words were spoken, he would be passing all control of the situation to her.

So what had he gained by keeping silent? Had he spared himself any pain? Was being in control of this misery such a prize? She still filled his heart, his mind, his soul. The only thing he had left was his pride.

And Jeff was discovering that pride made a very cold, lonely companion.

He glanced at the clock. It was almost two in the morning. Where was she? Whom was she with? The possibilities rumbled through his brain, increasing his pain rather than offering a respite.

He *had* to talk to her. How foolish he'd been to leave her without at least telling her how he felt. So what did he have to lose? Certainly not his heart. It was already lost forever. Certainly not a good night's sleep, because he hadn't had one of those since the last time she'd cuddled next to him and slept in his arms.

If he could just tell her how he felt, perhaps he'd be able to focus on his future. He needed to know whether or not that future included her.

That was it! He had to talk to her, face-to-face.

IT WAS JUST AFTER seven o'clock when Jeff drove into Crystal Creek. Fighting exhaustion, he stopped at the Longhorn, hoping a cup of coffee would revive him enough that he could talk to Beverly with at least some semblance of consciousness.

"Well, look who's back!" Dottie exclaimed as soon as he walked through the door. "You looking for Earl?"

Before Jeff could answer, Earl came out of the men's rest room and walked with a bow-legged swagger to the bar stools.

"Damn prostate ain't what it used to be," the older man grumbled. "I know where every bathroom in town is."

"Earl, isn't it a little early in the day for you to be out and about?" Jeff asked, sliding onto the stool next to the ranch foreman.

Earl looked surprised. "Early? Hell, the chickens have been up for hours, and I always get up before 'em. So, what're you doin' back in town? Got problems with the well?"

"No, everything's fine. I've applied for the permits, and I'm still working on lining up the crews and equipment."

Dottie put a cup of coffee in front of Jeff. "What can I get you for breakfast?"

He placed an order without glancing at the

menu. He wasn't really hungry, but he just wanted something to fill the time until he could go to Beverly.

"How does it look?" Earl asked, continuing their conversation.

"Great. I feel really good about this one. I'm hoping we have something going by the end of July."

Earl took a sip of his coffee, but his sharp eyes remained focused on Jeff. "Woman troubles?"

Jeff smiled. He doubted anything ever got by the old man. "Yeah, you might say that."

"Well, she's gone."

Jeff straightened, forgetting his fatigue. "Gone? Where?"

"I think I heard Val say New Orleans."

"Did she say why?"

"Something about being the new Belle model." Earl shrugged. "I wasn't *really* listening, but I remember hearin' she was stayin' at the Sheraton by the French Quarter."

"Damn!" Jeff muttered. He gulped the rest of his coffee, dropped some money on the counter and headed for the door.

"Ain't you gonna get some sleep first? You look like hell."

"Yeah, and I feel like it, too," Jeff admitted, dragging his fingers through his tousled hair. "But I won't feel any better until I see her. Talk to you later."

Jeff walked out the door and returned to his truck. After filling the dual gas tanks, he was on the road again, this time heading almost due east.

By the time he drove into New Orleans he was beat. He'd stopped only for lunch and arrived in the middle of rush hour. Inching through town in the heavy traffic, he finally reached the Sheraton.

"Can I get your bags, sir?" the bellboy asked when Jeff parked his truck out front.

"Don't have any." Jeff tossed the keys to the disapproving employee. "But you can get the valet to park my truck for me."

A glance in the mirror told Jeff why the bellboy had looked at him so oddly. A two-day growth of stubble darkened his cheeks and chin, and his hair was windblown and disheveled. His shirt was rumpled and his eyes bloodshot. All in all, Jeff knew he must look as if he'd spent a hard night on the town.

Oh, well, his mission was not to impress anyone except Beverly. What he needed right now was a room where he could take a shower, shave and generally get cleaned up. He signed in, picked up his key and headed for the gift shop to buy some essential grooming items.

But as he passed the bar area in the large, vaulted atrium, a flash of golden hair caught his attention. He stopped and took a step backward, wondering if his eyes were playing games with him.

Her hair, fashioned into soft, loose curls, was pulled up on top of her head. Her smooth, tanned shoulders were exposed by the strapless dark green gown she was wearing, and large diamond-and-emerald earrings sparkled on her earlobes. She was tilting her head back, laughing at something her companion was saying, and as Jeff watched, she leaned forward.

The man she was with closed the distance between them and kissed her on the cheek.

Jeff knew he should take that as his answer. Obviously, Beverly was a more skilled hunter than he'd given her credit for. She hadn't been in New Orleans but a few days and already she'd found a new boyfriend.

If he'd been thinking clearly, he would have just gone up to his room, got a good night's sleep, then headed back to Alvin the next morning.

Unfortunately, extreme exhaustion and a hint of a hangover from the night before rattled his judgment. Beverly was *his* woman, whether she knew it or not. How dared she go so quickly into the arms of another man when she already had a man who loved her to distraction!

Jeff stalked across the open reception area, not stopping until he stood in front of her.

"Jeff!" Beverly gasped. "What on earth are you doing here?"

"Let's go," he said, grabbing her by the wrist. "I want to talk to you."

Beverly glanced around at the people who had halted their conversations and were openly eavesdropping on hers. Spots of color darkened her cheeks. She looked back at Jeff. "What about?"

"I love you, Beverly. There, I've said it!" Jeff looked around the room and grinned sheepishly. "And I seem to have plenty of witnesses."

"Jeff—you've got more than live witnesses. You've now been filmed for posterity. I'm in the middle of a shoot here."

Way to go, Jeff. Make a complete idiot of yourself. How on earth did you miss the cameras and the lights? Of course, he knew how he'd missed seeing all the apparatus. He'd had eyes only for Beverly.

Beverly turned to the male model, who had placed his arm protectively over hers as Jeff had grabbed her. "Please excuse me." She moved into Jeff's waiting embrace. Neither noticed the round of applause that greeted their kiss. Only the popping of camera flashes finally drew them apart.

"Thank you, thank you." Jeff bowed playfully to the crowd. "It's been a pleasure, but we're leaving now."

"But…"

In a movement so quick it surprised them both, he leaned over and lifted her until she was lying bent over his shoulder.

"What are you doing?" she asked, clinging to him as he carried her across the lobby.

"We're going to finish this in my room."

He stopped at the elevator and pushed the button.

Once alone inside the elevator, Jeff let Beverly slide to the floor.

"That was an abrupt exit," she said, but her eyes were begging for a kiss, which he promptly gave her.

"I don't want to share you with anyone," he said when their lips separated again. "At least not for the next hundred years or so."

"That's going to be difficult in my line of work," she said.

"Your line of work?" he echoed. "You mean modeling?"

"No, I mean medicine. I've been thinking a lot about it the past few days, and I've decided to use one of my pageant scholarships to go to med school."

He smiled and kissed her again. "You'll be a wonderful nurse."

She laughed. "Oh no, I'm aiming higher than that. I'm going to become a doctor." Her hand lifted to the antique locket that hung around her neck. "Yes, I think it's something I can do well. And it's time I did something worthwhile."

"I can think of something else worthwhile you can do."

"Oh? What would that be?"

He pulled her back into his arms and gave her a warm, possessive hug. "You can tell me you love me."

"And how is that worthwhile?"

"If you do, you can take full credit for redeeming a scoundrel."

"What happened to all that 'listening to the wind' talk?" she asked, obviously still cautious. "I realize now the man who's perfect for me may not be rich, but I do expect him to be with me."

"When I compared listening to the wind against listening to my heart, I had to go with what my heart's saying." He looked deeply into her eyes, trying to convince her that his feelings were genuine. "Things might not always be easy for us, Beverly. But together we can make it. I can't be happy without you. I don't even want to try. You are my one true love."

All doubt melted from her eyes. "Is this a proposal?"

"It's a prophecy. I'll make you happy, and I'll love you forever."

"Then yes, Jeff darlin'. I love you and I'd be proud to become your wife."

The elevator doors opened as he leaned closer and captured her mouth in a long, loving kiss.

"Remember when I said there weren't any good men left?" Beverly whispered. "Now it's really true because I just got the last one."

Don't miss Ken Slattery and Nora Jones's story, The Thunder Rolls *by Bethany Campbell, available in November 2000.*

READER SERVICE™

The best romantic fiction direct to your door

Our guarantee to you...

The Reader Service involves you in no obligation
to purchase, and is truly a service to you!

There are many extra benefits including a free
monthly Newsletter with author interviews,
book previews and much more.

Your books are sent direct to your door
on 14 days no obligation home approval.

We offer huge discounts on selected books
exclusively for subscribers.

Plus, we have a dedicated Customer Care team
on hand to answer all your queries on
(UK) 020 8288 2888
(Ireland) 01 278 2062.

Escape into

Just a few pages
into any Silhouette®
novel and you'll find
yourself escaping
into a world of
desire and intrigue,
sensation and
passion.

Silhouette

Diana
Palmer

Beloved

Rebecca
YORK

Nowhere Man

The
Marriage
Bargain

Jennifer Mikels

A Husband
Waiting To Happen

MARIE FERRARELLA

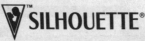

Warwick C

Death of an Angel

Pan Books
London, Sydney and Auckland

Warwick Collins is a yacht designer and the inventor of the Tandem Keel. In 1991 the 80-foot sailing yacht *Ocean Leopard*, fitted with one of his keels, established the all-time monohull record for the classic Round-the-Island race, breaking the previous record by twenty-two minutes. He is the author of *Challenge* and *New World* (both available in Pan), the first two novels in a yacht-racing trilogy, now completed by *Death of an Angel*.

First published in hardback in 1992 by Pan Books Limited

This edition published 1993 by Pan Books Limited
a division of Pan Macmillan Publishers Limited
Cavaye Place London SW10 9PG
and Basingstoke
Associated companies throughout the world

ISBN 0 330 32135 8

9 8 7 6 5 4 3 2 1

A CIP catalogue record for this book is available from
the British Library.

Photoset by Parker Typesetting Service, Leicester
Printed and bound in Great Britain by
Cox & Wyman Ltd, Reading, Berkshire

I feel myself suddenly invaded by doubt and ask myself if your heart is equal to your intelligence and spiritual qualities, if it is open to the tender feelings which here on earth are so great a source of consolation for a sensitive soul; I wonder whether the peculiar demon, to which your heart is manifestly a prey, is the Spirit of God or that of Faust. I ask myself – and this is not the least of the doubts that assail my heart – if you will ever know a simple happiness and family joys, and render happy those who surround you.

From a letter by Heinrich Marx to his son, Karl Marx.

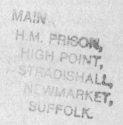

ACKNOWLEDGEMENTS

I owe a debt of gratitude to Chris Owen, my agent, for his far-sighted advice and encouragement; to Ian Chapman and Martin Neild for their faith in the Challenge trilogy; to Bill Scott-Kerr, my editor, and to Anna Pilkington for her help with the Russian background. Any remaining faults or inconsistencies are entirely my own.

One

No visibility to speak of.

Christian Parvu settled his hand on the wheel of *Livia* and stared over the doghouse into the mist. A light breeze was blowing. The white wall around him seemed to be changing shape slowly, breeding strange images; flying buttresses, the ramparts of esoteric castles, an arm outstretched. Beneath the tarred deck the single Lirov diesel rumbled quietly, so low he was only aware of its presence by the vibrations which permeated upwards through the soles of his feet. Nothing, no solid land or other permanence, gave him such reassurance as the purring of its six cylinders. The *Livia* might be old and worn, but at its core was an engine which he and Alt Vilde nurtured with infinite care.

Vilde stood at the side of the deck-house, on the narrow midship deck, propped by one hand as he stared forward into the mist. Parvu could see that he was nervous, if only because Vilde placed no weight against the deck-house, remaining instead balanced on the soles of his feet. The slow movements of Vilde's fingers, beating a soft rhythm on the deck-house side, were a further indication of his tenseness.

Parvu could feel beneath his own hands the occasional shiver, the feathery brush of the propeller, like snow falling off a branch. There was a deformation on one of the three phosphor-bronze blades, where it had once struck a piece of driftwood. It had been there for years. He only noticed it at times like the present, times of quietness and tension. As the boat eased forward at three and a half knots, the vibrations of the slowly running engine beat out like a heart against the wall of fog.

They continued on a course a few degrees south of east. Parvu eased the throttle back a little, until they were only ghosting.

The fog seemed to close and thicken. Occasionally, they could see the faint outline of the morning sun. The glare, and the movement of mist by the light breeze, gave the occasional impression of solidity and permanence. A shape suggested a wharf, the bow of a ship, a militia vessel. . .

Parvu tried to quieten his nerves. They had left their nets behind deliberately, so that if they were caught and searched there would be no evidence of any major fishing transgression. They had simply lost their way, he would claim. And the lines? Well, they had to pass the time somehow while they waited for the fog to clear.

Vilde turned his face sideways and tapped, slowly and deliberately, three times on the deck-house. Parvu responded by easing back the throttle. He found neutral, then used the existing way on the craft to turn into the wind. With her speed cut to hardly more than two knots, the *Livia* eased slowly forward.

Vilde moved towards the bow with the careful, slightly measured gait of an old fisherman. In the bow well he waited until speed had fallen off, then he released the pawl on the capstan. There was no hiding the noise as the chain rumbled out. The pressure eased and he knew the anchor had hit bottom. He eased some more, allowing the windage to pull the boat back, watching the coded lengths, white, green, blue, each colour a ten-metre. Then he tightened the lock a little, letting the wind pull her back, easing out a few more lengths of chain in rasping runs as the pressure came on. When he had let out forty metres he tightened fully and felt the anchor grip.

Parvu switched off the engine and began to set up fishing rods in the stern. Three rods were lucky. He pulled up the bait bucket and sat down on one of the

8

beam planks. Vilde came back to help him. Now that they had begun to fish they both felt a little easier. The activity spread its own small ripples of security. Even so, when a small stray swell struck the side of the boat, Parvu paused for a moment to listen.

Vilde said, 'This area hasn't been fished for years.'

'Just mined and depth-charged,' Parvu commented. And not so much of that, now that something like peace had spread across the globe. Russian naval budgets were not what they were in the heyday of Admiral Gorshkov, when both Parvu and Vilde had served their time as naval conscripts.

Not far away, when he was younger, Parvu had hooked a wahoo, a big one. No one knew what the fish was doing in the Baltic, an Atlantic predator. In moments like these he liked to recall that time, watching nervously the line streak out, the exploding energy of the fish, like catching a torpedo at full bore.

Somewhere a foghorn sounded, both near and far.

Vilde reached for the hook at the end of the line, releasing the tension on the reel.

'Old coaster at the top of the bay,' Vilde said, as if to reassure himself. Like a cow, he thought, calling for its calf.

'Maybe it's a militia vessel.'

'Militia vessel doesn't sound like that. Too much like a frog in the throat.' Vilde was right. You could hear a rattle as the old valve release on the coaster's foghorn shook. Some old coaster out of St Petersburg, exporting salted fish or cheap tractor parts. He could envisage the topsides high with rust, the seagulls watching the wake for spills, gold flakes above the surface fog. Somewhere out there.

But Parvu had heard another sound, another muffled, rasping growl; the teeth of an internal mechanism, the rattle of a winch.

Neither spoke for a few moments. Parvu said:

'Sound does odd things in this weather.'

Vilde put his feet down either side of the bait bucket. 'It's not the sound that worries me. It's whatever is making it.'

'You're nervous.' Parvu was determined to enjoy the expedition. 'We're outside the shipping lane. Let's see about those fish.'

Vilde stared out into the growing whiteness. Where the sun touched its edges the fog seemed to light up like phosphorescence.

'Something's out here with us.'

The fog came in waves over the bow, in places so dense it seemed like the sea.

'Maybe another pair of old fools like us, trying to take back some illegal fish.'

'Perhaps.'

But if he had heard it once, he had heard it several times now, the sound of a mechanism, the rasp of iron teeth.

Parvu rolled over the flesh with his forefinger to thread it on the hook. He tied on the strand of flesh with a piece of grey thread. The sound had gone now, stitched into a honeycomb of mist, sealed in one of those odd hollows.

The three lines were baited and let out. A wind-shadow aft of the boat made the water there appear as smooth as oil. In its centre three floats bobbed.

It had been quiet now for almost half an hour. Some of Parvu's apprehension had gone. Vilde had gone below to cook up some coffee on the diesel stove. From where he was sitting, Parvu could smell the coffee grains. With the onset of the morning, the temperature had risen a few degrees. Parvu put aside his heavy Siberian jacket. Mostly he enjoyed these quiet times. A certain ease began to enter his mind. As he threaded more baits he began to whistle tunelessly through his teeth.

'Coffee?'

Parvu hated it when Vilde crept up on him. He moved like a cat.

Vilde looked around at the fog. 'Still quiet?' he asked.

The coffee was good. A little fat Cuban, one of Castro's Angolan mercenaries who had settled in St Petersburg, sold sackfuls of beans from a corner shop on Suvorov Street. It was part of the new economics. Private industry, co-operatives. It came in sacks off the merchant fleet, part of that free enterprise culture that now flourished precariously like a flea on the carcass of a dog. You could buy beans from the Cuban and grind it yourself. The smell came up strong and dark, a magnificent scent.

One of the floats stirred once, as if animated by thought, but after a while it was still again. Something small perhaps had nibbled the bait.

After a half-hour Parvu hauled in the outer line to see whether there was bait still on the hook, or whether some fish had managed to detach it. The piece of flesh came up good and white; as it neared the surface, the refractions of the swells made it appear to flutter like a moth. He checked the bait and released the line again.

Some screams are silent. A triangular piece of fog seemed to detach itself, towering above them like a sudden cliff. Before they could react, before either could think or speak or even cry out, the two yachts were on them. With the hiss of a bow wave, a white prow slid by less than twenty feet away. Another crossed not much further away, on the other side. Orders were shouted, winches screamed, and it seemed to Parvu that he been flung, like a man falling off a cliff, into his own terror. The furious activity of grinding winches and the thunder of sails, the cacophonous sounds which now engulfed him were so unexpected that, a moment afterwards, they had wrung his soul of all fear, leaving him suspended. The first and then the second yacht tacked.

A wash from the closest yacht struck forcibly. *Livia* lurched, toppling Vilde's chair. Vilde was flung sideways, striking his arm. But he regained his balance against the side of the cockpit. Both men were standing now, unable to speak, as they watched the two Stars and Stripes on the yachts' sterns start to fade into the mist.

Before they disappeared, a weak sunburst touched one of the yachts briefly. The sails were made in some new cloth which shimmered like the wings of a butterfly, revealing through its opacity a complex and beautiful pattern of reinforced stress lines; these flowed from the corners of the sails as delicately as the ribbing of a leaf. The same beam of sunlight, penetrating through the mist, touched the top third of the second boat's sails, which glowed suddenly like a pulse of energy. The two yachts faded, leaving only the rapidly closing tracery of their wakes.

Livia rocked in the cross pattern of waves. Parvu's throat was so dry he could not speak. He waited until the saliva crept into the corners of his mouth before invoking God in whispered Estonian: '*O Issand!*'

It was spoken for both of them.

Two

Shaw had sensed the fog early that morning. It was not only the lowing of the big ships as they moved out of St Petersburg, but the whiteness of the light spreading through the small skylight above his and Maria's bed. It was in the peculiar quality of silence which surrounded him. He sensed it like a visceral presence.

It made him nervous. Like all sailors, he loathed fog. Beside him, Maria slept soundly. In the cocoon of their warmth he allowed his mind to float for a few minutes while he gathered his thoughts.

Raising the covers carefully, he eased himself out of bed, and stood quietly in the half-lit centre of the tiled wooden floor. The bare furniture and meagre contents of the bedroom came toward him and receded. He rubbed his eyes.

Moving quietly through the bedroom, he crossed the living area and the entrance porch, and filled a steel kettle. A cold-water supply had recently been fitted, but there was no hot water in the bungalow. He filled the kettle and placed it carefully on one of the stove's two old electric rings. Switching on the current, he watched the ring glow pink and then a deeper red.

From Jack's room he could hear his son's light snores, the faint catch of his breath as he shifted position in his sleep.

Shaw shivered and rubbed his eyes. The fog at the windows infiltrated the panes with a yellowish light. Its casual, deadening presence seemed to fill the room.

While the water heated on the stove, he crossed the entrance porch and entered the tiny bathroom, closing the door gingerly behind him. The basin was hardly more than a steel plate, the bath an old iron tub with claw feet. It was inconvenient from one point of view, but its distance from the bedrooms allowed him to close the door and wash without waking the others. Behind the door he heard the kettle begin to bubble quietly.

He poured cold water into the sink. The tap gave out a brief low squeal as it emitted faintly rusty water into the sink. Russian plumbing, he thought, suspended in the middle nineteenth century. He splashed cold water on his face. It seemed to wake his mind. He washed his face with soap and rinsed it off with cold water. He dried himself briskly with the towel, breathing out slowly.

13

Outside the door he heard the kettle begin to lift its tone from a bubble to a higher pitch. He opened the door and, intercepting it before it raised its voice to a scream that would wake the others, lifted it off the range.

It was a luxury to empty the sink, pour fresh water, heat it with water from the kettle. He spread a lather of soap over his face and, dipping his razor occasionally in the warm water, began to shave.

He could hear the lowing of the steamers in the distant fog. But there were other sounds, occasional faint shouts, sometimes a stealthy pounding as Vagir's early shift worked on *Leningrad* in the big shed sixty yards away. The fog took the edges off the sound, so that it seemed to come from far away.

In the small cracked mirror over the sink, Shaw watched his own face emerge from the foam. It was a face he had accepted, though he was not comfortable with it. His features were nondescript, but there was a sharpness about his eyes, an animal mobility which he found disturbing. Perhaps it was a consequence of this that he enjoyed the distorting effect of close quarter vision. He liked to place his face close to the mirror, so that all he saw was a line of jaw and one wall eye, like a Cyclops, or to move his mouth sideways to shave first one cheek and then the other in a series of demented, cartoon-like expressions. In the privacy of the bathroom, the propagation of this intense, silent mime was perhaps his only recreation during the day.

He had left his clothes neatly folded on one of the chairs in the living-room. It allowed him to dress quietly. He pulled on shorts, shirt, trousers, socks, strong deckshoes. He combed his hair in the mirror, and reached for the door.

In the half-light he saw Maria appear, pause in the doorway as she tied a dressing gown. One side of her face was lit by the adjacent window, the other was in

14

darkness. She was staring at him, but her eyes were curiously without emotion, as if she were looking through him. It was an expression that he always found desirable. It was too early to say anything. He opened the door. As the glare touched his face he saw her move gently towards Jack's room, a scented animal he hardly knew.

Three

Jim Shaw was working with Vagir on the final preparations of the yacht *Leningrad* when the news came.

He was sitting in the cockpit, checking through a list of final preparations. Vagir sat opposite him, board in hand, his heavy head on one side in a characteristic attitude of concentration. As Shaw called out, so Vagir placed a neat tick beside each item. They had covered eight pages and were almost finished. Through the great open doors of the building shed the sky was clear. It was seven thirty, one of those magnificent mornings when the light is not yet hard and shyly illuminates the day.

Shaw could taste the coffee still, the pleasant, bitter kernels. The tragedy of *Novy Mir*'s sinking in the third race against the Americans was now put aside, on a rack of memory to which he would later return. He felt, after two days' hard preparation, the subtle, inestimable satisfaction of work well done. Vagir, too, was hollow-eyed but cheerful.

Over Vagir's shoulder, through the open main doors, Shaw noticed the side door of the administration buildings open and close. From it emerged the short, square figure of Brod. There was a curious attribute to his walk. He was heavily built, huge in the shoulders, and generally he ambled with the genial power of a bull. But now his movements were more precise, as if he were in the grip of a strong emotion.

Shaw continued to call off the items, Vagir ticking each as he did so. With half his mind Shaw listened. Part of him continued to study Brod's movement across the short square. Now he had halted beside Soren Gir. Gir pointed to the open door. Perhaps he is looking for me, thought Shaw idly, and continued to work through the list with Vagir.

'Running backstay winches stripped, checked, oiled,' Shaw said. In Vagir's square fingers the pencil seemed tiny. 'Running backstay tackles stripped, checked, oiled.'

Brod was in the doorway now. His eyes partly blinded by morning sunshine, he gazed myopically upward into the dark interior of the building. He seemed to make out Shaw. Instead of coming forward, climbing the ladder to join Shaw and Vagir in the cockpit, he appeared to pause, as if what was driving him had caught up with him. He put out his hand carefully for support against the steel doorway, gathered himself, as if he were about to sing. For one absurd moment Shaw thought that was what he was about to do, to launch forth with his baritone into some operatic piece. Instead the thunder of his voice was not raised in song. It sent its echo into the empty building. Pigeons clattered off the roof. Only when the sound had died did the content of his cry remain.

Four

Illich was dead.

Brod did not use the phrase 'is dead', but the Estonian expression *on tapetud*, 'has been killed'. Shaw watched Vagir's face, as if he could find some explanation there. But Vagir's face had drained. The pencil stood still in his hand, arrested over the list.

Shaw stepped past him and half sidled, half slid down the ladder to the concrete floor. His heartbeats were loud, not only because of his sudden physical effort. He approached Brod, still standing at the doorway. Brod was breathing as if after some great effort.

What thoughts enter the mind at such moments? Three days earlier, in the third race of the America's Cup, the American yacht *Eagle* had rammed their defending yacht *Novy Mir*. It occurred to Shaw that Brod might regard Illich's death as another action by Shaw's American compatriots. More terrible than this, the thought that Brod might even be considering such a possibility made his mind run cold. For a moment it seemed that out of rage at life Brod might strike him, the one American who had joined this Estonian crew. In matters of life and death what counted was family, and whatever he might feel, whatever rage or sadness was building in his own heart, he wasn't part of this brotherhood.

So he approached Brod gingerly, half expecting one of those sudden, crushing blows that, on more than one occasion over the past six months, he had seen delivered to others.

In Shaw's experience, if someone is about to strike you, his white pallor, caused by adrenalin, gives notice of his intention. Shortly afterward, the parasympathetic nervous system launches its own chemicals into the

17

blood, and the flushed, reddened complexion is a sign that the crisis is fading. Their physical training instructor, Gustav Prem, a former sergeant in the paratroop forces, had told them to protract confrontations to the point where the parasympathetic nervous system has had an opportunity to dampen the opponent's aggressive response. 'Then what?' someone asked. 'Then *you* hit *him*,' Prem had said.

Brod was caught up in his own emotion, taking deep gulps of air as if emerging from underwater. Behind him Shaw heard Vagir's quiet tread. He had climbed down the ladder behind him and was standing at his shoulder, watching.

Brod said: 'Aegu phoned. It happened in Tallinn. Someone, an old woman, heard the sound of shots in the block of flats in Laidonner Street. She called the police. They had to break into Illich's flat. They found Illich had been shot several times. There was blood everywhere, on the walls and floors. He must have put up a fight. The assailant was wounded. A second trail of blood led down the fire escape.'

Shaw felt weak and sick. He said to Brod: 'But he went to Tallinn to see his wife. His ex-wife,' he corrected himself.

'Aegu's office said they have already phoned her. She was in Kharkov with her husband and family, and didn't know the first thing about it until the police informed her.'

Then who sent the telegram, thought Shaw, to bring Illich to Tallinn? The details made it real. He felt like being sick, and forced himself to think again.

'The telegram . . .'

'Illich took it with him,' Brod said suddenly. 'They found it on his body. It is being investigated.' Brod paused. 'Aegu said there will be a state funeral in ten days' time.'

But Shaw only heard part of the last sentence. He

18

moved past Vagir and out into the open sunlight. Blinded, his mouth full of salt saliva, he felt with one hand along the side of the building until he came to a patch of rough grass. There he was copiously sick. His bowels threw up everything. He hadn't been sick like that since his youth, when Jack Peabody used to beat him in races at summer camp so many years ago.

Almost immediately he felt better, even light-headed. Embarrassed, too. The grief remained, like the taste of coffee, but he would come to terms with Illich's death later. It was important to think logically, to concentrate.

Vagir produced from his pocket a thick ply rag to wipe his mouth. Shaw, no longer blinded by sunlight, leaned against the building. With a further sensation of embarrassment, he realized he was holding the rag to his mouth, hiding behind it like a child. He folded it carefully. With curiosity they watched him, Brod standing by Vagir. He realized that these two were now the heart of the Estonian team. Brod, navigator and crew boss; Vagir in charge of the shore operations. And himself, lost in his private circle of grief, somewhere outside both of them.

They watched him implacably, two short, square men, both curiously similar in build, Brod perhaps the darker of the two. Out of this uncertainty his thoughts slowly gathered.

'You should helm the boat,' Brod said.

Vagir nodded, as if it was decided.

'They wouldn't allow it,' Shaw replied. Though light-headed, he still felt weak. The sunlight danced on the open waters of the bay. Sometimes, touching the surface of a swell, it would gather power and send a tongue of white light towards him. He shielded his eyes. 'I'm American.' It was an instinctive reaction.

'And Estonian, too,' Brod replied.

Maybe it was true, at least in a technical sense. He had

19

dual passports. Aegu had seen to that. But the idea of an American helming the Russian defender was still a shocking, even a comical idea. Until he remembered who the rival team were. And what they'd done.

That, finally, was what decided him. The Russian defender, *Novy Mir*, had been salvaged from the sea bed the previous day, with the aid of tugs and flotation bags. She had been towed in, and like a broken sea monster, like some ancient bone-crushed fossil, tenderly raised and lifted ashore. Now, still decked with weed, she had been placed on a cradle beside the building shed. Her bow showed a hole approximately seven feet wide, peeled at the edges as if she been struck by a bomb. The aperture, ringed with fractured wood, seemed to stare at him. It had the dead look of a skull, with its single, staring eye. Like the rest of the crew, he was convinced that the American challenger had rammed them deliberately. He remembered the whoop of triumph when John Ericson, its skipper, heard the judges of the inquiry exonerate him for lack of conclusive evidence that he had deliberately caused the collision.

Brod and Vagir continued to watch him. He suspected that they took his agreement for granted.

Shaw nodded.

He saw an expression on their faces. Of what? Relief? Surprise? Sympathy?

'We'll tell the others,' Brod said. 'You should get some rest.' For the first time since the news of Illich's death, Brod seemed to gain back a modicum of his old, equable self. He added, 'We've had one shock. You've had two.'

Five

Maria was feeding Jack.

Without turning round, she said: 'That you, Jim?'

'Yeah.'

Shaw paused for a moment. His son, distracted by his entrance, had turned his face sideways and was watching him with his disconcerting eyes. Patiently Maria waited, spoon in hand, for Jack to turn back.

'Honey,' Shaw said, 'can I speak to you next door?'

She put down the spoon on the sink and followed him into the little bedroom. He closed the door.

Facing her, he said: 'Aegu phoned Brod this morning. Illich is dead.'

He watched the shock cross her face, and in some private area of his mind experienced his own enraged grief a second time. She turned away. He waited several seconds before continuing.

'Unfortunately, that isn't all. He was murdered in his flat in Tallinn. They think that someone must have faked that telegram from his wife to lure him there, then shot him.'

She turned back to him, her eyes quiet. He thought suddenly, Jesus, these Estonians.

'Do they have any idea who . . . ?'

'Not yet. There was a fight. The murderer left a trail of blood. Aegu's got half the police force working on it.'

Maria sat down on the bed. He let her sit for a while. In the next room he could hear Jack slapping the tray rhythmically with his chubby hands.

He opened the door, and reaching Jack just in time restrained him from throwing his plate of tapioca pudding across the room.

It was several minutes before Maria came through. He saw from the sudden startling redness in her eyes that she had been crying, crying privately while she leaned against the sink, her face turned away. He knew that to her, as to the others in the crew, Illich was more than a friend, a leader. Perhaps she too was thinking of the future, what would happen to them now. She asked: 'What about the rest of the crew? How are they taking it?'

'I've seen Brod and Vagir. Brod got the message directly from Aegu.'

'What will happen now?'

'That's the second bit of bad news. Brod and Vagir asked me to take over from him as helmsman.'

Her face was expressionless. He thought that she probably would not comment on that, it was too close. But he was wrong again.

'He would have wanted that,' she said finally.

'Maybe,' Shaw replied. It was curious how his own feelings didn't come into it, only Illich's. He'd recovered a little now from the first shock, and he wanted to give her time to do the same. He picked up the spoon from the sink, and started to feed Jack. He noticed how Jack's eyes, even while he ate, swivelled between him and Maria. Children, as intuitive as animals, are aware of atmosphere.

Maria had turned her face away from him, and was staring out of the window, over the tangled grass to the bay. He could see the concentration of thought in her back. It was calming for him, too, to feed Jack while the world raged outside.

Shaw tried to put his thoughts in order. Helmsmen are trained to concentrate on the crisis in hand, to set priorities coldly, to put aside emotion. The very essence of their occupation is to try to think constructively out of a disaster, never to give up even though the rival looks so far ahead. Perhaps his training came to his aid.

He had been through the arguments before with Illich and the crew. He must carry on now, now that

Novy Mir had been destroyed, and they would have to face their opponents in the older, slower *Leningrad*. The Americans would have a boat-speed advantage which would be almost insuperable. The outcome seemed inevitable. *Eagle 2*, the American second yacht, was an exact replica of their first. The American challenging syndicate had two other yachts in perfect condition, also replicas of their challenger, *Eagle*. The Estonians had only the older *Leningrad*, their trial horse.

The day before they had watched two American yachts, *Eagle 2* and her trial horse, practising in the bay, and it was like seeing a risen ghost. It came to him again how cynical the ramming incident had been, how utterly without mitigating feature. From one point of view the incident, in which both yachts were sunk, was a piece of the purest logic. Its cynicism was breathtaking. Some trace of its indecency moved inside him, causing a series of other movements which he did not fully understand. It was more than just a yacht race. Some day, someone with a mentality like that would have a red button under his fingers. Life to him, too, would be a game. He would want to win at all costs. It would look smart to sacrifice a pawn for another pawn, perhaps a rook for another rook, in some terrible, abstract game of dominance. The pawns would be military installations, the bishops would be cities. Was he over-reacting? Perhaps. At the same time he felt, on an intuitive level, that he was dealing with something that was more than mischief, closer to the casual simplicity of evil. Even though they were heading for almost certain defeat, a conviction began to grown in him that he must make the effort.

'How are you feeling?' he asked Maria.

'He was such a strange man,' she said. 'So unworldly.'

Use of the past tense, at least, was part of her initial acceptance of the fact of Illich's death. He knew it would take days, weeks, months, for them to recover, and that the real tragedy would come in on them when the action was over, when they were prey to memories.

'Only two more mouthfuls,' he said to Jack.

'Na.'

Jack puffed his cheeks like a balloon.

'Two.'

'Na.'

'Come on, eat.'

'Daddy eat.'

'Daddy will get angry.'

'Jacko angry.'

'He's had enough,' Maria said.

'You Estonians,' Shaw said. 'Always stick together. I had him going there. He was on the defensive.'

'Mummy smack Daddy,' Jack burbled.

'Daddy too fast,' Shaw said. 'Mummy not catch him.'

'Mummy catch him,' Jack said, with perfect assurance.

Maria took the plate quietly from Shaw, rinsed and washed it in the primitive metal sink.

'You sure you're OK?' Shaw asked her again.

He noticed the small, almost hidden flash of anger in his formidable wife, and he thought, You are now.

Outside the big corrugated iron repair shed, the Estonians had gathered around Brod and Vagir in the small square they used to exercise.

Brod was talking, making short stabbing movements of his hands as he emphasized a point. But the physical positions of the individuals within the group indicated to Shaw as much as he needed to know. They were the attitudes of men who are struck by shock. Several had sat on the rough concrete and, their knees drawn up, had adopted that almost foetal attitude of despair. Several others had drawn away and were looking elsewhere, lost in private thought.

A side-door in the building opened and Ilena, Brod's wife, who handled the secretarial side so effectively for Illich, ran out calling Shaw's name.

She paused so that she could catch her breath.

'President Aegu on the telephone. He wants to speak to you.'

He followed her into Illich's small office, with its neatly laid books, its air of austerity, and for a brief moment he felt his rage and grief flare again.

Ilena was holding out the receiver.

He said, 'Jim Shaw.'

'Aegu. You heard the news about Illich?'

'Yes.'

'We have virtually every detective and policeman in Estonia working on it. How are the crew?'

'Shell-shocked.'

'I expect so. But it is important that we try to continue as best we can in the circumstances. When I spoke to Brod, we agreed that he would ask you to take over from Illich. Has he spoken with you yet?'

'Yes.'

'What is your answer?'

'I'll do it if the others want me to.'

'Good.'

'What do you think about my American background?' Shaw asked.

'You have an Estonian wife,' Aegu said, 'and Estonian citizenship. Technically, your nationality is not an important concern. Besides, I do not like narrow chauvinism. My country has suffered enough from that already. Tell me, what do you think of your chances of winning with *Leningrad*?'

Shaw said, 'Zero,' then he added, because the statement was a fraction bald, 'Maybe a little less.'

'I always liked optimists.' There was a clicking on the phone, and Aegu spoke to someone in the background, giving orders in rapid affirmatives. The phone clicked again, his voice was clearer now. 'It doesn't matter if you lose. We have done well enough to beat the Russian Army yacht, and win two races against the

Americans. I merely ask you to do your best.'

You'll get that, thought Shaw.

There were several further clicks on the line. The Russian telephone system was still not good, despite the installation of a complex system from the West. For a moment he thought they were going to be cut off, then Aegu continued: 'The state funeral of Illich will take place in ten days' time, in Tallinn. I have resisted pressure that it should be held in Moscow. He was half Russian on his father's side. The military are pressing hard for him to be buried with military honours. Perhaps,' said Aegu drily, 'when I know you a little better, I will explain the irony of that.'

In the brief pause which followed, Shaw saw through the window Brod explaining something to the others, using his hands to make brisk, stabbing points.

'Goodbye, Mr Shaw,' Aegu said.

Shaw put down the phone. Outside the office he stepped into bright sunshine. He looked out across the bay. They would have been practising by now if Illich were still alive, he thought. The third race in the series was the following day.

In the small training area the men were still gathered. Several faces turned towards him as he approached. The buzz of conversation reduced and was replaced by a nervous, intense silence. Shaw had always hated social occasions. Physically he was small, slight, almost awkward. He carried the helmsman's powerful shoulders and strong forearms and sometimes, on the rare occasions that he thought about his appearance, he felt he resembled a small, big-clawed crab. By comparison, the men he now approached were giants. Gundar Arlof, the trial-horse helmsman, was standing with Brod and Vagir. They seemed to close ranks as he approached. Gustav Prem, their mainsheet man, the winchmen Berol Baltir and Graf Ulder, the trimmers Edvigs Tarku and Soren Gir, the forecrew Herman Maask, Stephan

26

Migdal, Viktor Kingissep. Beside these great sailors he felt small, insignificant. He might have been approaching the Argonauts.

They should have laughed, and indeed they were beginning to make a sound like laughter. Inside Shaw quailed. He wanted to disappear completely, to run away. But instead it was the clapping of hands that startled him. They started to cheer. Their hands were drubbing him on the back. He realized they were cheering him. Then, with a roar, their voices rising, they began to sing the 'Mu Isamaa', the Estonian national anthem.

Six

Brod would take over Shaw's former role as tactician. Gundar Arlof had now fully recovered from his injuries received during the rescue of the *Leningrad* from the Russian Army camp earlier that summer. He would become navigator.

Brod said to Shaw, 'There is someone who wants to see you.'

'Where?' Shaw asked.

'Follow me.'

Brod led the way into the few stark offices adjacent to the main shed. He and Shaw shared a small room. Brod opened the door and said, 'I asked them to wait here.'

Inside the office leaning against the walls, were two men of about sixty. Shaw knew enough about fishermen from his grandfather to guess what their trade was. He could smell the familiar heavy musk of the sea, like a seashore suddenly reached. But there were other signs.

The inevitable cuts on the fingers, the scars on the back of the hands, the peculiar depth of the lines on the face from screwing up the expression against the sun and wind.

'Christian Parvu,' Brod said, 'Alt Vilde. Jim Shaw.'

'The American,' Parvu commented. They had been expecting someone else. Illich, Shaw realized.

Brod moved in again to forestall embarrassment. 'They have some information.'

'Sit down,' Shaw said.

Vilde's eyes moved around the bare room, the unpainted walls. Maybe he expected something more glamorous of an America's Cup defence. For the first time that day, Shaw experienced a glimmer of something approaching amusement.

'Information?' Shaw suggested.

Parvu looked towards Brod, who nodded.

'We were out on the water this morning,' Parvu began.

'Early,' Vilde spoke unexpectedly, still examining the room.

'Sightseeing?' It was an innocent question, but Shaw couldn't help a note of sarcasm. He had other things to do that day.

He remembered the fog that morning, low on the water, thick. They hadn't been able to practise the sailing with visibility that tight. What would these two be doing out there early, in thick mist?

Parvu shuffled his feet. Vilde said suddenly, 'We were fishing.'

Brod and Shaw glanced at one another. A little to the north and west of the sailing course was a Russian naval exercise area. Strictly no fishing. Shaw could see a pattern emerging. Along with everyone else who owned or had access to a vessel, Parvu and Vilde had taken their fishing boat from Estonia to watch the America's Cup races. Shaw guessed that with a delay in the racing caused by the collision, the temptation to sneak out surreptitiously, using the fog as cover, and do a little extra fishing was too much. A chance of taking something back from Russia, which had taken so much and so often from them, even something as small as a few cod or mackerel. Psychological satisfaction. He was starting to get the picture.

'We caught nothing,' Parvu said, as if this altered something. Vilde nodded with approval.

'Information?' Shaw reminded them again.

Parvu shuffled.

'We were almost run down . . . by two yachts. American.'

He watched Parvu's eyes stray towards Brod again.

'In the fog?' His interest had risen sharply. He could sense Brod tense and go quiet on the other side of the table. Suddenly they were both listening. 'In deep fog?'

Parvu detected the interest in his voice, and perhaps the hidden disbelief. Perhaps it encouraged him, knowing that what he had to impart was important.

'Thick fog . . .' he emphasized.

'Visibility?'

'Thirty, maybe forty metres.'

'What were they doing?'

'The yachts? Sailing,' Parvu said.

'Not being towed? Not anchored? Not waiting for things to clear?'

'Sailing,' Vilde confirmed. He had finished his examination of the room. Now his eyes rested on Shaw, as if trying to work out his weight.

'How close were they?' he asked.

'To us?'

'To one another.'

'Close,' Parvu replied.

Brod breathed out. 'Practising at close quarters. A tacking duel. They can see one another in the fog.'

That meant radar. In itself that was hardly surprising

or remarkable. But when two boats are engaged in a tacking duel, a few feet from one another in almost impenetrable fog, it would require an extraordinary level of instrumental integration and sailing controls . . .

'What happened?'

Parvu said, 'One yacht went by us ten metres away on one side, the other yacht about the same distance on the other.'

Vilde nodded. Parvu, having imparted his information, merely stared at Shaw.

Changing the subject, he said mildly, 'How did you get into the camp?'

'They kicked up a fuss at the outside fence,' Brod intervened again. 'Raedu let them in.'

Shaw nodded.

'I'm sorry you were kept waiting. We had an emergency.' He wondered how much he could tell them. There were official aspects to the case, procedures, protocol. He glanced at Brod. Brod knew more about Estonian officialdom than he did. He would know whether the information of Illich's death was confidential. Brod nodded, as if to say, go ahead.

Shaw cleared his throat and said, 'Ivan Illich died yesterday. We only got the news this morning. A full investigation is under way.'

He saw again the sudden fervent disbelief that comes with bad news, a reaction that is like outrage. Illich was a national hero in Estonia, second only perhaps to Aegu. Shaw, the *parvenu* American, watched the colour drain out of their faces. He saw the way their eyes moved to Brod, a fellow Estonian, for confirmation. Brod nodded.

Parvu and Vilde had hoped to give their information to Illich himself. It was something they could have told their grandchildren. Instead this American was telling them that Illich was dead.

Brod said, 'It seems Illich may have been murdered.'

30

Shaw would allow them some silence, out of respect. In the former Soviet Union, where execution was for so long the prerogative of the ruling classes, death had a different meaning. In Western states, you suspected an individual, a legacy of free enterprise; in Russia, popular mistrust of officials meant that the first suspicion tended to fall on the authorities.

It was an impasse, which only Brod could break. After a few seconds Brod said, 'There is nothing any of us can do. We must wait until the investigation is concluded.'

Shaw asked quietly, 'Where are you based?'

'Narva,' Parvu replied, as if it was an effort to remember Shaw was still in the room.

'Thank you,' Shaw said to Parvu, to Vilde. 'Thank you for helping us.'

On the way out, Vilde swung towards Brod and asked unexpectedly, 'Why is your yacht called *Leningrad*?'

'It was built by the Russian Army,' Brod said.

'But,' Vilde objected, 'the city's name was changed back to St Petersburg more than ten years ago.'

'It was named after the battle, not the city.'

Vilde looked at Shaw.

'The Russian Army lives in the past,' Brod said, as if this explained something. He and Shaw watched the two fishermen turn and walk towards the periphery fence. Brod glanced at Shaw, then shrugged briefly, as if he too were perplexed by the conditions in which they found themselves.

That afternoon they worked on *Leningrad*. It was a psychological gesture more than anything, to give their minds something to think about other than Illich's death. By the time they started to sail, the mist had been burnt off the surface of the water. Now you could sense its former presence only by a dampness of the air. It was difficult to sail nevertheless. By the time *Leningrad* had been lowered into the water, and they were towed out

31

into the afternoon sunshine, the news of Illich's death had been widely broadcast, and their efforts to practise were dogged by a fleet of press and television craft. Despite the efforts of their towboat and tender, Shaw was forced to change course several times in order to avoid collisions.

All they could do was to check their wardrobe of sails. It had been Illich's policy from the start of their training programme that the rigs of *Novy Mir* and *Leningrad* would be identical, facilitating transfer of sails. They had cause to be grateful for this policy. Sail after sail seemed to fit well, and merely required the usual tuning. Without another boat to sail against, however, they had little idea of ultimate speed. The instruments provided an indication, but professional sailors know that to base performance upon instruments, however accurate, can lead to delusions.

The crew were still understandably subdued by the news of Illich's death. It remained on all their minds, lingering like the fog, deadening. They went through their paces with hardly a word being spoken.

When they returned to the dock in late afternoon, the camp was besieged with journalists. President Aegu, having foreseen the problem, had drafted in further Estonian militia to help keep the press at bay. There were demands to hold a press conference in order to explain Illich's death and the replacement of the great Russian helmsman by the renegade American Shaw.

The numbers of press continued to build, until the entire camp was ringed with a thick wall of bodies and cameras. Hardly a blade of grass in their camp had not been illuminated a thousand times by flash cameras. Under the cloud bank that had risen slowly out of the late afternoon they lifted *Leningrad* from the water and drew her inside a walled enclosure that would shield them from the eyes of the journalists. The extra militiamen were needed to prevent more determined elements from using wire-cutters or ladders to gain access. *Leningrad* underwent last preparations in the screened area of the forecourt. Vagir and his men were working on the fairing of the underwater sections, striving to produce a perfect finish. In the sail-loft, the final changes to their sails were being made. Shaw held a conference with Brod and Arlof about the weather conditions the following day. Moderate winds were predicted. They would have preferred heavier weather, but at least the conditions would not be light, allowing the Americans to use their superior computational facilities to predict and exploit fickle breezes.

Shortly after eight in the evening, when they had returned to camp, their patron Aegu phoned Shaw again.

'We have been obliged to issue a statement confirming that Illich was murdered,' Aegu told Shaw. 'The press will become even worse.'

'They're out there in force now.'

'Would you like to give a press conference?'

'Frankly, no. It would interrupt our preparations for tomorrow.'

'You have no deep loyalty, I notice, to the capitalist media,' Aegu commented drily.

'No,' Shaw replied by way of confirmation.

This was definitive at least. Changing the subject slightly, Aegu said: 'How are the crew?'

'We did a trial sail this morning. They're bearing up. As you might expect.'

'And you, *tovarich*?'

'I have enough to chew on.'

'Good. You have my telephone number. Phone me if you require any help or assistance.'

'Thanks,' Shaw replied.

The line went dead.

He returned to his conference with Arlof and Brod. Outside the sky was looking grey. The slow clouds were heavy, and the light outside the window had a strange quality of whiteness. Only after several seconds did he realize that the light was caused by the almost continuous flicker of flash bulbs at the camp perimeter.

Seven

That night, Shaw lay staring at the ceiling. He was aware that Maria, beside him, was also awake. He could hear the spare generator working while the sailcutters made their final adjustments to the light weather wardrobe in preparation for the following day. Occasionally the inside of the curtain would glow from the flashbulb of one of the photographers who kept a vigil outside the camp.

'You OK?' Maria asked.

'So-so.'

'Thinking about Illich?' She turned to face him.

'About the person who killed him, as a matter of fact. About his nationality, to be precise.'

Her hand came out of the dark and covered his mouth. She said, 'Don't say it.'

A few seconds later her hand withdrew. Shaw said, 'I'm not saying anything.'

'Then don't think about it.'

She had turned to face him fully, and her voice sounded in his ear. He always liked the pitch of it.

Somewhere in the night outside, Shaw could hear the hum of the sailcutting machine, the faint shout of a sailcutter as they moved a big sail around the floor for a final examination of stress points and seams, the flash and stutter of a press camera.

He turned to face her. They lay without touching for several seconds. He could have kissed her. He would have liked to. But she eased herself lower in the bed and put her forehead against his lips. She stayed like that for a while. He could sense that she was staring open-eyed through him, and he guessed that she too was thinking about Illich.

The following day there was a light sky, fleecy clouds moving north to south.

Prem, taking the exercises, shouted like a major-domo. Followed by showers, changing, breakfast at eight.

At the end of the meal, Shaw stood up. He hated speeches, talking into the empty air in front of him, and he knew he could not fool them. He waited until the room was silent. For a moment no one shuffled or coughed. Shaw said:

'Yesterday, President Aegu telephoned to say that every available resource is being brought in to find the murderer of Ivan Illich.'

He paused, glanced around him. They watched him without expression.

'You kindly asked me to take over as helmsman from Illich. Thank you. I am honoured. Sometimes a pygmy steps into the shoes of a giant.

'You know that in boats we are completely outclassed. We've got a new helmsman who isn't as good as the old. We've been given no time to practise or tune with our second boat. The fact is, the odds are heavily against us.'

They were silent. He could never tell with the Estonians. Individually, yes. Collectively, however, they seemed to operate like a hive of bees, using signals he could not understand.

'Because of Illich, we're two races ahead. We've got at most two races to learn, to roll with the punches. The key day will be the third from now, the fifth race of the series. The likelihood is that the score will be even. We'll move into it utterly demoralized, or with a certain amount of confidence. We have to build up towards the fifth race. Two races is all we've got to learn.'

Brod was the crew boss, the head of the Estonian crew, but Prem was its heart. He noticed that Prem nodded silently.

'That's all I have to say about racing.' Shaw looked round at the room. 'There's just one final thing, about Illich. I'm the last person who should write his epitaph, or even pass comment on his death. You all knew him better and for longer than I did. What I have to say is the opinion of an outsider. We all used to like to tease him. One day I caught him reading a newspaper. The article was about the fact that against the Russians and Americans, he hadn't lost a single race. The article ended that the man must be a demon or angel. I remember his embarrassment when I caught him reading it. He was laughing at the article. We all knew he was the least vain of men. The idea that he was anything other than an ordinary, vulnerable man was absurd to him.'

Shaw paused. Good orators hold audiences with their silences. Their silences are more heavily invested with their presence than their words. He was no orator, and his pauses were caused by the slow movement of his mind around unfamiliar words. He moved ahead as best he could.

'What they wrote about him wasn't all untrue. In hindsight, I realize there was something in what they said. If you think of what he did, of how he uplifted us, that there was no side to him, no greed, it seems truer of him than anyone else. He had many little failings, like all of us. But in the important things he moved through life in a way that was not quite human. We have an opportunity, a very slender opportunity, I admit, to do something for his memory.'

He'd come to the end, and was about to sit down. But

there was a shuffle of chairs, and led by Prem, the others rose to their feet. They stood for a silent minute in memory of Ivan Illich.

The wind was fourteen knots, several knots above that predicted, when the launch towed *Leningrad* out through the small harbour entrance into a chop. The course patrol vessels started to push back the press and spectator fleets with small rushes like sheep-dogs, clearing a path for their little convoy. Above the Russian flag at the stern, the huge blue, black and white Estonian tricolour flapped and thundered. Shaw and the others knew that the presence of the Estonian flag annoyed the Russian authorities whom they officially represented, but they flew it now in memory of Illich.

Shaw tried to gauge the number of boats out on the water. There had been a three-day lay-off since the collision of *Novy Mir* and *Eagle*. He expected that the majority of the fleet would have departed. But nearly all had been accommodated in one of the three great St Petersburg marinas, or in a naval area specially set aside. Beyond the line of the spectator boats were larger yachts and liners. Behind these were the grey of the warships. Helicopters moved like attendant bees between the naval vessels as diplomatic activity continued.

Towed at eight knots into the swell, Shaw and his crew were occasionally doused with spray. Below decks Herman Maask was making final preparations on the sails. Gundar Arlof was crouched on the cockpit floor, feeding final figures into the tactical computer. Brod had moved forward to discuss a tacking procedure with Prem.

Shaw looked out to starboard. Through the spectator fleet and the windblown diesel fumes he could see the American convoy that surrounded *Eagle* – a raft of huge motoryachts with, at its centre, a single tall mast. They had left their own vast shore complex and were heading out to sea on a parallel course.

The sky above was filled with aircraft, helicopters dipping like dragonflies, fixed wing aircraft wheeling slowly above them. Still higher above were the airships, helium-filled representatives of a great revival. Largest of them all, floating like a pike amongst minnows, was the Russian airship *Rodina*, sister-ship of *St Petersburg*, whose giant gondolas could hold a reputed 1,800 people. Shaw looked out to port. Behind the wall of spectator craft, a grey line of warships was anchored, between which launches shuttled carrying diplomats and politicians.

The crew started to run through its second check of the day, working through all the mechanisms, from winches to sheet leads. It was one of the primary rules of the America's Cup that, apart from the batteries required for the instrumentation, all the physical force required in sailing the yacht must come from human sources. Winches, blocks and tackles merely supplied different rates of gearing with which to harness and govern the huge loads.

The towing boat drew them forward towards the starting line. Heading directly into wind they were subject to less spray. The bows parted the waves neatly, and the bulk of the blown spume passed harmlessly on either side.

Patrol vessels continued to push back the spectator fleets. Russian course-patrol vessels, with machine-guns mounted in the bows, had a sinister quality which facilitated their clearing of the course of spectator craft. At last *Leningrad*'s towboat came to rest, using only enough power to keep her bows facing into wind. Occasionally its stern lifted clean out of the water, and they could hear the sudden growl of the propellers as they thrashed the surface.

In order to warm themselves the two main winchmen,

Berol Baltir and Graf Ulder, had turned up the friction lever on the coffee grinders and were putting in short bursts of grinding, standing back to flex their shoulders and breathe deeply in between. Gustav Prem was re-winding the mainsheet to take out a coil. Stephan Migdal and Viktor Kingissep, the forecrew, were at the mast, discussing with movements of the hand and occasional nods and shakes of the head a particular means of co-ordinating the hauling of a sail. It was a crucial skill. In virtually every leg of every race, it was normal to change the sails several times. Each sail change could count for precious seconds in the fight against the opponent.

This was the worst time, waiting. It was the classic time of nerves. No helmsman is immune. Coach Johnson, many years before, had told Shaw that pre-race nerves were simply the body chemistry readjusting. Sometimes a nervous storm hit him so strongly that he could look down and see himself shaking with fear. He was grateful that each of the crew had his own well-defined area of operation, his own problems to consider, and could leave him for the few minutes necessary to overcome his own internal terror.

The terror which affected him now didn't change so much as transmute itself into an emotion like anger. But it was not a hot-blooded anger, more a cold rage. His mind seemed to become clearer. After a while he stopped quaking and could begin to look around him.

Much of the course had been cleared. Shaw could see the *Eagle* convoy more closely now. The other great motor yachts which formed the convoy were in the process of departing, leaving *Eagle* with the single white palace of the Ericson launch.

'Wind steady,' Arlof called from the navigation console. 'Course laid. Twenty minutes to ten-minute gun.'

'Mainsail up,' Shaw ordered.

Migdal and Maask began to haul, pulling in alternate

39

loops. Once up, they tightened carefully. Halyard tension was critical to the efficiency of the sail. Prem, the mainsheet trimmer, was in charge of the great sail. Now he stood back to examine its shape, raising his hand, palm upwards for more tension.

'Cast off,' Shaw shouted. Kingissep broke the back of the bowline and the tow-rope snaked away.

'Genoa up,' Shaw called. 'Bearing away.'

Leningrad heeled to her mainsail. Migdal and Maask were hauling up the genoa which thundered slowly while the trimmers, Soren Gir and Edvigs Tarku, adjusted halyard tension. With a burst of power from Baltir and Ulder, the sail hardened in and the speed came on.

'Six six,' Brod said. 'Six eight, seven zero, seven one.'

With way on, Shaw could feather up slightly. Prem was easing the mainsail into shape. On port tack, Soren Gir trimmed the genoa.

'Seven six, seven eight . . .' Brod intoned.

'Gundar,' Shaw said. 'What's the wind prediction?'

'Steady. Increasing by two knots slowly in the next hour. Wind direction constant. Slight bias to port on the line, not significant.'

Shaw could see that *Eagle* also was under sail. One glance was enough to confirm that in every way she was like the early *Eagle*, from the shining gunsmoke-blue topsides to the perfectly setting sails. She might have been *Eagle* resurrected. It would take him a little while to get over it. Even her name had been changed to that of her predecessor – no '*Eagle 2*', merely *Eagle*.

A brief look at his crew indicated that they too had registered these facts. It was important to break out of the trance.

'Practice tacks,' Shaw shouted.

He put *Leningrad* through the wind a little faster than usual. The genoa thundered across, Ulder and Baltir pounding hard on the winches.

He waited twenty seconds while the boat settled and

picked up way, then pushed through another tack. And after that, another.

'Let's set her up on starboard,' shouted Shaw. On this tack it was Edvigs Tarku who was genoa trimmer. He wanted to give Tarku at least two minutes to tune.

'Twelve minutes to the ten-minute gun,' Brod said. The men had settled down better now. There were fewer glances in the direction of *Eagle*.

After two minutes they tacked on to port. Soren Gir worked with Prem to set up the mainsail and genoa. Prem, Gir and Tarku had their own boatspeed indicator on the mast; this was one of the reference points as the three combined to tune the powerful rig.

'Eight one, eight one, eight one, steady,' Brod said.

'Time to turn for the starting box,' Gundar Arlof suggested behind Shaw.

'Bearing away,' Shaw shouted.

As they reached, the speed rose to ten knots.

'Two minutes to ten-minute gun,' Arlof said.

On the other side, *Eagle* was moving fast towards the starting line, kicking up a line of white wake as she bore off and picked up speed.

In all his preparations, Shaw had forced himself not to think of *Eagle*'s helmsman. The mere thought of Ericson brought Shaw out in a cold sweat of anger. He remembered his face in the investigation of the ramming incident several days before, a face as cold and confident as any boardroom lawyer. He forced himself to think of the other boat as a single opponent, a combined unit, an enemy without a human personality.

'Closing with the line,' Shaw said to Brod.

Eight

'Nine, eight, seven, six,' Brod called out, 'five, four, three, two . . .'

They entered the starting box fast. It was now, when the two yachts were closing with each other, that Shaw experienced an unpleasant sensation of *déjà vu*. The last time they had rushed towards each other it had resulted in a collision. And here, like a risen ghost, was the same *Eagle* on a converging course.

'Ten five,' Brod said, 'ten six, ten six steady.'

He had an intuition that Ericson, not content with ramming *Novy Mir*, would make this one close, too. There was something about the fixity of *Eagle*'s course towards them that was unnerving.

Leningrad was on starboard, with right of way.

One hundred and fifty yards, closing speed more than twenty knots.

Behind him Brod was quiet.

One hundred yards. Under normal circumstances the yacht on port tack, *Eagle*, would have made a clear avoidance manoeuvre now, indicating whether it would pass high or low.

Seventy yards. Only seconds now separated them from a head-on collision.

Fifty yards.

Brod exhaled audibly. Then *Eagle* swung low, hard, picking up speed and swooping up towards them. Shaw flung himself into the wheel and *Leningrad* turned downwind.

Pandemonium struck as the two boats wheeled. The sails thundered as they crossed the decks, the trimmers screamed for power, the winchmen blasted into the coffee-grinders like madmen. A foot above Shaw the boom exploded across in the gybe with a squeal and clash of blocks. After three turns they were still even, their speeds down to only a few knots.

By means of mutual exhaustion, rather than consent, they broke away. Both teams of winchgrinders were struggling for breath. But Shaw was not displeased. At a first indication, though *Leningrad* was an older boat, she was not vulnerable in close-quarter duelling.

They were heading towards the port end of the line, picking up speed.

'Slight port bias maintained,' Arlof reported.

'We'll keep on this side. If they want to challenge for it, let them come.'

'I agree,' Brod said.

'Six minutes to starting gun,' Arlof called.

On the starboard side *Eagle* wheeled.

'What are their tactics, Brod?'

'They are convinced they have superior speed. They just found out they don't have easy manoeuvre superiority. So they'll stand off and try to blast us with their speed.'

Shaw had to agree. These had been *Eagle*'s preferred tactics throughout the series against other yachts. Lacking immediate contact with the other boat, they continued to tack back and forth as the minutes and then seconds moved towards the gun.

'Thirty seconds,' Brod said.

'Harden up,' shouted Shaw,

He swung the wheel slowly, keeping power on, so they would hit the line at a good speed.

'Ten, nine, eight . . .'

The genoa came in fast.

'Six, five, four, three . . . '

They tightened in sheets the few final inches. The start gun exploded and they crossed the line two seconds later.

'Eight three knots, eight three, eight four,' Brod sang out.

Eagle, on the starboard side of the line, was marching on a parallel tack, slicing the swells, her sails setting close to perfection.

Shaw turned away and concentrated on *Leningrad*. It was Brod's function as tactician to keep an eye on *Eagle*.

'Eight two,' Arlof called. 'Eight three. True windspeed steady twelve knots.'

On port tack it was Soren Gir who trimmed the genoa. His sail shaping was subtly different from that of Tarku, the port trimmer. Gir preferred a fuller, more powerful sail shape in comparison to Tarku's flatter, higher point- ing configuration. Prem, the mainsheet trimmer, adjus- ted his mainsail on each tack to suit these two different sail shapes. With Gir's full sail shape, he moved the boom a couple of inches down the track. With Tarku's tighter, flatter genoa, he moved the boom up the track and tightened the leech. The curious aspect was that the velocity made good to windward was almost exactly similar.

'Eight four,' Arlof said. 'Eight four steady.'

The waves were regular, and he began to pick up their rhythm as he tried to squeeze the extra twentieth of a knot from *Leningrad*. She was going as fast as ever she did. It was not only a matter of the numbers on the dials that gave encouragement, but the feel of the yacht, the subtle intuition that the hull was controlling its own motion through the seas, sliding fast, covering ground.

The crew were zombies in concentration, creatures in a trance. Only one thing worried Shaw, and that was Brod's silence. It almost certainly meant that *Eagle* was easing ahead. He disciplined himself not to look, con- centrating on the tune of the yacht.

After four minutes Shaw shouted: 'Tack!'

On the other side of the tack, Brod said: 'It's close. *Eagle* maybe a length up.'

Shaw expressed a touch of testiness:

'Goddamn, Brod, what's wrong with that?'

44

'Nothing, Excellency.'

'The old lady's moving well.'

They settled down again. Now *Eagle* and *Leningrad* were converging on the top mark.

Eagle was two lengths up as she slid around the mark, set a perfect spinnaker, and moved off down the run.

'Let's harass the bastards,' Shaw said. 'Port tack.'

If the yachts are within a few lengths, the trailing yacht can place itself between the wind and the forward yacht, obstructing the latter's wind. Above them the spinnaker set like a crack of thunder, and *Leningrad* accelerated after *Eagle*.

They began to hunt *Eagle*, searching for her wind, trying to sniff out vulnerability. Ericson manoeuvred to avoid them. They gybed and counter-gybed down the leg. But the contest was inconclusive. *Eagle* was still two lengths apart as the two boats rounded the downwind mark.

Shaw tended to be cautious in sail-changes. They dropped spinnaker several seconds before they rounded.

'Will they cover us?' he asked Brod.

'I think not,' Brod replied. Shaw agreed. For psychological reasons Ericson would try to demonstrate *Eagle*'s superiority by another show of speed.

Eagle continued on port tack.

Shaw desired clear air like a man beneath water.

'Tack!' he shouted. He swung the wheel and moved up to the windward side for better visibility. It was a good tack, *Leningrad* accelerating fast out the other side.

'Seven six, seven eight, eight zero, eight one,' sang Arlof.

Eagle continued effortlessly on her present tack, slicing away towards the starboard side of the course.

Sometimes a helmsman, announcing his intention to keep on a specific course, calls out 'Settle!' But glancing about him, Shaw could see that *Leningrad*'s crew were already in that silence when all that matters is the final fraction of a knot of speed. They were listening to the boat with all the concentration of tribesmen to the faraway beat of drums. The two boats moved apart as silently as spirits, leaving only their attenuated blips on the sensor screens.

Nine

Approaching the finish line, *Eagle* was four lengths ahead.

The gun exploded as her bow crossed. A phalanx of motor yachts poured towards her. The sirens of the American warships, anchored like a grey wall to the north, produced a blast of victory. The great nuclear aircraft carrier *Nemesis* made a sound like a bull roaring.

Shaw saw Ericson's arm held high in acknowledgement of his ovation. *Leningrad* sliced across the finish line behind *Eagle*.

A defeated crew usually collapse with exhaustion, but Prem, Tarku, Gir, turned round towards him. Prem, speaking for all of them, said: 'Congratulations, Captain. We're still in the game.'

The winchgrinders, Berol Baltir and Graf Ulder, who had taken the brunt of the punishment, would take longer to shrug off their tiredness as they waited for the towing launch to reach them. Around them the course patrol vessels began to beat back a path through the television and spectator craft. Shaw breathed silent thanks to these great sailors, magnanimous in victory, calm in defeat. And their defeat, he knew, must be taken in context. Entering the race, their fear had been that the elderly *Leningrad* would be so outclassed by *Eagle* that the race would be a humiliating procession. In fact, they had held on. There had been enough encouragement to keep their hopes alive.

The crew, defiant, ran up the Estonian tricolour, and were hauled back through the lumpy wash towards the shore. If they were taciturn and silent, it was because Illich's death hung over them. The day had turned overcast, though with that odd mixture of sun and cloud which sometimes produces rainbows. The mist and spray thrown up by the bow waves of more than a thousand craft seemed to produce the favoured conditions. On the way back to their base, they watched that conflagration of colours which emerges from refracted light but which rarely fails to strike its witnesses as magical.

At the base camp, Ilena was waiting on the harbour-side to tell Shaw that Aegu was on the phone. He walked up with her past the outlying buildings to the small office.

He picked up the telephone.

'Shaw here.'

Aegu was cheerful.

'A better result than you expected.'

'Yes.'

'You are pleased?'

'Pleased with the crew. Our boat is slower than theirs, but not as slow as I feared.'

'Do you hold out hopes of winning?'

'I always hold out hopes, but the chances are against us.'

'We have done well enough already. My congratulations for the crew's rapid recovery.'

Shaw said, 'Any progress with the investigation?'

'We are not making much progress. The evidence appears to be that the assailant was waiting in the flat when Illich arrived. Therefore it is likely that he arranged for the telegram to be sent. We have traced the source of the telegram. It is from an industrial agency in Kharkov, which is where Illich's ex-wife Anna lives, but the secretary who sent it does not have a clear picture of the person who gave it to her. Our investigations have run cold.

'The samples of blood are being analysed and checked against that of known criminals, so far without success. There is no sign of the murder weapon. Ballistic experts have identified from the bullets that the gun is a Makarov, an older version which is no longer produced. This is a controversial piece of evidence, and I ask you to keep this information highly confidential. It was a make of handgun widely used in the old Soviet Union and the former Eastern bloc states. Its origin may be entirely incidental, even an attempt by the assailant to mislead. For the time being, it may be that the murderer has no previous criminal record, in which case we are searching for a ghost. We have another strange piece of evidence, traces of vitreous humour – the fluid of the eyeball – on Illich's thumbs. It now looks as though the assailant may have been damaged or blinded in one or both eyes during the struggle. That is all we have to go on.'

'Thank you,' Shaw said.

'I hope these details do not disturb you too much.'

'I wanted to know,' Shaw replied.

There was a change in tone on the telephone, as though Aegu had put his hand over the mouthpiece and was speaking to someone in the room. His voice returned.

'I am sorry, I have a meeting shortly. I wish you luck with your further races.'

Shaw left for the quay to help move the sails onshore. He, Prem and Brod would hold a meeting with Anton Shuch, their sailmaker, to decide on adjustments to their sails in the light of the day's race. While the crew moved sails onshore, Vagir and his men hovered, ready to lift *Leningrad* from the water so they could prepare her for the race the following day.

In Vagir's hierarchy sailors occupied a particularly low level. He built beautiful yachts for them, maintained them to perfection, and every day they came back marked with the delinquency of the irresponsible children who raced them. Helmsmen were no better, perhaps worse.

Vagir moved aside aluminium parings, screws, pieces of old winches, and sat down on the bench. As a generous concession to his guest, he allowed Shaw the only chair in the room, a beaten plastic one. He made no attempt to shift the wood shavings that littered its seat like so many fallen leaves.

Vagir sat back on the cleared work-table and lit an Astra. You lit an Astra in hope and cynicism. The hope was that it would be no worse than before. The cynicism arose from the fact that it always was. There were two certain things in Russian life. The economy would never get better. And the next Astra would be even worse than the last.

As a consequence, Astra smokers tended to be optimists. They would inhale, and then you could see, from the initial look of astonished admiration, that their expectations had been confirmed.

Vagir settled back in his chair. 'What can we do for you?'

'Some advice,' Shaw asked.

Vagir nodded. His eyes had a slightly reptilian look which suggested an under-surface of thought.

'In the event of heavy fog, what could we do about radar?'

'We have a standard installation.'

'What does that mean, exactly?'

'Good at distances. At close quarters...' Vagir

49

shrugged. 'The standard installation is not designed for tacking duels.'

'At close quarters what can we do?'

Vagir put two fingers at his head like a pistol. He smirked.

'The Americans can duel in dense fog.'

Vagir nodded. 'I heard a rumour. Even in the dark, *Eagle* and her little friend can dance around each other like ballerinas.'

Vagir had gathered enough strength and resolution to draw again on his Astra. His eyes showed once again the reassurance of catastrophe.

Shaw was convinced that smoking for Vagir also had a social function. He used it to emphasize his special status as someone who did not have to obey the strict rules of fitness.

'You want a radar like the Americans. Yesterday if possible.'

'Tomorrow, perhaps.'

Vagir raised his eyebrows, as if he had just heard something incredible.

There was no point in talking further to Vagir. Shaw knew well enough that Vagir had received the information. To prolong his visit would be merely to subject himself to further caustic remarks, and the ordeal of the Astra smoke, which was already thickening the atmosphere around him. He was forced to beat an ignominious retreat. Vagir acknowledged his departure with a slight raising of his eyebrows.

Shaw slept reasonably well that night. He woke shortly before five. Restless, he climbed out of bed carefully, and moved quietly outside to examine the weather. The sparse grass was damp under his feet. He detected the smell of drying epoxy from the nearby building sheds. On these northern summer nights, there was enough light to see well, and he looked northwards out to sea.

The bay seemed calm, but a small, uncertain breeze was creeping in from the north. It would be sunny, and the heated landmass to the east tended to induce an onshore westerly breeze from eleven onwards, growing gradually into the afternoon. It was the pattern forecast for the day.

When he returned Maria was still sleeping quietly. He went into the small room. Jack had thrown off his outer blanket and lay curled in his cot, his knees drawn up, sleeping quietly. It was curious that Jack always moved upwards until his head gently touched the outside of the cot, as if this gave him reassurance. Shaw paused above his light, steady breathing.

Moving to the living-room, Shaw started to dress slowly and quietly. He wanted a final meeting with the sailcutters, nocturnal creatures that they were, before they retired to sleep. Then he would join the crew for physical exercise at seven, under Prem's unlovely tutelage. In the subdued light even the shadows seemed grey, insubstantial. It was a time of day he enjoyed, a time of almost perfect silence. Out of the opaque glass of their little house, no more than a converted shed, he could see the dawn glowing whiter.

Ten

'Fog,' Brod said. He pointed out beyond the line of the harbour wall.

Shaw looked out over the water. He could see traces of blue sky. But over the surface of the sea a grey mass extended like a glare. Inland too, the fog reached out, obliterating the pine forests to the south of them. It was thicker close to the water. Buildings on the coastline became ghostly excrescences, pitched roofs floating in air.

'How long do you think it will last?'

'If we're lucky, only the morning,' Brod said. 'But these Baltic fogs can be persistent. Perhaps longer.'

Shaw said, 'I think we'd better fit the radar.'

Brod nodded and walked away. Shaw could see by a curious precision in his stride that Brod was angry. He didn't like nature in support of Ericson.

Vagir was already on the mast in a bosun's chair fitting the forward-looking scanner at the first spreader. One needed a certain amount of height above the deck for the scanner, but not so much that the weight aloft became a problem. The increasing compactness of radar equipment made the weight of the scanner less onerous.

After exercising, Shaw walked down to *Leningrad*. Vagir was working with two assistants to fit the radar readout on the cockpit instruments. He had placed it so the helmsman had direct access. Now the scanner was operating, Vagir played with dials, invoking the local coastline.

The image was accurate and clear, and if studying the locality had been their intention, it would be adequate. But for purposes of close-quarter manoeuvre, one needed to know whether the other yacht was forty feet or sixty feet away. Twenty feet could make all the difference between safety and collision.

Vagir said, 'You turn this dial for contrast. Can you see the readout from the helming position?'

'Yes.'

Vagir looked out towards the sea and grimaced. 'It's thick out there.' He nodded with his head. Shaw saw that the two arms of the little harbour, less than a hundred feet away, had disappeared completely from sight. He felt dizzy looking at the white void.

52

'No lay days,' Brod said behind him. He had moved up silently behind Shaw. 'We have to race every day, whatever the weather.'

'What about the spectators?' Shaw asked. Brod shrugged in a typically Estonian gesture, hardly moving his shoulders, the expression of feeling by means of restraint.

The tow boat was manoeuvring forty feet away in the harbour, easing ahead of the yacht to tie up. Then it disappeared as if by magic into a white wall.

Brod adjusted dials, whistling tunelessly. Shaw wondered whether Parvu and Vilde, the two fishermen, were out there now.

'A political mist,' Brod said. Shaw almost smiled. You would have thought from Brod's expression that it had been produced expressly by the authorities, or perhaps that it stood for those huge white voids between what politicians said and what they did.

'An interesting article,' Irena commented when Shaw entered the little office.

He glanced down at the paper spread out on the desk. Shaw had taken to reading the British *Independent*. It was in English at least, and less likely than American papers to favour the American team. The article was headed 'Estonians show surprising form'.

In the resumed third race of the America's Cup (the previous third race having been abandoned because of a collision) we were witness to an interesting transformation. What was predicted has happened – the American syndicate has placed on the water a virtual replica of their previous yacht Eagle, *a replica in almost every detail, including the name. The yacht performed flawlessly, giving the Americans a well-deserved victory over the Estonian second boat, the veteran* Leningrad.

What could not be predicted was the performance of Leningrad *with her new helmsman Jim Shaw. The Estonian first boat,* Novy Mir, *and* Eagle *represent new generation yachts. It is widely accepted that there is a substantial performance improvement with these yachts over older generation yachts like* Leningrad. *Despite the Estonians' careful attempt to portray the new* Novy Mir *as slow, it is now known that in the later part of its tuning against* Leningrad, *its speed superiority was close to devastating. With Shaw now back in the old, familiar* Leningrad, *the remarkable thing is that she was in the race the whole way. Perhaps the difference between the performance of the new and older boats is still too much to bridge. But it must have been uplifting for the Estonians, and for Shaw, to see that after their double tragedy, the loss of* Novy Mir *and then, within a few days, the death of Ivan Illich, they have recovered to the point where they are still participants.*

'We'd better start,' Shaw said.

Amidships, the others were lifting the sails on board, storing them down below. Migdal and Maask were shouldering the heavy bales of cloth through the hatchway. Against the wall of white the crew took on a monumental quality, like Rembrandt's paintings of peasants.

They cast off. The towboat would rely on its radar to guide them to the start line. It was disconcerting to see the rope disappear into mist.

Half an hour of deadened sound, eruption of foghorns, the sudden emergence of vague shapes, occasional aoutbreaks of sunlight lasting only a few seconds. They watched their screens as the spectator boats moved past. Once the towboat was forced to halt by a passing launch, and they saw its halted stern rear out of the mist as their own momentum carried *Leningrad* forward. A few feet from contact the towboat kicked into forward and avoided a slow but potentially damaging collision.

The breeze was constant and about eight knots, moving the fog like fur against the skin. At last the towboat reduced speed to zero. They lay head to wind while they waited for the committee boat.

'Here they come.' Brod pointed to the radar screen. A group of boats was moving towards them with, at its centre, a single translucent blip that denoted *Eagle*. They were close, within a few hundred yards. But, except for the radar screen, *Eagle* and her entourage could not be seen or heard or sensed.

'Committee boat sets course 350 degrees,' Brod called. 'Twenty minutes to starting gun.'

The course-protection vessels were moving stray spectators off the course. Large open spaces were being created.

Shaw said, 'Hoist sail.'

Migdal started to haul on the halyard. The mainsail looped upwards into the white, then the top section disappeared.

'I don't believe this,' Shaw said to no one in particular.

'Genoa!' Brod called.

When the sails were up Shaw bore away to pick up speed. He could hear the hiss of the bow wave faintly deadened by mist. Looking up, the trimmers could only see clearly the bottom half of the sails. It was like staring into deep water. The upper tell-tales were mostly invisible. When they appeared their tails fluttered in the sky like small elusive fishes.

'Viktor,' Shaw called to Kingissep. 'Keep a lookout on the bow.' There was a problem of communication. Sometimes, as the waves of fog came over the bow, Kingissep would disappear into the white wall. 'Stephan,' Shaw called to Migdal, 'I need you as relay.'

One advantage was that the heavy air, freighted with moisture, seemed to give added power to the sails. On starboard tack they were settling down.

'Seven two,' Brod said. 'Seven three.'

On the radar screen they left the committee boat about sixty yards to port, gliding past it without even sensing its presence.

'*Eagle* begins to sail,' Brod said.

On the screen, *Eagle*'s support boats had eased back. The white blip at the centre began to grow brighter and to move. The additional brightness was due, Shaw suspected, to some reflective property in *Eagle*'s newly setting sails.

'Tack!' shouted Shaw. As they came through the wind the boom shook a cloud of water droplets on to his face. He bore a way a little to pick up speed, then feathered the yacht into wind.

'Six four,' Brod said. 'Six five, six six.'

The illuminated blip that was *Eagle* was moving on a collision course with the starting vessel. Shaw and Brod watched entranced as the two blips closed, then merged in a luminous detonation.

'Christ,' Brod breathed. Their own crude radar had registered a collision. But a few seconds later the two blips subdivided like an amoeba. *Eagle* moved off calmly, having deliberately shaved the starting boat by a few feet. It was, Shaw suspected, a gesture of intimidation towards *Leningrad*. It said, our instrument is better than yours.

'Two minutes to ten-minute gun,' Brod confirmed.

'Ease sheets,' Shaw shouted. Around them, he could see on the radar that the course was empty, except where the spectator fleets, shepherded by the course patrol boats, floated in massed ranks, often so closely packed together that they seemed a single luminous raft. A commentary was being broadcast to them over their radios. Somewhere the loudspeaker of a course patrol vessel sounded. The lowing of foghorns continued in the distance.

Mist pressed on his skin. The back of his hands on the wheel shone with moisture. His breath billowed thickly. It seemed they were in some strange medium between water and air.

On the screen he saw the blip that was *Eagle* move to the other side of the starting box. A rumour had come to him that *Eagle*'s radar could not only pick out *Leningrad* in some detail, but also the disposition of individual Estonian crewmen on *Leningrad*'s deck.

'Ten, nine, eight, seven, six,' Brod was calling out. The other blip was moving towards the starting box. 'Three, two, one. . .' The sound of the ten-minute cannon, so close, was startling.

'Port side slightly favoured,' Arlof called.

'We'll stay here a while,' Shaw replied.

He swung downwind, then gybed. Shaw looked at the screen, entranced. The blip that denoted *Eagle* was engaged in a curious manoeuvre, not loitering, but not heading directly towards *Leningrad* either.

Shaw watched the movement develop. Now *Eagle* was moving in a slow half-circle, taking up a position a few hundred yards away.

'Four minutes to starting gun,' Arlof called.

'What's he up to?' Shaw asked his tactician.

'Perhaps you know?' Brod replied.

'Do I?' Shaw asked in return. 'Ease sheets, we'll gybe again.'

After the gybe he swung his attention back to the luminous blip in the screen.

'Two minutes fifty seconds,' Arlof called.

'Is he risking a timed run?' Brod asked.

'No, I don't think so.'

'What, then?'

'My guess is he's going to come in close to us just before the start gun, and try to rough us up.'

'How will you respond?'

'Migrate,' Shaw suggested. 'Bias?' he asked Arlof.

'Unbiased line,' Arlof called.

'Here he comes,' Brod informed him.

The blip was moving directly towards him. Shaw said, 'We'll wait for him to close.'

'One minute forty.'

The distance between them had halved.

'One minute twenty.'

In the fog, the crew moved around like ice men. Swimming in the liquid air, Shaw felt time shedding seconds like dew.

'Sixty seconds.'

The distance between them had halved again.

Shaw said sharply, 'Tack.'

They slid through the wind. Moisture shaken off the boom and mainsail doused Shaw's face. Water streamed off the trimmers' gloves.

'Ease sails,' Shaw said, 'we're reaching off down the line.'

'Forty seconds.'

Shaw looked behind him. *Eagle*'s bow and most of her ninety-foot mast loomed out of the fog. *Eagle* was in dominant or 'pole' position. She could prevent any turn by *Leningrad*. But for the time being at least Shaw's manoeuvre of running down the line had neutralized Ericson's strategy of control.

'Thirty seconds.'

Eagle's presence both alarmed and reassured him. There was a visceral thrill in seeing the huge yacht emerge from the fog, transformed from a blip to an angry, pursuing presence.

'Twenty.'

It was going to be close. They were bearing down on the starting launch fast. There was a point at which *Eagle* would appear to merge with the starting launch. Shaw knew he would have to stretch his nerves.

Brod was glued to the screen. According to the radar they were about to collide with the starting launch. No one moved.

'Ten seconds.'

'Trust me, Brod.'

'Eight, seven, six . . .' The screen said they had already

58

collided with the starting launch. Shaw's nerves tightened up to screaming point.

'Harden up,' Shaw shouted. He swung the wheel. The winchmen hit the central grinder in a powerful, driving roll. Sheets screamed. Moisture burst from the tautened sails. The starting launch came out of the mist. They must have missed its topsides by two feet. For a few seconds it seemed they occupied the same space, that they were in a tunnel between the start launch and the other yacht as the cannon exploded a few feet away, dousing them in cordite smoke.

In the silence after the gun Brod said equably, 'A perfect start.' Maybe a little too perfect for Arlof, though, whose white face stared at Shaw in momentary disbelief at his callous treatment of time.

Eleven

Eagle was parallel, her initial advantage neutralized.

There was a brief howl of eased sheets, a thunder of sails from the other boat.

'*Eagle* tacks away,' Brod reported.

'We'll stay on this tack,' Shaw called. He wanted to give the crew time to calm down. You have to make amends, he thought, for hanging them over the abyss.

'Seven three,' Arlof said. 'Seven three, seven four.'

Far away they heard a sudden babble of shouting voices, and the unmistakable grinding of hulls as two spectator boats clashed in the mist far away.

On their own again, the men wiped the moisture from their faces and settled down. A brief burst of sunlight put lines of gold into the sails and mast. For perhaps seven seconds, they could see clearly the upper telltales on the sails, then the mist closed in again. On the screen, Shaw watched the blip that was *Eagle* move away. He enjoyed a brief retrospective moment of horror at the risk he had taken on the start line, then settled to watch the instruments.

Curiously, the fog allowed the crew to concentrate. The other boat had become a mere abstraction. They moved through the slow intensity of white.

'Tack,' Shaw called. *Leningrad* came about smoothly, with hardly an appreciable loss of speed. The sails thundered and quietened. Shaw blinked the moisture out of his eyes.

'Six nine,' Arlof said. 'Seven zero.'

'They're keeping to the other side of the course,' Brod informed him.

The mist curved past the sails, showing the transparency of speed at mid-section and vortices at the trailing edges – a beautiful, profound sight. The complex interaction between the sails in the area called the 'slot' had always been a source of speculation and debate. Now the behaviour of the transparent air was illumined by wisps of mist, like smoke in a wind tunnel.

'We're approaching the lay-line,' Arlof said. Beyond this point the boat would lose time if it did not tack for the mark.

'Tack,' Shaw called.

Eagle was approaching on the opposite tack, on starboard. The two boats seemed even. It was invigorating, but at the same time, it was precisely what Shaw had dreaded. They would have to give way to their rival and rely on the crude instrument of their radar. The important point was that it must be timed to perfection.

Brod's eyes were glued on the approaching blip. Water shone on his white cheeks and gathered on his heavy eyebrows.

The blip drew closer. Twenty tons of sharp-prowed

yacht approached them on a collision course in the mist.

The radar said collision was imminent. Gundar Arlof closed his eyes and turned away from the screen. Inside Shaw his nerves screamed to look out to port, to try and discern the giant shape bearing down on them. But if he could see the other boat, it would be too late.

'Tack,' Shaw said. They came through the wind and there, on their shoulder, perhaps forty feet to windward, was *Eagle* on parallel course, trailers of mist moving across her decks. On board *Eagle* Ericson stared ahead. Shaw felt a tremor of nervous response run down his back.

The windward mark was approaching fast.

'Hardening up,' Shaw shouted. He started to squeeze up, exercising right of way.

Twenty feet separated them. Shaw squeezed a little more. Fifteen, ten feet. If they touched now then by rights *Eagle* should be disqualified. But in the fog there would be no witnesses, merely Ericson's word against his. Ericson seemed to be acting on that premiss, refusing to budge. Shaw strained himself for the collision. But the buoy came up like a ghost on port and he could pivot round, leaving *Eagle* a boat length behind. *Leningrad*'s spinnaker filled with a punch and he felt the boat accelerate downwind.

Eagle's spinnaker bloomed behind them, a massive flower.

One of those rare sunbursts occurred, lighting up the two boats suddenly as if on a stage, forcing the trimmers to shade their eyes with their hands as they gazed upwards into the blinding luminescence of the sails. The sun was like a searchlight in darkness. Perhaps twenty seconds later *Eagle* was almost entirely enveloped in mist.

Shaw could sense the loss of power in their sails. Behind them, Ericson hunted for their wind. Sensing the others' alarm, Shaw knew he had to break out.

'Gybe!'

Kingissep swung out along the pole like a monkey over the sliding sea, until he could pull the pin and release the big sail. Migdal and Maask worked the spinnaker halyards to reset the pole. Kingissep swung inboard to reset the sheet. A few seconds later the huge sail was setting on port tack.

Behind them *Eagle* had gybed too, and was on the same course. Shaw felt the judder in his sails as Ericson again acted to cut their wind. On the screen *Eagle* was directly behind them, the two blips were touching.

'Harden sheets,' Shaw hissed.

Baltir and Ulder pounded the winches. Shaw changed course ten, fifteen, then twenty degrees higher. But on the screen the blip that was *Eagle* occupied the same commanding position. If it was true that Ericson's radar could give him *Leningrad*'s crew dispositions, Ericson could gauge Shaw's next move from crew movements alone. He could react to changes in course even before they happened.

Speculation was driven from Shaw's mind by events. Unable to see *Eagle*'s position on the screen, he knew suddenly that Ericson had found his wind. Above him, *Leningrad*'s spinnaker collapsed. A few seconds later, out of the mist emerged *Eagle*'s inexorable bow. With two more knots of speed, *Eagle* rolled past majestically. For a helmsman, to have one's wind taken by another boat is akin to the feeling of paralysis in a dream. Shaw would remember those moments for a long time, the crew staring helplessly around them as *Eagle* moved past them with all the stately certainty of a president's limousine.

Twelve

With the other boat's passage ahead, power returned to the spinnaker. Shaw tried to build up speed as rapidly as possible, swinging high to generate higher apparent wind. As trailing boat, they had one crucial advantage. They could strike back by intercepting the leader's wind. Shaw glanced down at the radar screen. The blip that should be *Eagle* had disappeared.

Brod said, 'The instrument's gone.'

But it was Arlof, looking at the whitened screen, who realized what was happening.

'Countermeasures.'

Shaw couldn't believe his ears. A crawling realization moved across the back of his mind. He said, trying to keep the shock out of his voice, 'That's illegal,' but that didn't make it untrue. The whole screen was active; but it was 'whited out' as if the fog itself had entered the instrument.

Shaw looked upwards into Arlof's face for perhaps half a second, and saw there his own consternation reflected. They had no idea of *Eagle*'s position and no chance of counter-attack. It was an eerie sensation. In match-racing, the fastest course to the next point is a secondary factor. Of foremost importance is the disposition of the rival boat. That entire source of information and tactics had been removed in one stroke. The fog had concentrated the opposing boat to a single blip on a radar screen, and now *Eagle* had cut off that final point of contact. Shaw heard at the back of his mind Ericson's laughter when the committee had cleared him of ramming *Novy Mir*.

He tried to concentrate. It was a matter now of making the fastest theoretical course to the next mark.

'Forget the instrument. Forget *Eagle*. Give me optimum course.'

Arlof punched instructions into the tactical computer. '235 degrees.'

'Concentrate on speed,' Shaw called out to the crew. The men in the cockpit would have heard their rapid discussions. He must bring them back into form, kick them out of their paralysis.

The screen was still whited out. Like a man feeling his way forward in a darkened room, he must function by instinct.

'Wind knocks two degrees,' Arlof said.

Somewhere out there was *Eagle*, watching their every move.

'Gybe!' called Shaw. Kingissep clambered along the spinnaker pole; Migdal and Maask prepared the halyards; Ulder and Baltir wiped the moisture from their faces as they prepared to grind. It was a fast gybe, swift and graceful.

Shaw checked the screen. It was still whited out. Somewhere in the fog he heard an American voice call out, 'They've gybed.' If Shaw had one source of satisfaction, it was that Ericson's forward position denied him the opportunity to interfere with *Leningrad*'s wind. A large potential weapon had been removed by circumstances.

'Look,' Brod said.

The screen had returned to normal. And it gave bad news. *Eagle* was ten lengths ahead at least, on starboard gybe to *Leningrad*'s port. The cessation of countermeasures was a further exercise in cynicism. Ericson had returned their radar just when he was effectively out of reach. Shaw had been through enough anger and outrage already. Nothing Ericson did surprised him. He wiped the clammy moisture from his eyes.

Brod turned to him and smiled. 'Your countryman,' he said.

'Yeah,' Shaw agreed. 'My countryman.'

*

With radar they found the downwind buoy easily, and rounded it some twelve lengths behind *Eagle*. The genoa had been raised before rounding. Now the grinders powered it in for the upwind leg, and *Leningrad* heeled to the increased breeze. Out of contact with the other boat, they concentrated on simple speed. At the top mark they were still ten lengths behind. *Eagle*'s lead increased on the downwind leg. The race became a procession.

On the final upwind leg they were nearly one minute and forty seconds behind. They heard the finish gun ahead of them as *Eagle* crossed the line, and the sudden whooping of sirens as the result was read out to her supporters in the fog. In the hanging mist *Leningrad* crossed the line, one minute forty-seven seconds behind.

As the soaked sails slid downwards, Shaw's body started to shake in the wet, though whether out of cold or long-suppressed rage it was difficult to tell.

Thirteen

As *Leningrad* was towed back through the fog, Shaw considered whether he should protest over *Eagle*'s use of countermeasures. He had inherited his grandfather's dislike of the polemic and verbal dexterity of protest meetings. He hated the predicament of the complainant, of someone who had been balked of victory on the water, and who sought reparation by other means. More than this, Shaw had a deep suspicion – hardly allayed by the finding of the protest committee in the case of the ramming of *Novy Mir* by *Eagle* – that the protest was too often the weapon of rogues.

Arlof had recorded the exact time during which their radar screen had been blanked out by countermeasures. Shaw and Brod and Arlof had discussed whether to pursue the matter. They felt that it was during the time of the countermeasures that *Eagle* had pulled ahead.

When *Leningrad* was tied up, Arlof said, 'If we were affected, then other yachts in the spectator fleet must have been affected.'

'But if other boats can corroborate they were blanked out at the same time, how can we prove the source of the disturbance was *Eagle*? It might have come from another spectator boat. There were several thousand other boats operating in the vicinity.'

Shaw had a vision of *Eagle*'s legal representative Mulvinney tearing their accusation to shreds. Mulvinney would accuse the Estonians of bad sportsmanship. Shaw smiled at the irony of it.

'No protest,' he said to Brod and Arlof. What did he see on their faces? Relief? A hint of condescension, perhaps, at his lack of aggression? The two Estonians turned away, and for the time being the matter was forgotten.

After each race, it was the custom for the *Eagle* syndicate to give a press conference. America's Cup custom over several decades dictated that both skippers were present. It was a ritual that pleased sponsors and fuelled the media circus. But Illich, who had no commercial sponsors, had refused to be present, and Shaw had decided to follow his example and not to participate. Ericson held the field.

When *Leningrad* had been raised from the water, and he had briefed Anton Shuch about the sails, Shaw sat down on the moth-eaten chair and switched on the black and white Ilyushin television set at the back of the offices.

An interviewer from CBS said to Ericson: 'You must have been pleased by today's race.'

Ericson sat with his father on one side and Mulvinney on the other: 'I think we're finally showing we're a better team than the opposition.'

'And what do you think of the performance of Jim Shaw?'

'He's lost two games in a row, now. I'd say I've got the measure of him.'

'You obviously outsmarted them in the fog.'

'Yeah,' Ericson said. 'I guess we did.'

Shaw liked to see modesty in an American hero. He was starting to enjoy himself.

'You've had experience of two helmsmen in this America's Cup. What would you say is the difference between Shaw and Illich?'

'Well. Illich was a hero, a patriot. I deeply respected him. What Shaw is doing is un-American. Frankly, Shaw is just a renegade.'

There was a silence. Ericson's father nodded beside him. On the other side of Ericson, Mulvinney stared ahead, expressionless.

'The score stands at two all. What is your prediction of the outcome?'

'I predict we will win four two.'

'Four straight wins against Jim Shaw?'

'That's what I said.'

Shaw switched off the set and stood up. He wondered what had changed that he was no longer affected by what Ericson said. Once he had attached a certain importance to the phrase 'un-American' or words such as 'traitor' or 'renegade'. But in the mouth of Ericson terms of abuse were like a double negative – they made him feel he was doing something right.

Shaw stepped out of a side-door and crossed to the small bungalow, hardly more than a shed, that he shared with Maria.

'Hurry,' Ilena said. 'He is waiting.'

Shaw felt a surge of anger at being summoned so peremptorily. He walked briskly with her to the main building. In the shadow of the offices a figure stepped out towards him, blocking his way. Another emerged from a slant of shadow beside the doorway. He had heard of the Kallas brothers, Aegu's guards. One of the men tapped him on the shoulder as an indication to turn. He was rapidly frisked. The men moved back so that he could pass.

Shaw stepped forward into his own office. One of the guards closed the door quietly behind him.

Aegu's short, square frame was seated in a chair. He had a former athlete's bulk in the chest and shoulders. Without looking at Shaw, he struck a match and the flame flowered in his hand. For a brief moment his heavy brows were lit up; the rest of the room was enveloped in the gloom light seems to make around itself. The discarded match rattled in the metal bin.

Aegu smoked Primas, a rough, non-filtered cigarette. His clothes carried their pungent odour. Shaw had seen films of gangsters, meetings in small rooms, formal ballets of heightened tension. He had an impulse to explode into derisive laughter. But something – perhaps simply the realization that the requirements of security were part of Aegu's normal life – prevented him. Drawing on his cigarette, Aegu seemed to notice him for the first time, and said amiably, 'Good morning, *tovarich*.' He indicated Shaw's chair with a smoke-stained hand, 'Please sit down.'

Aegu's insouciance was such that Shaw felt his rage escape. It was something he realized early, that would become customary. Aegu lived the natural life of an animal, of a man who has such natural power that he does not need to charm. He walked to his chair behind the old metal desk and sat down.

'I apologize for the security,' Aegu added. Shaw said nothing. Aegu, for his part, seemed to expect no response. He was reaching into his pocket, drawing out some object. He placed it on the desk and leaned back.

Aegu said, 'From Illich's pocket.'

Shaw studied it. It was a simple, cheap lighter, of American make. Lucky Strike.

'You recognize it, perhaps?'

Shaw took a deep breath. It stirred some faint trace of memory. Somewhere he had heard that one of the men, perhaps Kriis, had found a similar object on the base premises and had given it to Illich.

'I recognize the make, sure. It's about as common as sand.'

Aegu nodded.

'But no special significance? Given, for example, that Illich did not smoke.'

'I'd have to think about it.'

Aegu showed no disappointment. He inhaled and breathed out. As a prelude to making himself comfortable in Shaw's office, Aegu had opened the window. A breeze helped to dissipate the cloud of smoke that still lingered around him. Shaw knew he was being given time to reconsider.

Aegu said, 'There are no significant fingerprints on the lighter, apart from Illich's own. The police have recorded the precise nature of the object in their files. I will leave it in your safekeeping, as a reminder.'

Aegu stubbed out his cigarette and almost immediately reached into his pockets for a packet.

'Do you like Illich?' Aegu asked without warning, his eyes rising to meet Shaw's.

Shaw took several moments to recover. He said, 'I admired him.'

'Everyone admires him, *tovarich*.' Aegu brushed the statement aside. 'Who could not? That was not my question.'

Perhaps Shaw's discomfort was mitigated by the fact that Aegu knew Illich as well as he did. There was a certain complicity in the question.

'Maybe he was too remote to like easily.'

'Precisely,' Aegu said. 'Does one like saints? One admires, even worships them. I say this, even though you have not answered my question.'

Shaw felt himself stirred into something like anger by his insistence, not at Aegu himself, but the impossibility of answer. He felt an instinct to attack.

'Do people like me, Mr President?' Shaw's chest tightened in anticipation of his next question. 'Do they like you?'

He had spoken quietly, in polite enquiry, and for a moment he thought the question would be passed by.

Aegu paused. The smoke from his Prima moved about him. He reached forward to stub out the cigarette. He was laughing suddenly, a gravelly laugh that seemed to emerge from his lower chest or stomach and to fill the room. At the same time he raised himself off the chair with a powerful heave.

'Nearly all of them.' Aegu was on his feet, turning towards the door, his square fingers on the handle. He seemed to pause, as though something amusing had struck him. 'You see, I am rather far from being a saint.' He smiled briefly. 'I will find my own way out. Goodbye, *tovarich*.'

He closed the door behind him. Shaw heard the quiet footsteps of the Kallas brothers as they swung in behind him.

Ilena hurried to the door, knocked, opened it. Her face showed concern.

'I'm sorry I didn't give you any warning. He just appeared. A big car, bodyguards.'

'No problem,' Shaw said. 'He's a character, I think.'

'He is a terrible man,' Ilena confirmed, though from her intonation he recognized praise.

Fourteen

Maria looked up from drying the dishes. She removed her apron and put it aside.

'You don't look too down-hearted,' she said. 'I heard the result on the radio.'

Shaw shrugged. 'Where's Jack?'

'Ilena's looking after him. She's got him another hour.'

She came over to Shaw and put her arms around him. 'You sure you're not upset?'

She was taller than he. Her lips pressed lightly against his forehead. He could feel her breathing, the warmth of her body through her clothes. Shaw saw Ericson's face, flanked by his father and Mulvinney, shrink to a white point in the centre of a television screen as he clicked the switch. Increasingly he found he could do something like it in his own mind.

'Jack won't be back for an hour?' Shaw asked.

'A whole hour.'

After a while he said, 'Want me to prove it?'

'Prove what?'

'That I'm not upset.'

He could feel her back with his hands under the thin cloth of her summer dress, the line of her vertebrae.

'That sounds like a good idea.'

In *Leningrad*'s afterguard, it was Arlof who seemed most affected by the events of the race that day. Shaw had expected that Brod, with his explosive temper, might have been the one to watch. But in the debriefing that took place that evening Brod appeared taciturn, as if he too had become inured to Ericson.

There was, however, a second reason for continuing tension in Arlof. As navigator, he was most closely concerned with monitoring the weather. The weather reports for the following day indicated further coastal fog. What loomed in his mind was a repeat of today's conditions.

After the general crew debriefing, Shaw asked for a discussion with Brod and Arlof alone.

In his small office at the back of the shed, he addressed Brod first. 'If we have the same weather conditions, what could we do that's different from today?'

'Nothing,' Brod replied. 'That's the problem.'

Shaw glanced at Arlof.

'I agree.'

Shaw said, 'If we had protested, because we have no proof, Mulvinney would have torn us to shreds. Because we didn't protest, Ericson will feel he can use it again tomorrow if the conditions are right.'

Arlof looked glum. There was a psychological difference between them, Shaw decided. It seemed to him and Brod that if there was nothing they could do about something, then they must accept it. This acceptance produced a certain peace of mind. With Arlof, the same conditions seemed to gnaw. For Arlof's sake alone Shaw wanted at least to appear to take some positive action, even if its final effect was negligible.

'Maybe we should write a note to Vikunov at the protest committee, reporting that we were subject to electronic countermeasures today, and ask the committee to monitor the course tomorrow for any further outbreaks. At least, that way, if we want to protest tomorrow we aren't starting from scratch.'

Arlof seemed to relax slightly. Brod shrugged his shoulders.

'Arlof?' Shaw asked.

'It's the best we can do,' Arlof said.

'Brod?'

'I agree.'

'OK, I'll draft it and make sure it's delivered this evening.'

Shaw walked back to his office. Despite the open window, the room still stank from Aegu's Primas.

Ideally, Shaw would have asked Brod's wife Ilena, who acted as his secretary, to type it out. But he was grateful to Ilena for looking after Jack that afternoon. He pulled the cover off the old Remington and began laboriously to type using two fingers.

Alexei Sergeivich Vikunov
Chairman
Protest Committee
America's Cup

Dear Chairman Vikunov,
During the course of the race today, we on Leningrad *were subject to a 'white-out' of our radar screen from 10.23.06 to 10.28.52. During this period of approximately six minutes, we were unable to ascertain the position of* Eagle. *In this same period* Eagle *established an important lead. We have reason to believe this incident was not a fault of our equipment, which functioned perfectly for the rest of the race, both before and after the incident in question, but the result of external electronic disturbance. We feel it is important to establish that this disturbance was not deliberately planned, not least because deployment of such 'countermeasures' is against the rules.*

We did not protest today because we have no conclusive evidence that electronic countermeasures were used. However, in order to make sure that there is no repeat of such an incident, we formally request that if conditions of fog persist tomorrow or on another race, you will monitor the course for any further outbreaks of active electronic interference.

This message is confidential, and not a matter for general release. However, we feel it would be appropriate and fair, if you agree, to inform the Eagle *syndicate of the contents of this letter.*

Please contact me if you require further information.
Yours sincerely,
Jim Shaw

73

The ribbon had faded, and the typing was uneven, but it was legible. Shaw addressed the envelope by hand, then glanced at his watch. He had half an hour before the evening meal.

The number of reporters at the periphery of the camp was relatively low. The American press conference had drawn off the dwindling ranks of press and television journalists who vainly hoped for any information from him. Perhaps they too believed that the competition had swung decisively in *Eagle*'s favour. Behind one of the buildings there was a side-gate. A militiaman unlocked it. Shaw stepped out unobserved and made his way to the press and administration centre.

He attracted no attention. Small, nondescript, he walked through the lobby, past several groups of journalists, and into the reception area of the America's Cup protest committee. Livonia Paretna, the press officer, looked up.

He spoke first. 'Shaw, defence helmsman.'

She stood up.

'I have a letter for Chairman Vikunov.' He handed the envelope to her. 'It's important, I think, that the Chairman sees this letter today.'

'I understand. Unfortunately he's in a meeting right now. Would you like me to phone through?'

'No,' he said. 'As long as he gets it today.'

'He will. I'll write you a note now confirming receipt. Please sit down.'

'Thank you.'

Livonia Paretna removed a notepaper headed 'America's Cup Committee'. Shaw saw her write: 'I acknowledge receipt of a letter from Mr J. Shaw, on behalf of the defence syndicate.' She dated the letter and beside it wrote the time of receipt. He watched her sign it.

'Thank you.' Shaw folded her confirmation note and

put it in his pocket. He was about to leave when the hinge of the inner office door creaked and coughed. Vikunov emerged in company with a bearded man.

'Mr Shaw?'

Vikunov was huge, jovial. He felt obliged to turn and shake hands.

'This is an informal visit?'

'I came to deliver a letter.'

Vikunov's eyes moved down to the hand-addressed envelope on the desk. He said to Livonia Paretna, 'Anything further this evening?'

'No. All clear.'

'Would you like me to read it now?' Vikunov asked him.

'I'd be grateful.'

'Come into the office.'

It was large and bare. A Russian flag hung on the wall, suspended from two ceremonial brass rods. By contrast, the Estonian camp was relatively free of such formal regalia.

'Please sit down.'

Vikunov opened and read the letter. He placed it face down on the desk.

'If countermeasures have been used, it is a serious offence. You should have protested formally. We would have examined the issue.'

'Maybe,' Shaw said. 'But we didn't.'

'Why not?' Vikunov stared at him from under heavy eyebrows.

'Because we don't have proof.'

'You mean it isn't a clear-cut case?'

'I thought being rammed by *Eagle* was clear-cut. Our protest didn't do us any good.'

Vikunov said, 'On the contrary, it saved you from being disqualified.'

'Disqualified?'

Vikunov nodded.

'Yes. You didn't know the *Eagle* syndicate accused you of ramming them?'

Shaw was not usually lost for words. Vikunov leaned back.

'I am not breaking a confidence, I think,' he said. 'It is on the official record which will be circulated in due course.'

'It's a remarkable world, isn't it?' Shaw said.

Vikunov was silent, regarding his guest without apparent expression, his elbows on the desk, his fingers touching. At length he said:

'Your letter raises certain questions. You see, since you have suggested that I inform the challenging syndicate of the contents of your letter, I believe it is my duty to tell you that earlier this afternoon I received a communication from the *Eagle* camp, which claimed that at the time you mention in your letter, they were subject to electronic countermeasures. They suggested that the source was your yacht, *Leningrad*. If there is a further recurrence tomorrow, they requested that your yacht be examined.'

'Jesus,' Shaw whispered.

'Precisely,' Vikunov said amiably.

Fifteen

Shaw remembered something that his grandfather said. If you steal something as small as an apple, then you step over an invisible line into theft, and the only thing that separates you from bank robbery is courage. He was reminded of this now: if you are prepared in principle to break the agreed rules, then there is no end to it except the limit of your imagination. Standing in Vikunov's study, he tried to work out in his own mind how someone who has stepped so decisively across that boundary would think. He had ceased to be interested in Ericson's state of mind. Now it was a purely practical matter of attempting to prevent further damage.

'I suggest we discuss this matter, Mr Shaw,' Vikunov said.

'I guess we'd better.'

Seated in his high-backed chair, Vikunov seemed like one of those Russian village elders who administer a rough but implacable justice. Shaw waited for him to speak.

'You must understand that I am simply the representative of a committee. We must be as objective as possible. Taking that into account, I merely say to you that if you had not brought your letter to me, evidence of the use of countermeasures tomorrow would have resulted in the search of your yacht, not *Eagle*. Now that you have made your suspicion known, we will be obliged to search both yachts.'

'In the interests of objectivity,' Shaw said, 'could I suggest that you search both yachts immediately after the race, before they are allowed contact with any other boat?'

'On the face of it, that appears a reasonable suggestion, but I will seek ratification from the committee.' Vikunov wrote a note on a pad. While writing, he said, 'I will inform the *Eagle* syndicate of this precaution, and ask whether they have any further suggestions as to policing on this matter.'

Shaw struggled to control himself over the absurdity of Ericson's making suggestions about ensuring fair play. After a few moments he said: 'That seems fair.'

Vikunov stopped writing.

'Have you any further comments?'

'Yes. If it is possible, could you attempt to establish an exact heading for the source of the countermeasures, preferably from two boats well apart, so that a fix could be obtained on the position of the source at the time of the interference?'

'We will consider the matter. You must understand that we will be obliged also to pass on this suggestion to the challenging syndicate. Any further suggestions?'

'Yes,' Shaw said. A pellet of anger had hit him, and he felt a sudden desire to take the battle to the enemy. 'I suggest each yacht carries a witness, preferably from the committee itself, so that the witness can report back to the committee direct. We will accept any witness on our boat recommended by the committee. The witness can report back, for example, on the duration of white-out of the radar screen on each boat.'

'I note down your suggestion,' Vikunov said. 'You understand that the challenging syndicate has a right to refuse any outsider on their yacht, even at the suggestion of the committee?'

'It will be interesting to see whether they exercise that right,' Shaw said.

Vikunov was still writing carefully.

'Interesting in what sense?'

'As an indication of their attitude in this matter.'

'We are not interested in indications,' Vikunov said, 'merely facts. You understand that they have a right to refuse, and if they do the fact that they have exercised this right will have no bearing on the matter, or on any subsequent investigation?'

He stopped writing to look at Shaw over the top of his glasses. Shaw nodded. He had made his point, and he wouldn't press the matter.

'Any other suggestions?' Vikunov asked.

'No,' Shaw said. He was trying to adjust to a condition in which it was necessary to attack in order merely to defend. It was a state of mind he was familiar with on the race course. But it was clear that it was a state of mind necessary on land, too.

'Good,' Vikunov said. He put down his pen. 'I am pleased you visited us.'

He rose and they shook hands formally. 'No need to see me out,' Shaw said.

Livonia Paretna, the press officer, smiled at him on the way out. As he walked past, Shaw was aware of her surreptitious, flickering glance. She was ascertaining, he felt sure, how this small man could be the same intransigent demon Jim Shaw, the renegade American helmsman, who refused to give press conferences and whom the press (both Russian and foreign) described as an almost pathological recluse. Shaw guessed she expected someone stranger, someone with green teeth and perhaps the limp of a damaged predator. He was sorry to disappoint her.

'He said what?' Brod watched him across the table in open amazement.

Shaw preferred to be open with the crew, but he was concerned that if they knew the opposing syndicate's manoeuvres it might detract from their attention the following day. He had waited until the meal was over before inviting Brod and Arlof into his small office.

'I delivered our message to Vikunov personally. It was lucky I met him. He told me that the other syndicate has already lodged a formal complaint about our use of countermeasures.'

'Our use?' For a moment, Shaw enjoyed watching Brod's eyes flare in amazement.

'A case of pre-emptive defence, it seems to me,' Shaw said. He tried to keep the irony out of his voice. It was like one of those war-games in which he who strikes first wins. Assume the first step, the desire to win at all costs, and the rest follows neatly. Amongst all human activities, the application of logic produced perhaps the most surreal consequences.

Arlof, leaning against the wall, shifted restlessly. In

the absence of comment Shaw continued:

'We're facing a man who believes he got away cleanly from the act of sinking his rival right in front of the eyes of the world. After that, why shouldn't he think he can get away with just about anything he puts his mind to?' He didn't want to linger on the point. Once you accepted it, it had a certain banality. 'I suggested to Vikunov that both yachts should have independent witnesses on board. He accepted the suggestion, but he also said that as it wasn't a compulsory aspect of the rules, *Eagle* isn't obliged to take note of the recommendation, even if it is endorsed by the committee.'

'So we carry an extra weight, and they do not.' Arlof shook his head.

'Would you rather we didn't have a witness, so that they can accuse us again of using countermeasures in the fog?'

Arlof didn't reply. It was unlike Brod, too, to be so negative.

'You're Estonian.' Shaw looked from one to the other. 'How do you think I feel about this?'

In bed that evening with Maria, facing one another, Shaw said, 'It's interesting what people like Ericson do to your mind.'

'What?'

'I began to think that maybe they'd even be prepared to plant something on us, some little countermeasure device that the race authorities could find.'

Maria turned to face him in bed. He could see the curve of light on her face, the dark shadows of her eyes, but it was too dark to see her expression.

'That is horrible.'

'I even thought of asking for a special guard on the boat tonight.'

Maria, shifting slightly so that her cheek was against his, seemed to be staring through him or past him.

'And did you?'

'No,' Shaw said. 'In the end I didn't. I think maybe I'd prefer to lose than start to think like that.'

Sixteen

It was fog again.

Staring out of the window, Shaw could not even see the sea's edge. A heavy mist lay like a malevolent blanket. The tops of pines protruded at the water's edge. To the east, through the oblong of the window frame, he could see a slight lightening of the white sky. In the early morning, barely out of sleep, he was still vulnerable to emotion, and projected this naturally on to the fog that lapped against the grassed lawns and hillsides. It seemed to him lugubrious, turgid, menacing, slow. He felt his heart sink.

Vagir and his men were already on *Leningrad*, checking through her systems. Shaw could discern their vague shapes moving on deck as she hung suspended above the water by the crane.

He dressed as quietly as he could in his tracksuit, and let himself out of the door without waking Maria. Brod loomed out of a side-door.

'Same again.'

'Looks like it.'

On the forecourt the others were collecting, forming into lines to begin their exercises. In the early morning their blood seemed as thick and slow as reptiles'. Prem's merciless eye skewered the less enthusiastic. His barked instructions kicked them into life. His insults flowed with customary panache. They hated him with the same glowering rage that lions direct towards a tamer.

Apart from recent additions such as Edvigs Tarku, and Shaw himself, the average age of the Estonian veterans was over thirty. The stalwarts were Soren Gir, Berol Baltir, Herman Maask, Stephan Migdal – the solid fighting heart at the centre of the boat. In an intensely physical sport, they referred to themselves as the grand-fathers.

After training, the crew showered and collected at breakfast. Through the windows the fog glimmered like ashes. Shaw tapped his glass with a knife at the end of the meal and told them that they should expect a witness on board today to ensure fair play.

On his way to *Leningrad*, Shaw was called by Ilena to the telephone. A woman's voice sounded, then a gravelly male voice.

'Aegu here.'

'Shaw. Good morning.'

'I am phoning briefly to tell you something that may amuse you, or perhaps not.'

'I'm listening.'

'The military in Moscow appears to be taking great pleasure in the fact that the Americans seem on the road to victory.'

Shaw smiled to himself. He said, 'I never had much luck with the military.'

Static interrupted the line. He heard the echo of a woman's voice, earnestly asking for figures on trade conditions, then a return of Aegu's amiable voice.

'The politicians, on the other hand, are keen to foster trade with the Americans. They, too, are not displeased by the current turn of events.'

'Well, I appreciate that.'

'My point is that you seem to be pleasing more people by losing than by winning.'

'That's good to know,' Shaw said. 'How about you, Mr President, are you one of the pleased ones?'

'As a subversive, I am one of the few who hope you will win. I wish you luck, *tovarich*.'

'Thank you,' he said.

Aegu put down the phone.

Ilena called through the door: 'There is a man waiting to see you.'

Shaw recognized Nils Vaaren, one of the judges of the protest committee. Immensely tall and prematurely bald, Vaaren had a pleasant, lop-sided smile which off-set his formidable presence. They shook hands formally. Vaaren had the old Baltic aristocrat's habit of bowing his head in greeting, a nod towards tradition.

'I am here as a witness.'

Shaw nodded. Vaaren's English carried a Scandinavian lilt: 'I'll stay at the back of the boat, out of the way.'

'Hope we can keep you amused,' Shaw said.

Leningrad was ready to be towed off. Shaw introduced Vaaren to the crew. While Vaaren took up his position at the stern, Shaw looked out to sea. The mist seemed more luminous, less solid. Shaw stepped aboard. Slowly the towboat began to haul *Leningrad* towards the white conflagration.

'It may be less dense later,' Brod said, as they hit a solid wall of mist just outside the harbour mouth. Shaw was filled again with the claustrophobic sensation of travelling through some medium that was half water, half air.

He turned to Vaaren, standing several feet behind him in a part of the cockpit professional sailors sometimes called the 'owner's enclosure', because it was where an owner could cause least trouble to the operation of the boat. 'Did *Eagle* agree to a witness on board?'

'No,' Vaaren replied.

A phrase rose to Shaw's lips, but he held it back and merely nodded instead.

The moisture-laden air was heavy, so that for a given windspeed it contained more power. This required reprogramming the tactical computer for speed readouts at various strengths of wind. One advantage appeared to be that the wind direction of this heavy air was more constant. In turn this occasioned less delay while the committee boat organized the laying of the first upwind mark.

On the radar screen they could see the course patrol boats shepherding the spectator boats behind their lines. It must have been confusing out there in the fog. The spectator boats had diminished to those who had radar and were confident in its use.

Eventually *Leningrad*'s towboat turned into wind and they waited. On the screen *Eagle* and her entourage of large power boats gathered on the other side of the start box.

This was always a bad time for helmsmen, before the first pellet of adrenalin strikes the system. Yet Shaw noticed a qualitative change in his emotions. His dislike of Ericson lingered. But he felt oddly detached, and was prey to a sensation that somehow in the fog he could see his enemy more clearly.

'Radar's working perfectly,' Shaw said to Vaaren. 'No sign of interference of any kind.'

Vaaren came forward to study the screen.

'That's *Eagle*,' Shaw pointed to a blip at the centre of an expanding circle of blips, like a flower opening. 'You can see her fan club pulling away. The signal will grow stronger when she pulls up her sails.'

Vaaren nodded. He began to scribble down notes.

Shaw continued. 'If we get a white-out on the screen, and you want to make a note of the time during which it occurs, we can verify the times of start and stop on this dial here.'

'I have my own chronometer,' Vaaren said. 'You had

no signs of initial interference yesterday before the white-out?'

'None whatsoever.'

'And no other signs of malfunction before or after the race?'

'No.'

Vaaren scribbled. Around the bows the fog shifted. A wave of white moved across the foredeck.

'*Eagle* sets sail,' Brod called. The blip that was the other boat flowered gently into greater luminosity.

Seventeen

'It's time we started,' Shaw said to Vaaren. He nodded to Migdal at the mast, who began to haul up the mainsail in huge sweeps while Maask backed him on the halyard winch.

Kingissep broke the bowline knot and the bow rope was cast off. The mainsail was up now, being tensioned by Prem. Ahead of them the towboat made a half circle and then, like a conjuring trick, disappeared into the mist.

'Genoa!' Shaw shouted.

With the boom eased, they were drifting back gently. Prem tightened in the mainsheet and they began to accelerate.

The end of the period of waiting was a relief. Berol Baltir and Graf Ulder, the grinders, began to throw power into the winches. The genoa came in crisply. Shaw allowed the trimmers and sail-handlers a couple of minutes to trim. On the screen he watched *Eagle* circle.

'Twelve minutes to ten-minute gun,' Arlof said.

Brod had been right. The mist was qualitatively different from yesterday. Although visibility appeared just as limited, the mist itself had a luminous heart, as if it had trapped sunlight and was slowly releasing it, exhaling light like breath. Once, as they set up on starboard tack, a blast of sunlight had struck them from above. Looking up into golden light, Shaw saw two almost vertical cliffs of mist, and between them a delicate trace of blue sky. It was likely to be the only sight of the sun during the race, but it warmed some indefinable emotion.

'Two minutes to ten-minute gun.'

The mist had closed again. They were drifting like bacteria in their peculiar medium.

'Bearing away,' Shaw warned. He spun the wheel and they swung downwind.

'Gybe!' he shouted. The boom hesitated and then thundered across.

The previous day he and Brod had discussed tactics in the event of deep fog. They agreed that the safest course would be to keep away from *Eagle*, to retreat from her until they saw an opportunity for a timed run to the line. But as a helmsman, Shaw was a primitive; he trusted his emotions more than his reason.

'Brod, we'll change tactics. Let's go in and engage.'

Brod was attuned to his ways. As a rule, he tended to support the element of surprise. He nodded his agreement. Arlof merely kept his head to the radar screen. '*Eagle* approaches. Twenty seconds to ten-minute gun.'

They were drifting downwind to the point where they would enter the starting box.

'Ten, nine, eight . . .'

'Harden in. Power reach,' Shaw called.

'Five, four, three, two . . .'

The wall of mist seemed to bulge with the impact of the starting cannon. Then they were through, accelerating.

86

'Eight four, eight six, eight seven.'

Shaw threw a glance at Vaaren. At the decision to engage, he had seen the otherwise calm Vaaren's eyes bulge briefly with astonishment, his Adam's apple move down once as he swallowed. Now the outer edge of his hand and his knuckles shone white as he gripped the backstay for support. It was an image Shaw would cherish. To an outsider, it must appear madness to be thundering towards another yacht with nothing to separate himself from the other except the delicate image on a radar screen.

'Eight nine, nine zero, nine zero,' Arlof called. The fog was so close it gave an enhanced impression of speed. The walls of mist were like a tunnel through which they moved with the uncompromising power of an express train.

'Nine one, nine two.' Their closing speed must be eighteen knots. Shaw judged the time of collision to be about thirty seconds.

'White-out!' Brod shouted.

Shaw saw the screen fade, glow; a series of pulses moved across its face in patterns that looked like blank verse. Then it settled into a glowing blank.

Vaaren was pushing forward, craning his head down towards the bank of instrument readouts.

Fifteen seconds to collision, and they were running blind. Shaw tried to reassure Vaaren. 'We're on starboard; he must keep clear.'

He saw Vaaren's Adam's apple plunge again as his dry mouth tried to suck in moisture.

Eagle moved past them upwind at eighteen knots, twenty feet away, leaving only spray from the clash of the two yachts' hull waves and the sudden punch of her wind in *Leningrad*'s sails.

'Screen returns,' Brod said. *Eagle* was a dot moving away.

'Arlof,' Shaw called. 'Raise the protest flag.'

To Vaaren, he said, 'I find it a little strange that our screen whites out just as we were about to engage in a tacking duel with *Eagle*. I am speaking statistically, of course.'

'Of course.' Vaaren was writing carefully in his pad, wedged against the cockpit side for support. Shaw was impressed. Someone less assured might have scampered up the mast, teeth chattering like an ape.

Eighteen

They watched the glowing bacterium that was *Eagle* move across the screen away from them. It seemed to be attracted towards the port end of the line.

Setting aside the main aspects of the incident, Shaw wondered briefly whether the coolly writing Vaaren was receptive to the nuances of Ericson's action; that, for example, the particular timing of its use was designed for maximum psychological intimidation; even that the apparently flagrant use of countermeasures was in the nature of a challenge to the authorities to discipline the Americans.

The breeze seemed to have settled at about fourteen knots.

'Any bias?' Shaw asked Arlof.

'None. Wind direction constant.'

After the initial incident, *Eagle* too stayed at her end of the line, content to let the seconds tick down to the starting gun.

The occasional filter of sunlight gave the fog depth and solidity. Once, during a brief sunlit spell, a wall of mist moved by with the stateliness of an iceberg. The crew used the final minutes to tune. Approaching the line unhindered by the other boat, in the seconds before the gun Shaw reached along it in order to pick up maximum speed. Arlof counted out the seconds before the start gun.

'Ten, nine, eight . . .'

'Harden up,' Shaw shouted.

He swung the wheel and the grinders powered the sheets in. The start gun fired in the mist. He used the added momentum of the reach to build upwind speed.

Two seconds later they were over the line. It was a good beginning, safe and fast; they concentrated to maintain speed.

'According to the radar,' Brod said, '*Eagle* crossed the line three seconds before the gun.'

If one yacht is over, it is an international convention that the cannon fires once to signal there is a start line transgression, and to warn the culprit that he must return and restart. If two yachts are over, it fires twice for a general recall. But today there was no additional gun, and they knew that Ericson had escaped with an illegal start under cover of the fog. Shaw could have complained directly to Vaaren, but he judged him too competent an administrator not to have noticed. In addition, Shaw was certain Vaaren had heard Brod's comment, and would draw his own conclusions.

On the radar screen, *Eagle* kept to the starboard side of the course.

'Eight two, eight three, eight three steady . . .' Arlof called.

'*Eagle* tacks,' Brod said.

Eagle was tracking fast up the starboard side of the course, as if she had found a private corridor of wind. But if she was ahead, it was not by much.

Something else cheered Shaw: the occasional small breaks in the fog were becoming more frequent. Sometimes *Leningrad*'s decks would be doused by an unearthly light, as if by a spotlight from above; the metal surfaces would glow with a sudden irrational energy. It never cleared enough, however, for them to catch sight of *Eagle* until they were in the final stages of converging on the first buoy.

Driving for the mark, Shaw saw the buoy and their opponent almost simultaneously. It was one of those visions he would remember. *Eagle* emerged from a high wall of mist with no noise except a tumbling bow-wave, barrelling towards them on starboard tack with right of way.

'Ready to tack!' Shaw shouted.

Baltir and Ulder hovered over their winches.

'Tack!' he roared. They came through fast, faster than might have been necessary under other conditions. Now, hardly sixty feet from *Eagle*, they were on parallel course. Shaw bore away ruthlessly to pick up further speed. Neck and neck, the two crews fought for a foot here, a few inches there.

Shaw, as leeward helmsman, began to squeeze up, exercising right of way. For a few seconds more than necessary, Ericson seemed to be holding course in violation of the rules. Shaw sensed that while the fog obscured his actions from witnesses Ericson might try to shut *Leningrad* out from the buoy, but was probably dissuaded from doing so by the presence of Vaaren on board. He grudgingly eased upwind, allowing Shaw to exercise right of way.

The mist was clearing. Every extra second was valuable to *Leningrad*. The spinnaker pole was ready to hoist, the sheets led, the big full-bellied sail ready to soar upwards. In Estonian, Shaw called:

'We won't bear away for a while.'

The others understood. He intended to take the battle to Ericson.

The buoy was nearing. Shaw should have rounded, but the rules gave him right of way in this course. He saw Ericson swing the wheel towards him and then, realizing his mistake, veer upwind, losing a few seconds of power in the sails. Remorselessly, keeping within the rules, Shaw squeezed up. Locked in their respective positions, *Leningrad* blocked *Eagle* from turning.

Eagle's tactician scrambled on to the rail, put his hands to his mouth, and screamed. 'Turn, you dumb fuckers!' Rage turned his final tone into a high falsetto. Shaw tried to remember where he'd heard that tone before. An old Beach Boys number, maybe. Or Jan and Dean.

Shaw said to Brod: 'Did you hear something?'

'A seagull, I think.'

The two boats were thundering towards the spectator fleet. Shaw could see the dark mass of the spectator boats approaching. *Eagle* was unable to turn for the next course buoy without touching *Leningrad*, which in turn would have disqualified her. Around them the mist continued to clear.

The American tactician was on the rail again, screaming: 'Turn your fucking ass!'

'The people that one meets,' Shaw said to Brod.

'And the noise,' Brod said.

Shaw couldn't believe his luck. The motor boat they were approaching had an American flag. It wasn't *Eagle*'s tender, but it was one of her entourage. He could see her name. *Snow Bird*. A streamlined palace.

By squeezing *Eagle* upwind a bit more, Shaw calculated, he could drive her right into the side of the motor yacht. He squeezed.

Seventy yards, closing. *Eagle*'s tactician slipped back to the cockpit to take a rapid look at his instruments. *Eagle* would have to go upwind of the motor yacht. If it went upwind, it would lose precious distance . . .

With a sudden thunder of sails Ericson bit the bullet and turned upwind.

'Ease sheets!' Shaw shouted. He swung downwind while Migdal and the foredeck crew hauled the spinnaker aloft. The huge sail set with a satisfying punch. Behind them *Eagle*'s genoa fluttered as it fouled the pole, but even so the American crew's recovery was prodigious as they tacked and reset the pole. Behind him, Shaw could hear *Eagle*'s crew boss roaring, and the agitated shouts of the crew, then the powerful punch of *Eagle*'s spinnaker as it filled.

Shaw glanced up. His own spinnaker was setting well. *Leningrad* was pulling away fast. *Eagle* was up to full speed some six boat lengths behind. The speed and power of the American crew had transformed a disaster into a mere setback. Shaw, kicking *Leningrad* off a small swell to pick up speed, experienced a reluctant admiration.

They were approaching the same wall of fog from which they had emerged. In a few minutes visibility was down to a hundred feet. In his heart Shaw suspected that Ericson, his anger sharpened by Shaw's last manoeuvre, would use countermeasures in the fog. He knew there was a chance, but he didn't believe in his heart Ericson would be so blatant. On the radar screen Ericson was on the same course.

The fog rolled over them, as thick as a blanket. It took the shine from the surface of the water, so that the sea appeared to recede and they seemed to be suspended in its folds.

'White-out,' Brod said.

Shaw looked down at the screen. He glanced back towards Vaaren, who craned forward again to study the screen. Shaw said to Vaaren, 'We don't know where he is, and he can hunt our wind.'

Vaaren did not answer. He merely noted the time.

In their attempt to throw Ericson off their track, they gybed several times. It was after the second gybe that Shaw felt in the pit of his stomach that loss of control that affects helmsmen in their nightmares. The big spinnaker collapsed, filled restlessly, collapsed again. He glanced down at the glowing, blank screen.

'Gybe!' Shaw swung the wheel. Kingissep unleashed the big sail; they reset it on the other tack. He heard like a ghostly overlay the sounds of another yacht in the same manoeuvre behind them. *Leningrad*'s spinnaker filled, collapsed. Out of the mist behind emerged the colossal belly of *Eagle*'s filled spinnaker. Relentlessly they were overhauled. *Eagle* moved past them, her sheets straining with silent power.

Brod glanced at Shaw and tried to catch his eye, emotions swimming beneath the expression on his face. Shaw knew Brod wanted to say something to Vaaren, something about children who knew much about technology but little about anything else, or even something about the person of Ericson himself. Shaw shook his head once. Brod, whose fiery temper was legendary, lowered the corners of his mouth and merely shrugged.

Instead it was Shaw who spoke. He said to Brod, 'Now that he's achieved his objective, perhaps he'll restore our radar.'

Seventeen seconds later the screen cleared and they could see *Eagle*, a clear five lengths ahead, preparing to round the leeward mark.

Brod said, in a voice tinged with irony, 'Radar works again.'

Nineteen

A movement of white spaces; then the leeward buoy reared out of the mist.

At a shout from Brod, Kingissep swung out on the

spinnaker pole and wrenched out the snap-shackle pin. The huge sail fluttered and hauled down. Maask gathered its folds through the hatch. Shaw swung *Leningrad*'s wheel and the winchmen moved into a driving roll as they hauled in the sheets. They rounded out of sight of *Eagle* and began the windward leg, pushing forward into the swirling mist.

Shaw watched the other blip on the radar screen. Ahead of them Ericson tacked. They hit an area of deep fog, visibility down to sixty feet.

'Tack,' Shaw called.

The big yacht seemed to force aside mist as he flung it sideways. The boom crashed above him, sending a spray of tiny droplets down from the mainsail.

Shaw sensed the mood of anger on *Leningrad*. It was tangible; it demanded an outlet. Such considerations were part of the rhythm of aggression and defence that were fundamental to match-racing. Good helmsmen matched this psychological rhythm to the physical ebb and flow of the contest.

'*Eagle* tacks,' Brod called.

In the moment of tack, the blip that was *Eagle* showed a brief effulgence, as the curves of the loose sails caught radar reflections. On the new tack it settled again.

'What do you think?' Shaw asked Brod.

By following their manoeuvres, tack for tack, *Eagle* placed herself between *Leningrad* and the source of wind. Called 'close cover', it was effectively a stranglehold, one hand on the windpipe of the opposition. But the desire to choke the opponent's wind carried its own price. To maintain its stranglehold, the lead boat was constrained to match tack with gruelling tack. Each time the second boat tried to break away, the lead boat must tack again. This gave a certain power to the second helmsman who could, if he wished, initiate a match of strength against strength.

Brod knew the direction of his enquiry, and merely nodded his assent.

'Tacking duel,' Shaw called forward.

It was like the order to prepare for a broadside in an old battleship. Graf Ulder and Berol Baltir shook their shoulders and settled down, leaning over the big coffee-grinder winches. The trimmers Soren Gir and Edvigs Tarku pulled their gloves tighter. In the forward part of the huge open cockpit Stephan Migdal and Herman Maask temporarily set aside their roles of mastman and sail preparer, and now geared themselves to act as reserve winchgrinders.

There was an element of brutality in tacking several times in succession. One tack demanded flair and co-ordination; several demanded sheer physical energy and stamina.

Shaw watched the blip on the radar screen.

'Tack!'

They came through precisely, striving to minimize any loss of speed, bearing away as the sails came in to pick up power, gathering speed and slowly feathering higher into wind.

'*Eagle* covers,' Brod said.

'Seven four, seven six, seven seven.'

'Tack!'

The winchgrinders moved forward almost on to their toes and hit the pedestal, using brute force to bring the sail in fast, then clicked into higher gearing as the stress increased and they fine-tuned the sail in time with the helmsman's final feathering.

He waited until they reached seven knots before tacking again. The mist was uneven. Sometimes visibility would open up a corridor to a couple of hundred feet. Just beyond their vision Ericson on *Eagle* was trying to choke off their wind.

'*Eagle* covers again,' Brod confirmed.

After seven consecutive tacks *Eagle* continued to fight

manoeuvre for manoeuvre. Shaw watched the sudden incandescence on the screen as *Eagle* tacked in answer.

'Tack!'

Between sorties, the winchgrinders collapsed forward, breathing heavily. They were down to six knots between tacks, then five.

'We gain one and a half boat lengths,' Brod said.

'Tack!'

Bearing off to pick up power, Shaw glanced down towards the radar screen. *Eagle* continued on course without responding. Shaw used the short interval to build up speed.

He glanced at the screen again. The two boats were diverging now on separate courses.

'*Eagle* tacks,' Brod confirmed.

It was a subtle but important shift in tactics. Even though *Eagle* was now on parallel tack, Ericson's delayed tack meant there was too much distance between the boats to strangle *Leningrad*'s wind. Unnerved by a loss of lead distance during the tacking duel, Ericson had opted instead to apply a 'loose' cover.

'Settle,' Shaw called forward.

'Seven seven, seven eight,' Arlof sang out.

An oblong of mist shaped like a locomotive drifted past; then visibility opened up several hundred feet, accompanied by a burst of sunlight. A hundred yards away *Eagle* appeared suddenly, her sails translucent, running parallel. The sighting touched a nerve in *Leningrad*'s crew; it moved amongst them like a rumour in a crowd. They were in physical contact once again.

Vaaren was so quiet Shaw had almost forgotten him. As host, Shaw felt a responsibility for his guest. He swivelled briefly to glance at Vaaren. He was peering into the mist ahead.

The breeze had risen to fifteen knots. Shaw gave the order to peel the light headsail for a medium.

'Eight two,' Brod called.

At the top mark *Eagle* slid round five lengths ahead. Shaw followed, sheets were eased rapidly, they set the spinnaker and headed off in pursuit.

Ericson was wily. His downwind tactics showed a masterly appreciation of angles and close-quarter fighting. Try as he might, Shaw was unable to get closer. At the downwind buoy *Eagle* had extended her three-length lead to five lengths.

Spinnakers were doused. Around them the mist continued to clear. Sometimes Shaw could see the black masses of the spectator fleet. As it became clear *Eagle* was ahead on the final beat, there was a throaty blast of the siren from the US nuclear carrier *Nemesis*.

Appearing out of the fog well ahead of her rival, *Eagle* powered towards the line. A Japanese press photographer caught a magnificent picture of the yacht breaking away from the cliff face of fog, her sails burnished by fleeting sunlight, her bow slicing a crest. To those in the spectator fleet *Eagle* must have appeared invincible. Not for the first time, it occurred to Shaw that when Ericson wasn't trying to cheat, he was an extraordinary sailor. It was a strange psychological mixture.

Ericson swung into wind to shoot the line. The smoke from the finish gun had hardly cleared before it was followed by a series of exultant hoots from the warships on the horizon.

But the Estonians had their own consolations, not apparent to the audience. The final distance between them at the finish line was seven lengths. They had been ahead until countermeasures had been used. Even after the lead gained by *Eagle*, they had held on doggedly, hauling back several lengths until the downwind buoy. It was a curious elision of appearance and reality. The appearance was that *Eagle* had won three races, and was powering towards a clear and momentous victory. The underlying pattern was that her margins of win were being steadily eroded.

When the second gun sent its cloud of cordite across *Leningrad*'s decks, the Estonian crew stood up to shake the tensions of the race from their shoulders and muscles. Shaw saw none of that terrible exhaustion which a psychological loss visits upon racing sailors. The sails came down and were packed away by a crew which felt it had been balked of its victory.

Shaw turned towards Vaaren, their witness.

Twenty

'Do you have everything you require?' he asked him.

Vaaren nodded. 'An interesting day.'

Shaw remembered with a certain pleasure Vaaren's bulging eyes as they thundered towards *Eagle* in the mist with the radar screen blank and white as a tablecloth. He said, 'Not too interesting, I hope.'

The shadow of a smile moved across Vaaren's controlled features. He said, 'I will report my findings to the committee.'

One advantage of losing the race was that the yacht was not pressed by well-wishers. They were able to lower sails and stow the gear in more leisurely fashion. Ahead of them the coxswain of their tender flung a towing rope to Kingissep, who made fast on *Leningrad*'s bow. As the mist cleared, aircraft appeared out of the sky above them. Their shadows drifted across the surface of the water.

The scene reminded Shaw of the changeable nature of marine weather. Sunlight poured down in gold columns between banks of mist. Perhaps a thousand yachts and spectator craft left shining wakes on the surface of the water, made luminous by sunlight. Reflected blues and greens were flung upwards into the whites and gold of clouds. Bursts of spray as *Leningrad*'s bow sliced a crest were refracted into brief rainbow colours.

The shore appeared, a long, low bar. As the mist rolled back, he could see the rolling pine forests beyond. Course-patrol vessels cleared a path through spectator craft to the entrance of their own small harbour. Their tender towed them towards their mooring point until *Leningrad*, that bird with folded wings, lay gently against her fenders.

The press at the Estonian encampment was relatively sparse. Shaw guessed that the majority were already gathering at the Kunov media centre for the triumphal press briefing of the US syndicate. Behind the building shed protruded the blades of a civil helicopter. He saw the short, stocky figure of Aegu waiting on the shore.

They tied up and made fast. With *Leningrad* secured, Vaaren prepared to step off. As he stepped ashore Aegu moved forward and reached across to shake Shaw's hand.

'*Tovarich.*'

'Good day, Mr President.'

'I hear you are flying a protest flag.'

'Our radar screen blanked out in the mist at one or two crucial times. We think it might have been electronic countermeasures.'

Shaw picked up his sailing bag and stepped ashore. He allowed his eyes to drift through the crowd, but he could see no sign of Maria or Jack. Aegu said, 'Do you have a good case?'

He shrugged. 'A circumstantial one.'

They walked back along the quay towards the main buildings.

'You hold out no hope of success?'

'Very little. The Americans have a specialist, Mulvinney, an international lawyer. When they rammed *Novy Mir* Mulvinney managed to get them off the hook. What chance do we stand today?'

After a moment Aegu said, 'Do you think a former apparatchik and Estonian politician would be able to stand up to an American lawyer?'

When Shaw was young, he would madden his grandfather Sam Shaw by asking, 'Would a lion beat a tiger in a fight? Would a wolf beat a polar bear?' And Sam Shaw would tease him in return by replying, 'Well now, if the lion had a bad night, and the wolf had a wooden leg, let me see now ...' Was Aegu offering to defend *Leningrad*'s case himself? It was an unexpected suggestion, and it caught Shaw off guard. If only to humour him, he said, 'Could you spare the time from your political duties?'

'After all,' Aegu said, ignoring his question, 'I cannot do worse than lose on your behalf. And according to you, you will lose the protest anyway.'

'I can't argue with your logic,' Shaw replied.

'Good. I must make one or two calls from the helicopter about appointments concerning tomorrow. Perhaps we could meet in half an hour so that you can brief me on the circumstances of today's race?'

'Poor Jim,' Maria said.

In the bungalow Shaw put down his holdall and picked up Jack.

He looked him in the eye. 'Beaten three times out of three. What do you think about that, young man?'

Jack looked towards Maria, as if studying her response to his father's question. She smiled at him and he laughed back at Shaw.

'It's a terrible thing, isn't it?' Shaw said.

Jack laughed again.

He put him down and said to Maria, 'I have to debrief the crew now. Then I have a meeting with Aegu. Looks as though I'll be at a protest meeting this evening. Our radar blanked out again today.'

'You look tired.'

'I'm tired physically. Otherwise I feel pretty good.'

Maria came up to him and slipped her arms around him. 'You wouldn't have taken it this well a few years ago.'

'Win a few, lose a few,' he said. Praise still embarrassed him like nothing else.

Brod and Arlof were waiting for him in the little office. Shaw kicked off.

'Aegu's going to represent us at the protest this evening. I'm going to brief him on the incidents yesterday and today in a few minutes. Is there anything you wanted to talk about?'

Arlof asked: 'Tell us about Americans.'

'Americans? Americans are good people. They're mostly honest and they have warm hearts. They're ingenious and hard working. What else do you want to know?'

'Why aren't there any of those on *Eagle*?' Brod asked.

'Strange, isn't it?' Shaw agreed.

'Does it not upset you, this cheating?' Brod pursued.

'No,' Shaw said. 'Not any more.'

'Why not?'

'Because I don't care who wins. I think wanting to win too much is a poisoned cup.'

'Why are you here, then?'

'Because I wanted to do what I could to help Illich, and I like you.'

There was another silence. Arlof said, with understandable weight:

'It would help Estonia if we won.'

'And it would annoy everyone else,' Shaw said. 'You want to talk further about this? I have a family. I put a lot of effort into helping them. They are happy, I am

101

building something here. No one's getting annoyed. We've done well enough already. If we go out there and win, we make a lot of people mad. Is that what life's about?'

Brod glanced at Arlof. It was difficult to assess their precise feeling. Was it anger, frustration, or simply a matter of concern?

'Are you joking, perhaps?' Arlof asked.

Shaw continued. 'This protest meeting tonight, for instance. I'll do it, but does it matter, ultimately? Don't you think we're like spoiled children – all of us?'

He knew he shouldn't have unburdened himself. But the temptation to say what he honestly felt to two trusted colleagues was too great.

'You want to lose, maybe?' Brod insisted.

'No, I don't. I want to win like hell. But I can't justify it in any way. I can't see why winning is the most important thing any more. I'm not going to rip myself apart if we lose.'

Shaw looked from face to face. 'Are you guys worried about me? Think I'm crazy? Want me to step back so someone else can have a go?'

Brod shrugged his question aside. 'Without you, we wouldn't be here.'

But it didn't resolve the issue. Arlof said calmly, as if it were an accusation, 'You are our best helmsman.'

'After Illich, maybe. I do my best.'

'No,' Arlof said quietly. 'Since we are being honest . . . Illich was a better man, a much greater man. But you are a better helmsman.'

Now Shaw sensed their anger like a thundercloud. For several seconds no one spoke.

'Let's go,' Brod said. They walked out, leaving him to stare at the ceiling.

Twenty-one

'Comrade gentlemen . . .' Vikunov, chairman of the five-man protest committee, addressed the two parties with his curious combination of courtesy and bureaucratic tradition. 'I welcome you to this session of the protest committee. As Chairman, I shall ensure order at this session on behalf of my fellow members. Before we are seated, I extend good wishes to our American guests of the *Eagle* syndicate, whose spokesman shall be Mr Mulvinney. I also welcome the Russian defence syndicate, whose spokesman shall be President Aegu of Estonia.'

The two parties sat down on either side of the long pine table. Shaw looked across the table at the trio of Frank Mulvinney, John Ericson III, and his father John Ericson Jnr.

Shaw and Brod flanked President Aegu. Aegu lit a Prima. Exhaling, he blew smoke ostentatiously across the table.

Vikunov said, 'Before we proceed, there are two points which I announce formally. This meeting is convened because both parties have objected to the use of electronic countermeasures. Both parties appear to believe that the other is responsible, and have requested a full investigation. The second matter is that the defender *Leningrad* elected to carry on board one of our distinguished judges, Nils Vaaren, as witness to the proceedings of today's race. The committee is in receipt of his confidential report, and will take this into account amongst the other evidence.' Vikunov swung towards the Estonians. 'Will you speak first, President Aegu?'

Aegu nodded, inhaled, blew another stream of smoke at the Americans, put his cigarette in an ashtray with some obvious reluctance and, without hurrying, stood up. Across the table the three Americans regarded him like a rare animal that had crawled out of a lake.

'Thank you, Mr Chairman. I will be brief. During the last two races, most of the racing has been carried out in dense fog, with visibility often down to a reported hundred feet, sometimes even less. For much of the racing, the two boats were out of sight of one another. In these conditions, the installation of an effective radar was crucial to the performance of both boats.

'In yesterday's race, the radar screen of the defender *Leningrad* went suddenly blank. But it is important to denote what is meant by this. The screen did not recede to the familiar grey of a switched-off system. The screen was lit up, live, white. There was no sign of loss of current. But it showed no image. To be precise, from the time of 10.23 to 10.29 hours the image on the screen vanished. Those who are familiar testify to the fact that the effect described is typically generated by electronic interference of some kind. As a further vindication of this assumption, after the time given, the radar returned to perfect function. There appeared to be nothing wrong with the internal mechanism of the radar. Rather, the blanked screen appeared to be a response to outside circumstances.'

Aegu paused, turning his short, powerful frame to face the five judges.

'The exact timing of this interference is also important. It occurred as the two boats were running downwind in low visibility, when an appreciation of the other yacht's position is crucial. *Eagle* had overtaken *Leningrad* by taking her wind. By moving ahead *Eagle* herself became potentially vulnerable to precisely this type of tactic. However, in order for the defender to make such a counter-attack, it was crucial to know *Eagle*'s position. It was exactly then that *Leningrad*'s radar went white. When the radar screen returned, *Eagle* was ten lengths ahead and effectively out of reach.

'To summarize, there are two types of evidence which

104

point to the use of countermeasures. The first is that the screen showed the classic symptoms of electronic interference. The second is that the timing of the interference was such as to cause most damage to the chances of the defending yacht.'

Aegu paused again, glanced down at the transcript Shaw had given him, raised his head.

'Following this incident, *Leningrad*'s helmsman wrote a formal letter to the protest committee stating clearly that he suspected the use of electronic countermeasures by the challenge syndicate, and requested observation of the course to ensure fair play. At Mr Shaw's request, the committee passed a copy of this letter to the *Eagle* syndicate. The defending group felt that since conditions of fog and low visibility were predicted for the following day, additional action should be expedited. In a further meeting with the chairman of the committee, Mr Vikunov, it was suggested that witnesses were placed on both boats during the course of the following day's racing in order to ensure fair play. Mr Vikunov agreed. In the event, the *Eagle* syndicate exercised their right in refusing to be host to such a witness. *Leningrad* took on board a witness in the form of Mr Nils Vaaren.

'Despite the letter to the *Eagle* syndicate and the presence of a witness on board *Leningrad*, a similar incident took place today. On the second leg of the course, with *Eagle* behind them, the crew of *Leningrad* found their radar screen showed the familiar characteristics of electronic interference at a critical time. The interference took place between 10.34 and 10.47 hours. During this period, while *Leningrad* lacked any radar knowledge of their opponent's position, *Eagle* was able to turn a six-boat-length deficit into a four-boat-length lead.

'In summing up the case on behalf of the defender, I submit that there is a clear pattern of interference with the radar screen in a manner calculated to affect the

105

outcome of the races on both days. It is a pattern in which, I repeat, on two consecutive days the use of radar played a key role in the tactical outcome of the races. On both occasions *Leningrad*'s screen showed interference during a period in which such interference proved to be of maximum advantage to *Eagle*, and maximum disadvantage to *Leningrad*.'

Aegu had an orator's predilection for dramatic pauses. He examined his notes, then addressed his audience again.

'The fact that such interference took place on the first day is cause enough for a protest. But that it was repeated on the second day under the eyes of an independent witness appointed by the protest committee provides clear proof that a breach of rules took place. Accordingly, in conformity with the rules governing the competition, *Eagle* should be disqualified from both races.'

Aegu halted and sat down. Shaw felt he had put forward his case with considerable calm and authority, and with unexpected precision.

As Chairman, Vikunov said, 'Would you like to answer, Mr Mulvinney?'

Mulvinney drew himself up to his full height, extended a brief, sallow smile towards Aegu as if in professional acknowledgment of his advocacy, and removed his glasses to address the committee.

'Gentlemen, I listened with great interest to the case which has been made by our distinguished guest here tonight. Naturally, I am shocked by some of the imputations made, and I think it is important to consider all the issues relating to the matter. Before I answer these serious allegations in detail, I would like to make a few general comments.

'We are in a yacht race for the America's Cup, an insignificant sporting event in one sense, but in another an important symbolic event which unites our two great countries. I say this because it is extremely important that we make no hasty conclusions, and that the outcome takes all possible factors into account.

'In many of the cases with which I have been involved, the motive for an action is important. It provides a background for the action under consideration. It happens that, following the tragic collision of the two yachts, *Eagle* and *Novy Mir*, the score stood at two-nil. Since then we have had the good fortune to win the three races which followed, so that the score now stands at three-two. I do not deny that the competition has been close, but that is what we have come to expect from your fine sailors. Nevertheless, we could claim, with some conviction, that the tide is flowing strongly in our direction, and that since that tragic collision, we have proved to most commentators that we are the superior team. Now I should like to ask you, what reason do we have for cheating? What would be our motive? Why would we risk what we have already gained? I believe the gentlemen opposite should furnish us with a motive for doing what they have accused us of doing. Until they do so, I submit that their case is highly circumstantial.

'That is my first point. But it has a bearing on my second point. It seems that *Leningrad*'s radar suffered a temporary breakdown which appears to show the symptoms of outside interference, through the use of what are called "electronic countermeasures". I am not an electronics expert. I do not know what strange patterns of interaction and interference exist around us. But what I do know is that the race course was surrounded with a spectator fleet of more than a thousand marine craft from launches to cruise ships to military vessels, many if not most with active radar and telecommunications. In this huge swath of electromagnetic activity surrounding the course, is it not likely that there are patterns of interference?

'Thirdly, without a motive to deploy, I fail to see how

107

such activity can be ascribed to *Eagle* directly or to any boat in her entourage. Is it not far more likely to be the result of random or unattributable electromagnetic activity from the vast array of active transmitters in the close vicinity? I submit to you that we should apply the time-honoured principle of Occam's razor. Let us look for the simplest explanation first.

'Fourthly, gentlemen.' Mulvinney swung his glasses from his right hand gently. 'The pattern of interference must have been maddening for *Leningrad* and her crew. I am fully prepared to accept that the two sequences of interference occurred at difficult times in the race. But I have two comments to make on this. Surely in such a race, interference in the radar puts the boat affected at a disadvantage at almost any time? Not being able to detect the opponent is always a disadvantage. What I am saying is that whatever time it occurred the opposing yacht would have been able to take advantage of the failure of the instrument, so that the fact that an advantage occurred to *Eagle* at the time of incident does not prove that the timing was significant, it merely proves the general principle that the failure of an important instrument is a disadvantage to the boat affected.

'Fifthly, the "failure of an instrument" is an important phrase, and with respect I submit we consider its implications. The America's Cup competition has always been a confrontation not only of humans but of technology. The quality of equipment has always had an effect on the outcome. That is in the nature of the competition. Now it would seem to be the case that the US syndicate possesses radar equipment which is superior to the defender's. For example, it would seem to function better in the general race environment. It is not so readily subject to interference. That is a perfectly legitimate superiority. Gentlemen, I should like to ask you, in this contest of technologies, is that

108

anything to be ashamed of? And isn't this protest simply an understandable case of sour grapes?'

Mulvinney waved a hand.

'My summary is therefore as follows. In a court of law, a man is innocent until proven guilty. Can we say that there is a shred of evidence that, without any clear motive, the *Eagle* syndicate deliberately broke the rules in order to cheat when the game is going our way? Do you believe, if we had done so on yesterday's race, we would have the stupidity to do the same on today's race, when the committee has seen fit to place a witness on board *Leningrad* to catch us in the act? I ask you to grant us a little common sense and intelligence. If you will kindly do so, I think you will perceive that the allegations set out here today have no substance whatsoever.

'There is one final point which I should like to make. We are in the middle of a competition between our two nations, a competition based on rules which both sides are bound to obey. It is a very serious thing to accuse one side – any side – of attempting to break the rules in a cavalier fashion. It brings dishonour on us all. I believe it is a sad day that we should be called to answer such allegations. Gentleman, those are my comments.'

It was not merely the quality of Mulvinney's defence – which Shaw expected – it was the timing and tone, the weight of his delivery, the certainty of his conviction. In the earlier hearing over the ramming of *Novy Mir* by *Eagle*, Mulvinney had dazzled and intimidated. Now he was urbanity itself. Shaw knew that Mulvinney had buried their protest, that he had introduced enough doubt at every juncture. There were simply too many areas of doubt for any committee to uphold their protest.

Twenty-two

Mulvinney sat down.

Shaw glanced across into the face of Ericson. Ericson showed no emotion. He leaned sideways so that Mulvinney could whisper something in his ear. He smiled.

Vikunov stood up at the head of the table.

'President Aegu, is there anything you would like to say on behalf of the defence syndicate?'

'May I consult briefly with my colleagues, Mr Chairman?'

'Certainly.'

Aegu turned towards Shaw, and whispered: 'I see what you mean about American lawyers.'

Shaw said to Aegu, 'May I say a few words?'

Aegu nodded. To Vikunov, Shaw said, 'Comrade Chairman, I have a few things I should like to say in answer to Mr Mulvinney.'

Vikunov nodded. 'Please proceed.'

Shaw stood up carefully. 'I think I am old enough to accept that things will not always go my own way, and that is part of my training as a helmsman.

'What I witnessed out there were electronic counter-measures against our radar, on two consecutive days. Both incidents could not have been better timed to produce maximum damage to my syndicate's efforts. The second incident, and its effect on our performance, was witnessed by Mr Vaaren. During that interference, our six-length lead was transformed into a four-length lead by *Eagle*. Because of its timing, and its clear effects on two consecutive days, I have no doubt that this electronic interference was caused by the opposing syndicate, or by its agents. Whatever the source, it gave the *Eagle* syndicate an advantage over us, and directly influenced the outcome of the race.

'Mr Mulvinney says that the tide of the competition is moving towards the US syndicate. With all due respect, Mr Chairman, I submit that is misleading. The first interference occurred when the score was two-one to *Leningrad*. The second occurred when the score was two-all. If only one of the events in question affected the outcome unfairly, then we would be leading three-two. If the interference influenced the outcome in both races, we would be victors at four-one. So Mr Mulvinney's contention that there was no motive for the *Eagle* group to cheat because the series was swinging their way is inaccurate.'

Shaw paused. He knew he had lost the appeal, but the realization had a liberating effect. It cleared his mind, and he was determined to inflict what damage he could.

'Mr Mulvinney says that we have not furnished a motive for the *Eagle* syndicate to use countermeasures. One possible motive, I suggest, is to win the series, even if this means breaking the rules that are the essence of any sport.'

Shaw paused again. Perhaps in the long term he would regret what he was about to say, but it was something he had saved up a long time.

'Mr Mulvinney said that facts have to be examined in the light of the broader pattern. I should like the same leniency as him to describe this broader pattern. The broader pattern in which I view this incident is that two years ago I refused to sail with an American syndicate precisely because of their belief that to break the rules is fine if you can get away with it . . .'

Mulvinney was on his feet like a whiplash. 'Mr Chairman, this is an irrelevant slur. You cannot allow this man to proceed . . .'

Vikunov smiled. 'Why not, Mr Mulvinney?'

'It simply isn't germane to the case. And besides . . .'

'Besides?'

'Besides which Mr Shaw is a renegade who has left his own side. His evidence . . .'

'His evidence is therefore worthless?'

'My thoughts precisely, Mr Chairman.'

'Since you have now both exchanged insults, I consider the matter is evenly balanced. Please continue, Mr Shaw.'

Mulvinney sat down slowly. Shaw continued:

'Winning at all costs is part of my experience of the American syndicates in which I took part. I became so disheartened by this attitude, and the things that it brought about, that I deliberately turned back at the finish line of the last America's Cup as a protest . . .'

Mulvinney was on his feet again.

'Mr Chairman, this is outrageous. This is a slander not only against our syndicate but against the whole American nation.'

Vikunov nodded towards Mulvinney, and addressed himself to Shaw

'Mr Shaw,' Vikunov said pleasantly. 'Mr Mulvinney is right. We are adjudicating this America's Cup, not the previous one. Will you confine your evidence to the matter in hand?'

'I apologize, Mr Chairman. I am not slandering the American nation. I am attempting to slander Mr Mulvinney and the *Eagle* syndicate, who purport to represent America.'

'Mr Chairman . . .' Mulvinney was on his feet. 'This is disgraceful . . .'

Vikunov nodded amiably.

'Mr Shaw, please keep to the subject in hand.'

'I promise to confine my comments from now on to this series.' Shaw had the floor, and he paused. 'Mr Mulvinney was discussing the broader pattern of races in the series. He said that there was no motive to cheat. I am replying to that statement. The first protest we raised in this series was over the collision of the two yachts *Eagle* and *Novy Mir*. We said that *Eagle* had deliberately rammed and sunk *Novy Mir*. Mr Mulvinney argued that the accused was innocent until proved guilty, and that there was sufficient doubt to put aside our allegations. If we treat each of these incidents in isolation, in each one there is sufficient doubt to allow the accused to be declared innocent. But if we consider them together, we could say that they form a general pattern, a pattern of continuous and wilful transgression.

'I am a helmsman, and it is part of my function to weigh up probabilities. Suppose that in the first incident – the ramming of *Novy Mir*, the likelihood that the *Eagle* syndicate is innocent is ten to one against. And let us say, for the sake of the argument, that the second incident – the white-out of our radar screen – is the same. And the same is true for the third incident, when our screen was whited out again. In statistical terms, the likelihood of a transgression increases as a multiple of the chances in each individual case. As each successive transgression takes place, the likelihood that the *Eagle* syndicate is not cheating becomes smaller and smaller – infinitesimally small, in fact.'

'Mr Chairman . . .'

'Your objection?'

'Each case must be judged on its own merits. If you adjudge us innocent on previous occasions, then by normal principles of law, they are not material to the case.'

'Mr Shaw?'

'Mr Mulvinney challenged us to provide a motive for transgressing a rule. I am outlining a broad pattern of behaviour which indicates the presence of a consistent motive.'

'Please continue, Mr Shaw.'

'If you should ask, Mr Chairman, what is the statistical likelihood of the cheating, I should like to repeat that it

113

is a multiple of the previous likelihoods of cheating. This is a crucial point.'

Mulvinney stood up.

'Mr Chairman, if you allow Mr Shaw to break the normal rules by pursuing this line of argument then, with utmost regret, we will be forced to consider our position, and I will advise my clients to retire from this meeting and to declare no faith in the operation of the protest committee.'

Mulvinney sat down.

'Mr Shaw?'

Shaw said, 'I have made my point about probability, and I ask your permission to raise one more point which Mr Mulvinney himself has raised. He says that the *Eagle* syndicate must be treated as innocent until proved guilty.

'I question that principle. This is not a court of law. No one is going to prison. We are discussing whether someone is persistently interfering with the outcome of the races in a manner which transgresses the rules. It is not up to us to prove absolute guilt, but demonstrate whether it is more or less likely that what we believe happened actually occurred.'

Shaw had learned something about exposition. If you believe in your case, sometimes the words will come. If he had made a fool of himself, he couldn't do any worse now. Perhaps later he would feel ashamed at his own allegations, but now he felt cool and pure.

'I base my life on the assumption that the sun will rise tomorrow. But I cannot prove it beyond a reasonable doubt. We must weigh up the likelihood of whether or not that party is cheating. We are surely allowed to consider whether, in the light of three incidents in the same series, we have a consistent pattern.'

'Mr Chairman.' Mulvinney stood up to his full height, and turned to face Vikunov directly. 'As of now I am advising my client to consider his position. We will not participate in this protest committee further until I have consulted in private.'

Vikunov said, 'That is your privilege. In the meantime, your decision to leave us will not prevent us from continuing to hear the evidence from Mr Shaw.'

Mulvinney nodded, though it seemed to Shaw it was not with his usual grace.

Shaw did not wait for Mulvinney to leave the room before continuing.

'Mr Chairman and members of the committee, the America's Cup is a competition which means nothing if the rules are not maintained. The entire competition becomes reduced if we allow rule-breaking to occur. It is surely in our common interests to make certain that any reasonable likelihood of consistent interference with the rules is treated with the greatest severity. The principle is different from a court of law, where the accused is likely to go to prison or have his liberty curtailed. Here the main consideration is to maintain the fairness of the rules. I believe this should over-ride individual interests, or group interests.'

He halted. 'Thank you, Mr Chairman, for hearing me out.'

Vikunov waited until he had sat down.

'Are there any further matters relating to this protest that you wish to raise?'

'No.'

'Then, comrade gentlemen, if you would kindly adjourn to one of the waiting rooms, we will discuss the matter and call you when we have reached a decision.'

Twenty-three

In the waiting room Aegu's two guards took up position in the chairs on either side of the door. Aegu patted his pockets for cigarettes and said, 'I thought people who came from Maine didn't speak very much.'

Shaw smiled. 'We save it up for important occasions.'

'You should think of a political career.'

He didn't answer. There was a gulf between his and Aegu's perception. Aegu thought that he could advocate on any subject. Shaw knew his own brief articulacy was limited to the slender terrain of a subject on which he was both knowledgeable and passionate.

Aegu lit a Prima, exhaled, put his lighter back in his pocket. 'You did well. That Mulvinney is a formidable advocate.'

'They rely on him. They think he can get them out of anything. I know we've lost our case, but maybe it was worthwhile just to rattle the guy.'

'Perhaps one day he will over-reach himself,' Aegu suggested. 'It was a fascinating insight into the problems that face you. I am afraid I must leave you shortly. I am called to another meeting in St Petersburg this evening.'

'You did everything you could,' Shaw said. 'We're grateful.'

Aegu stood up. 'I wish you good luck.'

They heard him walk down the corridor, followed by the pad of his two bodyguards.

'Aegu,' Brod said. 'An elephant with a heart of gold.' He shook his head and smiled.

The committee deliberated for perhaps forty minutes. The two teams were called in to the main room.

Seated, Shaw studied the faces on the other side of the table. Ericson appeared calm, his albino eyes returning his stare. Mulvinney had regained his composure. Ericson's father was content to study the proceedings.

Vikunov said, 'Comrade gentlemen. We have reached our judgement. Our view is that sufficient doubt remains over the source of the electronic interference to reject the protest of both the defenders and challengers.'

Shaw watched a series of smiles move behind the eyes of the three men opposite.

'However,' he continued, 'we also accept in principle what Mr Shaw has argued. We believe that if one syndicate continues to throw suspicion on itself by its actions, the likelihood that it is breaking the rules becomes cumulative. We on the committee would like to make this clear. If there are any further transgressions which throw doubt upon the good offices of the *Eagle* syndicate, we will take into consideration its previous record.'

Despite the warning over future transgressions, it was a further victory for Ericson. The smiles didn't fade over the implicit threat. Shaw knew them too well. They were confident. They had taken risks to establish their lead, and it was paying off. The *Eagle* group were where they wanted to be, three-two up. One more win and they would take home the America's Cup. Shaw had a glimpse of the implications of future history. Everyone opposite him would bask in its glory for the rest of their lives. As winners, too, they would create their own historical version. Shaw would be cast as villain, the American renegade who not only had the audacity to support the rival team, but to impugn their motives. In their own accounts, Shaw would slander not just the *Eagle* syndicate, but the entire American nation. A glimpse of this future floated in front of Shaw's eyes. But it was not as shocking as the second insight, which moved beside the first. He couldn't give a damn. Something had happened to his own view of life's conduct. The only version he knew about was the real one, the one directly lived and experienced. His only reference was his own conscience.

'Comrade gentlemen,' Vikunov said. 'I thank you for attending.'

It was almost ten when the meeting adjourned. When Shaw returned to the bungalow, Maria and Ilena were sitting up at table. There were several cups of coffee on the sink. Shaw smelled the unmistakable odour of Prima cigarettes. Glancing at the table, he saw cigarette stubs in a saucer that had been used as an ashtray.

'How did it go?' Maria asked.

'They're still three-two up.'

'President Aegu's helicopter left half an hour ago.'

An image came to Shaw of the machine thundering into the air, its rotors blurred like smoke; Aegu's chariot, sweeping north towards St Petersburg.

'He called in here for a few minutes before he left,' Ilena said. She stood up to make a fresh cup of coffee. 'He told us we're doing excellent work here, running the camp. He knows where the real power lies, of course.'

'Of course,' Shaw said. 'He is an expert on power.'

He looked at Maria, setting out fresh cups on the stainless steel stand. She seemed preoccupied.

Ilena said, 'I must go. Brod will be wondering where I am.'

'Nothing at the office this evening?'

'Some calls expressing sympathy for the Estonian crew.'

'For being crushed by the American juggernaut.'

Maria and Ilena embraced. Then Ilena's arms were around Shaw. She hugged him strongly, then quickly left.

'What was that for?' Shaw asked.

'She's happy you've taken over so well from Illich. They all thought the Estonian team would fall apart.'

'We're not doing so well.'

'Aren't you?' Maria asked. 'I think you're doing pretty well.'

She faced him directly, with that candour of emotion that Shaw always feared in women. He said, 'I told Brod and Arlof I didn't mind losing. I'm starting to get used to losing.'

'How did your appeal go?'

'We lost that too.'

When Maria held him she swayed slightly, and he talked to cover up a savage happiness that came over him. He had lived his life in an ascetic, masculine household devoid of human contact. He could not explain to her the peculiar power of her embraces. It was not something he liked to dwell on. One of his favourite books as a child was Jack London's *White Fang*. He identified with a hero who was half wolf, half dog, who desired companionship but whose every nerve strained against contact with humans. One of his old girlfriends, Doris Schwarze, had given him Hesse's *Steppenwolf*, based on a similar theme. He had liked that too.

Maria turned away and began to wash up the cups in the sink. She said, 'I think Ilena's real reason for being happy is that Brod is not drinking. She's never known him so stable, so concentrated.'

'Maybe losing suits all of us,' Shaw said.

He moved towards the door, but he heard Maria say, so quietly she might have been talking to herself, 'I wish I believed you meant that.'

Twenty-four

Ilena had left the *New York Times* out for Shaw to see.

Eagle *leads the series 3–2 after today's race. It was a curious
match. Early mists hid the two duelling yachts. Sometimes one
caught sight of one of the huge triangular sails above the fog.
Much as if one had seen two dorsal fins above the surface on
some lonely sea, one deduced that the two monstrous machines
were fighting out there.*

At the first mark, the two yachts emerged neck and neck,
Leningrad *in the inner position. In a legitimate but ruthless
stratagem which seemed designed purposely to annoy his rival,
Shaw used his superior position to drive* Eagle *toward the
spectator boats. The maneuver forced Ericson to round up in
order to avoid collision with a large spectator craft, and resulted
in* Eagle *losing significant speed. With* Leningrad *leading the
two boats disappeared into the fog. When next seen, on the third
leg,* Eagle *had slipped into the lead and managed to maintain
it for the duration of the race.*

The overall score now lies three two to the US yacht. Eagle
*has won the last three races, and looks set to take the series
tomorrow. Shaw and the Estonians on* Leningrad *have fought
a good fight, and have not disgraced themselves.*

*It now appears certain that the US President will fly out to
watch the race tomorrow. Diplomatic sources say that a meeting
between the American and Russian Presidents has been
arranged for tomorrow evening in the staterooms of the US
aircraft carrier* Nemesis, *present at the races. The agenda is
likely to be a series of new trade deals which will be designed to
assist the improving but still shaky Russian economy. Although
certain former Soviet republics, such as Estonia, have shaken
themselves loose from the dead hand of the political bureaucracy
and established their indigenous free-market systems, most of
Russia still languishes under a centralized system which is*

neither communist nor fully capitalist, but seems to many observers to include the worst characteristics of both.

The current America's Cup presents a fitting ambience for the two Presidents to meet. America looks set to regain its amour propre after the loss of the Cup to the Russians in 2001. The Russians, for their part, unwilling to see the small, upstart Estonian republic establish itself on the international scene, are inclined to put a good face on the likely victory of the US.

In the few moments of relaxation after a work-out, Shaw put down the *New York Times*. He said to Brod, 'Looks like everybody's happy. All we have to do is go out there and lose.'

Brod did not answer. He was studying a weather chart faxed in from the weather bureau in Tartu.

Shaw said, 'You've changed, you know. You've calmed down, become more responsible. You look almost happy.'

Brod didn't look up. 'Age,' he said.

'No, I don't think so,' Shaw said. 'I think wisdom, humility, a recognition of life's deeper importance.'

Brod turned the page over to study a second sheet of ancillary figures. A thought occurred to him. 'Are you talking to me?' he asked suddenly.

'I certainly am. There's no one else here. I have to say I'm proud of you.'

'I begin to feel uneasy.'

'There's no need to,' Shaw continued. 'It's not only me I'm thinking of. You're a model to the others, too.'

Brod heaved his bulk upward from the chair and picked up the weather faxes. The door slammed behind him.

Shaw moved over to eat the toast Brod had left. He'd wondered how much of that Brod could take before leaving.

Eating the toast and holding the plate under him to catch crumbs, he walked over to the window. He peered out through the grubby glass panes. The bay was quiet, lit by sunlight. In the background a huge spectator fleet was already gathering.

Twenty-five

Leningrad kicked and plunged in the wash of the spectator boats as she was towed out to the sixth race. The weather was lighter than the previous day, though the breeze showed signs of increasing as predicted.

'Nine knots, occasionally gusting to eleven,' Arlof said.

The anticipation that this would be the final race had brought out the largest spectator fleet of the entire series. Under an almost clear sky the bay seemed black with craft. Although the coastline to the sound was relatively flat, on the few promontories of higher ground overlooking water, the crowds had returned. Like cobbles on the gently sloping land to the south they could see the reflections from the shining roofs of tens of thousands of cars.

Shaw wondered again that a mere yacht race could achieve such huge interest. Above them a dozen helicopters, each sporting television cameras, jockeyed for position. *Eagle*'s win the previous day had brought the score to three-two in favour of the Americans. The odds were now on the *Eagle* syndicate. And though Shaw did not regard himself as a political animal, he knew that much of the interest centred on the bizarre nature of the confrontation between the American giant and a group of Estonians led by a renegade American who today would receive his final justice.

Usually at this stage in the race Shaw was all jangled

nerves, but now, for some reason, he felt curiously steady. Part of it, he decided, was that he had full confidence in the crew. There was also the certainty that he was carrying on the good work of another. But a third cause was his inexplicable bout of nerves that morning, as if his body, having exacted its due punishment, would not do so a second time.

The towing launch reached the main course, and hovered under slow ahead, face to wind. *Eagle* emerged amongst her convoy of large motor launches and swung parallel. Her emergence was greeted by blasts from the horns of the great semi-circle of American warships anchored offshore. The course patrol boats began to clear the racing areas.

'Look,' Brod indicated the grey line of warships around the bay. 'Our political masters.'

Shaw noticed the movement of helicopters and launches between the warships. Diplomats, politicians, businessmen met their Russian counterparts in the staterooms of the warships and discussed policies, deals, mergers, and franchises.

'"The state,"' Brod said, '"is good at only two things. War and repression. And we want neither." Bakunin.'

Impressed, Shaw said, 'Brod the agitator.' Beneath the cynicism, there was a fiery side to his tactician. Shaw could imagine him on the barricades.

Brod pointed towards the helicopters that moved between the warships. As if to confirm his new status, he said, 'Like flies over shit.'

As the towboat reduced speed, there was a danger of *Leningrad* overtaking, propelled forward by a combination of her momentum and her fine, easily driven shape. Shaw swung the wheel so that their bow would miss the tow-boat's stern. The incident was short-lived. The wind in their mast and rigging soon eased them back until the rope tautened again.

In the waiting period before the race, *Leningrad*'s crew

123

took the opportunity to carry out a final check of gear. Berol Baltir and Graf Ulder, the winchmen, removed their tracksuits and began to warm themselves up with swinging arm movements and brisk deep knee bends.

A fickle breeze shifted direction constantly. The first leg of the course is traditionally directly upwind. Only once the wind has steadied can the windward buoy be laid precisely upwind so that the starting line is at a right angle to the wind, without 'bias'. They were forced to wait an extra half hour while the wind direction steadied and the course could be laid.

Arlof, listening on the radio, called: 'Wind now steady. Ten-minute gun in twenty minutes.'

Anxiety collected like sweat. You did not know it was there until for some reason you touched its clammy surface. 'Up sail,' Shaw shouted.

The mainsail began to rise in sudden, jerking rushes as Migdal and Maask swung on the halyard.

Viktor Kingissep cast off the bowline and moved back to the mast to haul up the genoa. Glancing at *Eagle*, Shaw noticed that there was no sign of her sails. He could see Ericson on board the single remaining tender, discussing tactics with his father. An unexpected wave of anger at their confidence went through him.

He swung the wheel and bore away to pick up speed. Prem was using halyard tension, kicker, outhaul, to persuade the mainsail into effective shape. The previous day it had been cut to remove some of its fullness. *Novy Mir*, with its unusual balance at high angles of heel, had been able to absorb the greater forces of a fuller main. With *Leningrad* it seemed more efficient, and a little faster, to heel less with a flatter main.

Prem turned back and made a sign for excellence, bringing thumb and forefinger together. He was pleased with the recut shape. They settled down to tune for several minutes on port tack, then swung on to starboard.

'Average windspeed has increased two knots to twelve,' Arlof called.

Shaw pointed to the still static *Eagle* and the tactical discussion on the American support vessel. 'What are they hatching, Brod?'

Brod's brown eyes took on an aspect of almost comical melancholy. He shrugged his shoulders, a gesture both impatient and dismissive. His emotions moved about inside him with the cumbersome power of a bull. Shaw realized that Brod's dislike of Ericson had become even greater than his own. It had reached beyond dislike into disgust. Now, even to attempt to think himself into Ericson's frame of mind was an exercise in sordidness.

'How to cheat and lie their way to victory,' Brod said. 'What else?'

'I'm not interested in their philosophy,' Shaw chided him. 'What are their tactics?'

Brod pulled himself together.

'Ah, tactics. Now that's different. My guess is that with one race up they will try and punish us. They will come in close.'

'At the start?'

'Not necessarily.'

'In a tacking duel, perhaps.' Shaw looked forward to the mid-deck, where the grandfathers were warming up. They would take most of the punishment in a duel.

Now that the sails were up, sheets were hauled in and *Leningrad* picked up speed. They tuned on port and starboard, tacked several times to warm up the grinders, and moved back towards the starting box.

'Thirty seconds,' Brod called.

Eagle was now also tuned and marching back and forth at the other end of the starting box. Shaw wondered whether the deliberate lateness in hauling up sails was not a psychological ploy on Ericson's part, a carefully contrived display of arrogance.

125

'Ten seconds,' Brod called. 'Nine, eight, seven, six, five, four . . .'

The starting gun went. They entered the starting box five seconds after the ten-minute gun. *Eagle* also entered, then began to move downwind at an oblique angle to them.

'Action at a distance,' Shaw said to Brod.

It seemed that on the start at least Ericson was intent on keeping away, aiming to blast *Leningrad* with superior speed.

'We'll play along, I think,' Shaw said.

He could see that Brod would have liked to engage *Eagle* directly. But he wanted to give Ericson room to make his play. He hovered at the end of the line, turning slowly, waiting for the minutes to climb downwards towards the gun.

'Two minutes,' Arlof said.

Glancing towards his opponent, Shaw saw that *Eagle* also loitered at her end of the line.

'How much time to reach her?'

Arlof fed the numbers into their tactical computer.

'About eighty seconds.'

'What do you think?' Shaw asked Brod.

Brod nodded. A pre-emptive strike.

'Let's go,' he said. 'We'll see if we can disturb their plan – whatever it is.' He swung the wheel to bear away on a reach. The tension rose inside him.

'Eight four,' Arlof called the speed, 'eight six, eight seven . . .'

Soren Gir trimmed the genoa, easing the sheet in and out with the gusts.

'Nine two,' Arlof called.

'One minute to the gun,' Brod warned.

Eagle was thirty seconds distant. She seemed to pause, watching the unexpected approach of *Leningrad*. It was too close to the start gun for *Eagle* to take avoiding action by moving away from the line. And Ericson

126

would be uncertain over *Leningrad*'s intentions. A fierce debate would be taking place inside Ericson. Was *Leningrad* moving over to their side of the course because of a potentially favourable wind, or were they about to engage directly in a duel? Shaw was determined to create ambiguity, and then play ruthlessly on any resulting hesitation. He drove at a slight oblique angle to *Eagle*, though his course meant they were closing fast.

'Forty seconds to start,' Brod called.

On board *Eagle* they had assumed the worst. Ericson had bitten the bullet, and was bearing off to counter-attack and pick up speed.

Ten seconds between them, a good two knots of difference in speed.

'Ready to turn,' Shaw hissed.

Parallel with *Eagle*, less than a boat length away, Shaw swung the wheel sharply.

'Thirty seconds to gun,' Arlof called.

Eagle had no choice but to swing with them. *Leningrad* gybed with a sudden thunder of sails and sheets, swung upwind savagely, tacked. Shaw felt the blood pumping as he swung the wheel. *Eagle* had responded well, but perhaps not well enough. Her two-knot deficiency in speed was being translated into a slower turn rate.

'Twenty seconds to the gun.'

Two more turns against the background confusion of the sails' thunder, the scream of winches and trimmers calling for power.

'Ten,' Brod snapped. He began to roar out the final count above the thunder of the sails, 'Seven, six, five, four . . .'

But they were on *Eagle*'s quarter and driving her away from the line, the Estonians angry and concentrated. The start gun exploded behind them. Brod ran forward to the mast to enforce right of way. There was no point in prolonging Ericson's agony, however. They had gained the advantage they sought. Shaw swung *Leningrad* upwind, hardened in sheets, and sprinted to the line. With a sudden thunder of sails and sheets *Eagle* followed, two boat lengths behind.

'Seven four, seven five, seven six. . .'

Shaw sailed full to pick up speed, treading the knife edge between power and pointing.

With flapping sails, *Eagle* tacked to clear her wind. Shaw tacked *Leningrad* to cover. Fifteen seconds later, *Eagle* tacked again.

'Tack!' he roared.

Between tacks Berol Baltir and Graf Ulder tried to shake out the stiffness in their limbs, leaning forward again ready to send explosive bursts of power into the winches. For perhaps ten seconds they drove hard, the veins standing out on their foreheads. In the final stages of the tack the winchmen changed gear, drawing in the final inches slowly as the boat picked up speed on the other side of the tack.

'They're tacking again,' Brod said.

In truth, Ericson had no choice. To linger in the turbulent slipstream of *Leningrad*'s sails would have caused them to slip backwards.

'Tell me when,' Shaw said to Brod.

It was important not to counter-tack too early, in case the boat behind engaged in a dummy tack, and could swing back to her original course.

'Now,' Brod said.

'Tack!' Shaw roared.

Behind Baltir and Ulder, the sewerman Herman Maask and mastman Stefan Migdal hovered as reserve grinders. But Baltir and Ulder were like dogs with private bones. They were beginning to find their own rhythm. Their heavy shoulders guarded the winch from interlopers. Between tacks they took huge gulps of air, then swung forward again with gloved hands to seize the winch-handles.

128

'They tack again.' Brod waited for the point of commitment. 'Now.'

'Tack!'

The flapping sails were drawn in and became still. He bore off a little to pick up speed, then feathered slowly up as the winchmen pulled in the few final inches at high gearing.

Twenty-three tacks up the first beat, a huge effort. *Eagle* had made neither gain nor loss. For the time being at least the Estonian winchmen had burned *Eagle* off. In the brief interval Ulder and Baltir, having proved their point, collapsed against the cockpit sides on the final tack, heaving for breath. Their respite only lasted a few seconds. *Eagle* was three lengths behind as *Leningrad* rounded the top mark and launched her spinnaker.

As soon as they rounded, *Eagle* started to fight back. American crew-work was never less than superb. Their speed in downwind tacking duels was legendary.

'Gybe!' Shaw called.

Eagle gybed with them. But the Estonians' blood was up. They counter-manoeuvred with the same cunning and ferocity shown on the first leg.

In the downwind leg the attacking position belongs to the boat behind. It is part of the rhythm of match-racing, as the initiative passes from one boat to the other. Shaw relied on Brod to keep him informed of *Eagle*'s movements. He did not need to glance behind to know, in almost luminous detail, the progress of his rival. Every time Shaw gybed he knew that behind him *Eagle*'s huge spinnaker would belly out for a few moments as the pole was ghosted from one corner of the sail to the other. Shaw could sense the powerful angle of her directional swing – a classic sign of confidence – and imagine, like a knife aimed towards his back, the acceleration of *Eagle*'s advancing prow as the sheet was tightened and she picked up a surge of speed on a swell.

At the downwind mark they were only one and a half lengths ahead. But it was enough to place a close cover on *Eagle*, and subject her to the same gruelling tacking duel as in the first manoeuvre. Shaw insisted that Migdal and Maask, the reserve grinders, take over on several of the tacks in order to preserve Baltir and Ulder for the final beat. *Leningrad* rounded the top mark once again ahead, by two and a half lengths this time. The Estonians launched their spinnaker.

'Now what?' Shaw asked Brod.

Brod did not take his eye off the other boat.

'They're gybing away.'

This was a reasonable tactic. All they could do was strive for speed and try to hold the other off, applying a loose cover so that they kept themselves approximately between *Eagle* and the downwind buoy. At the downwind mark they were one and a half lengths ahead. Once rounded, Shaw shouted, 'Close cover!'

The final beat was murderous. After thirteen tacks, Shaw ordered Migdal and Maask to take over as fresh grinders while Baltir and Ulder heaved for breath. The American grinders fought back with vicious strength. Shaw could hear *Eagle*'s crew boss roaring, and the thunder of *Eagle*'s loosened sails as they came through the tack.

At twenty-three tacks Baltir and Ulder were back in harness, snapping their wrists against the handles and punching the sails in. At twenty-eight tacks they seemed to have passed a threshold of pain and were starting to 'spin' on the body's own opiates.

Shaw glanced behind him.

Eagle hung on. Confident after three wins, the American crew showed spirit and aggression. At thirty-four tacks Shaw called for another change to Migdal and Maask.

'Tack!'

Baltir drifted back until he lay against the cockpit side.

Ulder sank to his knees, hauling in deep breaths. Compared to them Migdal and Maask seemed light.

Behind Shaw *Eagle*'s crew boss barked brief instructions, preparing his men for another tack to break out of *Leningrad*'s wind.

'Five two,' Arlof said. 'Five three.'

With a thunder of sheets *Eagle* tacked behind them, slicing hard through their wake. Shaw could feel Ericson's hatred, the intense co-ordination of his crew as they sought to grind back their lost lead.

The crew nerved themselves for another tack.

It was the American assumption of a moral right to victory that brought out a final rage in Shaw. He was within striking distance of the line. A cool line of reasoning told him to proceed without tacking, to take advantage of *Eagle*'s loss in speed induced by her final tack.

'Six four,' Arlof said. 'Six five.'

Shaw bore off to pick up further speed. The rhythm of tacking was broken. Through their exhaustion the crew tried to concentrate.

'Seven one,' Arlof said.

'*Eagle* tacks,' Brod called. Shaw heard the scream of sheets and the thunder of sails.

With increased speed, he could afford to feather up a little. Sensing his intention, Prem and Tarku hardened in main and genoa.

The committee boat was approaching. They were on a ramming course, aiming directly amidships. Shaw caught a glimpse of Vikunov at the stern, watching their progress. He saw the distinguished members of the protest committee moving back gingerly from *Leningrad*'s approaching prow.

Perhaps he left the final upwind break a few seconds too late. A helmsman's adrenalin narrows time. As he spun the wheel to shoot the line, *Leningrad*'s bow seemed to slice the air beside the committee like a knife descending towards cheese. They were too close for the cannon

131

to be fired without the prospect of damage from the blank charge. For a moment, while the loose sails thundered, the topsides of the two boats seemed about to kiss. It would have been the end of the race and a victory for *Eagle*. Tarku on port closed his eyes. For several seconds *Leningrad* seemed to occupy the same water as the committee boat. A few heartbeats later they were past.

In the silence Prem breathed out, a whisper of relief.

Belatedly, the cannon fired as *Eagle* sliced the line at the pin end. On *Leningrad* the sound of the finish gun drifted over the prostrate forms of Baltir and Ulder, the engines of their victory, as they lay like spent walruses on the cockpit floor.

Twenty-six

Maria was standing at the quay, Jack in her arms, when Shaw stepped ashore. Not usually a demonstrative man, he hugged them both until Jack, struggling to be set down, broke free of Maria's hand and rushed away through the crowd towards *Leningrad*.

Berol Baltir caught Jack and, raising him above his head, brought him back in triumph on his shoulder. After a few moments he passed the gurgling child back to Shaw. Lifting him back to Maria's arms Shaw saw, in the crowd of reporters and well-wishers clustering at the perimeter fence, the ghost of a familiar face.

The crowd at the fence was in turbulent movement as the reporters and cameramen jostled. Shaw's impression of the face was like one leaf blowing amongst others. At first he couldn't believe it. He took several steps forward and tried to call out, but his throat locked. The face, middle aged, somewhat haggard, seemed to recede. Shaw started to walk forward faster, then he lost control and broke into a run.

'Coach Johnson!'

A group of reporters was starting to move in parallel with him. Shaw was running alongside the perimeter fence, and the reporters and television men were shouting questions at him, halting to push microphones though the mesh. Angrily, he accelerated, trying to locate the familiar features. The hubbub increased. Along the outside of the fence the shouting, gesticulating crowd of reporters closed off his vision. Then, for some reason, they seemed to part for a moment. He saw the face again, this time sideways, the hawklike profile, the angry bush of crew-cut red hair. Shaw ran along the fence, shouting 'Coach!'

Once he caught sight of an old blue tracksuit, a limping walk, then the tide of journalists closed in again, and the image receded.

Ilena was signalling his attention. He saw her mouthe the word 'Aegu', and understood that their patron and protector was on the phone.

He kissed Maria briefly goodbye, and followed Ilena to the little office. She held out the receiver, then left, closing the door behind her.

'Shaw here.'

'My congratulations are superfluous. You must be pleased.'

'Yes, I'm pleased.'

'And of course,' Aegu said with a touch of irony, 'you still have no hope of winning the series.'

'I think the odds are still on their side. Since we lost *Novy Mir*, they've won three races to our one.'

In the pause which followed, Shaw heard the sounds of an office, a telephone ringing not far away. For several moments Aegu appeared distracted. Then he said: 'Despite our efforts, the investigation into Illich's death has made no significant progress. We have eliminated the primary suspects, but we still have no clue to the identity of the murderer.'

Aegu waited, and Shaw suspected that he was asking advice. He was prey to the suspicion that Illich's assailant had been American. Shaw said: 'Do you think he might be a foreigner?'

Aegu weighed his words carefully. 'What do you think?'

Shaw breathed out. 'I cannot imagine a worse thought.'

'I understand. It is a terrible thing to raise with you at this time. But perhaps afterwards, when the series is over, you will think about it, so that we can eliminate it from the range of possibilities. As far as I am concerned, you are an Estonian. It is not only your crew who trust you. Goodbye, Mr Shaw.'

The phone went dead. Shaw sat down in the tiny office on the old metal chair that had once been Illich's. He felt as if a tunnel had collapsed beneath him, as if the very ground he stood on was unsafe. He thought of the crew. They were as convinced as he that *Novy Mir* had been deliberately rammed. They too must have been prey to the thought that Illich's death could be connected to this manic desire to win at all costs. And they had said nothing but, as Aegu did, simply gave him their personal trust.

After the series was over, Shaw promised himself, he would dedicate himself to helping in the hunt for Illich's murderer. It was hardly a conscious decision, and one which required little deliberation. It was merely apparent that until the matter was cleared, there would always hang over the case the matter of American involvement, and he could not live happily with that. Ever.

He remained seated for several minutes while his mind cleared. When he finally left, still a little unsteady on his feet after the emotion of the race, he was clear about his immediate future. That was something, at least.

Twenty-seven

On the point of falling asleep that night, Shaw remembered a phrase Maria had used about losing. He detected a peculiar logic in what she had said. Ruefully, he admitted to himself that she exercised a decisive intuition in matters which affected her closely, and which he could only follow with lumbering reason. In the darkness of their small bedroom he tried to piece together his own understanding. The reasoning, it seemed to him, went something like this. If you win, you take on the identity that people expect of you. You become their object. They own you. When you lose, you reassert your own individual identity. You assume your own independence. Winning was adherence to a social convention; losing was an individual decision.

His reasoning solved nothing.

Maria breathed softly beside him. He stared up at the ceiling. In the distance he could hear the heartbeat of the spare generator as the sailcutters made their last adjustments before the final race.

Rising that morning he had experienced a moment of trepidation, not so much fear as a premonition of fear. Foghorns sounded out at sea. A familiar bluish-grey light hung about the room. Creeping to the window, he

135

could see a heavy mist hanging over the flat expanse of water. But it was close to the sea's surface, and in certain directions visibility was good.

But his nervousness remained with him while he shaved. The fear rose up inside him while he dressed, so that when he left the house for fresh air, he was like a struggling swimmer breaking the surface. Nothing had changed. The old visceral emotions were taking charge again. He stood in the open taking deep breaths, his palms sweating.

Vagir loomed out of the mist like a ghost, breathing a plume of white.

'The mist is clearing.'

'Looks like it.'

Vagir did not look at him directly, but perhaps he sensed his distress. Out of a curious respect for privacy he nodded once and moved away towards the shape of *Leningrad*. Shaw watched his square figure disappear, then walked to the office. In its small enclosed space he stood still for several seconds while his pulse hammered in his forehead and he fought for breath.

Ilena had left last night's weather fax on his desk. He glanced down at the ellipses indicating the depression that was moving through from the west. It was too far out to affect them today. The forecast was for sea breezes as the mainland air warmed, rose, and cold air from the sea flowed in to take its place. In the silence, for no reason he could think of, he felt his equability cautiously return.

Now, as the towboat drew them through the disturbed wash of the spectator fleet, the final ramparts of mist seemed to dissolve. What was left was the grey blur of several thousand diesel and petrol exhausts.

To avoid an especially dense raft of spectator craft which lay directly in their path, *Leningrad* was towed in a large semi-circle towards the starting line. A helicopter with a television camera swung low to film them, hardly more than a few feet above the mast. Shaw watched a second helicopter approach even lower from the side. Helicopters were a cause of anxiety. A swell from a spectator boat striking the side of *Leningrad* could easily cause the top of her ninety-foot mast to swing through an arc of thirty feet. It could happen in hardly more than a few seconds. On the water too, motor yachts drew in close for photographs, their washes cannonading against the yacht's shiny topsides. It was a curious sensation after the dense white fog of the previous races, to be exposed to this – like emerging from an experiment in sensory deprivation.

'What will he do today?' Shaw asked Brod while they waited for the course to be laid.

Brod said: 'Attack.'

Arlof programmed the tactical computer with initial course settings. Under *Leningrad*'s bow the towboat inched ahead on low forward revs, using just enough power to hold them into wind. Arlof listened on the radio for the signal that the course was laid and the countdown to the ten-minute gun had begun.

'Why?' Shaw asked.

'Because you caught him off guard yesterday.' Brod replied. 'He'll be out to prove something.'

A tactician is like the devil. It is his task to take the lowest possible view of things, particularly of human motives. A navigator, on the other hand, is like an angel. It is his function to point out the cool, pure arithmetic of distance and time. The helmsman, a human realist, listens now to his devil, now to his angel, and chooses his path, taking account of both.

'Windspeed eight knots,' Arlof said. 'Relatively steady now.'

Shaw looked towards *Eagle*. It was that eerie, magical moment when the course was almost cleared of spectator craft, and he became aware of the distances surrounding them. *Eagle* was partly hidden by her tender. The Ericson motor launch, all white geometric surfaces and stainless steel trim, hid most of *Eagle* from view except her mast.

Shaw had come to dislike white in boats. With the virtual extinction of wood in favour of fibreglass during the decades of the seventies, eighties and nineties, every marina was full of jaded fibreglass hulls, once white but now off-colour, like lines of old bathtubs. Fibreglass, once the harbinger of a new age, had an atmosphere of slightly soiled decrepitude. In the last decade, there had been a revival of wood construction. Protected by new epoxy resins, it was no longer subject to the ingress of water and rotting. Marinas increasingly were peppered with the wooden coachroofs of new wood-epoxy yachts, and sometimes their varnished hulls. Now, by a curious inversion of history, wood seemed modern and smart, fibreglass old and stale.

'Course set,' confirmed Arlof. 'Zero twenty-three. Twenty minutes to ten-minute gun ... now!' He keyed the computer clock.

'Sail up!' Shaw shouted.

Arlof took a childish delight in gadgetry. He tended his instruments like a mother hen her chicks.

'Tactical computer on. All instruments function.'

Brod, as befits a devil, was inclined, when angry or frustrated, to slam his palm against the side of the instrument panel with pent-up energy. Today, however, Brod said: 'We have a little surprise for you, Captain.'

Brod pointed downwards with his square fingers. In the tray beneath the instrument panel where they kept loose instruments was a set of militiaman's handcuffs.

'We are taking advance precautions against your unorthodox finishing tactics. If we are able to get into the lead, and you show any signs of turning back from the line, Arlof and I will overpower you and secure you to a cleat while one of us finishes the job. Naturally, I hope you understand.' Brod nodded towards Arlof. 'Arlof, as you see, is in agreement.'

Shaw looked at Arlof. Arlof nodded. 'Absolute agreement.'

It was clear to Shaw that he had not been the only one preoccupied about the prospect of losing. He said, 'I am touched by your confidence, comrades.'

'If,' Brod said, 'we are not able to overpower you, given your wiry frame and well-known animal instincts, Prem here will stun you with a heavy blow from a winch-handle.'

Prem held up the winch-handle in question. 'A small bump on the head, Kapitan. You'll feel nothing, then out like a light – what we call a paratrooper's kiss.'

'Very touching,' Shaw remarked. It was nice to feel wanted.

Brod shrugged amicably. 'We like to keep things clear.' He and Arlof turned back to their instruments.

The mainsail was being hauled up in giant loops. Kingissep untied the bow rope and released it. The final tensioning of the mainsail halyard was made while Prem, dark glasses shading his eye against glare, turned his careful attention to the shape generated in the mainsail. A few seconds later, the genoa followed.

'Bearing away!' Shaw shouted.

Leningrad heeled and picked up speed. By careful degrees he feathered her more closely into wind.

'Seven two,' Arlof called. 'Seven three, seven three.'

The crew set the yacht up on starboard tack as best they could. Shaw swung *Leningrad* through the wind, and the crew began to tune on port tack.

The sky was clear except for the shadows of helicopters, fixed-wing aircraft, and sometimes the huge, fish-like shadows of airships which drifted over them.

On the other side of the course, *Eagle* tuned.

'Three minutes to the ten-minute gun,' Arlof called.

The cameramen on the helicopters had gathered their shots or grown bored, and had moved away. Now *Leningrad*'s air was relatively undisturbed. They continued to tune. To Shaw the yacht was feeling good, moving forward in that strange, sliding rush which signals a finely honed machine. The sails had been further recut. Prem massaged the mainsail carefully into shape.

'One minute, thirty seconds.'

'Bearing away!' Shaw called.

They started to close with the starting box. On the other side, *Eagle* did the same. Shaw had trained himself not to become obsessed by the other boat, by the apparent perfection of her sails.

'Thirty seconds.'

They picked up speed as they headed towards the box, swung low, crossed six seconds after the gun, moving fast. *Eagle* came towards them on a direct collision course.

'What do you think?' he asked Brod.

'As predicted,' Brod replied.

He waited a few more seconds to ascertain *Eagle*'s intentions. She came on remorselessly, moving fast towards them.

'Bearing away.'

Always keep the opponent off balance, he thought. Attack when he doesn't expect it. By the same token, retreat when he wants to engage.

They were moving downwind, at a tangent to *Eagle*. She altered course towards them.

'Gybe!'

The boom crashed across the deck. The genoa was hauled across the foredeck. Now they were broad reaching away from *Eagle*.

For several minutes they remained on course while *Eagle* pursued them. Eventually *Eagle* swung upwind and returned to the line, circling warily. Shaw tacked and drifted back toward the line, keeping a respectful distance.

'Three minutes.'

There was a bias to port. Ericson moved over to the port side of the line to obtain the advantage, leaving the starboard side clear.

'Thirty seconds.'

'Hardening up!'

The winchgrinders tightened in slowly. They approached the line in a gradual arc, close reaching to build up speed.

'Ten seconds.'

Now they hardened in further.

'Six, five, four, three . . .'

Twenty-eight

Leningrad struck the line one and a half seconds after the smoke from the gun, moving fast. *Eagle* too had made a fine start, and was on parallel tack.

'Wind direction steady,' Arlof said.

'Tack!' Shaw shouted.

They came through the wind crisply, picking up speed well. Now they were on diverging tacks. He wondered if *Eagle* would follow them. But *Eagle* too seemed settled. The two yachts drew apart. After a minute on diverging courses they might have been on different planets.

It was on their own that Shaw had confidence in the Estonian crew. Perhaps it was their history, the history of a small state which had been entirely free of foreign domination for only a few years. Perhaps such a people developed inner resources not granted to others. The yacht became silent. Nerves were focused on minute adjustment of sails. Like somnambulists each man looked inwards, into the silent, breathing heart of the machine.

'Eight three,' Arlof called. 'Eight three. Eight four, eight four.'

Brod, as resident devil, did not like to move out of range of the other boat. He was quiet while he strained his eyes after *Eagle*.

'We're being headed one degree,' Arlof announced.

Others might have tacked, but Shaw felt the boat was going well. And the change of wind direction had a slightly ragged feel, difficult to explain. An intuition told him to keep on.

'Wind direction oscillating two degrees,' Arlof said.

Sometimes, Shaw remembered, this was followed by either a big header or a big lift.

They moved on, each in his own monk's cell of concentration.

'Lift two degrees,' Arlof said, 'three degrees, four degrees. Four, five, six. Steady six.'

Was it local?

Brod was silent. Thirty seconds passed. Clearly, it had not reached the other boat, or they would have tacked.

'*Eagle* tacks now,' Brod called.

Had the shift reached them in the form of a header, or were they getting nervous about too much distance between the two boats?

'We're being headed,' Brod confirmed. 'Two degrees. Two more. Five degrees.'

'Tack!' shouted Shaw.

It was like raising sleepers from a trance. He brought the boat through the wind a little more slowly, and they settled down on the new tack.

Thirty seconds. Then a minute.

'We're being headed,' Arlof said. 'Three degrees, four, four steady.'

'Tack!'

They settled down again.

Glancing out towards *Eagle*, a vague unease settled over Shaw. He carried in his head a geometric map of the course and the two yachts, and it could only accommodate *Eagle*'s position by distortion.

They were converging on the windward buoy.

'They're ahead,' breathed Arlof.

'How much?'

Hesitation under such circumstances is sinister. Arlof seemed to pause like a doctor about to pronounce on a patient.

'Seven lengths.'

Shaw breathed out. The nightmare of a helmsman is not of a sheet breaking, or some explosion of highly tensed equipment. It is this strange unease of one point on a map moving out of control. Afterwards, Shaw would try to work back to how that lead occurred, and when.

Now that they were closing fast with the buoy the difference between them was obvious. Less than a minute later *Eagle* swung round the buoy and launched a perfectly setting medium spinnaker.

Leningrad rounded and followed suit. Seven boat lengths was close enough to make the leader wary, but not sufficient to make him concentrate his full attention on avoiding action. In one of those decisions which seem strangely easy in retrospect, Shaw decided to strike out on the opposite tack.

'Gybe!'

Kingissep swung out on the pole, punched the spinnaker release, returned to the foredeck with the swiftness of a cat. The pole was swung, the spinnaker re-attached. A few seconds later the big sail was setting on the opposite tack.

Sometimes, Shaw knew, one can strike back. At other times one waits. He settled down to the rhythm of sailing high to pick up speed, catching the small face of a wave and using the extra speed to drive deep until the speed falls off and it is time to repeat the rhythm. But each sequence is subtly different, each wave face has a different shape. The tiny nuances of speed gain and loss take up different forms. It was absorbing, hypnotic.

It was an unspoken agreement that the navigator would inform him if the other boat was gaining significantly and he should revise his tactics. Arlof, crouched over his instruments, was silent. Brod, his eye on the other boat, watched for the faintest crew movements which would indicate sail changes.

'*Eagle* prepares to gybe,' Brod said at last.

On separate gybes, they were almost half a mile distant.

The distance between them was a mark of Ericson's confidence in his superior instrumentation and reading of the wind. It was a confidence amounting almost to arrogance. He ran the risk that *Leningrad*, on another part of the course, would pick up more wind. But he trusted his own complex sensors and instrumentation to warn of the likelihood.

In a surge of intuition, it occurred to Shaw suddenly what Ericson was seeking. Ericson would not be satisfied with a mere victory. He wanted to prove he could simply out-sail Shaw, that he could achieve victory without recourse to special effects. He would risk everything. It suggested to Shaw once again that, even with instrumentation that would do justice to a modern fighter aircraft, sailing is heavily invested with psychology.

'Gybe!' he called.

Converging now on the leeward mark he waited for Arlof to offer guidance on their respective positions.

'*Eagle* is ahead,' he said, 'by nine lengths.'

Again he had the impression of a race tilting out of

control. Although the gain in lead was small, it would fuel Ericson's confidence.

Ahead, *Eagle* doused spinnaker, rounded the downwind buoy, and began to tack up the second windward leg. An aeon seemed to pass before *Leningrad* could follow suit.

A peculiar fatality gripped him, an odd detachment now that the race seemed to be slipping away. *Eagle* had chosen the starboard side of the course. He felt there was more wind on port side. Now that he was on his own, he would trust his intuition.

'Tack,' he called.

The genoa was released, thundered briefly, came in fast on the other side. It was a good tack, crisp and fluent. The crew, too, seemed unaffected by *Eagle*'s big lead. Shaw sensed this detachment spread. They ceased to worry about the other boat and began to concentrate on their own. What was left, when the other boat was no longer in the reckoning, was something simpler, more single-minded.

'Eight three,' Brod called. 'Eight three steady.'

'Wind shift,' Arlof hardly moved from the instruments. 'Oscillating.'

A series of such oscillations often presaged a big directional movement. It was a gamble.

'Two degree knock,' Arlof said. 'Now lifting, lifting three degrees, five degrees. Seven, nine, eleven degrees.'

Shaw felt his own spirit rise, his adrenalin sing out. It was a huge shift in their favour. He allowed himself a half-second glance at *Eagle*, four hundred yards out to port, in what seemed an unassailable position.

'Wind direction steady,' Arlof called. 'Windspeed increases two knots.'

The boat became quiet as they held their breath and prayed, as a child may sometimes do at a party, that things would settle there, just like now.

'Eight five,' Brod said. 'Eight six. Eight six steady.'

It seemed they were in their own local corridor of wind. If it were so, they would climb on the shifts like a potholer ascending a shaft.

Small gusts moved across the water, kicking up a deeper blue in the surface. He feathered up in the gusts, bore away slightly in the lulls to maintain speed. The wind direction held steady.

They were in a trance. The hull kissed the swells, seemed to glide. He watched the instruments, the sails.

Perhaps half-way on the first leg Shaw suspected *Eagle* was behind, but he hardly dared admit it. At this stage it made little difference to their tactics.

'Lift,' Arlof said. 'Two degrees. Two degrees steady.'

'*Eagle* tacks towards us,' Brod announced.

It was a further indication of the changing relationship of the yachts as each hunted small gains. They were in entirely local shifts.

The Estonians were in gear. Two more tacks.

'What's the damage, Arlof?' Shaw asked. They were converging on the buoy. He breathed out deeply to remove some of the tensions in his chest.

'*Eagle* trails by six lengths,' Arlof said.

He felt his heart give off relief, a puff-ball shedding winged seeds.

As they rounded, *Eagle* was a full eight lengths behind. Inside, he couldn't help himself, a small voice began to cheer.

The spinnaker set with a punch that went through the boat, and they began to reach-tack down to the leeward mark.

'Twelve two,' Arlof called. 'Twelve four.'

As they headed away, *Eagle* was still tacking up to the buoy.

Eagle tacked towards them on an intercept course.

'I don't believe it,' Shaw said out loud. 'He's going to try to ram us again.'

'I agree,' Brod said.

Ericson had technical right of way, and was prepared to abuse it.

'Gybe!' shouted Shaw.

A change of course of nearly eighty degrees would carry them well out of range. It would also lose distance, but they had a small margin in hand. *Eagle*'s manoeuvre brought back a flare of anger. He wanted to humiliate Ericson. He concentrated to increase their lead.

On the downwind leg *Eagle* gained two lengths. Perhaps the Estonians too had been angered by *Eagle*'s manoeuvre, and had lost some of their fluency. Now they settled into their sleep-walking trance.

At the downwind mark they were one minute twenty-three seconds ahead. They moved into silence again on the final upwind leg.

Already the spectator fleet were starting to break ranks. Soon, he knew, they would be subject to disturbed water from the broken wakes. A gnat swarm of helicopters jostled for position above them. The shadows of fixed-wing aircraft flew by them like birds.

Tension slows time. As they approached, only the boat itself seemed to breathe. They suspended their belief. Swells moved against the hull. Strange nightmares rise, of being held for an aeon in the sea's mirrored mouth. Out of a sense of superstition, Arlof had ceased to call speed. They were approaching the launch end of the finish line, and Shaw could see the officials crowding the rail.

Shaw spun the wheel. With sails flapping *Leningrad* shot the finish line. Time unfolded its layers. The explosion of the cannon was a roar in their ears. A Russian course patrol vessel had detached itself from its background and was speeding at full throttle towards them. Silence lasted a few seconds, and then the Estonians broke out in a roar, embracing and pounding one another's backs. Shaw, who feared embraces, felt his hands held in Brod's heavy gorilla grip, and was swung around like a child in a parody of a sailor's dance. It was an asymmetric orbit, like a planet and its moon. For several full turns Shaw seemed to swing around Brod's powerful centre, his speed growing faster. Then without warning he was released, and found himself floating out over the water, folding into a splash and an explosion of cold on his skin.

For several seconds he faced down into the freezing Baltic. In a strangely light-headed experience of weightlessness he turned, rose to the surface and drew air into his shocked lungs. Spray moved away with almost leisurely calm from his hands and arms like birds taking off. Through watery eyes he saw the Estonians cheering from the side-decks as *Leningrad* slid by. Their genoa was being lowered. The culprit Brod had moved calmly to the wheel so he could circle under mainsail and pick Shaw from the water.

Alone, Shaw stared round at the horizon. He would remember that curiously surreal moment for as long as he lived. The surface of the water was clear. A long shallow swell gently raised and lowered him. While water still filled his ears he was aware of an absolute silence. Half a mile away the fluted bow-waves of the course patrol vessels were like statues as they powered in towards him.

The spectator fleets, held back a mile from the finish, were forbidden to approach the yachts until both had completed the race. But behind the lines of official vessels Shaw could see that same mass of spectator craft was already beginning to surge and charge against the instructions of the course officials.

With casual ease *Leningrad* swung away from him and gybed. In his goldfish bowl Shaw felt both central and vulnerable. Treading water, he turned slowly in the water to face back to the course. Events unfolded around him with a slow motion grace. A hundred yards away, *Eagle*'s mast towered above him as she thundered towards the finish line at the pin end. As her bow closed, no crewman burst into cheering, no great warship sent out a howl of triumph. Ericson swung into wind to shoot the line, and a few seconds afterwards *Eagle*'s genoa slid down. The crew seemed pole-axed. As the spectator fleet broke ranks and sped towards him, Shaw felt no anticipated sense of elation, merely a profound relief.

Two and a half minutes is a long time to wait for a competitor. By the time *Eagle* had made her approach and finish, *Leningrad* had completed the best part of a circle under mainsail and was approaching him from leeward, feathering towards Shaw to reduce way, mainsail flapping slowly. Brod's seamanship was precise. At two knots the topsides nudged him. Prem, with one hand on a stay for support, knelt to reach his hand down, seized Shaw's wrist in an acrobat's hand-clasp, and hauled him aboard.

Fresh from his own immersion, Shaw might have set about throwing the others in, beginning with Brod, but the approaching wall of spectator boats made it hazardous. As the water poured off his soaked clothes, they seemed to gather around him, as if he were some strange or unknown species. A few moments later he experienced another unreal moment of emotion and detachment. A Russian patrol vessel thundered around them in a wide circle on full power. Shaw, that renegade American whose appearance among them was as strange as if he had emerged from the sea, watched in surprise as the captain stepped from the bridge and in a spontaneous show of emotion punched both fists upward in victory.

In the few moments left before the final approach of the spectator fleet, they came forward to shake him by the hand one by one, with the peculiar solemnity and strength of feeling he had grown used to in Estonians; Prem, Brod, Arlof, Gir, Tarku, Baltir, Ulder, Maask, Migdal and Kingissep. Above them helicopters jostled. The roar of approaching power boats made any speech communication impossible. He was pleased that by now the motor boats were arriving. Swells from incoming wakes exploded against *Leningrad*'s topsides. Reporters were threatening to leap on board. The crew dispersed to protect the fabric of the craft and repel enthusiastic journalists. There had been reports in newspapers of Brod's strong-arm methods of dealing with potential boarders. The milling spectator yachts and press launches kept a wary distance, eyeing the infamous right fist.

Shortly afterwards their towboat arrived, swinging past and towards the bow. A tow-rope was hurled on to *Leningrad*'s deck. Kingissep made fast on the bow. The towboat began to ease forward to take up slack.

Well-wishers sometimes drew in close, to be firmly repelled by the Russian patrol vessels which had taken up station on either side. Less than a year after being fired on by a sister-ship, the Estonians were uncomfortable with such allies.

Shaw helped the others fold the mainsail on top of the boom, taking great folds with Prem, Arlof, Brod, then looping light tiers around it to hold it in place. Shaw turned to catch a final glimpse of *Eagle* as she too was towed away. Her grinders leaned forward over their winches. There was little life in the midship crew; only the bowman moved as he drew down the genoa. Shaw tried, before the intervening flurry of press and spectator boats obscured all view, to catch a clear sight of Ericson, but he was hidden by the surrounding American craft.

Twenty-nine

The crew had tied on the regulation Russian flag at the stern of *Leningrad*. Now they hauled the great Estonian tricolour up the backstay, hauling it tight on the halyard like a sail. Increasing its speed, the convoy proceeded southwards towards land. The Estonian yachts and launches formed a tight convoy, which with horns roaring, singing, and shouting, moved back towards the base. Now that the immediate danger of boarding parties had receded, the Estonians insisted that they lift Jim Shaw, the notorious American renegade and recluse, on to the boom. With one arm round the mast for support he posed warily for the photographers.

The base camp too was under siege by the press. *Leningrad* was forced to stand off while course patrol vessels cleared the small harbour mouth of television vessels. Perceiving a gap, the captain of the towboat moved into full ahead and they surged into harbour. The sudden acceleration on the yacht caused *Leningrad* to swing into harbour with too much momentum to easily halt in the confined space. Shaw swung the wheel hard. *Leningrad*'s bow missed the stern of the towboat and overshot until the bow-rope threatened to snap tight, hauling her in towards the tug. Acting with some presence of mind, Kingissep eased the tow-rope until the surging *Leningrad* came to a halt. The Estonian crew hauled the yacht back to her allotted quayside position and tied up. It was an unorthodox landing, but there was no damage.

The first person Shaw faced on shore was Aegu.

'*Tovarich!*'

Rendered speechless by emotion, he pumped Shaw's hand. Shaw, amused, glanced over his shoulder for

Maria and Jack. But speech had suddenly returned to Aegu.

'You won. You won against the greatest power on earth.'

'They did,' Shaw swung his hand towards the crew. 'And Illich.'

It was to him at least a statement of fact. But intense emotion caused an expression like pain on Aegu's face. He blundered past, blinded by tears, to shake the hands of the others.

Shaw looked around him. Vagir faced him. The support men and Anton Shuch and his sailmakers were lined up behind him. He knew that they were the engine of their victory. Hidden from sight, they had selflessly toiled to bring first *Novy Mir* and then *Leningrad* to peak condition. Intense gratitude and embarrassment formed an unholy cocktail of emotions. It was Vagir's turn to smile at his helmsman's discomfiture as he led him down the line so that he could shake hands with each of the support men in turn.

Aegu's helicopter stood on the empty training ground. Maria put Jack down and hugged him. Jack burbled 'Mummy catch Daddy.' They raised Jack up between them. He wanted to be lifted high in the air by the giant Berol Baltir, and they saw him, seated on Baltir's head, carried forward by the group of Estonians up towards the buildings.

He turned towards Maria.

'How does it feel?' she asked.

Something in her eyes troubled him. She put her arms around him, and he was aware, from the strength with which she held him, that she was crying.

John Herrick faxed his copy back to the sports desk at the *Independent*.

Russia has retained the America's Cup by beating the American Challenge four races to three.

Not surprisingly, in the final race Eagle *came out aggressively, looking for revenge after yesterday's defeat. We expected to see the fur fly. Unexpectedly, it was* Leningrad, *the defender, who shied away from physical contact.* Eagle *followed her like a charging bull, but she melted away, returning only to the line when* Eagle *had committed herself to starboard side. And then the giant Estonian crew simply sailed* Eagle *off her feet.*

We learnt again that the America's Cup is not merely about the sailing – though it is important – but the underlying psychological factors, the play of character, the hidden political influences. We are left with still unexplained matters such as the abandoned third race, when in the pre-start manoeuvres the two yachts hit each other with a force hardly less than an exploding bomb.

The jury who were sitting at that inquiry, five of the most distinguished sailing judges, were probably right in clearing the American syndicate of a deliberate stratagem to attempt to swing the race in their favour. Without absolutely certain evidence, it would be monstrous to end this series under that cloud. On the other hand, those who believe that the Americans were guilty of deliberation were treated to another incident today which gave a chilly reminder of that earlier one. At the end of the third leg, when Leningrad *had rounded the upper mark some eight lengths ahead of* Eagle, Eagle *tacked and seemed to aim herself at the other boat. As the upwind boat,* Eagle *had technical rights of way, and for a moment another dangerous incident seemed to loom. Wisely, Shaw gybed and gave* Eagle *a wide berth. It took* Leningrad *out of her way, and may have lost a couple of boat lengths of distance to the next mark, but by then she had some lead to spare.*

This incident highlighted what was perhaps the real crux of the racing. The series wasn't between two nations, but between two American helmsmen. On the one hand John Ericson – a fine example of American corporate man – is tough, capable and formed by the belief that winning is everything. On the other,

153

Shaw, independent, publicity shy, guided by his own lights, is an example of the old American virtues of honesty and independence. The first is a scion of a great commercial dynasty, the second the son of a Maine fishing family. There is nothing we like more than to lecture the Americans, the current international masters, about morality, and perhaps I fall into that trap. But those who think, like Ericson, that winning is everything, might take a little notice of these events. As far as I am concerned, the better American won. I just hope the American public will come to see this extraordinary series in the same light.

At the end of the series Shaw refused a press conference and simply disappeared with his wife and child into the stark buildings of the Estonian syndicate's camp-site. Luckily, the syndicate's patron, President Vajnen Aegu, was on hand to speak to the reporters on Shaw's behalf. John Ericson was also absent, though no doubt for different reasons. Initial reports indicated he was suffering from collapse, though his syndicate's formidable publicity machine assured the assembled press photographers that he was only temporarily indisposed. His father, John Ericson Jnr., stood in staunchly on his son's behalf. Beside him was his formidable associate, the international lawyer Frank Mulvinney.

The America's Cup was handed over by a minor official, representing the Russian holders, to President Aegu. The outcome had clearly left the Russian organizers unprepared. The handover took place in the great press building which had been specially built for this America's Cup. By a curious omission, the Russian authorities were hardly present. It is almost as if they are embarrassed by the success of the dynamic Baltic republic which has retained the Cup on their behalf. There was no visible representation from Moscow. In other respects, it was a fitting handover. Without President Aegu's full support, the Estonian syndicate would not have found funds or a base from which to function and develop. So, without either of the two helmsmen being present, the strange spectacle of the America's Cup was brought to an end.

154

Thirty

'Coffee?' asked Maria, as Shaw sat down at the small kitchen table.

'I'll make it,' he said.

She mixed Jack's food, adding hot milk. Shaw filled the kettle from the creaking cold-water tap and put it on the stove.

'What's it like to be without a future?' she asked. She tested Jack's food with a finger.

He looked out of the window of their little bungalow. He could see the side of the shed where Vagir and his men were preparing the wrecked *Novy Mir* for eventual storage in the nautical museum at Tallinn. She had contributed two victories to their final total of four. In due course, when Vagir and his team had made good the structural damage, she would be restored to her green-hulled perfection, then she would be placed in a museum. Children and old men would walk around her, like dinosaurs' bones. She would never sail again.

Maria reached for the kettle and poured the coffee, placing the cup on the pine table. Mixing the bowl of prepared food, she started to feed Jack. Shaw sat down at the table.

While Jack ate he watched Shaw carefully, studying how he drank his coffee, how he put the cup back on the table.

'He's not used to you eating breakfast with us.' Maria fed Jack another mouthful.

'Trying to figure me out,' Shaw said. 'Maybe he thinks I'm your new boyfriend. Don't you, Jack?'

Jack smiled beatifically.

Such domestic scenes had been rare. It was normal for Shaw to be up and exercising before the others were awake. Now he could see through the same window the pale morning shadows on the hillside behind the shed. From the window on the other side he could see a part of the bay. Two Solings were practising, tacking one after another, white sails shaking.

'You sure you don't want something to eat?' Maria asked.

Shaw nodded. He had decided to forgo breakfast. The big morning meal he and the crew usually ate was soon burnt up, if not by physical exercise, then by various kinds of stress and fear and rage on the water. Without that outlet he'd grow fat.

Shaw drank his coffee and stood up.

'Daddy not go,' Jack said.

'Daddy must go, Jack.'

Jack ate another spoonful and watched him, chewing slowly.

Maria said: 'There's a letter from America. For you. Postmarked from Weepeq Bay.'

She indicated with her empty spoon the plain white envelope on the stainless steel sideboard of the kitchen sink.

He picked it up.

It was Sam Shaw's writing. He recognized it from the straight-backed *l*s and *d*s. He read it out:

Dear Jim and Maria,

I read about Ivan Illich today in the newspaper brought up to me by Agnes, and wrote partly to say how sorry I was to hear about his death. He must have been an extraordinary man. The news brought back memories. I remember the race in the last America's Cup when you touched his yacht with right of way. He just turned aside without disputing that he was in the wrong and sailed back to his base, leaving you a clear course. I wished that one day I might have been able to meet him, just to shake hands.

The fishing here is getting better each year. Lobsters are the main thing, but even the bluefin are returning. And we're

*catching salmon again, not big, but healthy looking fish. There
are two younger guys helping me now with the business, Curly
Hale from Ramsden, and Ernie Fisher. They've bought third
shares. Your old grandfather has finally become a capitalist.
I've even got a few pennies to rub together in my old age.*

*My partners hardly seem to need me now. I wondered
whether, when the racing's all over, I couldn't come over and
see you both.*

Sam

Maria said: 'I hope he does.'

Shaw tucked the letter in his pocket and was about to
go outside. She said quietly, 'Where are you going?'

'I was going to check out *Novy Mir*.'

'Isn't that out of your hands now?' she asked. She
removed a dribble from Jack's chin with the spoon.

'Sure. But that doesn't mean I don't have an interest.'

'Well, I suppose we're interested in all kinds of
things,' Maria said softly. Her back was to him as she fed
Jack.

'Look, Maria, *Novy Mir* means quite a lot to me. . .'

'Why don't you write to your grandfather?' Maria
suggested coolly.

There was no answer. It was a reasonable suggestion,
it was a filial duty. To refuse would be churlish, and
once again she would get her own way.

So Shaw found a spare sheet of paper. He drew a
chair up to the tiny dining-room table, and under Jack's
careful eye he wrote in biro:

Dear Sam,

Got your letter.

*As you'll have seen by the time this gets to you, we managed to
keep going after Illich, not least because he set us such an
example. The Estonians are the best crew I've ever seen. We
will all remember Illich in our different ways.*

Right now, Maria and I are not too certain where we're going to be living. We've come to like Estonia, and we both want to stay at least a bit longer. We think we'll try and rent a flat somewhere not far from Tallinn.

Come over as soon as you like and stay as long as you wish. We'd like to see you wherever we are.

Maria sends her love.

Jim

Since he was responding on behalf of both of them, it was only fair that Maria should read the letter. She said:

'You people certainly go down big on the detail. I write five pages a week to my mother.'

'Your mother's a Russian,' Shaw said.

'What's that supposed to mean?'

'My grandfather's from Maine. We're not big on detail.'

'Oh, is that so?'

'Detail,' Jack commented, looking from one face to the other.

Since their little temporary shed still did not have hot running water, Shaw used the remaining hot water in the kettle to heat up some cold water in the sink. He poured some washing-up liquid into the water and worked the suds up with his fingers. He started to wash the plates with a steel-shafted brush.

There was a small window above the sink, hardly more than a ventilator, with clouded glass. He opened it now so he could look out. He felt again the obscure, luxurious pleasure of ordinary living. As he washed he could hear Jack complaining and burbling in the other room while Maria helped him dress. He liked the smooth feel of the enamel under his fingers, the gentle clink of the plates as he stowed them upside down on the steel sideboard to dry.

The window looked out on the hillsides. There was a road, newly made up for the America's Cup, from the shore up to a small complex of shops around the huge press centre. Sometimes he could see figures walking up there from the base camps to fetch food or papers. The press centre was a monument in concrete, designed to impress Westerners with its efficiency, but harking back to an earlier period in Western capitalism. It protruded from the hillside like a single giant tooth. Afterwards it would be converted into a hotel.

The traffic to and from the base camps reduced each day as the syndicates packed up and left. Most of the sailors had already departed, and now only the maintenance crews remained. The press corps too had almost entirely disappeared.

Maria returned from the bedroom, carrying Jack.

Shaw wiped his hands on the dishcloth, and was about to turn away, when he saw a figure walking away from the press centre. There was a familiarity in the limping walk.

Maria said: 'And now you've done the dishes, maybe you'd help me pack . . .'

He said, 'I have to go. I've just seen someone. I'll explain when I get back.'

'It better be good,' she called sweetly to him.

He was out through the doorway, walking across through grass to the compound fence. There were two militiamen patrolling the wire. One of them, seeing him, strolled forward to unlock the gate. It was an old lock, and it seemed to take ages.

'Thanks.'

The figure had disappeared in a dip in the road. Shaw walked fast, then began to run up the hillside. There was dew still on the grass, and it made the slope slippery. Occasionally he slipped in his haste, almost falling over. He found some old stairs, the flagstones lopsided; he ascended two at a time. At the top he was breathing hard. It was still about fifty yards to the road. He could see no one. But some way to his right he caught sight again of the blue tracksuit.

He started to run down the road.

Coach Johnson must have heard him approach, but he did not turn round. Shaw had a glimpse of the hawkish, lined face, the tight-mouthed grimace of discomfort as he drew his bad leg forward.

'Coach.'

Shaw had to cross in front of him, confront him, cause him to halt like an angry horse.

Coach Johnson looked at him without expression, standing in front of him, and for a moment he thought he would walk right through him. If he had, Shaw would have struck him down. Instead Coach Johnson allowed himself a half smile. Shaw saw how much he had aged. His hair showed areas of iron grey, his skin had deep lines down from the mouth. He seemed to hold himself upright with an effort, as if his thin frame was supported by an act of will.

'Told your grandfather you'd make a good devil.'

Thirty-one

If Sam Shaw had raised Jim, Coach Johnson had been a father. They still stood at loggerheads. But some of the anger seemed to go out of Coach Johnson. Perhaps he was grateful for the respite of standing.

Shaw said, 'We got a letter from him this morning. He's coming over.'

Coach Johnson paused, nodding as if to himself. He

sensed that he was thinking about whether to walk on, and deciding against it.

'I'm living down there.' He pointed down to the camp, at the small bungalow at the edge of the wire perimeter fence. 'You remember Maria Chednik? I married her.'

'Sure I remember.' Coach Johnson nodded. 'Fine girl. Knew her mind.'

At the thin line of sea, waves struck the shore in a rhythmic pulse. A seagull dipped and swung along the line of foam.

'Maybe you'd come and have coffee with us,' Shaw said. 'We're about to start packing.'

Coach Johnson looked down the hillside. Part of the camp was obscured by the fold in the hills, but you could see the perimeter fence and some of the rest of the buildings. Vagir's gear, piled together or in boxes outside the buildings, and several pantechnicons incongruously parked nearby, made it look like an old circus encampment, the kind that used to tour small towns.

'I have to get back.'

Jim Shaw would have blocked the road for ever. He would have stood like a dumb wall, and not even Coach Johnson's slicing beak of a nose would have cut through him.

Gulls had gathered around the rubbish tips left by the departing syndicates on the shoreline. Several flew overhead, dipping a wing to lean on the air-currents that came up over the folded hills. They did not mew or cry.

In the silence Coach Johnson folded carefully a telex message that he had picked up from the press office and was carrying in one hand. Carefully he put it in the upper pocket of his tracksuit. He looked at the departing gulls, as though studying their technique, and shrugged.

'I could do with some coffee.'

Walking down the hill, Shaw had to pause several times while Coach Johnson negotiated the stone stairs with his bad leg. There was a kind of recklessness in the older man's walk, something Shaw had not remembered, as though he were overcoming frailty with force. He was thinner now, and his only fuel seemed a form of abstract anger. Once he seemed about to fall. It was all Shaw could do to restrain himself from reaching out to support him. He knew the Coach would not have forgiven him for it. Instead, Shaw hid his concern by talking.

'We have a son now. Named Jack.'

They were on a small plateau of level ground. He thought he detected the trace of a smile on Coach Johnson's face.

'Wouldn't be named after Jack Peabody, would he?'

Shaw nodded and said, 'How is Jack?'

'He's OK. He finished law school and he's working in New York.'

'You've seen him?'

'Yeah, I tried to get him to join our outfit as second helmsman. But when he heard you were on the other side, he turned it down.'

'If you see him again, maybe you'd tell him we named our son after him.'

'Sure. He'd like that.'

Coach Johnson drove forward. They were approaching the perimeter fence of the camp. One of the militiamen moved in a casual, swaggering walk along the fence to open the gate and let them in. Bits of machinery were lying about, ready to be packed and transported – lathes, riveters, lifts, vices, mechanical saws. The camp, never a showpiece, looked even more ramshackle now. Shaw could imagine Coach Johnson thinking, 'How the hell could they beat us out of a place like this?'

Shaw knocked and pushed open the door of the little bungalow. Alerted by the unaccustomed formality of Shaw's knock, Maria stood up from the packing cases, smoothing down her dress.

'You remember Coach Johnson?'

162

Maria, a respecter of family ties, came forward to embrace Coach Johnson.

'I promised him a coffee,' Shaw said. 'I'll put the kettle on. Won't you sit down, Coach?'

Coach Johnson sat down carefully, holding his bad leg straight in front of him.

'So you're Jack?' he said.

'Don't encourage him,' Maria said. 'He's caused enough trouble this morning.'

'Is he an Estonian or an American?' Coach Johnson asked, eyeing Jack.

'Born in America,' Maria said. 'Estonian by adoption.'

'He could turn out a hell of a sailor.'

Maria was hostess. She pushed Shaw aside and poured the coffee. Shaw sat down opposite Coach Johnson across the bare pine boards of the table. For a moment Coach Johnson seemed tired. He breathed out deeply. Sometimes, Shaw remembered, he was subject to attacks of pain in his leg. In the past, Shaw had never felt sympathy, perhaps because Coach Johnson had never asked for it. But it was deeper than that. You couldn't separate Coach Johnson from his pain. It had become part of him, part of his nervous system. It gave him his vehemence and incisiveness. Perhaps Shaw also suspected that in some obscure manner the older man used his pain not only to sharpen his mind, but to establish his mental hold over others. When you faced Coach Johnson, his will and his pain functioned like allies.

'How's Charlie Grist?' Shaw asked. Grist was Coach Johnson's right-hand man.

'Happily married, two kids now, third on its way.'

'Still look after the summer sailing camp?'

'Still does.'

'And Ernie Stead?'

Stead had been navigator on *New World*, the best navigator Jim had ever worked with; a computer freak.

Shaw remembered reading the first list of *New World*'s future crew, and seeing Ernie's black face staring out of the dossier.

'Tried to get him on board the team too. He said the last America's Cup was enough for him.'

'What's he doing?'

'Lectures at MIT. Some fancy subject I always forget. Artificial Intelligence comes into it somewhere.'

There was a pause. Coach Johnson raised his coffee and drank. He put the cup down on the table, looked around him and said: 'No one who sailed on *New World* has ever come back to professional sailing again.'

It was a statement that would haunt Jim Shaw. Coach Johnson, seeing that he had said something that had an edge, added, as if to ameliorate, 'Sure, I hear of them now and again. Some regatta in Chesapeake won by someone, some guy helping with Admiral's Cup selection in St Petersburg, maybe. The odd bit of coaching somewhere in the country, on the Michigan lakes. They're around. No one came back for the America's Cup, though.' Coach Johnson paused here, and then added quietly, as if to himself, 'Except you.'

Shaw sipped his coffee, then said: 'And you.'

A slow smile moved across Coach Johnson's face. He shrugged his shoulders and drank down his coffee in quick gulps. He looked round the room, at the empty packing case, the few bits of furniture.

Maria, sensing the conversation had become dangerous, asked: 'Another coffee?'

'No thanks, I should be going.'

Coach Johnson patted his pocket, as if to remind himself of the telex he had stowed there.

Maria looked at Jim. Shaw shrugged, too.

Maria asked: 'What are you planning to do next, Coach? Another America's Cup?'

'I've been involved in two now which have failed, kind lady. Americans don't like losers.'

'Maybe that's their problem,' Maria said quietly.

'And mine too, I'm afraid.'

Coach Johnson raised himself to his feet. He remained still for a few seconds, waiting for the pain to subside.

'You sure you won't stay for another coffee?' Maria asked.

Coach Johnson smiled his roguish smile, and shook his head. He held out his hand to her, then he turned for the door.

Shaw accompanied him to the periphery fence. Waiting for the gate to be unlocked, he said: 'Do you still believe that the best helmsmen are devils?'

Coach Johnson looked at him with his hooded blue eyes, one lid slightly drooping. He smiled, as if in pride.

'I think you're the proof of that.' Coach Johnson turned to look up the hill, checking his path. 'No need to come any further. I can find my own way back.'

Shaw watched him climb the hillside, throwing his weight forward on his bad leg. Each movement was an act of anger and faith. Shaw watched him grow smaller as he climbed the hill in sudden bursts, watched him as long as he remained in sight.

Thirty-two

When he returned to the bungalow to help Maria pack, he saw by the unnatural clarity of her eyes that she had been crying.

'What's wrong?'

She didn't answer. He was inclined to let sleeping dogs lie, but he had come to suspect that, of all the slippery male vices, the one women despised the most was the unwillingness to confront emotion. So he followed her through to the kitchen and waited patiently while she scrubbed several dishes.

'I know something's troubling you.'

She continued to work away at the dishes. He knew he was expected to wait, so he waited. At length she said, 'He was almost your father. He made you what you are. You were just about at each other's throats.'

'He's a tough one,' Shaw said. 'He always was. He thinks I'm some kind of traitor.'

'You could settle your differences, if you both wanted to.'

'That's why I asked him here. I wanted to say, look, this business of you being on one side and me on another is all nonsense. But that's where we're different. To him it's not nonsense. To him that's still what counts.'

Jack said, 'Mommy smack Daddy.'

'Now don't you start,' Maria said to Jack.

'Anyway,' Shaw said. 'You told me that I'd started to change for the worse ever since Coach Johnson started to influence me. You said his influence made me base my whole life on beating other people.'

'That was a long time ago. You've grown out of that.'

'Thanks,' he said. 'But John Ericson hasn't. That's what gets me. Ericson just can't stand to be beaten. He's Coach's ideal pupil. And what has really thrown Coach is that he lost.'

'Did you really mean to make it up with him?'

'Yes, I did.'

'Why didn't you?'

She wiped her eyes carefully with her hands. He felt a desire to be honest, a dangerous urge.

'I don't know. Part of me wants to pin the old bastard to the wall and ask him whether they rammed *Novy Mir* deliberately.'

He could see by the expression in her eyes that Maria was horrified.

166

'I know, I know.' He looked out of the window. 'But he was their goddamn coach.'

Her eyes stayed on him. He knew that he had said one of those things that would be remembered.

'Maybe you're as bad as he is.'

Oddly, he felt better about her saying that. It wouldn't be stored up for later use, like one of those razor blades that prisoners stored in a crack in the wall. Shaw remembered, a little ruefully, what Coach Johnson had said when he left.

Shaw stood up, pushing the chair aside. He put his arms around her, and pushed her gently back against the kitchen wall. He placed his lips against hers, and she turned her face sideways, half resisting.

'Let's pack,' she said.

'OK.' Some other time, not now perhaps, he wanted to thank her for two things. She made him realize winning isn't everything. And she encouraged him to join the Estonians. Shaw had learned from Illich you didn't have to be like Ericson to do something well. You didn't have to distort yourself. It could come from inside.

They were standing awkwardly, like dancers after the music has stopped. She kissed him back, not passionately, because they had work to do, and there was Jack, and she was sensible.

On the radio, Shaw heard the announcer say:

'A new investment programme in the Russian rail system was announced by Minister of the Interior Kerasnikov.

'US sources today disclosed that talks were held on US warship *Nemesis* between senior American officials and their Russian counterparts over a wide range of trade deals aimed to redress the imbalance of imports and exports between the two countries.'

Shaw had obtained several large wooden packing cases from Vagir's storage shed which he had piled in one corner of the tiny sitting-room. Maria helped him lift one down. With a claw hammer he prised open the lid. Inside were wood-shavings and dust. He began to clear these into a paper bag.

In the background the radio announcer continued, 'Talks on the USS *Nemesis* were also held on a variety of other subjects, including arms reductions. It is understood that those present included, on the American side, General Marcus Walters and on the Russian side, General Valentin Chernavin. Both sides claimed substantial progress had been made.'

Shaw was on the point of carrying the paper bag outside to the rubbish bin when he paused.

Maria said, 'What's the matter?'

Over the sound of the radio Shaw said, 'The *Nemesis* has been anchored out there for more than two weeks. Those were some meetings.' He remembered glancing at the aircraft carrier's huge grey topsides as they were towed out to the course, and the constant movements of helicopters back and forth.

'Nothing you can do about it,' Maria said.

He closed the door behind him and carried the paper bag out behind the shed to a big open communal litter bin. He sent the bag sailing upwards over the top of the metal walls, and paused briefly to look at the bay.

As a child at Weepeq Bay he had walked along the seashore in the evening, looking for shells. There were foxes living in the deserted dunes, but in the dusk you rarely saw one. They lived outside the range of your own eyes. Sometimes he felt the same thing about politics. Things happened outside your range of knowledge.

The other warships had left the bay but *Nemesis* and several support ships were still anchored out in the roads. Shaw returned to the house.

'Are you thinking about Illich?'

'A little.'

'You admired him, didn't you?'

He remembered Aegu asking him a similar question. 'Do you like Illich?' he had said, as if he were still alive. A slip of the tongue perhaps, or a recognition of his pervasive presence. It seemed to Shaw that Aegu too recognized something unresolved.

'I'm going to find his murderer.'

He was half turned away from her, but he could sense her stiffen.

'Why?'

He was not inclined to answer.

'Why don't you just leave it to the authorities?' she insisted.

'Because it's personal.'

'What do you mean personal?'

Her voice was frightened, sensing some compulsion.

He said, 'I want to find out who would kill someone like that.'

'But why? Will that bring him back?'

He said, 'It better not be an American.'

She was silent, watching him. He felt obliged to speak again.

'Maybe it was just ... some psychopath, someone crazy enough to act on a personal grudge.'

In the quietness of the room, neither moved for several seconds.

'What if it wasn't?'

'Then,' he said evenly, 'I would like to know.'

He had turned to face her and she looked at him, slowly, moving her gaze from one of his eyes to the other. Shaw, usually in awe of her physical presence, appeared to stare through and past her. Perhaps she expected to confront some emotion, something that rose and fell. It was its absence that disturbed her. In the building shed someone struck metal against metal, rhythmically and repeatedly; they could hear its faint chime. She seemed to relax, to sigh almost, as if recognizing a palpable truth.

'I don't think I could stop you.'

'Not this time,' he said.

They put their few belongings into packing cases, the few items of furniture that had been shipped over from Maine when they knew they were going to be staying for some time. There were some large pieces: a pine table and chairs, several lamp-stands, a chest of drawers, a writing desk that Sam Shaw had given them. They put these to one side. In one packing case they placed sheets, rugs, blankets, and a faded Astrakhan rug; in another their clothes. By tacit agreement, neither of them mentioned Coach Johnson's visit.

Shaw spent the rest of the morning answering, as best he could, the mail that had come pouring in since their victory. Ilena replied to most of the letters on his behalf. She and Brod were still in the camp, along with Prem and his wife. Most of the crew had already left for Estonia to see their families and relations.

Shaw, Brod, Prem and their wives ate at the canteen together at lunch. It was a simple meal. Their respective children sat between them. Prem's wife, Elvira, was tall, fair, imposing. Shaw noticed with amusement how she quietly organized her ebullient husband.

After lunch Shaw returned to the little office that had once been Illich's to deal with remaining correspondence. Over lunch a telegram had arrived from Aegu, addressed to him:

Dear Mr Shaw,

We have arranged a flat for you and your family to live in indefinitely or as you wish — a small token of appreciation from our Estonian Republic:

3rd Floor
42 Rataskaevu St.,
Tallinn

The flat is available to you as from today,

We wish you a happy stay.

Aegu

Maria's aunt Liina had invited them to stay with her.
They had intended to put their furniture in storage
while they looked for a house to buy – Estonia's internal
laws had permitted ownership of private property for
more than a decade. Shaw carried the telegram over to
Maria. They pored over it together. It was fruitless to
speculate what sort of accommodation the flat would
provide, but at least it relieved her of the worry that they
might impose for too long on Aunt Liina. They could
arrange for their furniture to be dropped directly at the
flat the following day. He telefaxed back.

Dear President Aegu,

*We thank you for your kind offer regarding accommodation,
and will move our furniture to the flat tomorrow.*

Jim Shaw

Maria telephoned her aunt and explained their
change in fortune. Aunt Liina seemed disappointed.
She had looked forward to doting on Jack. Rataskaevu
Street, on the other hand, was only a few streets away
from her own small house, and dates for baby-sitting
could be arranged in advance. They wanted to be installed in the flat by the time of Illich's funeral, in three
days' time.

Thirty-three

On a strip of concrete outside the main shed, Vagir and his men were working on the hulk of *Novy Mir*. It had been stripped of all rigging, deck equipment and instrumentation. They had sawn away the destroyed bow, leaving a huge clean hole, and had stripped the paint from the local area preparatory to laying up new wood.

Shaw peered inside the shed. Lying on the floor like a mammoth's ribcage laminated wood-epoxy frames were being held in place by clamps as they dried. Shaw heard hammering inside the hull. He walked over to the giant hole and called inside.

'Vagir?'

The hammering stopped. Vagir appeared at the great void that had once been the bow, carrying a woodplane in his hand. Flakes of wood-chipping flecked his hair. He seemed distracted.

'Who ordered this?'

Vagir said, 'Written instructions from President Aegu's office.'

'What's the urgency?' Shaw asked. He assumed Vagir and his men would be allowed a holiday. But now his own work was over, he was no longer at the centre of things. Matters were moving outside his control. He was affected by a curious feeling of impotence.

Vagir shrugged. 'The hull must be capable of floating within three days. A transporter will take her to Tallinn.'

'What's happening?' Shaw asked.

Vagir spread his arms, palms upwards, in a gesture of doubt, as if to say 'who knows?' He merely followed instructions.

'Don't let me keep you,' Shaw said.

Without a word Vagir returned to the interior of the hull. The hammering had already started again, but now the plane joined it, like a sing-song duet.

It was a gusty day, but bright. Dappled cloud-shadows moved across the forecourt and the grass. Shaw returned to the bungalow.

Maria had switched on the television while she went about the packing. It was one of those strange times of momentous events. Everyone felt it, like an itch in the bones. The world seemed restless. You reached for a little switch that would turn on the news without knowing what you might hear next.

A few days earlier, Brod and Prem had insisted that Shaw take the small Ilyushin television set that had been used to monitor news during the course of the challenge. It had brought back a pang of memory. Illich and Shaw had surreptitiously gloated over the public sanctification of *Novy Mir*'s designer, Kalev Tammiste. They had watched his owl-like features as a swarm of reporters had asked inane questions about the design of the *Novy Mir*. Tammiste had watched as they interpolated this and that characteristic, building up a mythology of advantages which bore almost no relation to the truth.

'I couldn't,' Shaw said.

'Take it,' Brod insisted. He had protested but Brod said, 'It's above board, Captain. The crew bought it from their private funds and are donating it to you as a gift for your new home. Ask Prem, he organized the vote.'

He looked at Prem.

'Absolutely true,' he confirmed. 'I told them that anyone who disagreed would get a paratrooper's kiss.'

'You see?' Brod said. 'They were volunteers.'

'Then it must have been unanimous,' Shaw replied gracefully. He knew that Prem's volunteer system invariably produced 100 per cent agreement. That was its function, after all. 'I accept with gratitude.'

He carried away the little machine under his arm. It was a good piece of equipment. As part of the economic changes of the last decade, the Ilyushin aircraft factory had turned its hand to making civilian products; it was well known that amongst Russian production factories it was one of the best.

Entering the living-room, he saw Maria poised to place a piece of furniture. The little Ilyushin set was on in the background. His attention moved towards the screen. The announcer, a young woman with red hair, was saying:

'Today the Russian Defence Minister, General Chernavin, addressed the Congress of People's Deputies. His theme was the need for peace in the Russian republics, a priority which·in his view necessitated a strong military stance. He called for sacrifices on the part of the people for a new, stable order.'

There was a photograph of Chernavin. A handsome face, powerful, in his middle fifties, Shaw guessed. The red-headed announcer continued to extol his participation in the recent talks with the American President.

Maria turned to face Shaw. 'I didn't hear you come in.' She went back to her packing. Over her head, Shaw continued to watch the screen. Library footage showed Chernavin opening a factory and standing in front of a graduation class of officers as he raised his hand and beat the rostrum to emphasize certain rhetorical points. Shaw had reason to fear political animals. In his heart something told him this was a big one. You sensed his presence even on the screen, when his image was no more than a few lines of light.

'Why were you watching that guy?' he asked Maria.

'The newspapers say he's the strong man in the Russian leadership.'

Shaw tried to work out what it was that drew attention. Russian leaders, even more than other politicians, seemed to exhibit an animal vitality. Perhaps it was because they were at an earlier, more vital stage in their political evolution; their politicians had an older, more

174

primitive power. He had seen it with earlier Russian politicians, with Gorbachev and Yeltsin. On a podium with others, your eyes would swing towards certain figures for no reason other than an animal command. Watching Chernavin, it was not merely the energy which seemed to pour out of him, but a kind of focus, as if his concentration lit himself up. There was another shot of him, again out of library footage, walking through the streets amongst crowds several steps behind a group of politicians. He was merely one among several generals who were accompanying politicians around the Energeia factory which made space shuttles. Again the eye moved to the uniformed figure who seemed to generate around him his own psychological space, his own eerie gravity.

The news coverage switched to the troubled, volatile former Soviet republic of Azerbaijan. Maria returned to her packing. Shaw leaned forward and turned down the sound on the set. After a few seconds of silence he said: '*Novy Mir* is being repaired on President Aegu's orders.'

Maria did not respond. The matter was no longer in her sphere of interest. He admired her detachment, her focus on the present.

Shaw was already beginning to see, in vague outline, the nature of his retirement. Out on the sea you controlled at least to some degree your own life; you lived by your own skill and wits. On land you were submerged; you had no say at all. You saw orders transmitted you had no part in formulating and whose import you did not understand. You witnessed images on the television screen of frightening importance but you had no means of grasping their meaning. You tried to keep a low profile and pull together a few fragments of your life. With his eyes still on the television screen, he knelt down beside her and helped her pack.

'Jim?'

Maria's eyes were watching him as he placed various

175

items in the open-topped case. He smiled briefly but continued to keep an eye on the flickering screen. He suspected he was more of a hindrance than a help, but hoped it was the effort that counted.

She clucked with annoyance as he loaded in a delicate lampstand. It would be crushed under other things that should be loaded first. For some reason he could not fathom, he found her more desirable when agitated. He wanted to lean forward and – inappropriately in her present mood – kiss her on the cheek. He held these uxorious desires at bay. Another thought struck him. On land you were drowned not only by external events you could not control, but by gestures of warmth and solicitude which came from inside – by the surfacing of that good, loving human being who is every fine helmsman's most feared and hated enemy.

Thirty-four

The following morning a light mist had formed on the water. A few days earlier it would have represented a sinister threat. Now it was merely a physical phenomenon, an aspect of the early dawn. Even so a kind of claustrophobia gripped Shaw. He raised the bedcovers carefully in order not to disturb Maria and swung his legs out of the bed. Pulling on his trousers and socks, a feeling of lightness overtook him, a relief from weight.

It was clear from the empty grounds around the encampment that the media circus had moved on. Less than forty-eight hours after the America's Cup, there were no more journalists plaguing the inmates at the gates and fences. The previous day a few had remained behind, searching for post-mortems, aware that their elusive quarry was still on site. But by the second day the victory of the Estonians had faded. Stillness settled over the camp.

The only sound was the faint rasp and squeal of the electric tractor as Vagir and his men hooked up chains and hauled the shattered hull of *Novy Mir* into the shed for final repairs. Shaw knew they would replace the bow with the rapid, almost instinctive skill of ants. Less than a year previously, at the base camp at Khiuma, they had built the hull of *Novy Mir* in only a few days.

He looked out over the bay. Within twenty-four hours the two American yachts had been loaded and were standing on trailers. Now all he saw on the water were a few rafts of seagulls. The small bays were returning to their customary isolation.

A huge grey warship, the nuclear aircraft carrier *Nemesis*, was drifting eastwards slowly, as quiet as an elephant on a jungle path. Its lower areas were hidden by fog. Several helicopters hovered eerily above its bridge and upper structures like tiny, stationary insects. Not so many hours previously she had been host to the Presidents of the United States and Russia. Amongst the other high-level guests would have been the various Presidents of the former Soviet republics. Shaw knew that because of the Estonians' showing in the America's Cup Aegu would have enjoyed a certain additional status. The big warship moved away now, her upper decks and bridge towers as big as a city. He watched her go with a pang of guilt in his heart. He had caused America to lose twice now. The warship was the final elusive image of earthly power gathered at a yacht race.

And he, the victor, was nothing. A tolerated mercenary in his country by adoption, a renegade in his own country of origin. He lived in a kind of suspension, outside history. The thought was not a burden. Reality was moving away in the form of the great warship, slipping towards some other rendezvous. He decided to set out for a walk beyond the periphery of the camp.

He kept walking.

'When is Illich's burial?' Shaw had asked Prem shortly after the news of Illich's death.

'Not until the races are finished. He will have a state burial. In Tallinn.'

'How long would they keep his body. Ten days?'

'They will freeze him, I think.'

It was a morbid thought. They would preserve him in favour of a time which the state found convenient to bury his remains. The state had taken him over for its own grisly rituals. Perhaps Prem had guessed the direction of his thoughts. He said without rancour, 'Illich doesn't belong to us any more.'

Prem was right. Nothing belonged to them any more. Brief fame dried you like a tobacco leaf. It smoked you and passed on. If you were lucky some parts of you moved surreptitiously out of the cloud it made of your actions and you started somewhere else, out of sight, building your private life. If you were determined, if you were sensible, you left the old existence – the existence of a public man – like breath behind you.

Something inside Shaw had stopped moving, or moved into a different sequence. A score had been settled. Part of him had died.

Along the edge of the shore the other syndicates had left equipment they could not carry. Lathes, lifts, old keels that lay chocked up. Walking along the shore he could see, even at this unearthly hour, several men in overcoats moving slowly, almost contemplatively, between the rubble tips and the temporary sheds. Scrap collectors, metal merchants; at the same time, part of that ecological system which lay at the heart of natural processes. They would be from St Petersburg, that window on the West, with its free trade areas harbouring small businesses.

The men did not pay any attention to him. Russians, Shaw noticed, seldom worked alone. Even the small traders, scrap-metal merchants and local businessmen who were already moving over the remains worked in twos or threes. Several pick-up trucks had been parked outside the perimeter fences. Wirecutters had been used to break through strong-meshed security fences. They formed an efficient system of scavengers, recirculating the lead from keels and the titanium from broken masts and booms, even the stainless steel in winches. Much would be sold *ex officio* to the naval yards surrounding St Petersburg.

A part of Shaw hoped that Illich's killer was a Russian – not out of hatred, quite the reverse. A single killer, an Estonian or someone else, could lose himself like a sand-grain on a beach. But if it were a Russian, he felt intuitively there would be others; accomplices, an organization. There would be a path, a difficult one but a path, that could lead from one to another.

He turned and walked on. It was strange being out at this time of the morning. He thought he would be alone, but already there was a steady traffic of humans about the place.

At one end of the slightly sloping foreshore a white van was parked without identification marks. Its engine was running softly, leaving blue plumes on the moisture-laden air. A military policeman stood by while several bearded men in leather jackets moved what seemed to be a filing cabinet under a white dustsheet and placed it gingerly in the van. The military policeman smoked. Inside the vehicle two men sat, talking to one another and staring forward over the empty temporary docks to the grey sea beyond. Shaw felt, without knowing why, that the guard was edgy, that his taciturn poise hid an underlying nervousness. There were other signs, of a negative kind, that made him aware of the importance of the object they were guarding. The men in the van ignored his presence so steadfastly that he guessed they were concerned about him too.

Shaw sensed their unease and turned his face away, trying to make sense of what he had just seen. They were removing filing cabinets from what, until a few days ago, had been the Russian sailing base. The grounds were still fenced and spanned by electric fences. Even after the *Kirov* and her support yachts had been shipped away, the base continued to be guarded by police patrols with the red epaulettes of the MVD. When all personnel had gone, what remained to guard?

The long path on which he walked led inexorably towards the parked van. To turn off it would be suspicious now, and would be more likely to quicken their interest in his behaviour. The military policeman was putting out his cigarette, squeezing it between thumb and forefinger, a gesture that was both nonchalant and brutal, like crushing an insect, or breaking a bird's neck. As he drew abreast, the small white carcass of the cigarette fell like a warning at his feet.

Ahead of him the road split into several pathways. Shaw chose the one that would take him back towards the Estonian camp. Sensing, even at several hundred yards' distance, that the eyes of the military policeman were still on him, he did not look behind him.

Thirty-five

Their third-floor flat in one of the old merchants' houses in Rataskaevu Street was larger than expected. They had picked up the key from the white-haired janitor, and walked the two flights of stairs, Shaw carrying Jack on his shoulders. While he held on to Jack's ankles, Maria pushed the key in and opened the front door. For several seconds they paused on the threshold, nervous at what they might find.

Inside, at first they were silent. High ceilings, three large bedrooms, a bathroom in which the taps seemed to work, a big living-room and kitchen, and a view over a pleasant green garden at the back. As they moved from room to room, slowly their nervousness turned to pleasure.

Jack walked between them, holding one hand each. Like children, the three of them moved from room to room for a second time. Their few sticks of furniture would be lost.

Shaw opened a casement window on to the balcony to let in some fresh air and remove some of the heavy, flat smell of fresh paint. You could see over the roofs of houses down Viru Street, past Viru Gate, and out of one corner part of the nave of St Nicholas' church.

In the kitchen Maria leaned back against the sink.

'It's really ours?'

She looked around for places to put things, working out arrangements in her mind's eye.

'We'd better start moving things in,' Shaw said.

A militia truck, an old Benz lorry painted green, had brought their luggage and the few chests, and was parked beside the kerb with its engine running. The driver was a thin youth, asthmatic, with two high points of colour on his cheekbones. Wedged against the side-door, he roused himself.

'It's the right place?'

'Yes,' Shaw said.

The youth switched off the engine.

'I will help you with the furniture.'

But instead they sent him away to eat something. He had already driven for six hours non-stop. Coolly, he dropped from the cab, nodded, and walked down the street, his hands in his jacket pockets. Shaw and Maria began to lift the furniture piece by piece up the stairs. Jack sat on the steps leading up to the house. Together they carried tables, dismantled bed frames, and mattresses.

After the best part of an hour most of their possessions had been lifted. They paused so that Maria could feed Jack and make up his bed. Shaw used the screwdriver to set up the frame of their own double bed. Then they carried a few final items and stored them temporarily in the smallest bedroom.

Outside, in Rataskaevu Street, the thin youth had returned, knocking on the door, smelling of sausage and coffee. Out of gratitude for the long day's lift, Shaw gave him ten dollars. He reversed the old Benz truck in the road, and left waving, half his torso leaning out of the window. Shaw was certain he would mount the kerb and ram a lamppost. But he swung a corner sharply and disappeared with a squeal of tyres toward Pirita.

Tired, they returned to the flat.

It was starting to get dark. Inside the flat the shadows became luminous. Maria had brought a few eggs and some bread. She cooked a supper while Shaw worked at unpacking his few books from cardboard boxes and installing them in one of the two bookcases. It was ten thirty before they felt they had done as much as they could.

There was one final ritual. While Maria made the bed, under a bare, swinging bulb Shaw set out the instructions on the big Meeru central heating boiler in its kitchen recess. He lit the pilot flame, switched on the wall thermostat. With a thump like a spinnaker setting the gas heating came on.

It was a powerful machine, with something of the certitude of a ship's engine; in its efficiency and amplitude, typically Estonian. Shaw was overcome by tiredness. Maria was already in bed, breathing deeply. He undressed quietly, entered the sheets beside her. He closed his eyes and seemed to float backwards into sleep.

He liked the bareness, the largeness of the rooms, dwarfing the furniture. Their building had once been a medieval merchant's house, four storeys high, facing the street with its gable. The living quarters of the master had been on the lower floors. On the third and fourth floor were storage rooms. On the outside of the gable were the remains of a beam that had once been used to lift heavy objects upwards from the street. With the conversion to flats, new windows had been let in, but the original high ceilings remained.

Waking that morning, Shaw and Maria stood over the kitchen sink.

'You first,' he said.

She turned on the tap. Hot water burst out and steam rose in luxurious clouds from the stainless steel sink. They smiled broadly and inanely. In the background the Meeru boiler sighed and hummed. It was their first chance of a real hot bath after nearly a year of living with showers from dribbling cold water taps in sailing camps.

Shaw snapped in the plug and they watched the kitchen sink begin to fill.

While he shuffled around the apartment in his slippers, he could hear the sounds of Jack being bathed by Maria, the squeal as his body slid over the bath, the rattle of soap, his shouts as she scrubbed him.

Later that morning he walked to the post office and cabled his grandfather.

Dear Sam

We have been given a fine flat to stay in, courtesy of the Estonian people. Third floor, 42 Rataskaevu Street, Tallinn. It's bigger than we expected. We feel like peas rattling around in a pod.

There's a third bedroom that we've set up just for you. We reckon you'll cause about the same amount of trouble as Jack, so you'll even each other out.

Jim

The following day they received a return telegram.

Dear Jim

I can't guarantee to cause as much trouble as Jack, but I'm prepared to do my best.

I'm coming over on 18 September. No need to collect me, I can find my way there from the airport.

Sam

Maria bought new lampshades for the bare bulbs that hung from ceiling flexes, a carpet for the living-room, a new cot for Jack. The shopping arcades were as well stocked as any provincial Western city. She came home with two huge carrier bags full of food and toiletries. Shaw said, 'I'm going to have to find a job tomorrow.'

But Maria, in true Estonian tradition, controlled the finances, and there was enough in reserve to keep them going for several months, particularly since they paid no rent. It meant they wouldn't have to sell their small freeholding in Maine, at least for the time being. They had good neighbours, farmers who looked after their few sheep and hens, who kept an eye on the tiny wooden house. Their letters were reassuring and kind; it seemed the arrangement could continue for a while.

Prem called by in the afternoon of the following day.

They heard the doorbell ring and found him waiting on the landing, soberly suited, hat in hand. He seemed huge and out of place. He was like an actor come for an audition at a provincial theatre, feeling his way.

'Come in, come in,' Shaw said, standing aside.

Maria called, 'Who is it?'

'Gustav Prem himself,' he shouted. He took Prem's coat and hung it up. Maria appeared and hugged him. Prem lifted Jack up, looked into his eyes, and put him down.

'We moved in two days ago,' Shaw told him. Prem walked through, looking round. In the light he looked scrubbed and almost middle-aged. His untidy blond hair had been cut.

It was four-thirty. Shaw said: 'Something to drink?'

'Coffee, please.'

'Coffee?' He expressed surprise.

'Please.'

Shaw indicated the flat, the big, silent rooms. 'What do you think?'

'Excellent.' Prem was not at ease in houses any more. None of them were. Even with plenty of space, the walls pushed you inwards. It would take time to adjust.

He said, 'I came to tell you about the procession tomorrow. Illich's funeral.'

Shaw nodded.

'You will be one of the pall-bearers, in front with Brod. Soren Gir and I will be in the middle, directly behind behind us will be Maask and Migdal, then Arlof and Vagir.'

Shaw wanted to say, I know this is an honour and I don't deserve it, I'm just a latecomer. Maria looked at

185

him levelly, and he knew there would be no excuses. He said instead, 'Doesn't he have any relatives?'

'His parents are both dead. He had no brothers and sisters. There are his wife and children, of course. They will walk immediately behind the coffin.'

Prem carried a folded map of Tallinn with him. He laid it on the table. The route had been marked in arrows. He spread it out with his big hands. Like cloth it spilled over the sides of the table. He brought his finger down and talked them through the route. 'We lift the coffin off the carriage and carry it into the church. In the church we lay it on the floor of the aisle. A short private service for the relatives, perhaps twenty minutes. Then we carry the coffin back to the carriage and follow the carriage to St Olai's church. We lift the coffin down the aisle and place it on the catafalque in front of the altar. We stand beside it for the service, which will last nearly an hour. President Aegu will speak.'

Prem smiled briefly. Aegu always spoke; it was understood.

'When the service is over we carry the coffin back to the carriage. We follow it north along Lai Street, then right along Rannamae Street, and finally left again. After that, perhaps twenty minutes walking to the sea. There a launch will be waiting.'

He halted, as if to say, Simple.

Shaw was terrified. Prem, sensing this, for the first time showed genuine amusement behind the surface calm.

'You can forget entirely what I have said, just do what Brod does beside you.' Again he sensed Shaw's innocence of public occasion, and shook his head. 'Everything will be done very slowly. There is no one to hurry you.'

But despite Prem's reassuring words, Shaw was prey to more terrors about his role than he was about starting in an America's Cup race. When Prem left an hour or so later, he had visions about turning up the wrong road, separating completely. He feared Brod, following his instincts, might lead them not into the appropriate church, but into a public bar. He saw himself tripping and falling headlong in the aisle. He saw headlines: DRUNK AMERICAN IN BURIAL OUTRAGE.

In bed that night he was so restless with fear about his public role that Maria, trying to get an early night's sleep said: 'Look, if you're going to keep me awake, you may as well come over to my side of the bed.'

So their second day at the flat ended well, at least.

Thirty-six

On Saturday 18 September the bells began to peal in Tallinn at eight in memory of Ivan Illich. All around they could hear them, from the churches of St Nicholas, Holy Ghost, St Olai's, and the old Dome church, peals that flooded the city and its parks. From the ancient walled town on its hill the ringing spread out to the suburbs, from Toompea Palace to the stark new flat blocks of Mustamae, the carillons seemed to grow in strength, spilling over monuments and lakes, new shopping arcades, over the cold walls and ruins of the Pirita convent, until they reached the sea.

Shaw left the flat in Rataskaevu Street at nine thirty, giving himself ample time to walk to Voidu Square.

Despite the light rain, the park was dense with people, men, women and children. Shaw made his way through the throng towards the carriage at the square's centre. He hadn't expected to be recognized, but a call went up to make way, and hands patted him on the back as he made his way through. He found Brod, Prem, Gir and the others waiting in sober black beside the carriage with its six black horses.

He shook hands with them and they formed up in twos and waited behind the carriage. The light rain continued, though to the west the sky showed signs of clearing. Brod was unusually quiet. At nine the bells ceased their pealing, and only the great bell of the church of the Holy Ghost tolled slowly as they walked behind the carriage, two abreast, Shaw in front beside Brod, Prem and Gir behind him, then Arlof and Vagir, the others following; along Harju Street, through the open walls of the old city, between Assauwe Tower and Kiek in de Kok Cannon-Tower, the horses struggling up the incline. The route was dense with mourners as the carriage rolled past in silence, only the horses' hoofs sounding out above the tolling bell. Along Harju Street, past the church of St Nicholas, leaving the old Dwelling House at 1 Niguliste Street on the right. There was such a press as they neared the town square that the procession halted, and the horses waited while the road cleared and they could move into the square. They made their way around the Town Hall and its Old Thomas weather-vane on top of the tower, across Raekoja Plats, detouring around the old Town Council Apothecary, with its strange entwined symbol of healing. The carriage halted outside the doors of the church of the Holy Ghost. Shaw, Brod, Prem, Gir, Arlof, and Vagir moved forward to lift the coffin from the carriage and carry it through the great doors and down the aisle. In front of the altar they laid it on the tiles between them.

In the congregation were Illich's relatives, though Shaw had not met them. In the front right-hand pew was a pretty, dark-haired woman whom Shaw assumed would be Illich's ex-wife Anna, and the two girls beside her who were Illich's children. There were others who had Illich's long-boned features, with the hint of a family resemblance. Not far away was another woman, tall, strikingly beautiful, whom he had seen once before with Illich. This must be Lydia Teemant, he thought. He saw Maria and Jack sitting on a pew about twenty feet away on the left, Jack pulling at Maria's arm and pointing at him. Shaw turned back to look at the magnificent double-winged folding altar carved by Bernt Noltke. On its deep centre and on the sides of the wings were gilded woodcarvings. He allowed his eyes to be charmed by them, while the service continued.

The priest preached a simple sermon on the mortality of the body and the immortality of the soul, using as reference the beautiful clock on the outer wall of the church of the Holy Ghost, which bore the old Low German inscription:

ik sla rechte
der maghet als deme knechte
der vrouwen als dem heren
des en kan mi nemant ver keren

(I strike time correctly,
for the maidservant and the manservant,
for the mistress and the master.
No one can reproach me for that.)

At the end of the private service the pall-bearers raised the coffin and carried it to the waiting carriage.

The congregation of the church of the Holy Ghost gathered behind them. The procession moved on along Pikk Street, swinging left into Vana Street, then right into Lai Street, until they were at the doors of the great St Olai church. Shaw, Prem, and the others raised the coffin again from the carriage and carried it down the aisle of St Olai's for the public ceremony of mourning, laying it on the catafalque in front of the altar.

President Vajnen Aegu, sober-suited in black, stepped into the carved pulpit.

Aegu's sermon began with sober clarity. Ivan Illich, former colonel in the Russian Army, four times Olympic Gold medallist, helmsman and captain of the *Leningrad*, winner of the America's Cup in the year 2001, the greatest sailor of his time; half Estonian by birth, Estonian by loyalty, he had brought into being the yacht and the team that had successfully defended the America's Cup.

Aegu's voice in the nave swelled, reverberated, fell back, only to rise again. The techniques of secular oratory did not differ much from the religious. Ivan Illich was killed within a hundred yards of us, we the congregation who are here now. The assassin waited for the bells of the churches to begin pealing. The same bell tolled as in the procession, the church of the Holy Ghost, which could be heard even now tolling in St Olai's nave. And Aegu paused, while they listened to the single bell tolling and which would toll all day.

A man without pretensions, simple, direct, Aegu said. A fitting epitaph, he continued, would be that of Hans Pawels, merchant and art-lover, whose stone cenotaph was built into the outer wall of the adjoining St Mary's chapel. Translated from Low German, it read:

> What I have given has stayed with me,
> What I have had has parted with me,
> No one should think himself too high,
> Man's life goes by in a haze.

After the service, they lifted the coffin again from the catafalque, and placed it once more on the carriage. The procession moved northwards along Lai Street, turning right at Rannmae, and then left past the Great Coast Gate and Stout Margarete Cannon-Tower. A light rain began to fall, then cleared almost as quickly. The procession paused several times in its journey for the benefit of the children in its train. Stopping and starting, perhaps twenty-five minutes later they arrived at the harbour's edge. A space was gradually cleared, around which the huge crowd spilled. The pall-bearers gave the coffin its final lift into a waiting launch, then the launch's warps were cast off and it began its journey five miles out to sea.

Other vessels were waiting to carry the mourners out. Those of the crew who were not bearers were ushered by a militiaman on to one of the waiting customs vessels that had been seconded for the purpose. The congregation filled the other available launches. At the harbour entrance the funeral launch waited for the other boats to gather, then the convoy proceeded outwards to sea.

It had stopped raining. A watery sun occasionally showed itself behind clouds, putting dappled reflections in the waves and highlights into the shining wood and brightwork of the funeral launch. The wind seemed constant, Shaw guessed about twelve knots, and part of his mind registered that it was a good day for sailing. As they moved into the northerly swell the bow of the vessels kicked up the occasional sheet of spray, causing those on board to shield their eyes. Fine on starboard was the low wooded island of Aegna Saar. The convoy maintained five knots against the swell, then swung twenty degrees west towards the low, densely wooded line that was the island of Naissaar. When they arrived there must have been several hundred craft waiting in a broad hemisphere two miles to the east. At the centre of the hemisphere, rising and falling gently in the swell, was the green hull of *Novy Mir*.

Only then did Shaw begin to understand the largeness of Aegu's plan, the blend of the formal and the visionary, the peculiar fusion of imagination and calculation which informed his political actions.

Novy Mir lay at anchor, deserted, without mast or sails or rigging. The funeral launch approached, drew alongside her clear green topsides. Several boatmen and officials swarmed on board with warps to hold her fast. When the launch was securely held alongside, Illich's coffin was lifted aboard by the pall-bearers. Once they had slid the coffin on to *Novy Mir*'s empty decks, they climbed aboard themselves, ready to lift the coffin again as they regained their places on the yacht's decks. Perhaps ten feet aft of *Novy Mir*'s mast step, at the centre of the ship, a wooden platform had been constructed. The pall-bearers raised the coffin once more. Under Prem's *sotto voce* instructions it was carefully laid to rest on the dais itself. Dry wood had been piled against the lower part of the dais. Tarpaulins which had protected the wood against rain were now withdrawn. Shaw caught a whiff of petrol and, glancing down into the hull of the boat through the cockpit hatch, saw that the interior was partly filled with wood and dry rag. The entire yacht was a funeral pyre.

The choreography had been carefully planned. While the pall-bearers returned to the funeral launch, one of the two remaining officials on board *Novy Mir* lowered a detonator through the cockpit hatch on to the pile of flammable materials in the hold. He led the roll of insulated wire back to the launch. There it was connected to a plunger on the bow of the launch. The official clambered on board and the funeral launch reversed gingerly away, trailing insulated wire into the water.

Aegu, on board the funeral launch, nodded to the two priests who had taken both services. The priest of the church of the Holy Ghost began his last blessings. Stepping forward to the bow, Aegu pressed the plunger. Smoke issued from the hold of *Novy Mir*. Several seconds later flames appeared above the deck and began to move towards the coffin. The dry wood palings laid against the side of the dais began to light.

Shaw watched in awe. On board the funeral launch the detonation cable was severed with heavy wire-cutters; the launch continued to reverse slowly away out of range of the burning yacht. Flames now engulfed the coffin and dais in a concentrated conflagration. Other flames were migrating from head to stern. Occasional tongues of fire rose up high from the open hatches. Even from a hundred yards away, Shaw could feel the heat on his cheeks. Beside him *Novy Mir*'s Estonian crew were silent in concentration. Brod's face was wet with tears. Prem removed dark glasses from his pocket and quietly put them on. Suddenly the decks holding the dais collapsed and the coffin and its pyre descended into the intense white flames of the hold. Now the entire hull was burning. *Novy Mir* began to sink; flames hissed on the water like tongues. A rising pall of smoke hung above the silent boats. The priest of the church of the Holy Ghost gave his final blessing. Beneath his raised hand the yacht, weighted with its lead keel, breathed a sigh like an animal then slid slowly downwards into the green sea.

Shaw glanced at Aegu. His face showed no emotion. But he knew for certain that images of the violently burning, sinking hull would be on the front page of every major newspaper the following morning – that Aegu's final, calculated act would send the acrid smell of Illich's death to Moscow, even to Washington itself.

Thirty-seven

Only when the final few pieces of black debris had been released by the throat of the sea did the spectacle cease to hold them. It had been a Viking's funeral: primitive, powerful, and at the same time curiously cathartic.

Some residue of bitterness seemed to have been burned from their hearts. Shaw and Brod and Prem felt a peculiar lightness take hold of them as they journeyed back amongst the huge fleet. In the bow the two priests talked amiably. Aegu had gone below. Shaw saw him once, when the cabin doors were opened as an official emerged; he was wedged in a corner, a space around him, looking through the contents of a dispatch box and making marks with a pen in the margins.

'We should go somewhere,' Prem said. It was a euphemism. There was a general intention to get drunk that afternoon.

At the quay, they waited for Aegu to disembark to a waiting car. On shore, Brod said, 'I know a place.' Seven Estonian pall-bearers and one American, dressed in black and looking like undertakers, set out in a group towards the bar in question.

All industrial port areas are sordid; gantries and booms against a background of rusting metal and unused machinery. Ekaterina's was one of those small cellar bars that litter the seedier areas of ports. Swing doors, bare brick walls, nets with floats in them; a decor that was both sordid and familiar.

Ekaterina herself was huge. A Russian, her hair was red, her lips an exotic orange. She leaned over the bar towards Shaw as the smallest, as though to a child. 'Seven crows,' she said to him. 'And you.'

It was right that Shaw as helmsman should buy the first round. If there was to be mischief, he should lead the way.

'A bottle of vodka, please. Eight glasses.'

'Pull two tables together,' Ekaterina said, turning sideways towards the rows of bottles on her shelves. 'Make yourselves at home.'

There were two women at another table, one young, somewhat white faced; the other older. Shaw guessed the younger had a drug habit. The older was a calming

194

influence, and negotiated for both of them. Shortly afterwards the vodka came.

Prem undertook the ceremony, placing the glasses, all touching, in a circle. Concentrating, he poured continuously from one to another. They raised their glasses.

'To Illich.'

'Illich.' They drank. The vodka bit the back of Shaw's throat.

There was a silence.

'The grandfathers,' Brod called.

They drank again. Vagir was the only morose one. 'We worked night and day to get *Novy Mir* ready. Why? So it could be burnt.'

'It was a good fire.' Prem was inclined to be sympathetic. 'Usually, your beautiful boats are given to crews who are useless. A fire is surely a better fate.'

Vagir was partially persuaded by this truth. Prem said, piling on the arguments. 'Elderly army colonels, renegade Americans . . .'

'Former paratroopers. Another bottle,' Brod called to Ekaterina.

Vagir was close to seeing the advantage of having the boat burnt.

As a rule Shaw did not like large parties. Someone had said that the quality of conversation depreciated in proportion to the number of people at a table. This party was overdue, though. They had hardly had a chance to celebrate their victory before the camp dispersed.

Ekaterina came with a second bottle. It was Brod's turn to pour without spilling.

Something inside Shaw had turned. He had lost the taste for these hearty forms of male companionship. He would have preferred to be at home with Maria and Jack. The occasional urges to be out of the flat were minor compared with the feeling of claustrophobia which seemed to him to permeate these all-male

195

sessions. The fault lay not so much in the camaraderie, but in the way all life was reduced to a few basic common denominators. Women were objects to be pursued, seduced, dominated, but never treated as human. Heavy drinking was manly and sociable. It was the lore of male companionship everywhere.

'You look pensive, Kapitan,' Brod said.

Shaw shrugged. When there was a purpose in mind, a collective reason for existence, the group began to mean something. He suspected that the same isolation had separated Illich.

The seven Estonian undertakers began singing. Shaw was excused because he did not know the words of the songs, let alone the older songs that followed hard on their heels. While the rounds of vodka increased and the others became more voluble, so Shaw grew more detached. There was a collective movement to go to another bar, somewhere seedier, somewhere with more women of a certain type. Vagir knew of a place.

Getting to his feet, Shaw swayed alarmingly. He was not only out of practice in male company, he was also less able to hold his drink. He felt obliged to accompany them but Prem was kindly. 'Go home, Kapitan. You are no longer one of us.' Prem hiccupped delicately. 'Maybe none of us are.'

'Come and visit us, Prem,' Shaw said.

Outside it was overcast again. The seven Estonian undertakers shook hands with him and moved off down the road, arms over one another's shoulders, singing lustily. He watched them go, wondering whether he would ever see them together again.

Others had moved down to the docks, mostly men, mostly Finnish, mostly drunk. The Finns managed to achieve a level of inebriation which was, even to Estonians who prided themselves on such things, heroic. For most people drinking was a more or less steady movement towards physical incapacity. But for a Finn there seemed to be, at the end of incapacity, a kind of physical resurrection, a different form of life in which what reasserted itself was instinct. A drunken Finn was like the most primitive of animals, a being whose behaviour patterns were at the most basic; at the same time his continued function defied certain laws of biology and physics. There was a popular dance, called the Finnish Leg, a kind of sideways scuttle with arms hanging limply by one's sides, based closely on the movements of a drunken Finn.

There were other reasons for respecting Finns. They had a reputation for pulling knives in drunken brawls. Estonians preferred to admire their drinking from a safe distance. Shaw shared this cautiousness, and refused with as much tact as possible a bottle offered by a group of resolutely cheerful men crossing the road on Endla Street.

Carefully he made his way back. The fresh air went some way towards allaying his drunkenness. He had only reached that early stage of inebriation when the alcohol is like a vague mist on the senses rather than a heavy drowning presence. Walking fast, he took a longer route than normal to achieve at least a facsimile of sobriety.

Arriving back, he expected a lecture from Maria. The door was opened shortly after his tentative knock. Jack was sleeping quietly after the energies of his long walk behind the procession.

Maria had been crying. There is a stage beyond grief, a stage of exhaustion and reticence. He perceived, almost at the same moment, that she was more concerned to hide the extremity of her own emotions than to question his drinking habits. With a swiftness motivated partially by a genuine concern and partially by the instinct of predator Shaw changed his tactics and went directly on to the offensive.

197

'What's the matter?'

She closed the door quietly. Her grief extended to him. He knew instinctively that her anger included him. If he touched her she would have frozen.

'You men.'

He followed her through to the kitchen at a respectful distance. She sat down in a chair and rested her head in her hands. Shaw sat down opposite, taking care that their knees did not touch under the table.

Maria said, 'The way you use Illich's death.'

'That wasn't us. That was Aegu. I thought it was a good send-off.'

Her face came up fiercely.

'"A good send-off"? Is that all he means to you?'

Shaw tried to tread carefully.

'What would you have preferred?'

She didn't answer at first.

'Something suitable, something . . . quieter.'

Shaw paused, negotiating a difficult path.

'Whatever we might think, he was a public figure.'

'"Public"?' she sniffed. 'He was the most private man you could meet.'

Shaw knew that anything he said would condemn him. And if he didn't say anything, that would condemn him too. He preferred to be condemned for something really serious.

'I thought Aegu did right. He made a powerful public ceremony out of Illich's death. The others thought so too.'

'Men.' Sadness and compassion now, the full arsenal.

'I support it, but I didn't organize it personally.'

'Aegu is one of you. He is just more blatant. He is your representative. He does what you would like to do. That is why he has such power.'

Shaw was relieved and curious. He was impressed that a funeral could be turned into an attack on the callousness of mankind in general. He wondered fleetingly whether the others would be subject to the same criticism when they returned home to their own womenfolk, and what form it might take. He experienced a brief, comical vision of Brod returning, at a truly heroic, indeed Finnish level of inebriation, cowering in a corner while he was roundly harangued by Ilena.

It was a mistake to let one's mind wander, even for a moment. Maria was looking at him, as if for the first time. 'And you've been drinking.'

Thirty-eight

Shaw woke at his usual time and lay awake, watching a white dawn through the casement window which they would shortly curtain. Their bedroom was east-facing. Maria breathed deeply and softly.

He eased himself carefully from the bed, walked across the wooden floors to the bathroom. He washed his face and shaved slowly, then dressed. In his previous existence it was not the brevity of time so much as the pressure of events unfolding in his mind, the perception of possible crisis, that caused in him a continuous tension. Without a schedule to drive him, the mere passage of time seemed opulent.

He opened the door and went down the stairs into the street. Outside a Sunday calm held the city. There was no throng of early workers hurrying to factories, or the quiet return of late night shift workers.

He started to walk past St Nicholas' church. There was a newspaper kiosk at the corner of Niguliste and Harju Streets. Approaching it, he reached in his pocket to pay the old war veteran who sold papers.

An extraordinary sight met his eye. The development of communications technology and rapid print meant the newspapers could be printed locally. Tallinn received the major world papers simultaneous with their publication at source. He paused to glance down at the newspapers lining the stand. The front page of almost every paper, from *Stern* to *Le Figaro* to the *New York Times*, carried an image of the burning *Novy Mir*, flames rising about Illich's coffin. Several chose exactly the same picture – the hand of a priest raised in final benediction as the flames behind seemed to reach towards the white hand. Another showed the squat figure of Aegu from behind, his bull-like neck fixed in calm and fierce attention; in the background, *Novy Mir* was nothing more than a final effulgence of fire and steam on a surface already clotted with black debris. Shaw ran his eye along the headlines. 'ESTONIAN FIRESHIP', 'HERO'S FUNERAL', 'FINAL VALEDICTION', 'VIKING SALUTE'. On several photographs he could make out the tall figures of Prem and Soren Gir, even himself, minor bit players in an ancient drama of heroism and death. He felt an urge to buy half a dozen in order to gauge the response to Illich's life and departure, as if public expression could make sense of a private life. Already Illich was a public possession, a myth. If Shaw had not said goodbye to Illich at the funeral, he said goodbye to him now, standing alone at a kiosk on the corner of Harju Street.

Back at the flat, Maria said: 'Jack and I thought you did very well yesterday. We were quite proud of you.'

Shaw still had it in mind that she had suggested he and his crew had conducted a fascist rally on Illich's bones. He lay on the bedspread beside her, reading the *Washington Post*. He still liked to read newspapers in English. He said, 'I didn't drop the coffin. I didn't fall over.'

'I'm sorry about what I said.'

'I know you didn't mean it – I mean, about my being drunk.'

'Don't be facetious.'

He was facing towards the open casement window. He could sense her turning over in bed to face his back.

'Next Sunday,' she said, 'I'm going to start going to church, do what I can to help, try and meet a few people. Maybe I can get a part-time job somewhere. Aunt Liina will help with baby-sitting.'

Shaw turned the page.

'That sounds like good thinking.'

They lay in silence, knowing that the question that lay between them was what he would do, now that his sailing days were finally over.

The telephone rang at ten fifteen, loud in the big, empty rooms.

'Jim Shaw.'

In the silence which followed he knew instinctively who had called. He imagined Aegu at the other end, the receiver gripped between his shoulder and neck, as he struggled to light a cigarette. Over the intervening quiet he heard the flare of a match, a pause for inhalation. Aegu exhaled like a sigh.

'Good morning, *tovarich*. You are settled in to your flat.'

'We certainly are.'

'If you agree, I wish to arrange a meeting in order to bring you up to date on the various pieces of evidence regarding Illich's death.'

'I'd appreciate that.'

'This coming week I have too many duties to be able to see you. The following week I have three days of trade negotiations in Moscow, after which I travel to Vilnius. So two weeks will pass before I have a chance to discuss matters with you.'

Aegu inhaled and breathed out again. Shaw tried to catch the drift of the conversation.

'I'm not doing anything important.'

'Perhaps,' Aegu said, 'you would care to meet me at my house at 16 Kohtu Street.'

'I'll look that up on a map.'

'As I sit here I am looking down on the roof of your house from my study. Estonia,' Aegu commented wryly, 'is not a continent like America.'

To reach his official residence, however, it was necessary to follow a zig-zag path. Aegu outlined a set of directions. It was a few minutes' walk. They agreed to meet at noon. Shaw put down the phone.

'That was the great man.'

'Sounds like you were setting up a meeting.'

'He wants to meet at twelve so he can bring me up to date on Illich.'

'Be careful of Aegu,' Maria said. Her voice carried no emphasis.

'I'm careful of all politicians on principle,' Shaw replied. 'Even Estonian ones.'

Maria, rising from bed, threw on a dressing-gown and knelt over Jack, gathering his toys together so that he could disperse them again. Her dark hair had fallen in a single wave across her face, so he could not see her expression.

Thirty-nine

A sea mist had blown in, suddenly thick. Shaw could feel it clammy on his skin as he climbed towards Aegu's house.

A pedestrian path led upwards. He ascended as instructed the stone stairs from Rataskaevu Street to the Garden of the Danish King. Dense fog billowed down the passages like smoke. Once or twice he put his arm out for support on the walls, and noticed they were already moisture-laden. At the top of the stairs he found himself in an enclosed garden, laid with gravel paths. He made his way to Kohtu Street, and followed it as instructed until he came to Number Sixteen.

A single militiaman reared out of the thick mist to open the gate for him. He walked up the stairs and lifted the knocker on the heavy door. He heard the echo float away inside the house.

A slim woman opened the door, white-haired, with lively blue eyes behind metal-framed glasses. He had an impression of an academic. Somewhere he had heard that Aegu's wife was an historian.

'Mr Shaw?'

Shaw held out his hand.

'Linda Aegu.'

Her fingers were dry. The name Linda had a special provenance in Estonia. It was the name of the mythical mother of the nation. At her statue, in Hirve Park, had been held the first public affirmations of Estonian independence during the 1980s.

'Please come in. Aegu is in his study. He is on the telephone. He won't be long.'

She led him into an impressive, high-ceilinged sitting room. Shaw had noticed that, like other Scandinavians, the Estonians seemed to prefer their rooms uncluttered.

'Would you like a drink?'

He had the impression, difficult to explain, that she regarded the high formality of the house with something approaching irony. Already he had begun to categorize her. Her natural place was at a desk, surrounded by learned tomes.

'A whisky, please.'

She poured two glasses, handed him one, indicated a sofa, and and sat down opposite him in one of the high chairs.

'So.' She surveyed him. 'I expected a terrible monster, a wolf-man at least.'

The whisky touched the back of Shaw's throat. He replied, 'I'm afraid my howling days are over.'

'What a pity. My husband said you intend to retire from sailing.'

'That's right.'

'You look too young to be a pensioner.' Before he could reply, she said, 'You will have lunch with us, won't you?'

Upstairs a door was opened, and footsteps descended the staircase.

'My husband,' Linda Aegu said.

Aegu entered the room with his bull's energy, gripping Shaw's hand almost before he had a chance to stand up.

'Thank you,' he said to his wife. Before she turned and left for another room, she said, 'He is staying for lunch.' To Shaw she added, 'It will be simple, just a picnic.'

They took his acceptance for granted. 'Follow me,' Aegu said.

Aegu's study, at the top of several flights of stairs, looked east over the town. The casement windows were open, though the fog obscured the view. Piles of papers and official documents were scattered over the huge desk. Volumes were piled up on the chairs, spilling across the floor. On the corner of the desk was an ashtray overflowing with cigarette butts.

'We have to deal with the racial minorities question on an almost daily basis. It is our most important internal matter. As you know, there is tension between the indigenous Estonians and the waves of Russians, Georgians, and Azerbaijanis who migrate here. The Russians work in the factories, the Georgians are small traders, the Azerbaijanis run shops and taxis. Sometimes the activities of the minorities do not fall easily within the rules.' Aegu opened a cigarette packet, extracted one, lit it. 'It is said that the average Georgian trader keeps three sets of books; the first is for the taxman, the second for when the taxman says, "Where are the real books?" And the third are the real books.'

Aegu lifted a pile of volumes from a chair so that Shaw could sit down.

'The trouble with the primitive stage of capitalism,' he said, 'is that it is just as the socialists claim – seedy, exploitative, profiteering.'

'And the later stage?' Shaw asked.

'Ah, we shall see when we come to it,' he said amiably. He sat down opposite Shaw at his chair behind the desk. It was a fine desk, covered in green leather, with finely grained oak.

'You can always tell in a culture which are the points of tension,' he continued, 'by the subject of the prevailing jokes. With us it is the black economy. There is another about the new immigrants and the black market. The average new immigrant earns seven thousand roubles a year, spends ten thousand, and saves the rest.'

'A drink?' he winked, making a gesture towards the door which took in his formidable wife.

Behind one pile of volumes was a bottle of vodka, behind another a couple of glasses. Shaw was not averse to drinking, but he knew enough of Aegu's reputation to be aware that he would be expected, one day, to drink with him into oblivion. Aegu poured carefully, making sure the bottle did not touch the lip of the glass and cause a telltale chink which his wife would hear.

He put one glass in Shaw's hand, placed a finger across his mouth, and drank a silent toast to the spiritual world.

'Aegu,' his wife called up from the staircase well.

'Yes, my dear.'

'Only one glass before lunch.'

'Of course, dear.'

Aegu was like a schoolboy. He paused while his wife's footsteps moved away, threw back the vodka in one gulp, and refilled his glass. He gestured with the bottle towards Shaw. Shaw, out of some obscure sense of camaraderie, followed suit. Inside him the vodka paused. Then it hit his throat and stomach like fire. He blinked, tried not to cough and splutter, and held out his glass. Aegu refilled it.

'Now,' he said, taking up his formal tone. 'We come to the subject of the murder inquiry.'

Aegu picked up a pile of papers on his desk. 'These are photocopies for you to take away. In the meantime, I will summarize the findings.' He leant back in his chair.

'The investigation has pursued all lines of enquiry open to it. The first one was clearly related to the telegram which was found in Illich's pocket, sent by his wife. We sent a team to interview her in Kharkov. You know that several years ago they divorced and she married a professor of computer studies. A Russian Ukrainian. They live in Kharkov. She is a strong-minded woman. She used the loss of Illich's pension to enforce sole custody of the children.' He paused. 'The report of Inspector Saarinen cleared her of any active complicity on the basis of the available evidence. She had been in Kharkov during the time of the murder, and they obtained supporting alibis not only from her husband but from those who worked with her. There is no doubt she was in Kharkov. She denied all knowledge of the telegram. Saarinen and his men found no evidence to the contrary. For the time being, at least, that seems to be a closed avenue.

'What does that leave us with? The pathologist's report is also in the file. Illich was hit by four bullets in the chest area, fired from in front. There is evidence that this occurred during a struggle. A fifth shot was fired into the back of his head as he lay on the floor.

'Apart from traces of blood on the floor and walls, there was evidence of aqueous humour from an eye, belonging not to Illich but to the assailant. There was enough aqueous humour on the floor to indicate that the assailant had been blinded in at least one and probably both eyes. There were further traces of aqueous humour on Illich's hands, particularly on his thumbs, indicating that these were the means by which the assailant was blinded.'

Aegu paused, allowing him to recover. He poured himself another drink of vodka, offered the bottle with a raised eyebrow to Shaw.

He needed this one. The liquid was like a comet.

Aegu continued: 'The other strand of investigation concerned the janitor, Vladimir Irkut, a former paymaster's clerk in the Russian Army. He was on holiday with his family in the Black Sea. Inspector Saarinen mounted a full investigation of his case. There are no significant leads, but some points which may demand further investigation at a later stage. The preliminary report suggests there is little doubt that he was at the Black Sea. A team flew out there and alibis have been obtained. The suspicion remains that he may have known the identity of the murderer. Of course, he pleads total ignorance.'

'And your inspector doesn't believe him?' Shaw asked.

'Saarinen retains an open mind. So far, however, his suspicions remain unjustified – unjustified in terms of the material evidence.'

The door of the study remained slightly ajar. Footsteps came to the bottom of the stairwell.

'Lunch is ready!' called Linda.

'Thank you!' To Shaw, 'That is as much as we know at present. There are various other aspects of a rather speculative nature, but perhaps I had better deal with those after we have eaten.'

He placed the vodka bottle and the glasses carefully behind a pile of books.

'You'd better bring those glasses down for me to wash!' Linda called up the stairs. The schoolboy Aegu guiltily picked up the glasses, and Shaw followed him down the stairs.

A whisky followed by three vodkas on an empty stomach required the occasional assistance of the banisters as they descended. The soles of his feet seemed to free-float, to hover, before touching the next step. But he found himself at the bottom of the staircase in reasonable order, and followed Aegu through into the dining-room.

A large table had been laid with three places.

Linda held out her hand and Aegu handed over the used glasses with unabashed candour. Aegu seated himself at the head of the table, indicating the chair on his right for Shaw.

Linda returned from the kitchen, sat opposite him, and began to ladle out cold soup into plates.

'Please start.'

It was delicious. Shaw, determined to widen his knowledge from the narrow aspects of sailing, asked her what were the constituents.

'Zucchini, onion, celery, tarragon; would you like the full recipe?'

'Thank you. I can take it back to Maria.'

She looked at her husband, stirring his soup briskly. 'Food makes Aegu impatient.' It was true. Aegu appeared oblivious of them, swilling his soup at speed.

'I'm a peasant at heart,' Aegu commented, raising his head from the empty bowl.

'Nonsense,' Linda Aegu said. 'When he has an audience of socialists, he boasts of his baronial ancestors eating huge carcasses and throwing bones over his shoulder to the dogs.'

Shaw could see that these two built their relationship on a friendly balance of antagonism.

'Despite his table manners, my husband will have some more. May I offer you some first?'

'Thank you.' He must drink Aegu's vodka and have extra helpings of his wife's soup. It could have been worse; in certain parts of Africa, one ate sheep's eyes and grasshoppers.

She poured the remainder into Aegu's bowl. Aegu attacked the contents with the same unremitting ferocity.

'Of course,' he said, 'in Mr Shaw we have an Estonian hero. Yet we do not fully understand his political views.' Aegu made a sound like a tractor in his soup. 'We understand his father was a communist, yet in his own behaviour he exhibits an individualism which would do credit to a follower of Friedrich Nietzsche . . .' He broke with his strong hands a large hunk of brown bread into more manageable pieces and began to swab up stray puddles of soup from his plate.

'I am sure Mr Shaw was not expecting to be interrogated on his political views,' Linda Aegu said. 'Other people are not like Estonians, they are not obsessed about politics.'

'As a naturalized Estonian, he is qualified to become obsessed.'

Shaw finished his soup. 'I'm afraid I have no views.'

'You see,' Linda Aegu crowed. 'He is not obsessed like you.'

'Nonsense, my dear. There are certain people who are like *naïf* painters. They have political views, but they express that in action rather than words. They are . . .'

'*Naïf?*' suggested his wife.

'Thank you. As you see, Mr Shaw is a consummate politician.'

Linda Aegu left to fetch the second course. Aegu commented: 'It is difficult to describe one's position because of the constantly shifting terms. For example, as the demands for effective changes increase, so the labels undergo a further metamorphosis. Communism is now indelibly equated with conservatism. Capitalism used to be regarded as right wing. At the same time the move towards free enterprise is a form of "radicalism", a movement to the "left". How can we define our own difficult positions if the very words of political definition are themselves undergoing radical transformations?'

It was a rhetorical question, which Shaw did not attempt to answer. Linda Aegu returned with the second course, a huge plate of salads and a smaller one of meat, and sat down.

'If you do not mind, Mr Shaw, we will feed my husband first. It tends to put a brake on his political discussion. Pass me your plate, dear.'

Aegu did so but continued talking. 'It is possible, nevertheless, to detect an underlying trend, a glimmer of reason. Over the last thousand years in Europe the left wing, in my view, is the movement away from feudalism, from a centralist, conservative state, towards increasing decentralism of power. Now all our petty "isms" may be judged against this broad movement of progress. Clearly, communism and fascism are highly centralist, therefore they belong to the right of the spectrum. Capitalism and bourgeois democracy are, surprisingly, somewhat decentralist, and therefore to the left. Liberal or "pluralist" socialism is also on the left, though whether social democracy is more decentralist than capitalism is open to debate. Some of my colleagues assume too easily that it is.'

'Is he boring you with his political definitions?' Linda Aegu asked.

'Of course I am, my dear. You see, Mr Shaw, this

210

view places other major political developments in perspective. We speak of revolutions. Yet against the background of decentralization, did the French Revolution really constitute progress? Was not the "terror", in which vast numbers were killed at the whim of a small revolutionary clique, was not that an example of centralism rather than decentralism? The same is true of the Soviet Revolution. Power, which had begun to be dispersed into more democratic and liberal forms, was afterwards concentrated in the hands of the minority Bolshevik party, more particularly into the hands of Lenin and Stalin. Thereafter power was maintained in a small, self-perpetuating élite whose contempt for the ballot box, and the view of the masses, was total.'

'Meat and salad, Mr Shaw? My husband seems to have forgotten his duties as host. I will cut the meat.'

'Thank you.'

'If we look at the English Revolution, on the other hand, and the institution of democratically elected parliament, it would seem to be a genuine attempt to decentralize power. Thereafter the monarchy was subject to successive reduction of authority in favour of the elected assembly. That has more claim to a genuine revolution. The American revolution, too, with its clear separation of the powers of the executive and the law. A genuine revolution.'

'You are boring Mr Shaw.' Linda handed him a large plate piled high with salads, lettuce, tomato, radishes, beetroot. Aegu, pausing slightly at the clatter of the plate, surged on.

'The movement towards independence in smaller countries is clearly a movement of decentralization. We can call this movement progressive or left-wing. The difficulty arises in asking ourselves what sort of internal economy do we require? Shall we teeter delicately on the verge of liberal socialism, allowing a few sufficient reforms, or shall we introduce a complete free market?'

211

'Do please go ahead,' Linda Aegu said to Shaw. 'This table is a complete free market while he is talking. Salad dressing?'

'Thank you.'

'The question is, where do Estonian women fit into the equation? They prevent their husbands from talking about politics at lunch. They do not allow a single drink of vodka beforehand. Clearly, creatures of an extreme right-wing, centralist tendency.'

'And proud of it,' his wife commented.

Ignoring her, Aegu began to attack his plate of food, the meat first, sending pieces of lettuce scurrying off his plate on to the table. He paused briefly to add: 'Pride goeth before destruction, and an haughty spirit before a fall.'

'Since he gave the sermon yesterday,' his wife explained, 'he has become somewhat inclined to the Biblical. Tell me, Mr Shaw . . .'

'Please call me Jim.'

'Thank you. Jim. I ask you in all seriousness. Why did Illich inspire such loyalty? My husband, for example, was devastated by his death.'

She turned her grey eyes on him, and he realized this was perhaps the most serious question.

'I think I know what he means.'

'Why? Do you mind my asking?'

'I don't mind you asking, because it's a question I've asked myself.'

'Why, then?'

Perhaps it was the vodka that made him talk, that made him try to express something which words seemed to hide rather than disclose. 'Most helmsmen, as far as I can see, want to beat the other man. That's their motivation. I would say that was true of me. You want to beat your rival, so you train yourself to think that you are better, and to despise him. At the same time, you retain enough admiration for him to want to spend your life trying to beat him. At the heart of your attitude is a contradiction.'

'And Illich was different?'

'Yes.' Shaw struggled with expression. What he wanted to say seemed to lead him forward and hold him back. 'He wasn't obsessed about beating someone else. He was out to do the best that he could, independently of anyone else. You could say he wanted to beat himself. His point of reference was his knowledge of himself.' Shaw paused. 'I don't think I'm explaining this too well.'

'Carry on.'

'There is a British helmsman called Sinclair, a really fine helmsman; young, full of confidence. He beat Illich in a couple of practice races, before Illich got the hang of him. Illich could be annoyed, but it was only superficial. It wasn't his real motivation. His deep motivation had nothing to do with other people.'

Aegu's manic eating had slowed to a fast romp through the remaining vegetables. Shaw had the impression he was listening with at least part of his mind.

'That was the difference?' Linda Aegu encouraged him.

Shaw wondered what exactly he'd said. One effect of the vodka was that he was running parallel with himself, trying to keep up. The other effect was that it didn't seem to matter if he made a fool of himself.

'He was independent of other people. The closer you got, the further you were away. He was a little like a saint. I'm not good at analysing other people.'

'Better than you think, I suspect.' Like a good hostess, however, she did not press the subject.

'You see,' Aegu said, breaking in. 'He is a *naïf*, hiding behind false modesty.'

'Shut up, dear, and eat some more food. More, Jim?'

'Thank you,' he replied.

'And,' Aegu said, 'he speaks rather a lot, given that he comes from Maine.'

'Keep quiet, dear. Let's see how fast you can get through this plateful.'

She cut slices and prepared another huge helping for Aegu. Now she put the plate down in front of him with a springy, casual violence.

Aegu said to himself, in the lilting Estonian tongue, 'They only talk about fish in Maine, and here he is calling someone a saint.'

'Ignore him,' Linda Aegu said. 'How did you meet your wife, Jim? In Estonia?'

'No, in America. She lived close by when we were kids. She was the reason I came over here. She wanted to visit her relations in the old country.'

'She is a very pretty girl, with dark hair?'

'Thank you. She is looking for some way to help in the community. She has an aunt who likes to look after our son Jack.'

'And you? Is being a hero enough for you?'

'He is going to help me,' Aegu said, 'with the investigation into Illich's death.' He had finished his second plateful, and was investigating with a friendly finger a piece of lamb lodged between his teeth.

'I expect you want to return to the study,' his wife suggested sweetly. As a parting shot at Aegu, she said: 'You'd better take two clean glasses with you.'

Forty

In the study, Aegu said: 'There are a few other matters in the case which I wanted to discuss with you.'

Shaw sat back in the leather chair, a fresh glass of vodka in his hand. Outside the fog had cleared, except

214

for a few traces on the sides of buildings. A strong sun burned down. It was a magnificent view over the green trees of the slope to the red-tiled roofs and town squares. Threads of mist hung over them like white streamers. He tried to make out the roof of their own flat, and wondered what Maria was doing.

Aegu saw him staring out. 'Sometimes people state that a small country is economically not viable. The opposite is true. If one draws up a table of size against *per capita* income, the smaller the state, the higher the average wealth of the individuals within it. In Europe the larger states – Germany, Britain, France – are in only a moderate position compared to the Scandinavian countries, Switzerland, and then, higher still, Luxemburg, Liechtenstein, Monaco.'

Aegu gulped down a glass of vodka, and reached for the bottle. Shaw followed suit. Aegu sat back in his chair and changed the subject.

'I wanted to ask you a question which you may find embarrassing or painful. You do not need to answer it. One line of enquiry in Illich's murder concerns the American aspect.' Aegu paused. 'I understood from Illich, just before he died, that the Estonian camp believed that *Novy Mir* was rammed deliberately by the American yacht in the third race.'

Shaw nodded. 'I agree.'

Aegu watched him carefully, waiting for him to continue.

Shaw said, 'What you're asking is, having rammed *Novy Mir*, would they then try to murder Illich?'

Aegu waited patiently.

'My own feeling is that they wouldn't. For three reasons, none of them conclusive. The first is, by ramming *Novy Mir* and removing her from the equation, they believed they were back in the race with the best chance. They knew *Eagle* was much faster than *Leningrad*. There was no need to take the matter further with

215

such ... drastic action. The second is, American corporations are very tough in the way they deal. Takeover battles, some close legal deals, all kinds of pressure short of criminal blackmail, stretching the rules, that's all meat to these red-blooded boys. Murder is generally not a recognized method of pursuing corporate policy. It's not conclusive, but it's just something I feel.'

Aegu smiled. 'Continue.'

'Thirdly, Illich wouldn't have been their target. To them, he's a Russian pursuing legitimate interests. With the new economic conditions, those big corporation guys are all pally with Russia. When they weren't spectators, they were kissing Russian ass and making deals. Why shake that? If they were really feeling vindictive, I would have been more likely to arouse that type of feeling than Illich. I was the traitor who helped Illich get his team into final shape. I was the guy that pushed the Ericson faction out of the last America's Cup. So I'd be the natural target, not Illich. It just doesn't add up.'

After several seconds Aegu said: 'You are not arguing merely out of loyalty?'

Shaw shrugged. 'Let's say I'm an American patriot. One of the things that makes me want to help you in this is to find out whether there is an American interest. But you asked me whether I think it was likely. And I don't.'

Aegu stared out over the town. The threads of mist were clearing now. A bright sun shone on the red roofs and pastel-coloured walls of the old town.

'What you say seems cogent to me,' Aegu said. 'I am persuaded that unless further evidence arises we should place investigations into the American connection on one side.'

He threw back another glass of vodka, and Shaw followed suit. Aegu produced a second bottle from another pile of books and refilled their glasses. Swirling the drink in the glass, he leant back in his chair.

'I have had to make a judgement,' he continued, 'as to how much I believe you should know in order to help me proceed. I have now made my decision. All relevant information will be made available to you. That brings us to the final area of the investigation.

'The role of the Russian Army in this is unclear. I shall explain the background. As you know, the Russian defence was effectively controlled by the Army. It was intended to supervise this by means of a committee in Moscow, in which Army representation was partial, not total. The Chairman of the committee, Vitaly Pridilenko, was a senior member of the Russian ruling élite. He died recently in an accident under somewhat dubious circumstances. He was a personal friend.'

Aegu paused.

'There are indications that the Army was suspicious of Illich's loyalties in regard to the Russian defence. He is an Estonian citizen and it has been an unwritten rule that the officer corps of the Russian armed forces is composed of pure Russians, with a smattering of closely related ethnic groups – Byelorussians, Ukrainians. Balts like Illich are treated with suspicion. To rise in the hierarchy is not impossible, but it requires unusual ability and dedication. Illich was an exceptional officer and rose to colonel. The Army was proud of his sporting record. He was an ambassador for them, proof that Balts could be accepted, proof also of the sporting abilities fostered by the Army. At the same time they were nervous of his apparent independence. He was a hero outside the Army. In Russia, which traditionally prizes sportsmen and gives them the greatest privileges, Illich was a prince among heroes. He could have flourished outside the Army as a privileged member of the élite. There is a Russian word, *nash*, used by the Army. It means "ours", that is to say, wholly on our side. Illich was not *nash*. You said yourself that he was extremely independent.'

Aegu glanced at Shaw's half-filled glass, filled his own empty one, and took a gulp before continuing.

'A part of the Army hierarchy wanted to strengthen its grip on the defence. My old colleague Pridilenko was fascinated by the arcane symbolism of the America's Cup. He used to describe it as a bourgeois convention, but at the same time he recognized it as a highly prestigious competition. In the absence of a contest of arms, the Army also is fascinated by it, not least because it offered a chance to compete with American technology. The Russian Army had won the previous challenge, and gained considerable kudos. You might say they became – at an institutional level – somewhat possessive of this bourgeois Cup.

'With this background, the Army became increasingly uneasy that almost the entire team was composed of Estonians, led by a man, one of their own officers to be sure, who himself had dual loyalties. They would have preferred a Russian helmsman and a Russian crew. Accordingly, they introduced a younger helmsman, Pilnyak, and a new Russian reserve crew. Although the committee had agreed that Illich was to be the defending helmsman, the Army began to consolidate certain positions. Firstly, they built a second boat. Illich understood this was to be a trial horse against the *Leningrad*, but in fact it was an attempt at a superior new design. Significantly, the new yacht was given to Pilnyak and the second crew. It was clear that the Army authorities were intent on usurping Illich's and the Estonians' position. Illich was on the point of resigning.

'Matters reached a head by other means. He gave a lecture at Tartu University here, in Estonia, on the innocuous subject of yacht-racing tactics. An unexpectedly large crowd attended, composed very largely of people not interested in the esoteric subject. They began to shout and chant and riot. It was interpreted by the Army as the first sign of a militant

218

demonstration against their own remaining military presence on Estonian soil. The Army saw its opportunity. Illich was implicated. He was ordered to return to Moscow to face a court martial. Although he returned voluntarily, they proceeded to place him in solitary confinement prior to the court martial.'

Aegu drank from his glass, raised a bottle to fill Shaw's glass and his own, returned to his monologue.

'Pridilenko, the chairman of the America's Cup committee, had to fight tooth and nail for the Army to allow Illich to attend a committee meeting. There was a power struggle between the civil and the military, in which Illich was a pawn. I am boring you?'

'No,' said Shaw. 'Not at all, I just have to keep pinching myself to remind me that this is just a sailing match, a goddamn yacht race.'

'In politics,' Aegu said, 'there is the reality, and there is the symbolic value. In a famous statement, Stalin said one man's death is a tragedy, a million are a statistic. Forgive me. As a politician, I deal constantly with the symbolic function of actions. In this case, the Army had been proving itself a little too confident, and the political élite wished to teach it a lesson. Pridilenko, the Chairman, was incensed, perhaps rightly, because Illich was being court-martialled on a political matter. Political matters are civil, and thus outside the Army's jurisdiction. He mobilized the higher echelons of the political structure in his cause. Illich was allowed to attend a meeting of the America's Cup committee. After the meeting, he was taken from the Army's hands, placed on a plane to Estonia, and told to keep out of trouble while the internal crisis was resolved. Another drink?'

Shaw was so engrossed that he had forgotten his policy of matching drink for drink and waved 'no thanks'. He merely shrugged and poured himself another glass.

'Illich and I met to discuss what to do next. He had

effectively been barred from any other participation in the America's Cup defence. I explained to him that the *Leningrad* was owned by the Estonian Trade Delegation, and thus in law belonged to Estonia rather than the Russian Army. With characteristic bravery, Illich volunteered to return to the camp the following morning, take advantage of the confusion to join *Leningrad* on her daily trials against *Kirov*, and then abduct the yacht. I agreed to support him. The yacht would be sailed to the island of Khiuma. We would supply support from Estonian Customs vessels.

'It carried high risks. The sailing camp was officially under Russian military jurisdiction. If he entered the camp, he was likely to be arrested on the spot and returned to Moscow to face a court martial. He knew what these risks were, and decided to take them. During the operation he was fired upon. Gundar Arlof was badly wounded. The shot was almost certainly intended for Illich.' Aegu paused. 'What I am saying is that the Army not only has a motivation for the murder of Illich, it has tried to kill him once already.'

He sat back. Shaw, who had known something of the background from comments by the crew, reeled a little from the complexity of the story. Aegu waited for him to speak.

Shaw's mind felt light with drink. Following Aegu's invitation to comment, he moved forward cautiously.

'Assuming it may have been the Army who killed him in his flat, why would they choose the time that they did?'

'A good question,' Aegu agreed. 'But perhaps I could ask you. What other time would have been better? That is a rhetorical question, I agree. But let us try to place ourselves in the Army's position before the sailing events. Despite their efforts to stop him, Illich had achieved the abduction of the *Leningrad*. However, the

Army knew that *Kirov* was a faster yacht. They would continue without him. Pilnyak was a promising helmsman, and they had a well-funded development programme. When it became clear Illich had support from Estonia, and that his own programme was developing, they believed they were too far advanced in their own preparations to be caught. They believed this until they were beaten.'

Shaw said: 'Illich insisted we helped them to come to that conclusion by always allowing *Leningrad* to beat *Novy Mir* when they were observing us.'

Aegu nodded. 'So, they find their great *Kirov* is roundly beaten in the first race with *Novy Mir*. Then again in the second race. A pattern is becoming clear. *Novy Mir* is the faster yacht. Now, why not attempt to murder Illich after the first couple of races with *Kirov*? Clearly, they would be immediately suspect. It would have been unwise, to say the least. Better to bide one's time.'

Shaw once again felt he should pinch himself. Outside, the final strands of mist were being burned away by the sun. Aegu's logic appeared inexorable, but it was based on the predicate of the absurd importance of a yacht race. Aegu continued:

'Better to wait, perhaps, until the defender trials were over, and for the final America's Cup races against the Americans. Incidentally, however critical I may be of the Russian Army, I have never doubted its patience. The formal focus of an armed force is the enemy, but I know that to senior officers, the real preoccupation is a long game of attrition against politicians who wish to reduce their resources. What I am saying, *tovarich*, is that patience is a proven attribute of our prime suspect.

'Against the Americans, then, Illich won the first two races outright. Events took an unusual turn. The Americans appeared desperate to win, even to the extent, perhaps, of employing the dubious gamble of a deliberate collision. Clearly, at this stage in the races, if there was a political motive to eliminate their malign rival, Illich, it would belong to the Americans. The Army saw its opportunity to act.'

'But Illich was officially representing Russia. We were part of the defence.'

'But you had displaced and humiliated the Army. The Estonian yacht had beaten the Army's champion. After each victory, the Estonian tricolour was flown above the Russian flag. You must understand that to a traditionalist in the armed forces Estonia, with its movement towards eliminating all final traces of Russian Army presence from its own soil, is perhaps a greater irritant than America, with whom there is, after all, an increasing love affair. I agree that nearly all of what I have said is speculation, and that much of it would require support. But if you will forgive me for saying so, my life has been based on my judgement of political feelings. When I say that to the Russian Army, Estonia may present a greater threat to its strategic view than the United States, with whom it is increasingly content to share world hegemony, I have a reasonable basis for my suppositions.'

To Shaw these abstruse political considerations had as much solidity as the final strands of mist dissolving outside the window. Aegu was watching him carefully and perhaps judged his mood.

'Let us proceed,' he suggested, 'from these rarefied hypotheses to the practical necessities of the case.'

Forty-one

'Another drink?' Aegu asked.

Shaw's mind swam. Perceiving no fierce enthusiasm in his guest, he shrugged and poured another glass for himself. He opened a drawer and drew out a sheaf of headed writing paper. Taking a pen, he began to write briskly.

Shaw looked out at the town. The final mists had cleared. Aegu's pen scratched rapidly. Finally he said:

'I have written an authorization that you should be trusted with knowledge of all aspects of the case, and that for the time being at least you are to be considered my representative in this matter. You will report your findings to me directly.'

Leaning forward, he passed him the letter, on the embossed letterhead of the Republic of Estonia. Addressed to Chief Inspector Saarinen, it was written in a flowing hand:

From this date, please treat Mr J. Shaw as my personal representative in the investigation into Colonel I. Illich's death. Mr Shaw was a close associate of the deceased. I have confidence that, with his specialized background knowledge, he may be able to make a material contribution to the investigation.

I take personal responsibility for his full security clearance, and leave it to you both to make the necessary formal arrangements and to acquaint him with every aspect of the case.

Sincerely,

Vajnen Aegu,
President
Republic of Estonia

'Thank you,' Shaw said. 'I'll do my best to help.'
'I have transmitted an order to the Finance Department

of our Interior Ministry to treat you as a consultant to the police service, at a fixed salary for the next six months, renewable by mutual agreement. It will, I hope, pay for your living expenses.'

Shaw thought furiously. There would be obligations, too, a loss of freedom. He would be an employee of the state. But it would almost certainly only last for the first contractual period. It would be a pleasure to tell Maria that he had found gainful employment, if only for six months. It was the sort of breather he needed.

'Thank you again.'

Aegu raised his glass and drained its contents.

'Now, I am afraid, much though I enjoy your company, I have to attend to overdue paperwork. I told you I would be away for the next few days. If you should need to contact me, phone my office and they will give you a current telephone number.'

Aegu stood up and accompanied Shaw down the staircase. With food in his stomach, the effects of the vodka did not seem quite as pronounced to Shaw as on his first descent. He managed to reach the landing in a tolerable imitation of sobriety.

Linda Aegu appeared in the hall to wish him goodbye.

'Thank you for an enjoyable lunch,' Shaw said.

'Tell your wife if she needs introductions in the local community to come to me. I am quite active in the local churches.'

'Thank you.'

As the door closed, he heard her say:

'I am sure that poor man was a teetotaller before you corrupted him.'

'Nonsense,' he heard Aegu object. 'I had to struggle to keep up with him. He is from Maine. They only discuss fish and they have very few saints.'

The rest of their conversation was muffled by the closing of the door. In the heat of the afternoon, Shaw suddenly felt the force of the vodka. He walked out of

224

sight of the front of the house, then leant for support against portico while he tried to regain his balance. Several matrons, walking past from the direction of Toompea Palace, regarded him with charitable concern.

Shaw left his anchorage and swayed towards the direction of the Garden of the Danish King. He began the descent of the narrow stone path to Rataskaevu Street. It was hot, and he could feel the sweat prickling beneath his shirt. Loosening his collar, he paused several times on the way down to lean against the stone walls.

Maria opened the door of their flat.

'Hi, honey,' Shaw said.

'You've been drinking again,' Maria said, as if making a technical observation.

'I had a few. Hi, Jack.'

'You'd better lie down.'

'I think I'd better.'

Maria moved some knitting. Laid out on the couch the world stopped moving round and round.

'It was the President, honey. I had to make a decision. Was I going to be my usual sober self, or was I going to be sociable and accept the refilled glasses?'

'You're asking me to guess your decision?'

Jack was staring at him about a foot away. Shaw could see his pale gold hair out of the corner of his eye, like a small sun rising.

'Daddy sleep.'

'You could say that.' Maria picked him up. 'Daddy's first free day, too.'

'We're going to go and play in the park,' Maria informed him, 'while your father sleeps it off.'

'Play,' Jack said.

'Bye-bye, Jack,' he called.

When they had left Shaw slept uneasily. He dreamed he was in a large room, like a courtroom, an innocent and impotent witness to a drama he did not understand.

His mind echoed with Aegu's political statements about the Russian Army. Then Aegu harangued him from a pulpit about the evils of drink. He woke with a flat headache and the realization that two hours had passed. At least the room had stopped revolving. He felt a pain behind his eyes. He stood up and poured himself a glass of water from the kitchen tap.

Seating himself, he withdrew Aegu's letter from the top pocket of his shirt and placed it on the kitchen table.

Maria and Jack returned. Jack was asleep in Maria's arms.

'He exhausted himself in the park.' She carried Jack to his room, undressed him and put him in his cot. Shaw seated himself gingerly at the table and opened Aegu's letter. Maria, returning, stood behind him and read.

'The good news,' he said, 'is that I'm going to be treated as a consultant for the next six months. They'll pay living expenses.'

Maria bent down and kissed him.

'It was worth getting drunk for?'

'That's my excuse.'

'How's your head?' Maria asked. 'You look terrible. I'll make some tea.'

She filled a kettle.

'Aegu's probably done a full afternoon's work, that's what gets me,' Shaw said. 'He must have a constitution like an ox.'

But Maria seemed happy. She and Jack had found a place to play in the park. She had talked to several other Estonian mothers while he played. They had discussed kindergartens and crêches, doctors and dentists. Her head was so filled with information that she had to write names and addresses down on a postcard while she waited for the kettle to boil.

The tea helped. His head seemed to clear a little, leaving a dull flatness which was tolerable. His mind began to work on aspects of the investigation into Illich's death. Maria knew that he would immerse himself in it as fully as he did in sailing. She shrugged her shoulders and made her own plans.

Forty-two

Chief Inspector Saarinen's office in Kingissepa Street seemed much as other police offices – a strange mixture of tension and boredom, overlaid by routine. Even on a Monday morning, it already seemed filled with that odd, desultory activity which signifies local crisis. A telephone was ringing in a corner. Several detectives were talking to an Azerbaijani shop-owner about an armed robbery the previous night, ringed about him casually like accusers. A distraught elderly woman in a dressing-gown was being comforted by a young blonde woman police officer, as she repeated over and over, 'He was there when I last looked.'

The receptionist gave Shaw a card and asked him to sit in a waiting area behind some ropes, out of the way of most of the activity and movement. Notices on the wall advised vigilance, reporting of suspicious behaviour; another illustrated the grisly consequences of self-injection with used needles. There was an appeal for blood donors. The rooms carried the odour of official forms, coffee and cigarette smoke.

His eye was attracted to a picture of Viktor Kingissep, one of the founders of the Communist Party of Estonia, shot by a military tribunal on May 4, 1922. The initial purge of communist leaders had been replaced by a grudging acknowledgement of their place in Estonian history. Aegu, in one of his addresses, had said that

Estonia should digest its history, not attempt to sever limbs.

He waited for ten minutes before Saarinen emerged. His appearance was unexpected, not least because it was so quiet. He seemed to drift rather than walk, and was suddenly standing by his side; tall, balding, polite, with the economical smile of a man whose job places him under pressure.

'Mr Shaw?'

He stood up.

'Saarinen,' his host said. He shook his hand with a certain formality.

'You walked?'

'Yes.'

Saarinen nodded. 'President Aegu telephoned this morning to say you would be assisting us. Follow me, please.'

Behind was a warren of offices, filing-rooms, an area filled with display cases of strange instruments and exhibits. Saarinen led him down a corridor with green walls to an office a few doors from the end, and gestured for him to sit down. A metal desk was piled high with files. He picked up a stack of files and placed them on the floor.

Shaw pulled up a chair and sat down. Opposite him, Saarinen folded his hands on the desk and surveyed him without smiling.

'I was asked to give you this.' Shaw produced the letter from Aegu. Saarinen glanced at it briefly and then put it carefully to one side. Shaw had the impression he was displeased, or perhaps merely bored. Perhaps he didn't like the idea of outsiders on the case.

Reaching into his jacket pocket, Saarinen withdrew a pack of Mulhberg cigarettes, and offered one to Shaw. He shrugged briefly when Shaw refused, and lit one himself. In America a man about to light a cigarette would ask permission. Estonia was still at a stage of

228

conspicuous consumption. Here smoking was normal, and non-smokers were treated as mildly eccentric. Saarinen exhaled.

'Our investigation so far has not produced any significant clues. I understand President Aegu has kept you informed of the background.'

Shaw nodded.

Saarinen studied him briefly. He said, 'Comrade Aegu has taken a special interest in the case.'

Shaw struggled briefly with the nuances in the word 'comrade'. It was not unusual to use the word these days, but now it had a certain irony, perhaps an inflection of mild disapproval. It seemed to Shaw there was something formal and officious in this disapproval, the cynicism of a professional man towards a politician.

Saarinen smoked quietly, focused on the middle distance. In another office there was a briefly rising voice, then the slamming of a door. Someone walked with loud strides down the corridor outside.

Watching Shaw listen to this distraction, Saarinen smiled his dry ghost's smile.

'You are familiar with police work?'

'No,' Shaw replied.

Saarinen continued to smoke. His disapproval floated upwards in small, grey clouds. Shaw guessed there was some other dimension to this casual antipathy. There were several to choose from. Firstly, he was an outsider, an American. Secondly, Illich himself was half Russian, therefore a figure of some ambiguity to an Estonian suspicious of all things Russian. Thirdly, there was Aegu, an interfering politician, demanding early results in a case which was set about with difficulties of a special nature. Finally, there was perhaps even a matter of personal dislike. In some part of himself, he was suspicious of officialdom of any kind. Perhaps he himself gave off a subtle scent of suspicion. There was at least one advantage in pariah status, however. You had nothing to lose.

Shaw said, as casually as he was able, 'Would you prefer me not to assist on the case?'

Saarinen's eyes snapped towards him. The swiftness of that movement gave Shaw his first small satisfaction of the day. He had said something dangerous, confirmed his outsider status.

He continued, 'I get the impression you don't approve of my being here. That's fine by me. If you wish, I'll leave just as soon as you say.'

Saarinen was watching him now as if he were an unusual animal, with a certain fascination. Shaw felt a compulsion to press ahead.

'There'll be no comeback on you,' he continued. 'I give you my word. I'll tell President Aegu I decided the issues were too complex, and on reflection I didn't think that I could contribute anything. I'll say I have no further wish to be involved in any way. Just tell me I'm not needed, and this will be the last you see of me on this case.'

He waited. The smoke from Saarinen's cigarette moved upwards, spreading out thinly. In another office a telephone rang. Saarinen studied him without moving, casually smoking, as if assessing his performance.

Saarinen exhaled, seemed to make up his mind, then said quietly: 'We have tried to investigate as closely as we can the possibility that the killing was not an assassination. Perhaps the victim came upon a thief, who fired in self-defence. There are several problems with this assumption. The first is that there would appear to have been little of value in the flat. We checked with the janitor Irkut, and by other means. The victim's wife and children had left him a year before, removing nearly all the furniture. The flat was almost empty. There was no sign that anything had been stolen. We found an inventory compiled in the process of the divorce proceedings, a list of the articles remaining ...' He pulled out two sheets of paper from a pile on the right of his desk and pushed them towards him. 'We checked the contents of the flat against the inventory. Not a single item missing. It is possible there may have been a box for personal effects or some such other item which we have overlooked, but we found no signs of a search. All the signs of violence in the apartment were specifically related to the murder.'

Saarinen paused to draw on his cigarette. It seemed to Shaw that he used his smoking to build in a certain rhythm. At certain stages he inhaled and exhaled, as if allowing pauses for comment. At other times he lowered his stained fingers to the table and pressed ahead.

'There were no signs of a break-in. The murderer entered by the front door and left by it. He had access to a key. The lock was not a complex one. It would have been easy for someone to open. In theory, the only one who had a key to the apartment, apart from Illich, was the janitor. We questioned him repeatedly over several days. We can establish that on the day of the murder he was in Jevpatorija, on the Black Sea, with his family. We checked the hotel at which he and his family were staying, the flights they used to get there and back, the currency cheques he cashed at the local bank, amongst other things. I repeat, there is no doubt that he and his family were at Jevpatorija during the time of the murder, and that he is cleared from a direct physical involvement. This,' he added, 'leaves the question of the key.

'Irkut kept the spare keys of Illich's flat behind his door. When Illich was away for extended periods, he routinely checked the apartment, piled the mail, and made sure there were no leaking taps or other problems. Irkut was certain that he had locked the door to Illich's apartment. During the early stages of our investigation of his possible role in the affair, we took advantage of Irkut's absence on the Black Sea to check on the evidence closer to the site of the murder. Using a search warrant, we broke the lock on the front door to his flat in order to check the interior. We can confirm that the spare keys of the flats – including that of Illich – were hanging on their pegs behind the door, as the witness claimed during the interviews which followed. We also took advantage of the access given by the search warrant to investigate Irkut's own flat for any sign of a break-in, but we found nothing.'

Saarinen leant forward to crush the Muhlberg in a metal ashtray. Casually, he opened a drawer and drew out a second packet.

Shaw looked more closely at it. It was the familiar deep red. The smoke was heavier, more pungent. He understood. The Muhlbergs were for foreigners. For himself, Saarinen preferred unfiltered Prima cigarettes. In this at least, he resembled Aegu.

'You have never smoked?'

'When I was younger.'

'You thought about your health?'

'No, my wallet. I lived on a smallholding in Maine. Down to my last resources. No luxuries.'

'No luxuries?' Saarinen was sceptical. To his mind the West *was* luxury. He saw that he would always be dealing with this image that Saarinen had of Americans.

Saarinen lit a fresh Prima with a silver lighter of delicate shape, in odd contrast to the plebeian roughness of the cigarette. The incongruity of it fascinated him; some sort of present, perhaps?

'In my experience,' Saarinen continued, 'keys have a habit of multiplying. A spare is left on top of the doorjamb for emergencies. A relative or friend is given a copy just to "check up" on the flat occasionally while the owner is away. The assumption that the spare key of the janitor must be the only other key is therefore a weak one.'

The smoke moved upwards. It was thicker smoke

than the Muhlberg, tinged with blue, frankly pungent – a forest fire of a cigarette.

'We checked on the ownership of the flat. The property is not owned by the Estonian authorities. It is in Colonel Illich's name, but was originally owned by the Russian Interior Ministry. Illich was given the use of it as a gift or reward of the Russian republic for his sporting achievements on their behalf while a member of the Russian Army. The old rules governing such allocations stated that it should revert to the State on his death. As you know, the new laws on ownership of property allow it to pass to the family of the deceased. We found an envelope in a drawer in Illich's apartment which contained his personal papers. He had made a will some time ago leaving all his effects to his wife. There appear to be no subsequent wills since his divorce, so the will is presumably in force. The matter may be complicated by the fact that Illich left the Russian Army without remuneration. Perhaps in the eyes of the Russian authorities this alters his previous heroic status. We are currently seeking clarification from the Russian Interior Ministry as to the ownership of the flat while we continue with our tests.'

He paused, as if waiting for Shaw to comment.

'Returning to the key,' he continued, 'it may be that the Russian Interior Ministry retains the original key in its own files. Given the habitual secrecy of the Interior Ministry in such matters, we have found it difficult to obtain confirmation. I am forced to repeat that the attempt to work out how entrance was gained by means of a key is exceptionally difficult. Perhaps,' he added, 'as you were a close friend of the victim, you could assure me that you yourself did not have access to a key.'

'I had no knowledge of a key,' Shaw said. Something troubled him about the assumption that he would know about the key, so he added, 'I don't think I could call myself a close friend of Illich. I'm not sure that he had any. I was his tactician on the yacht.'

Saarinen's detached eyes surveyed him. He said, 'He was a very private man.'

For several moments Saarinen stared not at him but past him to a point on the wall behind him. He tried to guess what was passing through his mind. If he couldn't give personal information, if he was not a close friend of Illich, what use was he on the case? Again, the question of his presence arose. Saarinen's silence was like a comment.

Shaw experienced, not for the first time, a surge of frustration. He knew that what he had said sounded defensive, a denial of responsibility. But how could he explain Illich's peculiar detachment, his almost monkish distance? He didn't like Saarinen's attitude. On the crew of the *Leningrad*, he had become used to standards of personal directness. Racing at that level, one couldn't afford to play politics. Each man was sure of his contribution and his place in the team. With Saarinen, once again, he was facing the prejudices of a professional policeman.

'How do you think you can help us?'

Saarinen's question was neutral. But Shaw felt the force of his resentment, the weight of his doubt driven home. Saarinen was a professional. To him, Shaw was a kind of gilded drone. Shaw knew. He had his own view of professionals. Sometimes, institutions like the Army or the police put a crew on a racing yacht, financed and trained it to perfection, and expected it to beat the crews of motley individualists who faced them. They were tough men, physically and mentally. They came from organizations with a record of valour. They had discipline. They could work in a team. Almost without exception it was a failure. No one knew why. It was difficult not to assume that it lay in the individual psychology of the crew. Yachtsmen felt they knew.

There was something about people who could live in institutions, that could stomach being told what to do, that did not respond to that final loneliness in which only an individual's nerve functions. A yacht stretches the institutional to breaking point. Perhaps an institutional crew lacked the final inner fibre of individual motive. Shaw looked across at Saarinen across this gulf of distrust. It was a stalemate.

In Saarinen's studied hesitation Shaw felt he recognized institutional prevarication in the face of a quantity which was unknown. Perhaps Saarinen had never met a mere civilian who was not intimidated by his professional superiority. In a case like this, Shaw would have operated on instinct. He said: 'Look, you didn't answer me a little while ago. You obviously don't believe I can be of help on the case. Why don't you just say so, and I'll go somewhere else?'

Saarinen's eyes moved towards him casually. Shaw continued amiably enough: 'I'm not trying to annoy or provoke you. I meant what I said. I get the feeling you don't much like the prospect of being my shepherd. Frankly, I don't much like the prospect of being shepherded. No offence, I've just got better things to do.'

For a moment he thought Saarinen was finally going to tell him to get out of the office. His jaw tightened and Shaw waited for the terse rejoinder, the call for a subordinate to show him out.

Placing his Prima on the lip of the metal ashtray, Saarinen stood up almost casually, walked round the table, put his hand on the doorknob, and then paused. Shaw was determined not to move until Saarinen asked him to leave. He wanted him to make that final move.

'You are right, Mr Shaw,' he said. 'I do resent your presence on this case.' He could sense from the tone of his voice that he had recovered. 'Particularly since we seem to have made no progress, and the lines of

235

investigation are closing. Frankly, I do not see how you can help.'

That was enough, Shaw thought. He stood up to leave.

But Saarinen faced him, looking him straight in the face. There was something about his attitude, opening the door, that irritated Shaw It was the feeling that Saarinen had confirmed to himself that he was dealing with a spoilt Westerner, someone who left at the first sign of difficulty. Shaw merely shrugged and turned towards the door.

But before he reached it Saarinen raised the palm of his hand. Shaw halted. Saarinen turned and moved through the open doorway ahead of him with surprising speed, calling to an assistant across the corridor, asking him to bring files. He turned back.

'You will stay for coffee?'

Shaw paused. Saarinen's hand was on the handle of the door, his head turned sideways. He was neither assertive nor pleading. A neutral question, a neutral response.

'A sincere question,' Saarinen said. 'From an Estonian policeman.'

Forty-three

The coffee arrived.

'My assistant, Johan Vares,' Saarinen said. Vares had a long horse face set in a serious expression, one of those Scandinavian faces which appear permanently middle-aged. Shaw guessed he was in his early twenties.

Vares left, closing the door. Saarinen stubbed out the cigarette and said: 'We have found what appear to be fibres from the murderer's clothes, dislodged during the struggle. We sent several to the pathology laboratories at Kiev. As a precaution, we sent another batch to our laboratory at Tartu. Professor Ernesaks is the Tartu pathologist. We await his report.'

This, at least, was interesting. Kiev was outside Estonia, Tartu inside. Why would Saarinen send a second sample to Tartu for any other reason than that he did not trust the report from Kiev? Shaw would consider the further implications of this later. He suspected it would be inadvisable to enquire further, at least for the time being. Saarinen had given him as much information as he wished. Shaw said: 'I understand you also checked the alibi of Illich's ex-wife.'

'We followed that up in detail. We are satisfied that she was in Kharkov with her family at the time of the murder. She spent the entire day at work, and left at five thirty, arriving back' – he checked a file – 'just before six, which was when the murder occurred. Her husband gave evidence. The report says when she heard of his death later that night she began to cry. She refused to speak for several hours. Later she told us she had no knowledge of the telegram whatsoever.'

'Do you believe her?'

An odd smile spread across Saarinen's face, as if he had been asked an improper question.

'I tell my men, belief is a religious concept, not a police officer's. I merely say we could find no means of disproving her claims.'

Saarinen removed the packet from his pocket, and lit another of the pungent cigarettes with a graceful arch of flame from the silver lighter. He expelled breath upwards.

'We checked the telegram. It did indeed come from Kharkov, not from her but from a commercial agency. The girl who received the instruction by telephone said she believed it was a man's voice. She could not remember enough to comment on accent or other distinguishing features. It was a day before, and she had taken dozens of other messages since. She only remembered it because it was "personal". Nearly all their messages are of a technical nature. Yes, she was certain it was a man's voice.'

With his free hand Saarinen reached towards the pile of files. He ran his finger down a list of titles, withdrew one, and flipped several pages in a white-fronted official dossier. Having found the page he sought, he pushed it towards Shaw. He saw the telegram, the original. It was battered. Once it had been folded into Illich's pocket; perhaps it had suffered during the struggle, and afterwards no doubt it been handled by the investigators in the search for fingerprints. It was already yellowing now. It occurred to him that nothing seems so dated as an old telegram, an amalgam of urgency and history. Beside it, like a ghost, was a copy, but with additional numerals and markings in the top right-hand corner. Embossed on this copy, on the left, was the official stamp of the Interior Ministry. 'Limited access' in red in the cyrillic Russian alphabet. Beside that 'Confidential' in Estonian.

Saarinen said: 'Although it is not admitted officially, all telegrams in Russia are monitored. First Secretary Aegu used his influence with the Interior Ministry to obtain a copy of the telegram. It was sent at 4.33 p.m., the day before the murder. It was traced to the same machine at the agency. We tried to find out if the Interior Ministry had a recording of the instruction. Even with Comrade Aegu's authority, we could get no further.'

Saarinen drew out a fresh file and began to leaf through the pages quickly. Although their personal relations might be suspicious, he increasingly gained the impression that Saarinen's professional enthusiasm had taken over. Now he was filling in details, opening and closing files, sketching in a picture here, using a notepad to draw something here.

The layout of the murder was next. Saarinen pushed

forward a map of the interior of the flat. The position of Illich's fallen body was marked on one side of the living-room. On a replica drawing, the movements of the two protagonists prior to the shooting were marked in arrows.

Saarinen took a swill from his coffee and said: 'We were able to work out the position from which the bullets had been fired. The assailant was standing here, in this part of the room. The likelihood is that he was already there when Illich entered. Illich would have turned to face him. We have worked out from the direction of the bullets that he began firing from this same position. This makes sense, by the way.' Saarinen paused. 'When firing, you tend to stand with your feet apart.' He stood up to demonstrate. 'The changing disposition of the cordite stains on Illich's clothing shows that the first shot was fired at a distance of about ten feet, the second at about eight feet, the third at five feet.' He looked up. 'All three shots were in the chest and lungs. It was a very determined rush. Analysis of the cordite stains shows that the fourth shot was fired with the barrel of the gun held right against the chest. The victim had closed with the assailant. We found traces of aqueous humour on Illich's hands – on his thumbs. We think that just prior to this shot, Illich had reached forward and driven his thumbs into the eyes of the assailant. The shot occurred. Illich fell to the floor. The assailant, blinded and in some pain, knelt down and must have felt with his hands the position of the fallen victim's body, then fired a fifth shot into the back of his head at point-blank range. Then the assailant somehow made his way to the door, down the first flight of stairs to the fire escape door. He opened this escape door and moved down the fire escape to the private courtyard, where we deduce there was a car waiting. The trail of blood ends in the forecourt. We assume there must have been a driver because the blinded assailant could not drive.'

Shaw found himself struggling for breath. It was not the murder itself, the firing of the gun, but the sense of emotional hatred of the two opponents which seemed to rise from the occasion like disturbed dust. He could feel this dust clinging to him, and felt an urge to go outside into the fresh air. He wondered afterwards whether this was possibly Saarinen's own vision of the murder, but it seemed to him that Saarinen described the murder as best he was able, in language that was accurate.

Out of kindness, perhaps, Saarinen gave him a few seconds to absorb the details.

'We have sent out requests to all hospitals and medical establishments in Estonia asking for details of individuals who have been blinded or who have received major eye damage. There have been three possible cases. Officers were sent out to investigate. Two were bona-fide industrial accidents. The third was a chemical accident, but detailed investigation showed that in this case the patient actually entered hospital in Narva two and three-quarter hours before the time of the murder. There is absolutely no sign of our man. We have an alert to all hospitals to report to us immediately if any such accidents are reported.'

'What do you make of his disappearance?'

'The man was bleeding badly and required urgent medical attention, particularly if he was to have any chance of saving his sight. He must have received medical treatment.'

'A single doctor?'

'The diagnosis and treatment is well beyond the normal scope of a doctor. He needed modern hospital facilities, expert surgery.' Saarinen paused: 'And you, Mr Shaw? What do you think?'

'When you say you alerted all hospitals, does that include military hospitals?'

Saarinen smiled his moonless smile. 'Not all. Russian military hospitals are outside our area of official

240

operations. The list of patients in military hospitals is a matter of Russian State Security. The same restrictions also apply to politically sensitive non-military installations, such as nuclear plants. The quality and type of injury is also sensitive, by the way. Radiation burns, for example, are automatically subject to a different classification. The Interior Ministry have their own system of hospitals, their own staff.'

'Are there such hospitals in Estonia?'

'Several. The Russian military garrison at Khiuma has its own hospital. There is also a large nuclear power plant near by. That too has its hospital. As far as I am able to tell without further investigation, there is also a Russian research centre outside Tartu, staffed by Russian nationals. Like the nuclear power station, that has its own health and medical facilities.'

'Can't we check those places?'

'Perhaps I could explain something to you, Mr Shaw,' Saarinen said. He leant back. 'Those places are outside our jurisdiction. The attempt to obtain a report from them would be politically sensitive. There would be an implied suggestion that they are deliberately harbouring a murderer.'

'I'm just a simple civilian, Chief Inspector. I thought the suggestion of any investigating case is that those interviewed may have something to contribute. What's wrong with pursuing that line?'

The faintest of smiles moved across Saarinen's features. 'There is nothing wrong in pursuing that line, but not into the military. These are the official restrictions within which I work.'

'Part of the reason Aegu has asked me to become involved is to clarify any possibility of American involvement. That isn't some kind of deadly insult. It's just something that should be considered. If I'm supposed to keep an eye on that, why can't we investigate possible Russian involvement?'

'It is politically sensitive.'

Shaw finished his coffee and put the mug down on the iron table. He said: 'To me that sounds like you're frightened.'

He thought for a moment he had gone too far. Saarinen's face showed no emotion, but he was still as if listening. Several moments passed. Eventually Saarinen said: 'In your stay in Estonia, Mr Shaw, it is unwise to suggest to an Estonian that he is frightened of the Russians.'

Shaw waited a little longer for Saarinen to calm down. He looked physically fit. Shaw had noticed he had that peculiar poise which is common to athletes and sportsmen, of balancing slightly forward on his feet. He guessed he worked out in a gym.

Saarinen had turned almost sideways in his chair and was looking at a map of Estonia on the wall. Then his eyes travelled upwards, as if he were considering some abstruse problem.

'Supposing we were to pursue the matter further,' Saarinen said. 'What do you suggest?'

'That letter I gave you from Aegu describes me as his representative.'

Saarinen inclined his head. He was still staring thoughtfully into space, studying some private area of possibility.

Shaw glanced at him, and pressed on. 'Let's say I interpret that literally. He told me to do everything possible to find Illich's murderer. So why shouldn't I suggest that you go ahead? Try and get the lists. I'll take responsibility.'

Saarinen almost smiled.

'What's wrong with asking?' Shaw said. 'This is an important murder inquiry. All possible leads are being followed. There are no signs of any casualty in the civilian hospitals. So do you have anyone with injuries answering to this description?'

'It may alert them,' Saarinen said softly. 'They may move him.'

'Could we put a watch on their movements?'

'It is expensive. It uses men. How many weeks, months, would we wait?'

Shaw bit the bullet. He'd have to assume they would move him almost immediately.

'Three days. That's all I'm asking. Put a watch for three days on each of the establishments to report suspicious movements. See what we flush out.'

Saarinen gave another brief, mirthless smile. He lit a further cigarette, and smoked quietly.

'You will take responsibility?'

'My guarantee. Want me to put it in writing?'

'No,' Saarinen said. 'No, I accept your word.'

He reached for the telephone.

'Vares? Ask Inspector Anvalt to come to my office. Yes, now.'

To Shaw he said: 'We'll file our request to the three institutions tomorrow. Today and tomorrow we'll work out a plan of surveillance. We'll have teams of plainclothes officers watching all three hospitals for twenty-four hours throughout Wednesday, Thursday and Friday. On Friday at midnight they will be pulled out.'

Shaw watched Saarinen stand up. To the left of the wall map there was a small window, with internal bars for security. A pane was left open for ventilation. Saarinen stood looking out into the street. He added quietly: 'You will also take responsibility if our President considers I have exceeded my duties?'

Saarinen seemed to expect no response. Instead he pointed to the wall.

'On the map there are certain blank areas. It is not formally written into our instructions as police officers, but those are the Russian military establishments. At Uus, for example, there is an entire Soviet motor-rifle

243

division, a community with its own shops, schools, hospitals, occupying several square miles. At Vara is a huge servicing facility for armoured vehicles and military engineering equipment. It is part of our mutual obligations. The Russians pretend they are not there. We pretend they do not exist. It is a policy of selective blindness by mutual agreement.'

Saarinen smoked quietly. 'In Estonia, we do not dismiss people for an error unless it is a serious crime. We are Scandinavians, we believe in security of tenure. The only exception is a political error. That too is part of our history. We must not disturb the great neighbour.'

Shaw said, 'I have one final favour to ask. May I trouble you for a key to Illich's flat?'

Saarinen leant back and opened a filing cabinet, producing a set of two keys with a white label.

'One is for the outer door into the hall and stairs, the other is for the door to his flat. If anyone uses the keys, it is our rule to sign for it so that we know who currently holds it.'

Shaw signed the list. Saarinen handed the keys across the desk.

'I'll see myself out.'

Saarinen stood up and nodded curtly, then sat down again. Shaw left Saarinen in the same place, staring into space. Contemplating what? he asked himself. It was enough that he should think about the motive of the killer, without trying to fathom Saarinen's complex mind.

Forty-four

Leaving the Kingissepa police offices, Shaw walked up Lembitu Street, passing the plinth of what was once the statue of Lenin. Shaw had seen the statue in photographs of the period, before it was pulled down following the 'coup' in August 1991. The unoccupied plinth remained. Like much else, it had subtly changed its meaning and had become instead a symbol invested with irony. There had been various standard positions of the Lenin statues in the former Soviet Union: Lenin striding forward into the future ('fleeing his wife'); Lenin, his jaw thrust forward, haranguing the crowds ('complaining about the State sausages'), Lenin raising his fist ('hailing a taxi'). This one had been Lenin 'holding down the lid'. His left hand gripped the lapel of his jacket, his right arm was extended forward, level with his stomach, as if restraining a lid from blowing off. Estonians liked to joke that it was the news about pollution in their country. They cited the huge Russian-built shale industries in the north-east, which poured their wastes into the surrounding countryside, and the formerly 'secret' nuclear power station not far from Narva, in whose immediate vicinity children had developed mysterious skin discoloration and lost their hair.

There was a light skein of cloud, causing a glare, though the day was warming rapidly. Sometimes the sun would emerge. Walking north, he could feel its shy heat on his back. There had been an unusually late summer. Red dahlias filled the flower beds in what was once Lenin Boulevard, though they did not ameliorate the ugly grey-brown concrete building that had once housed the Tallinn City Committee of the Communist party. Walking swiftly past the porticoed mass of the

Estonia Opera and Ballet Theatre, Shaw made his way north.

He turned into Harju Street. Hardly a hundred yards away, in Rataskaevu Street, Maria would be feeding Jack. He was tempted to detour by way of them, but was impelled forward by curiosity to see Illich's flat. Across Town Hall Square, along the narrow Bread Passage to Pikk Street, number 32. He halted in front of what had once clearly been a noble's house, with gables and the high window, on a third floor, through which provisions had once been hauled. He knocked on the door and heard the echo move away, as shyly as a cat, into the interior.

At first he thought no one was in. The building seemed echoing, empty. A few yards down the street, several small girls played a game like hopscotch on the paving stones. Shaw knocked again and heard the shy movement of sound in the empty interior. A car, a black Toyota, started up down the street and moved away from the pavement. He put the key in the doorway and was about to turn it when the door was drawn suddenly back. A man of medium height, broad, casually dressed in a white shirt and baggy trousers, watched him from the shadow of the doorway. The door had creaked as it was drawn back. Shaw's own heartbeat was an echo, sliding away.

Shaw held out a hand. The man neither came forward nor stepped back, but merely examined him and his outstretched arm. It came to him suddenly who this must be.

'Mr Irkut?'

No change came over the janitor's face at the mention of his name. Shaw said, 'I came to see Ivan Illich's apartment,' but his attempt at introduction made no impression. The keys had been pulled away from him as the door had been opened and were now out of his reach. Irkut had not moved. But now he reached forward around the door. His broad fingers found, then slowly turned and removed, the key in the door. Standing still, Irkut cast his eyes down to examine the two keys in the palm of his broad hand. Shaw experienced a heightened sense of his own importunity. It seemed he might put the keys in his pocket and close the door. Shaw tried again. 'I knew Illich.'

At first there was no reaction. Irkut's face rose from his examination of the keys and fixed expressionlessly on him. When he thought his way permanently barred, Irkut drew back the door and, still watching him carefully, stood aside so that he could step through. In the darkness of the hall, Irkut examined him from under his heavy brows. Shaw felt obscurely guilty about the keys still in Irkut's hands, as if they might be evidence against him.

'Thank you,' Shaw said. He pointed up the stairs. 'Second floor?'

Irkut gave an almost imperceptible nod and held out the keys. He retrieved them, but because of the janitor's lack of response to verbal communication, did not attempt to speak. Shaw nodded to him, and began to walk up the staircase. Four broad flights of stairs, lined by the heavy original oak banisters. Irkut watched his progress from the hall below. Turning the first flight, he looked back and saw that a child, a young girl with button brown eyes, had put her face around the door of Irkut's flat and was watching him too.

On the second floor landing Shaw faced a tall wooden door with white painted panels and varnished wooden cross-braces. He inserted the second key in its lock. The tumblers swung smoothly. Shaw pushed. The door opened easily. Shadows moved away across empty floorboards. The flat was bare but clean, as if someone had recently swept it. It was a big flat, if anything larger than his own, and as he moved forward it echoed with his steps. The living-room stretched away on both sides, without carpets and with a few pieces of furniture, two chairs covered in white dust-covers, a pine table. Light poured in through tall casement windows.

He had a good memory for maps and diagrams, and he turned and looked about the room, beginning to make his calculations on the disposition of the body, and from that, the positions of assailant and victim. On a section of the floor furthest from the entrance, some way back from the windows, there were still chalk traces on the floorboards of the outline of Illich's body. This gave him the orientation he needed.

He stood where Illich must have entered, turned and seen the intruder. The intruder was standing perhaps fifteen feet away, a certain distance from the windows so that he would not immediately be seen. After a certain time Illich had closed the fifteen feet or so separating them, had got close enough for physical contact in the final exchange of hands, eyes and bullets.

The flat smelt of paint. One of the casement windows had been opened to aerate it, but the smell was still strong. It reminded him of the paint smell which still lingered in his own apartment. From his memory of the diagrams of the killing in Saarinen's files he knew there should be bullet marks on the wall behind him where two of the slugs had passed through Illich's body and struck the plaster. He turned to look for signs of the impact behind him, but the impact craters had been plastered over and painted. There were no signs of the sprayed blood from Illich's wounds. For some reason the speed of its cleaning disturbed Shaw, though he knew his reaction was irrational. He wondered whether Irkut had been responsible for this additional work on the flat. The actual murder was now fourteen days old. Much could happen in fourteen days.

He must have lingered for half an hour, opening the doors to the bedrooms and bathroom, the kitchen, allowing the layout of the flat to seep into his mind. All

Illich's personal effects had been removed. Some of them, he knew, were in storage in the police offices in Kingissepa Street. He would ask Saarinen if he could go through them. Had Illich's wife also returned? In the echoing silence, he went again through the sequence of actions, the final rush of the victim towards his assailant under the devastating fire of the murderer.

He was preparing to leave when the phone rang.

Its tone was so clamorous in the empty rooms that at first he thought it was a fire-bell beginning its alarm. He had assumed, if he had thought about it at all, that the phone would have been disconnected. It was situated in an alcove of one of the casement windows. He picked it up.

'Mr Shaw?'

A woman's voice; a secretary.

'Yes.'

'President Aegu's office.'

Shaw breathed out. There was a click as the phone was put through to another. Over the silence Aegu said: 'I telephoned Saarinen. He told me he had briefed you and that you were on your way to Illich's flat. You had a good meeting?'

'It was informative.'

'I should perhaps have warned you. He is a hardened investigating officer.'

'I was starting to get used to him.'

Without changing his tone of voice, Aegu said casually: 'I understand you have authorized a major political investigation into the Russian secret medical establishments, with the object of initiating a serious diplomatic and political crisis.'

Sometimes ambiguity of tone is an ambush, designed to smoke out an opponent. Aegu's statement hovered between humour and threat.

'That's right. I suggested to the Chief Inspector that he should issue a request for information on any patient

249

with serious eye wounds recently admitted to the non-civilian medical establishments. I said as your representative I would take full responsibility for the request.'

There was brief silence at the other end of the line. Shaw said: 'As you know, I come from Maine, and we have a very simple outlook in that part of the world. When you said "let nothing stand in your way", I took that literally.'

'So I see.'

Shaw could hear his own heart beating in the shell of the telephone receiver. His mouth went dry. There were several clicks on the line. Aegu spoke to someone in the background, but the voices were unclear. He heard the sound of a door being closed. Perhaps Aegu had put the receiver down on the desk. Now it rustled as if it was being picked up again.

Aegu continued: 'I confirmed approval of the request for details of patients with eye wounds, including the necessary accompanying actions.'

Shaw was beginning to understand how things operated. He guessed that Aegu was unwilling to make a direct reference to the plan for three days' surveillance of the hospitals in case it breached security. In Estonia these assumptions over what was secure or insecure were automatic. He would have to get used to them.

'Thank you,' Shaw said. The shadows moved around him in the room.

'Perhaps you could telephone at the weekend to keep me informed of any action which may result.'

'Certainly.'

'Goodbye.'

The phone went dead.

Shaw leant against a wall, and did not move for several seconds. Behind the bonhomie, he knew he'd been warned off taking other initiatives. The arrogance of his action brought a cold sweat to his forehead and palms. At least he'd unstalled, for a few days, an investigation that was starting to run cold. What was done was done. The silence settled again. Once he heard, above him, the sound of voices – a man and a woman's – raised, perhaps in argument. They seemed to be speaking in Russian, and he always assumed that Russians were arguing. He completed his exploration of the flat, then returned by the staircase to the main hall.

Forty-five

In the hall, Irkut emerged from the door of his flat. Shaw said, out of courtesy, 'Thank you.'

But Irkut was trying to communicate something, moving towards Shaw with a peculiar sideways gait, like a crab. He was holding out a Russian language newspaper of several weeks earlier. In its sport pages was a picture of Ivan Illich, and beside that, one of Shaw. It must have been shortly after Illich's death, when the mantle of defending helmsman moved from Illich to Shaw.

The picture of Illich must have been an old one. He was in Army uniform, with that unnatural blandness with which Russia, even in its previous liberal-socialist phase, retouched the portraits of its heroes. But Irkut was pointing to the picture of Shaw, moving the index finger of his right hand from the photograph to him, as if to say, 'This is you.'

Shaw nodded. He wanted to leave, but Irkut was insistent. Shaw had no Russian, but he recognized once or twice the words '*Novy Mir*' in Irkut's excitable outpourings, and sometimes the word '*Mir*' on its own.

Irkut spoke no Estonian, that was clear. He was aware that some members of the Russian-speaking minority in

Estonia took pride in speaking only Russian. It was a residue of the old Soviet imperialism. But these thoughts were pushed to the back of his mind. Irkut was excited about something.

'*Droog*,' he was saying, pointing to Shaw's photograph. Shaw tried hard to grasp the Russian: '*Droog*,' Irkut repeated, '*Droog*.'

He remembered the popular Russian dog-food '*Droog sobaka*'. *Droog* was Russian for 'friend'.

'That's right,' Shaw replied in Estonian. 'I'm a friend of Colonel Illich.'

But Irkut did not understand his affirmation, or if he did, desired something more in the form of recognition. While he gestured at the photograph and at Shaw, he continued to move sideways across the floor towards his visitor, talking fast and excitably. Shaw noticed the huge size of Irkut's hands, the dirt under the fingernails, the wobbling chins as he gestured and expostulated.

Carefully attempting not to excite him further, Shaw backed towards the door. He had the feeling Irkut intended to embrace him like a warm, friendly bear. Irkut, seeing his quarry escaping, stopped in his tracks. A series of expressions passed across his face. Disappointment, incomprehension. Irkut gave a sad smile, made a grotesque little bow. Shaw stopped. Irkut advanced again. When Shaw was through the door, walking down the steps, he looked back and saw Irkut waving goodbye from the portico, like a child from a hospital. Then he closed the door suddenly, as if exhausted by his efforts.

Outside, in the preternaturally bright sunlight, the oppression of the flat still clung to Shaw. Irkut's sudden display of emotion had embarrassed him. At the same time, Irkut's dumb-show of communication was curiously moving.

Shaw's watch showed two-thirty. He wondered where the morning had gone.

*

Maria was washing up. She glanced around at him as he came in the door.

He said, 'Hi, Jack.'

Jack was in his high chair. His surveillance of his father was unnervingly close, as if he, too, were checking for signs of the demon drink.

'How was your morning?' Maria asked.

'Uneventful.' Shaw would have liked to have told her that he'd just sparked off a diplomatic crisis with Russia, that he'd jeopardized the good will of Aegu, that he'd nearly been embraced by an affectionate bear. But somehow he felt Maria was not in the mood for these trivialities. Her practicalities had a way of dominating the household. His own preoccupations seemed curiously inconsequential compared to the importance of helping to dry the plates. He picked up a plate and began to dry it.

'How was your day?' he asked.

'You really want to know?'

'Look, if I didn't want to know,' Shaw said, 'I wouldn't ask.'

Maria paused, rinsing the suds from a plate and setting it thoughtfully in the rack.

'You can ask out of courtesy.'

'Me?' Shaw asked. 'Courtesy?'

Shaw wiped a dish and placed it on the wooden washstand. He realized, not for the first time, that the greatest difficulty in his new life would be the ordeal of waiting, and the patience required to deal with it. Seated in his chair, Jack continued to survey him with quiet objectivity.

'Would you like to eat out this evening?' Shaw asked.

On his way through the town he had looked at a couple of restaurants. Tallinn's cellar restaurants were famous. One called Vanatoomas, at 8 City Hall Street, was celebrated. But others had sprung up to rival it.

Maria paused and put another plate on the side.

'Where?'

'I thought maybe Floria.'

Maria seemed to know about Floria, just as she seemed to pick up almost everything about the city.

'Muurivahe Street,' Shaw added. 'Easy walking distance.'

'I'll see if Aunt Liina can baby-sit.'

She dried her hands and went through to the living-room to the telephone. He heard her footsteps echo through the big empty flat.

He turned round to look at Jack. Jack's eyes met his. Shaw stepped sideways, fast, only about a foot, leaving Jack's infant eyes to catch up with him. When Jack's eyes met his again, he stepped back, just as fast. Jack frowned, then, unable to hold this pose of hostility, started to gurgle with laughter.

'Are you sure?' he heard Maria ask Aunt Liina. 'That's fine.'

Jack had managed to return to his former poise and was regarding Shaw with a ferocious frown. He moved sideways again. Jack's face split into a grin like a ripe pear. He tried to cover it with another frown. In the other room there were some further exchanges about shops and food.

'Are you teasing Jack again?' Maria called from the other room. Hastily Shaw returned to drying the dishes. Jack returned to his frown. Everything was as it should be. Maria's shadow crossed the doorway.

'Aunt Liina can come,' Maria said.

'I better reserve a table.'

'I already did. Seven o' clock.'

'Oh, you did?'

'Well, I thought you wanted me to.'

Perhaps sensing his mental restlessness, Maria said, 'I brought a newspaper home for you. I forgot about it. There's a bit on the Ericson group.'

She pointed to the *Herald Tribune* lying on one of the two chairs. Picking up the paper, Shaw sat down on one chair, and hid himself behind it. It was a little while before he found the item. Page 5. A brief headline: AMERICA'S CUP AFTERMATH:

The Ericson group today drew a discreet silence over the rumours that John Ericson, the America's Cup helmsman defeated 4-3 in the recent series, was receiving treatment for a mental condition at an expensive private clinic near Philadelphia. Rumours had begun to flow that Ericson had been subject to some kind of mental relapse after his defeat by Ivan Illich and the 'renegade' American helmsman Jim Shaw. The unwillingness of the Ericson camp to comment on these rumours fuelled further speculation.

The defeat of the American syndicate, the most lavishly funded and highly organized of all time, has led to an outbreak of litigation amongst the sponsors. Several of the larger companies are demanding a refund. They say their association with the loss has caused them 'negative publicity', and this, they argue, runs against the spirit of the sponsorship deal. It is the first major legal action of its kind, and if the litigants are successful, could throw the future of sports sponsorship into turmoil.

What has added fuel to the fire is that the Russian victory was effectively the effort of the small, semi-independent republic of Estonia. The sponsors point out that this effort had relatively low funding, started nearly two years late, and was undertaken under difficult conditions of disapproval by the Russian authorities. Something went drastically wrong in the organization of the American challenge, say the sponsors, and they are asking for a full inquiry. Battle lines appear to be forming. The Ericson group are about to hit back, claiming that the sponsors have not paid the full amount agreed in the original contract. Lawyers are currently advising both groups.

Shaw was transfixed. He asked: 'Have you read this?'
'I glanced through it.'

'They lost, so they're tearing each other apart. They're such wonderful losers.'

Maria did not comment. She removed her washing-up gloves and poured the bowl of hot water down the sink.

'There's another article,' she said, without looking up.

'Oh?'

'A bit about Coach Johnson. On the back page, I think.'

He picked up the newspaper again. Several articles down the page, there was a small item:

FAMOUS US SAILING COACH RETIRES

Coach Hal Johnson, US National Sailing Coach, whom many regard as responsible for American dominance of the sport of sailing over the last two decades, particularly in the Olympics, has decided to take early retirement.

Always known simply as 'Coach', this hawklike, somewhat ascetic figure walked with a constant limp from an old wound in Vietnam. He trained and brought forth a new generation of American sailing talent. Within the sport, Johnson was held in almost universal respect. He was straight-spoken, and his ideology, that good helmsmen were more devils than angels, was a source of humour and pride to those whom he coached. His only two 'failures' were the America's cup of 2001, when the American yacht New World *turned away from the finish line on the point of completing a successful defence, and the most recent American failure to win back the Cup. Not given much to public pronouncement, Johnson was asked which of his many achievements was the one of which he was most proud.*

Johnson mentioned the various Olympic campaigns which he had coached. Like the seasoned campaigner that he is, Johnson declined to comment on the latest US America's Cup effort. Some indication of his views, however, may be gained from one question put to him. Asked which sailor he felt most proud of coaching, he said Jim Shaw. When asked why, Johnson declined to comment further.

'I'm going for a walk,' Shaw said.

Outside, in the street, his emotions once more under control, he made his way down Noukugude to the deer park, then crossed to the more open reaches of the Toompark, walking beneath the high walls of the castle.

It was still sunny. Now that September was coming in the nights were coming earlier, and he could feel a chill in the air. He walked for what seemed only a few minutes, caught up in his thoughts, but when he looked at his watch, he had been away almost an hour.

Forty-six

Shaw's restlessness moved him forwards amongst the fallen leaves. He sat down at the serpentine Toompark lake. While his mind was preoccupied, in some part of himself he had worked out what he would do in the next six months. He would build a boat out of wood and epoxy resins. It had been an idea, an idea that had been so close to him that he had not recognized it. It had grown from some deep personal need, and now he had time to do it. Once, sitting inside the hull of *New World*, he had looked into the flames of the wood, and he had known that one day he would construct a boat himself.

It was curious how well the mind operated under conditions of emotional turmoil. Once the idea coalesced it seemed that it had been there for ever. He needed a hull lines-plan, drawings of coach-roof, keel, rudder and sail-plan. He would undertake the building himself. The interior would be sparse, merely a place to sit or sleep against the living walls of wood. Amongst his few books he kept the classic of the Gougeon Brothers. He had spent half his life around boats, beginning in McLuskey's shed, shaping, repairing, fitting. His experience would find its way again into his hands.

Building in wood appealed to a certain notion of asceticism. With a wooden boat the structure itself was warm and beautiful. You did not need to line the interior with some other material. All the less reason to fill the boat with furniture and luxuries. He would fit in the few bunks, and leave the varnished wood exposed. Long ago at school he remembered a phrase in his textbooks, one of the echoes of his basic education. An architect, perhaps Mies van der Rohe, that unlikely progenitor of the American skyscraper, had said that the most elegant designs were those in which structure and decoration were the same.

The same principles distinguished wooden boats from other constructions. If you built the hull in fibre-glass or aluminium or steel, you felt constrained to cover the cold surfaces with a lining, perhaps even wood. Accordingly the yacht contained two types of hull – the structural outer hull and an inner decorative shell. The elegance of wood construction was that the two were fused into a single function. The outcome was lighter, stronger, and – since the retired helmsman Shaw was not entirely averse to the occasional competitive sailing – faster.

The yacht's size he knew beforehand. Thirty-five feet. Long enough to take offshore. Small enough for one or two people to handle with reasonable ease. You could get full headroom on a thirty-five footer, and still be long enough to be sleek.

It would be a boat for cruising, not for racing. Yet

like all cruising men, Shaw knew he would be obsessed by performance. There was only one designer who came to mind, the designer of *Novy Mir*.

Forty-seven

That evening Maria dressed in a simple green dress that showed off her fine figure, with a single necklace of artificial pearls. When Aunt Liina arrived to look after Jack, and they stepped out of the door, he felt the same catch in the throat that he had felt when they were courting, a combination of tenderness and fear.

In the hallway Maria checked her handbag. Noticing him watching her, she looked directly at him, staring straight through him. She put her arm firmly through his and they walked down the stairs to the hallway. The evening air was soft. In the walls and buildings the stones seemed to glow with the day's heat.

They walked at a leisurely pace down Rataskaevu Street, turned into Niguliste. Maria halted to look in a window full of children's clothes. He could feel the force of her concentration as her eyes passed over the little clothes and shoes. They strolled down Niguliste, crossed Harju, and then turned right along Vaika Karja. There were few people about, a few wanderers, the occasional amiable drifting drunk.

In Muurivahe Street they found Floria's. A simple blue sign, with an arrow pointing down to the basement. It was a big room, spare, with large wooden tables and chairs that reminded him of church pews, and metal lights. The decor was simple, a little Spartan and wholly to Shaw's taste.

The *maitresse*, Madame Laht, a handsome woman in her forties with hair drawn severely back in a bun, showed them to a table at the far end.

It was the first time they had eaten out since they had joined the syndicate early in the year. They studied the menu. Madame Laht returned. Maria wanted to try the local speciality of *sultc*, jellied veal. Shaw, whose puritanism reacted against gourmet appreciation, put his prejudices aside. He would try *taidetud basikarind*, roast stuffed shoulder of veal. For starters they agreed on *rossolye*, vinaigrette with herring and beets. In the wine list there was listed a Lithuanian drink, Black Balsam. Prem had claimed that the fumes alone could fell an Estonian shot-putter at two hundred feet. This was a claim he wanted to test. Since they were both walking home, they decided to try a bottle.

Seven was early, but the restaurant was filling already. In America, he fell into an easy, perhaps facile classification of the people around him: businessman, farmer, lawyer, blue-collar worker. Here, the patrons were less easy to identify. Although he had been in Estonia for nearly sixteen months, he was aware of the cultural divide, of how much he had to learn about his newly adopted society.

He liked the movement around him, the customers arriving with an awkward self-importance, the *maitresse* and her two waiters moving backwards and forwards, the hum of conversation, the smells of cooking that issued from the kitchen door. Maria's eyes held his own. Just as certain animals cannot look a human in the eye without growing nervous, so he found the candour of her attention intimidating. Her focus on him made him feel light-headed. It caused in him an obscure desire to show off, to start juggling the condiments and saucers, even (if he could) to tap-dance on the table.

He tried to tell her of the week's extraordinary occurrences, not so much the events themselves as the strange see-saw of his emotions as he tried to immerse himself in the details of Illich's death. He would have liked to say that Illich's life and death seemed to grow more distant as he grew to know the details better. But for some reason he felt reticent. Instead he tried to describe the atmosphere of the police station, like all police stations, a calm which hid an underlying hysteria. He outlined his impression of Chief Inspector Saarinen and tried to give some idea of his moonlike, humourless smile.

He preferred Maria to talk. It was not so much what she said, though he tried to show polite interest, but the pitch of her voice. Listening to her talking about Jack and the necessities of the household exerted the same fascination as listening to distant breakers on a shore.

The Black Balsam arrived and was poured. Maria drank hers first, without hesitation. In his heightened state this excited him. There was something about her absolute lack of fear. He recalled that Eve had eaten the apple first. He tasted his own. At first acquaintance it seemed innocuous enough. Maria smiled, a smile both knowing and wicked.

'Want to continue racing?' she asked.

'I don't know.'

She waited for him to continue, and he said: 'After this everything might be a letdown.'

'You could teach, if you wanted to. Like Brod.'

He could, too. And there were attractions in it. But there were demons lurking. His great model of a teacher was Coach Johnson. Did he want to teach youngsters the same things – to be independent, implacable in their ambition, to sharpen their hatred like a knife?

The *rossolye* arrived.

He couldn't tell her directly, but it began to seem to him that there was a frightening conundrum which he had to pursue. Illich had not been a devil. He was the absolute negation of all Coach Johnson's imperatives.

Yet Illich, the incipient angel, had been brutally murdered, and he, Coach Johnson's favourite devil, was alive, honoured and free, sitting here with the most beautiful woman in Estonia.

Already the Black Balsam was having an effect, an effect not unlike vodka, a weighted kick at the base of the brain. He sensed a slight shift in mental state. Drunkenness did not release emotions in him. Drink did not reveal an underside of extroversion; it tended if anything to make him more introvert, more melancholy. Maria, on the other hand, seemed to thrive on it. With alcohol, her cheeks and eyes glowed, her gestures became both more pronounced and precise. This increased her allure, and her own awareness. Normally taciturn, one of those cold beauties whose attraction is a barrier, she became more confident. Perhaps it was the effect of the drink on him. Changing position slightly, he felt her knee nudge him under the table.

Pieces of conversation drifted towards them. At a large table to their right, several smart middle-aged Latvian matrons were discussing the fashion houses of Estonia, talking of a designer called Virtinu, another called Eesak, comparing the colour sense of the former with the eye for shape of the latter.

'What are you thinking about?' Maria asked.

This brought him back to earth. He had been thinking about whether he should return to Saarinen's office the following day. Perhaps it was better to stay away, he thought: let them call me if they need me.

'I was thinking about tomorrow.'

Maria raised an eyebrow.

'How best to deal with Saarinen.'

He felt obscurely guilty for not keeping his mind on the present. To deflect attention from this lapse, he asked: 'How long have you had that dress?'

'Since college. You've just never noticed it.'

'I bet you bought it today. Probably paid a fortune for it.'

'Not so much.'

For a moment he believed her. The sweat broke out on his forehead. Of all the terrors of the married male the world over, nothing quite matches the intimation of a wife at liberty in a clothes shop. The fact that later that week he would substantially reduce their funds for the design of a yacht was, of course, in a different category.

At another table, beneath one of the smooth sculptural wall-lights, an elderly couple were discussing the beneficent effects of mud baths at one of the several sanatoriums in the coastal environs of Parnu.

The empty *rossolye* plates were cleared away. The food in his stomach seemed to have soaked up some of the effects of the Black Balsam. Approaching an almost gleeful sense of abandon, he refilled Maria's glass, then his own. They clinked glasses.

The main course arrived. The events of the day had given him a gargantuan appetite. A trolley laden with vegetables – legumes, broccoli, cabbages, leeks, beetroot – was wheeled by. Their plates were full.

'My mother might be visiting us next month,' Maria said.

Shaw, still recovering from the prospect of the designer dress, felt almost blasé about this new announcement.

'She can keep Sam company,' she explained.

Through the Black Balsam Shaw's mind swam. He detected a plot. This was matchmaking at its most cool and blatant. Sam Shaw had avoided marriage since his first wife died twenty years earlier. Maria had that demure look which was a certain danger sign. Shaw took another swig of Black Balsam. He needed time to regroup. The drink hit the back of his throat.

'Well, that sounds real nice.'

'He'd get bored on his own,' she said.

He would, would he?

'Where's everyone going to sleep?' Shaw asked.

'Well, if Jack moves in with us, then they can each have one of the other rooms.'

Their big, echoing flat was starting to seem quite small. It looked as though he'd been outmanoeuvred. He'd have to let Sam Shaw fend for himself.

For dessert Shaw had Alexander Torte. Maria, protesting about becoming too fat, had coffee. She wanted to get back reasonably early so that Aunt Liina wasn't kept up too late. He attended to the bill.

It was when they stood up that Shaw felt the full effects of the drink. The room grew larger and smaller. Curiously, by means of a kind of remote control, he managed to walk reasonably steadily to the door after Maria.

Outside, the fresh air helped. It was chill. They linked arms and began to stroll back along Muurvahe Street. This time they went by Viru Street, crossed the Town Hall Square. They passed several parties of inebriated tourists. Maria seemed as steady as a ship beside him. Her hip moved against him as they walked.

At the flat Aunt Liina answered the door.

'He's been as good as gold,' she said to Maria.

In other words she'd allowed Jack to run riot. But the flat seemed tidy and undisturbed. Aunt Liina had been knitting. She packed her wool into a bag. From Jack's room they heard his shallow, even breathing.

At the doorway Aunt Liina and Maria hugged. Aunt Liina had driven her small car. She would have walked, but was nervous of the parties of well-meaning but legless Finnish tourists who roamed the town looking for their hotels. Shaw saw her to the car, despite her protestations.

They went to their bedroom and closed the door. They helped one another undress. He expected the intake of Black Balsam to fell other parts of him, but the evening appeared to have given him the instincts of a mating weasel.

Maria said, 'Let's get into bed first.'

Undressing, his mind drifted to their conversation at Floria's. Soon the flat would be full of their relations. He was determined to make up for when Sam and Agnes Chednik were staying with him. He moved into bed beside Maria. She was already breathing in that precise, emphatic way which, though not passion itself, preceded passion as thunderclouds precede rain.

Forty-eight

'Mr Shaw?'

He was used to Saarinen's tones by now, level as a grave. Strangely, he had expected Aegu.

'We have not heard from you for twenty-four hours. I am checking that you are all right.'

'I'm fine,' Shaw replied. 'I'm touched by your concern.'

He imagined, at the other end of the line, one of those brief mirthless smiles.

'Perhaps you could visit us. We have prepared our plan. Since you were its initiator, we would value your approval.'

'When would you like me to call by?'

'As soon as you can, please.'

'I'll be there in quarter of an hour,' Shaw replied. He put the phone down and turned towards Maria.

'I haven't entirely blotted my copybook. Saarinen wants me to check something.'

Maria did not turn round.

'You'll be back for supper?'

'Well before then, I hope. I shouldn't be more than an hour or two at most.'

Before leaving, he put on a white, waterproof jacket that had once been almost smart. Maria's eye glanced over his jacket. He had the chill premonition of a new wardrobe for him. Outside, a weak sun had established itself. He walked down Harju Hill, through Victory Square towards Kingissepa Street.

Vares was waiting for him in reception, and accompanied him through to Saarinen's office. Pausing briefly, Vares knocked once, and opened the door.

Saarinen was seated at his desk. With a telephone at his ear, he gestured towards a chair opposite. After a few moments of rapid conversation, he put the phone down and extended a hand across the table.

'We have investigated the positions of the non-civilian hospitals. Before the investigation, I had believed there were three, but the resiting of the Russian military garrisons means that two have now amalgamated into the Russian Estonian Military hospital. The second hospital, the Military Engineers hospital, is within the grounds of the Tallinn Second Garrison ten miles south of here. It is in the country. As you may be aware, the Russian Army presence over the past decade has been resited to what are called "areas of minimum impact". It was a policy developed in the 1990s, after the troubles. We have already looked at the site, in so far as Army security permits.'

Saarinen withdrew from his desk a piece of foolscap paper on which someone had drawn a crude map in pencil.

'It is illegal, as you may be aware, to show Russian Army positions on any map. It is also illegal to sketch outlines such as these of Army installations. However, due to a subvention by President Aegu, this case is now under a special category, and we are empowered to take certain steps.'

Under pressure, Saarinen seemed to grow colder, more precise. Behind his reserve, Shaw detected a certain degree of excitement. Perhaps excitement was another drug; under its influence he did not seem to need to smoke. Shaw supposed the operation was a change from the usual preoccupations of the Estonian Criminal Investigation department – petty thieving, small-time racketeering, drunkenness and prostitution. He stood up and walked to the wall. A mobile radio telephone hung from the wall. He switched to an open line. A voice said, 'We are proceeding south-east along Talev Street, but we cannot see the lorry yet. Can you check its number?'

Saarinen returned to his desk and sat down. On the radio-telephone the voice of the controller said, 'It was last seen on the Parnu highway, travelling west at ninety kilometres. Saab diesel, light blue body.'

Saarinen leaned forward across his desk and lowered his voice. 'Security. Let me tell you a brief story. The Communists loved statistics. During the final phase of the Soviet Union, the guide to the Viru hotel used to tell his audience, "The Viru hotel, a monument to Soviet construction. Sixty-three per cent concrete, fifteen per cent steel, ten per cent glass, five per cent listening devices."' Saarinen half smiled, as if he were discussing a melancholy fact of life. 'It is one thing to install such devices, another to remove them. It is expensive, for one thing. To remove all one would need to demolish a building. Maybe the Viru guide was right, perhaps they contribute to the structure itself. Who is to say that all those bugs have been removed from the walls of official buildings of the state of the Estonian Republic?'

He studied Shaw's face. 'When we wish to maintain security, we switch on an open line as background noise. You understand?'

Shaw nodded.

With his big square hands Saarinen swung the map

around on his desk so that it faced Shaw. Carefully, he tapped a series of concentric squares with his right forefinger.

'This is the outline of the military establishment. The line here represents a high security fence. Luckily, this presents no obstacle to observation. The main entrance to the military hospital is about fifty yards back from this fence. Unfortunately for our observation team, the hospital itself is enclosed by a high wall. By careful positioning, however, it is possible to gain a clear field of view through the security fence, through the open gates, to the main disembarkation point of ambulances. The observation point in question is a copse of trees, still in leaf. We have positioned two watchers here, both with powerful binoculars and listening devices.'

He looked up.

'Comrade Aegu asked me to make plain to you the implications of this operation. Firstly, if the Russians detect the two observers, and it is found that they form part of an Estonian police operation, there will be a diplomatic incident. He wants me to make clear the consequences if the operation goes wrong. If that should arise, then he will step in and handle the matter personally. The criminal investigation will cease for the time that it is necessary to deal with the crisis.'

Shaw said, 'I'm warned.'

Saarinen paused, then began to speak again in low tones.

'Secondly, I must explain to you that there are security precautions which must be maintained at all costs. Some are merely routine, but it is my duty to remind you of the main principles. Do not speak to anyone about this operation, including your wife, even in your sleep. In communication with me, assume all telephone conversations are tapped. In practice, the Estonian Republic has had a new telephone exchange, and the incidence of direct monitoring is reduced as a part of commercial liberalization. But remember the story of the Viru hotel. Thirdly,' Saarinen added, 'no direct references to the operation outside this office, either in writing or in conversation. Officially it does not exist. I hope I make myself plain.'

He looked directly at Shaw. Shaw observed a certain coldness in his eyes.

'Finally, the requirements of security are generally considered by outsiders to be somewhat unnecessary. It is useful to bring them home by means of an object lesson. In your case, I note with amusement the description you gave of me in the Floria restaurant last night.'

Shaw felt a slight sweat on his forehead and the palms of his hands. He tried to recall what exactly he'd said. Something about his smile. He felt a blush on his cheeks. Saarinen added: 'Some further information of a harmless kind. Your wife's aunt left your apartment at 10:27 last night, and drove in her Fiat registration OND455, to her home, arriving at 10:33.'

He considered Shaw with that studious seriousness which sometimes hides amusement.

'So far, harmless observations, as I say. A little plainclothes surveillance. But perhaps I make my point. You can be easily observed; so in future please keep to the security precautions.'

Saarinen leaned back. Then he stood up, walked to the window, glanced out briefly, and returned. Seated again, he permitted himself a cigarette. Lighting a Prima, he waved away the cloud of smoke. One drug deserved another. He said: 'You look to me like a man who could do with a coffee.'

Saarinen dialled Vares. 'Two coffees.' He put down the phone.

On the open line a patrolman said: 'I see no sign of the female pedestrian. Can you give me any further information?' There was a click of a second party returning. A second voice came on the line. 'She is

269

blonde, taller than average, and is reasonably well dressed.' More clicks. The patrolman said, 'Thank you. I will arrest every woman in Estonia.' A buzz followed, a hiss of static.

Saarinen allowed himself a brief smile. 'Patience and cynicism, the policeman's two companions.'

Vares entered and put the coffees on the table. Saarinen gestured perfunctorily for him to sit down. He drew up a chair. Saarinen leant forward again, so that their three faces were close; he addressed Shaw directly.

'In any future dealings you will not take any matter into your own hands. You will report all matters relating to the case to myself or to Vares. You will maintain contact with us at least once a day. You will not deal with any Russian officials without first consulting us. You will not interview any person relating to the case without our express approval. Do you understand?'

Shaw inclined his head.

'Vares is witness.'

Close up, Vares' long horse face showed no sign of amusement.

Saarinen paused. 'The second hospital is a small non-military establishment for Russian diplomats and bureaucrats who visit Estonia. It is about eight miles away, to the south-west, in the gardens of the Russian residential complex at Hadriarga. Although there is only a skeleton staff of one doctor, a general surgeon and several nurses, it has facilities for emergency operations. Our problem is that the complex is situated behind a high brick wall in a very flat area without vantage points. There is a housing complex about five hundred yards away, but a belt of trees prevents direct observation. It is not enough to observe the traffic to and from the gate. We need to be able to view the disembarkation point, to see who is being placed in an ambulance. In this case, because we cannot directly observe the place of embarkation, we are restricted to observing traffic to and from the diplomatic complex through the main gates. We will be putting two observers there as well.'

A knock sounded at the door. The three men sat back as though they had been discovered in a gambling game.

'Come in!' Saarinen called.

A policewoman appeared.

'The enquiry you made earlier. A fax message has arrived from Pskov.' She placed the message on the desk in front of Saarinen.

'Allow me to introduce you,' Saarinen said. Shaw stood up. 'Sergeant Ulle Rana, Mr Shaw. Sergeant Rana had an enjoyable meal in plainclothes at Floria last night.'

Broad cheekbones, clear eyes. Her expression held a trace of amusement. He thought he remembered her face from a table about twelve feet away.

She left, closing the door.

'That's rubbing it in,' Shaw said.

'Precisely.' Saarinen gave another of his swift mirthless smiles. He opened a file marked 'Strictly confidential. For office use only'. Turning it towards Shaw, he said: 'This is a copy of a letter that is due to be delivered by hand this afternoon. Please feel free to read it.'

It was on the official headed paper of the Estonian Department of Criminal Investigation.

Colonel V. Suvolov
Commandant
Tallinn Military Garrison

Dear Colonel Suvolov,

We are currently engaged in an investigation of the circumstances of the murder of Ivan Illich, formerly Colonel, Russian Army. We have reason to believe his assailant may have suffered serious eye damage. In pursuit of information regarding this case, we have requested information from all

271

civilian hospitals. In addition, however, we would be grateful if you would notify us immediately if any personnel treated for serious eye damage since the date of August 18, 2003, have been registered in your own internal hospital.
We urgently wish to interview such personnel.

Yours sincerely,

Chief Inspector S. Saarinen
Estonia Department of Criminal Investigation

'There is a copy of another letter beneath that,' Saarinen said.

Shaw looked. It was identical in content, except that it was addressed to *I. Imanta, Superintendent, Kirov House.*

'Kirov House?' Shaw asked.

'The name of a residential complex for senior Russian officials. It has no official title. The Moscow *vlasti* still have access to many such complexes all over neighbouring states. They are used for diplomatic negotiations, for residential stays when a senior official visits an outlying republic, sometimes for holidays or rest periods. They appear on no maps or civilian lists. Their telephone numbers are not recorded. Their security is overseen by a central department of the Russian Interior Ministry. That letter, too, will be delivered by hand this afternoon by one of our plainclothes officers.'

'When are you going to start observation?' Shaw asked.

'It is unlikely that the institutions would react within a few hours. After the message has been opened, senior officials would be consulted. If a patient with serious eye damage is housed there, and the staff are made nervous by my letter, alternative arrangements would have to be made for his transfer. This will all take time. However, you asked a direct question.' Saarinen consulted his watch. 'The first watch of both teams should be in position in fifteen minutes' time.'

An idea suggested not much more than twenty-four hours earlier was already a functioning operation. It was impressive; perhaps a little eerie.

On the open radio-telephone line someone sang a few tuneless words of a pop-song. A switch sounded. A long buzz of static, a cheeping sound like birds or bats. A voice cut in. 'Patrol car E17, move north to support D3.'

Shaw said, 'What do we do now?'

'We wait,' Saarinen replied.

Vares stood up to leave, shook hands with Shaw. Saarinen nodded briefly to him.

'Any questions?' Saarinen asked Shaw.

Shaw shook his head.

Saarinen stood up to switch off the radio open line. The room was silent, as if after rain.

Shaw finished his coffee.

'You have the keys to Illich's flat?' Saarinen asked.

Shaw nodded. He signed the register confirming that he had returned it. Saarinen signed a confirmation beside it. Shortly afterwards Shaw left.

But he was too restless to go home. He walked along Lembitu Street towards the plinth that had once housed the statue of Lenin across the Boulevard that had once been named after Lenin. He hovered there, as if in unconscious acknowledgement of the official efface-ment of memory. From there he detoured to Voidu Square, where he again hesitated briefly. It was in Voidu that Illich's funeral procession had started. The mem-ories were still fresh in his mind. Then the square was full. Now a few tourists took photographs. Crossing the square, he walked up Harju Street, then turned left along Noukogude Street. The grey walls of Toompea castle rose on his right. He walked into the deer park, past the cumbersomely named Monument to the Dele-gates of the 1st Congress of Estonian Trades Unions. The sun was still shining brightly, lighting the first autumn gold of the leaves. Shaw walked among the trees towards the lake, once part of the old moat. Pedestrians, mostly tourists, drifted about the park. An old woman was feeding ducks. Two youngsters were playing with a model yacht. One path led off to the right. Sections of the park were thickly wooded. On an impulse, he turned back, making a semi-circle back to his original path. He looked along it, but could see no one, apart from two elderly men.

Why did he think he was being followed?

After several minutes he strolled towards Vaksali Street. Through the thick trees he occasionally caught glimpses of the Baltic Railway Station. A white dust of pigeons fluttered from the high Toompea walls. Reaching Vaksali, he climbed upwards around the castle complex to Rataskaevu Street.

Forty-nine

Lying beside Maria in the early dawn, Shaw turned over quietly. Her regular breathing seemed to fill the room.

There had been a fall of rain earlier that evening. He had looked out over the shiny streets and red-tiled roofs and wondered whether the second group of watchers had taken over from the first. Now there was light on the window sill, the first traces of dawn through the partly drawn curtains. He wondered again whether a new shift had taken over.

Maria moved in her sleep, and for a few moments her breathing ceased, as if she too, were listening. Then it asserted its rhythm once again.

Half awake, half sleeping, it struck him as comical

how vastly different were his roles inside and outside the family. Outside he had suggested to a sceptical police inspector that the non-civilian hospitals should be watched, and two teams of watchers were out braving the cold and the rain. Inside the family he was an accessory, whose function was to screw in curtain rails where indicated.

On her side of the bed, Maria's breathing was like a tide, moving in and out over the room. On his own, the ticking of a little clock asserted its small mechanical regularity.

That morning Shaw left the flat for the Maritime Museum. It was a brisk, windy day, with rapidly passing clouds. He could smell the Baltic. From Rataskaevu to Lai Street, right along Vana, left at Pikk Street to the grey-walled cannon-tower called Stout Margarete, once a prison. A strong gust of wind drove along the street, causing women to hold on to their headscarves and hold down their skirts.

He pressed down the heavy handle on an outside door. The door opened and he found himself in a dark, cool interior of flagged stone. His instructions were to knock on a door marked 'private' on the right of the entrance. A short woman in a scarf came to the heavy oak door. He gave his name, and she ushered him in, calling out to Doctor Vader in an inner office.

Vader was tall, bearded, with glasses. There was something fastidious in his clothes, the well-tailored suit, the perfectly positioned handkerchief protruding from his top coat pocket; a touch of the dandy.

'Good morning, Mr Shaw.' Vader inclined his head in Estonian solemnity. They shook hands. 'Please follow me.'

A wrought-iron spiral staircase led upwards. A second-floor room had been set aside as an America's Cup display. Shaw had never seen this room before. At its centre was a magnificent tenth-scale model of *Leningrad*. In a display case behind it were several fine colour photographs of *Leningrad* and *New World* racing in the 2001 series. Shaw was plunged into the past. There was a deck shot of *New World*, with Shaw helming, Jack Peabody as tactician. Ernie Stead, the navigator, stood in characteristic pose over the instruments as the sails threshed the decks during a tack. Shaw moved along the photographs in a trance. One sequence followed another as the races unfolded. He halted, suddenly breathless. There was a photograph of *New World* swinging away from the finish line, spinning fast on its axis with the boom already well eased out. A curved wake behind it showed – like the trace of a particle in a cloud chamber – the history of the manoeuvre; history written in water. With that single explosive turn he had lost the race and the series; he had settled on his life as an outcast. Next to it there was another photograph that seemed to drain the final breath from him. *New World*, having turned, slid past *Leningrad*. The two great yachts passed in opposite directions. Shaw moved a single step closer to the photograph. On the sidedecks of *Leningrad*, Ivan Illich raised his fist and roared out his spontaneous salute.

There was a caption below.

Ivan Illich raises his arm to New World *in the final race after the American helmsman deliberately turned away from the finish line in one of the most enigmatic gestures of America's Cup history.*

He had not imagined that the victors would show that aspect, let alone display it as a central feature of their exhibition. Did it not remove some of their glory? There was something else that he would need to reconcile. It was an incident that was buried deep inside him, like a neurosis with which he would always live. Vader was standing at his elbow. Perhaps sensing

Shaw's consternation, he said: 'I am an historian. I believe history should be as accurate as possible.'

For a few moments Shaw could not speak. He could only nod and smile.

There was a large framed photograph on the wall — Illich as the world had seen him, sleek in his colonel's uniform, the eyes hooded, expressionless, the fair hair sleeked back. This was the first image he remembered, a construct of his imagination; Illich as adversary, ruthless, unfeeling, implacable. Several times in his life he had seen this strange transformation of another's character in the light of his own greater knowledge. Illich, once known, was less a soldier and more a monk or priest in the peculiar purity of his will.

This was the most moving and eerie aspect of the photographs, not the historical record preserved in disconcerting detail, but the transformation of the human players under the pressure of time and events. In the photographs of *Leningrad*, the Estonian crew had seemed demonic in their professionalism and determination, as detached as samurai. Now that he perceived them in the light of their extraordinary diverse characters, the magical quality of their cohesion was more, not less, impressive.

Shaw tore himself away from the photographs with difficulty. Vader stood politely at his elbow.

'How can I help?' Shaw asked.

Vader said: 'We have a series of new photographs of the America's Cup, the most recent event. We need to make a selection. I have marked those which I believe are most illustrative.'

He showed Shaw to a desk in an adjoining office, laden with paperwork. There was a pile of photographs, coloured, each ten inches square. Shaw started to work through. The first was a fine one of *Novy Mir* slicing the line ahead of the Soviet yacht *Kirov* in the defender trials. A second showed *Novy Mir* crossing the line on the

final race, her jib in tatters from the low-flying helicopter.

'What happened there?' asked Vader.

'Russian Army helicopter,' Shaw replied. 'Appeared
out of nowhere, seemed to be going at full speed, about
two hundred knots, hardly more than a hundred feet
up. Went straight over the top of our mast. Our jib
disintegrated in the downwash from its blades, so we
had to shoot the finish line under mainsail alone, relying
on our momentum to keep up speed.'

'Worth exhibiting?'

'Yes,' Shaw said. 'Fine by me.'

There were others that he paused over.

'We have selected four photographs showing the
sequence of the collision of *Eagle* with *Novy Mir*.'

Fear, anticipation, exhilaration moved through Shaw.
They were mainly aerial shots, taken from a helicopter
or low-flying aircraft. The first showed the two yachts
approaching on a reach on a collision course; the second
the impact, the two bows disintegrating at a combined
closing speed of thirty knots. The third showed the two
fatally crippled yachts, both still entangled, both sinking
rapidly by the head, their broken masts in the water; on
deck the crews tried to break free of fallen ropes, rigging and sails. It was a miracle, he thought, that the
worst injury was a minor concussion, that no one was
killed. Anger flooded him again. The fourth photograph showed merely turbulent water where the two
boats had sunk; two groups of bobbing heads on the
water, a few floating objects where both yachts had been.

'It brings it back,' Shaw said.

'You have no objection to our choice?'

'No. That's how it was.'

Vader nodded. 'We have a model of *Novy Mir* currently being built. It will occupy centre stage. As a maritime historian, I am interested in your opinion of her.'

'A great yacht. Fast, beautifully balanced, with

astonishing windward speed when pressed.'

'I understand you did not like her when you first saw her.'

'Who told you that?' asked Shaw.

'I have my sources.' Vader smiled.

'You're right. She had such strange stern sections. It took us several months to realize how to sail her best. It was Illich who persevered. Frankly, I would have abandoned her after the first few races. Illich had faith.'

'Fascinating. Thank you for coming to see us.'

They stood up. Vader accompanied Shaw to the entrance hall.

On his way out, Shaw lingered for a few more moments at the photographs of *New World* turning away from the finish line. He said: 'I'm surprised you didn't ask me why I did that.'

'You'll tell me in your own time.'

Out into the silvery sunlight. He could start to feel winter in the breeze. Pikk Street was the main approach from the sea. Today it was filled with tourists. Shaw paused while the emotional after-effects of the photographs stirred him.

He set off along Rannamae Street, turned left into Lai Street, past the three walled towers of Laboratiumi Street. In Tornide he paused for no particular reason at the bronze statue of a bearded Mikhail Kalinin on his high pedestal. About to cross Vaksali Street into the Toompark, he paused again.

Fifty

It was her beauty which finally caused him to remember, beauty of a cold, Nordic type, in the set of her fine eyes, her broad cheekbones. She walked deliberately, as if deep in thought. There were several groups of people, tourists, in her path. They parted quietly to let her pass and glanced after her, as if she had been a famous actress. If only because he had seen her in photographs, and tried to seek her out at the funeral, he recognized Lydia Teemant, Illich's mistress. Although not facing her directly, he found himself on a converging path. She drew closer, and he felt his palms moisten as he continued to walk, hands in pockets, while the distance between them closed. She did not recognize him (why should she?). As she drew closer he noticed she was wearing flat heels, but she must have been over six feet.

He experienced one of those intense sensations of embarrassment which he had almost forgotten, along with adolescent pimples. He wished desperately to talk to her but could think of no immediate means of introduction. She was almost past when she seemed to turn.

'Mr Shaw?' In English, with a slight Scandinavian lilt. She stopped and was facing him.

Shaw halted and turned back towards her. Her accent was quite formal, almost stilted. She was standing in front of him now, with the sun behind her. 'I recognize you from photographs. Lydia Teemant.'

She held out a hand.

Her dry palm was abstracted, even in greeting. Shaw experienced a second wave of embarrassment. The sun was over her left shoulder, and all he could see in its white blindness was her outline. They each withdrew hands politely, as if from some charged border. Shaw said into the halo of sun and hair: 'I was going to sit in the park and watch the ducks.'

When he thought about it later, she too would have been turning the traces, hunting for some reminders of her lover, perhaps searching for him in his friends. A gaggle of tourists went past. Seeming to sense his discomfort, she moved quietly out of the sun. Her face emerged as if rising out of water. He became aware of cheek, mouth, a fairness of hair that was almost white or silver.

Shaw had a deep suspicion of such beauty, not only of beauty itself but his own reaction to it. The ambivalence it generated was, in its own way, intrusive. He despised himself for awe. At the same time he recognized that by some curious alchemy her very self-possession made her beauty her own.

Keeping a careful distance, he walked beside her through the trees to the lake that was once the old moat. Set back from the water, on its own small plinth of stones, was a concrete bench, of the type beloved by park authorities everywhere. The bench was old, with traces of green moss on the back. She sat down, straight-backed, not looking at him but directly ahead at the surface of the dark green lake on which several mallard drakes were manoeuvring beside a placid female. He suspected that her stiffness was not embarrassment but a certain formality that was part of her personality. He seated himself beside her, with the sun behind and the ducks in front, and waited for her to speak.

Several groups of tourists wandered by. A small child played with a dog. Behind the lake the steep grey walls of Toompea rose into a sky that was now almost clear of cloud. If he had one advantage, he was not afraid of silence.

'My father advises President Aegu on legal matters. I

was told by him that you are helping in the inquiry into Ivan Illich's murder.'

Shaw nodded.

On a second bench two middle-aged women were sitting, their eyes closed, their faces turned upwards. Scandinavians can be struck into silence by the summer sun, their faces drinking sunlight like pale flowers.

'I understand that the inquiry has not progressed very far.'

He could not work out immediately whether she was making a statement or asking a question.

'That seems fair.'

She paused again.

'May I ask you: how are you helping?'

He hadn't expected such a direct question, and for several seconds he waited. She was a lecturer in child psychology, and had the reputation of a formidable mind. Even though she was seated beside him, looking over the lake, her curiosity seemed to search him out.

'There are no obvious leads. I try to provide whatever background I can.'

'Background.' She seemed to breathe it out; pronouncing it without any inflection, but he could sense her frustration with the word, with the concept perhaps. She would not elucidate further, so he said: 'You think we're not looking in the right direction?'

The thought seemed to amuse her.

'It is more of a general consideration. People used to believe in the old days that background in scientific research was the most important thing. If you know the empirical facts, the explanation will emerge of its own accord.'

'And that isn't so?'

'I don't know about criminal investigation.'

Shaw was determined not to lose the thread. He said: 'I thought perhaps you were talking generally.'

'In the experimental sciences we know now that the

282

most important thing is the foreground, the theory. If you do not have a theory, nothing makes sense. You do not even know where to look. Sometimes even a flawed theory is better than none.'

Two of the mallard drakes, in a parody of male aggression and vanity, were squaring up to one another. The third drake, surreptitiously, seemed to be making off with the female. Shaw wondered if there was a moral lesson.

'Do you have a theory?' he asked.

'Not a theory, so much. Some views, perhaps. Illich was an Estonian. He lived here most of his life without danger. Perhaps those involved were . . . from outside.'

Behind the lake, rising behind the oaks and birches of the park was the tower called 'Tall Herman'. Cloud appeared above it like puffs of smoke from a chimney. A single Estonian tricolour moved lazily at its summit; blue, black, white. She appeared to be waiting for him.

'You think it might have been an American, for example?' Shaw asked.

He was getting used to her silences now.

'No.'

'A Russian?'

This time he was not so much off guard. He could wait.

She was silent, so he took the initiative and pressed ahead in a way which he would not dreamed of doing if she had not asked him first about the inquiry.

'Might you know anyone, Estonian or foreign, who harboured some kind of personal animosity against him?'

'No.'

It was a firm response, unyielding, and Shaw wondered whether he had provoked her somehow; perhaps it was a matter of loyalty. We can't walk without treading on something, he thought; extreme Hindus sweep ants from their path with little brushes.

'No one with a personal motive?'

'Motive,' she repeated, and smiled quietly to herself. 'I am a psychologist. A person who kills doesn't necessarily need a motive.'

He was starting to feel out of his depth.

'Don't you think one must be ... abnormal to kill, a little obsessed, perhaps?'

'Psychologically disturbed?' She smiled. 'Perhaps we all wish to kill at one time or another. The question is, what makes some people do it?'

He was firing loosely, and he knew it. But just as she had greeted him unexpectedly, so now a part of him hoped she might bring the conversation back on to course. He tried again: 'You knew Illich better than I did. Do you think he inspired personal animosity?'

'He wasn't a person who held personal animosities himself.'

It was not so much an answer as a mild rebuke. She seemed to reject his line of questioning. She continued to sit quietly. Without knowing why, Shaw was already feeling alarmed. Were her silences deliberate? Did she use them as actors use pauses, to create an effect? There was something unnerving about these long inter-missions.

'Then we have nothing more to go on.'

Yet he was aware of the concentration of her thought. Peripheral vision does not register detail, but it is sensitive to movement. She sat absolutely still.

Shaw looked out across the sward to the lake. Two youths were throwing a ball for a dog. An elderly woman was standing by the side of the lake, feeding the ducks. Briefly the sun disappeared behind clouds. The surface of the water turned grey.

'Perhaps it was political.' She spoke softly, almost reluctantly, like an expulsion of breath. Nervous of pressing her, he watched the ducks on the water. Their shining V-shaped wakes seemed to him like arrows of

284

death. How long did he wait? A few seconds? A minute? After that she would not speak. There was a barrier between them. He felt that she knew something important, was now surer of it than ever.

He said: 'The investigation is at a sensitive stage. If you could do anything that could give us a lead . . .'

She had been watching the lake, but now she stood up with such conviction that it might have appeared sudden if it had not also been so calm. She stood facing the water. In some way, he suspected, he had disappointed her. There seemed no point in walking back with her.

'If some new line of evidence came up,' Shaw said, 'would you like me to contact you?'

She withdrew a card from her handbag.

Dr Lydia Teemant
16 Gargarin Puiestee
Tallinn

She wrote her work and home telephone numbers on it. Then she turned to face him directly.

'Goodbye.'

'Thank you for your help,' Shaw said.

She shook hands with him formally and he watched her walk away. The sky had become overcast. The ducks' wakes were now turbid squiggles. He sat down again. After a few minutes he stood up and walked to Vaksali Street, finding his way back to the flat. He glanced at his watch. Twelve thirty-five.

Maria was looking composed after her shopping expedition. At first, there were no suspicious signs of hatboxes. She handed back the chequebook.

'Did you have a good morning?' Shaw asked.

'Yes.'

He looked at the stubs. There were only three figures entered there, but they made him break out into a sweat.

285

'Just two dresses, two pairs of shoes, and a couple of other things.'

'Uh-huh.'

It was bad, but it wasn't necessarily disastrous. He'd run a few provisional calculations and with a little luck, they might still be solvent.

'Other things?'

'Well, I needed a business suit, for when I go part-time job hunting.'

'Oh, right.'

'And a couple of accessories.'

Well, we all need accessories.

'And how was your morning?' she asked.

'My morning? I saw the display in the Maritime Museum. Doctor Vader seemed a nice enough guy. They've got really excellent photographs in there.'

'That all?'

'I went for a walk in the Toompark, and I recognized Lydia Teemant. Do you remember Illich sometimes sneaked off over weekends to see his girlfriend?'

'I thought he had several.'

'Maybe,' Shaw said. 'But I think that one was serious.'

He thought: That one would be enough. But her name had triggered memories for Maria.

'I think Ilena mentioned her. I seem to remember being told she's engaged to someone, but she was having an affair with Illich.' Maria paused to raise Jack into his high chair. 'Ilena said she was also Aegu's mistress.'

Shaw was still for a moment.

Maria was helping Jack put his legs through the slots in his high chair, preparatory to feeding. Her back was to him.

'Whose mistress?'

'President Aegu. Your friend.'

Maria helped Jack's legs through. He put his elbows on the little flip-table, and stared ferociously forward. She began to mix some food in a little blue bowl.

'Ilena told you?'

Jack ignored the proffered spoon. Like a small mystic, he was more interested in his own thoughts.

'She said it was common knowledge. One of those recognized unofficial relationships.'

Maria, who had her back to him, walked around the other side of Jack's chair so that she could approach the problem of feeding him from another angle. Facing Shaw now, she said: 'You look as if you've seen a ghost.'

'Do I?'

'Have I just said something?'

'I didn't know about Aegu.'

Maria halted with a spoon raised towards Jack. Jack, ready to repel, was disconcerted by the spoon's halted progress, and for the first time gave it his attention.

'What's going on?'

'Nothing's going on. It was just something she said.'

'Who? Ilena?'

'Lydia Teemant.'

Jack was snapping at the spoon with his mouth, pretending to be an animal, but it was just out of his reach.

'You sure she hasn't got to you?'

Maria was studying him directly.

'What has got to me,' Shaw said carefully, 'is what you've just told me about Aegu.'

Maria looked at him a little while longer; then, without any change in her expression, she turned her attention to feeding Jack.

The most important things are hidden, he thought.

Fifty-one

Kalev Tammiste put down the phone. His face hovered for a moment between incredulity and laughter. His astonishment was so great that he consciously made an attempt to steady himself for a few seconds.

His wife Margarita was outside in the garden. He opened the back door of their wooden A-frame house and walked out between two rows of fuchsias. She was tidying up the vegetable garden, her solid hands preparing the soil for planting the following spring. She paused between piling old beans and peas on the compost heap.

'The American phoned.'

His wife said nothing.

'Jim Shaw. He wants me to design a yacht.'

'A racing boat?'

'No, a cruising yacht.'

'That is very strange.' Margarita paused for a moment, and shrugged, before going back to stripping off the old bean plants and piling them on the compost heap.

It always pleased him when his wife showed no reaction to the latest outrage of owners and sailors. Her stolidity was the perfect foil to his highly strung astonishment at their shifts and changes. It was not the cruising yacht aspect which had taken him by surprise. Shaw had suggested to Illich that he scrap the great *Novy Mir* when it was first launched. And here he was returning for a second design.

'Perhaps,' his wife said, 'he thinks you can only design cruising boats.'

It was a good rejoinder. But Tammiste believed that a good cruising boat was, if anything, more difficult to design than a good racing boat. The demands were more complex, the compromises more subtle and intractable. In the configuration of racing yacht the designer faced the rule to which he must conform. He designed against the artificial simplicity of a man-made construct. Like a solicitor searching for flaws in a contract, he searched for loopholes which add a fraction of sail area here, a small reduction in weight there. In designing a cruising yacht he designs against the sea itself, against the classic propinquities of wave and wind.

There were other differences, too. A racing yacht, crewed by a dozen young, fit men (sometimes referred to in the trade as "gorillas") could be built light and unseaworthy, without sufficient ballast, in the knowledge that a powerful and expert crew will manhandle the yacht through dangers. In a cruising yacht, the boat itself must look after the short-handed owner and his wife and family. In this sense, too, the cruising owner appeared the more exacting client.

'You seem pleased,' Margarita said.

'More amused than pleased.'

Margarita paused momentarily, then went back to stripping the climbing beans from their poles.

Since *Novy Mir*'s victory in the America's Cup, Tammiste had been flooded with work to design racing yachts, so much so that he could pick and choose his design commissions. It would be perfectly easy to refuse, amicably of course, and recommend another designer. But he liked the sound of the boat. It would be simple in conception, uncluttered by internal furniture, built for strength and seaworthiness. If there was a type of yacht which did not excite Tammiste it was the floating cottage, a yacht filled with every modern convenience, one designed never to leave a marina. This was clearly not one of those.

'Will you do it?' Margarita asked. She paused to brush a strand of hair from her eyes.

Tammiste was preoccupied.

To build in wood coated with epoxy, the American had said. It was intriguing, at least. In his own view, simplicity was the essence of seaworthiness. The sea had a way of testing equipment to destruction, and the fewer things there were to go wrong the better. He decided he would do it. He would generate the lines-plan in the old way, by hand, fairing up the curves with strips of paper. It was so long since he had done so that he experienced the pleasant apprehension of a challenge.

Margarita watched him. He had forgotten her question. Shrugging, she went back to her work.

When he sat down to it several days later, it was a surprisingly satisfying process, shuffling the lines into fairness, using the brush to clear away rubbings, while the little strips of marking paper gathered in a pile at one side of his drawing desk. Slowly the lines-plan emerged. He explained the salient points to Shaw: 'You can see from the profile the deep forefoot; it draws out the hull wave and makes the boat faster. The bow waterline entry is narrow; a combination of narrow entry and deep forefoot reduces slamming into a sea.'

Shaw, standing beside him at the drawing board, knew that racing boats with shallow forefoots slammed unmercifully in a seaway. He nodded.

'I've given the stern sections some tumblehome,' Tammiste continued. 'Not as extreme as *Novy Mir*, because you lose living area. But it helps to make the hull exceptionally well balanced. There shouldn't be much increase in weather helm when you heel.'

The tumblehome added a certain attractiveness, too. But Shaw wasn't going to say that now.

'The transom almost touches the water; long waterline: shallow deadrise; good for surfing off waves downwind. There are eight laminated frames at metre intervals.'

Without understanding the detailed intricacies, Shaw

liked the look of the boat. The coachroof seemed in harmony with the hull. The cockpit was big, but it drained directly out through a letter-box run at the back – one of the few useful innovations from racing yachts.

He wrote out a cheque for six thousand five hundred roubles – a substantial sum, but one which he felt was worth it. To absorb the shock of the cheque, Tammiste offered Shaw a cognac. They sat down in one of the designer's low chairs.

'Is there any news on Illich's murder? No suspect yet?'

'Not much progress,' Shaw replied.

'I hear you are seconded to the police force.'

'I do what little I can to help.'

Tammiste had a nervous blink. His spectacles gave him the look of an owl.

'Will you be racing again?'

'I don't think so.'

'You gave it up once before,' Tammiste said slyly.

Fifty-two

Sam Shaw stood on the landing, a single suitcase in one hand, a plastic shopping bag in the other. He looked frail. His neck had the same skinny look as the wrists that protruded from his worn cuffs. There was a ring of red in his eyes. He wore an ill-fitting suit which his shrunken frame had made too large. If Shaw had seen him in the street, he would have thought he was a peasant farmer come to town.

Compared to Russians, or even Estonians, Shaw was not a demonstrative man. But he lifted Sam Shaw off the ground in a bear-hug, and practically carried him inside. He could smell the old man's protesting breath, like mothballs, and once again was aware of his age. Maria was behind him, Jack in her arms. Shaw dreaded to think of the emotional scenes if Jack had not been there as a barrier.

In the first instant of a meeting one glimpses people as others see them. Sam Shaw had the self-sufficiency of the truly detached. A curious glint of happiness seemed to rise out of his face, like a Buddhist monk or elderly abbot. He smiled around at the apartment.

'How are you, Jack?'

Jack, made nervous by adult emotion, reached up towards his mother's hand. Maria lifted him up. He surveyed their visitor from an equal height.

'Sit down,' Shaw said. He took Sam's suitcase from the landing into the second room.

Maria was asking through her tears, 'How was your flight?'

'Easy. The taxi driver brought me straight here. This is really a fine place.'

He looked around at the rooms almost empty of furniture, the bare white-washed walls, the way voices echoed into an infinite regression, the flavour of cold-ness or distance between things. It seemed he felt at home.

'Let me hold the little devil,' he said. 'Got his mother's good looks, I'm glad to see.'

Jack sat on his knee. 'A great-grandchild. That's really something.'

The old man had lost weight. There were indenta-tions in his cheeks, blue veins in his chin, the begin-nings of a tremor in his fingers. Rocking Jack on his knee, he suddenly looked tired. Physically, he gave the impression of absence rather than presence.

'Your bed's made up if you want to sleep,' Maria said.

'I'll have plenty of time for that.'

'Coffee?' Shaw asked.

'Black and strong, please.'

'Did you see Coach Johnson?' Sam Shaw asked his grandson.

'We saw him quite recently.'

'He OK?'

'Seems to be. We didn't see him long.'

'Guess he's upset about losing.'

'I expect so,' Shaw answered.

He kept in mind that his grandfather did not own a television, and did not read newspapers. Mercifully, he thought, although his grandfather knew of his involvement from the beginning, he would have been protected from most of the barrage of media comment on the fact that the successful Russian defence of the America's Cup was assisted by an American helmsman.

'What do you think of Estonia?' Shaw asked.

'All those shops, all those cars on the streets, all those well-dressed people. I expected somewhere grey, full of smoking chimneys.'

'You sound disappointed.'

Shaw had a notion his grandfather was disoriented. Maybe he imagined high billboards with workers shoulder to shoulder and slogans commending the dignity of labour.

'Estonia is politically independent.' Shaw knew he sounded like a tourist guide. 'Economically it runs itself. The Russian military still has a foothold here, but they keep in the background.'

Jack was starting to get restless. Maria lifted him off Sam's knee and took him through to his bedroom.

But Sam Shaw wasn't so much disappointed as disconcerted. He'd looked forward to those chimneys everywhere, the feeling of austerity, hardship, honest toil. Instead he saw Japanese cars, people dressed in Italian designs, tourists with cameras. He observed the gloss of prosperity and high consumption.

With coffee, he started to revive. It had been chilly outside, the first chill of autumn, and he gathered his thin fingers about the cup. Through the casement window the city lights were coming on. Maria, returning from putting Jack to bed, switched on the lights.

Maria started to cook, arranging things on the side-table: red peppers, pearly white slivers of fish. She poured vegetable oil into a pan and heated it up on the Gralu gas stove.

While she cooked, Shaw said: 'We like it here. Not just the flat, I mean. The place. Estonia. We're going to be staying a while.'

'What are you going to do?' Sam Shaw asked him.

That was the most difficult question. Would his grandfather accept that he didn't know? He shrugged his shoulders. 'I'll find something.'

Sam changed the subject. 'I hear Agnes is coming over.'

'In a week or two, I think,' Shaw replied.

He wondered whether Maria had heard that. She was putting the fish into a casserole dish lined with vegetables, grating a layer of cheese over it with quick movements of her elbow, her head tipped to one side with concentration. She had heard, Shaw knew.

'That'll be good,' Sam replied. He was studying a Japanese print of storks taking wing, big birds rising like white tablecloths towards a grey sky. He didn't like pictures on walls but he had a liking for certain Japanese prints, their simplicity and power.

To change the subject, Shaw said, 'I'm thinking of building a boat.'

Fifty-three

The phone shrieked out in the night. At the second ring Shaw had rolled over and was beside it like an anxious parent over a child, shaking, breathless. His eyes blinked with rage and sleep.

'Mr Shaw?'

'Speaking.'

'Saarinen. I apologize for ringing. It is urgent.'

'Go ahead.'

'At 3.17 a.m. an ambulance drew up at the Stavere hospital outside Parnu. A man was carried on a stretcher to the ambulance. One of the two watchers saw bandages over his face.'

'Goddamn.' Shaw shifted the receiver from one hand to another, and half rolled, half slid into a sitting position with his feet on the floor. Down the phone line he could hear a background of shouted orders, another phone ringing shrilly. It sounded as though the police station were fully staffed. His eyes grew slowly accustomed to the darkness. He could make out the face of the small traveller's clock beside his bed; its arms indicated 3:22.

'The ambulance moved west towards the border then north,' Saarinen continued. 'Car 18 is tracking them. I have a car waiting outside the police station. I will call for you in one minute's time.'

'I'll be waiting.'

Shaw put down the phone. There was enough light through the window to see by. Carefully, he picked up his clothes and moved through to the sitting-room. He began to dress; shirt, pants, trousers, socks.

He did not hear Maria rise from the bed. She was standing in the doorway, her arms folded, watching. He could see the hollows of her cheeks, but could not see the expression in her eyes.

'Saarinen,' Shaw explained, putting on his shoes. He tried to kiss her but she merely stood aside so that he could move past her into their bedroom. There was enough light to see; neither wanted to switch on a light. He put on his watch, then searched the cupboard with his hands for a sweater.

Shaw hauled on the sweater. 'Don't wait up.'

Maria seemed to lean against a shadow. Her feet beneath her shift were bare. In the hall Shaw put a waterproof jacket over the sweater, unlocked the door, and descended the uncarpeted stairs.

Outside the door, Saarinen's police Volvo was already standing against the kerb, engine running. Approaching, Shaw could just make out the shadowy shapes of two officers in the front, their collars drawn up against the cold. Vares moved out with a certain litheness and opened the back door for him. When he was inside the door was closed peremptorily. A few seconds later the front door was slammed and the car accelerated fast away from the kerb, as if the driver too was angry at being out at this hour. Saarinen's moon-face turned towards him in the glowing darkness of the interior. The shadows of buildings moved across his eerie grin.

'We may have hooked a little fish.'

The Volvo was being driven fast on full headlights. They thundered down empty streets. Shadows lay across their path as solid as timber. Now the anger of the driver knew no bounds. They two-wheeled around corners and broke through traffic lights. Once they crossed an old freight yard, full of disused wooden loading docks, piled high with barrels of chemical dye. Out through wide gateposts, across a ramp, on to the open road. On the radio a patrolman's voice was saying: 'Moving north, towards Tallinn, Motorway 12. Driving a hundred and twenty kilometres.' In the passenger seat Vares studied a map by the light of a small hand-held torch. Beside his hand the car's instrument panel glimmered like phosphorescence.

'The ambulance seemed to be going west at first, then it turned north.' Saarinen scanned the road ahead. 'It is likely they will be coming towards Tallinn. They could take Motorway 11 to the border and into Russia at Narva. Technically, we are not allowed to pursue across the border without prior permission. It is an unfortunate aspect of our independence.'

'How long would it take to get permission?' Shaw asked.

Saarinen simply shrugged, as if to say 'too long'.

'Intercept estimate eighteen minutes,' Vares called.

Ahead of them, a policeman in the civil guard flashed a powerful torch at them. The driver raised and lowered his headlights in three quick flashes.

'Who was it?' asked Saarinen.

'Erlak,' the driver suggested. 'Maybe Gurlof. He's the same size.'

The car cut through a narrow siding, then they were out on the highway, up to one hundred and sixty kilometres. Before they hit the open road, Shaw had seen militia gathered in one of the small courtyards, perhaps fifty or sixty men standing at ease, blowing on their hands.

'What's going on?' he asked.

'A political crisis,' Saarinen observed. 'The militia have been called out on exercise.'

'Political?'

'Sometimes it happens.'

'Still heading north,' came the voice on the radio, 'Motorway 12.'

'Radio silence unless route changes,' snapped Saarinen. He too was tense. Shaw wondered whether he was spooked by the militia alert.

Vares repeated his instruction on the car radio.

'Intercept estimate twelve minutes,' Vares confirmed.

'All right,' Saarinen said sarcastically to no one in particular, 'we can count.'

No one spoke. Shaw thought Saarinen might have smoked, but he sat hunched in his jacket, staring resolutely ahead. Occasional desultory headlights passed them on the highway, the Fiats and Zhigulis of drowsy Russian immigrant workers returning from night shifts to the dormitory flats surrounding Tallinn; sometimes the big round owl eyes of trucks on overnight deliveries.

The three officers were starting to study with interest the vehicles coming the other way. Ahead of them, on the horizon, they could see the faint glow of Parnu.

'That was it,' said Saarinen. The two officers in front looked behind them at the shape of the ambulance receding. About four hundred yards later another set of headlamps. The driver dipped his headlights once.

'Car 18.'

There was a grass verge between the motorways. They went on for another thirty seconds, then slowed and pulled over the fast lane hard shoulder. The Volvo jumped and squealed as it climbed the grass verge, sliced a flower bed, throwing up two plumes of black soil behind them. With a howl of burning tyres they swung on to the motorway and accelerated after the other two cars.

In the distance ahead of them they could see the red tail-lights of car 18.

'Keep your distance,' Saarinen said.

They trailed them for about eight minutes.

Ahead of them, car 18 passed the turn-off to the circular road around Tallinn.

'They're not going to Narva, sir,' Vares commented.

Saarinen didn't answer. Car 18 was continuing north. Then it detoured right unexpectedly.

'A boat maybe?' Saarinen asked. 'Break radio silence,' he snapped to Vares. 'Tell car 18 to close up.'

Vares issued brief instructions.

'Let's close up ourselves.'

'Looks like the airport,' Vares said shortly afterwards.

'The airport,' Saarinen repeated. A crackle broke through on the car radio.

'Turning right to airport. Military section.'

'Damn,' Saarinen hissed. 'I don't believe it. A special plane out of the military section.'

To their right they could see, behind high, barbed-wire mesh, the shadowy shapes of Antonov transports. The field was lit up. In the mist of lights it was alive with men.

'What in God's name is going on?' Saarinen asked. 'What is all this activity?'

The radio crackled again. 'Car 18. Quarry has halted at military security.'

'Slow down,' Saarinen ordered.

They would have had to slow, anyway. Ahead of them, about fifty yards, glowed the tail-lights of car 18, almost halted. About a hundred yards ahead, the bland, blind rear of the ambulance waited beside the guard-house while two Russian military police, on the passenger's side of the ambulance, checked identifications.

'Tell 18 to stay put,' ordered Saarinen. 'Cover us. Let's get that ambulance!'

Torson hit the pedal. The car wheels screamed as they rode up on the kerb to pass car 18. They seemed to plunge forward and upwards on two wheels. The Russians checking the ambulance had turned towards them, were unshipping their guns.

Saarinen roared out of the open window, 'Police!'

The car swung, plunged, seemed to float for several seconds, then came to a halt against the curve.

'Stay here,' Saarinen told Shaw.

All three investigators jumped out. Behind the military policemen the lights on the airfield glowed. Where night mists met the light there was an eerie territory of ghosts. The airfield military police were nervous. They stood against the lights of the arc-lamps, watching figures approaching out of the darkness. A sergeant called 'Halt!' in Russian.

'Police!' Close to, Saarinen's voice was more statement than shout. He held up the fat green card of Criminal Investigations in the sodium lamps. Advancing, keeping their hands away from their bodies, the three officers spread out naturally, as if they merely sought space in which to breathe. Their shadows, flung backwards, made them seem huge.

Shaw could hear the safety catches come off on the guns of the military police. But the three investigators continued to advance steadily into the light.

Vares had reached the further side of the ambulance. Technically, it was still on Estonian territory. The barrier had been raised. If it pulled through it would be on Russian military soil. Perhaps someone inside the ambulance was aware of the distinction. The ambulance shook as its engine started. Vares, in a gesture almost casual, struck upwards from the hip in a single flow, shattering the side-window glass with his elbow; in almost the same movement, he reached in and snapped off the key. The ambulance kicked forward a few inches and halted.

Somewhere, inside the compound, an alarm sounded, the noise started to climb.

In the lights, Saarinen's figure dominated. Holding up his card, he must have seemed an image from the past, the Lenin of a thousand fallen statues. The two military policemen facing him edged back and took up a crouched position, ready to fire. On the other side of the ambulance Vares and Torson were feeling for the side-door of the ambulance. Saarinen slowed his walk, standing still in the full flood of the headlights, his officer's card held high in the sodium light. In the distance the alarm went into a higher register.

Hidden from sight on the other side Torson and

300

Vares, like two hoodlums, were breaking the locked door-handle with an almost gleeful violence, using heavy blows of their boots. While his men were breaking in on one side of the ambulance, hidden from the view of the military police, on the other side Saarinen was talking like a tamer to wolves, invoking peace and co-operation, his voice too quiet for sanity.

Boots were running across the airfield. The door handle finally gave under Vares' and Torson's attention. They leapt to the side. Torson called out: 'It's full of armed men!'

Saarinen spoke softly, 'We have reason to believe that the patient in the ambulance is a witness to a murder. We request that you hand over the patient. We will take him to a civilian hospital for further treatment. Tell the men in the ambulance to throw out their guns.'

The two military policemen did not move.

Another voice was shouting. An officer was advancing out of the floodlights. Behind him were more men than could be easily counted.

'Torson, Vares,' Saarinen said softly, without changing his tone. 'Move back to the car.'

To the military police, he said, 'Our article 43a, Estonian Code. Aiding a witness in resisting arrest.'

The officer shouted, 'Stop them.' But the military police, transfixed in their firing position, made no move as Saarinen backed slowly to the car. He was on Estonian territory and acted as if he owned it. The car heeled and shook like a small boat as the three investigators climbed back inside. Torson punched the starter, released the brake and the car surged, mounted the kerb, and swung back in the direction from which they had come. In front of them car 18 did a three-point turn.

'Don't look back,' Saarinen said to Shaw. 'People in that state are like animals. Don't show fear or nervousness.'

They followed car 18 out slowly.

'Tell the others to return to base.'

When they were several hundred yards away Vares said, 'I think I've crapped in my pants.'

'A good policeman has so many layers of crap in his pants,' Saarinen said quietly, 'you can tell his age like a tree.'

But the two younger men were high on adrenalin, and if Saarinen had not been there, they would have sung.

'Pull up,' Saarinen said.

The car swung to the side of the curve. Behind them the airfield was lit up. Forms moved back and forth like the set of a film. The ambulance could no longer be discerned. Saarinen's anger was an expulsion of breath.

'What did you see inside the ambulance?' Saarinen asked.

'About four shiny gun-barrels.'

'Pistols?'

'Machine pistols. Blackened faces.'

'Interior ministry?'

'Army. Spetsnaz.'

'Impressive,' Saarinen commented. 'No wonder you crapped your pants.'

Vares continued with his account. Inside the ambulance there must have been half a dozen men hunched beside the stretcher; they seemed like a single bristling machine.

'What can we do now?' It was almost the first time Shaw had spoken.

'If we go back, we'll be shot.'

'But you're policemen.'

Saarinen smiled without mirth.

'That doesn't matter. At a military base, all unauthorized entrants will be treated as enemy aliens, and shot. Military bases are effectively Russian territory, even now. It is the regulation.'

Ahead of them car 18's lights drifted over a ramp in the darkness.

Shaw said, 'That was our goddamn man.'

'Vares,' Saarinen said. 'Tell base to telephone Priority One. Put it on scrambler code.'

'Sir.'

Saarinen said without rancour, 'Now we'll see what President Aegu can do.'

Fifty-four

A few minutes later the radio crackled through.

'Priority One contacted. Requests you call by at his house.'

'Understood,' Saarinen said. 'Ten minutes.'

Vares transmitted a brief message to the other car. Car 18 peeled away down a side-street.

On the way back they saw more militia, standing in the darkness like the armies of the dead. Their own car hit high speed, switching to back lanes, pausing only to assure no other vehicle was coming down the narrow streets before accelerating again to jump lights. Over a hogback in the road, the wheels howling and the car suspension jack-knifing. Down a one-way street, almost brushing an elderly night-watchman aside, Shaw caught a glimpse of his white face in one of the side mirrors as the car swept past.

Into the old town, along Naukogude Street, turning right into Toompea. They came to a halt outside 16 Kohtu Street and Saarinen sprang out, moving quickly to Aegu's gate. A plainclothes man opened the door. Shaw recognized him as one of the Kallas brothers who guarded Aegu. Shaw followed Saarinen up the steps.

The officer knocked on the door. Aegu received them in his dressing-gown, his eyes red. An artery in his temple visibly pulsed. He led them through to a ground-floor office, gestured them to sit down.

To Saarinen, Aegu said: 'The ambulance disappeared?'

'Tallinn military airfield,' Saarinen replied. 'They were preparing to shoot us. They must have a special plane waiting.'

Aegu picked up the telephone.

'Colonel Bulgayev, please.'

There were several clicks. Aegu put his hand over the mouthpiece.

'How certain are you our man was in the ambulance?' he asked Saarinen

'Certain.'

'Colonel,' Aegu said into the phone. 'You have an aircraft about to take off from the military section at Tallinn. It is carrying an individual with eye-damage. We would like to interview this man.'

The reply was indistinct.

'The charge?' Aegu said. 'First-degree murder.'

There was a brief silence. Shaw tried to imagine a Russian colonel, perhaps woken from slumber, his aide standing by.

Aegu put his hand over the telephone again.

'He's consulting with someone.' He moved his hand from the mouthpiece. Aegu was relentless. 'No one answering that description? A flight carrying back an officer? Which officer? Why is he travelling at this time of night? Why on a special plane?'

Shaw strained to hear the static of the answer. The conversation was mostly in Russian. Aegu took advantage of the officer's halting reply to press home his interrogation.

'Colonel, if the flight proceeds, if the man is flown off, we will bring a criminal charge against you personally.'

Aegu's square hand covered the mouthpiece. He whispered to Saarinen.

'Can we do that?'

Saarinen breathed in and looked upwards towards the ceiling.

'What is the name of the officer? Why can't you tell me his name, if you have nothing to hide? I order you to tell me his name.'

The phone went dead.

'He cut me off,' Aegu said. 'My only hope was to keep pressing him while he was drowsy. He'll have collected his wits in ten minutes and will phone back to apologize for the fault in the line. Meanwhile he'll be phoning Moscow.'

It was at best a rearguard action. Each of them knew that their suspect was even now airborne and on his way into the Russian hinterland; that he had flown out of their area of restriction and they had no means of recall; that for some reason he was being protected by the Russian military. And they knew, finally, that this in turn posed fearful problems – civil, diplomatic, military – to any attempt to bring him to justice. Even so Aegu was pleased.

'We got something. The killer exists. We sniffed him out. The man on the stretcher is an officer. For a special plane, my guess is it's a senior officer. We have a suspect, gentlemen.'

Saarinen turned towards Shaw. For the first time Shaw detected a trace of warmth in that moonlike smile.

A few minutes later, when Saarinen stood up to leave, Aegu said to Shaw, 'There are some matters I would like to discuss with you.'

Shaw saw Saarinen hesitate.

'Shall we wait for you?'

'I can walk home,' Shaw said to the policeman.

Saarinen nodded and shook hands with them both.

They heard his car draw out from the kerb and the sigh of its wheels as it moved down Kohtu Street.

'So,' Aegu said.

In one sense Shaw could be pleased. His initiative had flushed out a suspect. He had risked his neck and it had paid off. But he was haunted by the prospect of the murderer escaping beyond their reach.

Aegu withdrew from his desk a bottle of vodka and two glasses, filled them, and pushed one towards him. It was quiet outside. He could hear drops of dew falling from the window ledge.

Aegu threw back a glass, and filled his glass again. He sat back. Overwork showed in the shadows beneath his eyes. Bearish, he sprawled in his chair; his mouth turned down as the first slug of vodka hit his stomach.

'You know the story of the child who rode on a tiger's back? We seem to be riding such a tiger now.'

Shaw suspected he was in for a long session. He took a gulp of his own drink.

'Over the last few months we have been renegotiating our defence pact with Russia. Russian troops are allowed here as part of our strategic agreements. The current treaty allows a limited build-up of the Russian Army in Estonia as defence reasons dictate. We have stipulated, as part of the process of developing relations between our two countries, we should be informed of any troop increases and should ultimately exercise a right of veto. It is a contentious issue.

'There are some strange developments in the Russian republic. Not recent ones, I hasten to add, but longer term movements which are now entering what old Marxists used to call the critical stage. It is a crisis composed of several strands. Each strand is innocuous, but they twist together slowly until they form a hangman's noose.'

Aegu had been drinking on his own, perhaps to douse some internal pain. 'It is interesting to talk to you. I am forced to reconstruct the picture, so to speak, from its components.'

Shaw drained his glass. Aegu reached forward to fill it.

'The first strand is the continuing economic crisis in Russia itself. It was hoped that an independent Estonia, by proving successful in its free-market economy, would show the way. But something, some strange pride, prohibits Moscow from following full-heartedly.' Aegu settled back in his chair and stared at the ceiling. 'They make small reforms, and raise expectations, but little occurs. The problem with Russians is that they are led by the heart, by great ideas, by reality-defying plans. The market, on the other hand, does not like to be led. It sets its own terms. It works slowly, day and night. We Estonians are a more sober, more phlegmatic people. We have the patience to allow the market system to work.'

This seemed like a ramble to Shaw. But it was Aegu who had given him the chance to work with the police. He felt he owed it to him to hear him out.

'There is a diminishing likelihood that they will achieve their economic goals. There continue to be shortages despite all the changes. The country has no deep democratic tradition and wild rumours are beginning to fly. They demand a dictator, a benevolent one of course, to carry out the necessary re-ordering of society. If they allowed the market to develop their economy for them, perhaps a crisis could be averted . . .'

The phone rang suddenly. Aegu put down his glass of vodka and picked it up.

'Yes.'

It was a man's voice, giving what sounded like a report. Aegu merely pursed his lips. 'I see.'

He put down the phone. 'Colonel Bulgayev phoning back. He apologizes for being cut off. The individual in the ambulance and the officer who is being flown out are separate people. The individual in the ambulance is a technician from their military installation at Radu who was repairing a power cable when he fell.'

Anger rose inside Shaw. He said, 'If he's a technician, why did he have an armed guard?'

'You saw inside the ambulance?'

'Torson and Vares did. One stretcher case and at least four armed men.'

'They will put in their report, and my committee will study it in detail. I am afraid there is nothing that can be done now about the officer. By now he is almost certainly out of Estonian territory.'

'Can't we check where he's going to land?'

'No,' Aegu replied. 'It could be one of a hundred military airfields. I am afraid that for the time being our friend has been lost.'

'He killed Illich.'

'I agree with you, and we must now try to identify him and pursue him by other means. But for the time being we must accept that, physically speaking, we are powerless to follow him into Russia.'

Shaw knew Aegu was right. But he had sat in a police car thirty feet away from the murderer, and now he had escaped. He couldn't help but feel frustrated. Aegu refilled both glasses and continued.

'If something is wrong, the Russian population demands human scapegoats. That is how it has always been. It is the instability which is the problem. One of the means of reasserting authority is to divert attention. This brings to mind the second cause of instability. There is a dangerous breed of militarism which is asserting itself again. Its proponents are increasingly inclined to impose order using the old methods. It could suspend the democratic institutions by calling a state of emergency. Free of criticism, it would be in a position to reassert its grip over the former territories.'

Aegu was leaning forward. Shaw could see the strain

in his face, the artery still moving in his temple. His eyes were blood-red. He hadn't slept for days.

'Perhaps you noticed the military airfield at Tallinn. The lights were on. Troops were everywhere, aircraft taking off and landing. The military garrison is being reinforced. Why?'

Shaw felt his heart begin to pound. At first he thought it was a joke, an exaggeration. But there were other signs that night. Groups of militia standing at crossroads.

'It's happened before. An exercise. But we used to be warned of exercises. When the beast stirs, and puts out its limbs, it sometimes strikes a smaller creature. We are simply that smaller creature. But the animal is moving. It is raising itself off the ground. It has happened before, and then it fades away, leaving us nervous. Perhaps it is conditioning us.'

'You should get some sleep,' Shaw said.

'Yes,' Aegu agreed, and poured himself one more drink. He offered the bottle to Shaw. Shaw raised a hand in polite refusal.

'Go back to your house, *tovarich*.'

Exhaustion was taking hold of Aegu. He rose to his feet with difficulty, and called out. The plainclothes officer opened the door.

'Goodbye,' Aegu said.

Outside the officer asked, 'Would you like me to arrange a car?'

Shaw shook his head. 'It's a few minutes' walk.'

It was just after five in the morning. On Kohtu Street, the vodka warming his insides met the adrenalin coming down. Like two rival police forces, they confronted one another, then settled into uneasy accommodation. What was left was plain fear. He hadn't felt so frightened for a long time.

Fifty-five

'Not again,' Maria said softly.

She was standing in the doorway. One side of her face glowed white in the light from the landing; the other was covered with a flow of dark hair and shadow. It was five thirty-eight and he guessed she hadn't slept.

'Aegu,' Shaw said, as if this explained the alcohol on his breath.

She let him past, pulling her nightgown around her against the cold air that had come in with him. In the shadows he could sense her musky warmth. Despite the alcohol he felt desire.

He undressed in their bedroom. Behind him he heard the bedsprings move as she slipped between the sheets. He turned out the light. She had turned away from him, and he knew no explanation would suffice. She would assume that he and Saarinen and Aegu had used the excuse of a night's emergency to drink themselves to stupefaction. In the darkness the room revolved slowly. From the other side of the bed Shaw could sense Maria's disapproval. He was too exhausted to care; he shut his eyes and felt sleep close over him like water.

When he woke sunlight streamed through the partly opened windows. He looked at the travelling clock and saw, with astonishment, that it was after ten. In the sitting-room he could hear Jack laugh, and the murmur of conversation between Maria and Sam.

He washed and shaved. In the half-lit bathroom a memory returned, of an airfield swarming with personnel at four in the morning, of Saarinen holding up his Criminal Investigation card in the white sodium light while the military police faced him like nervous animals. He dressed in the bedroom.

The air in the sitting-room seemed pure, golden. The casement window was open. Maria stood at the sideboard, preparing something. Jack sat beside her in his high chair, his legs dangling down.

Shaw sat down at the dining-room table.

'I hear you're wandering at night,' Sam commented. 'I don't suppose you're inclined to tell us what you did get up to?'

'You wouldn't believe me if I told you,' he replied. I go out and howl at the moon, he thought.

'Coffee?' Maria asked.

The previous night's vodka was a dull pain behind the eyes. But the coffee was good. It woke him up. Maria said: 'Chief Inspector Saarinen phoned. He wants you to call when you've come to.'

Finishing his coffee, Shaw went to the phone and dialled. A receptionist put him through.

'You have recovered?' Saarinen asked.

'You could say that.'

'Could you kindly visit us?'

'Now?'

'As soon as possible,' Saarinen replied evenly.

Fifty-six

'We have called off the other watchers,' Saarinen informed him.

Shaw faced him across the desk. Saarinen looked surprisingly well after the previous night's foray, as if such jaunts were normal.

'What will happen now?' Shaw asked.

Saarinen shrugged.

'I am sending out renewed requests to all medical facilities in Russia to report to us.'

'Including military hospitals?'

'Comrade Aegu is directing that aspect. It will be in the form of a request from the Estonian Council of Ministers to the Ministry of Defence in Moscow.'

'Think they'll respond?'

'It is a political matter,' Saarinen replied grimly.

'So what do we do now?'

'Wait,' Saarinen replied. 'In the mean time, there are a few other aspects.' He buzzed Vares. Shortly afterwards Vares appeared carrying three large files.

'We received the analysis returns from the two laboratories – Kiev and Tartu – on the fibres we sent them from the assailant's clothes.' Shaw glanced at the official designation 'confidential'. On the notepaper of the Kiev pathological laboratory report, the summary was in Russian.

'I will translate the conclusion,' Saarinen said. '"The fibres belong to a coat which is not that of the victim, and would thus appear to be that of the assailant. The fibres belong to a group widely used, impossible to trace. The dyes are normal chemical dyes, also widely used."'

Saarinen drew forth the second file.

'From Tartu. "Summary. The fibres in the sample belong to a widely used group of man-made fibres. The dyes are distinctive. Without doubt they are characteristic of certain types of military uniform. Investigation of the source of the dyes reveals that they came from the clothing factory of Jaroslavl." Below this is a note. "We point out that the factory is a supplier of military clothing and that in particular it makes coats and uniforms for senior officers of the Russian Army, in the rank of colonel or above."

Shaw breathed out quietly. Even now, the Russian administrative élite were supplied from different sources. Specialized factories, shops, medical services. It was part of the extraordinary stratification of society inherited from Communism. Apply a sprinkling of democracy, allow a limited free market; but inside that structure the renamed government institutions remained huge, and within them the *vlasti* exercised their customary power and privileges.

Saarinen lit a Prima and exhaled a plume of blue-grey smoke.

'Does President Aegu know about these reports?' Shaw asked.

'He does now,' Saarinen replied amicably. 'We sent a copy of both reports to his office this morning.'

'The rank of colonel and above,' Shaw repeated. 'That narrows the field, doesn't it?'

'It also indicates,' Saarinen said quietly, 'the difficulties of the case.'

'Difficulties?'

'The seniority of the accused makes it a political, rather than a civilian, matter.'

'Why?' Shaw asked.

'If he is a colonel or above, he is likely to have been a local garrison commander. In our society that is a political role. It is a sensitive issue.'

'So it's out of our hands?'

'Not entirely. It means that in order to pursue the matter, we must gain political authorization.'

Shaw said, 'We've established a lead that he's a Russian officer, that he's a senior Russian officer. That cuts down the field. And because we've now established that, we are forced to hold back?'

'Precisely,' Saarinen said, without apparent irony.

Shaw understood. He had an intimation that negotiations could take months, even years, before some agreement was made to extricate the officer in question and bring him to trial – even if that were possible. In order to avoid a sensitive political scandal, officials would not labour unceasingly to bring the case forward. Instead, the entire affair would drift from the investigative to the bureaucratic.

Saarinen handed him a form.

'We would like your report of the events of last night. It will assist us in any matter of future corroboration.'

'What about all the activity on the airfield? Should I report that too?'

'No,' Saarinen replied. 'That also is a political matter.'

'Anything else you'd like me to leave out?'

Saarinen smiled his mirthless smile: 'I would appreciate return of the form by this evening.'

Shaw nodded. He stood up and left. On the way out he almost collided with Vares, drifting tall and pale about the outside office, who raised the palm of his hand in amiable mock salute.

In another brief vision, Shaw saw the months of waiting stretch ahead, his impatience and irritability growing. After he had filed his report, he would wait for political and diplomatic negotiations to take their slow course. He would know nothing of the content of these negotiations, only that time was passing. He looked at Vares, who was studying him with a half-smile, watching him pause by the door.

That was when Shaw decided he would begin to build his boat as soon as possible. But there was a matter that had been preying on his mind, a missed opportunity that he would attend to first.

Fifty-seven

He pressed the doorbell. A few minutes later, a child's face appeared at the window. Then that of a man, Irkut.

He heard Irkut's shuffling walk in the hallway. The door was drawn back. The janitor stood looking at him, his arm raised against the light like a man warding off a blow. His eyes were puffy, as if he had just woken from sleep.

In Estonian Shaw enquired, 'May I come in?'

Irkut hesitated for several further seconds. He had thrown a ruffled jacket over a T-shirt. With a shock Shaw realized that the face emblazoned on the shirt – the moustaches curling out beneath Irkut's fleshy pectorals – was that of Stalin. It was a brief glimpse into the isolation of Irkut, his defiant Russian identity in this land of middle-class Scandinavians. Irkut stood aside and Shaw stepped inside.

In the hallway Irkut paused again, hovering outside the door of his flat.

'May I ask you some questions?' Shaw asked. 'About Colonel Illich?'

Irkut did not seem to understand. For a few seconds he paused. Then he called through the open door of his house, 'Nadia!'

A short woman in a bright yellow dress came to the door. Irkut said something to her in Russian. She turned to Shaw and enunciated in slow but reasonable Estonian.

'My husband does not understand what it is you want.'

'I would like to ask some questions about Colonel Illich.'

She translated. Shaw watched the expression on Irkut's face change. Studying it was like watching the surface of a lake in which fish are swimming. One might see a fin, a flickering tail, a disturbance at the surface, but one could only guess at the creatures beneath. Without emotion, Irkut indicated the open door of his flat. Shaw, following his invitation, walked inside.

With elaborate ceremony Irkut bolted the door. Shaw thought he looked nervous as he led him through to a small sitting-room. In Russia, he knew, Irkut would be considered privileged to have a single flat. Those who had privileges were servants of the State.

He was invited to sit on a sofa beside a low pine table.

A samovar was bubbling in the kitchen. 'Tea?' asked Irkut's wife.

'Thank you.' Shaw waited until she had returned with three cups and sat down beside her husband.

The tea was strong, acidic. He began his slow questions.

'How long have you lived here?'

'Four, no, five years,' Nadia Irkut translated. She spoke slowly but clearly. He suspected she had been a teacher.

'You were here when Illich's wife lived here.'

'Yes, the first three years. Then they were divorced and she left with the children.'

'That was two years ago?'

'Yes.'

'Did you get on well with Colonel Illich?'

'He was an easy man,' Irkut's wife translated. 'Very quiet.'

'Few friends?'

Irkut looked briefly at his wife.

'Some female friends.'

Shaw smiled.

'Pretty?'

Irkut nodded.

'One in particular?'

'A tall blonde woman. I didn't know her name. Very smart.'

'Estonian?'

'Yes.'

'Did Illich have any personal enemies that you knew of?'

Shaw watched her translate and saw Irkut shake his head. It was an adamant movement, and his hopes began to grow. He was defending Illich. He had a suspicion that there was a core of admiration in his attitude.

'You and your family were on holiday at the time of the murder?'

Irkut nodded.

'Was there anything, looking back, that indicated to you such a thing might happen?'

He was surprised at the response. The question was translated. Then a sudden argument seemed to break out between Irkut and his wife. Since Shaw did not understand Russian, it might have been a perfectly normal exchange. In this household, in which Stalin was a hero, he didn't know what was normal. He listened to Irkut's nasal chords, his wife's higher pitched voice.

Nadia was shaking.

'Nothing.'

Irkut was talking to her still. She put her hands over her ears, and shook her head. Irkut continued to talk in that whining nasal Russian which Shaw recognized as emotion, but if anything she became more adamant. When their argument seemed to reach its height Shaw decided to gamble, to play a single card.

'We know for certain that Illich's murderer was an officer, a high-ranking officer of the Russian Army.'

Nadia Irkut stood up. Her small face was set, her fists clenched.

'It is better if you go.'

Shaw glanced at Irkut, and for a moment he feared for her. Irkut's whine had something of a cat in it, a cat who is about to break into violence.

'Please,' Shaw said, 'could you tell me what he is saying?'

'He is saying nothing. Please go.'

Shaw looked at Irkut; his face appeared suddenly anguished, as if some strong and terrible emotion had been stirred to the surface. It was a popular myth that Russians were supposed to beat their wives, but Irkut clearly was afraid of her.

Shaw stood up. Nadia Irkut followed him to the door and unbolted the locks. Her husband hovered in the gloom of the passageway. Shaw said, 'Thank you.'

In the background Irkut smiled weakly.

Shaw crossed the open hall to the main door. As he opened it the door of Irkut's flat was slammed shut and he heard renewed argument break out behind it. He let himself out into the street.

Cold gusts of wind were coming in from the west, blowing up Pikk Street, swinging the signs as he walked down Rataskaevu Street. He put up his collar against the blasts and cursed himself for losing an opportunity which would never be presented again.

Fifty-eight

Several days passed without incident, several clean autumn days in which Shaw could show his grandfather the beautiful city of Tallinn. The phone rang without warning early one morning. Shaw answered it. At the other end, Aegu said, 'I would like a meeting.'

'Sure,' he replied. 'Shall I come to your office?'

Aegu said, 'I am tired of the inside of offices, committee rooms, official receptions. We will walk in the country, I think. I will call for you at three.'

'Three it is.'

'Fine autumn days are too few,' Aegu said. He withdrew a packet of cigarettes from his pocket. 'I will tell you about Chernavin.'

In the untilled field behind them the Zil stood empty, shining like an undertaker's hearse. A few yards off, the Kallas brothers casually talked in low voices.

Aegu put a Prima between his lips. 'A caricature, but a strong one. A Russian manifestation of strength.'

'How did he come to power?' Shaw asked.

'In the absence of alternatives. Nature abhors a

318

vacuum. How did a certain General Jaruzelski come to power in Poland in 1980? To occupy the empty space left by the Communist Party.'

Shaw sensed a degree of exasperation.

'Russians don't understand democracy?'

Aegu paused. 'It is deeper than that. Russians worship strong leaders. Leaving aside their numerous virtues, they are a self-indulgent people. They know and fear this in themselves. You remember the character Oblomov? Every Russian is aware of the fat Oblomov inside himself. He fears his greed, his lassitude, his capacity for a kind of swinish contentment. A figure like Chernavin is the antidote. Chernavin is the whip that will keep Oblomov at bay.'

Aegu stood still while the flame from his match touched the tip of the cigarette. A plume of smoke emerged from the side of his mouth. 'A Western liberal looks at Chernavin and visualizes cruelty and suffering.' Aegu flicked out the match and threw it away. 'A Russian looks at such a man and envisages human suffering, certainly – but also a purification of the spirit.'

They began to walk. They were skirting woodland, mostly pines. Behind them the Kallas brothers ambled. Alongside Aegu, Shaw seemed subject to the same tensions, his mind turning on nothing. This was not a pretty exercise in philosophy. Chernavin was like a shadow who fell over them. Shaw wanted something to grasp. Perhaps sensing this, Aegu said:

'A Slav is an extremist. He lives life to the edges of experience. There is a charming side to his character. He does not censure others. He is extremely tolerant of faults. At the same time he feels he must pay a price for these faults – an extreme price, a truly Russian price. You can see it in the Russian admiration for another typically Slav figure, Boris Yeltsin. His faults were tolerated precisely because he paid for them so extravagantly in suffering and in personal hardship.'

Phrases that seemed real, then dispersed like cigarette smoke. Shaw said, 'So what does that tell us about Russian political life?'

'The Russian political system must be able to accommodate figures such as Yeltsin. If liberalism has a future in Russia, it is because it is capable of giving freedom to these extremes of character.'

'Why isn't it secure?'

'Liberalism? Because it takes time. Russians are intolerant of waiting. The condition of liberalism may give them what they want, but they cannot wait for it, and therefore it eludes them. They are like a child constantly digging up a plant to see whether it has grown.'

'We have to wait too?'

'Estonians can wait,' Aegu said. 'Among our numerous faults, we can wait.'

'How long?'

He shrugged. 'Who knows? That is what true waiting is – not knowing. Russians suffer. Estonians wait.'

'I don't see much suffering in Chernavin.'

Aegu smiled. 'That is why Chernavin will not last. He does not have this largeness of soul. He represents only one side of the Russian personality – fierce discipline. He is a corrective; that is why he is tolerated. In the end he will be forced to make way for another, another Yeltsin.'

'How long do we have to wait?' Shaw asked. 'Five years? Ten years?'

'Patience. We have to let history run its course. Patience, the most difficult course of all.'

They crossed a tract of grass lined by silver spruces and elms. The Kallas brothers had dropped back and now talked quietly to one another. There was a small rise ahead; beyond that a scatter of trees with white shadows.

'Look at that,' Aegu pointed with his arm. 'Our Soviet past.'

320

They were on a slight rise and it gave an advantageous view.

The residential district of Vaike Oismae was a monument to the old age of Soviet corporate planning, a paean to the absolute power of the human will. It was a series of huge barrack-like blocks built around a lake which was in turn a perfect geometric circle. The buildings had begun as white blocks but Shaw could see they were already showing signs of discoloration. Amongst the geometric design, regularly spaced high rise buildings stood like watch-towers. Inside the barracks the enclosed spaces were like prison yards. The huge complex had been constructed on a semi-rural site adjacent to the shore, but there had been no attempt to blend the design into the beautiful site. Instead, it was as if the implacable man-made geometry had landed there like a colony from outer space.

Surveying it, Aegu said, 'Soviet architecture is now an historical style, like Gothic or rococo or classical. It is an attempt to numb the mind by sheer scale. You could say, I suppose, that it is characterized by a combination of scale and absolute inhumanity. There is no sense of a human being at all. The individual is crushed into one of those walled spaces.'

Aegu drew on his cigarette.

'Illich had a girlfriend who lived in one of those flats. A girl called Vera. I forget her surname. A Russian. Saarinen has a record of her address.'

Aegu dropped the ember from his fingers and stubbed it out with his heel. Before Shaw could question him further he was already beginning to walk down the incline, his head down, as if he were once again afflicted with personal thoughts.

Fifty-nine

Vera Olgarkova looked at Shaw once, then drew open the door so that he could come in.

Her features were not striking or memorable; you would have lost her in a supermarket uniform. The ambience of her flat was far from the Estonian standard of clean white surfaces and cool colours. There were icons on the walls, a large wooden cross. A white and gold Uzbek carpet hung on the wall. Bright colours burned in the furnishings, a series of florid designs most Scandinavians would have found too rich. It was like the gold sandals and heavy make-up which some Russian women were reputed to wear – a clash of aesthetics based on different cultures.

'You would like some coffee?'

'Please.'

She moved about the apartment with particular grace, pausing to pour water and click a switch. Casually she leaned against the counter, her arms folded, while the electric kettle came to the boil.

'You came by car?'

'By bus,' Shaw said.

She made a movement of her lips, as if trying to assess the significance. Perhaps she imagined Americans always travelled in cars. Behind her he could see through the window out to the other barrack-like buildings that reared upwards. A group of children and a dog wandered across some waste ground between the buildings. They walked slowly, not speaking. One of the youths kicked a ball thoughtfully ahead of him, like someone who has time on his hands.

Vera Olgakova prepared two cups, pouring in a teaspoon of instant coffee.

Shaw said, 'Have you lived here long?'

'Three years,' she replied. It was a matter of pride and good luck. A single woman without a family was a low priority for such an apartment.

Shaw reminded himself that Estonia represented a kind of secular heaven to Russian workers and their families. The stolid conscientiousness of the Estonian authorities ensured relatively good municipal services. There was a genuine choice of food in the shops. Acclimatized to the slowly improving but often shoddy material goods of their own country, Russians regarded even a moderately furnished flat with systems that worked as a special reward and blessing.

The kettle whistled. She poured boiling water into two cups.

He had studied the notes in the file at Saarinen's office. The entry was sparse. Olgakova was a manageress of a large department store. She was single, and lived in Vaike Oismae. From the notes Shaw had an impression of that new phenomenon in Russia – the independent career woman.

Her Estonian was good, though the Russian came through in a series of lilts and the occasional odd emphasis. She sat down opposite him.

'Colonel Illich,' she said, as if reminding him. She sipped her coffee and waited. Shaw felt an instinctive liking for her, for her independence. He said: 'His assailant was a man, according to the evidence. Who might have had a grudge against him?'

She shrugged. 'The others asked that question.'

'Saarinen?'

'The bald one, yes.'

'What was your answer?'

'My answer was that I do not know anyone who does not have enemies. I am not sure I would like to know anyone who did not.'

She shrugged again. Shaw sensed boredom. No, something else, something like disbelief. It occurred to

323

him suddenly that it was a strange question to a Russian. Everyone had grudges. Russians lived their lives with passion, and passion created enmities as it created friends. Who did not know people who wished to kill them? Who was so poor that he was without enemies?

She smiled again. Shaw experienced a further charge of sympathy for her, and embarrassment at his question. He recalled Lydia Teemant's cold refutation of the view that Illich was the subject of personal animosity, and wondered not for the first time at differences in culture. According to one, Illich had no enemies. According to the other, a surfeit. Both were praising him in their own terms.

Shaw tried a different tack; he shifted from the motive to the act itself.

'Who actually might have pulled the trigger?'

Something about her changed. It was a movement of posture, hardly noticeable.

'The authorities.'

She was holding her coffee in her hands, sitting forward on her chair. Shaw felt a trace of nervousness or anticipation pass through him. 'Which authorities?'

'The Army, maybe.'

Shaw paused. 'Who in particular?'

She looked down at her hands, folded in her lap.

'I didn't know his superiors.'

'You think it was an Army superior?'

She didn't answer. Instead she turned her eyes on him and studied him directly, as if challenging him to find his own answers.

It was something he had never considered. Until now he had assumed a dichotomy between several possibilities. The assailant was either an acquaintance, or the authorities. The authorities were a faceless presence. Yet there was something about the killing, the way the assailant had found his way into the flat, that was personal, based on direct knowledge. And the terrible ferocity of Illich's charge as the bullets punched into him and he reached forward with his final life in his hands to blind his attacker . . . It was someone he knew, someone who betrayed him.

His face must have expressed his feelings. She had registered his turmoil. Now she was watching him with detached interest as he returned to the room.

'Your coffee is all right?'

'Yes,' he said, nodding as if to anchor himself in the room again.

'If you will forgive me for asking,' he began again, 'for how long did you know him?'

'You are asking me, perhaps, how well I knew him.'

'Yes,' he admitted. 'I imagine I am.'

She paused and then asked, 'How well did you know him?'

It was the first time she smiled, and he could see why Illich had liked her.

At first he thought she was mimicking him, but he had an intimation why she was asking the question in reverse. He had a further impression – one of those understandings which occur suddenly – that she would answer according to how he himself answered.

'I was his tactician. I worked with him for up to ten hours a day over more than a year. How well is that?'

She merely repeated her question.

'And how well did you know him?'

'Not very well,' he agreed.

She nodded, drank her coffee, and he saw that he had given the answer to his own question. She said quietly, 'He was a beautiful man. Very . . .' She hesitated. 'Very detached.'

'And he didn't confide much?'

'Not about colleagues or acquaintances.' She shook her head.

'Nothing that would concern the inquiry?'

'No,' she said. 'Nothing like that.'

She was watching him without expression, as though waiting a decision. Shaw was an opportunist and predator. But he had a duty, as much to his own loose notion of self-respect as his idea of faithfulness, however fragile that might be.

He said, 'Thank you for seeing me at such short notice.'

She was not offended. She almost smiled, but nodded briefly instead. He wanted to ask her whether, if he thought of any more questions, he could phone her again, but decided it might have been misinterpreted.

She showed him to the door. He turned round and caught sight of her again as she closed the door. In the corridors there was no sign of the graffiti that he would have expected in, say, the municipal flats of a Western city whose citizens might be more inclined to take their housing for granted. He walked down the stairs and emerged into the open sunlight.

Sixty

Sometimes, when they walked down early to the shed, out through the Pikk Street gate, Sam Shaw would pause to gaze in a shop window and shake his head. Smart clothes, elegant suits, furs, accessories, perfumes, Japanese televisions and stereos.

'Will you look at that?' he'd say, while Shaw patted his gloves together in the cold, and waited for him to catch up. 'These people are selling their birthright. They had something fine here, something collective. Education, welfare, decent employment, housing. Here they are chasing all that capitalist crap. They complain like hell about pollution and then bitch about not enough in the shops. Those things are related, you know.'

Shaw said, 'Are we walking, or are we talking?' In practice, however, he enjoyed his grandfather's diatribes against capitalism. They were an antidote to Aegu's hymn of praise for the free market.

The boat came first as a pile of pale timber, Western red cedar cut into lengths, mahogany for the laminated frames, spruce strips for the longitudinals. It was important to keep the moisture content stable. They made joists on which they could pile the wood to keep it above any dampness on the floors and allow air to circulate.

The heating plant was unreliable. It produced gouts of hot air and then, with a strange creaking and cracking, would grow reticent. They stripped it down and put it together again, working without a manual and relying on Sam Shaw's mechanical aptitude. When the boiler was working again its irregularity had, if anything, increased. Now the unexpected efficiency of its sudden heat output was daunting, its frosty silences agonizing. They were forced to confront the thermostat. They struggled with the strange intricacies of its internal structure for several hours, then bought and installed a new one from a central heating plant supplier in Pirita.

'Under communism, you would have waited three months for that, and had to bribe some officials for it,' Shaw commented.

'You would have appreciated it when you got it,' Sam replied.

They fixed down a thin skein of wooden boards and lofted the linesplan on to it, using wood battens to make the curves. The builder grows intimate with the linesplan as he lofts: the full-size shapes emerge under his fingers, against which he can place his own dimensions; hand, forearm, torso.

Over the following weeks they cut the mahogany veneers for laminating the wooden frames, fixing the shapes

327

with clamps until the resins had hardened. While they waited for the resin to dry, they worked on setting up the main and subsidiary bulkheads for the yacht.

They cut, shaped and planed the laminated frames to shape.

The hull would be built upside down, as was customary. The first part of the build consisted of setting up a jig on the floor to attach the frames and bulkheads. Two weeks later they began to lay the longitudinal cedar strips over the frames and bulkheads. The shape of the yacht began to appear under their hands. Working from port side they moved to starboard until, five days later, the hull was entirely covered.

Now, as the winter came on, the hull occupied the shed like a live animal. Each evening, before they left, they swept the sawdust and leavings out, so that the dust would have time to settle overnight. Each morning they walked down cold streets in the dark, having left the thermostat on overnight. They punched the light-switch in the gloomy shed and after a few flickers of the fluorescent tubes the hull would rise out of the shadows. The shed was warm. They removed their coats and gloves, boiled up a kettle of coffee, talked through the day's tasks for a few minutes while their blood warmed, then they set to work. Mostly they worked through the morning with hardly a stop. They broke off at midday. Maria made them a sandwich lunch with hot soup. Then they set to again, cutting and working the wood. Most days became the same.

After laying the first longitudinal strips, they made two further layers of diagonal veneers. The alignment of fibres would make for a hull far stronger and more rigid than equivalent weights of fibreglass. They covered the outside with a single layer of heavy glass sheathing, not so much for strength but abrasion resistance. Each day they worked Shaw tried to forget the nervousness that walking

328

with Aegu induced, the obscure frustrations of Illich's murderer.

Saarinen phoned one evening.

'We have followed through your suggestion following your interview with Vera Olgarkova. Perhaps you could call by.'

'Now?'

'I am at the office. If it is not convenient . . .'

'I'll be there.' Shaw put down the phone. He said to Maria, 'I have to speak with Saarinen.'

Maria gave him a cool, appraising look. Shaw walked the short distance to Kingissepa Street in the cool of the evening. A receptionist showed him through to Saarinen's office.

Saarinen shook hands with him and went through the procedure of turning on the radio. He gestured to Shaw to sit down.

'You enquired about Illich's senior officers?'

Shaw waited.

'You must understand that it is difficult to ask detailed questions about senior personnel without arousing suspicion.'

Shaw nodded. Saarinen paused. 'Illich's commanding officer was a certain Major-General Stephan Vorolov. Our enquiries indicate that he left for Moscow in August, at approximately the time of the murder.'

'That's some coincidence,' Shaw said.

'The authorities say that he was due to leave at the end of Russian involvement in the America's Cup. He had fulfilled his duty in organizing the training camp.'

'You believe that?'

On the other side of the desk, Saarinen's expression moved into the dry rictus of a smile. 'I have mentioned before what an investigator thinks of belief.'

'How did he leave?' Shaw asked. 'In an ambulance guarded by four men? Did they tell you that?'

'We have some additional information. Our informal enquiries into the schedules of other senior military figures have so far indicated no other senior officer leaving his post at the time of Illich's murder. These inquiries are far from conclusive. On a purely circumstantial basis, however, Major-General Vorolov would appear to be a suspect.'

'Any way we can find out about Vorolov?' Shaw asked. 'Where he's posted to? What sort of condition he's in?'

'That is difficult. I detected some defensiveness in the authorities' replies. It is difficult to say why. But I am forced to repeat something else to you. Even more so than previously, the seniority of the officer in question introduces a political dimension. I have already informed Comrade Aegu.'

'Sure, I get the picture,' Shaw said. 'Every time we make progress in the investigation, we can do less about it. One day we'll get to the point where we know everything and will be able to do absolutely nothing.'

'Perhaps,' Saarinen suggested, 'that is true of life in general.'

Shaw didn't speak. Saarinen took advantage of this to add:

'Major-General Vorolov is now a suspect. That is all.'

'Thank you. I appreciate your calling me.'

Sixty-one

The boat was progressing well. When the longitudinal strips of cedar had been laid on the hull, they laid down two further diagonal cross layers of mahogany veneers.

Maria had warned Shaw to keep an eye on his grandfather, to make sure that he didn't overstress himself. When he told his grandfather he'd been warned to look after him, Sam Shaw nodded his head, as if acknowledging a melancholy fact.

'Sure sign,' Shaw said.

'Sure sign of what?'

'She's got plans for you,' Shaw said with satisfaction.

'Plans?'

'She's going to marry you off to Agnes.'

There was a moment's awed pause. It was the big plans which stunned the mind, the ones which presented you with something so large it hit you like incontrovertible proof.

'That so?'

'I'm afraid you don't stand a chance. I'd give in now, if I were you. Tell Maria you're coming out with your hands up.'

Marriage was like communism in its early phase, Shaw thought. It polarized the thought processes. You had to take up a position for or against, and woe betide you if you were against.

They rubbed down the surface to a reasonable fairness for several more days. It was gruelling work. They wore face-masks to protect themselves from the dust that floated everywhere. It was amazing the places the dust could get to. One night after work Shaw, undressing in the bathroom for privacy, glanced in the mirror and saw that his hair was white, his eyebrows and eyelashes too were snowy, his skin had the chalky pallor of age, and as he took down his trousers even his pubic hair appeared white. He looked like a statue of Father Time. A hell of an outfit to go to a fancy dress ball.

An entire morning was spent sweeping and cleaning the premises of dust. They took the afternoon off while the dust settled, and went with Maria and Jack to the gardens at Kadriorg.

'When's the wedding date fixed, just so I know?' Sam asked.

'Oh, she'll have it marked down somewhere,' Shaw said contentedly. 'Maybe it's not public knowledge exactly yet, but my guess is she's sent out the invitation to her friends already.'

The following day they put on rubber gloves, mixed the epoxy resins again, and began the task of laying down the final outer later of glass.

After fairing, they sprayed the outer surface with a filler paint, faired, sprayed again. After spraying, Shaw and his grandfather would go to the Grulte, a working men's cafe on the side of Vasa Street, while the acrid paint fumes dispersed.

They had installed a pool table in one of the side rooms of the *Grulte*, and underneath the old ship beams (it had once been a storage shed for Hanseatic merchants) they took their turns in circling the table and striking the chipped balls.

'If only Maria could see us now,' Sam commented.

'Enjoy your freedom while it lasts,' Shaw said.

The following week they attached chains to the roof-beams of the shed and slowly turned the hull over. Upright on her cradle the boat looked like a boat at last.

Now Shaw could see the influence of the designer more easily. From fine prow to powerful square aft sections the hull looked purposeful.

'How's she seem to you?' he asked Sam.

Somewhere the boat had turned from an 'it' to a 'she'. It was difficult to say where that point was. In evolution, at some point apes became human.

'Fast,' he replied.

It is a convention that well-designed hulls tend towards beauty. Triremes, Viking longships, coracles, dhows, junks, canoes, everything that has plied the water and served its human masters, possesses beauty. There were traces of *Novy Mir* in the yacht, but whereas *Novy Mir*'s hard chines were sharp, the little yacht had more softened curves so that the radical tumblehome in the aft sections looked almost traditional.

It sometimes seemed to Shaw that a yacht, made to inhabit the constantly changing motion of the sea, feeding off the currents of air and water, was the closest thing to a living being that human beings could make. The most simple and mysterious of shapes, eloquent in its silence. To Shaw at least there was nothing, no great column of dinosaur's bones, no bronze sculpture, which inhabited space quite like a hull. A well-shaped hull did not simply live in its space, so much as create its own, as if its dynamism spread out like a mysterious penumbra. Around it, all other objects became still, static, ephemeral.

'I could leave the country, of course,' Sam said.

They knew this was the last resort. The imminent threat of marriage took hold of the mind, it changed you, it didn't matter where you were.

Sixty-two

In his evenings after work, Sam Shaw liked to read the English language version of the Russian weekly *Argumenty I Fakty*. It was the magazine with the largest readership in the world, but his own interest was the letters column. He obtained an abbreviated English language version and would spend his time poring over the letters that poured in: ironic, earthy, brilliant, banal, the entire fauna of human life. For example, there had been a long-running debate over the nature of heroes. It was a debate relished by its hundred million or so readers. The argument consisted of occasional sniper shots from Smolensk, or the odd hand-grenade from outer Mongolia. But sometimes it flared up and became a truly enthralling crossfire in which whole sections of the community were represented, from combine sub-managers in Irkutsk to postmistresses from Saratov.

In his spare moments, Shaw too had taken to reading surreptitiously the English-language version of *Argumenty I Fakty*. There were other reasons for fascination. Shaw had not realized how deeply embedded Ivan Illich was in the hearts of the people. That, too, was a revelation.

I am a veteran of the Second World War. I write to ask what is going on. Ivan Ivanovich Illich was one of our greatest sportsmen, a winner of four Olympic gold medals, a feat only surpassed by one or two people in our history. He was a professional soldier, a colonel in the Russian Army. He served with valour in Afghanistan. In 2001 he won the America's Cup. Rightly, he was chosen as our helmsman in defence of the following America's Cup. Then he was arrested, fired upon by the Army, and forced to set up a challenge in Estonia. Despite this, he beat the official Russian defender, Kirov. Now, after winning two races against the Americans, he is dead from an assassin's bullet.

I would like to ask, has politics entered sport, or has sport entered politics? Whatever the answer, I do not like the result.

A. Racusuyev, doorkeeper, Leningrad

On 2 January, I, together with my colleague S. Validev, was due to come back from Moscow by Aeroflot Flight No 762. We had attended the congress of tractor manufacturers in Tallinn. The captain was pilot first class Yasarov. Validev and I took our seats with another one hundred and thirty-seven passengers. The plane did not take off and no reasons were given. We waited a half-hour, then another hour while other planes took off. After a further delay we were informed that the weather was bad. All around us other planes continued to take off.

There were nine empty seats at the front of the aircraft, three rows of three each. During our third hour of waiting there appeared a certain Colonel Ivan Illich, accompanied by two other men. At the time the newspapers were full of accounts of the riots he had fomented in Tartu. Ignoring the others, this Illich sat down in one of the nine seats, and the two others sat down beside him. It was obvious to all one hundred and thirty-nine passengers of Flight No. 762 that we had waited solely for him to appear. At no time did this arrogant individual say anything to the others, including his colleagues. Of course, suddenly it appeared that the weather was clear and we could take off.

Is it any wonder that he proceeded, by virtue of his arrogance, to steal a yacht from the Russian Army, and through certain other incidents, eventually come to his own tragic death? In former days we had true heroes, who gave their lives for their country, not the type of individualist which the former Colonel Ivan Ivanovich Illich represents. I do not see why we should mourn the passing of someone who lacked all humility and who in his life has acted more like a Western pop star than a representative of the Rodina.

L. Stekhanov, tractor manager, Rostov

'Probably an official letter,' Shaw said to his grandfather, 'from the Interior Ministry. You can recognize them. They don't lie outright. What they do is research an incident and then put a particular slant on it.'

Colonel (then Major) Ivan Illich was leader of the sailors in the 1996 Olympic team. He was an example to us all. Kind, modest, helpful to those who looked up to him. In my own recollection, he personally intervened on my behalf as a Finn sailor during a dispute over certain aspects of training with the senior coach of the team. The dispute was settled amicably and constructively. It was during those same Olympics he won his fourth gold medal in the Flying Dutchman class, a record for a Russian sailor.

I have a picture of him receiving that medal with his

crewman Sergei Linkov, on one side the rising Americans Shaw and Peabody, and on the other the great Germans Zimmer and Zeit.

A. Moptorin, sailing correspondent, Odessa, Ukraine

We have heard so much about the 'black colonels' in the Congress of People's Deputies — politicians in uniform, who have done nothing personally for this country — that the death of a real hero comes as a tragedy.

V. Baronovich, on behalf of the staff of school no. 27, Gorky

Is it true that the Interior Ministry has a special department of letter writers to Argumenty I Fakty? *There are those who say that the late Colonel Ivan Illich was an alcoholic and womanizer on such an heroic scale as to defy any single man, no matter how dedicated to these pursuits. For example, two letters from A. Volgarkova and V. Semyova in the issue of the week ending May 17 last year claimed that Colonel Illich was simultaneously molesting women in the same three days in Pskov and in Chabrovsk, which is to the north of Vladivostock, despite the fact that the scenes of these violations of Russian womanhood were several thousand miles apart.*

I would like to complain that the Interior Ministry letter-writers department is not fulfilling its proper function, is badly coordinated, and is making an ass of an important Russian institution which, as we all know, labours ceaselessly in the cause of patriotism and truth.

L. Alekseyev, Frunze

Sometimes I feel that I and my sister Ludmila are the only women in Russia who were not the subject of the late Colonel Illich's fervent attentions. In spite of this, we mourn his passing.

Kamarova, Minsk

We gain the impression that the hero is supposed to be a true example of sobriety and clean living, someone who does not touch alcohol and who spends his life helping old ladies across the road. Yet at the same time we all know, historically speaking, that every attack on the propriety of the former President of the Russian Federation, Boris Yeltsin, resulted in a huge increase in his popularity. I understand that since those heady days the Interior Ministry has changed its policy. Those it wants to render less popular it now paints as white as snow, and those it wants to render popular it hints at all kinds of peccadilloes. Is this a sign of modern times? If so, I prefer the old system.

S. Moltov

I read V. Kuznetsov's letter about the Interior Ministry's 'white propaganda' tactics and frankly I am worried on behalf of my friend B. Yashenkov. For the last several years, despite all his efforts to the contrary, B. Yashenkov's reputation has been getting better and better. He used to pride himself on his reputation as a drinker, and women used to say they would not trust their young, marriageable daughters with him. Now, he says, he is trusted by everyone, including their daughters.

B. Yashenkov has written to me asking, what has gone wrong, where can he turn? Above all, he asks, can the Interior Ministry be to blame?

A. Solevich

Shaw's refuge was the yacht that he and Sam Shaw were building on the harbour front. Working, they went into a kind of trance down there, with the heating on just sufficiently to prevent their hands from freezing. The wood shavings accumulated on the concrete floor. They mixed epoxy in small jars as they needed it, using rubber gloves to insulate it from the skin.

Every piece of furniture that went into the yacht strengthened and stiffened the overall construction. The epoxy glue join was stronger than the wood. Shaw loved this aspect of the construction. Somewhere he had read that design elegance arose out of the marriage of aesthetics and function. He looked at the pale cream hull walls, the living, subtle shades of spruce.

Agnes Chednik had arrived. For Sam Shaw it was his opportunity to plot against the coming marriage. There had to be some way out of it. Shaw liked to comment on the movements in the battle. That morning, for instance, Maria had pointed out how much weight Agnes had lost. It was true. Agnes had always carried her weight well, but now she looked positively healthy. Her skin seemed radiant. Her eyes sparkled. She had always dressed with a certain attention to detail, but now the details seemed to cohere and she looked genuinely elegant. Shaw had seen them out shopping one day, and before he had fully registered who they were, he had asked himself who these handsome women were, this mother and daughter. Maria and she had the place so organized a man could hardly breathe.

In his comments on the inevitability of Sam's marriage, Shaw liked to point out that Jack had started calling Agnes 'grandma', and used the combination 'grandma and grandpa' to describe the two guests in the house. It was a subtle point, of course, but it was the subtle points that could effect the largest emotional pressure, and they needed time to consider the implications. It was like being surrounded. Each day he was being conditioned, Shaw said, like a pig being driven towards a net. For the pig, the end of the net represented the spears of the hunters – for Sam, the extinction of his independence.

Sixty-three

What was he hunting in Illich's women?

On a day in winter he telephoned Lydia Teemant from a public callbox, using the number she had given him in the park. With unexpected luck she answered directly, and listened to his suggestion that they meet as if she had expected it.

He suggested a coffee house, but she said, 'Come to my flat.'

'Now?'

'Later this afternoon. Four o' clock.'

'I'll be there.'

He had spent his life attempting to control and direct his fear, but now it seemed to rise inside him. Outside the callbox he paused. He had an hour and a half to kill. Lembitu Street seemed quiet. A spring breeze with a certain concealed warmth moved beneath the bare trees. He began to walk through the outskirts of the city, across the empty pavements. His feet seemed to carry him regardless.

Her flat was on the Gagarini Puiestee, overlooking the Toompark. He pressed a bell and heard the calm movement of her bare feet across the floors. She was dressed in a simple white dress, a dress to work in. She stood aside to let him in. Inside the flat was small, hardly more than a large study. But it faced east across the park, filled with the light preferred by painters.

'Coffee?'

'No, thanks.'

Shaw, like a reluctant adulterer, did not allow himself to think about her features until she was seated opposite him on the divan. But facing her directly she exuded a kind of calmness. Her eyes had a directness that made him nervous. He wondered why Estonia had such a sexual ambience. He seemed to be constantly rearing back from attractive women, guilty and afraid, suppressing an awareness of their physical composure.

He had some kind of status here, but it was ambiguous. He was regarded as an eccentric recluse. Shaw wondered why he was suddenly susceptible to women – not merely sexually, which had always been the case, but emotionally. This susceptibility caused fear in him, and in some odd way it drove him towards further solitude. He suspected he was changing, that hidden parts of the character unfolded. Perhaps that was why he had come to Estonia, following some unconscious desire that he would find himself in a society which was itself in flux, that was attempting to change itself for the better.

He began, 'We have a suspect. I can't disclose who it is, but I remembered you said you considered it would be the authorities.'

She nodded.

'Since you seem to be right about that, is there anything else you can give us – any information?'

'Give you?' she smiled.

He waited.

'I think I mentioned that in science it isn't the information that matters, it's the theory which pieces the information together.'

'Perhaps you could help with the theory.'

'My theory is that the authorities were involved.'

Shaw found himself floundering.

'Nothing more . . . explicit?'

She shook her head. 'No.'

It should have been the end of the interview, and perhaps it was. She was looking at his face, studying him objectively, not bothering to hide her interest. It was curiosity, but curiosity of a heightened, emotional kind, and in a woman that is the equivalent of desire. He realized that she wanted him. The knowledge was tempered by the fact that he suspected it was Illich whom she sought. That was how, in the immediacy of her flat, he came to terms with the implacable intensity of her interest. She was searching for something inside him that would give a clue to Illich, to his elusive personality and ambiguous presence. People are haunted not by the deceased person, but what was missing in the person in his life – by what remained mysterious and outside their knowledge. A ghost is not a presence but a kind of intense absence.

For a moment he thought he saw something like passion in her eyes, or a refined impatience which might have shown as anger, as if he had not realized the nature of their discussion, or was questioning the nature, the depth of her relationship with him. But whatever it was that showed, she let it take its course and go by, so that when she next spoke she was back to her normal self, her steady, didactic self. He realized that words – their precise usage – were her profession, and that to say something was to subject himself to a relentless study. Yet when he began to speak her eyes clouded, went vague, as if she were staring past him to some further landscape.

Shaw said, 'Did Illich ever speak about his commanding officer, General Vorolov?'

'Not directly, not in person.'

'But he spoke about his seniors?'

'Sometimes. He talked about what he would do under certain conditions.'

'What did he say exactly?'

She had none of those displacement gestures, smoking or sweeping hair back with a hand, or any other movement which denoted nervousness. It was this absence of pretence which made her own presence so direct and powerful.

'Why should I tell you?'

'You don't have to. Why should I ask? Maybe I couldn't give a damn anyway.'

She considered this too. He looked at her eyes again and saw that she was regarding him with amusement. It had always frightened him how far blatant directness went with women. You felt instinctively you had to use ploys, but it seemed all they wanted from you was a clear statement of intent, nothing more or less, as if by some internal logic their fierce souls would forgive anything but prevarication.

341

Her eyes never left him.

'Illich did talk to me once or twice. He said he only understood his life as a preparation, a preparation for the time he would be tested.' She continued to watch him. 'He said one day he would be ordered to kill someone, someone who was not threatening him. Slowly, he said, he had resolved what he would do.'

Shaw felt his mouth go dry. He wanted to ask but something held him back. He suddenly felt absurd, asking someone questions when naked. He allowed her to settle into the forms, the recesses, of the answer she would give in her own good time. At last he said: 'What was that?'

'He would kill the man who gave him the order.'

'His superior?'

She looked at him from the recesses of her thoughts, as if not understanding his question, and he would have asked her again except that he realized with a sudden clarity, as transfixing as a bolt through the heart, that she had given her message, disposed of her answer, that outside this sequence of communication he did not exist. Having told him what she wished to say, he had lost his significance. He could stand up now and leave, and she would remain where she was, lost in her own thoughts.

Shortly afterwards, she stood up, accompanied him to the door, and closed it firmly, as if a chapter of her life were past.

Sixty-four

Winter came on. A thin wind blew the shadows of clouds along the streets.

They fitted the bulkheads and additional hull frames,

laminating them carefully. Set in clamps, they seemed messy, the epoxy spilling out from the joins like an overfilled sandwich. But the finished frame, planed down to its wood and varnished, unfolded its magnificent golds, reds, and browns. Shaw, working with it every day, believed that the curious value of wood is that even an error has its beauty. The closer one came to wood, the more one became immersed in the geometric contours of its grain, its flames and radials.

They had allowed themselves the frozen winter, from the end of November to late March, to complete the interior ready for a launching in April. The work proceeded steadily. The keel floors were fitted in; designed to spread the load of the keel up the hull, they were the ribs of the animal. They cut the interior furniture out of high-grade marine ply and fitted each in place. Tammiste had designed the furniture to form part of the structure of the yacht. The forward berths reinforced the bow; the settee berths formed a box structure providing support for the keel floors.

They worked on the coach roof separately. Decks were laid. Suspending a chain from the main roof beam, they raised the engine on pulleys and lowered it into the hull recess until it could be fitted.

Cold weather removed the final leaves from the trees and winter frosts followed. Each day they walked down to the yacht in freezing temperatures. They spent a jovial Christmas.

A nervous Sam kept out of the way of marriage plans. In the temporary haven of the shed, Shaw and his grandfather could plot counter-moves. During the height of the Cold War, in the battle for strategic control, the Soviets used the sinister phrase 'the correlation of forces' to describe the accumulation of military and strategic factors. Shaw felt that correlation of forces was moving against them. The other side was essentially offensive, and carried with it the implacable desire to win. It was a bitter battle, and it swayed back and forth. The fact that the battle turned on tiny details – the placement at table, the uses of phrases such as 'Sam and Agnes' as if they were already a pair – did not reduce the intensity of the engagement. The lines were never still. Redoubts were held, but they had the impression that the opponent seemed always to have broken through up the line somewhere. Faced with strategic superiority, with an opponent whose every move seemed calculated to throw them off balance, they had to move back into the hinterland.

'I think we've lost control,' Shaw said in February. 'I believe we may be forced to recognize certain realities.'

'A married man is a pinioned duck,' Sam said. 'You told me that.'

'We may have to concede ground on one or two points.'

'You mean give in.'

'Revise a few of our assumptions.'

'Admit defeat.'

Agnes was going to return to Estonia permanently. She was about to move lock stock and barrel. But in the midst of defeat there is sometimes a reprieve. To complete her move, she was going to return to America to oversee the sale of the store and flat. Weepeq Bay was becoming a tourist resort in the summer, and land prices on the Highton coast were high. She'd need several months to pack things up, sell the business, and organize to the point where she could return with a clean slate. To encourage foreign capital, Estonia was offering to returning former nationals the opportunity to invest in government bonds with a high rate of return. Her intention was to deposit her savings in bonds and wait for the right time to invest in a home. Shaw and his grandfather knew what that meant – a merely temporary stay of execution.

Sixty-five

What could one say about television?

The Ilyushin set that had been a gift from the Estonian crew seemed to record a public nightmare. In its glowing fish-tank they watched the news, trying to read the signs of the tension that was creeping through Estonia.

They saw pictures of Aegu entering negotiations with the Russian leaders, tight-lipped faces, handshakes and bear-hugs sometimes a little too emphatic, flash bulbs producing flat angles and bones in their faces like skulls, except for the smiles.

At news time, broadcast from the station at Tallinn, they nervously switched on the set. Even Sam, that inveterate hater of all things of the modern world, who had cut himself off even from electricity in Maine, sat down in the chair, shifting a little uneasily as he settled, his face turned sideways suspiciously.

It was early February, and cold blasts of wind sometimes filled the streets. Maria told Jack stories from her mother and grandmother about how the Baltic sometimes froze all the way across to Denmark, how family skating parties would go on the sea, uncles and cousins and aunts and all who were physically capable of the journey, wrapped in greatcoats and scarves, their leggings so large they looked like bears. With the slow stateliness of circus animals, they would skate across the Gulf of Riga from Parnu to the Latvian capital itself, driving off one leg and then another, skating through the morning and pausing only to stand on the ice like some strange colony of polar animals while the slow ones caught up, the sun flaming the surface, and setting off again until they arrived at their relation's house with its fluted roofs. There they would drink and eat around a huge table, beginning in the late afternoon, the lights flickering, and continuing through the evening. The uncles, as they fell asleep, would push their chairs away from the table so that they could snore, and afterwards the younger members would help their inebriated elders up the winding stairways, of which there were half a dozen in that house, until the early morning found them sleeping in the rooms heated by a great heated stone in the basement which circulated air upwards into the attics where the children slept, and then they would return the following day, in white sunlight, as they skated away the effects of hangovers and rich food.

Shaw saw in the television the slow images of dread. The nightmare was unfolding not in Estonia, but in Russia. Like witnesses at an accident, they began to watch the Russian television broadcasts. He noticed the pretty features of the newscaster stiffen as she read out the news. There was a cabinet crisis. The resignation of certain ministers followed. They were never interviewed. The reasons for their resignations were given in the ponderous phrases of ill-health, heart attack. The list was relentless. Always there were pictures of a single man, impressive, grey-haired, the Minister of Defence Valentin Chernavin. He too seldom gave interviews. But Shaw saw him give occasional broadcasts, talking to the camera like a man to an unwelcome guest.

'Russia is entering another crisis,' Aegu said to Shaw. 'From centralized state to early democracy. Then what? A new era of freedom? Or a new military dictatorship?'

It had been several weeks since Aegu had phoned or had imposed upon him one of his impromptu monologues. Once Shaw had seen newspaper accounts of Aegu in discussion with the Minister of Defence over what were called 'strategic matters'. There was no report on the substance of those talks. Shaw remembered the image of the short, square Aegu approaching Chernavin cautiously, shaking hands for the cameras, avoiding the great bear-hug beloved of Russian politicians.

Aegu was angry. Estonia might be economically free but it was increasingly 'Finlandicized'.

'The Russian military machine intimidates to the point where the victim exerts a self-censorship as rigorous as any which could be directly imposed in order not to inflame the great neighbour.'

Aegu had called in the afternoon and asked to see him that evening. Shaw, used to the ways of Aegu, expected nothing but a monologue, in which he was merely an audience for the articulated fears and frustrations of a politician whose natural environment was uncertainty. In its waters Aegu seemed to survive, though it took its toll.

'Vodka. A bottle, two glasses.'

The bar Aegu had chosen was the Sarov, a dingy waterfront place. Shaw waited while a tired girl served them.

'Chernavin heads the military faction. A man who offers a clear lead, who promises to end corruption and profiteering. He calls himself a socialist, of course.' Aegu drank quickly, with the effortless ease of someone for whom the hand has become merely a conveyor.

'The flaw in socialism is the central role it gives to the state. It is this which allows authoritarians like Chernavin to use its sacred name. It allows him to invoke the needs of society against the individual. It justifies his oppression of rivals.'

Around them groups of dockyard workers were singing. But Estonians on the whole tended to be quiet, even in their carousing. Aegu raised his voice and continued with his harangue.

'The concentration of power in the state always corrupts. Socialism begins as the best political system and ends as the worst. Capitalism begins as the worst and ends as the best. Unfortunately, the Russian system is at an early stage of capitalism. How is your family?'

'They're well.'

'Your son is becoming a true Estonian?'

'Can't hold him back.'

'I sometimes think I miss children. But my wife has always said there is no room in the house for children while I am around. She has her consolations – her career. I have mine.'

Amongst both his numerous failings and virtues, Aegu lacked rectitude. He was open about both his drinking and his womanizing. Rumours and stories circulated, but in some curious way it immunized him to criticism. What the population appeared to dislike above all was hypocrisy. Whatever else he might be, Aegu was no hypocrite.

'You know Lydia Teemant?'

What did Shaw sense behind that question? An attitude that was more than mere idle interest, that was proprietorial? He felt a sudden nervousness.

'Yes.'

Aegu poured himself himself a vodka. Shaw's glass was still almost full. Aegu shrugged.

'An interesting word, "yes".'

Aegu drank, throwing the entire contents back and pouring himself another.

'Part of your investigation into Illich's death, of course.'

Shaw did not reply. His defensiveness had given rise to calculation, even a certain amount of aggression. It was the alchemy of a helmsman, turning his fear into attack. What special rights did Aegu think he held?

'Illich's mistress,' Aegu commented. 'As such, of natural assistance in the investigation.'

'And your mistress too, I understand.'

How did he expect Aegu to react? Aegu had stopped drinking suddenly. The movement of vodka from bottle to glass to mouth halted. He placed his hands on the table and interweaved the fingers. His hands seemed to interest him more than the surroundings. After a few moments he smiled, and continued to drink.

*

She was a tall girl, Byelorussian, Shaw guessed, and she walked out on to the stage with the grace of a former dancer. The lights were doused, and a single spotlight picked up her figure.

Shaw asked, 'Why does Chernavin appeal to Russians?'

Aegu seemed to have returned from his contemplation. 'Chernavin reminds them of a character from Russian mythology: the *bogatir*, a giant who is clumsy of speech but accomplishes mighty deeds, and grows stronger whenever his enemy strikes him. A stage is reached when the momentum of such an individual is so great he merely cows the opposition into acquiescence.'

Aegu offered him a cigarette. Shaw refused politely.

'You think he's reached that point?'

'Perhaps.' Aegu shrugged. A light flowered at his fingertips. The tip of a cigarette glowed. He flicked away the match and continued:

'In the past Russia has been like a pirate ship. It has not directed its primary resources into agriculture or civil industry. Rather, it invested them in armies and weapons. It believed that with this policy it could obtain what it required by intimidation and blackmail. It has a kind of commercial logic, but it is a dark one. In the old days, the Soviet Union could justify its massive investment in the military as an attempt to export socialism. But now that the old Soviet system of socialism is universally rejected . . .' Aegu breathed out, letting the sentence trail out.

'Chernavin doesn't say that to his audiences.'

'No, of course not. He talks about selling out to capitalism, about Russia's hasty abandonment of the great cause of socialism. He rejects the influence of Lenin, but hankers after his spirit. Whereas military might used to be justified by socialism, now Chernavin will use his socialism to justify his military agenda.' Aegu paused. 'Let me explain it this way, comrade. Chernavin is drawn to the idea of socialism in the same way a termite is drawn to a wooden house. He needs the structure to live in. He is not a socialist himself, but the rotten wood of socialism sustains him. In the end perhaps he believes he is a socialist.'

On the stage the dancer was about to drop her final, flimsy clothes. The band seemed to have come to life. Under the spotlight her shoulders were a creamy white. Her breasts swung forward as she leant down to push down her panties. The band seemed to halt and in silence the audience watched. She stepped back naked, her fingers in front of her pubis. The music rose again.

Aegu's voice dropped an octave. 'One thing is puzzling. The politicians who have witnessed his assault on the political establishment cannot understand Chernavin's ascent to power. They cannot explain the timing or the content of his brilliant campaigns. Who is backing him? Who is advising him? Who writes his speeches? Who tells him to say one thing to the American ambassador, and another to a group of mineworkers in Omsk? He is a bear, a huge powerful bear. Yet he dances on the political stage like a ballerina.'

'Do you have an explanation?'

'His deputy is General Vadim Soludov. But they say the real power is another general. They say he is not in Moscow, that he lives in a dacha amongst telephones and secretaries. Or perhaps on an island in St Petersburg. They say that Chernavin treats him like a prince, like an heir. It is rumoured that not long ago this general suffered a terrible accident.' Aegu swallowed his vodka. 'They say, my friend, that he is blind.'

Sixty-six

Aegu said: 'I am shortly to go to Moscow. There may not be much time, a few weeks, a few months.

'Allow me to tell you about Vorolov. Since he was a colonel, even a major, he was earmarked for the highest command. In the armed services there is a certain route to highest command. In Comrade General Vorolov's career, we witness this golden path. He was one of the officers in the office of the chief of defence staff. At a higher level, his path was clearly set when he became chief instructor of the College of Strategic Rocket Studies. The young prince moves from one position to another with apparent ease. His juniors hold him in awe. Senior commanders pay polite attention to his opinions. It is a strange, perhaps mystical procedure, like anointment. Those who know about these things will be able to point to a certain captain and say, in twenty years' time he will reach the highest levels of command – not with absolute certainty, you understand, because nothing is certain in this world, but with an alarmingly high probability.

'I am interested, *tovarich*, in this mystical development, because to some extent it is a self-fulfilling prophecy. The young prince reacts to his circumstances in an understandable and predictable manner. His elders take him seriously, even defer to him. He becomes more confident. This confidence distinguishes him further from his peers. He grows, so to speak, into the role.

'It is a mutually advantageous relationship. The king will choose someone whom he believes shares his concerns and will carry out his wishes. Perhaps he looks for a younger version of himself, I do not know. Whatever his motives, he believes that through his successor, his strategies will be perpetuated and developed. He regards his investment in the prince as his own best means of securing his own future.

'That is how you must understand Vorolov. He is a crown prince, the next in line. He was Chernavin's chief of staff. He has known for much of his adult life that his function is to carry out his superior's wishes, and in the process to make as few mistakes as possible. If he fulfils his obligations to his best ability, he will rise to the highest position.

'This brings us to the matter of Illich. If Chernavin were to wish for the execution of an officer, who would he turn to to undertake this mission? Who would have most to lose by disobeying an order? The crown prince.

'Chernavin wishes to discipline Illich. He entrusts Vorolov to do so. Vorolov carries out his mission, but in the course of it, the unforeseen happens. The unexpected ferocity of Illich's response catches him off guard. He is blinded. Vorolov leaves active service at immediate short notice. He disappears into the hinterland.'

Shaw said, 'How can you be certain Vorolov is our man?'

'All truth is tentative. But allow me, *tovarich*, to complete my analysis. Supposing Vorolov has committed the crime in question; what is his current position? Is he in disgrace? Is he under arrest, perhaps? Will he be tried, as they tried to court-martial Illich?'

Shaw did not answer. The questions seemed rhetorical, designed merely to set out a pattern of consequences.

'I know the Army. Like all institutions, it is intolerant of those who disobey. But in the Army this is taken to an extreme. Illich's crime was that he no longer belonged. Vorolov's virtue is that he not only belongs but is prepared to sacrifice himself for the institution. He did his best to carry out his orders. His wounds will be treated as honourable wounds. If anything, his status will be improved.'

'Even now?' Shaw's consternation showed.

'You are a Westerner,' Aegu said. 'You do not yet

understand Russia. There is a part of Russia that is Asian, that is cold, rapacious, absolute. It is the West which brings Russia her culture, but it is the East which ensures her survival. If Russia was merely a Western state, it would have been conquered by Napoleon, it would have been over-run by the Nazis. It is not merely the Asian hinterland into which Russia retreats, but her Asian soul. It is this Asian element which finds its final refuge in the Armed Forces.

'We must welcome these developments, *tovarich*, because they will play into our hands. If Vorolov was a minor functionary, he would be pensioned off and the matter would be forgotten, at an official level at least. But he is not. He is someone who is destined for higher command. It is not in the nature of the prince to hide. He will re-emerge. He will exercise power. Then we will see him. In the mean time we must be patient and wait.'

Shaw experienced at least momentarily that sensation of belief which it was Aegu's privilege to impart. Aegu stood up from the table, swayed. Shaw saw the Kallas brothers emerge from a background of tables. Aegu raised his hand to halt their proffered assistance. To demonstrate his sobriety, he turned a full circle, his hand raised in gratuitous valediction. Then he left, moving slowly but with impressive consistency, his two bodyguards at a respectful distance.

Sixty-seven

The big-bellied Antonov floated down through an afternoon light that was heavy with industrial pollution.

Shaw looked out over Kharkov and saw the buildings

lean in a summer haze of heat and industrial smoke. The thin thread cutting from north to south was the Lopan river.

At the airport he was forced to wait for one and a half hours while an official – a young man with soulful eyes and a thin moustache – stepped into an adjacent room and behind a sound-proofed glass front made what seemed an interminable phone-call. Shaw was not searched, or subjected to the other mild humiliations sometimes imposed by officials on those of whom they are suspicious, but he was certain his background was being checked with some senior official.

The walls of the waiting room were lined with posters of the Ukraine, showing rolling farmlands which reminded him of the American Midwest, others of the magnificent old seaport of Odessa, and yet others of Kiev's beautiful cathedrals and churches. It was interesting what the posters left out. Kharkov did not feature at all. Shaw looked out of the plateglass window. Two hundred miles to the west was Chernobyl.

The young man with the thin moustache returned with his passport.

'Are you staying for a few days?'

'I have a flight booked out tomorrow.'

Shaw took his passport and turned away. He felt the official's eyes follow him down the main stairs.

Outside the early afternoon light was golden. Shaw found a rank of old taxis, and took one towards the centre of town.

'Enjoying your visit?' his driver asked in Russian. Shaw noticed an old picture of Yeltsin, full face, posted with tape beside the glove compartment. The driver glanced at him in the window. Shaw nodded, but he was shy of trying to converse in his halting guide-book Russian. He preferred to look out of the window into the huge, wide streets. They were approaching the outer suburbs, the blank rises of worker flats.

Kharkov was a monument to Soviet giganticism, a great industrial city built to a vision of old style communism. The scale itself was inhuman, except perhaps to bureaucrats. Scale was everything in the workers' paradise. Shaw felt a visitor's reticence about criticizing the colossal squares and buildings that opened out as they passed down the huge streets: even in the privacy of his own mind it seemed oddly heretical. He wondered whether it was the type of city Sam Shaw might approve of. It had no luxury, no comfort, a planner's monument to utility. But whereas Sam was an ascetic, the huge façades seemed a special kind of indulgence from a former era. There was something sterile and forbidding in its power. He would have liked his grandfather to see it, if only to goad him over his beliefs in a system which enshrined the political solidarity of workers but gave so little thought to their individual needs.

The taxi came to a halt outside a row of terraced houses.

'Roubles?' Shaw asked.

The taxi-driver shrugged. Dollars would be better. But Shaw, conforming to his own obscure beliefs, preferred to deal in roubles than in black-market American currency, even though he lost out a little in the process.

He knocked on the door of Anna Varileva's apartment and heard a woman raise her voice briefly inside. The answering voice was that of a child. To his Maine ears, Russians were as noisy and ebullient as Italians. The brief exchange whose higher syllables reached him sounded like an argument but was probably an arrangement for dinner, or an injunction to a child to do her homework.

The door opened suddenly and unexpectedly. A striking woman faced him. In her early thirties, slender, by no means tall, she had the poise of a ballet dancer. Her blonde hair was drawn back into a severe bun. Her eyes were wide, her cheekbones high, her broad mouth severe. She wore no make-up. Raised a step above him by the entrance porch, she looked down into his eyes with a steady gaze.

'Jim Shaw,' he said. He smiled but she continued to stare. Shaw sensed this was someone with whom it would be useless to force the pace. He felt he should apologize for arriving at the wrong time and might even have done so when, as if she had seen all she needed, she stepped back, opening the door for him to enter.

'Please come in.'

She chose to speak in English, even though he had spoken in Estonian on the telephone.

Inside, she did not shake hands, but walked ahead of him through a spacious entrance hall to a large living-room. It was a big, comfortable apartment, the apartment of a member of the *vlasti*. There were mohair and Astrakhan rugs on the wall, a series of three small abstract oil-paintings on the wall, low divans, a thick white pile carpet. Whatever child she had been talking to had disappeared. Shaw had an impression of a highly regulated household.

She swung round to face him, and he was aware again of her implacable composure.

'Please sit down.'

Shaw sat down on one of the divans. She stood facing him, staring down at him with her intense eyes.

'Would you like some tea?'

'Thank you.'

She disappeared towards the kitchen, leaving him alone in the sudden quietness of the large living-room.

Shaw's only connection with her was through Illich. Vaguely, he tried to imagine an emotional relationship between his formidable hostess and the detached, floating warrior that was Illich. It would be fraught, he suspected; it would have its tensions. The quietness of the flat encouraged reverie. His mind turned away from particulars to more general aspects.

Anna Varileva returned with the tea, set out the tray on the table.

'Lemon?'

'Please.'

She handed him a cup. He saw she had adapted to her new life. The style of tea was Russian. Lemon, not milk. If you wanted sugar, you did not dissolve it, but put a lump in the corner of your mouth and sipped your tea.

Shaw said, 'Thank you for seeing me at such short notice.'

She shrugged with a certain lightness, and poured herself a cup from the high kettle.

He said, 'This is not an official visit. We've made some recent progress on narrowing down the suspects. I hoped I could ask you about some background details that would help us a little more.'

She nodded cautiously, watching him steadily. He noticed how lightly she leaned back against the sofa, her spine poised.

'Would you say Illich was ever in conflict with his superiors?'

He detected the faint trace of a smile.

'Conflict?'

'Did he express himself in disagreement with them?'

She paused before replying.

'He hardly recognized their existence. He was a sporting hero. The Army regarded him as a popular ambassador, its human face. After the end of communism, the Army was keen to preserve its popular image. It gave him leniency to pursue his career.'

'He lived almost without supervision?' Shaw suggested.

She nodded briefly.

'Then suppose,' he said, 'he found himself in a different situation, one in which a superior was put in charge of the sailing camp – someone who was also a strong character.'

She did not answer immediately, though he suspected

357

he was being given tacit permission to continue with his line of questioning.

Shaw turned over in his mind what Aegu had told him, that the second boat after *Leningrad*, *Kirov*, was a new design; that the Army authorities had given this ostensibly superior yacht to the second crew, an unprecedented move.

Shaw said, 'Suppose the function of this superior was to impose Army rule over Illich, to organize his programme.'

Anna Varileva said, simply, 'Conflict.'

'Suppose there was conflict, then. Illich was not the sort of person to back down.'

'No.'

'What would have happened if there was conflict, and if his superior refused to back down either?'

'Illich would resign, I think.'

'No attempt to compromise?'

'No.'

He watched her, and she for her part coolly studied him.

'The tea is cold,' Anna Varileva said. 'I will make another kettle.'

It was not an official visit, and Shaw felt constrained not to press his case, to observe the formalities. When she returned with a second kettle, she said, 'You took over from Illich as helmsman?'

'Yes.'

'You knew him well?'

'As well as most of the crew, I think.'

He wanted to say, how much do we know of anyone? And in particular, how much does one know of a leader, someone who, almost by definition, presents only his stronger side? She handed him another cup.

'You did well,' Anna Varileva commented.

'You mean we won,' he replied.

There was a difference. She smiled, almost with bene-

358

volence. It was the first small sign of warmth in her disposition.

'Illich won two races,' he continued. 'I lost three races and only won two.'

She finished pouring her own tea and sat down opposite him:

'You don't seem unhappy.'

'Why should I be unhappy?'

She half smiled again. He saw she could be beautiful. In the calmness of the flat he was aware of traffic as a distant hum, hardly discernible.

'I have some other questions,' he said.

He had a vice: he was too lazy to dissimulate. The result was honesty. He said: 'I am an American, as you know. I have a vested interest. I want to make sure that whoever killed him was not an American.'

'Ah.' What expression flitted across her face. Surprise, perhaps, tolerant condescension?

'What if he were?'

'I would be unhappy,' Shaw said carefully. His second vice was understatement.

'I see. In order that you are not . . . unhappy . . . what can I do to assist you?'

'I wanted to ask about some other aspects of Illich's life. I hope my questions won't distress you.'

He looked at her directly, sitting on the chair, and she shrugged her shoulders in a brief gesture of acquiescence, not so much to the question as to the situation in which they both found themselves.

'Did you know anyone with an obvious motive to kill him?'

'Apart from half the women in Russia?'

There seemed to be no bitterness in the remark, merely a statement of fact.

'I don't think it was likely to be a woman,' Shaw said. 'When Illich entered the flat, his assailant was already waiting for him. The investigators thought he might have known the assailant personally. He had a gun. There was a struggle. The powder stains on Illich's clothing from several shots show that the gap was closing between each shot. You don't fire while running towards a person. So he must have been doing the running. He was charging the assailant down. Would one do that with a burglar, for example? It seemed as if he knew whoever was firing. It seemed he didn't like him.'

She closed her eyes. He saw tears emerge from under her lids, from a face that was in other respects perfectly composed.

Shaw said, 'I'm sorry. That was stupid. There's no need for you to know all the details.'

He had never seen someone cry so quietly, without moving, only the tears rolling from beneath her eyes.

But she recovered quickly, with an eerie power of will he found almost disturbing. When she had recovered, she asked: 'Your first time in the Ukraine?'

Shaw said, 'Yes. My first time.'

What could he say in the silence that followed? He struggled to express something of what he felt. Because of its tragic history the republics of the former Soviet Union exerted a peculiar alchemy on the emotions of the visitor, the outsider. At the same time he suspected that the average citizen would despise him for this view, this American who could romanticize their suffering, then fly out to another existence in a fast, comfortable jet. It was wiser to say nothing.

Perhaps she sensed his struggle. She seemed about to say something but was interrupted by a phone ringing. She stood up to pick it up. Shaw gathered from her tone that it was her husband. There were no greetings or preliminaries, her voice seemed merely to adopt a register of familiarity. She put down the phone and sat down opposite him again.

'You like Kharkov?'

'It is impressive.'

It was true. Shaw supposed there were other places like this, monuments to departed ideals. You looked at a Greek statue, and saw a vision of humanity. Kharkov was not like that. It was like the pyramids. You didn't imagine happiness. You imagined a hundred thousand slaves.

He wanted to return to the subject of her husband. But she said, 'Are you married?'

'Yes.'

'And children?'

'One boy.'

'How old?'

'A little over two years.'

She wiped her tears and blew her nose.

'And you sail.'

'I came over to visit my wife's relatives in Estonia and took the opportunity to meet Illich. Illich asked me to sail the trial boat. At first it was simply as practice helmsman, someone Illich could tune up against. After that he asked me to be tactician.'

'You accepted?'

He nodded.

'And your wife agreed?'

He smiled. 'She insisted, in fact.'

Anna Varileva had held her handkerchief in her hand. Now she tucked it into a pocket of her jacket.

'It was a happy decision?'

'Yes.'

She seemed interested in his answers, as though referring to her own life.

'Why?'

He said, 'We admired Illich, I suppose. We were willing to be led by him.'

'Admired.' She smiled and sniffed. The thought seemed to revive her. 'He could lead others, but not himself.'

361

Perhaps she dared him to answer. But if she did dare him, he did not respond.

In the course of his short life, Shaw had formed a loose impression about relationships. He suspected that those who most regretted the passing of loved ones were those who had had unsatisfactory relationships, that the real pain was the pain of the unfulfilled. He pushed these thoughts aside and began again.

'The Investigation Department in Tallinn have already interviewed you about the telegram which was sent to Illich in your name. They accept that you had nothing to do with it, that it was a hoax. I simply wanted to ask you if you have any idea about who might have perpetrated it.'

A factory hooter started in the background, far away. It was a disturbing sound, like an air-raid siren. It was over quite suddenly, leaving the room silent. He was aware of a change in her, as if she was once again on difficult ground.

Eventually she said, 'What good will these investigations do? They will not bring him back.'

'I agree. But someone killed him. Someone sent him a telegram from his wife and then waited in his flat to murder him.'

'If I knew, I would tell you.'

He felt she was telling the truth. But there was a more ambiguous aspect.

'I'm not asking whether you know. I'm asking who you suspect.'

'Suspect?' She shrugged, a curiously revealing gesture. He sensed almost a mild derision of this American who thought of things in such simple terms. He began to sense again the depth of a cultural divide. In a country only recently freed from a conspiratorial regime, at an official level at least one suspected everyone.

He realized he must keep still, that he must not disturb

her. Left on her own, perhaps she could tell him something.

But she did not respond further to his question. After a few seconds he said: 'Mrs Varileva, I appreciate what you say. I have no more questions. Thank you for seeing me.'

Perhaps she had expected him to persist. 'I am sorry you have come a long way for nothing.'

He shrugged. 'I'm glad I met you. It was interesting to see Kharkov.'

'You would like another tea before you go?'

'Thank you,' he said. 'One for the road.'

'For the road?'

'An American expression.'

'Ah yes, for the journey.'

She leant forward to pour out the tea. He was aware of the silence of the flat, the concentration of her presence within it. Sometimes in such stressful circumstances a woman will gather her husband and family around her. But she had wanted to face him alone. Now she said with warning:

'He liked America, you know.'

'Illich?'

'Yes.'

She handed him another cup.

'Not for the usual reasons. Not for its wealth, or its power, you understand. He hated that.'

'For what, then?'

Shaw leaned back on the sofa.

'For its individuals.'

Shaw could get used to the Russian style of drinking tea. The lemon slice floated like a half moon. It leached its taste into the clear brown fluid; the liquid grew more bitter as it cooled. When you reached the bottom of the cup you found a body of bitterness almost pure.

In the silence, he nodded and smiled.

'You think I am angry about him. I am not. I was

foolish in believing I could own him, or that anyone could.'

She drank her tea. It seemed to him that she had forgotten him, that she addressed herself.

'Wives know their husbands' weaknesses. They believe that underneath men crave security, safety, peace. He did not. He was only happy in some struggle which consumed him. Then you saw him achieve something like peace.'

She smiled to herself.

'It was a peace outside his family, or anyone else. He needed no one else. That is what was most difficult to face. There was nothing to hold him. I think he realized it himself, poor man.'

She halted.

'The last time he met me, he agreed that he would exercise no further rights over his daughters. He didn't say so, but it seemed to me that he felt he was going to die.'

'He knew he was going to be murdered?'

She looked at him, as if he had misunderstood.

'No,' she smiled sadly. 'You don't understand. It was nothing to do with anyone else, with me or his murderer. He was cutting attachments. All his life he was cutting away what held him.'

A fly buzzed in one of the windows. Outside Shaw could see a line of smoke from a series of chimneys, smelters, archaic industries, winding together like a rope.

He said, 'He went back to Tallinn because he hoped to find you. He had reached a decision, I think.'

He remembered the force of Illich's joy when he had received the telegram, as if it were something for which he had prayed.

'A decision?'

'To give up everything. To return to you.'

She smiled sadly.

He felt impelled to continue. 'I had the impression that something had changed inside him, but I couldn't be sure about that. Maybe it happened when *Novy Mir* was rammed by *Eagle*. Maybe he realized that competing against people like that wasn't worth it, it wasn't worth the effort or the loss of everything else.'

She smiled again and shook her head.

He said, 'It happened to me. It happens suddenly, like a weight being removed.'

He thought that what he said had not affected her. And for a moment he hoped that this was true. She sat upright, almost rigid, with that strangely empty, contemplative look which occurs when the mind is full of memories. Perhaps she had not heard him; or, if she had, what had been said was already relegated to some other part of her mind. He put his cup back on the saucer and for a few moments his attention wandered to the window and the pall of smoke outside. When she moved there was something oddly resigned about the way she let herself fall, like a marionette. She seemed to fold forward, as neatly as a jack-knife. She was leaning forward over her knees, and was crying. He felt a sudden horror inside him at what he had said.

She was repeating something over and over in Estonian, her native language, and he struggled to hear what she said. Her crying was terrible. After a while she said, 'The only time he came to me was when I wasn't there.'

Sixty-eight

Shaw listened to her sobbing, frozen, unable to offer consolation, knowing that he had trespassed on some private area, had blundered on some insupportable grief. He supposed it had been a few seconds, but it seemed to go on until without warning the front door opened and he heard footsteps in the hallway.

She heard too, and the speed with which she raised herself was another revelation of her character. He had never seen such an effort of pure will. Her face was drained, but she was once again in control. Paralysed, rendered speechless by these transformations, he listened to someone opening another door or hallway cupboard, pausing to hang up a coat, then further footsteps in the hall. A voice shouted, 'Anya!'

'Here,' she said.

Professor Stefan Varilev was of medium height, thin, white-haired, with the beard of a Russian patriarch. His skin had a fine white transparency, his blue eyes were so pale they almost lacked colour. He halted when he saw Shaw stand up, staring at his guest with an expression so direct it might have been hostile.

'Jim Shaw,' Anna Varileva introduced them in English. 'My husband.'

Now Varilev turned his disconcerting gaze away from Shaw and looked towards his wife.

'Are you upset?'

'It isn't his fault,' she said. 'He tried to help me.'

Varilev looked towards Shaw, and said with a certain control, 'Please sit down.'

'I was about to leave,' Shaw said. 'I think I've overstayed as it is.'

'You have to catch a flight?'

Even Varilev's casual question expressed a form of authority. The truth was that he had intended to check in at the Intourist Hotel at Sverdlov Street for the night, then fly out the following morning.

'No, not today. But your wife has been kind enough to see me for longer than I hoped.'

'Please stay a little longer,' Anna Varileva insisted, standing at her husband's side.

366

Varilev glanced at his wife, at Shaw, then indicated a chair. 'Please.'

An obscure guilt made him sit down again. Varilev positioned himself next to his wife on the sofa and put his thin, bony hand over her shoulder protectively. Shaw looked towards her. She was as silent as bone china. It took Shaw several moments to adjust to the fact that she had not told her husband that he was expected. Or that if she told him, she had not mentioned the purpose of his visit.

Varilev inclined his head, as if at something that had already been said. 'You came to discuss Illich?'

Shaw nodded.

'An official visit?'

'No, not official. I'm helping the Estonian Investigation Department with some details about his death. I hoped I might clear up some background information.'

'He is also a friend of Illich,' Anna Varileva interposed. 'A good friend.'

In spite of Varilev's uncertainty towards him, Shaw instinctively liked him. He too had had to live in the shadow of Illich. It was one thing to be exposed to the personal history of his wife's former husband, another to know that he is considered by his countrymen to be a hero amongst heroes.

Shaw's discomfort increased. He had wanted to tell this admirable woman what Illich had sacrificed to see her, in the hope that it might comfort her, only to see it cause terrible pain. He should have guessed the effects of his words. He should have known that in the strange alchemy of relationships, a message of personal comfort could turn into its opposite. Now he wished he had been more insistent about leaving earlier.

Shaw said again, 'Your wife has been very generous with her time. I don't wish to take up any more of it.'

Varilev nodded, though he did not move.

'The Estonian Investigation Department sent you to see Anna?'

'No. They are satisfied that there is no further information your wife can give them. I was hoping to ask questions about his relationship with the Army.'

'Are they making progress with their inquiries?'

'I believe so,' Shaw said.

Varilev studied him dispassionately. Shaw felt a tension in the air, as if Varilev was turning something over in his mind, was preparing to speak.

'You have a suspect?'

Under Varilev's stare, Shaw considered how much he should say. But the matter was removed from his hands, because Varilev suddenly said:

'An Army officer?'

Shaw experienced a sudden fear, the fear of powerful intuition, of knowledge which is suddenly displayed.

'We have a suspect.'

Varilev studied him with implacable eyes.

'Perhaps you should question me,' Varilev said quietly. 'My wife only has personal knowledge. Mine is more general. I am a Russian, though I choose to live in the Ukraine. Perhaps I could tell you about the nature of Russian institutions.'

Shaw said: 'Maybe I could ask a few questions then, for my own information.'

Varilev nodded.

'What makes you think it's someone in authority?'

Varilev paused. Shaw had the impression his reactions were being studied.

'In the Ukraine,' he said, 'we have similar problems to the Estonians. We too are nervous of the new political developments in Russia.'

Shaw nodded. But now Varilev did not seem to notice him. He seemed to have made some private decision. He started to speak slowly, forming each word carefully in a foreign tongue.

'I left Russia precisely because I am nervous of her

institutions, or more precisely, of the role of those institutions in her history. Perhaps,' Varilev said quietly, 'we have a similar enemy.'

Shaw let the silence settle. The Ukraine had been the industrial heartland of the Soviet Union. Estonia was a tiny republic perched on the periphery. The statement carried a peculiar, though ambiguous, weight. Behind Varilev's head he could see, through the clear glass of a plate window, a horizon lined with factory roofs and high chimney towers.

He said, 'What institutions would those be?'

Varilev half smiled.

'Until recently, Russian expansionism was based on three institutions: the Communist Party, the security apparatus, and the armed forces. The first of those institutions was effectively disbanded more than a decade ago. The security forces were reformed, and their power is severely curtailed. That leaves the armed forces.'

Shaw waited in the silence. Varilev continued calmly: 'You know that in Moscow the military increasingly hold power?'

'Yes.'

Varilev's pale eyes seemed to search him for a further response.

'You are searching for a murderer, an assassin. You are surprised, as a Westerner, that I should question the role of the armed forces.'

'I wish we had talked earlier.'

'In Western society, you have the authorities and the criminals. In Russian society, the authorities have lost their former ideological principles. That is the terrible thing about Russian history. Everything so easily becomes its opposite. The authorities and the criminals have become the same thing.'

Shaw was still not used to the ponderous directness, the sweeping generalizations of political discussion in the former republics of the Soviet Union. He had the impression of people who felt that they were on the threshold of a new society, that what they said mattered, that they were discussing fundamentals. Perhaps this had always been so with Slavs. Shaw was determined to return to Illich.

'Are you saying in Illich's case the prime suspect must be the armed forces?'

'Specifically his branch of the armed services, the Russian Army.' Varilev paused to give his word emphasis. '*Da*.'

The Russian affirmative was more powerful than the Russian negative, '*niet*'. In English, the opposite was the case; the negative 'no' was more insistent and clear than the more tenuous, serpentine English 'yes'.

'The function of the Army also concerns you, perhaps?' Varilev asked.

Shaw nodded. In older democracies there was a certain complacency about the political processes, an assumption that if you let the system alone it would let you alone. Here, he had noticed, such assumptions had no validity. Every subject had a political dimension. Every independent act was a political confrontation.

Shaw noticed something else about his hosts. He felt uneasy in an environment of moral ambiguity and tension. But they, curiously, appeared to feel at home. Perhaps they were made of tougher material than he. Perhaps, to someone living in this society, it was the norm. Varilev interrupted his thoughts by saying without warning: 'My wife is haunted by Illich. I do not believe that I can ever replace him. Her problem is that she has no framework in which to place him. She does not see that he is part of a culture, even a tradition.'

'Tradition?' Shaw was curious.

'My wife thinks she married an Estonian who caused her great unhappiness.' Varilev smiled at her. 'I do not view him in quite the same way. To me, he was not an

Estonian. He was a Russian. The best type of Russian. Brave, sincere, driven by some internal conscience, detached from this world. Maybe a kind of saint, like Tolstoy. You understand?'

'Not exactly,' Shaw said.

'He was the type of Russian who always comes into conflict with the authorities.'

Varilev shrugged.

'Tolstoy's wife was an unhappy woman. But she at least had an advantage. She knew she had married a Russian.'

Anna Varileva was looking directly at her husband. There was affection in her gaze: 'My husband admires Illich as much as I did, though he doesn't easily admit it.'

Varilev drew down the corners of his mouth, as if in reluctant agreement.

Anna Varileva said: 'My husband as usual is trying to protect me. My real problem is that I divorced a great Estonian helmsman in order to marry a Russian saint.'

'If that is true,' Varilev said, 'then we really are in trouble.'

It was a cause for smiles, if not laughter. Shaw, slightly awed by the power of the couple who faced him on the sofa opposite, felt he had been let off the hook.

'Will you stay for dinner, Mr Shaw?' Anna Varileva interposed. She had been quiet on the sofa beside her husband. Now she asked with composed, clear eyes.

Shaw might have prevaricated. But he felt lighter now that the subject had been changed from the anguish his personal message about Illich had caused her. He could say 'yes' in English at least, not being confident enough in his welcome to use the Russian '*da*'.

'Politics, politics,' Anna Varileva said. 'Who cares about American foreign policy? The important thing is to concentrate on your own life. If everyone did that, everyone would be happier.'

371

Shaw was relieved at her intervention. He finished his second plateful of *kolbasa* sausage. Inside he felt the whole rich dinner turn over casually like cement in a mixer. He patted his stomach and managed a satisfied smile at his hostess.

Anna Varileva it was who cleared the plates again. Russian marriages might include a degree more liberalism than previously, but at meals the patriarch was still waited upon like a household deity.

Shaw tried to remember when he had eaten *vareniki* – small dumplings filled with sour cream – before. It occurred to him suddenly that he had sampled them at a dinner with Illich and Brod after they had beaten the Russian Army yacht *Kirov*. Maria and Ilena had cooked it in the small bungalow that he and Maria had shared for several months. It seemed years ago.

'Tell me,' Varilev said, 'what is it that makes a good helmsman?'

'What makes you think I can answer that?'

Varilev smiled. 'Come now. Modesty is a pose. You are, after all, a Russian hero.'

'Am I?' Shaw asked. 'I'm regarded as a renegade by the sailing community in America. In Russia I'm regarded with suspicion, I would say. Even here, you should have seen the customs when I landed.'

'Officials,' Varilev said. 'Suspicious by nature. You have not answered my question about helmsmen.'

'My coach, Hal Johnson, used to tell us that good helmsmen came from the infernal regions.'

'You believe him?' Anna Varileva asked, suddenly interested.

'Sure,' he replied. He might have used Illich as a counter-example, but he didn't want to raise the name again.

'You think of yourself as a devil?' Varilev asked.

'Absolutely,' Shaw said. 'Wholly without redeeming features.'

372

'But your wife likes you,' Anna Varileva insisted. 'You cannot be entirely bad.'

'The nicest women like the worst men, is my observation.'

'An inescapable truth, I think.' Varilev came in heavily but amiably on his side.

Varilev raised his glass. 'To good women and bad men.'

'I'll drink to that,' Shaw said.

But Anna Varileva's attention was somewhere else. He suspected that the conversation had raised again the memory of Illich.

For dessert, they enjoyed another delicacy, *medivnyk*, a spiced honeycake. Shaw couldn't remember when he felt so full. The food was not only abundant, it was rich, too. Shaw fancied he could feel the heavy sausage curled up in his stomach like a sleeping animal.

On the principle that heavy eating makes one popular with Russian hostesses – whose ideal guest, Shaw suspected, would consume the plates as well – he believed, somewhat tentatively, he had scored a small initial success with Anna Varileva.

The three of them stood up. At the door she embraced him. Varilev opened the door. Shaw feared the distinguished professor might also embrace him, but instead he reached out a fine-boned hand and shook his with warmth. Anna Varileva said, 'You must bring your wife and family to visit us.' Shaw nodded, unable to speak. On the pavement, a mixture of emotions overtook him, relief and terror at the power of the past, something like astonishment at the generosity of people who, once they accepted him, treated him like an old friend.

Varilev had offered to drop him off at the Intourist hotel on Sverdlov Street. But he had no wish to take further advantage of their hospitality. A taxi had been called, and was waiting for him in the street. He was transported to his hotel, checked in, and was shown to his room. He was more than tired, he was exhausted. In sympathy with Anna Varileva, his emotions had been wrung to the extremes of pity and admiration. It had been an episode of tears and laughter, overeating and drinking, of intense moralizing and confession – in other words, he increasingly suspected, a more or less average Russian evening.

Sixty-nine

'We missed you,' Sam said. 'I didn't personally, but everyone else did.'

'I missed everyone too,' Shaw said, 'except you.'

He was glad to be back. The boat was ready for final decking. Despite the expense of the material, Shaw had decided on teak decks. It was still the best and perhaps the most durable non-slip surface. In conventional teak decking, the deck was just a finish, placed on a rubber compound which held it to the deck and filled in the spaces between the planks. The advantage of wood-epoxy building was that the teak was bonded to the ply decking by epoxy resin, so that the teak planks became part of the structure, contributing to its strength and stiffness. Instead of rubber compound, they used epoxy mixed with graphite which provided the traditional black lines dividing the planks.

Once the pieces had been laid, and the king-plank installed, it took them two days to lay the teak decks. Shaw enjoyed the labour, despite the fact that he worked with heavy rubber gloves and protective overalls. The decks looked messy at first because of the inevitable overspills of black wood-epoxy, but when they were power-planed back they looked fine.

It had taken five days in all to lay the decks. The two of them admired their work. Shaw and his grandfather walked backward and forward, testing the teak under their soles. It felt good. They collaborated on fitting the deck gear. Sam worked slowly but consistently, pacing himself, and Shaw was content to move at that rhythm.

He had read in the Gougeon brothers' classic account of wood-epoxy boat-building that one did not need to bolt the winches through the deck, that one could rely on the strength of the glue join. On the one hand, the Gougeon brothers had not only pioneered wood-epoxy boat-building, but were themselves responsible for building a series of fast and highly successful racers which had amply demonstrated their dedicated construction technique. On the other hand, the rule of thumb with a cruising boat was to be as conservative as possible. Shaw had been in a quandary.

Perhaps it was the influence of the Varilevs. Shaw would keep faith with the brothers. He said, 'Let's use epoxy alone. No throughbolts.'

'It's your boat,' Sam Shaw said.

'What was Illich like?' Sam asked, when they were working late.

'Illich? He wasn't someone that you'd notice immediately.'

'Like you,' his grandfather suggested.

'Yeah,' Shaw said. 'Like me.' It was important not to flinch at one of Sam's gibes. The best technique was to let them float past.

'There was something almost faceless about the guy, something that was ordinary.'

'Guess you could identify with that,' Sam Shaw commented.

'Guess I could. He had these cold eyes, like a wolf. He lived on the inside, if you know what I mean.'

'Would I have liked him?'

'I think maybe you would,' he said, considering. 'But I'm not sure whether he would've liked you.'

In the course of his work, Shaw was subject to sudden and intense bouts of happiness. They were as inexplicable as anxiety or terror, and sometimes they made him nervous. He moved from Maria and Jack at home to the boat in an atmosphere of joyful concentration. Perhaps it had something to do with the use of the hands, with making something. It seemed to strike an ancient chord in him, as if each act of making was a private confession of peace.

The days were lengthening as spring approached, but they were up at five and walked down in the early pre-dawn to begin work before six. Every time Shaw reached across the rough brickwork for the lights in the ramshackle shed in the early morning and his fingers struck the switch, the little hull rose out of the darkness. Its shape was curiously affecting, its mere existence an affirmation of faith.

They worked for two weeks fitting on genoa tracks, mainsheet tracks, eyes, stanchions, bow-rollers, pulpits, pushpits, a forehatch and several ventilators. They fitted a series of standard lights into the side of the coachroof. The stainless steel shroud bases were delayed for a week. Even in the simplest boats, it was surprising how much gear was fitted.

In the interior they worked on lowering the small auxiliary engine through the hatch and on to its base. The aim of beginning so early was that they could leave in the early afternoon and Shaw would have the rest of the afternoon and evening with his family. But sometimes they were still there when darkness closed in, hardly speaking, working in unison in the fading light on the fit-out of the interior. Shaw would say, 'We're late again,' and Sam Shaw would grunt; they'd put in another half-hour by the lights before closing down and walking back up the streets towards the house.

There came the final days of rubbing surfaces down with fine sandpaper before the last coats of paint and varnish. Shaw preferred to paint by hand with a brush, rather than to spray in a suit with the mask against the toxic droplets floating in the atmosphere of the shed. The finish was not quite as even as if sprayed, but it was good enough for his purposes. He had decided in the early stages of the design to paint the hull, but to varnish the coachroof sides. With the final paint finished, they set to the final small jobs, to cut away paint runs, to add an extra coat of epoxy in certain areas which might have been missed or which would be subject to special usage.

Seventy

'What are we going to call her?' Sam Shaw asked.

Shaw had lain awake at night considering that.

'I've thought of something.'

'Have you now?'

'I remembered something Illich told me about the words *Novy Mir*. It means "new world". But he said *Mir* has other meanings.'

'Is that so?'

'It means "peace",' Shaw said.

'Well, I'll be.'

'It also means the village community, the *Mir*. I thought maybe calling a boat a combination of "peace" and "small community" might just do us pretty well.'

'You're a persuasive little devil, you know that?'

'Well, hell.' Shaw was modest. 'I guess I just have that gift.'

'Have you discussed it with Maria?' Sam asked.

'She's OK about it.'

'Well, then it looks as though it has to be *Mir*.'

'It reminds me of *Novy Mir*, too,' Shaw added. 'It's just shorter.'

'I don't know where you get it from,' Sam Shaw said.

If there was one prejudice that Shaw had held in common with Illich, it was a hatred of elaborate launching ceremonies. Their shed was perhaps three hundred yards from the shore. They would launch *Mir* in the harbour. First, they had to hire a crane from the Meeri construction company. The keel was a single steel casting, with an integral bulb and wings.

Putting the keel on was a procedure they knew was difficult. They mixed a thick pot of epoxy glue and laid it along the top flange of the keel like icing on a cake. Then the crane lowered the yacht on to the keel.

Fortunately, the crane driver was expert. Shaw guided the yacht by hand-signals and some pulling on ropes until the keel bolts from the keel fitted upwards through the ready-made holes in the hull and the flange fitted the recess. The excess epoxy was squeezed out and they trowelled it away before it set. They laid a ladder against the hull and went inside. Tightening the keelbolts gently they 'nipped' it against the hull to squeeze out any excess epoxy. Then they tidied the flange of excess epoxy and they could relax for a while. The remaining epoxy would take several hours to set really hard. The hull was left sitting on the keel overnight in the slings of the crane while the epoxy set. When it was set you knew that the hard epoxy would provide a perfectly-shaped medium between hull and casting.

It was an elaborate procedure but it meant the keel was comfortable with the hull, and vice versa. Few castings are perfect. A few years before Shaw had seen at Weepeq a yacht being fitted with a keel. Some minor distortion of the keel while cooling had meant that it did not fit precisely into the flange recess. As the keel bolts were tightened the huge forces of the tightened bolts hauled down the hull on to the unyielding keel. With a sound like a rifle shot the keel-floors split away from the main bulkhead.

The following morning was fine and cold. The yacht hung in its slings. Climbing aboard on a ladder, they undid the keel bolts one by one. Into each bolt-hole they poured liquid epoxy. Then they put on washers and nuts and tightened them hard, just short of cracking the wood. They moved from bolt to bolt, undoing the nut, pouring, tightening. The epoxy poured into the keel bolt holes would set hard into a perfect watertight join. That was a keel that would remain in place for fifty or a hundred years or more and not let in a drop of water. It would be a little difficult to remove, maybe, if you wanted to get it off for any reason. But it was a price worth paying.

With the keel bolts tightened they could chock up the boat and the crane could leave. They let her sit for a day while the epoxy dried.

On the day of the launch they hired a flat-bed trailer and truck. The crane lifted the boat on to the trailer in the early morning, before there was traffic on the streets. Under a light blue Baltic sky they watched the boat leave on her journey the few miles down to the Pirita yacht basin where a launching Renner lifted her and hung her over the water, bow pointing inland. Shaw and his grand-father picked up Maria and Jack from the flat in the old Lada. They drove to Pirita in mute expectancy, without talking; only Jack burbled merrily in the back of the car.

The launching ceremony was as swift and as simple as Shaw could wish. Maria said, 'I name this boat *Mir*. May

379

God bless her and all who sail in her.' Shaw gripped a champagne bottle with her and they broke it against the metal stemhead fitting. The Renner lowered *Mir* slowly into the water. They watched her descend without looking at one another, until she floated and the slings came loose. Shaw noted with relief that she trimmed more or less to her marks, with the bow up an inch or two before loading. They pulled her to shore and tied her up. Sam was quiet; Shaw knew that he couldn't believe a boat they had built could float, just like that, upright and without turning turtle or sinking directly to the bottom. They opened a second bottle of champagne and filled plastic cups. The driver of the Renner accepted a cup of champagne. He said, 'A good boat, I think.'

'I think so,' Shaw said.

A few minutes later Shaw went to a public phone booth and dialled Tammiste.

'Your design floats,' he said. 'I wanted you to know that.'

'That is always a good start,' Tammiste commented.

Seventy-one

Launching is only a small part of preparation and commissioning. The mast, fitted with halyards and rigging, had been delivered several days earlier to the Pirita yacht club. Shaw and his grandfather used the nearby hand-crane to raise the mast, swing it over the deck, and lower its base through the coachroof until they could chock secure the heel above the keel. Shaw insisted on rigging the boat himself. Stainless steel rod rigging was normally used on racing yachts, but it was what he was used to and he wanted a rig that was stiff.

By mid-afternoon the main rigging was in place and suitably tensioned. Towards evening they threaded halyards and reef lines through the boom. Sam worked uncomplainingly. Every hour or so Shaw would go below and raise the floorboard to see how much water had entered the bilges. The only leak they could find was from an outlet pipe. The open plan of the boat meant the leak was accessible and was easily put right. The rest of the boat seemed dry.

At seven that evening they relaxed for half an hour. Maria returned in the Lada with the cushions and they admired their cool grey and blue colours. They had sandwiches on the saloon table. Shaw fitted the calor gas into its isolated drained locker at the aft of the boat. Maria cooked soup in the galley. The two saloon lights, switched on, showed the glowing pale gold of the spruce interiors.

'Absolutely the best,' Maria said.

Shaw trial-ran the engine for half an hour and then they went home, like children from an elaborate picnic, Shaw and his grandfather too exhausted to talk.

The following day they prepared to take *Mir* on her maiden sail. It was overcast, with the promise of a force five in the afternoon. The sea had a flat grey glare. They shipped sails on board early and motored northwards into Tallinn Bay. Sam took the helm while Shaw hauled up the sails.

In all his years of receiving advice from his grandfather, he had never seen him sail.

'Bet you don't what to do,' Shaw teased him. 'I don't think you've ever been on a sailing boat.'

Sam Shaw took the helm and ignored him.

'I believe that advice you gave me was all moonshine,' Shaw said. 'No wonder I can't sail.'

Sam held the tiller and peered into the distance.

'If anything goes wrong, turn into the wind,' Shaw said. 'If you know where that is.'

He hauled the genoa up first. That directed the flow so that the fully battened main could be hauled up with greater ease. He hauled in the genoa sheet and then attended to the main.

Sam bore away a little to pick up speed. *Mir* heeled and started to show the chuckle of a bow-wave. Maria came up on deck and looked round.

Sam feathered up a little.

'You're doing great, Sam,' Maria said.

'That genoa has to come in a fraction,' Sam Shaw said. 'I can see I'm going to have to train you up.'

Shaw clipped in the winch-handle and hauled in the genoa a little. He could sense the strength of his grandfather's concentration.

'Call that a mainsail?' Sam Shaw said.

It looked a little shapeless, Shaw had to admit. He worked on the flattener and outhaul a bit.

'It must have been those magazines you read,' Shaw said. 'You maybe picked it up from there.'

Shaw looked down at the speedometer and wind speed indicator dials.

'It's amazing what people can pick up,' Shaw said. 'I read in this newspaper once about this girl who shot her boyfriend with a .38 revolver. They had a quarrel, so she went into the bedroom where he kept his gun, came back into the living-room and shot him clean through the heart. The judge asked how she knew anything about firearms. She said she saw it on the TV.'

In eight knots of true wind they registered six and a quarter knots hard on the wind. Shaw looked out at the wake, unwaveringly true, with its edges folding neatly. The boat seemed to be sliding forward effortlessly, picking up in gusts, moving and sliding. He tried to work out what he'd do different. Not a great deal. Shaw looked back at the wake again, flat and glimmering and straight as a die. He said: 'The judge said that was some TV.'

Seventy-two

The phone made a sound like a child. Shaw reached to pick it up out of his own shy darkness.

At first no one said anything. He would have put it down, but in the background he heard voices, voices that seemed angry because they were controlled.

'Aegu,' the phone said suddenly.

Shaw said 'Yes,' as if he'd been expecting it. He could make out the face of the small travelling clock. Four twenty-three. In his cocoon of warmth he was nervous, fearful, fatalistic.

More background voices, someone issuing instructions patiently, setting things out one by one, someone else talking in that persistent gentle way which denoted tension.

'Aegu again,' it said. 'Could you meet me as soon as possible? A car will come for you.'

The phone went dead.

Shaw replaced it on the receiver and for several moments he could hear his heart above Maria's breathing. He lay on his back and turned his head to face her. In the dark he could make out the glowing side of her face, her lips parted. Attuned to Jack's call, at the first sound she would rise from sleep into an unconscious watchfulness. Awake, he could feel the tide of her waiting. He experienced an intense and urgent desire for her.

Slowly he drew back the sheets and slid from the bed to

the cold, bare floors. He put on his clothes carefully, methodically.

Outside a car drew up, lighting up the room momentarily with its headlights. The lights were doused. In the bathroom Shaw urinated, then splashed cold water on his face. Perhaps Maria had fallen asleep again. It would be better to wake her up now, he thought, than leave an empty bed and a penned message.

He put his face close to hers and was about to whisper when her face floated towards him and her lips met his. Again he felt that overwhelming desire, the darkness moving around inside him.

'You're going?'

'Aegu called.'

She sank back. Perhaps she knew there was one reason that he would call at this hour. It was some form of crisis. But it was too early for exasperation. It was the time the mind seems quieted by depth of feeling.

On the landing there was enough light to feel his way down the stairs, pull the locks on the outside door, step into the street. There was only one man in the waiting car. Shaw knew who it would be. He rapped gently on the side-window and felt the cold metal strike into his hand as he opened the door.

Saarinen's moon-face stretched into a brief smile that was like fear as he pushed the key into start and the engine rolled over. Shaw got in. The car, warmed by previous recent journeys, floated away from the kerb, picking up speed through the various gears.

Saarinen was silent. There was white frost on the road. Street-lamps blinked. They accelerated down Harju Street, to Voidu Square, swung right into Suvorov Street and ascended the hill. Saarinen, driving, manipulated the gears and wheel with a detached efficiency, a displacement of other emotions.

In Kohtu Street they parked. There were other cars there, three police cars, a militia van. Several men, police and militia, stood in a group at the end of the road near a street lamp. It was damp. In the light their breaths were like cigarette smoke.

Saarinen got out and Shaw followed. Saarinen's burly back moved ahead thirty yards or so until they came to Aegu's house. A militiaman stepped aside. Saarinen raised the heavy door knocker. Another militiaman came to the door, a man with a heavy moustache.

Saarinen showed his card. 'He is cleared,' he said, indicating Shaw. The militiaman led them down a passageway and knocked. A voice called, 'Come in.'

Aegu was in his dressing-gown, seated in a heavy wooden chair, looking dishevelled. He had been up all night. There was an empty vodka bottle beside him, and several glasses. He had a telephone in his shoulder. He reached forward and kicked a chair for Shaw to sit down. Saarinen nodded to Aegu and left without looking at Shaw.

Aegu said, 'It has begun.'

For several minutes Shaw waited while Aegu spoke rapidly into the telephone in Russian. Although he could not understand much of what was said, it was plain from his tone of voice that he was negotiating, commanding, wheedling. He was trying to reach certain figures in Moscow through other figures. Shaw had a vision of certain senior political figures being woken in their beds, stumbling out answers, searching their minds, sometimes in anger accusing him or denying him, once or twice even putting down the phone.

Aegu replaced the receiver finally, drew the back of his hand across his forehead. He had been sweating and his face was shiny. He said to Shaw: 'The Army has established control in Russia. I cannot appeal to my civil counterparts because they are as confused as I am. No, that is not right. I am confused, they are merely in ignorance.'

'The Army?'

Aegu seemed to rise out of his own reverie. He smiled at Shaw almost sympathetically. The question seemed to bring him out of some depth or personal region of thought. With a sweep of his broad fingers he sent the empty vodka bottle into the metal wastepaper bin.

'Chernavin. The Army. What does it matter? Every street corner in Moscow has soldiers on it. There is a state of emergency. Would you like a drink? I can ask for another bottle.'

Shaw groped blindly. He said, 'That's happened before.'

'This time it is entirely at the behest of the military. The civil authorities have not even been consulted. The main civilian telephone exchanges are being disconnected. Even while I was making calls I was being constantly cut off. In half an hour the entire civil communication system will be paralysed.' Aegu seemed vitiated by emotion. He had reached a plateau.

'Over the last three days, reports of increasing troop concentrations moving in east from St Petersburg and Novgorod. Yesterday they were gathering at Kingissep and Pskov. "Routine troop movements." It is like a dream. You recognize the pattern but cannot do anything about it. Yesterday afternoon and evening convoys two miles long massing at the border. The Russian forces in Estonia are on full alert, all leave cancelled. Full call-up for the *kadrirovannye* battalions. No special alarm from the civil authorities in Moscow. "The Army is testing certain procedures." What procedures? "Civil disorder procedures." What civil disorder? "For the future, comrade." Well, the future has arrived.'

Shaw gained an impression of Aegu's night – not only the unceasing tension, but the harangues with others. He guessed he had been up the entire previous evening, increasingly alarmed and angry.

Aegu lit a cigarette, a Prima. He seemed curiously unperturbed, like a man recovering in a ward after an accident.

'What will they do about you?' Shaw asked.

Aegu smiled, exhaling, as if the thought amused him.

'At first, they will not even bother to arrest me. They will simply cut the string between the people and the elected authorities.'

The phone rang suddenly and Aegu reached for the receiver.

'Yes. Thank you.'

He leant back.

'There are troop movements in the town. I have ordered our militia to show no violent resistance. The same is happening in Latvia and Lithuania. We are entering a period of Russian madness.'

'Why did you call me?' Shaw said.

'I wanted to ask you, as an American, whether you have any idea what the United States will do. I am not asking you about policy. I am enquiring about instinct. We have arrived at the time of instinct.'

Shaw could guess. But he didn't like to answer. He felt an enormous helplessness.

Aegu glanced at him briefly and continued to smoke.

'The Russian Army offers a return to order and discipline in a region which has become unruly, which threatens to split into a thousand small chaotic states. I imagine that is attractive to a superpower, to whom the worst possible alternative is disorder.'

'Maybe.'

'I was visited perhaps two weeks ago by a delegation of Americans.'

Shaw waited without speaking.

'It was one of those groups who do not carry official status, but who nevertheless appear to wield influence. Perhaps you have heard of them?'

Shaw shrugged.

'General Marcus Walters, Senator Hickstead, Tom Stuttaford.'

In the silence, Shaw was only aware of the muted voices of the militia talking outside the window.

Seventy-three

'What did they want?' Shaw asked.

'To discuss the future of the region.' Aegu drew on his cigarette. 'To offer advice.'

Shaw waited. He thought of Maria lying in bed. He thought of the tanks moving around the outskirts of Tallinn in the early morning, creeping forward like beetles, their tracks tearing the tar surface of the main thoroughfares. The room had only a small window. There was the faint hum of an air-conditioning unit.

Aegu said, 'I must start to prepare myself to announce the new conditions.' He rubbed his eyes. He stood up, surprisingly steadily, and went to the door. Opening it, he said to the younger of the Kallas brothers: 'Bring me some clothes.'

There was a washbasin in the room. Certain personal belongings had collected there as if it was a hotel room, or the small flat of a bachelor. It was Aegu's lonely outpost for his night vigils. Facing the sink, he dropped his dressing-gown and turned on the tap. Shaw was aware of the Minotaur's ugly, powerful body. Aegu poured water into the basin and began to wash his face with a sudden anger, splashing his shoulders. He spread shaving foam on his face and picked up in his left hand a cut-throat razor. Before he began to shave, Aegu said: 'They had no official capacity, but they seemed to be sure of themselves. I gave them an hour or so of time, if only out of courtesy.'

Aegu began to shave slowly. To most men the ritual of shaving is calming. This was his moment of privacy before the day, and Shaw was not concerned to press him. After a while Aegu said, 'They talked about stability in the region, the importance of order. It seemed vague, and it did not trouble me at the time. They were expressing views which, broadly speaking, I know the American administration holds. It was one of those meetings which returns to haunt one in the light of subsequent events.'

Aegu continued to shave. He shaved the left side of his face first. Shaw had read somewhere in a magazine, in the welter of information which makes up the background to a modern world, that in the mornings Picasso would spread shaving cream to give himself the huge white mouth of a clown. Aegu paused to study himself, as though assessing briefly his identity. One side was masked, the other clear. Then he began carefully to shave the right side of his face.

Aegu said, 'I quoted Lenin to them. "The interests of socialism are above the interests of the rights of nations to self-determination." With those words Lenin justified the imperialism of the Soviet Union. I asked them whether they agreed that was a good motto for the new Russia under Chernavin.'

It was perhaps five twenty in the morning. Outside, there was the faintest trace of the coming dawn. Shaw could hear occasional whispers in the hall, and the quiet movement of feet. Somewhere a telephone was ringing. Aegu removed the cream from the other side of his face.

'It occurred to me that, although the terms of our discussion were general, they were warning me of a specific event.' He paused briefly to study the result in the mirror. 'It was as if they knew in advance. I ask myself now, would I be right in deducing that they knew about the Army's coup? And if they knew, were they colluding,

389

encouraging the Army to establish stability?'

In the early dawn Shaw could hear pigeons cooing, a sound of peace. Aegu said: 'They informed me that what is required for stability is a strong man who can hold Russia together. "Stability",' he repeated to himself, as if wondering about the word. 'They told me there is a new force, rising behind Chernavin, a younger general whom the armed forces will follow. They say he has made his temporary headquarters in St Petersburg, in the Peter and Paul fortress.'

Aegu spoke casually, but Shaw knew that now he was listening intently for Shaw's own response. Lowering his head towards the basin, Aegu rinsed his face slowly with cold water, and rubbed his face with a towel.

Shaw couldn't speak. His mind was running along the thread of the connection, his emotions in turmoil.

Aegu cleaned his teeth vigorously, spitting into the basin, raising a handful of water to his mouth to rinse. He seemed for the moment to have forgotten Shaw. Or perhaps he was merely content to allow him the privacy of introspection. While Shaw considered, Aegu dressed in silence. Underclothes, clean white shirt, pressed trousers, braces, tie, like a man going to a wedding or a funeral. In the mirror he combed his hair.

Shaw noticed there was more light now through the small window, a white dawn cross-hatched by cloud. He thought to himself: A day like any other.

Aegu persisted, 'I am not asking you for an interpretation of American foreign policy. I am asking you for a feeling, an instinct. These are your countrymen.'

Shaw said, 'I think those people are capable of anything.'

Aegu paused for several moments. 'Including nothing? Suppose this general, who they believe is necessary to ensure stability in Russia, decides that it is in Russian strategic interests to place certain of the independent republics of the former Soviet Union under military control. Would they act to prevent that?' He looked at Shaw in the mirror, then made a final adjustment to his tie. He nodded, almost to himself, as if in melancholy confirmation of Shaw's silence. 'Thank you. Go home.'

Shaw stood up and walked to the door. At the doorway he turned. 'Good luck.'

In an Estonian farewell, Aegu said, '*Haad Aega.*'

Seventy-four

Outside it was humid.

Shaw paused outside the door of 16 Kohtu Street. He could see the huge district of Mustamae, that monument to former Soviet architecture, an entire district laid out on geometric principles, a heartless vision of human existence.

There was a sea mist. He began to walk down the slope. A thin line of smoke or dust alerted him to a column of tanks in the east. They seemed motionless at this distance, but he guessed they were moving forward steadily to cut off the perimeter roads. That morning the populace would wake to the new presence in the streets.

Inside, Shaw felt almost calm. Aegu's resilience had reassured him. There is a security in inevitability. Soldiers and militia at the end of Kohtu Street shifted aside to let him pass. For security reasons, they guarded the narrow passage that led down to Rataskaevu Street. Shaw decided to take the longer route, past Toomkali. There were more militia at the intersection with Naukogude Street – a lorry was drawn up and they stood around smoking. He felt their eyes study him casually.

Conscious now that he must remain calm, he descended Naukogude without hurry and swung left into Harju Street. Militia were gathering everywhere, perhaps in an attempt to seal off the hill. He had to pause at Niguliste while a troop ran past, harried by a sergeant.

Aegu, on one of their walks, had told him that the whole posture of former Soviet citizens had changed during the years of *perestroika*. The years of fear had caused people to hunch over their own fears, to hold in their terror until the very shape of their bodies came to reflect their inner state. To an outsider they moved slowly and deliberately, as if any cheerfulness was an ostentation which would attract unwelcome attention. In Moscow, Aegu said, you could recognize foreigners at a distance, long before their clothes gave them away, merely by their posture. Shaw himself had never felt that peculiar animal terror which is heightened by the consciousness that fear itself will draw attention. He had never lived in a society which makes an axiom of seeking out this fear in others, which operates on the principle that fear alone is proof of guilt.

He reached the entrance to the flat. Once inside he ran up the stairs, drove the key into the door, and opened the flat.

Shaw closed the door behind him and experienced a certain relief. From his position he could see through to the kitchen. Maria, standing at the stove, turned to glance at him and then, reassured by his presence, turned away to pour milk into a bowl. Struck by a sensation of completeness, he moved forward, fascinated by the way that the light touched her back in the kitchen.

His grandfather was seated at the table, drinking coffee. Shaw sat down alongside him. For several seconds he was unwilling to break the silence. Finally he said: 'There's a military crackdown. Tanks are coming into the town.'

'Russians?' He sensed rather than saw the trace of the old atavistic fear as Maria turned to face him.

Shaw nodded.

'It's important you all stay inside today. We'll have to wait and see what happens.'

Inside himself, he felt a strange combination of anger and reassurance, as if the worst had happened, and somehow it could be negotiated. You remember days like this afterwards, he thought.

'What about Aegu?' Maria asked.

'Aegu's preparing himself for what's coming. He doesn't seem unduly concerned. He says it's a matter of being patient.'

Seventy-five

'What about you?' Maria asked. He felt the fine cutting sense of her intuition.

At times like these, Shaw thought, it was best to be direct. He sensed the rising force of her anger, but could do nothing to explain. He could not explain to himself. As Aegu had said, these were times of instinct.

'I'm going to St Petersburg.'

'Why?'

He could only stare at her.

There was a stage when he thought Maria's calm would explode, that she would turn into a demon of imprecation, screaming and snarling at the stupidities and vanities of men. She merely turned away.

Sam said: 'How will you get there? You won't be able to use the roads. The borders must be closed.'

'By sea,' Shaw replied.

*

Packing oilskins into his bag, he turned away from the silence Maria was directing against him. He could hear her washing Jack, speaking to him in a calming, patient voice. He busied himself in preparations, filling a small box with items for the yacht; hand-bearing compass, signal flags, spare tools for the engine.

They had enough food in the flat for at least ten days, possibly two weeks. He hoped, he prayed, he would be back by then. He hated to leave them. But Maria was resourceful. Sam Shaw would help. There was unlikely to be civil fighting. The Estonians were not given to violence in pursuit of their political aims, if only because it raised the temperature and gave their invaders further excuses for draconian action. They must keep indoors; the dangers would be out on the streets.

Flares for an emergency, a waterproof torch, the few odds and ends he had collected if he were to make a longer voyage. Somewhere he had planned for this. In their hearts, yachtsmen make silent calculations for voyages. There was enough tinned food on board for several days at sea, stored in the bilges. There was fresh water in the tanks. He had a chart of the Gulf of Finland. The diesel tanks for the auxiliary engine were only half full. That was a pity. Now was not the time to consider filling them. If there was no wind, he would be forced to drift, to conserve fuel for the final approach to St Petersburg harbour.

A few final items; heavy pullovers, vests, extra trousers against the wind, seaboots. Shaw snapped them together into a holdall and walked out into the hall. At the bathroom door he paused.

Maria stood up and turned around. Shaw held her. He said, 'It will be quiet for a while. Just stay inside. Promise me.'

Her anger made her stiffen. Shaw too was coiled and wound tight. They drew apart. He shook Sam's hand.

Shaw glanced at his son. Perplexed by all this

embracing and shaking hands, Jack sat with a bar of soap in both hands, holding it like a live fish, staring up at them. Torn between hugging him and not wanting to disturb him further, Shaw said, 'Goodbye, Jack.'

Seventy-six

Rateskaevu Street was curiously deserted. The same was true of Lai Street. On Vana several groups of militia were hurrying towards Olevimagi. Shaw made his way towards the waterfront and began to walk towards Pirita. It had been a dry summer; the early morning mist was the dust-cloud of tanks that had broken through the borders at Narva the previous evening and advanced on Tallinn through the night. It was a curious expression of military intimidation and pragmatic civil respect. Tank tracks would have torn up the highway, so the tanks and motorized rifle brigades fanned out through country lanes and fields, raising clouds of dust like a forest fire.

Shaw pressed on, keeping to side-roads, but making no show of hiding. He walked east towards the tanks, into a pale sunrise. There were other figures that could be seen now, factory workers going to work, postmen and others determined to shoulder off the arrival of the Russian Army by normality. He passed two women talking on a corner. Walking fast, he moved eastwards along the coast road.

The city seemed set in an equable calm. It was three miles to Pirita. Shaw maintained a brisk stride. With occasional excursions, it took him the best part of an hour. He was approaching the quayside at Pirita when from the city the high walls and ramparts bells began to chime and resound, at first a few high-pealing bells, then the low sonorous chant of the bigger bells, as if in answer, proclaiming a calm defiance that would last throughout the morning as the motor-rifle divisions circled south to surround the capital. The strength of the invading forces would be rendered by contrast both absurd and unnecessary. The sound of the bells increased and pressed him forward. Turning a corner Shaw's breath froze. Several tanks were gathered on the road ahead, fifty yards away from the beach. He guessed at once they were from local garrisons which were waiting for the invading forces to join them. Their guns were pointed in the direction of Tallinn. In the open turret of one an officer in camouflage uniform casually smoked a cigarette.

Shaw felt their eyes scrutinize him. He saw the officer lean down and say something. He continued to close with them, determined to show no sign of haste or fear. Drawing alongside, he waited for a call to halt, to turn back, but the officer continued to smoke in the quiet morning air. Ahead of Shaw was the beach, a spur of shingle.

Mir lay at anchor in a small harbour behind a sloping protective wall. Several upturned dinghies lay like seals on the beach. He turned over his own pram dinghy. He had decided at the last moment to leave the oars at the flat in case they too closely identified his destination as he walked through the town.

Pushing the dinghy out over the gravel, he forced himself to move slowly. Carefully he pushed into the water. Lying down, facing forward, he used his hands to paddle slowly across the fifty yards of water to *Mir*. He did not look behind him at the tanks. Touching the yacht's topsides, he hauled himself up over the side and pulled his holdall after him. On *Mir*'s decks he walked forward with the painter of the dinghy and attached it to the mooring line.

He looked at his watch; seven thirty-five. A few cars

were moving along the inland roads. Occasionally he caught a flash from a windscreen or side-door. Behind them the bells of Tallinn continued to peal. A slight breeze from the west puckered the surface of the water. Rather than risk the sudden sound of the motor, he would leave by sail. Sail was innocuous. He suspected the soldiers were country boys who would associate sail with leisure and short distances. It did not matter that for aeons it had shifted men and cargo around the globe.

Mir lay head to wind. He unclipped the sail cover and stowed it below. Then he hauled up the mainsail slowly with a winch, studying the shape for leech tension, allowing the boom to swing out so that the sail had no power and would not drive the boat forward over her mooring. Forcing himself to pause, he carefully unfurled the roller-furling headsail.

On the shore the officer flung his cigarette out in an arc and casually turned to watch him. Avoiding the flapping foresail, Shaw moved to the foredeck and untied the anchor rope from the main cleat. He eased it over the side. Standing up, he backwinded the jib to swing the bow around. He was on a pivoting deck. The boat was swinging its head slowly. Even with sheets eased, it began to pick up speed. The dinghy, attached now to the mooring, bumped once against the topside and fell away to port. Shaw went to the stern, hauling the tiller up to weather, allowing the mainsail to swing out. He tightened the foresail sheets; the jib gathered wind and he could swing the yacht in the limited confines of the little harbour until her bow was heading towards the entrance. A small gust touched the surface of the water and he heard the ruffle of the bow-wave as he slid through the entrance.

On shore the officer was shouting something to another soldier, a joke or order or greeting. Shaw heard the reply fade as *Mir* picked up speed and he headed her for the open sea.

Seventy-seven

On a close reach *Mir* began to pick up speed, heeling slightly and accelerating. Shaw tightened on the genoa sheet and eased the main traveller to reduce weather helm. The speedometer showed four, then five knots. He steered *Mir* a little west of north, leaving the densely wooded island of Naissaar to port and aiming to shave Aegna Saar to starboard. Behind him, the bells of Tallinn tolled out across the water, travelling with him across the bay, receding into a light morning haze.

By nine he was abreast of island of Aegna, smaller and higher than Naissaar but as densely wooded. He could see the Aegna Light, with its red framework tower above a flat expanse of water. Out of sight of the shore a long westerly swell reached him from some former wind pattern. A few minutes later, calculating that he was clear of the Aegna shallows, he swung north-east between the rocky reef known as Tallinnamadal and the Kuradimuna shoal.

Now *Mir* rose and swung on a slow, quartering swell. He was heading into the Gulf of Finland, into open sea. For the rest of the daylight he would be clear of shoals and hazards. To the north, just beyond his sight, lay the land mass of Finland itself.

Leaving Kuradimuna to starboard, he swung almost due east, aiming towards St Petersburg. Then he went below to study the chart and plot his next course.

As the wind freshened it seemed to go more northerly, and became colder. By noon he was again on a close fetch. There the wind steadied. It was a relatively fast point of sail, the speedometer reading six and a half knots. He saw the occasional ship at a distance. With a clear seaway he decided to put in a few hours of sleep before night came on. The wind had shifted a little ahead, so that *Mir* was a few degrees off close hauled. He used one of the genoa sheets, attached to a winch, to secure the tiller, and spent a few minutes increasing or decreasing the length of rope between the tiller and the windward winch until he had achieved the right degree of weather helm.

The course was set on seventy-one degrees. *Mir* was tracking well, sometimes moving five degrees up or down off course. Shaw went below and wedged himself in a leeward bunk, propping a sweater under his head for a pillow. A second compass, set into the bulkhead, allowed him to view the course from his position without moving.

He drifted off for hardly more than an hour at a time, waking at intervals to check the course and wind velocity; but he was able to doze until the late afternoon. At five fifteen Shaw put his head above the hatch. Two merchant ships were passing to the north. *Mir* was approaching a shipping lane. Feeling hungry, he ducked below and searched the bilges for something to eat. He started the gas stove and cooked himself a tin of soup. Every few minutes he went up to check the course and the shipping. He spent the next half hour stowing bits and pieces. Occasionally *Mir* would punch into a swell and he could hear the hiss of spray along the lee deck. Before going out for what would be a full night's watch, Shaw put on oilskins to keep off the colder, northerly wind.

At a few minutes before eight in the evening he began to see the white light of Ostrov Rodsher. Before the sun set behind him he could plainly see its red octagonal tower, set on an isolated rocky islet. Keeping the light to starboard, he knew he was entering the main shipping lanes south of the six-mile-long island of Ostrov Gogland. Before the darkness began to rise, the island's flat black shadow appeared on the port bow, the Mys Lounatrivi Light a faint blink on its southernmost shore.

The wind became lighter, and from the north-west. Visibility decreased. Shaw decided to edge north, keeping south of the main shipping lane. Too much southerly would take him towards a Russian Navy prohibited area. The sun settled in a skein of bright clouds. After sundown, he saw a wall of grey approaching to the north-east. Not long afterwards, a light mist enveloped the yacht. In the brief interlude before the white wall closed around him, he decided to give himself sea-room and struck a more southerly course away from the main shipping lanes. Leaving the prohibited area sufficiently far to be safe, he maintained a parallel course to the shipping channel. His last sight was the lights of a large cargo vessel steaming north-east on an approximately parallel course.

Seventy-eight

Most yachtsmen fear fog more than bad weather, particularly in well-travelled coastal waters. A gale is active, but fog is passive, like paralysis. It is an eerie sensation, a combination of sensory deprivation and fear. Around him he could hear occasional horns and sirens of big ships. He assumed they were to the north, in the main shipping lane, but sound in fog is deceptive. He could only wait, alert, as the sirens called through the night. Several hours later the dense mist lifted, moving away in a solid wall to the south.

At night the sea is as strange as the jungle. The night is black and fervid, all-surrounding. Sea and sky merge. The lights of passing ships float like moths, or the eyes of nocturnal animals, giving no hint of the travelling mass of the objects on which they form tiny outposts — faint illuminations attached to the massive bulk of ruminants. He remembered the little rhymes which form the rules between life and death.

Green to green and red to red,
perfect safety, go ahead.

If to starboard red appear,
it is your duty to keep clear.
Take the action fit and proper,
port or starboard, back or stop her.

Plaintive nursery rhymes that lived in the mind because they formulated the rules between life and death; fireflies blown by the wind.

If upon the port is seen,
a steamer's starboard light of green,
there is not much for you to do,
for green to port stays clear of you.

Here the mind floated, suspended, in the vivid darkness. Beneath his eyes, like a small constellation, the faintly lighted orb of the compass.

Before midnight he saw lights out of one of the portholes and with consternation moved out to the hatchway to see a big liner moving west, a quarter of a mile north in the shipping lane. Broadside, it seemed like a city with a thousand lights. He felt the beat of his heart recede. The traffic on the sea is endless, like the procession of life and death.

Darkness closed in entirely shortly after midnight. The wind continued to drop. Out of the north-east a wall of white appeared. Soon all traces of ships' lights had disappeared. By one fifteen in the morning the breeze was down to a few knots; the long swell raised and lowered *Mir*, but without way she would suddenly plunge, kicking out spray.

Partly to allay his nervousness, he made coffee on the gas stove, returning every few minutes to stare around him from the hatchway and to check the course. Perhaps half an hour later, his eyes straining ahead, the entire wall of fog seemed to move; he heard a sound like the swishing of water, the low, heavy thunder of a huge engine, and the alarmed mewing of lost souls. For several seconds Shaw's heart migrated north into his mouth. It was a flock of gulls, sitting on the water, suddenly disturbed by his silent approach, flapping hugely in the grey ahead. For those seconds, as they struggled upwards, their wings hammering the mist, they must have been as frightened as he was.

Towards three o' clock he was still in thick fog, with the uncomfortable sensation of craft moving around him. He could still hear foghorns and sirens. He strained his eyes and ears to the north. *Mir* was making barely two knots in the light breezes. He was too concerned to leave the tiller for more than a few seconds. To ensure speed in the case of emergency manoeuvre, he put the engine key in the starter and kicked the engine into gear. He ran it for half an hour to recharge the batteries, then switched it off. A slight increase in breeze meant that he could progress at just above three knots under sail. The fog-horns continued to the north as the big steamers plied the shipping channel. Shaw's nervousness made him curiously light-headed. Standing in the companionway, he glanced round, then went below to check the position on the chart.

Returning, he saw that the mist had begun to lift. Suddenly he was aware of the amount of shipping around. Wherever he looked there were lights. Although the fog had lifted, the night was pitch black. A whole new sense had opened. He could see the surface of the water in the slight glow from the steaming light. There was no sign of wind and he continued to ease *Mir* carefully east. A long line of lights stretched out along the south, in the area of the islands of Moshchnyy and Malyy.

Another one of those strange phenomena held his attention. A dark hand was moving along the lights of Moshchnyy, turning them out. It was as if someone were playing with the switches that controlled the lights. He was fascinated. The sea felt flat calm. His only explanation was that in the absolute dark there were swells sufficiently large enough to rise between himself and the lights to the south. He could not see such seas, merely deduce that they existed from the strange behaviour of the lights.

At five the dawn was showing, and with a little breeze. More lights appeared. By now he had gained a second wind and was able to stay on watch in the cockpit. A breeze appeared. He felt *Mir*'s speed increase. It was a pleasure to experience again the sensation of movement, and listen to the swells against the hull. He bore off a little to pick up way. Forward momentum helped to fill the sails. *Mir* accelerated and proceeded at four knots in just enough breeze to fill the sails.

The island of Ostrov Seskar, low and wooded; a cloud above like an exhalation of the land. He could follow the safe-water posts. Seskar's western lighthouse combed the dawn. The island gradually rose, fell, and slipped behind.

Seventy-nine

A cool, metallic morning.

The breeze filled slightly and *Mir*'s speed started to touch six knots, gliding over level grey water. Although he had been without sleep the previous night, the prospect of reaching shore in daylight hours gave him confidence that he could hold out. Sleep was a drug on his nerves. After the night the wind seemed to grow out of the mongrel whiteness, causing the boat to heel and produce occasional brisk explosions of spray as she punched through a crest. Looking through the galley porthole as he checked the course, he could see the horizon on all sides as a line of grey.

Course ninety-five degrees, almost due east, towards St Petersburg. Tiredness had refined his senses. He was hungry but not starving. Leaving the yacht to steer herself for a few minutes, he went below to check his chart for identifying marks as he neared St Petersburg Bay.

Two hours later *Mir* was approaching the constriction of the Stirsudden and Ustinsky headlands, barely fifteen miles apart. The breeze was moderate, freeing a little to a more northerly direction. Self-steering on a reach was more difficult than on the wind; now he could only leave the helm for a few seconds at a time. His tension had assumed a certain lightness. He was a good mile to the south of the main shipping lane. In daylight the danger of collision seemed remote. It was an opportunity to sail the yacht as well as he could. Trimming the sails, he settled down to steer, using each of the quartering swells to drive forward and pick up speed. Between swells he bore up into wind to retain drive until the next wave. He became mesmerized in the actions of helming.

There was driftwood on the surface, packing cases, oil drums, sometimes large planks – the paraphernalia of a polluted seaway. The water moved heavily, as though thickened with human flotsam. A quick expulsion of air surprised him. He glanced to port and saw a body rise from the surface, a graceful curving sweep that seemed like an arm rising but turned into the fin of a dolphin. The colour of the dorsal fin and back was almost pink, like that of human flesh. It left no trace except a rapidly disappearing series of ripples. Travelling across the bow of the yacht, it should have passed perhaps thirty yards ahead. Straining his eyes, Shaw kept a search on starboard for its reappearance. One minute passed to three; then four, five. He never saw a trace of it again. Perhaps it changed course under water. Perhaps it used its full lung capacity to strike off a long distance away from the yacht. It was another of those strange sensations thrown up by the sea, that single sight of a dolphin with a skin the colour of human flesh, in the polluted waters of St Petersburg Bay.

At the Shepelevskiy light the land was flat, but it started rising towards Krasnaya Gorka. Occasional bursts of sunlight moved over the water and illuminated wave-crests.

The sea-traffic began to increase. To the north, three Russian warships out of St Petersburg or Lomonosov moved majestically west, a big *Kirov*-class battle cruiser and two *Udaloy*-class destroyers. Shaw wondered whether they were destined to anchor off Tallinn as part of a carefully orchestrated intimidation. He felt both detached and absurdly vulnerable. As they passed broadside, the cruiser leading, they began to accelerate, throwing out white wakes above which hung numerous gulls like snowflakes. He could see the name of the cruiser: *Frunze*. He imagined officers studying *Mir*'s tiny radar image. At thirty knots, the three warships moved west with implacable power.

Local Russian harbour rules demanded that all entrants to St Petersburg take aboard a pilot at the Light buoy. Shaw calculated it was still five miles away. A stream of grey naval vessels, supply ships and fuellers, emerged ahead of him and crossed into the starboard shipping lane. He searched the horizon to the north.

The naval patrol vessel that approached him must have moved along the coast before swinging out to intercept him from the south. His attention was so absorbed by the traffic out at sea that he only saw it five hundred yards away; two bow-waves standing out like flutes. In hardly any time it had swung across him forward and revved back, settling in the water dead ahead of his bows. To avoid collision he was forced to swing *Mir* into wind, sails shaking. On the patrol vessel a blue-uniformed officer came to the rail, raising a loudhailer to call out '*Stoi!*'

Shaw folded away the roller-furling genoa, then moved forward to release the mainsail halyard. He piled the sail on to the boom and secured it with tiers. Without the steadying effect of sail, *Mir* was lively in the swells. Shaw had to hang on as he went about his business. It was important to work methodically and fast. Aboard the patrol vessel a group of sailors lowered a launch under the orders of a non-commissioned officer. The officer loud-hailered again:

'*Idyom na abordazh!*'

Shaw went below to stow any loose gear. Not long afterwards the gunwale of the launch touched *Mir*'s topsides and the boots of the sailors moved along her decks. He heard the thud as they descended the companionway. He was facing sideways, stowing charts and navigational implements in the chart table locker when several men entered the cabin. Shaw glanced up and, determined to keep calm, turned sideways to close the drawer. It was then that someone, perhaps the officer, struck him with the butt of a gun on the side of the head between cheek and ear. It was the slowness of the gesture that caught Shaw off guard; the graceful loop of the blow in his peripheral vision seemed no more than a casual shift of movement, a spreading of weight. A fiery pain moved through his skull, and he felt himself sliding downwards.

Eighty

Waking, Shaw thought of the flesh-coloured dolphin rising amongst the debris in St Petersburg Bay.

He was lying on a stretcher in a room. A single bare bulb provided the only light. At first the room was shadowy, the bulb like an indeterminate sun. As his sight improved, he saw that the ceiling and walls were a uniform grey-green.

'An Estonian hero,' a voice said.

He closed his eyes against the pain that seemed to move across his skull like a slow burn. He heard footsteps approaching him across empty floors. A tall figure was standing over him.

'Major Archem,' the voice said.

Shaw could not see his face against the light. Perhaps because he had assured himself that Shaw was conscious, perhaps out of concern, Archem moved back a step.

'You took a risk, approaching St Petersburg at this time.' Archem seemed to search for words. 'There is an international alert. We are nervous.' He waited a few seconds and when Shaw did not speak, he repeated simply, 'A risk.'

Shaw's tongue felt huge, and he tasted the metallic tang of dried blood, as if he had bitten himself when he had fallen. His mouth was dry. He tried to move. Staring past Major Archem, he moved his eyes cautiously around the room. To his right there was a single small window, no more than an embrasure in walls that were several feet thick.

Archem was holding out a cigarette. Shaw said, 'No thanks.' Archem shrugged, replaced the packet in his pocket. Without taking his eyes off Shaw he took several steps backward and leaned against a wall.

Carefully Shaw rolled on his side. Archem watched his

progress. For several moments Shaw waited for the pain in his head partially to subside, then swung his legs out over the floor and slowly raised himself into a sitting position.

Archem pulled a short wooden table across the floor towards Shaw. On its surface was a stainless steel bowl, half filled with cold water. A towel lay beside it. Archem moved back quietly, and sat on a chair facing him.

Sitting on his bed, Shaw felt on the point of vomiting. Salty saliva filled his mouth. But perhaps because his stomach was empty, his nausea passed. After a few minutes he leaned over the basin and splashed his face with cold water.

Archem watched him with detachment.

'You can walk?'

Shaw dried his face on the towel that lay beside the basin. He pushed the table forward and stood up, leaning on the table for support. At first his legs felt weak, but as the seconds passed, he felt able to stand without support. Across the right side of his head and ear, stretching to the jaw and the upper part of the neck, he felt a soft and sickening pain, like toothache. For a little while his vision came and went.

Archem allowed him to stand for a little longer while he regained his balance. Then he tapped on the metal door. A key moved from the outside moved in the lock; the door swung open noiselessly on its heavy hinges.

A subaltern stood facing him. Shaw saw a young Slavic face, intense blue eyes; lean, big in the shoulders. The officer saluted him. Reaching forward, he seized Shaw by the shoulder and pulled him out of the door. In the corridor, he spun Shaw roughly. Shaw waited until he had his back to the subaltern. They were of similar height. When he calculated the man least expected it, he quietly drove his left elbow backwards into the officer's solar plexus. It might have been an accident. He heard a grunt. Pivoting, Shaw used the whole weight of his body to swing his right elbow into the surprised face. He could feel the explosion of force in the officer's jaw and cheek-bone. As he sank, the colour seemed to drain from his face. The remaining guards rushed forward in a body, driven by a collective hunger; he knew he could be trampled like a child in a football crowd.

'*Ataydi!*' Archem was shouting in Russian. '*Nye tron'!*'

Reluctantly, the guards drew back. Shaw leant against the wall, breathing heavily. Beside him the subaltern had sunk to his knees, holding his face.

Archem was talking evenly to the others, issuing commands. Two of the guards helped the young officer to his feet, supporting him under the shoulders. They moved away down the corridor.

Archem appeared to show no emotion. Perhaps *Dedovshina*, the beating and brutalizing of recruits, was still too much a part of the services' habitual routine for him to show surprise. Shaw himself had been struck, and perhaps he was entitled to retaliate. Now that order was restored, Archem showed no embarrassment, merely a brief concern over the nature of an incident in public.

Shaw was leaning against the wall. The effort of striking out had drained him, almost as much as if he himself had been hit.

Archem motioned the guards to stand back, and waited patiently while he recovered, then said in English, 'Follow me.'

With Archem in front, the guards following, they moved down lines of corridors. For Shaw the first few yards were the most difficult; then the rhythm of walking took over. He lost count of the turnings. Sometimes a clerk or messenger would go by, half at the run. Guards were stationed at the end of each corridor. Shaw sensed the curious exaltation of crisis. They passed through several further security checks. Archem used his authority to drive through. They seemed to be in a part of the building devoted to administration. Several of the doors they passed now had individual guards stationed outside them.

Archem paused beside a door painted in official green and spoke briefly to the sergeant and two guards. They frisked Shaw automatically and quickly. Archem knocked on the door, opened it, stood back, and nodded coolly at him. Tentatively, Shaw stepped through into darkness.

Eighty-one

The door closed behind Shaw, and for several seconds he imagined they had merely transferred him to a different cell. The only light was from a small embrasure window in the furthest wall. At first he thought he was alone.

He was sitting at a desk, partially hidden against the dark corner. Shaw could see from the angle of his head on his powerful neck, and the way his head listened, that he was blind. He stared like a statue in the faint light from the tiny embrasure. In this light the dark glasses that hid his eyes seemed superfluous. He sat in his own darkness, listening.

Dressed in Army uniform, he waited for the scratch of Shaw's shoes on the wooden floor. For a few seconds Shaw tried to imagine the unimaginable, the world of permanent darkness. Each day sensation gathered at his fingertips. Sound gathered in his ears. But no sight. He absorbed the world with different senses.

Shaw waited. He wasn't prepared for the precise but heavily accented English.

'Mr Shaw?'

Shaw said, 'General Vorolov.'

Vorolov showed no emotion. He seemed to be studying the sound of Shaw's voice. After a few moments he said: 'Please sit down.'

How long did he wait in the semi-darkness, sitting opposite Vorolov? A few minutes, a few seconds? The furniture of the room seemed to gather the gloom around itself and rise towards him. Vorolov appeared to be listening to his breathing, or perhaps he was waiting for the silence to settle.

Vorolov reached towards a packet of cigarettes. Shaw watched the strong, square fingers touch the pack of Primas, gather it into his palm. He had the veteran soldier's habit of raising one cigarette from the packet with the thumb and forefinger, lifting the packet to his mouth to place the cigarette between his lips. It came from having a gun always in the other hand. Vorolov replaced the pack on the desk top.

'Illich had a method of progressing, one step at a time. Make things the same, he used to say, change only one thing. That was how it was. We were the same, except for one thing. I had not prepared to answer for myself.'

Vorolov reached towards the box of matches and struck one carefully. For a moment his face lit up. Under the brief intensity of the flame Shaw saw, through the dark glasses, Vorolov's empty eyes. Smoke drifted around his head. He exhaled.

'I believe he prepared himself psychologically. He prepared himself for the time when he would be asked to harm or kill another man who was innocent of any crime. He knew for certain that he would die rather than do such a thing. When he decided that, he was no longer part of the Army, no longer ours.' Silence moved around his head in the dark. 'The rest followed naturally.

'There are certain decisions which we can only make on

411

our own. It is our conscience which separates us from the animals. In killing him, something passed to me. Not at first, but later. I began to understand a little.'

Vorolov breathed out contemplatively. Smoke drifted in the thin light of the embrasure window. He turned his head sideways, as if he were listening to Shaw's response. After several seconds he began to speak in an even voice, not lingering, but choosing his words carefully.

'Russia changes but is always the same. You think it is sinister, this reversion to the old ways? We cannot simply eliminate eighty years of history, eighty years of living, eighty years of accumulated experience. It is more than our official history, it is what is buried in ourselves.

'We can airbrush official history, but not our own lives. Our memory does not simply disappear a few years ago. Each of us has roots in our Communist past. Our experience stays with us.'

He moved slowly, at his pace, formulating his thoughts in a foreign language in which he was expert but unpractised.

'That is something the West does not understand. Communism grew out of the Russian soul. We always had a hierarchical society, first monarchist, then Leninist. We have always had direct rule, a secret police force. The names change, but the institutions remain. To a Russian, these things are so obvious that he does not need to mention them.'

Shaw watched the dry movement of smoke around Vorolov's head.

'We have always relied on strong leaders. It is not the dictator who imposes his will on the community, but the community which insists on the strength of a leader. Chernavin is a manifestation of this ancient will. But he too will go.

'Russia returns to herself. In a few years it will be over. We simply accept the process of another change of leader. We cannot be repressed for ever. Perhaps there will be other cycles. Who knows?'

412

Shaw waited in the silence. Vorolov felt with his fingers for the ashtray, then stubbed out his cigarette. Having performed this small task, slowly he leant back.

'Physical pain goes. It leaves physical scars, disabilities, visible signs of its presence. But psychological pain, spiritual pain, shows no signs. If the mind which holds it is able to accept it, then it purifies like water. That is why I believe in Christ, Mr Shaw. He was a vessel for this spiritual pain.

'I have experienced a small measure of it. I killed a man, a man who was better than I. Only later did I understand the meaning of what I had done.'

Far away Shaw heard a shouted order, perhaps a change of guard in the corridor. It hardly reached into the silence of the room. It did not touch Vorolov's concentration.

'In certain respects we were like twins, two ambitious Army officers. But set on different tracks.

'Illich is dead. I killed him. He was the purest kind of Russian. Absolutely courageous, not of this world. He was one of those who challenge our institutions, sometimes not even consciously. Our society produces people like him. We demand them, just as we demand dictators. There is a young poet, Nevsky, who wrote a poem about those people, people who are born and teach by example, people who were on this earth only to rise through their own death. "Angels", he called them.'

Vorolov paused. Shaw watched him reach towards a drawer, fumble with the catch for a moment, then withdraw something square and heavy. At first Shaw could not make out the blunt shape half hidden by his fist. Vorolov put it down with a heavy thump on the desk, and with a sudden powerful thrust sent it trundling across the desk towards him. Shaw would remember the heavy, flat sound as it skidded towards him. It might have been a tram-car, sliding on wheels, showering tiny points of light.

Before it came to a halt in front of him, perhaps even before it had left Vorolov's hand, Shaw knew what it was. A blunt automatic pistol, a Makarov. Vorolov put both hands, palms down, on the table in front of him. He appeared calm.

'It is loaded. You may check.'

Shaw hesitated for a moment, then reached forward to pick up the gun. On its handgrip was a five-pointed star, old Soviet Army issue. Its squat weight felt like the heavy shadow of death.

Vorolov said: 'It would serve justice. I have become reconciled to my death. Like Illich, I am detached.'

Carefully Shaw raised it, moving the blunt barrel towards Vorolov. The muzzle was only two feet away from Vorolov's chest. Shaw knew that any pistol is a notoriously inaccurate instrument, particularly in the hand of an amateur. But even an amateur could kill at this range.

Illich's murder had been a brutal one. It was the struggle of two men, one fighting for his life, the other shooting mercilessly.

'What will happen to me?' Shaw asked. 'If I pull the trigger?'

'You will be tried for my murder.'

'What are my chances?' Shaw asked. 'Mitigating circumstances, maybe? A reduced sentence. You killed my great and admired friend.'

'A good chance, I think,' Vorolov said equably. 'You were invited to kill me. I gave you the gun that killed Illich. You participated in my suicide. It would be convincing because it is true.'

Shaw swung the heavy barrel across Vorolov's chest, from one armpit to the other, and squeezed the trigger. For several moments he was blinded by the discharge and deafened by the sound of the shot. Cordite filled the room; his ears rang.

The silence roared in his mind. In the darkness Shaw

could see where the bullet had struck the wall beside the window embrasure, producing a crater in the soft brick, spreading debris and powder over the floorboards beneath. Vorolov sat unmoving on the other side of the desk.

Shaw said, 'I wondered if it was loaded.'

After a while Vorolov's lips moved and he seemed to smile, as though understanding something.

'A suspicious American. We were discussing matters of the heart. A Russian would have taken me at my word.'

Shaw heard the door punched open behind him. He sat still as heavy boots approached across the bare floor. He was certain he would be struck from behind with the heavy butt of a gun. Inside he quailed.

But Vorolov was waving an arm, saying firmly, '*Stoi!*'

The gun remained suspended above him. Shaw had read once that flies can detect a movement of electricity before the hand begins to move. He sensed the muscular suspension, a pyramid of force gathered to break his skull.

'*Da!*'

Major Archem reached forward and lifted the Makarov Shaw had set down on the desk. He snapped on the safety catch. Vorolov held out his hand. Archem placed the gun in Vorolov's fist.

Boots moved across the floor. The door was firmly closed.

In the darkness, Vorolov slid the gun into a drawer and closed it. After a moment's pause, he said, 'We were discussing detachment.'

Shaw waited. Vorolov said: 'You pursued me. You waited patiently until you discovered my whereabouts. Then you followed me into Russia.' Hearing no response, he continued: 'What is your interest in Illich's death?'

'My interest is whether Americans were behind it.'

'A patriot,' Vorolov said, 'after all.'

415

Shaw's ears still echoed from the pistol shot in the confined space. He said: 'It seems now they weren't.'

Vorolov shrugged, a slow animal movement of doubt and distaste. 'No more than usual. There are some things I cannot tell you. But Illich's death was an internal matter, if that is any reassurance.'

'It is,' Shaw said carefully. 'It is some.'

Eighty-two

Shaw remembered a sentence of Aegu's. 'In Russia, power moves in the darkness like an animal.' In the darkness it seemed to have moved to Vorolov, at home here without light, detached. He had been invited to kill Vorolov, to carry out some notion of personal justice. Now his function was over. It seemed he was waiting for him to go.

Shaw said, 'If I left, I would go back to an occupied country.'

Vorolov said, 'Russia is in its agony. It is transforming itself. It reaches out to its friends.'

'With tanks?'

Vorolov paused, as if in faint recognition. 'When it comes to neighbours, we have a limited vocabulary.'

Shaw struggled to say something, something terse and bitter. He had lived with Estonians for several years, and he knew the ferocity with which they desired to preserve their own small culture.

'You should stay with us,' Vorolov said quietly. 'We have suffered together.'

A series of vague answers moved in Shaw's mind. In Russian literature, the husband beats his wife, drinks

416

away his earnings, abuses her and the children, then finally begs her for forgiveness. It was the old family tragedy; it was absurd and at the same time it was heartfelt. But the Estonians did not wish to play the part of the wife.

'Our vocabulary is also limited. Maybe we don't understand tanks.'

Vorolov did not reply. Perhaps his mind had moved on to other things. After some time Shaw stood up and moved carefully through the darkness towards the door. He turned round once. Vorolov sat unmoving in his chair. Shaw tapped on the heavy steel door.

Almost immediately it was drawn open. Brightness crashed against his eyes. Hands gripped his shoulders. He was pulled through the doorway, turned and spun hard against a wall, frisked, turned round again. A gun barrel drove against his stomach, causing him to cough in pain. A figure – Archem – moved past him through the doorway and was speaking with Vorolov. Shaw could not hear what was being said. Vorolov was communicating in short sentences, issuing orders. The door was closed. Archem faced him. Shaw could see the strain in the tall major's face, the strain of waiting while a single shot rang out in a dark room. Archem said, 'Follow me.'

The guards on either side forced Shaw into motion. Fighting for breath, his eyes blinking against the brightness of bare lightbulbs, he was marched down corridors, past other guards. The party was moving down stairs, through further corridors. They turned a corner and he was halted by a hand on his shoulder. Two of the guards opened a small side-door. Shaw was pushed through into open sunlight.

They were in a small square enclosed on all sides by high walls. Kropotkin had been interned here, he remembered. They moved ahead, then halted again. Two large doors were opened with a rattle of hinges. Outside the fortress, the attitude of the guards seemed to change. Now they walked smartly beside him like companions, Archem ahead. Brilliant spring sunlight touched the roots of his eyes. They were walking to the edge of the small pier that was washed by the wakes of river boats and the big Raketa hydrofoils that traversed the Neva.

They came to the edge. Shaw could see *Mir*'s mast. The yacht rose and fell against the landing. He felt space open around him.

On the river, perhaps a hundred yards out, a tug was towing with heavy chains what seemed a huge black underwater obstruction; an immense block of ice that had come down on the Neva, blackened now with river dirt and diesel oil. It was being towed out of the main passage into shallow water where it could melt. Shaw wondered briefly how many such hidden icebergs he had missed during his night's passage. The guards stood aside so that he could climb downwards on to the yacht.

He descended the metal ladder carefully. On the deck he turned round. Reaching forward to hold the lifelines for support, he saw that his hands were shaking. Above him Archem's great height made him seem a statue against the sky.

'*Povorachivai na zapad*,' Archem said. 'Go west.' Then he added, 'Goodbye.'

They turned and moved out of sight. He heard the martial strike of their boots on the heavy wooden planks of the quay.